Praise

'Brooks' mischievous retelling [of Chaucer's *The Wife of Bath's Tale*] dials up the feminist themes — and the fun — to 11.'

—*The Canberra Times* on *The Good Wife of Bath*

'Astonishingly good — an instant classic. Certes 'tis a tale for everywoman.'

—Tea Cooper, bestselling international author, on *The Good Wife of Bath*

'So damn readable and fun … This is the story of a woman fighting for her rights; it breaches the walls of history.'

—*The Australian* on *The Good Wife of Bath*

'Brooks' Wife is as vital, crude and strong as in the Tales … an intriguing character study.'

—*The Sydney Morning Herald* on *The Good Wife of Bath*

'It's the language of this bawdy tale that tickles.'

—*Australian Women's Weekly* on *The Good Wife of Bath*

'Karen Brooks' funny, picaresque and clever retelling of Chaucer's "The Wife of Bath's Tale" is a cutting assessment of what happens when male power is left unchecked. It's a rich, rollicking yet ultimately important read that finally reclaims Eleanor's story for her own.'

—*Better Reading* on *The Good Wife of Bath*

'Eleanor is a warm and funny heroine and while she might be centuries old, her story is still relevant to women of today. Established author Karen Brooks is a powerful storyteller who skilfully brings a minor character to the fore.'

—*Family Circle* on *The Good Wife of Bath*

'Gleefully bawdy, delightfully irreverent, this vibrant novel not only invokes empathy for the struggles of women in Chaucer's times, it resonates with women's experiences today.'

—Darry Fraser, bestselling Australian author, on *The Good Wife of Bath*

'Historian and novelist Brooks shows her research and imaginative chops in a luscious and astonishingly affecting chronicle of family scandal, political unrest, and redemptive hope in 1660s London.'

—*Publishers Weekly* on *The Chocolate Maker's Wife*

'Brooks masterfully deploys surprising plot twists, deftly pacing the opening of closets to reveal hidden diaries and family skeletons … A charming and smart historical novel from a master storyteller.'

—*Kirkus Reviews* on *The Chocolate Maker's Wife*

'*The Darkest Shore* is meticulously researched, taking a real historical event, and [Karen Brooks'] academic experience and merging it with exceptional storytelling. The characters are complex and compelling … a powerful novel, at times brutal, but always enthralling, *The Darkest Shore* is a major achievement for Karen Brooks.'

—*Better Reading*

'Karen Brooks has handled such a dark history with care and empathy … I can't recommend this one highly enough, it's a brilliant read.'

—*Theresa Smith Writes* on *The Darkest Shore*

'A compelling, fascinating, and disturbing historical fiction novel … Beautifully written, with authentic characterisation and vivid description … a captivating, even if sometimes confronting, read.'

—*Book'd Out* on *The Darkest Shore*

'… a completely absorbing historical novel.'
—*Other Dreams Other Lives* on *The Darkest Shore*

'Moving, tragic, frustrating and inspiring. *The Darkest Shore* is yet another triumph from historical specialist Karen Brooks.'
—*Mrs B's Book Reviews*

'Sensual, seductive, bold … A rich indulgence.'
—*Booklist* on *The Chocolate Maker's Wife*

'The latest from Australian author Brooks is an excellent option for reading groups that enjoy multigenerational tales and historical fiction … Your late middle English vocabulary will be sumptuously rewarded.'
—*Library Journal* on *The Chocolate Maker's Wife*

'Meticulously researched and historically compelling … this fast-paced novel is a dramatic spy thriller that shines a spotlight on the inner workings of Elizabethan England.'
—*Books + Publishing* on *The Locksmith's Daughter*

'Brooks's attention to historical detail instils the novel with authenticity by including many historical figures and events, while Anneke's lively voice keeps a strong grip on the reader as she works to overcome societal prohibitions against women in business and find happiness and contentment. Brooks's immersive page-turner does not disappoint.'
—*Publishers Weekly* on *The Brewer's Tale*

'Karen Brooks's writing is simply superb, thrusting you immediately into Anneke's world with her use of all the elements of a good historical fiction novel, such as significant period detail, authentic settings, characterisation and tone, rendering a colourful portrait of a heroine bound by the politics of her time and showing us the real difficulties that woman of that era experienced and the dangers they faced.'

—*Book Muster Down Under* on *The Brewer's Tale*

'... a gripping rollercoaster of an escapist read!'

—*Bookloons* on *The Brewer's Tale*

Karen Brooks is the author of fifteen books, an academic of more than twenty years' experience, a newspaper columnist and social commentator, and has appeared regularly on national TV and radio. Before turning to academia, she was an army officer for five years, and prior to that dabbled in acting. She lives in Hobart, Tasmania, in a beautiful stone house with its own marvellous history. When she's not writing, she's helping her husband Stephen in his brewstillery, Captain Bligh's, or cooking for family and friends, travelling, cuddling and walking her dogs, stroking her cats, or curled up with a great book and dreaming of more stories.

Also by Karen Brooks

Fiction

The Brewer's Tale
The Locksmith's Daughter
The Chocolate Maker's Wife
The Darkest Shore
The Good Wife of Bath

The Curse of the Bond Riders trilogy

Tallow
Votive
Illumination

Young Adult Fantasy

It's Time, Cassandra Klein
The Gaze of the Gorgon
The Book of Night
The Kurs of Atlantis
Rifts Through Quentaris

Non-fiction

Consuming Innocence

The ESCAPADES of TRIBULATION JOHNSON

A WOMAN WRITES BACK

KAREN BROOKS

First Published 2023
First Australian Paperback Edition 2023
ISBN 9781867227229

THE ESCAPADES OF TRIBULATION JOHNSON

Published by
HQ Fiction
An imprint of Harlequin Enterprises (Australia) Pty Limited (ABN 47 001 180 918),
a subsidiary of HarperCollins Publishers Australia Pty Limited (ABN 36 009 913 517)
Level 19, 201 Elizabeth St
SYDNEY NSW 2000
AUSTRALIA

Map by Alex Hotchin

A catalogue record for this book is available from the National Library of Australia
www.librariesaustralia.nla.gov.au

Printed and bound in Australia by McPherson's Printing Group

This book is dedicated to my amazing, kind, patient and generous sister, Jennifer Farrell. Throughout the hardest and saddest year for our family, she continually showed the depth of her compassion, love and fortitude.
She is the best of women; the best of people; the best of siblings.
I am so very blessed you are mine, Jenny.

CONTENTS

Explanatory Note xvii
Prologue 1

ACT ONE: *From Bride to Bridewell or, Preferment Postponed, Winter 1679–Spring 1679* 13

Scene One 15
Scene Two 25
Scene Three 35
Scene Four 44
Scene Five 51
Scene Six 64
Scene Seven 69
Scene Eight 74
Scene Nine 86

ACT TWO: *'Jealousy, the old worm that bites' or, Promptly Employed, Spring 1679–Autumn 1679* 97

Scene One 99
Scene Two 110
Scene Three 122
Scene Four 125
Scene Five 137
Scene Six 146

Scene Seven 159
Scene Eight 169
Scene Nine 179
Scene Ten 188
Scene Eleven 203
Scene Twelve 213
Scene Thirteen 219

ACT THREE: *From Teaching to Reaching or, Improper Spheres of Activity, Winter 1680–Winter 1681* 233
Scene One 235
Scene Two 242
Scene Three 248
Scene Four 253
Scene Five 257
Scene Six 264
Scene Seven 272
Scene Eight 277
Scene Nine 282
Scene Ten 290

ACT FOUR: *From Proof to Punishment or, The Crooked Piece of Man, Spring 1682–Autumn 1682* 297
Scene One 299
Scene Two 305
Scene Three 313
Scene Four 321
Scene Five 328
Scene Six 336
Scene Seven 345
Scene Eight 352
Scene Nine 365
Scene Ten 371
Scene Eleven 377

ACT FIVE: *From Loving Absence to Scorning Presence or, Such Short-Liv'd Happiness, Winter 1682–Winter 1689* 385

Scene One 387
Scene Two 396
Scene Three 402
Scene Four 407
Scene Five 416
Scene Six 422
Scene Seven 431
Scene Eight 440
Scene Nine 450
Scene Ten 454
Scene Eleven 466
Scene Twelve 477
Scene Thirteen 486
Scene Fourteen 497

Epilogue 503
Cast of Characters 513
Plays Performed or Mentioned Throughout Novel 521
Author's Note 523
Acknowledgements 535

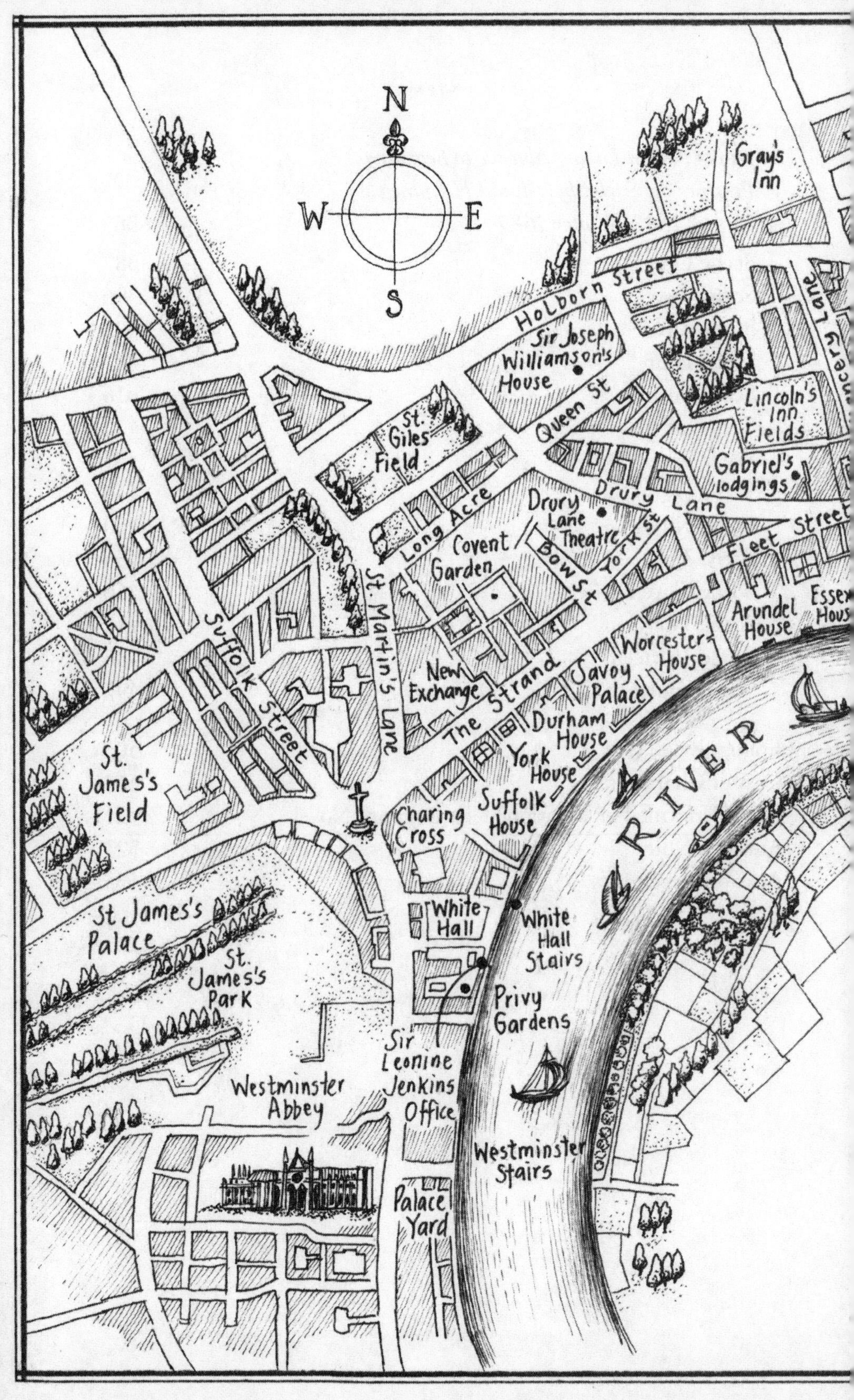
N
W
E
S
Gray's Inn
Holborn Street
Sir Joseph Williamson's House
Queen St
Lincoln's Inn Fields
St. Giles Field
Gabriel's lodgings
Drury Lane
Drury Lane Theatre
Long Acre
Covent Garden
Bow St
York St
Fleet Street
Arundel House
Suffolk Street
St. Martin's Lane
Worcester House
New Exchange
The Strand
Savoy Palace
Durham House
York House
St. James's Field
Suffolk House
Charing Cross
RIVER
White Hall
White Hall Stairs
St James's Palace
St. James's Park
Privy Gardens
Sir Leonine Jenkins Office
Westminster Abbey
Westminster Stairs
Palace Yard

TRIBULATION'S LONDON
1679
Long Lane
Thanet House
London Wall
Bedlam
Moore Gate
Bishop's Gate
Alder Gate
Fleet
River
Newgate
the Gun Bookshop
Old Bailey
Coggin's House
Ludgate Hill
Aphra's House
Cheap Side
St Pauls Churchyard
Cornhill St
Fish Street
Dorset St
Tudor House
Dorset Stairs
Dorset Garden Theatre
Steelyard
Thames St
Tower St
THAMES
London Bridge
Billingsgate
Borough High Street
Southwark
To Gravesend

EXPLANATORY NOTE

Throughout this period, 'Missus' or 'Mrs' were terms of address applied to women who, regardless of their marital status, warranted the social distinction of not being called 'mistress' — a title which carried rather unsavoury connotations. Hence, Tribulation Johnson, despite not being married, is called 'Missus' or 'Mrs Johnson'. Other single, widowed and married women in the novel are also accorded the title 'Missus'.

PROLOGUE

An honest man, being troubled with a scold,
Told her, if she continued so bold,
That he would have a case made out of hand,
To keep her tongue in, under his command

Anatomy of a Woman's Tongue

The potshotten woman tangled in the sheets beside me looked and smelled like a corpse. Paler than the moon which, against nature, still sat in the heavens, and colder than Papa's stare, she lay unmoving, mouth gaping, arms and legs akimbo. It wasn't until I nudged her a few times and she emitted a foul-smelling groan that I saw with no small measure of relief she was alive. I knew where the blame would have fallen had she indeed gone to meet her Maker.

I squinched out of the bed, scratching and wriggling in my night shift, which was now inhabited by the fleas that called the mattress home. The innkeeper had sworn this was his best room. Easy to declare — even honestly — when standards were so low.

Before I washed, I checked my travelling companion once more, pressing my fingers to her scrawny neck. A pulse knocked the tips. What was I supposed to do? We'd a tilt boat to meet.

My mind chirped and wheeled, much like the swallows outside, who rose in a mighty flock to greet the dawn. First breaking through the ice coating the washbasin, I quickly dragged the frigid cloth over my face and under my armpits, rinsing my mouth and rubbing my teeth for good measure.

'God save me.' The words rasped like a blacksmith's chisel.

I swung around and faced the relic stirring in the bed. Abstinence Gumble. A widow and distant cousin of the Bishop of Canterbury, she'd been paid to accompany me to London. With her chicken-coop hair, bleary eyes and shaking hands, she wouldn't have been able to accompany a hymn let alone a person. Why, when a person has been cursed with a Puritan name, did others assume the appellation defined them? The only thing Mrs Gumble had abstained from as she drank the thirsty sailors under the table last night was any modicum of self-control.

Then again, I was called Tribulation and, for some reason, trouble always followed me.

Or, as Papa repeated *ad nauseum*, I caused it.

If you asked me (and no-one ever did), it was really a matter of perspective rather than truth. Though if I hadn't said what I did, when I did, I wouldn't be banished from Chartham and here, at the Gull's Cry in Gravesend, en route to London to live with a relation I'd never met.

With, let's not forget, a tap-shackled beldame in tow.

'Oh, my head, my head,' wailed the tap-unshackled beldame, fingers pressed to her temples. One eye cracked open. 'Please, please, child.' Mrs Gumble pouted. 'Fetch me a posset. A tincture of herbs from an apothecary — anything to stop the raging storm in my skull, quell the churning ocean in my stomach.' With a whimper (and a ripe toot from her rear end), she pulled herself into a sitting position and looked about, smacking her withered lips together.

'Here,' I said, with less sympathy than I should. 'Drink this.' I poured the remnants of wine from a jug into her goblet.

With wide blood-crazed eyes and a canny smile, she gulped it down. 'Good girl,' she said, wiping her mouth on the sheets. 'If you could procure some more, I'll be right in a few hours. The inn-keep will oblige.' She began to ease herself back under the covers.

'But, Mrs Gumble.' I went to the window and pushed it open. The air was redolent with fresh frost, fish, barnacles and bilge water. 'We don't have a few hours. The boat will depart with the tide.' I pointed at the river and said craft.

Already the docks were busy. Men from the East India Company crawled over the rigging of anchored ships, and on the smaller wharves fishing boats were mooring while the tilt boat to London was being prepared for passengers. Whistles, shouts and even a song cleaved the air, giving the day an urgency my ailing chaperone clearly did not feel.

I summoned an authoritarian voice. 'We must make haste, Mrs Gumble.' I flung the cloth back in the water and began to rummage through my burlap. What I donned today was important. I needed to make a good impression.

Mrs Gumble waved a careless hand. 'Haste? Why I can barely move.' She adjusted the pillows and gazed about, blinking. 'It's not so bad here. I'm sure your cousin won't mind if we're a day or two late.' She began to yawn. It turned into a belch she didn't even try to disguise. 'Nor your father for that matter. I mean,' she said, slapping her chest a few times to loosen whatever adhered to the inside then dragging the covers up to her chin like an invalid, 'he hardly needs know.' She winked, as if we were conspirators. 'Let's remain here.'

I stopped midway through pulling out a gown. 'Here? A day or two?'

She nodded amiably and shut her eyes.

I wanted to shake her. Mrs Gumble had seemed so respectable yesterday when we left Canterbury. All smiles and prayers and 'yes Reverend Johnson, no Reverend Johnson' as Papa gave her instructions on where to go once we reached the city and listed his expectations regarding my behaviour. She was especially humble when he gave her coin to cover our expenses, but the moment the coach left the city walls and we were no longer observed, she produced a small leather flask and tipped the contents into her mouth.

I continued to stare at this woman who was supposed to deliver me safely to my cousin's door in Bridewell.

When I was forced to leave Chartham, the village in which I'd spent my entire life, my sister, Bethan, pointed out I should be pleased. I was always threatening to go. But, as I said to her, it wasn't the leave-taking causing me distress as much as the manner of it.

Nevertheless, Bethan *was* right. I'd always dreamed of leaving our small village and seeing London and many more places besides. Maybe the stories I relished had given me ideas that had no place in my head (or any woman's, for that matter, according to Papa), but it was also because I'd always felt there had to be more to life than simply listening. For that's what women did. From the moment we entered the world, we were compelled to keep our lips sealed and ears primed so our fathers, brothers, other men, God, could pour their wisdom into them. So they could tell us what to read and eat, when to retire to bed and attend church, when to speak and, most of all, when and whom to marry. All the while, we had to smile and nod, regardless of our opinion on the matter. 'Yes, sir. No sir. As you wish, sir.' Through it all, we had to be agreeable, lest we upset some unspoken law or rule or, worse, offend the men.

Bethan might have been content to abide by the directives that bound us, obey the constant instructions, but I was not. It required a docility and silence I simply couldn't endure, nor even pretend to. Papa always said I was unnatural — that I'd too much to say for myself. He said a great many other things besides, all of which included the prefix *un*: ungrateful, ungodly, unguarded, unlike other girls.

I oft wondered, especially as I grew older and seemed to forever land in scrapes, if a part of me was broken — the part that would enable me to be more like Bethan and the other village girls, accept what God and our fathers willed.

When Papa first decided I must leave, he hadn't known where to send me. The Bishop of Canterbury had even been consulted. Could I be a teacher for young ladies? A governess? Companion to one of our titled cousins? Anything that didn't involve me remaining in Chartham.

Every suggestion left my blood frostier than a winter morn.

Christmas had been a miserable affair, made worse by the fact that I knew the negotiations for Bethan's nuptials were stalled. The business of removing me took on fresher urgency.

Then, a bolt from the blue. Bethan announced she'd heard from a relation. Though they were once close, time had created a distance between them that, magically, was suddenly bridged. A solution presented itself. I was to board with this lady. Letters went to and fro and finally arrangements were in place.

During this interminable season I seriously contemplated running away, becoming one of those Missing People advertised in the news-sheets all the time, rather than wait for others to decide my fate.

What changed my mind was Bethan.

A few weeks before I was due to leave, my biddable sister came to my room and sat on the bed.

Thirty-three years of age, which made her sixteen years older than me, and having suffered the loss of our many siblings in between, Bethan was so sensible, so obliging. It was as if every negative attribute a female could possess had been distilled into me to abnegate her cooperation. (That's what I overheard Papa saying one day. I was ear-wigging. Again.) She was also ridiculously lovely, with thick chestnut hair and large brown eyes. No wonder Sir Marmaduke had proposed — until he retracted his offer, having, in his mind, found a better alternative.

Surprised at Bethan's temerity (had not Papa forbidden anyone to talk to me?), I determined not to mention her suitor.

She began our conversation like so many others between us — with a long sigh. 'Oh, Tribulation. How often have I warned you to hold that uncouth tongue of yours?'

The question was, I assumed, rhetorical.

My sister, her back straighter than a schoolmaster's cane, hands in her lap, bestowed her usual look of sad remonstrance. 'And still, you never learn.'

'But I do. I just refuse to accept the lesson.'

'Life is not a series of escapades, Tribulation,' she said impatiently, quoting Papa, 'but a matter to be taken seriously. Nevertheless, you've been given an opportunity. What you choose to do from hereon is entirely up to you.'

'If it was up to me, I wouldn't be travelling to London to become a companion to some old woman and her widowed daughter.' I was unable to keep the derision out of my voice.

'Shush, you little fool,' snapped Bethan. It was most uncharacteristic of her, even when dealing with me. 'I never thought it a mistake to surrender you to Lady Adeline's influence. Alas, she put injurious ideas in your head that you allow an unhealthy encouragement.'

I swallowed the sadness thoughts of Lady Adeline always conjured.

After our mother died, followed closely by Bethan's husband, my sister, who up until then was unknown to me as she married when I was but a babe, was forced to return to Chartham. This was mainly so she could take up my care but, over the years, I heard tattle. Bethan's marriage had been conducted in such unseemly haste, it was only once she became Mrs Pratt that she discovered her sweet-faced carpenter husband, Joseph, preferred fists to embraces. Not only that, his death left Bethan in such debt she'd no choice but to return, Papa grudgingly paying her creditors so she could put the past behind her.

I vaguely remember her homecoming. Excited to think I'd have a sibling to bother, especially an older one who could answer the many questions forever spinning in my mind, I was disappointed when she first spent a great deal of time holed up with Papa in his study and then, when free, was so quiet and unassuming. I began to wonder if we were even related. Able to affect the role Mama once held by managing the household, when it came to me she remained remote, barely offering a word. She treated me as if I were a vase she afeared to break, or an exotic pet to be studied. She'd order the maids to dress my hair, prepare food, ensure I learned my letters and repeated the catechism. Together we would attend church and occasionally the market, but we were rarely alone. It wasn't until she'd been back a few years that she started to come to my room when I was abed and spend time reading with me. I loved those moments.

Perhaps feeling sorry for Bethan and the manner of her return to Chartham (or maybe it was that she had to return at all), Lady

Adeline invited her to the manor on a regular basis. Ever since I could remember, milady had lived alone outside the village. When her duties at home were complete, Bethan would oblige, offering the old woman companionship. As I grew older, and no doubt more demanding, Bethan passed the task to me, stating it would keep me from mischief. Each day, I would walk across the fields and, propped in a comfortable chair in Lady Adeline's parlour and, later when she grew ill, by her bed, read a host of stories, plays and poems all from her vast library. As milady said, I may not have had the same education my brother received (for all the good it had done him), but through our reading, I learned not only about history, gods, goddesses, mighty and poor rulers, but many other important lessons: ones only the ancients, the philosophers and poets, could impart.

'And the correspondents,' I added, gesturing to the news-sheets that, unbeknownst to Papa, I also read to her.

Lady Adeline had laughed. 'Correspondents are not poets, nor do their words carry weight — or much truth. Remember that, dear child.'

I remembered that and a great deal more, especially the time we read a play by William Shakespeare. It was called *The Merchant of Venice* and I recall being thrilled — not by the love story or Shylock's misguided intentions, but by the heroine Portia's ability to control her own fate, even donning masculine attire to do so. When I said this to Lady Adeline, she smiled. 'Ah, Tribulation, this is but a feat of imagination to be performed on stage. Only there can a woman be whatever she wishes. Only then is a woman heard.'

'On stage? Or in the imagination?'

'Both,' said Lady Adeline. 'It's why some women pick up the pen.'

I'd run home and burst into the parlour, puffing and panting from my exertions. 'I want to be an actress,' I declared. *Or a writer.* It was an afterthought, but no less potent. Encouraged by Bethan and milady, I was always scribbling down thoughts, inventing tales of derring-do, battles, and even love.

Bethan had begun to rise from her chair. With a mere look, Papa forced her to sit.

'What did you say?' he asked quietly, putting down his Bible.

I repeated my declaration, striking a martial pose to drive the point home.

Papa's eyes blazed. In three strides, he'd crossed the room, and struck me so hard across the cheek I fell to the floor. He stood over me, a rabid dog, barking and slavering. His fury was intense; he could see nothing, not even me. 'As long as you're *my* daughter, you'll not step foot on a stage, do you hear? We've enough shame to bear without you contributing more.'

His reaction was so unexpected, so harsh, I never questioned it. But it stayed with me.

'What makes our cousin different?' I asked Bethan as my memory faded, trying not to let disbelief inflect my words.

'She makes a living from writing.'

I glanced at Bethan suspiciously. 'What does she write?'

Bethan faltered. 'My understanding is she mainly writes on men's behalf.'

I took a moment to drink that in, then frowned. 'What does Papa say? You know how he feels about women who write, even under a man's name.' Or holds opinions, thinks for herself, talks too much. 'And what about her mother?'

A little spark of defiance appeared in Bethan's eyes. 'Truth be told, I haven't been entirely honest with Papa.'

My mouth dropped open.

With a smile, Bethan used a finger to push my jaw back into place. 'Her mother lives nearby, but not under the same roof. I believe they're estranged.'

I regarded Bethan curiously, unable to escape the notion something more was amiss. Certainly, she couldn't meet my gaze.

She rose, patting me on the shoulder. 'You must keep what I've just told you a secret. If Papa learns our cousin lives alone, he'll never agree to send you.'

I could scarce believe it; Bethan was both defying *and* lying to our father — not by telling falsehoods exactly, but by omission. What else was Bethan hiding? And what did she mean by *mainly* on men's behalf? It was this more than anything that not only reconciled me to the plan but allowed me to anticipate the future.

'What's our cousin's name?' I asked.

'Aphra,' she said, peering into corners and lowering her voice, as if she'd conjured an evil sprite. 'Aphra Johnson. At least, that was the name she once went by.'

A tiny thrill raced through me. *Aphra* … Where had I heard that name before?

'Bethan,' I asked suddenly. 'Why are you doing this? Sending me to someone of whom Papa would scarce approve?'

Her face twisted into something unrecognisable, as if some internal wrestle was occurring. Then, her features regained their usual composure.

'Because, for once, I'm being allowed a say in your future.'

I stared at her. 'What about *my* say? What *I* want?'

Her eyes flickered over me. 'Tribulation.' There it was. Another sigh. 'Until you leave here, I fear you won't have a future. Not the kind you deserve.'

She was right about that, but before I could quiz her further, she'd left.

A volley of moist coughs jerked me back to the present. Right now, I had to persuade Mrs Gumble to rise and board the tilt boat tied to a Gravesend pier. Best I was dressed for that. My hands landed on a piece of clothing I'd almost forgotten I'd packed. Before leaving, in a rush of sentimentality, I'd gone to the attic to see if there was anything I wished to take. Apart from a few books, gifts from Lady Adeline that Bethan had made me hide, the best discovery came when I opened a chest to find my brother's old clothes.

Though Fabian died before I was born, fighting against Cromwell in Scotland, I'd grown up hearing about him. Like me, he'd been inclined to defy authority, to land in trouble all the time. It was why he'd gone against Papa's and Mama's wishes and joined the Royalist cause in Scotland. Bethan said, despite their reservations, our parents had been proud. After he died, they were just sad.

I often wondered if they'd used up all their happiness and pride on Fabian, hence there was none left for me.

So I took some of Fabian's clothes in the hope a little of his spirit, his courage, would rub off on me.

I drew them out of the burlap, and another thought crossed my mind. A woman travelling alone would draw comment, unwanted attention and even censure. But a young man — well, no-one would look twice, would they?

Did I dare?

As Mrs Gumble swooned and beseeched me to fetch more drink, I dressed in Fabian's clothes. Being tall for a woman, and unfashionably slender, all I had to do was roll sleeves, tuck shirt and tie hose, then bind back my mop of dark curls and pull down the wide-brimmed hat. The large frilly collar concealed any hint of breasts as did the long, wide-lapelled coat. My own boots served. When I peered in the mirror, I was pleased. If one didn't look too closely, I passed for a fellow quite well.

I sniffed loudly, scratched my non-existent crotch and spat for good measure. Oh, that was ghastly. I fetched the cloth and wiped it up. Next, I'd be pissing out my breeches.

The entire time I was dressing, Mrs Gumble watched, her uninterested gaze slowly turning into round-eyed disbelief.

'What are you doing, Mrs Johnson?' she asked as I turned first one way then the other before the small mirror.

'Playing the breeches part.' I'd heard about actresses who oft played men's roles, causing great excitement. Shakespeare's Portia did — and look how well things turned out for her.

'What on earth for?' she asked.

I sat heavily on the bed, swinging one leg up over the other and clutching my ankle as I'd seen the sailors do last night. 'Well,' I began, drawling and deepening my voice, 'it's like this, Mrs Gumble. You may not wish to make haste, but I do. The way I see it, you were asked to escort me to my cousins' door. Now —' I said, holding up my hand to stop her objections '— you can either do that today, as agreed — even though you're in no fit state to rise, let alone leave the room. Or I can pay what you're owed and you can remain here.'

'What about you, Mrs Johnson?' she asked, eyes on the purse I held in the palm of my hand.

'I'll make my own way to London. I've the directions. I've the fare.' I patted a pocket.

'What about your father?'

I smiled. 'As far as I'm concerned, Mrs Gumble, you may consider your duty discharged. I don't see any reason to inform Papa conditions changed, do you?' I placed the purse in her hand and curled her fingers around it.

She returned my smile, her thin lips retreating over large grey teeth. 'Oh, not at all, Mrs Johnson. Mum's the word. You can count on me.'

I heaved myself off the mattress. 'Thought I could.'

I took one last look around to make sure I hadn't left anything, then threw the burlap over my shoulder and hauled the chest filled with my belongings upright by its sturdy handle. Lord, it was heavy.

'Good day to you, Mrs Gumble, and thank you for your … companionship. I hope your megrim improves.'

I made for the door, dragging the chest. It was going to be quite the nuisance.

'Oh, Mrs Johnson … I mean, *Mr*,' Mrs Gumble said in a sly voice. 'You couldn't see it in your heart to send an old woman up some ale or wine, could you?' She fluttered her lashes. 'Maybe, both?' God help me. 'Remember,' she added, '*Mum's* the word and all.'

She wasn't above a threat.

With a long sigh, I nodded and tugged my hat. '"And only drink'll drown 'em,"' I muttered as I lugged the chest down the rickety wooden stairs and ordered enough ale to not only fell a sow but ensure an old woman forgot I was ever there.

ACT ONE

Winter 1679–Spring 1679

From Bride to Bridewell or, Preferment Postponed

… when a Woman has once lost her Modesty, she is fit for all sorts of Mischief.

Thomas Dangerfield's Answer To A Certain Scandalous Lying Pamphlet, Entitled *Malice Defeated or, The Deliverance of Elizabeth Cellier*, Thomas Dangerfield

The penalties and discouragements attending the profession of an author fall upon women with a double weight …

Public Characters, Anonymous

SCENE ONE

An old maid is now thought such a curse as no metric fury can exceed, looked on as the most calamitous creature in nature.

The Ladies Calling, Anonymous (Richard Allestree)

The wherry pitched wildly against the water stairs, causing me to stumble as I leaped off the craft. I found my feet and quickly turned to slip a coin in the oarsman's filthy palm, colliding with other passengers who cursed and pushed past me roughly. Once the last person disembarked, the waterman signalled me forwards and, together, we heaved my wretched chest out of the boat and carried it up to the landing.

Before I could thank him, he was back in the prow, herding a fresh flock of customers on board.

Forced to stand aside, I took in my surroundings with a little frisson of satisfaction. Against the odds, I was here, in the ward of Farringdon Without.

Before me rose the magnificence of Dorset Garden Theatre. I could identify the building because, as the wherry steered towards the stairs, a couple of passengers had begun a heated debate about which of the two London theatre companies was better. There was the

Duke's Company (named after the King's brother, James the Duke of York) based at Dorset Garden Theatre — the structure looming before us — and also the King's Company, whose members performed at Drury Lane. In the end, the passengers couldn't agree which company provided better entertainment but decided both buildings, at least, were deserving of admiration. Not having seen Drury Lane (yet), I had to admit, Dorset Garden was most impressive. Built of white stone, it comprised three storeys and was capped by a little domed tower replete with flagpole. Large windows captured views of the Thames behind me. The two higher levels were jettied, protecting the many patrons milling in front of and upon wide steps that led to a grand entrance.

There were women in flounced dresses and velvet capes, wearing pattens over their pretty shoes. Their faces were artificially pale; some wore black patches upon their cheeks and breasts. These included star shapes, a crescent moon and even a horse and carriage galloping across a generous décolletage. The poor beasties, forever plunging into a fleshy canyon. Jewels glistened in the grey afternoon light: rings sat atop satin gloves, dripped from ears and adorned white necks. I'd never seen so many bedizened people in one place, not even at the bishop's ball in Canterbury, where church men strutted about in their religious finery worse than peacocks.

The men were just as ostentatiously garbed. Frills and laces burst from necks and the ends of sleeves, and towering periwigs made them seem impossibly tall, as did their brightly coloured heels. I wished Bethan could see them and was ever so glad Papa could not.

A nearby group threw some pointed looks in my direction, laughing. I tried to ignore them, lifting my chin and smoothing the lapels on my coat. Fabian's clothes might be outdated, but they'd allowed me to travel unscathed. Dressed as a man, I'd enjoyed a liberty the likes of which I'd never experienced and suspected I'd forever envy.

Barrows and carts set up to trade everything from hot chestnuts to fans and crude vizards shared the space outside the theatre. Between a couple of flaming braziers stood two young women selling oranges out of woven baskets. It wasn't their oranges that caught my eyes so much as the way their breasts balanced on the brinks of their necklines, threatening to burst their linen banks. At least three carriages and a well-worn sedan chair pulled up as I gawped, setting down more theatregoers who swiftly ascended the steps.

Time for me to move as well. I found the note with my cousin's address.

Dorset Street, upon Dorset Rise, next to the sign of the Quill and Ink.

Flakes of snow began to spiral from the heavens and a chill wind rose from the water. I shivered. The sunshiney promise of the morning had dissolved into a typical wintry day. If only my stomach would settle. My fist flew to my mouth as I stifled a rather unpleasant belch. Dear Lordy, my belly was rioting worse than a London apprentice.

What did I expect after purchasing oysters from a dirty-looking urchin? When the tilt boat disgorged its Gravesend passengers at Billingsgate Dock in the heart of London earlier, allowing those continuing upriver to change craft, I'd been starving. Keen to put Mrs Gumble behind me, I'd foregone breaking my fast, determined to be at the river on time. Clearly, oyster-girl had seen a mark. The creatures may have just been shucked, but they weren't fresh. No wonder she'd disappeared the moment I paid her. They were slimy and very metallic. Since then, my stomach hadn't stopped protesting, and not just because the wherry careened side to side the entire way to Dorset Stairs.

Still, there'd been a great deal to distract me. While I'd heard and read so much about London, it defied expectations. Having come from the country with its expanse of sky and fields and small clusters of houses and shops, the city was just so … so … full. Seeing it crammed with buildings, people, animals, vehicles, sound, smells and so much more, I was reminded of an adult trying to don a child's gown and finding the seams split or the length wrong. It was bursting with life, all wreathed in thick grey and brown smoke. Even before I caught a glimpse of the capital, I could smell it. With every push of the oars, the air had grown denser, thicker. It coated the roof of my mouth, filled my nostrils. The smells of piss, shit and a ripeness like rancid meat hung in the air, as if London were a corpse that hadn't yet been buried.

A line from one of John Donne's poems sprang to mind: 'In that the world's contracted thus.' Aye, that was the city, the bridge and river too. Cramped, crowded. Noisy. There were the frenzied shouts of watermen trying to avoid slamming into each other. Dock workers directing cranes and crawling across decks, yelling as cargo was unloaded. The grind and screech of carriage wheels, carts, the endless tolling of church bells, the cacophony of thousands of voices all competing to be heard. There were white faces, red and black ones, brown too. People with arms missing, eyes, a man with a wooden stump where his leg should be. There were chickens clucking, swine snuffling, a herd of sheep, some ribbed cows. Skinny dogs, tails-awagging, tongues lolling, darted between legs, thrust their noses into snow, buckets, barrels, groins, barking joyously or whining in fear.

Wherever I looked (and my head was like a weathervane in high winds), it was pungent, heady. No market day in Chartham, Wye or even Canterbury could compare.

It was bloody marvellous.

A bell then a whistle sounded, making me jump. Suddenly, all the milling people headed in the same direction, towards the wide theatre doors, where a withered man waited, rattling a large box. I had to decide — to see the play or not to see the play? I struck a pose (a rather provocative habit I'd developed, according to Bethan, only matched by my tendency to use 'ripe' language now and then; one can't live in the country without harvesting some), holding my chin, the other hand on my hip, frowning.

Before I could reach a decision, a young man in a long coat and dark hat approached.

'May I be of assistance, sir?' he asked warily.

My arms fell to my side.

He offered a weak smile. 'I can tell you're not from here.' He was too polite to reference my clothes directly. 'And, since you're not going inside —' he gestured to the theatre '— I'm guessing you might be lost?' He doffed his hat. 'Timothy Shale, publisher, at your service.'

Mr Shale waited patiently as, playing for time, I lowered the burlap back to the ground, fussing when the strap became caught in a dangling coat sleeve. As a woman, it was most improper to speak to this gentleman … but then, I wasn't a woman. Not on the outside. Better still, for the first time in my life, there was no-one to tell me what I could or couldn't do or say, let alone rebuke me. Nor did I have to wait to be introduced. I could speak to whomever I damn well pleased. This nice man seemed very pleasing.

It was then I realised the flaw in my plan. I couldn't reveal my sex. It would cast aspersions upon me and, worse, upon my cousin, that she could house such an improper female. Someone who boldly strutted about the streets like a common slut, pretending an authority to which she'd no right. For her sake and my own, I had to maintain my façade.

'My name is … Howell Johnson … errr …' I'd told the curious passengers on the tilt boat I was a student going down to Oxford. A flapping poster, advertising a past performance at Dorset Garden and stuck on the nearest colonnade, caught my eye. The name, Thomas Otway, stood out in bold letters: he was identified as author of the play *Friendship in Fashion*. Dare I?

'I'm a writer,' I finished.

Well, I did write. Most of it execrable. All of it in secret. Poor efforts I never kept long before burning, lest Papa found them. Well, Papa wasn't here. I was. I could claim to be whatever I wanted; may God forgive me.

There was a burst of excited laugher. A woman with long feathers sticking out of her hat and a decorative vizard hiding her face slapped a man in a frock coat with her fan, before he swept her through the theatre doors, flapping and squawking. They were like dressed chickens.

'A writer,' repeated Mr Shale, indicating we should move further away, especially as more carriages and chairs arrived, unloading people faster than a Three Cranes docker. He grabbed the other handle on the chest and carried it out of the way with me. 'It's a pastime I indulge in on occasion myself. What a stroke of luck you being here. Though,' he said, lowering the trunk, 'not really. After all — theatre —' he gestured to the building '— writer.' He flipped his hand towards me. 'Made for each other; like chocolate and cinnamon.'

It so happened I liked the combination very much.

Mr Shale jerked his chin towards the theatre again. 'It's almost three of the clock. Play's about to start, though I've seen it already.' He rocked backwards and forwards on his heels as he spoke, like an excited child. 'To see Mr Thomas Betterton strutting the stage, declaiming in that voice of his, well … His turn as Goodville,' he pointed to the poster from which I'd borrowed an occupation, 'was exceptional. The current production, *The Libertine*, is excellent and will test the sourest of critics' minds. And believe me when I say, some are so very, very sour.' Was the man preening? 'Though I can't help but feel a great deal of disparagement arises from the fact that the plays are being performed by the *Duke's* Company, what with the King's brother being so out of favour with the Commons because he's Catholic and in line to the throne now the king has failed to produce a legitimate heir. It all just adds to fears of a Papist resurgence, doesn't it?' Upon seeing the expression on my face, he paused. 'Forgive me, Mr Johnson. I shouldn't be saying things like that — about the royal succession and such — not with the mood in the city so volatile, especially with all this Popish Plot business.'

I'd heard of the Popish Plot. It was impossible not to, even in Chartham. The news-sheets reported little else: how a former priest named Titus Oates had told the King and Privy Council about a dreadful plan, concocted by Jesuits in league with many powerful English Catholic nobles, to assassinate his Majesty and place his brother, the Romish Duke of York, on the throne in his stead. As if to prove Mr Oates's claims, the magistrate who'd taken down his evidence was murdered. Since then, there had been many arrests and executions. It was said Newgate was bursting at the seams with Papists and plotters.

And here I was outside a theatre that claimed a Catholic as royal patron. Papa would have conniptions.

The crowd had all but moved inside and the reluctant snow turned into steady sleet. Icy shards hurled themselves to the ground, lodging in cheeks, sticking to clothes. I glanced up and rubbed my face.

'We must escape this foul weather,' said Mr Shale. 'Pray, Mr Johnson, who *are* you here to see?'

The whole time Mr Shale had been talking, and thank goodness he had, my mind was working swiftly.

'Actually,' I began, 'I'm here to see Mrs Aphra Johnson. Do you happen to know her? I have her address …' I reached into my pocket.

Mr Shale's face altered. His smile disappeared. His wide grey eyes grew colder than a fish's fin. 'Mrs Johnson? *Aphra*, you say. Hmpf.'

Was that a disparaging noise?

'She's my neighbour.'

This *was* a good sign.

Mr Shale's eyes narrowed and not just because of the bitter flurries. 'Are you *related* to her?'

'Indeed,' I said, marvelling at how such a promising word sounded so ill upon his lips. A wave of nausea clenched my stomach. It made my next utterance sharper than intended. 'I'm her cousin.'

'I'm sorry to hear that.'

'*What?*' My belly began to rumble and the feeling of discomfort grew. An unexpected wave of empathy for Mrs Gumble accompanied it. I decided to ignore Mr Shale's sardonic tone. I needed assistance and fast. 'I'm uncertain exactly …' I waved a casual arm '… which direction to head in.'

Mr Shale sighed wearily. 'Since you seem to have arrived ill-equipped to deal with your —' he gestured to the chest '— luggage, and your destination is next door to mine, I feel obliged to help you.'

'Oh, *please*.' Sarcasm shaped my response. 'Don't discommode yourself on my account.'

'I must.' He glanced skywards. 'We should try and make it there before the storm breaks.'

The day had darkened and not just because the sleet was thickening. Bulging slate clouds glowered above. In the distance, there was a long, low growl, much like I'd heard as the boat drifted past the Tower. Only this was no lion. I mended my tone somewhat. 'I'm very grateful, sir.'

'Let us tarry no longer then.' Mr Shale clamped hold of one end of the chest, waited until I hefted the other, and headed quickly towards the street to the left of Dorset Garden Theatre.

Houses of stone, with fine glazed windows and snow scattered like dandruff on their stoops, stood side by side with narrow, ramshackle buildings. We squeezed past men outside a tavern, crowded around braziers, hands in fingerless gloves waving to and fro above the flames. Further along, women young and old stood mithering behind carts and barrows half-filled with day-old offerings. I studied them, collecting the sights the way a tinker did cast-offs. There was a woman with no teeth, a child with a stump where his arm should be, a man with a twisted foot. There was a broken window in a heaving tavern, poorly mended with pigskin. Mould adorned the window of the book-seller. A contented cat with a black patch over one eye licked its paws beneath a costermonger's cart. A little girl with pink cheeks sat wrapped in a shawl beside it, sharing her vittles, sticking out her tongue to capture the flurries. Days-old snow had gathered in crevices and corners, barely disguising filthy walls, veined with the same soot and grime marking the faces of those who paused to inspect through curious eyes the stranger linked to Mr Shale by a battered old chest.

Though I was able to cope with the fusty stench of unwashed bodies, ordure and damp, squalid corners, it was the smell of cooking meat that almost undid me. Just past an ordinary, I was forced to stop. I gripped my middle as bile rose.

'Are you alright, Mr Johnson?' asked Mr Shale.

'I ate something that didn't agree with me.' I was afraid if I named the culprits, I'd not be responsible for my actions.

Mr Shale put down his end of the chest and took the burlap from my shoulder, transferring it to his. 'Let me ease your burden.' He considered me. 'You're very pale. Can you walk a little further? The house is just up this hill.'

The hill took on the proportions of Mount Olympus, but I grimaced and nodded, praying either the house or a privy (and preferably both) would materialise soon.

Sure enough, less than a minute later, Mr Shale stopped. 'Your cousin's house, sir.'

Together, we lowered the chest to the ground.

Four storeys high, jettied from the first storey up, looking like a gust of wind might topple it over, the house rose just above its neighbours. It was completely unremarkable, even in a street filled with unremarkable.

I stood beneath the curtain of sleet, unable to move, blocking the thoroughfare.

People pushed past, muttering abuse, spitting, looking over their shoulders, raising brows at Mr Shale who, swiping moisture from his face, shrugged.

Finally, he cleared his throat. 'That's me.' He signalled the business next door. 'The Quill and Ink.'

I tried to thank him, I really did. Reassure him he need not remain. My limbs began to feel as if they no longer belonged to me, as if I was a puppet with severed strings.

'Shall I?' asked Mr Shale impatiently, and, when I didn't budge, he rapped on the door.

There was a rattle, the creak of a handle, and the door swung open.

A woman with dark, coffee-coloured hair threaded with silver, deep hooded eyes and a rosy complexion stood on the threshold. She wore a generous smile. The moment she saw us, it vanished.

'Oh,' she said, disappointment rearranging her face. 'It's you, Mr Shale.' Her eyes swept over me. 'I was expecting …' Her voice trailed off.

Mr Shale waited for me to speak, but I couldn't, daren't.

'Good evening, Mrs Behn.'

Did he say *Behn*? Surely this couldn't be *the* Aphra Behn?

Mr Shale sniffed somewhat disapprovingly, and reluctantly doffed his hat. 'May I present your cousin, Mr Howell Johnson? I found him at Dorset Stairs.'

'*Howell* Johnson?' said the woman, frowning, studying me top to toe and back again. 'I may not have seen him for almost twenty years, but this person is *not* Howell Johnson.'

Mr Shale's face blanched. 'Forgive me, Mrs Behn. I didn't … I wouldn't … He told me he …' He huffed and blew. 'You scoundrel,' he said.

'My name is —' Pain tore through my belly. I clutched it with both hands and fell to my knees. A great guttural groan escaped. God was paying me back for abandoning Mrs Gumble, making her complicit in my deception.

For treating life as another escapade.

'Oh, my lord,' said Mrs Behn, bending to assist.

Before I could utter a word of warning, I erupted. A river of hot human lava, chunks of undigested oysters spewed forth on a stream of breakfast ale, splattering my brother's breeches, Mrs Behn's skirt and Mr Shale's stockings. It poured across the doorstep and melded with the downpour.

Mr Shale vaulted out of the way with a yelp that made the dog opposite scramble to its feet. He stared at the mess upon his shoes, his hose, wrinkling his nose.

Mrs Behn didn't shriek, nor attempt to move. She simply stared as I purged and purged.

When nothing except a couple of empty burps issued, I calmly wiped my mouth with the back of my sleeve.

I'd so wanted to make a good impression, win my cousin over with manners, cleverness, wit and daring: ensure from the outset she'd no cause to regret taking me in.

Instead, dressed like a cavalier of old, I'd cast my insides all over her doorstep.

All over her.

I rose on shaky legs, one hand resting on the doorframe. Determined to muster what remained of my dignity, I smoothed the coat, the aged jacket and large collar, tugged the stained lace cuffs and tried to pretend everything was as it should be.

I raised wet lashes. 'I *am* family, Mrs Behn.' I glared pointedly at Mr Shale then turned back. 'I'm your cousin Howell's youngest daughter.'

Mr Shale looked me up and down with undisguised revulsion. 'God's truth! You're a maid.'

'Tribulation.' I spat, and wiped my mouth again. 'Tribulation Johnson.'

'My, my,' said Mrs Behn finally, hands on hips, looking from me to Mr Shale to the mucilaginous mess. 'Haven't you been aptly named?'

SCENE TWO

A learned woman is thought to be a comet
that bodes mischief wherever it appears.
Bathusa Makin — ran a school in Tottenham
High Road London in the mid-1600s

Little more than an hour later, I was washed and wearing clean clothes. I sat in the parlour, a filled wine glass beside me, and a bowl of delicious chocolate (with cinnamon) cupped in my hands. An elderly woman with grey hair peeping beneath her cap, a large nose and kind hazel eyes, introduced as Nest (if I didn't know differently, I would have thought her Mrs Behn's mother), had seen to my every comfort, even insisting the two young housemaids, Millie and Molly, took my clothes to the laundress — after they'd cleaned the stoop, that was.

They were not happy.

While Mrs Behn tended the fire in the small, smoking hearth, I studied my surroundings. Teetering piles of books and papers rested against damp-sullied walls, sat upon tables and chairs, and reclined along the mantelpiece. There were plates of half-eaten food, replete with lumps of hard cheese and smears of grease. Bottles lolled on a threadbare rug and any number of drinking glasses were toppled on the scattered tables and even reclined in the larger cushioned chairs.

Stains marked all the furniture — as did deep scratches, which had either lifted polish off the wood or rent the fabric into shreds. The latter was likely the responsibility of the large ginger cat splayed across the top of one of the chairs. I saw her claw the headrest before she stretched, yawned to reveal a row of tiny daggers, and then settled herself down. She kept one golden eye upon me.

Nest gestured. 'That be Hecate.' She rubbed the top of the cat's head. I swear Hecate growled.

'And a right little witch she is too,' said Mrs Behn, throwing herself in the chair opposite. 'But don't tell Jonathan I said that.'

Jonathan Cross, I was to learn, was an apothecary and one of the three lodgers who shared the house with Mrs Behn and Nest. The other two, brothers Michael and Robert Tetchall, were scriveners. There'd been another gentleman, Roger, a printer. About to get married, he'd left to prepare rooms at his parents' house for his new bride. His absence was one of the reasons my presence was possible: they needed another lodger to share the rent monies.

Mrs Behn lamented the state of the parlour. 'However,' she said, scanning the room with a frown, 'I refuse to apologise, which implies I'm somehow responsible for it. This is the men's doing. I've told them, they can either clean it themselves or pay Millie and Molly more to keep it in order. Alas, as you now witness, they do neither.' She swiftly explained that even in its current disarray, it was still more comfortable than the draughty kitchen. More importantly, it was away from the curious stares and talkative lips of the maids.

Two large windows faced the street, admitting a great deal of the silvery afternoon light. Sleet struck the windows, which rattled with the occasional gust. Dust coated the tables; cobwebs festooned the candles and corners. Yet, despite the dirt and lived-in appearance, never mind the odour — wet socks, bodies that had an aversion to soap, rancid meat and cat — it was cosy.

If Papa knew the kind of house he'd sent me to — one in such shambles let alone shared with three men — he never would have allowed me to step outside the manse, never mind Chartham.

Papa might not like it, but if I'd been a lanthorn I would have glowed.

'Are you feeling better?' asked Mrs Behn, tucking her legs under, and rearranging her skirts.

'I am, thank you. And again, I'm so sorry —'

'Hush, hush,' she said. 'No need to keep apologising. Though it's not an entrance I'll forget in a hurry.'

Nest snorted. I couldn't help but laugh. 'Nor me.'

'Now, let me have a good look at you.'

With the smuts and vomit removed and dressed as a woman once more, I must have seemed a different person. 'Well ...' She exhaled, considering me with a peculiar intensity, then appeared to stop herself. 'I confess, I'd never heard of your existence before Bethan's letter. I was most astonished. The last I heard from her ... oh, it must be almost twenty years ago — before you were born.'

'I confess, Mrs Behn, up until a few weeks ago, I'd never heard of you either.'

'Is that so?' She appeared puzzled.

'Not as a relation. No ... But I have to ask,' I began hesitantly. 'Are you by chance *the* Aphra Behn, the playwright?'

I held my breath.

'Indeed, I am.'

I began to fizz with excitement as thousands of questions rushed into my head. Before I could even consider what to ask first, what to say next, Mrs Behn held up a finger to forestall me. 'Right this minute, the only topic I want to discuss is *you*.' She studied me keenly. 'You've a most unusual name, particularly as you're not of Puritan stock.'

I sighed. My name was often a whip used to lash me. 'I console myself at least no-one forgets it.'

Mrs Behn chuckled. 'Which can work both for and against one, can it not? Mine's the same. Believe it or not,' she said, 'there's a St Aphra. The patron saint of female penitents. She was a prostitute who found Christ due to the ministration of St Narcissus. From whore to martyr via a popinjay — quite the journey. Speaking of which.' She rapped a hand on the arm of her chair. 'Tell me all about yours, and why you arrived dressed in Fabian's clothes.'

I'd already given a rushed explanation as I changed, but this time I gave both Mrs Behn and Nest the story in full. I didn't hold back about Mrs Abstinence Gumble either and was gratified when both she and Nest laughed heartily.

'What's in a name?' asked Mrs Behn and, reaching over, she plucked my wine glass from the table, pushing it into my hand. 'A toast,' she declared. 'Welcome, my dear. May all your tribulations be behind you, now you are before us.' We raised vessels and drank.

Over the lip of my drink, I caught Mrs Behn regarding me with that strange expression once more. It made me catch my breath. She wasn't simply looking *at* me, but *inside* me. It was fierce, yet also filled with a kind of yearning. When I thought I could bear it no longer and must ask if something was awry, she turned away.

After a while, and as our conversation wandered, I thought I must have imagined it.

We spoke of my impressions of London, Dorset Garden, how the family in Chartham fared. Mrs Behn revealed she and Bethan had spent a great deal of time together as children, when our families all lived in Canterbury. Then, she relocated to London and, much to her bafflement, a couple of years later, our family left Canterbury. She never did learn where the family had moved to or why, as all communication ceased. It was a subject never spoken about at home either. I hadn't allowed it to concern me.

She shrugged. 'We lost the connection. It happens. I didn't know Bethan married. Or was widowed. And I was so sorry to hear of Jacquetta's passing. That must have been difficult for you, losing your mother so young.'

I lowered my head. Difficult didn't begin to describe it.

'So,' continued Mrs Behn, 'imagine my surprise, when, out of nowhere, a letter from your sister arrives asking if you can come and board.' She paused. 'And Bethan's getting married? Again?' She patted her hair which, uncovered, fell in thick, soft waves framing her forehead and cheeks. I liked her hands: long-fingered with little calluses where the quill must rest. 'She was always so very beautiful. Your father must have chased suitors away.'

'Hounded, more like.'

There wasn't anyone of our acquaintance who didn't express surprise Bethan wasn't married again; they publicly put it down to her godliness in assisting her widower father while privately saying her experiences with her first husband likely put her off matrimony for life. Papa declared it had taken years, but she'd become the embodiment of the Bible's ideal woman — silent and disinclined to assert herself or usurp authority over a man.

It was only when Sir Marmaduke moved into the neighbourhood that Bethan's apparent reluctance to wed again and Papa's inexplicable accommodation of this altered.

'I'm guessing there's a story to be told,' said Mrs Behn softly, assessing my every expression. 'If you're willing, I'd like to hear it.'

'The real reason I'm here?' The moment had come. Truth would out.

'Please.'

And so, I told her.

Ever since I could remember, Sir Marmaduke (or Sir M, as I called him), was a presence around the village. He was yet another Puritan volte face who, after his Majesty returned from exile to take the throne, became more Cavalier than the King's spaniels. A distant relation of Lady Adeline's, once he discovered the estate was his to inherit, he became a fixture. Or 'something to be endured, like a canker' as Lady Adeline would say. On rare occasions, he'd visit the manse. I'd always been kept out of the way, as I usually was when anyone of note called. But you don't grow up in a big rambling house without knowing all the nooks and crannies and places to listen and spy from. Two wives the man had chased to the grave (or so Cook said). After listening to Sir M, I was convinced he'd bored them to death.

Then, on a cool, grey October day last year, a few months after Lady Adeline died, plunging me and Bethan into despair, Papa demanded we join him, Mr Walter Parker (Papa's quietly spoken and kind curate) and Sir Marmaduke for dinner.

I tried to look on the bright side. Sir M might be ancient and inclined to hawk and spit regardless of the company, but he'd travelled. Hopefully, he'd have a treasure trove of tales. As I dressed, I began to gather questions — not that I dared ask them. I wasn't a complete fool.

After being appraised as if we were cattle en route to market, Bethan and I greeted Sir M and took our seats. The afternoon wore on and, as I suspected, Bethan and I may as well have been vacant chairs for all the notice we received. We were there merely to bear witness to the men's erudition — I just wished they'd hurry up and reveal some.

Papa and Sir M stuffed their cheeks and grunted approval at each other, oblivious to anyone else. Only the laden dishes captured their interest, and then only for as long as it took to empty them.

When he'd had a sufficiency, Sir M sat back, hands linked atop his swollen belly, and began to regale us. Far from entertaining, he was duller than a block of wood. On second thoughts, wood at least has splinters. He droned on about his newly inherited estate, the rents that were due, how he intended to enclose more land for sheep and remove the tenants, punctuating his diatribes by hawking great globs onto the floor.

It took all my willpower not to shudder. Mr Parker wasn't so successful.

The afternoon grew cooler, the fire was stoked and more candles were lit. I'd counted the number of fleurs-de-lis bordering the arras opposite (fifty-seven), the number of crumbs decorating the tablecloth in front of Sir M (three hundred and two) and began plucking at a loose stitch on the waist of my gown. I started to imagine the entire thing unravelling, so when I stood, my skirts dropped to the floor. How would Papa react? And what about Sir M? Would that give him pause?

I pulled harder at the thread.

I stifled yet another yawn, my eyes watering, wondering why I was there …

My ears finally pricked when I heard the word 'murder'. Papa, Sir M and Mr Parker were discussing the death of a London magistrate, Sir Edmund Berry Godfrey, who'd been found stabbed at the bottom of a hill. The men picked over the details like the servants would later the carcasses of the pigeons.

Then, in a bold gesture, Papa threw down his napkin and declared his Majesty foolish to offer one thousand pounds for information leading to the prosecution of Sir Edmund's murderers, as it would attract any vagabond with a tale.

'A thousand pounds!' cooed Sir M.

'That's a great sum,' said Mr Parker, who was inclined to state the obvious.

However, it was also incorrect. The amount was a falsehood I couldn't allow to go unchallenged.

'It's not one thousand pounds, Papa,' I blurted. 'It's five hundred.'

There were sharp intakes of breath. Sir M's brows rose so high up his forehead, I thought they'd take flight. Bethan shot me such a look of dread I should have keeled over. Mr Parker stared at the table. I'd not only spoken without being bidden and revealed I'd read Papa's news-sheets without permission; worse, I'd corrected Papa. In company.

There was silence. The deep, solid kind that crushes you with its weight.

A trapped fly buzzed against the window. In the distance, I heard a door slam. One of the servants cracked his knuckles.

But then, the unexpected happened. Papa pushed his plate away and stood. 'I'll deal with your impertinence later, Tribulation. For now, there's a far more important matter to deal with. I'm not going to allow a mere garrulous chit to spoil it.'

What could be more important to Papa than chastising his child? And in public.

Papa rearranged his robe and began to strut around the room. 'Over the last few weeks, Sir Marmaduke and I have held many a discussion about how we can best preserve — how shall I put it? The ideals of the past — which are at serious risk of being lost forever.' He folded his hands behind his back. 'One of the ways to ensure they're maintained is through family. Right, Sir Marmaduke?'

'Indeed,' grunted the squire.

Papa looked at his curate. 'Mr Parker?'

'A-aye, sir.' Mr Parker dabbed his upper lip with a napkin. 'Family is the masterpiece of God's creation.' He flashed a meaningful look at Bethan.

I was watching her too, for Papa had come to a stop behind her chair and, hesitating a fraction, rested his hands on her shoulders. She stiffened.

'That's why —' Papa leaned over '— I'm pleased to inform you that my dear friend, Sir Marmaduke, a pure soul with a pure purpose —'

I coughed. Let's not forget two dead wives and ousted tenants.

'— has asked for your hand in marriage.'

Bethan lowered her head.

She knew.

'Naturally, I've accepted. Come summer, Bethan will be Lady Marmaduke Babcock. The new lady of the manor.' He beamed. 'What an honour for us. What an honour for *you*, Bethan.' He tightened his grip, forcing agreement.

Bethan paled and winced. Mr Parker sucked in his breath. Sir M parted his greasy lips to reveal a row of slate stumps. Then, he spat.

The trapped fly beat itself to death against the glass.

My head was filled with broken shards. I couldn't move. Sir M? Bethan as Lady Marmaduke? Sleeping beside that corpulent, spitting, ponderous old windbag? That was no honour — that was a travesty. Well, if Bethan, the paragon of womanhood, wouldn't say anything, I bloody well would.

I leaped to my feet. 'Nay.' My chair toppled back and struck the floor. A servant raced to right it.

'What did you say?' Papa's hands slithered from Bethan's shoulders.

'Nay.'

My voice was a bell. 'Nay. Nay. *No.*' I stared first at Sir M then, showing a defiance I'd never dared before, Papa. As I was taller than him by some inches, he was forced to tilt his head to meet my eyes. 'I won't have it.'

Papa guffawed. '*You* won't have it. Oh, that's rich, that is. Fortunately, it's not up to you.'

Mr Parker made to move.

'Sit down, Parker,' snapped Papa. The curate slowly sank back. 'As for you, Tribulation, I may have promised your dear mother I'd keep you under my roof until such times as a suitable preferment be found, but I do *not* have to tolerate your insubordination. You'll be sorry you ever —'

'Wait,' said Sir Marmaduke, holding up a hand. He levered himself upright using the table, his stomach almost preventing him. 'Just wait a minute.'

Papa's mouth snapped shut, but his eyes fired with an arquebus's precision. 'What is it?' he all but snarled at the squire. You didn't interrupt when he was in the middle of disciplining his household.

Unfazed, Sir M continued. 'The girl has a point.' Thick fingers paddled in my direction.

Maybe the ancient dullard wasn't so bad after all.

'She does?' Papa was as bewildered as a newborn foal.

'Aye,' said Sir Marmaduke, and he began to lumber towards us. 'After all,' he panted, 'why would I take the older, used one when there's a much younger, unbroken version of the same? Eh?' He chuckled. 'Tell me that, Howell?'

There was a beat when no-one spoke.

Then Bethan, who I'd never heard raise her voice, shouted, 'You take *me*, Sir Marmaduke. Your agreement is for *me*. Papa —' She turned and clung to Papa's robe, staring at him imploringly. 'Tell him, please. You promised …'

I don't recall too much after that as Bethan and I were bundled from the room by Mr Parker and a footman.

What I do remember is later that night Papa came to my room, brows beetling, anger rising from him like steam off freshly baked bread. A decision had been made. I was to be sent away.

'At least until Sir Marmaduke comes to his senses,' he said. It was then I saw Bethan loitering in the doorway. Her eyes red, her face swollen.

'How can he come to what he lacks?' I asked.

Papa's eyes narrowed. 'And you,' he added.

'Never,' I said, the defiance of earlier having not yet run its course.

'So be it,' said Papa, and he marched out of the room, Bethan, with one last forlorn shake of her head, eyes aswim, in his wake.

SCENE THREE

Wit in women is apt to have bad consequences; like a sword without scabbard, it wounds the wearer and provokes assailants. I am sorry to say the generality of women who have excelled in wit have failed in chastity …

Elizabeth Montagu

'And that's why I'm here,' I finished, my shrug an attempt to mimic an indifference I didn't feel. 'I'm to be kept out of the way so Papa can secure this marriage.'

Mrs Behn stood to draw the curtains, and when she returned, she surprised me by bestowing a fierce hug. I wondered what for. Rigid at first, unaccustomed to being embraced, I slowly melted. It was nice. Better than nice. She smelled of roses and musk.

Curled in our chairs, we continued to talk as evening drew its dusky curtain. Nest went to an ordinary to purchase food. Six bells had not long resounded when, in a rush of noise and cold, the boarders arrived home. First were the scriveners, Michael and Timothy Tetchall. Both had unruly strawberry thatches, freckles across their cheeks and almost no lips. Michael, older and shorter, barely reached my breasts. The top of Timothy's head came to my shoulder. After welcoming me, they excused themselves, whispering to each other. Not long after,

Jonathon Cross, the apothecary, bowled into the sitting room and made his way straight to Hecate, who he bundled into his arms and showered with kisses. The feline purred so loudly it was like an anchor chain being raised. It was only when he put her down that he noticed the rest of us. He took a step back.

'Mrs Behn! What news?' Then he saw me. He slapped his forehead. 'What day is it? Oh. Damn. You must be Mrs Johnson. We didn't expect —' He looked around the room and screwed up his nose. 'Ah. My humblest apologies. Michael and Timothy have neglected to tidy up.'

Mrs Behn blinked.

Before she could say anything, Jonathan continued. 'I'll have a word with them — again, Mrs Behn, I promise. You mustn't think we're always like this,' he said to me, while flicking a snowstorm of cat hair from his jacket.

Mrs Behn mouthed, *They are.*

I pretended to clear my throat.

He weaved his way between the chairs and stools with difficulty, as he was quite portly — Jonathan's size was matched by his wide, twinkling smile. He thrust out a hand and I put my own in it. He exacted the most elegant bow, spoiled only when his arse knocked over a vase. He didn't stay long either — not even to salvage the vase — as he had a dinner engagement. With a wave to Mrs Behn and another kiss for Hecate, he left.

'There now, you've met the lodgers,' said Mrs Behn.

Nest returned with hot eel pies. I ate cautiously at first, but with each mouthful my insides felt warmer and more settled. The wine helped. When Nest began clearing our plates, I went to assist but was shooed away.

'Talk to the missus. You've catching up to do.'

'We do indeed,' said Mrs Behn, passing Nest her plate. 'Though it doesn't all have to be accomplished in one night. Friendships take time, do they not?'

How did I admit I wouldn't know? I'd no friends, not really. I knew the village children, but I was always the vicar's daughter, set apart in their eyes, God's and Papa's. I had to be better, smarter, cleaner, more obedient, and they knew it and loathed me for it. No more than I loathed myself. Hence, I was always getting into trouble, brawling, using language that would make the angels blush, taking up dares to prove I wasn't different. But I was. Dear Lord, the village children had too much sense to do or say half the things I did.

Wind battered the windows, and the room shrank as the growing shadows enveloped us, pools of candlelight our only solace against the night. Mrs Behn was staring at the window, and I had the strongest feeling it was my reflection she was scrutinising.

Nest returned and, picking up a basket of sewing, huddled near the hearth, sharing a chair with Hecate while she repaired some lace on one of Aphra's gowns. Mrs Behn explained it had been torn when she alighted from a hackney on her way back from White Hall a few evenings earlier.

'White Hall? Where the King lives?'

She smiled. 'The King and many, many others.'

'Please,' I began, those questions I had smothered earlier seeking air, 'tell me about … everything. About *you*.'

Despite claiming she couldn't chronicle something so varied as her life in one night, she became quite loquacious, relating stories about the places she'd recently been, the people she spent time with. Just hearing 'White Hall' and the 'New Exchange', never mind 'Cheapside' and 'St James's Park', pepper Mrs Behn's conversation made my head reel. Likewise, the names that tripped off her tongue, names I'd seen mentioned in the news-sheets or upon printed material as authors or even as subjects of poems, plays, proclamations or tracts I was reading, were startling — like a painting coming to life or a statue moving. Actors' and actresses' names were scattered before me like petals in a breeze, as were the names of well-known publishers. Mrs Behn counted John Wilmot, the Earl of Rochester, among her dearest friends. She oft dined at his London house and they occasionally shared work in progress. Likewise, the King's favourite mistress, the former actress Nell Gwyn, was a favoured companion. But the name mentioned most often was Mr John Hoyle — a lawyer at Gray's Inn. My cousin was almost coy when talking about him, and I wondered what he meant to her that her cheeks flooded with colour. Nest arched a brow and ceased stitching when his name was said thrice in a short space of time, before returning to her needlework with a long sigh. Regardless of who this man was (and I was reassured I would meet him), what was evident was my cousin counted many important people among her acquaintance. It was both an exciting and daunting prospect. I said as much.

She laughed, a delicious sound that burbled from her throat, like a songbird in full voice. 'It's hardly surprising, considering what I do.'

'You write.'

'I do. I'm a writer by trade.'

The profession I had borrowed by the water stairs returned to haunt me. Nay, *taunt* — and with a vengeance. Why, I'd read all her plays, poems, tracts and public letters. She was one of the reasons I'd dared to defy Papa and write clandestinely. She was the woman who attracted such opprobrium, such disapproval, such awe. Who was, if what I'd read was to be believed, possessed of a reputation that would make a whore flush. When Bethan said I was going to live with the widow, Aphra *Johnson*, who mainly wrote on men's behalf, I'd imagined her an aged spinster with a crooked nose, wrinkled cheeks and pendulous breasts. Not this rosy-cheeked, chuckling vision who wrote for herself and Dorset Garden Theatre, sipping wine and entertaining me with tales of famous rakes, authors and louches.

Did Papa know? He couldn't. Never would he have sent me here.

But Bethan knew *exactly* who our cousin was.

Ha! I could scarce credit she'd not only allowed me to come but arranged it. Why? To what end? Had she listened to my anguished laments and desires? Sought to rescue me from a hideous marriage and ensure the seeds of my hopes were at the least sown? Or was it to ensure her nuptials proceeded?

Regardless, bless you, dear sister, bless you!

Mrs Behn was still talking, her deep, mellifluous voice animated. I marvelled that here I was, Tribulation Johnson, the daughter of a country vicar, tucked into a threadbare chair in a London parlour, my belly settled and sated, a glass of perfectly drinkable wine in my hand, opposite one of the most notorious women in the country.

Drum roll. Sound the trumpets.

The Aphra Behn. My bloody cousin.

Tiredness fled my body, leaving me feeling more spirited yet contented than I could ever recall.

If this was to be my punishment, then please God let me be naughty for evermore.

'How old were you when Jacquetta died?' asked Aphra, halting my capering thoughts.

'I was six.' My memories of Mama were vague. Mostly soft pinks, yellows. Roses, violets and jasmine. I remember tears, some raised voices too, and yet also her arms around me. Because she so oft cried when she held me, I'd resist her embrace for fear of hurting her. Maybe that's what made her sad. Or maybe it was me …

'It was the Great Sickness,' I said. I was sent to Lady Adeline's while it raged throughout the land. In my mind, Lady Adeline and my mother often blurred. They hadn't looked unlike — slender, fair-haired, with dark eyes. Then, Bethan came. She rarely had time for me, Papa kept her so busy, but she did encourage Mr Parker to admit me to classes at Petty School. As a consequence, the usual activities at which a young woman should excel — sewing, music, painting, dancing — were neglected. I could neither sew neatly nor play an instrument unless blowing a few notes on a flageolet counted. I could draw after a fashion and often sketched people and trees in my notebook, between my silly scribbles, as Papa called them. As for dancing, any time I tried, Papa erupted in gales of laughter, claiming I looked like a six-legged mower — a cow.

Bethan would console me at night, whispering that there was more to being an accomplished woman than dancing. Easy for her to say when she was more graceful than a swan.

Over time, I hardened myself to Papa's mocking laughter, the constant barbs, the torments of the children, and sought consolation and escape in stories, other people's words and, later, my own.

'The Black Death took too many,' said Nest, reminding us she was listening.

'It did indeed,' said Mrs Behn. Later, I would learn it took her husband, Johannes Behn, and after only a year of marriage. 'You would have been born before the King was restored?'

'Just after.'

'Hmmm.' Mrs Behn went quiet. 'That mark in your eye.' She dusted her fingers across her cheek. My eyes, which were a bright turquoise, were oft a cause for comment. As much as my name. My left one was stained with a dash of amber. She shook her head with a half-laugh. 'I once knew someone with a similar spot. Did you notice, Nest?'

'I did,' said Nest. 'Quite lovely, really.' She paused. 'I wouldn't be making more of it if I were you, Mrs Aphra.'

Aphra gave an uncomfortable laugh. 'I'm sure you're right.'

Who did I remind her of? I wondered. Mama? Papa? Bethan? Unlikely. I returned Mrs Behn's gaze, trying to see something of myself in her, my cousin. She turned her face aside.

It was hard to imagine my sister and this woman as friends, let alone relations, never mind my father. They were worlds apart: not just in the way they lived, but in how they thought, what they did. Already Mrs Behn showed more interest in me than Papa ever had.

She leaned forwards and refilled her glass. Her movements were elegant. She added more wine to mine as well, even though my head was quite giddy. I wasn't accustomed to drinking so much.

'Now,' she said, 'before we're utterly cupshotten, it's time to get down to business. Unless you're too tired?'

Business? Should I be alarmed?

'I'm not.' I was filled with buzzing bees and biting ants, drunken ones.

'In her letters,' said Mrs Behn, settling back into the chair, 'Bethan mentioned you should be put to work, maybe as a companion or even maid. Frankly, the notion of someone dogging my footsteps and doing what I'm perfectly capable of is the last thing I need. And, as you have seen, we already have maids. But neither can you be idle,' she continued. 'Despite what the gentry think, idleness is not an occupation. So, I ask, Tribulation Johnson, what would you *like* to do?'

No-one had ever asked me that before. Was it a genuine query or a test? Should I tell her my fervent hope was to one day be like her and write for a living? To compose poems, articles, pieces that were printed and published and which people paid to read.

Too embarrassed to reveal my longings, afraid of the mirth such a flight of fancy would elicit, I erred on the side of caution — or maybe it was cowardice. 'London is so much bigger, grander than I anticipated. I can't begin to imagine what I might do,' I lied. 'I've no wish to be lax. If you could help find me something to do, a purpose, I'd be very grateful.'

Mrs Behn replaced her glass on the table slowly. 'They're not necessarily the same though, are they? Something to do and a purpose.' She frowned. 'What do *you* think your purpose is? And call me Aphra, please.'

'Aphra.' I flashed a shy smile. 'If you ask Papa, my womanly purpose — nay, my God-given duty — is to marry well and have a family.' I paused. 'Fathers and daughters, men and women, oft find disagreement on what constitutes "well", don't you think?' Sir M's image ballooned in my mind.

'I do.'

'I hope that being here —' my arm swept the room '— I'll find one. And by that, I mean a purpose, not a husband. I don't want to be anyone's wife or helpmeet, not yet anyhow. In my opinion, it's the same as being indentured in miserable slavery.'

It wasn't really my opinion. Lady Adeline had said it and, when I repeated it to Bethan, she'd given me such a look and said, 'So's being a daughter.'

Or younger sister, I'd silently added.

'My, my. You're far too young to be so cynical. And yet, I cannot disagree.' She rose and began to trim the candles. 'You don't *have* to work, you know. Your father is paying me an allowance for your upkeep.'

'I want to.'

She sighed. 'It won't be easy. Not unless you wish to be a nursemaid.' She glanced at me. 'I didn't think so.'

She resumed her seat.

'I just want to make my own way … like you,' I whispered.

Aphra gave a wry smile. 'I might earn a living, but it's an uncertain one and not just because I'm a member of the fair sex. I can support myself and Nest but look around.' Her eyes travelled the room. 'Does this look like the kind of place someone who "makes a living" would choose? I make enough, most weeks, to pay my portion of the board and for our maids' service — such as it is. The men you met wouldn't be my first choice of house-mates.' She flagged the half-empty glasses, pipes spewing out ash upon tabletops, books with bent spines and dog-eared pages. Her expression softened. 'Nor, having grown fond of them over the years, would they be my last.'

'They're a vast improvement on that lot in Grubb Street,' said Nest.

'My last residence,' explained Aphra. 'Correspondents, the lot of them, and the most self-centred crew you're likely to meet. I adored them.' She laughed.

Correspondents. I thought of what Lady Adeline said.

My hands withdrew into a snarl on my lap.

'What I'm trying to say, very poorly,' said Aphra quietly, 'is when you work, it should be to flex your abilities, build upon them, gain experience, *and* earn a proper wage, no matter how small. Use the skills you possess, whatever they may be. In other words, do more than follow the advice of Hannah Woolley. I assume you've read her?'

I nodded. Who hadn't? *The Gentlewoman's Companion* was compulsory reading for all young ladies.

'She said that if young women don't find places as waiting maids, then they'll either become whores or steal,' said Aphra. 'What's your inclination?'

'Stealing.'

Aphra smiled.

It was easy for her to make light. She *was* successful, regardless of what she said. She'd a purpose.

'Though,' she continued. 'If one reads the late William Davenant's play, *The Wits*, he argues the only honest work for a single woman if she wants to avoid whoring, is to —'

'Teach children in a dark cellar or work coifs for cracked groats and broken meats.' I knew the play.

'My, my,' said Aphra. 'You *are* well read.'

'If I am, it's thanks to Lady Adeline … and Bethan.' Unexpected sorrow welled. The exhaustion I'd managed to keep at bay struck me like a wet sheet. The wine and Aphra's frank words took their toll. I wanted to find my bed and crawl into it. I began to imagine climbing the stairs, opening the door into that small, dank room with its curtained bed, hearth, chair, rug and table. It called to me. Only, that would be admitting defeat, failing to find a use for *any* skills. What were mine anyhow? I could read, aye. I could write — but as to the quality of my words … I winced. I loved poetry and knew swathes of Shakespeare, Ben Jonson and Christopher Marlowe's works as well as Sophocles and Aristotle. I knew some Etherege, Wycherley, Davenant and most of Aphra's plays. Since Lady Adeline passed, I'd been forced to perform all the parts.

A small idea blossomed, swiftly growing. Once upon a time, I'd wished to be an actress … I resisted the urge to rub my cheek.

Papa wasn't here. He would never know. Bethan had made it clear I was to create my own opportunities.

'Aphra,' I began, as a deliciously terrible, horribly disobedient, completely unnatural notion took root, 'do you think there might be a role for me at Dorset Garden Theatre?'

Why had Bethan sent me to a playwright if not to indulge a fancy?

Aphra started as if I'd announced I was a Quaker. 'In a play?'

'Aye,' I said cautiously. 'Perhaps a small part? Though I've no experience, I can read, I've a good memory, I love reciting lines —'

Aphra held up her palm to silence me. The fire crackled and spat; the sleet had turned into heavy rain which slapped the windows. Blasts of wind forced the curtains to perform half-hearted billows.

We locked eyes. 'Imagine what your father would say,' she said with mock severity.

'Aye,' I said, breaking into a wide grin. 'I am.'

SCENE FOUR

One man in his time plays many parts …

As You Like It, William Shakespeare

As Gabriel Freeman listened to King Charles II's spymaster, Joseph Williamson, carefully explaining his latest commission, he had to work hard to repress his resentment. After years at sea, captaining ships, chasing privateers and those who would evade taxes, all while carrying important messages and collecting valuable information regarding the French and Dutch, not to mention exposing traitors, he was to be given a job that would see him rooted in place for what could be a long time. The mission itself was not the problem: it was the fact he was being asked to remain in the city he'd once sworn never to return to.

He stifled the objections that naturally arose, pressing his lips together and concentrating on Williamson's instructions. He was to report to the Duke's Company at Dorset Garden Theatre. Prior to that, he had to visit Drury Lane. There, the manager of the King's Company, Thomas Killigrew, a former intelligencer himself who still controlled a group of men ferreting out information for Williamson and whoever else might be paying, would ensure his introduction to the

Duke's Company went smoothly. Killigrew would also serve as a point of contact if needed. Not that Williamson expected anything to go wrong. Gabriel's role was very clear: infiltrate Duke's, identify friends and contacts of recently arrested Papist actor Matthew Medbourne, and see how far his involvement in the Popish Plot extended. Were others at Dorset Garden implicated? Who were they and what were their connections and intentions? He would be given other tasks as they arose — as the information uncovered demanded.

As Williamson continued, Gabriel's thoughts took flight. Where better to plot and plan, pretend to be someone you weren't, hide secrets, tell falsehoods, put words in others' mouths, than the place that made a profit from doing just that — a workplace that legitimated the very act of deception?

How easy would it be to strike at the heart of the monarchy from the stage? From the Catholic Duke's own Company no less? He felt a trill of disquiet course through him at the thought of spying in such a manner. Yet, knowing he wasn't to remain permanently at the theatre, that he had a job to do, meant he could welcome it wholeheartedly — until such time as he quit its sight.

And what would his partner in everything, Solomon, make of this? Why, he'd be pleased, though less inclined to show it. The thought made him smile. While he was busy performing, Solomon could deal with Williamson's other duties, help maintain his cover. For, as Williamson warned, this was to be a protracted mission, one that required complete immersion to succeed.

After he'd finished explaining what was required, Williamson fell quiet. Then, with a disgruntled sigh, he rose and came around to the other side of the desk, perching his arse on the edge, looking down his considerable nose at Gabriel.

Unruffled, Gabriel returned his master's gaze.

Williamson was a saturnine man with ruddy cheeks and thick black brows; he was diligent, meticulous and suspicious — a good combination in someone charged with keeping the realm and King safe. He was also deeply unpopular because it appeared he was above bribery. There was nothing those at court, let alone wealthy merchants grazing on the profits of corruption, loathed more than a man they couldn't buy. Over the years, Gabriel had learned to both respect and trust him. Nevertheless, what Williamson said next took him by surprise.

'From here on, Freeman, you won't find me here, at White Hall.'

'Sir?'

'Thing is —' Williamson gave a dry half-laugh. 'I have it on the best authority I'm about to be dismissed.'

Gabriel remained silent.

'Robert Spencer, the Earl of Sunderland, will be installed in my stead.'

Practised at dissembling, Gabriel's response was steady. 'I'm sorry to hear that, milord.'

'Not half as sorry or relieved as I am. You heard I'd been thrown in the Tower?' Williamson seemed remarkably unperturbed for someone about to lose their position, never mind have their reputation impugned. All those years of dedication and for what?

'I heard rumours to that effect,' said Gabriel. Gossip had crawled over the docks and taverns, burrowing its way into his ears the moment he'd berthed — and not just about Williamson's situation.

Even before the ship reached Gravesend, Gabriel heard whispers of the Popish Plot, of those who'd already been found guilty of involvement and executed. Since he'd been in the city, it was all folk talked about. Fingers were being pointed, accusations levelled. Suddenly, calling someone a 'Catholic' was no longer merely an insult, but a prelude to something far more deadly.

Williamson grunted. 'Then you heard I was accused of harbouring Papist sympathies and worse?' He levered himself off the desk and strode to the window. The jingle of harness and tack carried. Voices too. He stared at whatever was happening outside then turned around. 'If *my* arrest on specious charges of being a secret Catholic, of commissioning Papist officers with intent to stage a coup, doesn't prove this plot of Titus Oates's is a complete fabrication, I don't know what will.' His finger became a weapon he levelled at Gabriel. 'This was Lord Danby's doing, mark my words.' He returned to his desk and sat back down. 'It's designed to undermine my position and my authority and test my nerve. Revenge upon me because I married the woman he'd picked for his son.'

Something jogged loose in Gabriel's mind. He'd heard Williamson had remarried — the widow of his closest friend, Henry O'Brien, Lord Ibrackan. Not only had the marriage elevated Williamson, a former clergyman's son, into the gentry and thereby earned him the eternal enmity of lords who felt he didn't deserve a place among them, it had set tongues wagging. O'Brien had only been dead three months when the nuptials took place. What was her name again? That's right, Catherine. Same as the Queen.

'Despite Danby's efforts to be rid of me,' continued Williamson, pouring himself another drink from the jug, offering the same to Gabriel, who declined, 'I'll still be running this investigation.'

'Sir? I don't report to Sir Henry Coventry then? Or Sunderland?'

'You do not. They have their own men they'll deploy; I'll have mine — and that includes you and the blackamoor.'

Gabriel shifted uncomfortably in his seat. This was going in a direction he hadn't foreseen. A part of him was relieved he and Solomon would still be working with Williamson. Better the devil you know. 'I see.' He gazed about the room. It might the last time he was in this office. He couldn't imagine Sunderland being content with such a dark space, close to the kitchens and where couriers often loitered. Williamson had made it his own, what with the portraits on the walls, the tapestry of a hunt by the window, the elegant statuette of a pagan goddess reclining over some scattered news-sheets and reports on the table. Over the years, he'd spent a few convivial evenings here. And many he'd prefer to forget. 'If you're not here, where will we find you, sir?'

'It wouldn't do for you to come to my house,' said Williamson. 'It'll be watched. With that in mind I've taken some rooms in Holborn.' He picked up a quill and scribbled on a piece of paper. 'You'll find me next to the sign of the Golden Alligator.' He passed the paper over. 'Far away enough to alleviate suspicion, but close enough.'

Freeman glanced at what he'd written. *Robin Woods Court, off Dean Street.* He didn't know it. 'Close enough for what, sir?'

'To observe whatever the Earl of Shaftesbury and his underlings are up to.'

'You think Shaftesbury has something to do with this plot then?'

'Him, the Duke of Buckingham, and the disaffected Parliamentarians who follow them like starving pups. If they're not spreading fears of Popish rule, they're claiming the King intends to abolish Parliament and rule without it. A claim that, despite it being all teeth and no body, still manages to bite.' He shook his head. 'I know they're using this Popish Plot and any other that will no doubt arise under the cover of Oates's wild stories for their own duplicitous ends. Have you seen the pamphlets?' He scrabbled among those lying on his desk before giving up. 'They're full of nothing else. All they do is give credence to Oates and his cronies. For while everyone is looking out for vengeful, hateful Catholics, no-one is watching anyone else. It's the perfect façade. Invent a dreadful far-reaching plot; accuse; make arrests; and, in the meantime, the real plots and plotters go undiscovered. It has Shaftesbury and his sycophants at the Green Ribbon Club written all over it.'

'You don't think this Popish Plot is real then?'

'Oh, I think there are Catholics in the city, the country, and certainly among our enemies and allies who have long desired to wrest us back to Romish ways using whatever means at their disposal. Do I think Oates's plot is the way they intend to achieve this? By assassinating his Majesty? No. But that doesn't mean there isn't some truth in what Oates is saying or that those he's accused aren't guilty of harbouring seditious intentions.'

He pushed the tips of his fingers into his temples, rubbing. 'Whatever I think, for now we must go along with it. With Oates.' He stared at Freeman. 'Remember. What works as a cover for any other plotters also works for me. For us. For those I hire to find proof of the existence or otherwise of this Popish Plot or any others being devised.'

Gabriel considered his master's instructions. At Dorset Garden, he'd have access to some of the most important nobles as well as those who consorted with them. 'May I ask, sir, if you're about to be dismissed, why are you doing this?'

'For the same reason I've done everything, Freeman. For King and country.' Williamson gave a wry laugh, holding up a hand. 'Before you think me virtuous, it was his Majesty's idea. Discredit me publicly so I can continue my work without the inevitable scrutiny that comes with this office. Unofficially, I'll be doing what I've always done, only without being bound to the rules.'

Gabriel was about to add, 'When have you ever been?' but thought the wiser of it. 'So, his Majesty knows about . . .?' He pointed to himself and waved the bit of paper.

Williamson nodded. 'He does. Along with a select few.' He didn't provide names. 'The next time we meet, Freeman, it will be in very different circumstances. Until then, go and play your part — on the boards and off them. I'm relying on you.'

And the fifty others you'll have given the same speech to, Gabriel thought grimly as he took his leave.

'Oh, and Freeman —' Williamson crossed the floor and rested a hand on his shoulder. 'I want you to know how sorry I was to hear about Wait-Still and your daughter.'

Gabriel stared and blinked. His wife's name, the evocation of his child, their unexpected deaths when he was absent — again — still possessed the power to rock him. He stood a moment, not seeing, not hearing, though Williamson continued to speak. Finally, he mumbled something, turning away from the pity in his master's eyes.

Out in the corridor, he pushed his sorrow aside, grateful he'd something else to fill the yawning chasm in his heart, his soul, his head. It was a clever move to discredit the soon to be former Secretary of State and spymaster, make the likes of Shaftesbury and Lord Danby think they'd bested him. They didn't know Williamson very well, clearly: the man was more cunning than a plague rat.

A group of giggling maids bustled along the hallway, one making sure to meet his eye. She was a pretty thing with dark curls and a full mouth, so he gave her a smile — and then dismissed her from his mind. He needed to be on his guard.

Outside, he kept his hat pulled down and his head low and adopted the slouch he used to hide his stature. Ignored by the guards and courtiers passing through the gates, who'd paused to stare at a vision in a fur-lined cape who'd just been admitted into a coach, he slipped past. A courier chose that exact moment to arrive, the horse's hooves kicking mud onto his breeches. He cursed loudly. Heads turned and a group of apprentices loitering by the coach house jeered. Damn. He brushed the mud, spreading it further. He should have waited until it dried. *God's balls in a vice.* It had been a long time since he auditioned for the stage, let alone a place in a Company. And while success was all but assured, thanks to Killigrew, appearances also counted, unless the profession had changed markedly since he last took part.

He walked slowly towards Charing Cross, admiring the new buildings, noting the formal gardens, most looking forlorn in their winter dress. Wait-Still always loved this time of year.

He shouted to attract the attention of the nearest sedan chair, whose bearers were trying to pretend they hadn't seen him. It hadn't drawn to a complete stop before he hastened into its confines. It was a bitterly cold day and the wind had picked up since he left his lodgings early that morning. Snow was threatening, from the look of the low-slung clouds. He negotiated the fare then pulled back the little curtains. Despite the chill, he wanted to look where he was going, reacquaint himself with the city he once loved and which, unable to face, he'd been absent from for far too long. He settled back as he was rattled along The Strand to Drury Lane, then it would be on to Dorset Garden and a new role — one he was keen to sink his teeth into.

SCENE FIVE

Frailty, thy name is woman.

Hamlet, William Shakespeare

Daubed with make-up meant to resemble boils and suppurating wounds but looking more like I'd overturned a bowl of stewed fruit upon myself, and smelling like I'd rolled in pig fat, I glanced down at the stained white robe. As a plague victim, I should be crawling into bed, not onto a stage. Yet, here I was, little more than a week after arriving in London, in the wings of Dorset Garden Theatre, about to make my debut as an actress.

I'd spent the last six days trying to persuade myself being on stage didn't spell ruination. Despite my eagerness to tread the boards, Papa's warnings rang in my ears as regularly as the city bells. Words like 'slut', 'strumpet' and 'whore' echoed and rebounded. That the other players didn't hear them astounded me. No young lady of good family would dare consider acting. Only, the actresses I'd met thus far seemed perfectly respectable … well, mostly. And the theatre was where Aphra made her living … mostly.

Anyway, the defiant part of me (the greater part, Bethan would say) wanted to forge ahead regardless. What was treading the boards but a way to make myself useful? Earn a wage and contribute to the household? From the moment I suggested I might take a part in a play, events had moved swiftly.

The day after I arrived in London, after a sleepless night in a strange bed, the noises of the house and street constantly nudging me from slumber, Aphra took me to Dorset Garden and presented me to the theatre manager, Lady Mary Davenant. My manners flew out the door and raced along the corridor to hide themselves in a cupboard as I stood before her, mouth agape, forgetting words, to curtsey, my name. I stared, completely stunned. *She* was the manager? It was as if I'd arrived in an inverse world where all the parts usually assigned to men were suddenly women's. Short, tow-headed, with a booming voice, Lady Mary was also forthright. She looked me up and down a few times, tilting my chin first one way then the other.

'You're uncommonly tall for a wench, aren't you?' She stepped back.

I wanted to retort, 'Maybe, but you're uncommonly short.' Despite being deserted by courtesy, I managed to still my tongue.

'I suppose people say that to you all the time,' she finished with a lopsided grin.

I knew then I was going to like her. 'Ever since I can remember.'

Words like 'ungainly', 'awkward,' 'ugly', 'monstrous' oft attended me, and that was just Papa. When we'd travel to Canterbury to purchase fabric for gowns and shifts, the mercers didn't try to hide their glee when they spied me, imagining the swathes of cloth needed. Likewise, tailors and seamstresses would tally up the hours with undisguised joy.

As I grew — older and taller — making my own clothes became as much a pecuniary matter as it was a woman's task. Bethan would bemoan how untidy my stitches (try holding a tiny needle with my hands). When my feet grew larger than Papa's, she would exclaim how my boots were better suited to Farmer Whittle (his feet were positively enormous). I was always chosen to be the highwayman or a Roundhead in games when I was younger, forced to chase the other children, who would scream and run away or, more often than not, turn and fight me — reminders I didn't fit in.

Naturally, this meant I wanted to belong more than anything.

It didn't help that one eye was tainted either. At least, that's how Papa described it. Lady Adeline was much kinder, saying when God painted my eyes, a streak of amber from another brush left an impression. Bethan never mentioned it.

'Still,' said Lady Mary, lifting my skirts to examine my legs, 'you'll do very nicely and not just in breeches parts.' She nodded approval at Aphra, who in turn smiled at me. 'Welcome to the Duke's Company, Tribulation Johnson.'

My heart sang. Before I could thank her, she called to another actress, who came bouncing over.

My care was handed to one Charlotte Butler. Ordered to show me around, she looped her arm through mine and dragged me away. I glanced back at Aphra, who gave a reassuring wave.

Charlotte had been with the Duke's Company a few years. Slender, she had long, honey-coloured hair and sparkling amber eyes. She also had the most mischievous chuckle. First, she took me backstage to meet the prompter, John Downes ('Most important person in the Company,' she whispered).

Of middling height with big ears and long fingers, Mr Downes also had a delightfully husky voice. He stood beside me, craning his neck in an exaggerated fashion. 'Lovely,' he said and sat on his stool. Well, that was a word never applied to me so I liked this man immediately — even better than Lady Mary. Only later did I learn that his approbation was because I was standing next to a pulley he found difficult to reach.

Next, I met the stage manager, Mark Danvers. Stocky, with short-cropped brown hair and a great gap in his left brow where he'd been burned by a footlight, he was gruff but not unkind, making sure to offer welcome. He was assisted by two brothers — Nicholas and Tom Brown. A young boy with a shorn head, Michael Mortimer, was a junior stagehand. He had no front teeth and the cheekiest grin. There were others too, who I'd eventually meet. There was also a young man who claimed he was an artist.

Charlotte leaned over and whispered. 'A right shit, that one. He's only doing scenery, but you'd think he counted the Duchess of Portsmouth among his clients.' Another artist, Evan Marbury, was away painting flats for a court performance. 'Now, he can wield a brush, if you know what I mean.' Charlotte winked.

I didn't — but I could guess. Years spent reading with Lady Adeline had given me some understanding in these matters. A small snort escaped.

We squeezed past enormous decorated screens, swathes of glittering fabric, artificial boulders, tombstones, crosses and piles of ropes, sandbags and chains. There was a musty smell in the air — stale tobacco, mildew and newly applied paint. The plinking of tools echoed while the heavy grind of gears beneath us made the floor shudder and forced Charlotte to raise her voice to be heard. Whistles resounded.

We plunged into a dark corridor where long stretches of canvas were rolled to one side.

'Prop rooms,' said Charlotte, rapping her fist against the first door we passed while simultaneously shoving a ladder closer to the wall with her shoulder. 'Costumes are stored in this one.' She struck the next. 'Along with headpieces, wigs and all sorts. You'll see.'

Voices grew louder as we approached two open doors.

'The Tiring Rooms,' said Charlotte as we entered the first. 'These are where the cast assemble, change and prepare to go on stage and where we *entertain* certain patrons.' A nudge in the ribs, a roll of the eyes and a grin. I swallowed, as Papa's unkind assertions about actresses began to toll in my head. I tried hard to muffle them.

Windows admitting a great deal of light revealed adjoining rooms filled to the brim with half-clothed men and women, discarded shifts, numerous tables, mirrors, chairs and all manner of objects. A doorway in one wall led to the second Tiring Room, where I could see still more people. The noise was deafening as the performers conned lines, chatted, read aloud from news-sheets and news-books, and reached to grab things off adjoining dressers or tables, all while having costumes fitted, hair done and make-up applied.

'Breath like a rancid onion,' declared one woman loudly.

'Had his prick in his hand and was playing it like a flute,' laughed another.

'She promised me ten ducats if I'd only —' began one man before lowering his voice.

Perfumes filled the air, as did the ubiquitous smoke from lit pipes, and the musky fragrance of sweating bodies and dusty garments. It was so colourful, loud, and unlike anything I'd ever seen.

'Attention all!' shouted Charlotte suddenly, arms raised. Much to my embarrassment, she pushed me forwards. One by one, everyone fell quiet, sponges and brushes halted halfway to faces, bodkins part-inserted into wigs, clothes clutched (or not) to breasts and chests. Those in the adjoining room squeezed into the doorway. 'This,' announced Charlotte with a flourish, 'is Tribulation Johnson. *Aphra's cousin*.' There were some intakes of breath, arched brows and looks of appraisal. 'She's joining us for *Oedipus* and, hopefully, beyond.'

There were some merry hails, waves, a few furtive looks, while most regarded me curiously for a second then returned to what they were doing. Charlotte said they were used to new actors and actresses coming on board. Happened all the time, especially with big productions, and *Oedipus* was considered a colossal one. Charlotte took my arm and led me to an empty dresser.

'Here,' she said, shoving the gee-gaws littering the surface to one side. 'You can use this. Beside me.' I was swiftly introduced to the nearby performers. Names crowded my head, some of which were well known, such as Thomas and Mary Betterton, Henry Harris, Elizabeth Barry, Elizabeth Currer and Susanna Mountfort (she was striding around in breeches and I couldn't help but admire her legs). There was even a little girl, Anne Bracegirdle, weaving in and out of the players, trailing a blue ribbon. Other names were thrown, as were glances, grins and dismissive waves. A few ignored me altogether. Whispers began — not that the actors were good at keeping their voices low.

'Didn't know Aphra had a cousin.'

'You couldn't miss the wench, could you?'

'Taller than a maypole.'

'Did you see her eyes?'

'Never acted before …'

'We all have to start somewhere.'

'Nice for *some*.' The last was said with volume and such venom I half-expected the speaker to reveal a forked tongue. It was a skinny woman with lovely flame-coloured hair.

'Prisca Smithton,' said Charlotte, noticing where my gaze landed. 'Ignore her. Most of us do,' she added loudly.

I prayed I'd remember who was who. There was also a rangy, broad-shouldered man hunched over a dresser, a script open before him. He'd neither acknowledged me nor looked in my direction.

'He's new too,' whispered Charlotte.

Perhaps I'd have an ally. Someone to share experiences with.

Charlotte dragged her stool closer. 'Jonathan Rickman. A principal actor. Only arrived yesterday. Replacing Matt …' Her voice caught.

I touched her arm gently. 'Aphra told me about Mr Medbourne.' How, on the testimony of Titus Oates, the man holding all of London if not England to ransom, Matthew Medbourne had been arrested on charges of being part of this Catholic plot to kill the King. He'd been thrown into Newgate.

Charlotte's face fell. 'Aye. Poor Matty. The only thing he'd be plotting is where to go for supper.' She shook her head sorrowfully. 'This Popish Plot … it's terrifying. So's the power this Oates fellow has.' She lowered her voice. 'Some say the man's a fabulator of the worst kind. A liar who, in the past, was accused of blasphemy, drunkenness and sodomy.'

I'd heard the same. 'Perhaps that's why he's accusing so many of being Catholics and whipping up fear. He's trying to detract from his own sins.'

Charlotte nodded. 'Aye, well, it's working, ain't it? He claimed Matty's a bloody captain in some Jesuit army.' She glanced about. 'We all knew Matthew was a Papist … he's not the only one. But he's no murderer. Don't misjudge me. I hope they catch all those planning to kill the King, I really do. But they've made a mistake with Matty.'

I threw a sympathetic look but remained silent. Charlotte wasn't alone in believing errors were being made: that so many of those Mr Oates accused were innocent. But it made not one whit of difference.

'I tremble for him,' continued Charlotte quietly. 'Matthew's all alone; terrified. Worse, we're all being watched lest we make contact with him. After all, our patron is none other than the *Catholic* Duke of York which, in some minds, tars us all with a Papist brush. Did you see those two ruffians loitering by the water stairs?'

I had. Aphra pointed them out to me when we arrived.

'They appeared three days ago,' said Charlotte. 'If they're oarsmen, Lady Mary said, she's Queen of the Blackamoors.' She emitted a puff of air. 'They've been ordered to watch us. Anyone entering this theatre is being noted. Which means you will be too.'

I shrugged. 'They can watch me all they like. I've nothing to hide.'

Charlotte snorted. 'Really?' Her eyes raked me top to toe. 'You'd be an exception, Tribulation Johnson.' She thrust her chin towards the new actor. 'Next you'll be telling me he's got nothing to hide either. Yet, he arrived just as panic was setting in about who would replace Matthew. If that's not suspicious, I don't know what is.'

I followed Charlotte's gaze, considering Mr Rickman. Long dark hair fell over much of his face, though not enough to hide a slightly hooked nose and a thick pair of neatly curved brows. He was in desperate need of a shave.

'Apparently, he's a sailor — or was,' said Charlotte, rising and inviting me to continue our tour of the theatre. 'More like a pirate if you ask me. Grumpy cove, whatever his reason for being here. Doesn't talk much.'

'Maybe he just wants to act,' I said.

Mr Rickman chose that moment to raise his head. A pair of dark eyes met mine and his forehead furrowed before he returned to his script. No-one was sitting near him.

As we left the Tiring Rooms, whispers started again. 'Aphra's cousin, you say? Could be useful.'

'Looking for favours again, Samuel?'

'Aren't we all?' said a woman.

There was laughter.

''Ware who you befriend here, Tribulation,' said Charlotte quietly once we were out of earshot. She had a lovely way of saying my name, rolling the 'r' and making it sound like a song. 'Some will seek friendship merely to further their own ends.'

'Why?' We headed back to the stage and Charlotte looked pointedly towards Aphra, who was deep in conversation with Lady Mary. 'Oh.'

'Aye,' she said, her slight accent revealing her northern origins. 'There's those here who'd befriend Mephistopheles if it would land them better parts.'

I thought over Charlotte's initial words of caution as I waited to make my debut. Last-minute adjustments were being done to the set. Mr Danvers and the stagehands, Tom and Nicholas, aligned the painted flats into the grooves on the wide stage, while Michael and another man scampered along the walkways above, checking ropes, adjusting sandbags and hauling upon pulleys. Bells and whistles were used to communicate, as was the occasional frustrated shout. Mostly, hand signals were deployed. Across from where I stood in the wings with Charlotte and another actress, Katherine Herbert, I could see the lambent glow from the lanthorn on the prompter, John Downes's table. He was conversing with Jonathan Rickman.

Katherine nudged me in the ribs. 'Rude bastard, isn't he?'

I mumbled something. I was much too nervous to consider Mr Rickman closely. Though I had to agree: in the few days I'd been there, I'd reached the conclusion that surly didn't begin to describe him. He barely exchanged a word unless it was scripted. Most gave him a wide berth, though a few continued to try and draw him out — unsuccessfully. Unkind words were being said, and assumptions made, especially about his appearance which was unorthodox for an actor, so the women said, what with all the scars on his face and tattoos on his arms. How quickly these people were to judge. I feared to think what they said about me.

'Well, whatever he is, he's a mite early to be in the wings annoying Mr Downes. His entrance isn't for ages,' said Katherine.

'No harm ensuring he gets it right though, eh?' said Charlotte.

We all stared.

Maybe he was just there because it was impossible to hear oneself think in the Tiring Rooms, as cramped, crowded and noisy as they were.

This had been made worse earlier when, about an hour before curtains, in a flurry of tobacco smoke, pomade and chatter, a group of well-dressed men burst in. I'd reached for a shawl to cover myself, but no-one else sought to hide their state of undress. On the contrary, some flaunted it — even Charlotte.

Charlotte saw the look on my face. 'Better get used to it. There's always some cove in 'ere looking, groping. Or more,' she added as Mary Lee slapped one man's roving hand away with a fan. 'Sometimes, it's worth it.' She pulled a face suggesting otherwise.

Mr Downes appeared soon after, warning us we had fifteen minutes until curtains opened. There was a frisson of excitement, and a lance of utter fear tore through my chest. Polly, another new actress, reached over and squeezed my hand.

'May there be lots of shit,' she said.

Fortunately, Aphra had explained this odd expression the night before as we sat in the kitchen chatting over some mulled wine. Meant to offer good luck, it originated from the French, the idea being the more people who arrived at the theatre, the more mud and horse dung outside, which bettered the chance of a full house. So, performers always wished each other '*Beaucoup de merde*' or 'lots of shit'.

'Lot and lots,' I agreed, summoning a grin. As the visitors were ushered out of the Tiring Rooms, I tried desperately to remember all the other little things I mustn't do or say. The theatre was such a superstitious place. I wasn't to place shoes on a table, or whistle (only stagehands were allowed to do that). No real mirrors were to be brought onto the set as they could reflect light into the performers' or audience members' eyes. And if anyone dared utter the name of Shakespeare's Scottish play (I daredn't even say it to myself), they had to spin three times, widdershins, leave the room, spit, and all other manner of peculiar things.

It was all quite marvellously silly.

As I waited to take my place on stage, I tried to list them all. Then, it struck me. Before I'd even seen a London play, I'd be taking part in one.

Thank the Lord Papa didn't know. It didn't bear consideration. By now, my previous bravado had well and truly deserted me.

With bare arms, a flimsy tunic, and sandals with leather thongs criss-crossed up my ankles and calves, it wasn't just the cold making my entire body tremble. It was knowing hundreds of people were pouring into the theatre to watch me perform. Well, not *me* exactly, but try telling that to my heart, which jumped about like a moon-struck hare. From the other side of the curtain, there was the growing thud of feet, deep voices hailed one another, and the swell of conversation grew.

'Lady Mary will be pleased,' whispered Mary Betterton, joining us suddenly. 'Looks like we'll come close to full.' A woman of medium height with a slim waist, she had a round, pleasant face, small twinkly eyes and a buttery voice. She was also one of the most famous actresses in London, according to Charlotte. I didn't doubt it as her name had even reached Chartham. She looked regal in costume, a floral wreath upon her dark hair like a queen of old. She was playing Jocasta — wife to her real-life even more famous husband, who was playing Oedipus.

For days, Mrs Betterton had guided me and the other newcomers through our movements and cues. Aphra said she was not only a very good actress, but an exceptionally kind woman. The Bettertons lived above the theatre and had four other actresses and young Anne Bracegirdle boarding with them. Five days a week, Mrs Betterton ran morning classes for aspiring performers. Maybe I could avail myself of them, study the craft and, one day, be like Mrs Betterton herself.

'Want to take a peep?' She indicated the curtains.

Did I?

Hand in hand, Charlotte beside us, we went to where the large velvet curtains were drawn across the stage and opened them a fraction. It took my eyes a moment to adjust as it was much lighter beyond. Though I'd seen the auditorium each day, I'd been too focussed on learning to pay much attention to that cavernous space. Candles burned along the edges of the long forestage and in the chandeliers hanging from the moulded ceiling, causing a haze of smoke to roil and twist. Plump-faced plaster putti pouted at the people below. Rows and rows of benches covered in green cloth ran across the space at floor level; rising around three sides were more seats in boxed sections, tiers of them — the topmost so high they were cast in gloom. Each one was divided by a hip-high wall and would seat about eight people. The topmost tiers wouldn't have a very good view, but those on the sides would have excellent vantages as would anyone occupying the benches, which was a great many people.

Men and women wended their way along the aisles, filling the seats around the projecting forestage as well as above it. Scents floated — lavender, rose, ambergris, cloves, the faint odour of unwashed bodies, musty boots, coats and tallow. There were towering periwigs, some divided in the centre to form the equivalent of devil's horns. Women in flounced and hooped skirts with patched faces laughed loudly, or pretended indifference, their chins — and some possessed a few — held high. Many wore bejewelled vizards, the only indication of life the glint of eyes. They opened and closed their fans, their eyes, their arms. It was all an exhibition, a show.

The great and small took their seats, waving to those they knew, climbing over barriers to shift closer, offering up powdered and pock-marked cheeks, wet lips and gloved hands to be kissed, blatantly ignoring a greeting or even turning aside so as not to see someone. Arguments broke out over where to sit and next to whom. Some slurped and burped down drinks, others chewed and swallowed. The noise grew.

Mrs Betterton pointed out some people. 'See that man there?' she whispered. 'The pudgy one in the gaping ruby waistcoat? That's Samuel Pepys, Secretary of the Admiralty. He loves the theatre. Loves the actresses even more. Watch him, my dear. Or, should I say, watch out for him.' She made pinching gestures with her hands. 'Charlotte knows what I mean. She's come in for particular attention of late.'

Charlotte gave a good-natured grin. 'Sam's not as bad as some.'

He sat in a box near the stage, beaming and nodding at all and sundry, appearing to enjoy himself enormously. He was joined by a tall thin man with white hair that curled around his collar.

'That's John Evelyn,' shared Mrs Betterton. 'Excellent writer.'

There was a grandly dressed crook-back who, using a cane, forced people aside. 'Anthony Ashley Cooper, Earl of Shaftesbury. Dangerous gent.' Mrs Betterton frowned. 'Some believe he's the man protecting Titus Oates and promoting this Popish Plot so he can rid himself of any political rivals. Oh, look. Lord Grey's with him. Dear God, so's the Scottish vicar, Robert Ferguson. Mark them well, Tribulation. These men spell trouble and not just for us women.'

What a contrast they made, the older man with the bent back, the younger with his naturally curled russet-coloured hair and rather cherubic face, and the thickset preacher with a crop of auburn curls.

We were soon joined by other cast members, who added their commentary to Mrs Betterton's, pointing, sniggering, gasping, whispering. It was enormous fun, as if we were schoolboys observing the master when he wasn't looking. It was lovely to be included, to feel a part of something so … naughty, but it was also what the cast members were clearly accustomed to doing. It reduced the threat the audience posed — after all, the play's fortunes and thus the Company's rose or fell depending on whether or not they enjoyed the performance — and, to a degree, settled my nerves. Perhaps that was the point.

'Who's Aphra with?' I asked, spying her at last. A slender man in a golden periwig plonked himself beside her.

'That's the notorious John Wilmot, the Earl of Rochester,' said Mrs Betterton. 'I fear he's out of favour with the King — again.'

Ah … Aphra's friend. I'd heard many stories from her about him since arriving — he'd done all manner of deeds from kidnapping an heiress to breaking the King's precious sundial and even, after being exiled from court, returning to London and disguising himself as one 'Doctor Bendo' and actually treating women for medical problems. Even when he was exposed as a charlatan, his patients had continued to seek his services. He was also known for his salacious verses, a few of which Lady Adeline and I had read.

'The other gentleman is John Hoyle,' continued Mrs Betterton.

I took a second look. The man whose name peppered Aphra's conversation like seasoning in a salat. The man who made Aphra blush. If ever I was asked to draw seething anger, I would sketch this man.

Women carrying baskets of oranges, like those I'd seen the day I alighted from the wherry, wove their way through the press of people, selling them. The women were squeezed, grabbed, forced onto laps; there were scuffles and shouts and much laughter.

'Are they always like this? The audience?' I asked.

'What?' asked Mrs Betterton. 'So badly behaved?'

I hesitated, not wanting to give offence. Charlotte gave her rich laugh. The other actresses smiled indulgently.

'Oh no, dear.' Mrs Betterton chuckled. My shoulders relaxed. 'Usually, they're much, much worse.'

Another bell sounded.

'Five minutes,' called Mr Downes, striding past.

Charlotte squeezed my hand. 'Lots of shit,' she said and raced away with another actress, Margaret Collins, to take up position before I could return the phrase.

I took one last look through the curtains. 'All the world's a stage,' I murmured.

'And *all* the men and women merely players.' Mrs Betterton nodded towards the auditorium. 'Remember that. We're all acting. Only difference is, we're paid.'

Suddenly, the music altered. Instead of playing melodic tunes, suitable while everyone found their seats, the musicians started plucking their viols. A drum beat. It was hollow, eldritch. One of the instruments whined, like wind howling down a chimney. The lights fluttered and dimmed as if blown by an unseen wind. Or divine breath.

The audience hushed.

My body quivered. It was time.

I found where I was supposed to be, near a wooden tree, stretched out across a fake headstone. I lay down, draped my garment over my legs, then rested my head on one arm and closed my eyes. I may have been acting deceased, but I'd never felt more alive.

Ever so slowly, the curtains parted.

SCENE SIX

... A poor player, That struts and frets his hour upon the stage, and then is heard no more ...
Macbeth, William Shakespeare

A drum rolls and Mr Harris, one of the principal actors, dressed in a fine coat and large, plumed hat, enters stage left. I watch through half-closed eyes as he steps over recumbent bodies and walks around the aimless others, plague victims all, before he passes out of my line of sight. There's a sonorous clap from the heavens. A woman in the audience screams. Someone giggles.

His voice booms as he delivers the prologue like a carnival roister.

'... And wit from wisdom differed not in those, But as 'twas sung in verse, or said in prose. Then, Oedipus, on crowded theatres, Drew all admiring eyes and listening ears ...'

I can feel the vibrations of his footsteps as he paces the forestage, arms outstretched, body taut like a fletched arrow.

When the prologue finishes, the audience falls silent. There's a cough. Someone blows their nose. Another hails an acquaintance. A low swell of chitter begins.

Aware of eyes boring into me, I resist the urge to roll over. At least with my back to the audience I can watch what's happening upstage.

I admire the painted sky — a mixture of pending storm and blue promise.

Players shuffle out from the wings, frail, emaciated, their arms outstretched, their moans just audible. Plague victims of Thebes. Among them is Charlotte. The wind whines; the beat of soldiers' drums (or is it just my heart?) intensifies. Shadows lengthen. The music changes again, jarring, like a baby's suffering wails.

Caught up in the magic, I almost forget to breathe. Onto the stage struts Thomas Betterton as Oedipus. His lines are beautifully enunciated, even if they're sometimes thrown back by the odd acoustics. His voice is lustrous, mesmeric.

I almost cheer when Mary Betterton appears. Unrecognisable as the woman who stood beside me gossiping about the audience, she beseeches her husband and the gods, pleads with and for her children. Castigates herself. The audience boos, cheers, whimpers, protests.

The lights dim, the scene changes. It's my cue. I scrabble to my feet and with the others run to the Tiring Rooms. There, amidst excited chitter, Finnola, the plump seamstress, tiny Juliet, and grizzled Jacob, the man I'd seen holding a box outside the theatre door the day I disembarked, help us change.

Minutes later, I wait in the wings, no longer a plague victim, but this time a spectre.

Enter Mary Lee as Eurydice, Creon's wife. With every word, every gesture, her pain, anger and anguish are apparent. Susanna Mountfort, the one with shapely legs, plays her maid.

The audience is captivated. The scenery is astounding — from a tangled forest to the interior of a grand castle room to a riverside and the edges of Hell. The music, which plays throughout, burrows its way under the skin, alternately setting teeth on edge and soothing fraught souls.

When Jonathan Rickman appears, playing the war-hero Prince Adrastus, it's as if the audience catch their collective breath. Some women gasp as he strides to the very edge of the forestage, the sloped floor making him loom over the distant painted city. He speaks to the audience — not as a group, but to each individual. The silence is tangible, heavy. Charlotte grabs my wrist so tightly I wince.

'Good God, he might be a boor, but what a man,' she sighs.

Having little empirical experience in that regard, I say nothing. Though I must admit, while I can barely tear my eyes away, it's my ears that are most effected.

If Mr Betterton's delivery was unctuous, like rich gravy, then Jonathan Rickman's is akin to a wild beast's — a deep, rich purr that takes up lodging in my centre and travels south. Heat floods my cheeks as the unfamiliar but exquisite sensation lingers. I cast a quick glance sideways, praying no-one notices. Good God. Where did *that* come from? Judging by the look of Charlotte and the others waiting in the shadows, I'm not alone in feeling it. Some of the women fan themselves: a couple of the men too.

Finally, it's time to make my entrance. My chest is tighter than a mistress's stays. Nevertheless, holding my breath, I follow Charlotte, lifting my feet high, arms outstretched as instructed by Mrs Betterton. I'm one of six wraiths, ghosts who must ignore the speakers and weave our way between them, keeping mouths open as if the music — which is haunting — issues from between our gruesome lips.

It was easy in rehearsals when the auditorium was empty. When daylight beamed through the windows and all the stagehands crawled about the place, hammering, stomping, dragging. When Lady Mary and even Aphra and the Bettertons were interrupting, halting the performance, insisting lines be repeated over and over, that we redo the action. When little Anne was skipping between us with that damned ribbon.

At first, it isn't hard. I float onto the stage, eyes fixed on Eurydice, Mary Lee, whom I've been directed to taunt. It was thought having me whirl about her tiny figure would emphasise the threat. I circle, arms rising and falling, mouth moving. Then I spin and face the audience.

Rows and rows of eyes fix upon me like gimlets. Grim faces, worried faces, half-smiling faces: they all lock onto me.

Frozen into place in the middle of the stage, in front of Mary Lee, who's delivering lines, I become a tree, sprouting roots that burrow through my sandals and into the stage floor, securing me to the spot.

Someone points and whispers.

Mary Lee steps around me and continues. The other cast members go on as if nothing is amiss, as if I'm doing exactly as directed. This is the scene where a fight breaks out between the villain, Creon, and hero, Adrastus. The other ghosts drift off stage in preparation for the duel and the music plays on.

I can't move.

My arms slowly drop, my shoulders droop. I begin to tremble like a wet cat. The canvas of faces grows dark around the edges, slowly contracting until there's just a bright light glowing in the centre. In that light is a woman with a large, feathered headdress. Her head is thrown back, her finger a spear ready to impale me. She laughs. Others point and chortle — not at the action, but the inaction.

At me.

I'm vaguely aware of my inner voice screaming, *Move, move, you dolt!* I'm ruining everything, but however hard I try, I simply cannot. I become so hot: a candle, burning from the inside out. I will myself to melt — a great wax puddle scraped off and thrown away.

The laughter grows.

Someone shouts, 'Oy, long-legs, give us a jig!'

'Say something for yourself, dell.'

'What was that? We can't hear you!'

More laughter. More words.

'She's a monument!' shouts one wag.

'To what?' asks another.

'The King's inaction,' cries another, to gales of laughter and angry shouts.

Then, I'm swept up in a pair of burly arms.

'Thine, say'st thou, monster!' The voice is chasmic, vast. It echoes, filling the void in my mind, the theatre, silencing the shouts, the taunts. 'Shall my love be thine? O, I can bear no more.'

It's Jonathan Rickman.

He carries me to the wings and deposits me in outstretched arms before swinging back onstage, drawing his sword.

I can scarce stand. Hands brush hair out of my eyes. There are kind whispers, strokes to my face, rubbing of my cold, cold arms, and whispers of solace. Why is everyone being so cursed nice when I've let them down so badly?

Up until then, the play was going well. The performances were outstanding. I want to crawl into a closet and remain until I'm old and wasted.

I want to say sorry. To everyone. My audacity — that I thought for even a moment I could do this: count myself among these seasoned performers. It was beyond foolhardy. I fumble for words, but shame drowns them.

Too soon I'm abandoned as the cast continue to play the parts they've been given — on stage, off stage.

The show goes on.

Sans me.

SCENE SEVEN

Obey'd as soveraign (sic) by thy subjects be,
But know that I alone am King of me.
Conquest of Granada, John Dryden

Absorbed in my misery, I didn't hear Aphra enter the Tiring Rooms. It wasn't until she slipped into the chair beside me and placed a warm hand over where my icy one rested that I became aware I was no longer alone. She didn't say anything. She waited for me to make eye contact, to speak, weep, though the state of my face paint must have announced the last action was well under way.

Corridors away, the play reached its climax. The crescendo of music, the thump of the performers crossing the stage, the clash of swords and the cries of the dead and dying reached us. There was the grating sound as flats shifted along the grooves. A dull whistle, a shout; there was a burst of applause. 'Bravo! Brava!' Cheers, cries of 'Encore!'

'I thought I'd ruined it,' I said. My voice was grainy, as if it came from far, far away.

'Ah, my dear,' said Aphra gently. 'Your part was too small, the show too great for that. Though you won't easily be forgotten.'

A laugh that sounded suspiciously like a sob sputtered. 'I make a habit of that, don't I? Spew all over you the moment I arrive, freeze the moment I set foot on stage. Cause nothing but trouble.' I gave an unladylike sniff. I reached for a rag and began to wipe the grease paint from my face.

Aphra took the cloth from my hand and, first dipping it into a pot of milky-coloured unguent, adjusted her chair so she faced me. Then she began to dab my cheeks. 'What happened isn't uncommon,' she said. 'Ask Elizabeth Barry. Susanna Mountfort, Mary Lee. Even Thomas Betterton. They've all had similar experiences. Forgotten their lines, been seized by panic and rendered unable to move. Some worse, some not.'

'Nay!'

Aphra nodded vigorously. 'Happens to the best of them.'

'Really?'

She folded the cloth and dipped it in the cream again. 'There's even a name for it.' She rubbed hard at my lips. 'Stage-fright.'

'Stage-fwight?'

Aphra focussed on my brows, which had been thickened and lengthened. 'Ah-ha. Before he wrote fine plays, Thomas Otway — you've heard of him? The author of *Friendship in Fashion*? Yes, well, he tried his hand at acting. I cast him as the old king in my very first play — *The Forc'd Marriage*.'

'I never knew he acted.'

'He didn't. Stood there like a stunned coney, then gibbered some lines — nothing I'd written.' Aphra chuckled. 'Lucky for him, he found his forte. Unfortunately, he also developed a great passion for Elizabeth Barry.'

'Oh?' I knew Aphra was trying to distract me with gossip. I was both grateful and, I confess, entertained.

'It was unrequited. The poor man had no choice but to watch as the woman he loved fell into the arms of the Earl of Rochester.'

I pictured the man in the blond periwig in the audience beside Aphra. I couldn't imagine him and Mrs Barry as lovers and said so.

'You're not alone. Yet, they had a daughter, Izzie. It wasn't to be though. Dear Rochester, as we all knew he would, abandoned Elizabeth. I know. I know. Just because he's my friend doesn't mean

I like *everything* he does. She was only ever good enough to be his mistress. Otway hoped that in her misery she'd turn to him. He clearly didn't know Elizabeth. Dear Tom isn't nearly wealthy enough and thus had his heart broken all over again. Maybe that's what makes his writing so poignant. Maybe that's what all us writers need.' Aphra paused, the rag midway to my cheek. 'To suffer.'

I glanced at her reflection in the mirror and for just a moment saw Aphra's own travails mapped upon her face. Before I could express the compassion I felt, Aphra resumed her ministrations. My turn to distract her.

'He never acted again?' I asked.

Aphra shook her head. 'No — nor tried. But cease your worries. You'll find the next time easier.'

I regarded her in horror. 'Next time? There cannot be a next time. What if I do it again?'

Aphra smiled gently. 'Firstly,' she said, 'the cast are now alerted you might and will take measures. Secondly, it's very unlikely. If Otway had just given himself a chance, he may have found he enjoyed performing. He lacked courage. Fortunately for us, as he became a fine writer,' she added. Aphra put down the cloth. She stood up behind me and, resting her hands on my shoulders, levelled her face so we could see each other in the mirror. 'What about you? Are you brave enough?'

I looked from Aphra to myself and back again. My cheeks were red from rubbing. My eyes were still bright from unshed tears, but within their depths, something sparked. 'I'm no coward.' As if to bely my bravado, my voice shook with every word. 'Do you think the cast can forgive me?'

Aphra squeezed my shoulders. 'There's nothing to forgive. Anyway, they understand that, for all it appears easy, acting is hard. This life is hard. For many reasons and, as you know, mostly for us women.' She reached for my clothes. 'You may as well get changed.'

I sighed in agreement.

'I hope you'll still join us in celebrating a fine opening. It's tradition. A few drinks at the Bishop's Whelp — a nearby tavern.' Aphra hesitated. 'Speaking of women — how are you getting on with the others? They seem to have made you welcome. Charlotte especially.'

I stripped off the simple gown, making sure to hang it carefully. I began to pull on my stockings. 'Charlotte's very nice. In fact, most are. But I suspect that's because of you.'

'What? You're not worth being nice to?'

I gave a half-laugh. 'They admire *you* and want to remain in your graces so you write a good part for them in your next play. Hence, they're nice to me too. For the time being, at least.' I paused. 'But I admit … they're different from what I thought.'

'What was that?'

My face grew hot. 'I don't want to say.'

'You're referring to what's sometimes written in the news-sheets? In pamphlets? Gossip? Or do you mean things your papa said?'

'More the latter than the former,' I admitted, unable to look at Aphra. 'If you believed half of what was written and said about actresses, let alone what Papa used to sermonise, you'd think the road to Hell was paved with them.'

'Well, if not that, then certainly Satan's boudoir.'

I burst out laughing then just as quickly ceased.

'Tribulation.' Aphra sat back down. 'I pray I've done the right thing, introducing you here, helping you find work.' I went to speak, but she continued, leaning over, rearranging the bits and bobs on the dresser. 'The peculiar thing about this life — on stage and off — is that it brings all sorts together — high born, low born, those with wit, those with none. A shared love of words, performance and performers but, above all, it's a world held together by artifice.' She met my eyes in the mirror then and drew her breath in sharply. It was a moment before she spoke again. 'Be cautious, whatever your reasons for wishing to strut the boards. Stay true to yourself. Your principles. Don't let these people, even those who appear to have good intentions, sway or seduce you. Few here are who or what they seem. In fact, as much as I adore them, most people of my acquaintance are not. They're quite simply great pretenders.'

'Mrs Betterton said something similar just before the play opened. She said, "We're all actors."'

'Wise woman, Mrs Betterton.' Aphra straightened a brush, then pushed the lid back on the cream. 'And what of the hero of the hour, Mr Jonathan Rickman?' began Aphra slowly. 'What do you think of him? He certainly knows how to command an audience.'

On stage, aye, I thought. While off stage he did all in his power to avoid one.

Before I could answer, the door flew open. I tried to stand, meet my critics. There was a rush as the players gathered around, slapping me on the back, asking if I was well, reassuring me.

Those wretched tears began to gather again, this time in relief. Relief and something warm and altogether agreeable. When the Bettertons and Mary Lee appeared, dragging over chairs, recounting their own stories of stage-fright, I locked eyes with Aphra and shared a smile.

Aphra was right. My stage-fright, whatever the reason for it, was forgiven.

But not, as I was soon to discover, forgotten.

SCENE EIGHT

... The whole world was made for man, but the twelfth part of man for women. Man is the whole world, and the breath of God; women the rib and crooked piece of man.

Religio Medici, Sir Thomas Browne

As much as it pained me to recall what a harecop I'd been opening night, it was important I thank Mr Rickman for what he did. I tried when I saw him in the Tiring Rooms immediately after, but he didn't hear above the adulation and congratulations being showered upon him like summer rains — not only by his fellow thespians, but by members of the audience who stampeded the rooms, trampling us lesser performers in their eagerness to rub shoulders with the hero of the hour and the Bettertons. Mr Rickman was transformed into a holy artefact who would elevate those who could but lay hands upon him to some higher plane. I could have sworn I saw him shaking his head in disbelief at one point. What I didn't see was him smile, though he did bear the sycophants and their ridiculous attempts to stroke and catch his attention with grace if not good humour.

Certainly, he barely acknowledged me that night or any other. Thank the Lord, I didn't give a repeat of my initial performance.

Imagine if he hadn't acted (ha!) as he did when we premiered? Carried me off stage? Why, I'd probably still be there, stuck, gawping like a fish brought to land. A very thin, hungry and no doubt smelly one.

Thanking him became even more imperative when an anonymous reviewer in the *London Gazette* claimed Mr Rickman's actions had saved the play from disaster. The words were as sour as our disapproving neighbour, Mr Shale, claimed they could be.

Ouch.

Still, the play was a huge success and in no small measure due to Jonathan Rickman. Men and women flocked to the theatre and, after, the Tiring Rooms hoping to catch a glimpse of him. Mr Downes wryly noted that if we could but charge entry to the changing area, never mind for being within arm's reach of Mr Rickman, we'd make a fortune. Invited to suppers, dinners, walks in St James's Park and to attend the wealthy in Covent Garden, Mr Rickman had become an attraction unto himself. Lady Mary and the other shareholders were delighted as night after night there was enough *merde* to fertilise Smithfield. The playwrights, Mr Dryden and Mr Lee, were full of glee as their Author's Benefit, the takings from every third performance, exceeded expectations as the play ran for ten days. (Not all plays ran that long — three to five shows was considered acceptable, any longer a triumph.) Even performers who'd been ready to cast aspersions on Mr Rickman's character off stage were now singing his praises, declaring quite openly they were prepared to overlook any degree of surliness if it came packaged with such talent.

I confess I was a little bit grateful that every time I tried to thank him his gaggle of admirers made it impossible.

Night had well and truly wrapped its velvet arms around the city before the cast managed to gather in the tavern to mark the final performance of *Oedipus*.

While the principal actors, shareholders, Lady Mary, her sons, Charles and Alexander Davenant, and the playwrights, including Aphra, were enjoying celebrations at the Earl of Rochester's London abode, the rest of us made do with the Bishop's Whelp. To me, it was the best tavern in the world, with its smoky interior, wide benches, crackling hearth and jolly wenches. The fact that my judgement might not be sound, as it was only the second tavern I'd ever been in, I chose not to admit — not even to myself.

The place was crowded with theatregoers, river men, local vendors and some provincials who were spending the evening this side of the wall in preparation for market day on the morrow. I pushed my way through the tightly packed bodies, slapping wandering hands and one man who grabbed me about the waist, waving at Charlotte who was kneeling on a bench and gesturing me and a few of the other stragglers over. A fugue of smoke sat under the rafters and the smell of cooking meat made my mouth water. The floor was sticky with spilled ale, something a large hound was trying to help with, licking up a great puddle caused by a broken bung in a barrel. Music drifted over the hum of conversation — three minstrels were sat in a far corner playing ballads. After removing my cloak, I sank onto the bench, forcing Charlotte to move up.

A brimming tankard was placed before me and, as I raised it to my mouth, I looked around at the by now familiar faces in something close to contentment. I might be, as the critic in the *London Gazette* claimed, 'better suited as a prop than a performer', but I was still a part of this Company. Granted, a very small part, I thought as I rubbed a smear of make-up I'd missed from my wrist. Never having really belonged to anything before, I was like an early spring flower enjoying the sunshine. I turned my head this way and that, grinning, and when John Downes offered me another ale I gave cheer and drank heartily.

I caught Prisca watching, her lip curled. Of all the Company members, she'd been the most unwelcoming. To her, I was a piece of dung carried in from the outside: a hidden stink. I resisted the urge to pull a face and instead tried not to let her evident distaste destroy my mood. Inclined to level snide barbs in my hearing, she had been emboldened by the review, which, much to my horror named me (and I could guess who provided that piece of information). Whenever a nobleman or merchant appeared in the Tiring Rooms and laughingly asked Mr Rickman which of the actresses he'd carried off stage opening night (he refused to answer), she took great delight in pointing me out.

Charlotte had reassured me she was jealous I'd appeared in print. I'd snorted. 'She's welcome to swap places.'

Exclamations of horror had followed from those within earshot. What a thespian desired most was notice — didn't matter if it was couched in cruel terms, it was still attention.

'Means you've been seen!' said Charlotte, dusting herself liberally with powder.

'I'd rather be heard,' I whispered in a voice so small no-one did.

Another part of me prayed Papa was still averse to reading the 'less edifying' sections of the news-sheets — the parts that advertised and reviewed the theatre. If he saw my name, I'd be summoned home or, worse, he'd fetch me himself. Fire and brimstone were nothing next to Papa's wrath. I began to imagine him dragging me, protesting, out of the house in Dorset Street. Aphra would be pulling one arm, he the other. I'd be torn asunder, like a medieval criminal bound to horses. But as the days had passed and he didn't appear nor a letter materialise, I had begun to relax.

Margaret chose that moment to arrive at the tavern, wrapped in a shawl of icy air which she spread over the rest of us. She sat down and grabbed the tankard awaiting her.

'Cheers everyone.' We clanked rims.

'What was the ruckus outside the Tiring Rooms earlier?' she asked, wiping the back of her mouth with her sleeve.

'Aye, what *was* that about?' Charlotte pushed her fist against her mouth, trying to stifle a burp. 'Cleared the coves faster than someone shouting "gardi loo".'

''Twas the Earl of Shaftesbury,' answered John Downes from further down the table. He was referring to the man with the crook-back I'd seen in the audience the first night. His lordship oft frequented the Tiring Rooms, along with his coterie. He'd certainly taken to Mr Rickman; they were forever hunkered down in conversation.

'Again?' exclaimed Margaret. 'Why, he's worse than Hamlet's father's ghost. What got up his arse this time?'

'The same as every other,' said Mrs Herbert. 'Accused Samuel Sandford of making a mockery of him, then turned on Mr Dryden.'

There were a few sniggers. One attacked the poet laureate at great risk. He could cleave a person in two with a phrase.

'Dryden did insist Samuel play Creon with a hunchback and limp,' said Finnola, tucking some white wisps back under her cap. She tsked. 'I said no good would come of such an obvious likeness.'

'Don't piss off the author, he'll write you as a villain and then kill you,' said Mr Downes.

'Or she,' I murmured, thinking of Aphra as everyone laughed.

Chatter washed over me as I brooded. Some audience members — mainly merchants and a group of blacksmiths — entered the tavern and joined the other end of the table, buying rounds, determined to toast a successful show. They were welcomed like old friends, albeit badly behaved ones.

I doubted I'd ever become accustomed to the audience's rowdiness. Raised a reverend's daughter, all I'd ever known was the demure and phlegmatic behaviour of congregations (or perhaps they were just bored?), where even a cough or a sneeze drew condemnatory looks. The Company was far more indulgent, almost resigned about the way patrons not only spoke loudly while actors were performing, catcalling and jeering, but wandered around the theatre, hailing one another, and even throwing objects (usually half-eaten oranges). The other actors had been both bemused and amused by my disgust.

After one performance, I'd barely made it back to the Tiring Rooms before I aired my feelings. 'I saw two gentlemen in the pits combing their periwigs! They simply removed them halfway through the play and began delousing them.'

'That's not unusual,' said Elizabeth Barry, with a quiet smile.

'And,' I'd continued, in high dudgeon, 'I saw at least three men leave with the same orange-seller at different times, returning in the middle of an act, pushing and shoving, calling out to their companions, uncaring of what was happening on stage.'

'Funny, I thought the audience was meant to be watching us, not the other way around,' snapped Prisca.

'I noticed that too, Tribulation,' said Mary Lee quickly, as Finnola unclipped her gown.

Prisca turned away, muttering.

'Wait until they start telling bawdy jokes and drown out the actor,' said Elizabeth, fastening the buttons on her sleeve. 'Remember last time that happened?'

'Oh, good Lord, yes,' said Aphra, who'd not long arrived to escort me home. 'That was during the run of *Madam Fickle,* wasn't it?'

I stared at them in horror. 'They spoke *that* loudly?'

'Oh, they didn't just speak, dear,' drawled Mary Lee. 'They *performed.*'

'The Duke of Buckingham and George Etherege do it all the time,' said Aphra, helping Elizabeth remove her peruke.

'But they're playwrights,' I objected. 'Shouldn't they know better?'

'Aye,' said Elizabeth, unfastening the net constraining her real hair, lustrous locks of deep auburn. 'But if they can upstage and disrupt another playwright's work — especially the female one —' she patted Aphra's arm '— trust me. They will.'

So much for having your voice heard.

Billows of smoke rolled through the tavern as more wood was thrown on the large fire, mingling with fumes from the many pipes. The musicians changed their repertoire, a viol and dulcian being added, and someone pushed a table against a wall to create room for dancing. Mr Downes grabbed Finnola, Tom reached for young Anne, and soon there was clapping and stamping of feet to accompany the music as skirts swirled and coats flapped. After finishing her drink, Margaret bade the group farewell. She had a small child at home and wanted to get back to him.

I'd only just topped up my drink and Charlotte's when she elbowed me so hard in the ribs, half my ale spilled. Before I could try to wipe it, she did it again. I followed the direction of her chin.

Jonathan Rickman.

'What's he doing here?' pondered Charlotte. 'Thought the nazy-cove would be boozing with the gentry.'

I did too. By now, the other players were aware who'd joined us. Chatter lulled.

Mr Rickman hesitated, dark eyes roaming. He looked a little harried and I imagined him fending off admirers. The smell of him alone would have attracted them. Bees to a bouquet. If I'd reached out I could have touched him, he stood so close.

Here was my chance to thank him properly. No-one else was speaking to him. Ambivalent, they were pretending they weren't pleased he'd joined them by refusing to acknowledge him immediately, giving a dose of his own treatment to the man who barely said a civil word in the Tiring Rooms yet left the distinct impression he heard every single one.

For a moment, I felt pity. I knew what it was like to be the odd one out.

'Excuse me, Mr Rickman,' I began, sliding to the edge of the bench and tugging gently on his coat. I rose and stood beside him. Because of the wall and a post, never mind the crush of people, I was nearer than was comfortable. 'I don't know if you remember me …' His head swivelled. I lost my words. Christ in a basket, but his eyes were like ink. Obsidian pools. He had a long thin scar travelling across his right cheek, as if a nail had been scraped across his flesh, or a very sharp dagger …

In a rush, what I wanted to say, needed to, poured out. 'Forgive me, sir, but I just wanted to say thank you for what you did opening night — not just your performance, which was magnificent and has been ever since, but for — well, you know.' I widened my eyes, opened my mouth slightly, became rigid and stared straight ahead unblinking. 'That.' I resumed my normal expression and prayed he could tell the difference. 'I owe you both a huge debt and an enormous apology. I've said sorry to everyone except you. I almost ruined your first night. I don't know what came over —'

'Silence,' he said, and pushed his finger against my lips. The touch was so unexpected, so intimate, I stiffened. I'd never been touched by another man, not in such a manner. Why, Papa had only ever hit me. The curate Mr Parker had occasionally patted my arm. Mr Rickman's finger was callused and firm. I wanted to pull away; dear Lord, I wanted it to remain. I grew very, very warm.

'Why do women prate so?' purred Mr Rickman, his voice coming from somewhere in his boots, transforming his rude observation into something less insulting. Nevertheless, a flicker of anger sparked.

How dare he — and when I was expressing gratitude? 'Mrs Johnson, you've no need to apologise.' He removed his finger. Slowly. 'I think you should dismiss it from your mind. Satan's turds, I know I have.'

Perhaps he wasn't so terrible after all. Perhaps the man was just misunderstood.

'If I hadn't acted as I had,' he continued, 'you wouldn't have just ruined first night but jeopardised the entire run. And I couldn't afford that — no-one in the Company can.'

My face began to burn. My entire body followed.

'As far as I'm concerned, you should never have been on stage in the first place. And, if I had my say, no amount of nepotism would enable you to set foot on it again.'

Everyone at the table was listening, but before I could summon a retort, he casually turned away and, through the gap that opened before him the way the Red Sea did for Moses, left.

'Did I hear the knave aright?' said Charlotte, staring at his retreating back with eyes that had they been daggers would have drawn blood.

I sank back down next to her. 'I think everyone did.'

Nepotism. Well, that was working well for me, wasn't it?

Smiles were flashed, some sympathetic looks, smirks as well.

Charlotte flung an arm around me. 'How dare he! The glimflashy knave needs a lesson.' She punched her fist into her palm to demonstrate the kind she meant, almost strangling me in the process. 'A good floggin' and a reminder that, if he can't be civil, to keep that grunting cheat's tongue in his head.'

'Shouldn't sledge a man who speaks the truth,' said a nasally voice.

'Truth?' Charlotte practically snarled at Prisca. 'Truth is he's nothing but a queer cove who's forgotten his place.'

'Forgotten it,' said Prisca, rising, inviting Mr Crosby to join her. 'Or finding it?' As she squeezed past the tables and closer to me, she leaned over. 'Something the new chit's yet to do, eh? Nepotism or no …'

This time, it was my eyes shooting daggers. Sadly, truth or no … they missed their mark.

'He said *what*?' Aphra's breath came out in streams of white as we entered the street. She'd come to fetch me from the tavern. Though I'd assured her I'd find my own way home, she insisted on escorting me. After my encounters with both Mr Rickman and Prisca, I was grateful. I was shaken by their words, their veracity, and though I was trying hard not to let them bother me, they did. Greatly.

Aphra could tell something was wrong. It didn't help that Charlotte had kept shooting her conspiratorial looks and then insisted on relating the whole incident to her.

'Now, tell me again what exactly was said. It was hard to hear in there.' Aphra had waited until we were outside to have me confirm Charlotte's account. Fortunately, she'd hired a link boy to walk us home. He was waiting in the cold, wrapped in mufflers and a thick coat, looking miserable, though his pitch torch offered a decent flame. The night was dark as coal, illuminated by lanthorns set above the shop doors and burning braziers dotted up the hill, a series of fallen stars casting crazed shadows on the faces gathered around them. Some carriages and sedan chairs, lights swinging, rolled slowly through the fallen snow. More link boys lit the way for couples and families. Children darted between them, two dogs scampering after a young girl who was unaware the chicken carcass she carried was half out of the bag. A beldame was crouched in a shop doorway, her pipe clamped between wrinkled lips, the smoke swirling about her like a miniature fog.

With my arm wound through Aphra's, I drew her closer. 'He said women prate too much.'

'Did he?'

'And he only carried me off stage to save himself and the play's run. And —' I paused. Aphra leaned heavily upon me. The smell of sac was sweet on her breath. 'If he had any say, I wouldn't be allowed to act again.'

Aphra stopped dead in her tracks, forcing me to halt. 'Rude bastard.'

The link boy looked over his shoulder and, seeing we'd halted, scurried back.

I shrugged. 'That's what Charlotte said as well, in her way. But he's right. I've no place on stage.'

'Rubbish,' said Aphra. 'After a … bumpy start, you've acquitted yourself very well. And it's too late. You're cast in the next few productions.'

Much to my relief and no small satisfaction, I was. Minor parts, but it was still a wage.

The link boy cleared his throat. We started up the hill again.

'I don't know who Mr Rickman thinks he is,' said Aphra. 'He may have proven himself an asset, one that has swiftly accumulated support in high places — in the theatre and outside it — but he's no right to talk to you like that.'

'What if he asks for me to be dismissed?'

'That will *not* happen,' reassured Aphra as we arrived home. She began to fumble in her purse for a coin to give the link boy. She paid him, then watched as he was hailed by two men stumbling out of the tavern across the way. 'Better still, I'll have a word with the upstart. No?' she added, when I clutched her wrist in horror.

God. It would simply confirm the worst of what Mr Rickman had levelled at me.

'Very well,' she said reluctantly. 'I'll resist rebuking him — this time.' Aphra patted my hand reassuringly. 'Lest you forget, cousin, Mr Rickman may have his admirers, but he's not the only person the Duke's has to accommodate. If they want more plays, they must also look after me.'

She was about to unlock the door when it opened. The welcome face of Nest and a wave of warmth greeted us.

'And I must look after you,' Aphra added, giving Nest a peck on the cheek as we entered.

'You don't have to,' I said, also kissing Nest. The old woman helped Aphra with her cloak while I unclasped mine.

'Let me put it another way,' said Aphra, holding my arm for balance as she removed her boots. 'I don't *have* to look after you — you're perfectly capable of doing that. But, for some unfathomable reason, Tribulation Johnson, I want to.' She cupped my face and gave me a kiss on first one cheek then the other. 'If there are those at the Duke's who choose to call it nepotism, let them. How often can we women use that to our advantage, eh? I call it a brief balancing of very skewed scales. A kind of justice, only done with eyes wide open. *My* eyes. *My* justice.' Then, with a somewhat silly smile, a floppy wave, and instructions to Nest to bring more wine to her room, she flunked up the stairs.

I watched her with a growing grin, my heart swelling.

'She likes you,' said Nest, hanging our cloaks.

'And I her,' I said. 'Very much.' I thought more on this as I helped Nest retrieve wine and glasses to take upstairs while I quickly ate some leftover pie from the night before.

I did like Aphra. More than I ever expected. She treated me with respect, allowed me to find my own way, and yet also let me know she was there if I faltered — like opening night. Like tonight.

Likewise, she readily shared her opinions and sought mine on matters Papa would have been shocked to discover even entered a woman's head let alone came out of her mouth. Though she was troubled by Catholicism, Aphra was far more disturbed by the virulence and hatred directed towards those of Papist faith. She strongly felt the throne should pass to the rightful, legitimate heir, the King's brother, no matter what religion he served. Not a day went by when she didn't express frustration at the browbeaters in Parliament who were using whatever means at their disposal — Titus Oates and the Popish Plot or the King's illegitimate but Protestant son, James Scott, the Duke of Monmouth — in an attempt to place someone they could control upon the throne. There were even those who sought a return to a Republic, like the country had been under Oliver Cromwell.

In the short time I'd been in London, I'd learned about the constant struggle for authority between the King and the power-brokers within his Parliament — namely Shaftesbury. I read the news-sheets, listened to the conversations swirling around me, absorbing what they meant, how the smallest actions on the part of his Majesty or his Parliament impacted those who relied upon them for leadership and governance. Aphra never hesitated to discuss what she'd read, witnessed or heard. It was both enlightening and flattering.

Already she was becoming more than simply my landlady, my guardian.

She was fast becoming my mentor.

There was a time I sought to cast Papa in that role. Instead, from as early as I could remember, he'd been more of a *tor*mentor.

I dressed for bed and crawled under the covers, listening to Aphra move about her room, musing upon how one word could contain another, yet alter its meaning entirely, turning something so positive into something cruel.

As I drifted off to sleep, I wondered what had happened to transform my father from one into the other, why he never offered me the benefit of his wisdom let alone love, his face looming large and distorted in my dreams.

SCENE NINE

Who is't that to woman's beauty would submit
And yet refuse the fetters of their wit?

Prologue to *The Forc'd Marriage or, The Jealous Bridegroom*, Aphra Behn

Aphra was unusually silent as we headed down the hill towards the theatre. Yesterday, she'd left the house early to meet with Lady Mary, returning a short time later. I'd scarce seen her since as she'd kept to her room. I was about to ask if anything was troubling her when Mr Shale appeared. Unable to avoid us, he fell into step, offering a curt greeting which we returned. While the Shales refused to publish Aphra, they'd readily print her detractors, including that dreadful anonymous critic who took great delight in lampooning many of the Duke's plays, but Aphra's especially. They even inflated the prices of their supplies when Aphra was short of paper or ink, just to discourage her purchasing from them (not that she needed to be).

The sky was pregnant with grey menace. As if on cue, a steady spitter began, the kind that when it strikes clothing, seeps through the weave to leave the wearer sodden and cold. Wind off the river snapped and bit.

So did Aphra. 'You'd be wise to get those indoors before they're ruined.' She bobbed her head towards the sheaves of paper tucked under Mr Shale's arm.

'Undoubtedly,' agreed Mr Shale. 'Yet, they'll have to withstand a moment or two longer.' He rearranged his cloak over them and, cross at having been forced to engage with us, bid a gruff good day, and increased his pace.

'Ridiculous little man,' sniffed Aphra.

I couldn't disagree.

We walked without speaking the remainder of the way, concentrating on keeping our hats in place and cloaks together. When we reached the theatre, I hesitated. 'Are you alright, Aphra?'

'Why do you ask?' She wrenched open the rear door.

'You seem quite distracted. Ever since your meeting with Lady Mary …' I waited for her to recognise the truth of my statement. She didn't. 'Forgive me, cousin,' I continued after a beat. 'Is it something I've said or —?'

'No.' Aphra plunged into the darkness of the corridor and disappeared.

With a sigh, I shut the door and followed. I consoled myself she must be worried about her play, but a little mouse of doubt began to gnaw at my peace. It wasn't only Aphra who'd been uncharacteristically quiet since that meeting. I could have sworn Lady Mary had spent yesterday avoiding me.

A short time later, rehearsals for Thomas Shadwell's *The Virtuoso* were in full swing. He was rather a florid man with a love of lavish periwigs and the company of the Earl of Shaftesbury. No friend of Aphra's, Mr Shadwell had written that Aphra's work was not only inferior but the result of plagiarising (poorly) the men's.

Shadwell's play had first been performed by the Duke's two years earlier and, with its story of ill-fated lovers, some rather dark cross-dressing and a fruitless and ruinous search for the Philosopher's Stone, had been so successful, the company staged it again and again. Lady Mary and Mr Betterton thought it would be good to run between the other stock plays and Aphra's new one. I'd been cast in the small role of a maid.

The final run-through went well with everyone remembering their lines, which was just as well as the prompter, John Downes, hadn't yet made an appearance. It was most out of character.

By the time we retreated to rest and change for the afternoon's performance, he still hadn't arrived. When the musicians took up their positions and began to play, and some merchants bowled into the Tiring Rooms, there was still no sign of him. Panic began to set in.

Lady Mary sent Tom to the nearest tavern. Alexander, her son, took his valet and went to Drury Lane. John Downes was oft in the vicinity on a Sunday, visiting old friends, drinking in local ale-houses, trying to find out how the King's Company had fared for the week. An old gossip, he loved to be the bearer of any tidings. When it came to the Duke's rival company, the worse, the better.

Fully dressed and with make-up applied, I did what I could to assist the others. Close to the Tiring Rooms' door, which was ajar, I was helping Finnola get Elizabeth Barry into costume when I heard the unmistakable burr of Aphra's voice in the corridor.

'I haven't had a chance.' Something in the tone, the cautious way she spoke, made me shift nearer the door so I might hear better. Have I mentioned my fondness for ear-wigging?

'If you don't feel you can tell her, I will.' It was Lady Mary. 'I'll explain we don't have the means to keep her on. Not when her, you know, isn't the calibre of those with more experience …'

Oh dear God. They were discussing me. My acting ability. Or lack thereof. And I'd thought I'd improved. I had. Not enough, it seemed. The room swam. If my mouth hadn't been full of pins, I would have laughed. Or wailed. So that's what the meeting had been about. The reason Lady Mary evaded me and Aphra was reticent — she didn't know how to tell me. Of course the Company couldn't continue paying me a wage. Not when, as Prisca reminded everyone, and John Crosby and Margaret Collins oft commented, all I did was wander on and off stage. It wasn't as if acting was my real passion. I'd simply fallen into this, as Mr Rickman insisted, through nepotism.

And yet, as I gazed about, knowing it soon must end, my pragmatism dissolved. I would miss it — this — the camaraderie and intimacy of the Tiring Rooms, the shared anticipation as we waited in the wings, the fond mocking of patrons and above all, the tired but exhilarated reflections upon the performance afterwards. The understanding and appreciation that naturally arose from working together and creating. Even the backstage barbs, the aloofness and spite from some quarters (I did my utmost not to look at Prisca) were worth tolerating.

Chartham was closed to me. From what Papa and Bethan said in their brief letters (Papa's were more instructions and Bethan's, while filled with village goings-on, made no mention of forthcoming nuptials), it would be for a long time yet.

I batted away the moths of sadness swooping and fluttering, but they were persistent.

'I think it needs to come from me, don't you?' said Aphra. She sounded sad, resigned. 'After all, I introduced her to this.'

'At her request,' said Lady Mary softly. She was right.

'Still …' said Aphra, determined to wear a portion of blame when there was none to don.

'I just wish there was another option.' Lady Mary sighed. There was a rustle of fabric. 'Numbers are thin again. When we find John — where *is* he? — he can tell us how Drury Lane is managing. This plot business isn't good for them either and, what with Thomas Killigrew and his son at each other's throats all the time … they're lucky they're able to mount anything let alone drag audiences in.'

'It's never good when fathers and sons argue. And, as I've had cause to reflect of late, fathers and daughter either …'

The women moved away.

Oh God. Was Aphra regretting taking me in? Had Papa written to her? Had she written to him?

'How can you help me standing over there?' rebuked Finnola, clicking her fingers. 'Are you going to swallow those pins or pass them to me?'

I scurried back to the dresser, held the fabric fast over the base of Elizabeth Barry's spine with one hand and extracted a pin from my mouth. 'Here,' I mumbled.

'Gawd, Mrs Barry,' said Finnola. 'You been dining at the palace regular or something? This fitted last time you wore it.'

Mrs Barry struck Finnola with a fan. 'Cheeky harridan. That was months ago! The dress has clearly shrunk.' Elizabeth glanced at me for support. 'Do I look …?' She paused and stared at me hard. 'Are you alright, Tribulation?'

'Forgotten her lines,' snapped Prisca as she passed.

There was some sharp laughter. Everyone knew I'd none to con.

I didn't have time to retort as the stage manager, Mark Danvers, appeared, ringing the bell usually tolled by John Downes.

'Fifteen minutes!' he called.

The room erupted. There were shrieks, orders for help with laces, perukes, last-minute adjustments. The merchants were hurried out of the room. I ran from one dressing table to the next, fastening shirts, applying a dusting of powder, securing a headpiece, making sure a feather in a fan was straightened, grateful to be doing, not tangled in my wretched thoughts. Before I knew it, the second bell rang, the cast were crowded into the wings and the curtains opened.

For the first time in the Duke's Company memory, a production started without John Downes perched on his stool. Instead, Lady Mary sat there, head bent over the script, the candlelight making her nose look huge and her eyes glimmer.

Lady Mary was right — the audience wasn't large and no-one of real note attended except Samuel Pepys and John Evelyn. They'd been hoping the King's current interest, Hortense Mancini, or even his old flame Barbara Castlemaine might attend or, better still, some of the Wits. The Wits were a raucous, attention-seeking group of men — mostly writers and some nobles, rakes and louches the lot, according to Nest, so called because they were renowned as much for their debauched frolics as they were for their sardonic repartee and poetic works. They enjoyed the King's favour (and thus were tolerated by everyone) even though they were more likely to skewer their liege for everything from his fondness for women to his inability to sire a legitimate heir than honour him. Charlotte whispered that Lady Castlemaine was in Paris, sent there in disgrace by the King. As for Hortense Mancini, it was agreed that wherever his Majesty bided, she was likely by his side. Most blamed what Aphra was calling 'the Oates effect' for the low attendance. People were cautious about being seen mingling, even inadvertently, with a suspected Catholic, let alone entering a venue patronised by a noble one, lest they were thought sympathisers. Still, those brave enough to risk accusations — including false ones — and appear were appreciative and there'd been many laughs and spontaneous moments of applause, especially when a sheep's tail magically grew out of a man's arse and the character Sir Nicholas tried to swim on dry land.

Only Mr Pepys and a pox-scarred noble whose silken jacket was embroidered with mythical beasts came to the Tiring Rooms afterwards and they didn't remain long. Mr Pepys was not his usual self, barely flirting and inclined to the doldrums. Despite Lady Mary and Mr Betterton congratulating us, everyone was despondent. It may only have been Monday, but in past runs, Mr Shadwell's play had sold out every performance. Thank goodness he wasn't present to see the poor takings. He'd a tendency to blame the actors. This didn't bode well for the coming days.

Didn't bode well for me either, I thought selfishly.

Aphra excused herself from chatting with Mary Lee, giving Jonathan Rickman, who'd not only been extraordinary but had wished me *beaucoup de merde* before he left the Tiring Rooms earlier, a congratulatory squeeze as she passed him. 'Tribulation,' she said quietly. 'I need a word.'

Securing my brightest smile, I patted the seat beside me.

Aware Mr Rickman was watching, something he was wont to do, I gave him a pointed stare. I didn't want any witnesses, especially not one inclined to choler and who believed I'd been given a position in the Company because of bias alone. Not that he was entirely incorrect. With a cavalier rise of his shoulders, he swung back to the mirror.

Before Aphra could sit, there was the thump of boots, a shout in the corridor. Alexander Davenant burst in, his face red and shining. 'Mother? he cried.

'Alex?' Lady Mary flung aside the dress she was holding. 'What is it? What's wrong?'

At once the chatter died. In the ensuing silence, we exchanged concerned looks. Alexander untied his cloak and tossing it aside bent over and held his knees, breathing like the Greek soldier Pheidippides arriving in Athens from Marathon. Though, from the expression on his face, he wasn't about to announce a victory. Mr Sandford, Mr Smith, Henry Harris and Mr and Mrs Betterton appeared in the doorway to the second Tiring Room. Questions shaped everyone's expressions. Questions and more than a little bit of fear.

This was worse than waiting for the curtains to open.

Recovering slightly, Alexander straightened and, daubing his forehead with a kerchief, took stock of who was present. The laces on his shirt had come undone and the ribbon holding his hair was loose, causing strands to fall about his face and stick to his sweaty cheeks. 'Listen up.' He waited until he had everyone's attention. 'There's been a terrible accident. John Downes has been badly hurt.'

There were gasps.

'How?'

'What's happened?'

Alex waited until the chitter ceased. 'Last night, John went to his usual haunt in Covent Garden.' There were some murmurs. 'After a few drinks, an argument broke out between him and some of the actors from the King's Company.'

Disapproval surged and subsided.

'According to witnesses, John was pushed and staggered against a brazier. The whole thing toppled and —' Alexander swallowed and grimaced. 'His clothes caught fire.'

There was a burst of talk. 'Dear God, no!' exclaimed Lady Mary. Elizabeth Barry swooned. Charlotte and Lily gasped. Mary Betterton turned to her husband, Margaret Collins and Katherine Herbert to each other. I sought Aphra's hand and held it tight. She'd been close to Mr Downes. 'Is he … did he …?' Lady Mary couldn't quite say what everyone was thinking.

'He's alive.' There were collective sighs of relief. 'But he's badly burned.' Alexander gathered his mother against him. 'His hands and arms took the worst — he tried to beat out the flames. It wasn't until one of the King's men heaved him into a nearby trough that they were doused. The doctor said it likely saved him.'

'You've seen him?' asked Aphra.

'Briefly,' said Alexander. His face told us more than words.

'I must go to him,' said Lady Mary, extricating herself from her son's arms.

'Me too,' said Aphra, letting go of my hand and rising.

'And I,' said Elizabeth Barry and Mary Lee in unison.

Everyone began talking at once. It was decided Lady Mary, Aphra and the Bettertons would visit and report back. The performers began dressing swiftly, the mournful mood replaced by a grim one, but also a sense of proportion. What did poor attendance matter when the life of one of our own hung in the balance?

'What about tomorrow's performance?' asked Mary Lee suddenly. 'I mean, I know you sat in John's seat today, Lady Mary, but you can't be there all the time.'

'She's right,' said Mr Betterton. 'We're going to need someone to replace John. Urgently.'

'Aye,' said Mrs Betterton. 'Especially with a new play about to open.' She glanced at Aphra.

Alexander Davenant rubbed his cheeks and sighed. 'I'll speak to Charles. We'll see if there's anyone who can fill John's considerable shoes.' He glanced towards Mr Rickman. 'Who knows, perhaps Killigrew can come to the rescue again. Don't worry, Mother. Leave this with me and Charles.' He addressed the room. 'If anyone can think of someone in the meantime, please, come forwards.'

There were whispers. A few names were thrown about and immediately discarded. Voices increased as debates started: anything to take their minds off what had happened to their prompter.

'Wait,' said Aphra loudly as people began to leave. She'd already donned her cloak.

'What is it?' asked Alexander, half out the door.

'You've the perfect replacement right here.'

'Who?' The word echoed throughout the room. It was as if a parliament of owls had taken roost.

'Tribulation.'

I could not have been more astonished had she announced my betrothal to a chair.

There was a burst of laughter before it quickly died. Aphra wasn't joking.

My face grew hot, my mouth dry, as everyone stared. The light in the room became so very intense, faces blurred.

My heart began to tumble. Bells clamoured in my ears.

'Tribulation?' Prisca's nasal tone was sharp.

Murmurs of incredulity swelled to audible protests, filled with doubt and more than a little disdain.

'Your cousin?'

'A wench?'

'Why she knows nothing of the theatre, of the craft.'

'She's no experience.'

'She's been here less time than it takes to spend half a hog. Why should she get such a position?'

'What about Henry?'

'What about Underhill?'

'I don't want it.'

More names from within the Company were bruited about, but they either couldn't read or write well enough, or were needed on stage.

Slowly, the discussion died. Gazes became inquisitive, considered. Some regarded me with a hostility I would never have attributed to them before.

'Why not Tribulation?' said Aphra loudly, her question a knife that sliced through the rising babble. 'She can read beautifully, write too. She has a fine memory. I've heard her helping many of you with your lines.' A great silence met her claims. Mr Sandford folded his arms, Henry Harris and Jacob as well. Cave Underhill regarded me curiously. Alexander stood there shaking his head. Mary Lee was whispering something in Elizabeth Barry's ear. 'At best,' said Aphra, nonplussed, 'she can take John's place until he's better. At worst, she can fill in until someone else is found.'

No-one said a word.

'For God's sake!' Aphra's cheeks grew red. Her eyes flashed. 'You can at least give the girl a try. Just because you *might* find someone who can read or write, doesn't mean they know the stage, the plays, or *you*. Or do you think because she has a quim, or she's dimber, she's incapable? Incompetent? You who work side by side with clever, talented women every single day? She might lack experience, but just as she's grasped basic stagecraft, she can learn what's required of a prompter, can't she?' She dared someone to correct her.

Mr Betterton lowered his eyes. Mr Sandford plucked the stitching in his sleeve. Aphra sighed. 'You've nothing to lose if you give her a chance. Keep looking if you must, if you're so foolish as to let her sex or relation to me —' her gaze rested briefly on Jonathan Rickman '— be the cause of your reluctance. But I'm telling you, you're not punishing anyone but yourselves and the entire Company by not giving her a chance.' She locked eyes with Lady Mary, who turned and stared at me thoughtfully.

A part of me wished a hole would open, like the one in the stage, and devour me.

There was a lull and then everyone began talking at once, examining me, as if I were an insect on a pin. Aphra returned to my side.

'Trust me,' she murmured. 'Hold your chin up. Remember what I said. Half the battle in convincing people you can do something is pretending you can.'

'I think it's a splendid idea,' said a deep, gravelly voice.

A stool scraped and with his hair a hotchpotch on his head, his make-up only half removed, Jonathan Rickman towered. If I hadn't been seated, I would have fallen. 'Tribulation helped John a few times with annotations, perfectly remembering the changes Mr Dryden insisted upon after our fifth performance of *Oedipus*, don't you recall?'

'She helped me with those bloody Latin phrases I had to master,' said Mr Underhill.

'She's a dab hand with costumes,' added Elizabeth Barry. There were a few murmurs.

'And anything else that needs doing, unlike you lazy lot,' said Charlotte, waggling an admonitory finger.

'And,' continued Jonathan Rickman, 'as Mrs Behn says, she's helped more than a few con lines — for our current play and the rest of the season.' He should know, I'd even helped him. 'She's a good choice.'

'Who are you to say?' said someone loudly. It was James Nokes, Prisca sneering beside him. 'You've only just made an entrance.'

There were nods of agreement.

'And yet I'm given better roles than you,' parried Mr Rickman, eyes flashing.

There were gasps, some disbelieving laughter.

'Touché. He has you there, Jimmy.' Henry Harris chuckled.

Chatter broke out until Lady Mary clapped her hands. I almost leaped out of my flesh. I wasn't the only one. How she managed to make such a loud sound with such small, thin hands confounded me.

'Whether Mr Rickman's been here ten years or hours matters not, James Nokes,' she snarled. 'I would have thought better of you.' She fixed her gaze upon him then Prisca. Only James lowered his head. 'You too, Mr Rickman.' He did not look away. Lady Mary took a deep breath. 'Aphra's right. For the time being, using Tribulation is a good solution. It doesn't stop Alexander or Charles continuing to search for a replacement. What say you, Tribulation? Will you step into John's shoes?'

Once again, all eyes latched onto me.

'Her feet are bloody big enough.' Prisca snickered.

Guilt that someone's terrible misfortune presented such an opportunity and the fear that taking it would divide the players further warred within me, but then I recalled the conversation in the corridor, what Lady Mary had said: 'I just wish there was another option ...'

Well, one was being presented. Who was I to refuse? I did what Aphra advised. I ignored the naysayers and doubters (including myself), lifted my chin, and just like that, answered.

'I will.'

ACT TWO

Spring 1679–Autumn 1679

'Jealousy, the old worm that bites' or, Promptly Employed

I here and there overheard a coxcomb cry,
Ah, Rot it — 'tis a woman's comedy,
One, who because she lately chanc'd to please us,
With her damn'd stuff, will never cease to tease us.
What had poor woman done, that she must be
Debarred from sense, and sacred poetry? …
As for you half-wits, you unthinking tribe,
We'll let you see, what e'er besides we do,
How artfully we copy some of you:
And if you're drawn th' life, pray tell me then,
Why women should not write as well as men.

Epilogue to *Sir Patient Fancy*, Aphra Behn

Plots, true or false, are necessary things,
To raise up commonwealths and ruin kings

Absalom and Achitophel, John Dryden

SCENE ONE

Pan, grant that I may never prove
So great a Slave to fall in love,
And to an unknown deity
Resign my happy liberty

'Song', Aphra Behn

The Tiring Rooms were all but empty, the performers having gone to the Bishop's Whelp. I wasn't invited. Ever since I'd taken over from poor John Downes weeks earlier, those I'd thought friends had become adversaries. Not Charlotte or Elizabeth Barry, Mr Smith, Mr Underhill or the Bettertons: they didn't avoid me. It was the rest of the players who not only altered their manner, but repeated any unkind words being said, most oft in my hearing.

While Finnola, Juliet and Jacob, the backbone of the Tiring Rooms, made a business of tidying up Elizabeth Barry's dresser and reorganising the costumes on the rack, I roamed about, collecting a page of script here, another there, delaying joining Lady Mary, to whom I reported after every performance. Eventually, only Finnola remained.

Even the backstage crew wore their resentment openly, deciding I'd been given a role I didn't deserve (whether it was because I was female or inexperienced or both, I remained uncertain; to them, it was simply unfair, and apart from instructions issued during rehearsals and production, they mostly ignored me). The only exceptions were Finnola and Mark Danvers. They remained helpful and respectful and, like Aphra and Lady Mary, oft guided me when I erred. I was very grateful.

Even Pascal, Evan and the musicians, who used to flirt with me, whisper salacious words, attempt to grope me in the corridor, treated me like a leper. I never thought I'd miss their attentions. I didn't. It was what caused them to cease that gave me pause.

To most of the company, my daily ascension up the stairs to Lady Mary's office was simply another reminder of the lofty heights to which I'd unjustly risen. I was Judas with a halo. If only they knew I worked harder than a waterfowl's legs to keep myself afloat and learn the tasks required of me. If they only knew the number of mistakes I'd made, and the hours I'd spent fixing them, they may have been more generous.

Aye, and kittens grew into lions.

When I said that to Aphra, she smiled. 'Sometimes, they do.'

Turns out, cueing missed or half-forgotten lines in rehearsals and during performances was a fraction of what a prompter or, rather, book-keeper, did. The keeper of the book (the master script) called rehearsals, timed them, and kept the pace when they flagged. He made certain actors were present each performance. If someone was late or ill, it was the book-keeper's duty to find a replacement. He checked copy for posters advertising the next production, made certain they were in the hands of publishers and printers in time and pasted in prominent positions about the city. He also managed the shareholders' correspondence. This included all the Davenants, Mr Betterton *and* Mr Harris. It was time-consuming, even when Mrs Betterton dealt with hers.

I was tired beyond measure; my days were long, but also full and very rewarding. Aware of how I'd come upon the work and its temporary nature, I determined not to let anyone down, no matter what was voiced or done behind my back or to my face. Not that the disgruntled players confronted me with all their gripes. Nay, they also mumbled and moaned behind hands, doors, curtains, before mirrors and in corridors. If I happened along, I was slapped with a smile as false as Tom Otway's periwig, especially when it was evident I'd heard every word.

When the lock on the script box was tampered with and key pages of a play went missing, I didn't say anything. I simply wrote them out that night from memory. I told Aphra what happened, as I had to borrow paper and ink from her (I replaced both the following day — not from the Shales' shop). She was furious and told Lady Mary. In turn, she must have said something to the Company, because after that, they were surlier and more furtive than ever. Two days later, the master script was wet when I retrieved it, the pages stuck together, the writing smudged. Actors arrived late and lines were missed that never had been before, keeping me on the tippiest part of my toes. There was never enough done to damage an actor's reputation, but ample that, if things had gone wrong, the blame would have fallen squarely on my shoulders. I determined it would not.

Instead of ceasing their torments or respecting my efforts (and the fact I never tattled), those keen to thwart my endeavours just resented me more.

I grew sleepless, sorrier than a sow's teats, and lost my appetite. Aphra tried to draw me out, but I was in no mind to share my torment, not after she made it hers and told Lady Mary. Instead, when we were together, I steered the conversation onto less choppy topics — the latest news, her writing, antics of our neighbours, the court, even the audience: anything but the backstage machinations of the Company.

If I'd known I'd lose the fellowship I'd so enjoyed by accepting the position, would I have been as eager to jump into Mr Downes's shoes? I was treated worse than an excise man, excluded, mocked, kept at arm's length, as if this was war and I the enemy. It was Chartham all over again. The performers would send out scouts to warn each other if I approached, fall silent, turn away, but not before sibilant whispers and looks were exchanged; sneers delivered with glacial stares. I may as well have been wearing bells.

Or horns.

Weren't we all on the same side? Didn't we have the same goal? Mr Downes always had one foot in management, one with the actors. Why couldn't I?

Was it because I was a woman? One who didn't know her place? Or, worse, refused to accept it. Or did this happen to anyone who dared rise above their station? Those who were granted opportunities and then made the most of them.

My heart lurched as I thought of the players roistering in the tavern, and I was filled with an unexpected longing for open fields, fresh, fragrant air, a slow-moving, reed-lined river, Lady Adeline, her books, and Bethan. I doubled over, leaning on a dresser.

Finnola gave me such a sympathetic smile I almost lost what little control remained. I ducked so the mirror shielded me, checked my face (cheerless and ashen, hair falling out of pins), took a deep breath, tidied myself, and went to find Lady Mary.

I ascended the staircase slowly, noting how each step creaked under my weight. Pale light from a dirty window cast grey stripes across the wood, highlighting the cobwebs garlanding the beams and forming starbursts beneath the handrail. Paint was peeling off the walls and the faint odour of stale beer lingered. God's balls, but the theatre was a different place when it was all but empty, when the audience had left and there were no lights or make-up or grand, colourful costumes and sets, never mind the arguments, catty chitter and drama of the performers to focus upon — and that just off stage. I peered over the banister at the props stacked in corners below: the closed doors and draped furniture. Filled with grotesque shadows, solid shapes resembling nothing like what they were, it really was the stuff of nightmares.

There was the reassuring scuffle of feet and a merry call as I knocked on Lady Mary's door and was admitted by a servant.

'Ah, Tribulation. I was wondering where you were,' said Lady Mary, pushing past and beckoning me to follow. 'Mr Dryden has made some changes to *The Spanish Friar.*' She indicated the pages in her hand. 'I thought we'd run through them. Best do it downstairs.'

Grateful none of the cast remained to see me trailing in Lady Mary's wake, I followed her back the way I'd come, through the corridors, and across the stage. Once we reached the prompter's table, she pulled up a stool, dropped the pages she was carrying and, when I didn't remark or reach for them, looked at me. 'Are you quite well, dear?'

Kindness was harder to bear than bitter words. I was almost undone. 'I'm fine,' I said, flipping a hand to prove how easily trouble could be dismissed. Ha.

Lady Mary sighed. 'I wish I could tell you they'll get over their envy.' She nodded towards the Tiring Rooms. 'Facts are, they won't. And the better you do the job, the worse their malice will become.'

I'm damned if my eyes didn't well.

'They're a fickle lot, actors. I know. I've spent my life around them. They're all hale and hearty and come hither my friend until someone is elevated, given a better role. Then they watch you like a rat a crumb, waiting to steal it out from under you or, better still, poison it so you can't enjoy the fruits of your talent and labours.' She leaned over, put her arm around my shoulders and drew me against her. Much to my shame, a tear escaped. 'There, there, sweetling. Once John returns, they'll discover someone new to focus their spite upon. Pity that person, for they'll not have your skills or the friends you do possess.'

'I don't have any friends,' I sniffed, trying to find my kerchief so I might blow my nose, stopper up the snot of misery.

'Don't you? I can think of a few. Me for a start; Aphra, of course. But also, Charlotte and Finnola. Mark Danvers. The Bettertons, Cave Underhill and Mr Smith. Jonathan Rickman has been singing your praises of late. And I warrant he doesn't make friends easily.'

I couldn't answer.

'Come, it's late. Dry your eyes and let's get on with this.'

And so, Lady Mary patiently took me through Mr Dryden's changes.

An hour later, we'd finished. Lady Mary retreated to her rooms. I made sure everything was in position for the morrow. I was about to lock the script away when I changed my mind. After all, it wasn't as if I'd be welcome at the tavern.

Among the many things I'd learned was that the prompter's script was very different from the partial one a performer was given. Not only was it annotated with changes, but often stage directions, timings and so much more. Best go over them again; make certain I knew them by heart, if for no other reason than I'd be familiar with them if they were tampered with overnight. I stood up and arched my aching back. I eyed the empty sofa downstage, a prop from the current play, George Etherege's *Man of Mode*. It looked far more comfortable than my stool.

I picked up the lamp and, carrying the script, dragged a small table towards the sofa. If only I had an ale, this could be quite the occasion. I patted the dusty cushions, coughing as motes billowed, and commenced reading.

'Thought I might find you here.'

As if to compensate for the way the other performers treated me, of late Mr Rickman had made a point of seeking me out. Ostensibly, it was so I could help him con lines: after all, he had to learn the stock plays. It was easy for the Bettertons and other company actors as they'd been playing the same characters for years. But Mr Rickman had to learn many different parts in a matter of weeks. I'd been a bit reluctant at first — he wasn't my choice of companion — but when Charlotte was busy (often with Mr Pepys), Aphra at home writing or visiting Mr Hoyle, the Earl of Rochester, or Sir Roger L'Estrange the publisher, and the rest of the cast were comfortably ensconced at the Bishop's Whelp, any company was better than none.

To my surprise, when he wasn't being grumpy, or 'glimflashy' as Charlotte called it, or trying to ingratiate himself with nobles, he wasn't completely unpleasant. Sort of like a bruised apple; you just ignored the horrid bits. We even shared some laughs.

Together, we conned lines for *Othello*, where Mr Rickman played Cassio, Iago the villain's loyal servant, followed by *The Spanish Friar*. Currently, he was playing young Bellair in *Man of Mode*. We'd also worked on Dryden's *Troilus and Cressida*, and Aphra's *The Feign'd Curtezans*. He almost had the part of Julio down. I read the other roles.

Without the pressure of an audience aside from Mr Rickman, I began to enjoy being someone else, many someones, even for a brief time. As we rehearsed, Mr Rickman would occasionally ask me to repeat the line, only this time I was to emphasise sorrow, sarcasm, increase the pause, the pace, say the line more flirtatiously, with extra anger. Add a gesture, step forwards, backwards, crouch, bend, laugh or swoon. If I hadn't known better, I'd have said he was training me in stagecraft. I began to anticipate our time together.

'Hello, Mr Rickman,' I said, torn between wanting to be alone and gratitude for the distraction.

As he sauntered over, his jacket swinging against his slender thighs, I wondered why this irascible man was being kind to me.

'I thought *you* might want to go through the script.' He tapped the pile of pages on my lap. 'I heard Dryden made changes. I can assist if you like.' He flashed a smile. 'It's the least I owe after all you've done. Mind if I …?' He didn't wait for a response, but flopped into the space beside me. His leg brushed against my thigh. 'Not that you need help. You're one of those annoying people with exceptional memories and who are good at whatever they put their minds to.'

A compliment. From Mr Rickman. Wonders will never … and all that.

'Only because I know when to give up.'

He glanced at me. 'Well, you haven't yet, despite others' efforts to make you.' He dropped the script he'd been carrying on the table and dusted his hands. 'There's a lot to be said for that.'

I half-turned on the sofa. He'd taken off his coat and the frill of his shirt cascaded over his waistcoat, revealing a broad chest and dark curling hair. A puckered bit of skin peeped. Another scar. According to Charlotte, who made a habit of looking, Mr Rickman's torso was riddled with them, as if he'd been repeatedly whipped with barbs. As she said, what kind of actor carries such mementos? No-one dared ask, though many persisted in guessing what he'd done before Dorset Garden. From what I'd heard, he'd been a slaver, slave, executioner, soldier (which would explain some of the marks), prisoner in the Tower and even a banished regicide. He was far too young for the last. And that was on top of the initials claims he'd been a spy, sailor or pirate. Dear God, whatever he'd been, he smelled good. Musk, ambergris and the lingering odour of tobacco.

'Hey,' said Mr Rickman softly, studying my face. 'You've been listening to gossip.'

'Don't we all?' I said wryly.

He lifted a hand as if he might place it over where mine rested on my knee, then changed his mind. 'While this is easy for me to say, Mrs Johnson, try not to. At least, not so it chips away at your confidence, undermines your courage.' He waited until I met his eyes. 'You possess that in spades.'

'How can you say that? You don't really know me.'

'I know you well enough. Who was it stepped back on stage after coming undone opening night? You didn't let that daunt you —'

'I did.'

'You went on the following night and every night after.'

'Only because with everyone on alert there was no chance of me ruining anything.'

'There was every chance,' he said with a twinkle.

'So you made very clear.'

Mr Rickman began to laugh. 'At last. The mouse roars. I was unaccountably rude. Forgive me.'

'Squeaks,' I corrected. 'A mouse squeaks. It's the lion that roars.' I paused. 'And just so you know, I do forgive you. I can hardly hold you to account for speaking the truth.'

Mr Rickman stared at me for a long moment before he spoke. 'And thus, I stand by what I said that day in the Tiring Rooms. I knew you'd be an excellent replacement for Mr Downes. I hear his recovery is slow.'

I nodded sadly. I'd been to visit him. The unfortunate man was abed, swathed in bandages, barely able to utter a word.

'Your cousin was both prescient and wise in putting you forward,' said Mr Rickman softly.

I gave a very unladylike snort. 'Not all would agree. But she is an excellent person.' Thoughts of Aphra made me smile.

'And a talented one.' Mr Rickman wriggled into a more comfortable position. 'Her writing is quite remarkable — and I don't just mean her plays. Her other work is very fine and I'm not the only one who thinks so. I hear she's in great demand in certain circles.'

I stared at Mr Rickman in astonishment. Whilst it was true Aphra had supporters and she was paid to write by certain nobles and publishers, like Sir Roger L'Estrange, her critics were many and vociferous — Mr Shadwell, for example. But Mr Rickman made her sound as popular as … as … William Wycherley or Mr Dryden.

'The Earl of Shaftesbury is one of her patrons, I believe,' pressed Mr Rickman, determined to stay on topic. 'Commissions work from her.'

'Is he? Then you are in possession of facts of which I am ignorant, sir.' What a strange conversation. Why did he want to know who Aphra wrote for?

'Perhaps I've the wrong man. Maybe it's someone else?'

'Why are you asking me? I'm not my cousin's keeper.' I went to rise, but the sofa made me about as graceful as a newborn calf. I fell back into the cushions and tried to pretend it was what I intended all along.

'No, you're not,' said Mr Rickman agreeably. 'Just trying to get to know members of the Duke's Company better. Something I'm accused of neglecting.'

I looked at him a little suspiciously. If that was the case, why didn't he ask about me? Then again, I was as interesting as a wooden dagger. Still, this sudden loquaciousness and curiosity were a far cry from his usual brusqueness. I should humour, not scold him.

'Anyway, *when* Mr Downes does return,' continued Mr Rickman, 'he may need help. At the very least, you'll be in the best position to offer it.'

The performers' angry words, aimed at me only a few days earlier when I called an extra rehearsal (at Lady Mary's behest), echoed in my head.

'A doxy scarce off her mother's teat being given such responsibility.'

'If she fucks up, we all do.'

I tried to silence the voices by changing the subject. If Mr Rickman could seek to get to know members of the Duke's Company better, then so could I. 'Have you always been an actor, Mr Rickman?'

At first, I didn't think he was going to answer, then he leaned back, stretched out his long legs, threw an arm along the back of the sofa, and stared into the darkness above. I followed his gaze, noting the fragile-looking walkways, the garlands of ropes and pulleys emerging out of the gloom.

As I suspected, he wasn't going to answer.

'Not always …'

Well, well, well. 'What else have you done? The Company amuse themselves trying to guess.' I was glad he couldn't see how red my cheeks had become.

'My, you're a curious mouse tonight.'

'No more than you, sir. Are you going to satisfy me?' He was so very close. The width of a finger — a babe's — away. He turned his head and those dark eyes latched onto mine, refusing to be shaken loose.

'Depends.'

'On what?'

'What you ask next.'

I tried desperately to conjure a question, but all I could think upon was how, if I just raised my hand, I could touch his chest, feel that hair. Aware of his arm resting behind my head, I could have sworn I felt something gently tugging the little curls along my nape. All it would take was for me to move a little closer and … His eyes were magnets, pulling me forwards.

'And what scene is *that* you're rehearsing?' Finnola strutted across the stage, dragging a length of shimmering cloth in one hand and holding a lanthorn aloft in the other. 'It's dark as pitch in here.'

Grateful yet again for the umbra, I bounded off the sofa — successfully this time. Mr Rickman rose with a great deal more elegance behind me.

'Come away, the pair of you. You know this is how rumours start — a man and a woman alone in the semi-dark. Anyway, Aphra is looking for you, Tribulation. Said you're expected at the tavern.'

I glanced at Mr Rickman out of the corner of my eye. 'I'm afraid we'll have to practise another time.'

'Is that what we were doing?' He grinned mischievously. What had got into him this evening? I wasn't sure what to make of his … his … playfulness.

Finnola threw the fabric upon the vacated lounge and shooed us away with her free hand. 'Just as well Prisca's been telling folk you be a man-lady, Mr Rickman, like Matthew Medbourne, or Tribulation here would be the subject of more nasty gossip.'

Mr Rickman didn't miss a beat. 'A man-lady, am I? That's a malicious rumour indeed.' Humour laced his words. 'Next she'll be saying I'm Catholic.'

Finnola shook her head in admonishment. 'Now, Mr Rickman, don't be saying things like that.'

'Though,' said Mr Rickman, holding up a finger as if a thought had just dawned, 'we could start rumours of our own, could we not? Cease the nasty chitter about Tribulation and cozen those with twisted tongues, give them something much more interesting to discuss.'

'Like what?' asked Finnola.

I began to retrieve the script. I didn't want to know.

He looped one arm through Finnola's and tried to catch mine. 'That far from being a man-lady, I'm a ladies' man. Yours.' He included both of us.

Finnola struck him lightly, giggling like a giddy maid. 'Get away with ye.'

I gathered the pages to my chest with one arm and grabbed the lamp with the other. I'd no intention of playing this game. He raised a brow and his lip curled as my rejection registered. 'Make that, *this* lady's man then.' With slow deliberation, he turned his back on me and escorted Finnola from the stage.

And in one fell swoop, Mr Rickman was back.

In a bubble of titters, Finnola allowed herself to be led away, leaving me to follow behind.

He could be quite the charmer. Or churl, depending on the audience.

Aphra's warning about actors flew into my head. *Learn this now: few are who or what they seem … they're great pretenders.*

Well, Jonathan Rickman could pretend all he liked. He didn't fool me.

SCENE TWO

Faith, sir, we are here today, and gone tomorrow.

The Lucky Chance or, The Alderman's Bargain, Aphra Behn

Despite the absence of his Majesty and the always lurking spectre of the Popish Plot, the house was almost full. Aphra's new play *The Feign'd Curtezans or, A Night's Intrigue* was about to open. It portrayed good Catholics and bad Catholics and a couple of stupid Englishmen — the aptly named Mr Signall Buffoon and Mr Tickletext (the latter, many were convinced, based on Titus Oates) — whose fears of Popery, in the end, are revealed as grossly misplaced. Thrilled to see so many clambering over the stalls, waving and hailing each other from the boxes and pits, I couldn't keep the smile from my face as I peeked through the curtains one last time.

'It's going to be alright,' said a deep voice.

'I hope so.' I smiled at Mr Betterton, who'd joined me.

'His Majesty mightn't be here tonight, but look, there's Nell Gwyn.'

The King's favourite mistress and Aphra's friend. The play was dedicated to her.

'And,' continued Mr Betterton enthusiastically, 'if I'm not mistaken, that's the Duke of Buckingham and the writer Charles Sedley either side of her.'

His excitement was catching. 'Aphra's sat directly behind. And look, is that William Wycherley just below the musicians?'

''Tis. Next to him is John Dryden, Samuel Pepys, and the Irish alchemist, Robert Boyle. He's a founder of the Royal Society, no less.'

I knew of the Royal Society from Lady Adeline. Notices about their meetings and lectures on natural philosophy and all kinds of scientific experiments at Gresham College in London appeared regularly in the news-sheets. I regarded Mr Boyle with some interest. Far from looking like an esteemed scientist, he resembled a hungry bird. His sable periwig, full and lush like a pampered hound's coat, served mainly to highlight his sunken cheeks and sallow complexion.

Mr Betterton sealed the gap in the curtains. 'They may not be royalty, but they're as close as you can get when his Majesty isn't around. Bless Drury Lane for shutting its doors a time, eh?'

Drury Lane's takings had been so poor of late they'd been unable to pay the actors and were forced to close. The glee that infected the Duke's Company once the news reached us would have been most unbecoming had it not also been infused with terrible hope.

He tweaked the end of my nose. 'Cease your worries, Tribulation. You cannot be damned for a full house.'

Caught by his kind reassurance, the knowledge he knew what I endured in slights and fault-finding, it took me a moment to realise Lady Mary was signalling.

Horrified I'd almost missed the five-minute warning, I swiftly pulled out the small bell from my décolletage and rang it softly. 'Five minutes!' I ran on fleet feet about the stage.

I was about to dart into the wings and ensure Tom was letting the actors in the Tiring Rooms know, when I noticed Mr Rickman. Beside him was Prisca. They were whispering hotly.

'Five minutes,' I repeated, noting the way they broke apart. What had they been talking about? From the smug look on Prisca's face, like she'd found the Holy Grail, I feared my apparent failings were the subject. My heart sank. Not Mr Rickman too …

I strode towards the prompter's table, trying to put the image of them together out of my mind, forcing myself to focus on the performance ahead and not the man left standing behind. The man who, despite his arrogance and laconic manner, I thought supported me.

Not only was the audience almost impossible to quiet, but the swell of music presaging the start of the play failed to work its usual magic. Some took the strains of the viols, oboes and lute as a cue to commence shouting. A range of insults were exchanged, which caused bursts of laughter and even threats to be levelled. Just when I wondered if we could even start, Mrs Currer, who was delivering the prologue, ignored the ruckus and glided downstage.

The music ceased.

The prologue was the moment the author, through the performer, spoke directly to the audience — usually with great élan and daring. The playwright didn't always pen the introduction to their play, nor the epilogue, sharing the spotlight — for better and worse — with another writer. Everything from the monarchy, to science, the latest scandal and, of late, the Popish Plot, to what was reported in the news-sheets, was included. For this play, however, Aphra had written both herself.

At first, the crowd refused to hush. Aphra's beautifully crafted words would be lost.

Honestly, they were worse than sailors reaching a tavern after a long voyage. I knew who'd be blamed. Already, dark stares from across the stage were trepanning fresh holes into my skull. Satan's hairy scullions (aye, I was learning some rich curses — I blame Charlotte). The audience grew noisier, and I took satisfaction from imagining banging heads together.

But, when Mrs Currer began, completely undaunted, only venturing closer to the footlights so her voice would carry over the din, I watched those sat closest to the stage. Gradually, men and women did a double take, clutched their chests, frowned, shushed and nudged each other into silence and, finally, turned their attention to the actress.

After all, she was talking about what was utmost in everyone's minds: the Horrid Popish Plot and the royal succession.

'... The Devil take this cursed plotting age,
'T has ruin'd all our plots upon the stage;
Suspicions, new elections, jealousies,
Fresh informations, new discoveries,
Do so employ the busy fearful town,
Our honest calling here is useless grown;
Each fool turns politician now, and wears
A formal face, and talks of state affairs.'

There were loud objections. This prologue didn't demur from insults, calling those who sanctioned the Plot or called into doubt the Duke of York's right to the throne upon his brother's demise a bunch of simpletons. Half an orange landed on the stage, the pith and peel bursting on impact. Mrs Currer didn't even flinch. There were boos, and a couple of cheers which were quickly drowned. In the crowd's mind, the writer was accusing them not only of being buffoons, but of fearmongering and putting theatres out of business by creating a bigger and (by implication) more farcical plot in real life than a playwright ever could.

Who was it that said the truth hurts?

It wasn't Mrs Currer the crowd was challenging — she was merely a conduit. As far as the audience were concerned, it was Aphra Behn they were jeering. Heads turned to seek her out, necks twisted, fingers pointed.

I tried to spot her again, but from the prompter's table, it was impossible. She'd known her words were provocative, but also hoped to tweak the public's scruples. Tweaked their wrath more like.

Then, the play proper commenced. *The Feign'd Curtezans* was audacious, especially in its sympathy towards Catholicism, but with its volatile themes and dialogue, and considering the changes Aphra kept incorporating depending which news-sheet or pamphlet she read or which of her friends she'd spoken to, she was treading on very dangerous ground in more ways than one.

Only the night before, I'd gone to her bedroom, having finally plucked up the courage to raise my worries.

'I've always believed,' said Aphra firmly after I finished, indicating I should pull up a chair, 'plays ought to be political — especially when the times call for commitment. As a woman, I cannot argue in Parliament or even in a coffee-house. I cannot vote in a guild nor run for office. I cannot take arms but I *can* write. My plays — the words I put in the characters' mouths, the plots, and themes, whether they are couched in comedy or drama, are like secret instructions to the people: instructions in things it's impossible to insinuate into them in any other way.'

Pages of scrawled notes, drafts of new plays and other writings fanned the surface of her desk. 'You see yourself as teaching the audience, giving them lessons they don't even know they're having,' I said as understanding dawned. Some plays were so silly, so salacious and outrageous, and yet Aphra was right. Just because something was humorous or bawdy didn't make it less profound. That was the shallow dressing in which deeper meanings were buried.

Aphra smiled. I loved her smile, the way it made her eyes glimmer, dance in the soft light of candles. The way her lips parted to reveal her even, creamy teeth. 'That's certainly one way to consider it. Maybe what I do is *reach*, rather than teach. That's at least something, don't you think?' She placed her hand over mine. 'Name one other way women can do that.' She waited. 'No. neither can I. Through words — words *I* write, and which actresses like Elizabeth Barry, Mary Lee, Elizabeth Currer, your Charlotte and the rest perform — we speak to the audience, to other women especially. The hear *us*. They see *us*. It's one of the reasons I make sure there's plenty for my female characters to say. There's a strength in numbers, Tribulation. Every general knows that. What's life but a constant battle for women? We must recruit others and join forces where we can. It's only when we unite we have any might, that our voices are heard and maybe even listened to. It's why men work so hard to keep us apart, sow discord, interrupt, call us abhorrent names, sully reputations before they're even made. They try to silence us, turn us against each other because they're afraid of what we'll achieve if we work together.' She shifted on her chair, grimacing as the leg that sometimes ached caused her pain. 'I've said it before, and I'll say it again. Fear makes men angry. Those they fear the most bear the brunt of that fury.'

'They must be terrified of you.'

Aphra gave a droll look. 'Perhaps. Mind, there are still women who perceive females like me, like those in the Duke's and King's Companies, like Nell Gwyn, Moll Davis, the publisher, Joanna Brome, like *you*, as enemies. They take the men's part, become willing warriors for *their* causes, take up arms against those they should fight beside. In my experience, women can make the very best of allies, but also the worst of adversaries.' She sighed. 'It's hard to forge ahead when you're always watching your back — as you've had cause to learn of late.'

I took a deep breath. 'From here on in, I'll watch yours, Aphra.' It was a vow.

Aphra cupped my face. I froze, then relaxed into it. 'And I yours, kitten.'

It was her new pet name for me, the implication being that I would one day turn into a lion — or, rather, a lioness.

I liked it.

I thought hard on what Aphra said as the play continued its run over the next few days, and listened to the invective hurled at first Mrs Currer, then the cast and, finally, at Aphra — and not only from the pits. New-sheets, tracts and letters flew off the presses condemning her. Rotten food was flung so often during performances I was forced to calculate how long it would take Tom and Nicholas to clean it between scenes. I had to believe Aphra was not only being heard but listened to — that her words were reaching the right ears as well as those who preferred to stopper theirs or ensure their discrepant views were louder and more far-reaching.

Day by day, the audience grew. Rumour spread that a piece of Catholic cant was being performed and so the play went into its fourth, then fifth day. While this effected a solid Author's Benefit for Aphra, it also meant the theatre began to fill with friends of Titus Oates, Justice Scroggs, the publisher Henry Care and a host of other anti-Catholic men. They didn't come once, but many times. Beside them sat those who thought the Popish Plot an aberration and likely a fabulation, who were convinced Titus Oates was nothing more than a cunning puppet. These were mainly Aphra's friends, Sir Roger, Henry and Joanna Brome, John Hoyle and even some of the better-known Catholic and Protestant nobles.

Dorset Garden became kindling; the people filling its seats, firewood and coal; the play the spark that could, if we weren't careful, set off a conflagration.

On the sixth day, my worst fears were realised.

The play was attended by none other than William Bedlowe, one of Titus Oates's cronies and another rabid informer whose far-fetched testimony and endorsing of Oates was responsible for many arrests and executions. Dressed in a new coat and a large hat, he made a noisy show of arriving, some rough-looking fellows beside him, smirking at whoever glanced in their direction.

Just when I thought it couldn't get any worse, a group of novices from the Catholic College of St Omer entered. Accused of being part of the Popish Plot by Titus Oates, why they were at the theatre, I couldn't fathom. Perhaps to prove they'd nothing to hide. Or perhaps to prod. They positioned themselves directly opposite Bedlowe and his group.

As the audience grew rowdier, I thanked the Lord Aphra had a megrim and had remained at home.

It all began well then, midway through the play, a quarrel broke out in the pit.

No-one knew who started it, though it was suspected the first insult was flung by Bedlowe. It was followed by the lobbing of a large stone which struck one of the novices in the forehead. He keeled over, bleeding, crashing into a lady who fell against her husband. He bellowed like a bull.

Filled with fury, and taking advantage of the confusion, Bedlowe and his men jumped over the benches, rats swarming. There were screams as folk were skittled, punched to the ground. Shouts filled the auditorium, drowning the dialogue on stage.

The actors were forced to surrender; they simply couldn't compete. Instead, they reversed their usual roles and became the audience, gathering downstage to watch the action. The musicians stilled their instruments, peering over the balcony as men brawled in the box seats and benches. Women were tearing at each other's vizards, ripping bodices, tugging hanks of hair, kicking and slapping anyone who ventured near. Periwigs sailed through the air like crazed clouds; kerchiefs fluttered like sick birds. As if launched from a trebuchet, a lone cane completed an arc before striking a column and breaking in two.

I ordered the curtain drawn and began ushering the performers behind it. My first duty was to protect the Company. The audience, as far as I was concerned, could be damned.

The actors didn't share my views, nor did Mark Danvers or the Brown boys. When they realised the curtain was being closed, they went behind it, but only to drag some of the props downstage. At first, their intentions weren't clear. Ordering Tom and Nicholas to fetch some ale, a few of the players sat upon sofas, stools and a gilded throne facing the auditorium. Slowly, the other performers joined them. Mr Rickman looked at me, shrugged and took a seat beside them.

'A palpable hit!' shouted Mr Betterton from his chair, clapping enthusiastically as a stocky man in a filthy coat landed an upper cut on a nobleman's jaw, felling him. From the stage, cheers and applause erupted.

Oh, what the hell, I thought, and plonked myself next to Mrs Betterton, just as two oranges splatted into the stalls, the pulp raining over three well-dressed women who shrieked as if it was the contents of a jordan.

Another man, a butcher by the look of his apron, clambered on top of a fallen gent to pummel a man who was swinging his arms wildly, his periwig having slipped over his eyes. It was as if a hairy beast was devouring his face. A man and two women were clawing each other's clothes — to what end was unclear.

The Company whooped, stomped, booed and laughed uproariously as someone tumbled over a kneeling woman, his wooden teeth flying out of his mouth. The theatre was turned into an arena of old. The musicians picked up their instruments and began to play a merry tune. From our raised vantage point, we gave the audience a dose of their own medicine.

When swords were drawn, the steel blades catching the light, the laughter and gaiety ceased abruptly. Mr Rickman bounded off the stage, followed by the actors carrying an assortment of props. Not even Tom and Nicholas could be discouraged. The pair threw themselves on Bedlowe's men, who'd drawn nasty-looking cudgels. Mr Rickman waded through the throng, trying to reach the novices, who were cowering, bleeding and shaking, against a column. They were not fighters. One of Bedlowe's companions, an old fence with a scar cleaving his left cheek and a terrible squint, hefted a truncheon. With a blood-curdling yell, he raised it above the head of a kneeling novice. Before it could descend, Mr Rickman knocked the weapon from his hand and punched him hard. The man struck a bench, splitting it in two, throwing the occupants into a huddle of terrified men and women.

Blood, hair and more teeth flew. The din was tremendous. I was on the brink of ordering Tom to fetch the constables when Mr Betterton, his costume torn, his hair a shambles, climbed back onto the stage. He stood behind the candles, threw back his head and thundered, 'For the love o' God, peace!'

It was enough.

Everyone stopped and stared, slack-jawed and disbelieving. The music ceased. Noses dripped carmine. There were cuts and grazes, swollen cheeks, eyes and jaws, torn clothing, hair askew and garments ripped. A sword clanged to the ground, echoing like an out-of-tune instrument. It broke the spell. Suddenly, there was a wild rush for the exit. Folk were dragged back, climbed over, pushed out of the way. Threats were shouted — not at Bedlowe or the novices, or at those preventing escape, but at us.

'I'll never set foot in this godforsaken ruffin-space again,' cried one man.

'I demand a new periwig!'

'You'll hear from my lawyer!'

'A pox on you Papist-loving poltroons,' spat another.

Fists were shaken in our direction, and more missiles lobbed at the stage. A shoe, a book, a silver buckle, the head of a cane. The damn stone that started the fight crashed at our feet. That was our cue to flee, which we did — behind the curtain. Not before a few footlights shattered, releasing melted wax and the theatre's greatest threat; fire.

'There be a glimmer!' cried Mark. 'Bring your stampers out here.'

I grabbed a bucket of sand, the others whatever they could — costumes, cloths, blankets — and using feet and everything at our disposal, we doused the flames.

Only once the place was emptied could the real damage be assessed. Surrounded by a haze of smoke, the sweet wafts of fruit and perfume and the less appetising ones of sweat and blood, I stood beside Lady Mary, Caesar gazing upon the Rubicon. Mr Betterton, Mr Harris, Mr Rickman and some of the other men wandered about, righting seats, picking up cleaved benches, lumps of fruit pulp, scraps of fabric, feathers, gloves, locks of hair, broken glass, even a crushed boot. The forestage was scorched.

Some of the younger performers, while accustomed to a roisterous audience, had never seen a fight of that magnitude. Overcome, they sat back on their arses and cried, comforted by the older players. It was all I could do to hold my own tears at bay. I needed to be strong, to help Lady Mary, the Bettertons. I took my lead from them and began to use a cloth to wipe the stage. Without waiting to be told, Mark, Tom, Pascal, Evan, Nicholas and Michael ran backstage and fetched besoms, mops and the bucket I'd used, found more rags and began to clean. They were joined by Jacob, Juliet and Finnola.

Afterwards, when what couldn't be salvaged was lugged out into the alley and what could was taken to the workshop at the back of the theatre for repair, Mr Betterton insisted everyone go to the Tiring Rooms for a drink, going so far as to send Jacob and Pascal to the tavern for more wine and ale. Then he addressed us. By now, the initial shock and excitement, the incredulity of what we'd borne witness to, had subsided. We sat slumped in chairs, on the floor, exhausted, forlorn. Mr Betterton reassured us we were blameless; responsibility lay firmly at the feet of Mr Bedlowe and his stooges, who'd come for no other reason than to stir up trouble. But he didn't stop there.

'This is Titus Oates's doing as much as it's anyone else's. He's burst onto the scene like a comet, or one of the villains in an Etherege play, frothing and burbling, causing no end of strife. He's turned the world as we know it upside down.' He lowered his voice and pointed towards the street. 'Not even our Dorset Garden or Drury Lane for that matter have been spared his evil folly. As it is —' his eyes swept the room, taking in the shattered, disbelieving faces, broken swords and pikes, the pile of torn costumes near Juliet '— let us be grateful all we have to do is repair some minor damage to our theatre and to our reputations, and think upon those less fortunate — those whose lives will never be the same again.'

Matthew's name was whispered — reverently, sorrowfully. Never far from anyone's thoughts, he still languished in Newgate, becoming frailer and more despondent by the day. Today's fracas brought home, in every sense, the precariousness of the Company, the cost of being aligned with Papists, even if it was only through royal patent, performance and make-believe.

Lady Mary quickly added her consolations to Mr Betterton's. They both thanked me for having the presence of mind to shut the curtains but also for allowing the cast to make fun of the tumult.

A few even added praise. Mr Rickman, a cut above his brow, raised his tankard in my direction. At least no-one sought to hold me responsible.

Before long, the ale and wine, combined with relief we were safe, did its work and we not only relaxed, but began to see some humour in what had happened. When Mr Sandford, Mr Underhill, Elizabeth Currer and Charlotte re-enacted moments, the laughter was loud even if somewhat forced.

When seven bells struck, we swiftly drained our drinks and left the theatre, farewells more poignant and lingering than usual. For the blink of an eye, we'd been united in adversity.

Of William Bedlowe, his men, and the young novices, there was no sign that night or in the following days.

But in shadowy corners, darkened streets, well-lit ale-houses, taverns and coffee houses, fantastical and true accounts were given — some even by those who'd been present — about the great ruckus at Dorset Garden Theatre. Mr Shale and the Bromes were repositories of information in that regard as the news-sheets and pamphlets rushed to print. Whispers were exchanged, words hissed behind hands and into ears. When a detailed and prejudiced version of what unfolded appeared in Henry Care's publication, the oddly named *The Weekly Pacquet of Advice from Rome*, a few days later, the volume increased so everyone could hear.

Even as far away as Newmarket.

The place where the King — London theatre's greatest patron, the man with the power to make or break a city, a country, the Parliament and, it so happened, a Company — currently dwelled.

SCENE THREE

The Weekly Pacquet of Advice from Rome

Monday, 3rd April 1679

We live in dangerous times, it must be said, especially when swords are drawn and blood is shed at the theatre. Not, as custom allows, on stage, but in and by the very audience come to be enthralled.

Perhaps enthralled is too generous a word to describe the goings-on in a play that is unapologetically a sentimental piece of Popish Puffery. *The Feign'd Curtezans or, A Night's Intrigue* claims to be comedy. The only thing feign'd here is talent. The only laugh to be had is that a female had the effrontery to scribble such a nonsense. Ostensibly set in Italy (presumably to flatter the Papist Duchess of York who, though she hails from Modena, has found it expedient to retreat, royal husband in tow, to Brussels), where Romishness flows in the veins and taints the very air. The only intrigue to be had was in the pits, where Catholics and Protestants mixed and melded in rancorous disharmony.

Who thought to mount such an incendiary production? Why, a woman, of course. None other than the petticoat author, Aphra Behn.

Repulsed by what they were witnessing, a play where Papists held centre stage and dared to steal stout Protestant women's hearts, loyalists in the audience took offence and released their rage upon the only suitable target — a group of Catholics.

Novices from St Omer, the same academy where our leading light in uncovering this Horrid Plot against his Majesty, Dr Titus Oates, studied, garbed in their religious regalia, were also spectators. What an affront they posed to any decent Englishman! By their presence alone, they did mock our desperate search for the deadly traitors who would murder our liege and overturn our country's faith. It was more than Mr William Bedlowe, he who, at great risk to his own safety, did turn King's evidence and support Dr Oates in his shocking claims, could bear. Without his testimony — and that of Israel Tonge, and the other brave men who came forward at great cost to themselves — the murderers of that most noble of magistrates, Sir Edmund Berry Godfrey, would yet be roaming city streets unshackled and unaccounted for, never mind the already convicted plotters who would still be alive to instigate their wicked plans.

Yet, this would be the preferred outcome, according to our Politician of Pretence, the Feign'd Femme herself, Mrs Behn.

Upon witnessing what was indeed a night's intrigue at Dorset Garden Theatre, Popish Apologia by any other name, Bedlowe did demand the players cease their hour upon the stage. Met with protests from the novices in the form of drawn weapons, what could the brave man do, but seek his own defence and that of the realm.

When the hurly burly was done, the battle was neither lost nor won, and the play untimely finished.

This is what happens when a woman dares to trespass upon what is man's domain. Dorset Garden has become *un paradis pour les chattes*. After all, it has a Lady manager, a vile woman writer and, apart from the actresses whose fame does spread as far as their legs, a woman book-keeper too. One with a name that dost tempt fate: Tribulation, thy name is Woman.

What prompted such a foolish move as to appoint another wench in a man's role? Doing so has proven as calamitous as the *femelle* playwright's factious efforts. The shareholders should know better. One has only to look to the Bible to be forewarned. Did not a doxy, abetted by a serpent, transform the Lord's Empyrean into a wasteland? 'Twas she who ensured man was forever cast adrift in this world. Must we always suffer for women's sins?

Best the members of the Duke's Company reassess their womanly parts before they too are cast out and doomed to wander the wilderness of ignominy for eternity. Or until Drury Lane opens its doors once more and seeks to hire surrogate thespians.

Altogether, this work by an alleged writer provided less A Night's Intrigue and more an example of dells who truly lack wit, talent, or honour, but feign all.

Once again, it has taken a man to put things aright and see justice served. The finest man in all the land. His Majesty has, by royal decree, ordered that Dorset Garden Theatre close its doors. A move of sense that will, hopefully, allow the Duke's Company to come to theirs and at the very least, evict these driggle-draggle morts, beldames and whores by any other name, so they may learn their rightful place and male authority be restored.

Anonymous

SCENE FOUR

But now the woman (Pandora) opens up the cask,
And scattered pains and evils among men.
Inside the cask's hard walls remained one thing,
Hope, only, which did not fly through the door.

Works and Days, Hesiod

Apart from some clangs in the kitchen, the house was still. No doubt the Tetchalls were hunkered down in a coffee-house somewhere; Jonathan Cross, the apothecary, would still be at work. A rash of spring coughs and running noses kept him busy of late. Aphra had gone to see her publisher, Jacob Tonson, in Newe Street. She was owed money for the publication of *The Feign'd Curtezans*. Though it had caused so much strife, dedicating it to Nell Gwyn had gone some way to mitigating the losses she'd incurred by not receiving a second Author's Benefit, the performance having been so rudely interrupted. Not only did sweet Nell pay ten whole pounds for the privilege, but Aphra hoped Tonson would pay nicely as well. Not as nicely as he remunerated the men (and no amount of arguing the injustice was able to sway him to part with more), but at least, as Aphra said, it would keep the wolves from the door awhile.

I imagined said door, with its swollen wood and peeling paint, huge beasts in a semi-circle outside, hackles raised, jaws slavering. The situation wasn't quite so dire … yet. And, thank God's bunions, in an act of unprecedented generosity, Lady Mary, Mr Harris and Mr Betterton had decided to keep paying the actors and stagehands … and me. Accustomed to unexpected closures — they made mention of the plague and fire, never mind the King's mercurial mood, which had both Companies shutting and opening more often than his bedroom door — the Duke's had a small contingency set aside. Not that it would last long. At least I had a wage — however meagre. For now.

I tried to concentrate on how I was going to pay my share of the bills from here on in, but it was to no avail. Something else, something far more unexpected and distressing, took centre stage in my thoughts, making no allowance for other parts.

Thus, I failed to hear Aphra come home, failed to hear her and Nest greet each other, lament the weather, discuss various vendors' demands for payment. I failed to hear her climb the stairs. I was too busy composing a dirge. It wasn't until the bedroom door creaked open, an arrow of light from the landing piercing the gloom, that I understood my wallowing had acquired an audience. I stifled a sob.

'Have those blasted poltroons at the theatre been making your life a misery again, kitten?' Fury propelled Aphra to my side in four strides.

'Please.' It was as if all the sorrows of the age had been filtered into one word. 'Leave me.' Like an Elizabeth Barry heroine, I was cast across the bed, head buried in the pillows. My hair was loose, my clothes crumpled.

Aphra sat gingerly on the mattress, her weight forcing me to roll slightly towards her. 'What's happened, kitten?' she asked, stroking my back.

I jerked my shoulder, trying to deter her. Though I'd longed for her to return, I didn't mean for her to see me like this. So undone. Aphra simply pressed more firmly, keeping her movements slow and steady. 'Pray, what is it? A burden shared is a burden halved.'

If I could have summoned a laugh, it would have been more bitter than a Spanish lemon. 'Not this one. This is mine alone to bear.' I pushed my face back into the pillow. When Aphra didn't answer, but remained, still massaging, I turned my head to the side. 'You'll persist until I tell you, won't you? Or start purring.'

'I will,' said Aphra.

I heaved myself into a sitting position with a great shuddering sigh, forcing Aphra to cease her caresses. Swallowing hard, I swiped my sleeve across my nose like an urchin, and began to rummage among the bedclothes. The letters were here somewhere.

'Wait,' said Aphra, standing and pulling back the curtains. The evening sky was admitted in all its rosy radiance, casting a pastel light over the bed and exposing my state: swollen eyes, runnels on cheeks, bitten lips and a red nose sore from blowing it repeatedly.

'Oh, Tribulation,' said Aphra, with such pity fresh tears welled.

It would not do.

Before she could fold me into her arms, I found the sheets of paper and thrust them against her chest. 'These came,' I said.

Aphra took the pages from me, slowly smoothing them out upon the bedclothes. 'Letters? From whom?'

I made a strangled noise.

'May I read them?'

'If you want to know why I'm —' a hand swept my body, my face '— then, you must.'

Without moving from where she sat, except to tilt the pages towards the light, Aphra read the first brief note. A page had been torn from a book or Bible and was smudged, the writing difficult to make out, even though the hand was both familiar and, to me, beloved.

Dearest Sister,

Papa's fury knows no bounds and my anguish cannot be described. I must own the fault does not lie with you alone, but all Johnsons.

Forthwith, I'm forbidden to write and must cease all contact.

I pray the Lord will forgive me my trespass and that one day you will too.

With His blessings and my love,
Bethan

Aphra released a long sigh.

'Wait,' I cautioned. 'Read the other before you utter a word.'
The paper was rumpled, but the ink clear and dark.

Mrs Tribulation Johnson
Near the sign of The Quill and Ink
Dorset Street
Farringdon Ward Without
London

St Mary's Manse
Chartham Green
Kent
30th April 1679

Tribulation,

Recently, I was given an edition of The Weekly Pacquet. *Whereas I would usually eschew this news-sheet as ungodly and unnecessary, this one was handed to me with admonition I read a particular section: a theatre review. Much to my incredulity, what do I find but mention of you. At first, I thought there must be some error in the printing, or someone had stolen your identity to protect their own reputation. Alas, further investigation has proven this a false assumption.*

You always were a disobedient and wilful child — a Pandora who has knowingly opened a box of wickedness and released what lies within so those closest to you will do naught but suffer further shame and humiliation.

Not only have you been made a public mockery by some canting correspondent, but you have taken up an occupation fit only for whores and strumpets. You have deliberately traduced both your own and the family name. You are now reduced to a theatre-harlot by any reckoning. This shocking revelation did send your sister, who advanced the notion you abide in London, into apoplexy. When the village began to ask if the woman mentioned in the article was our Tribulation, I did deny it.

Any hope I held of redeeming your character through prayer and penance is forever lost. Fortunately, Bethan has sworn to compensate for her sins and will work towards salvaging our ruined esteem. Unlike you, your sister understands the duty to family by which a true daughter is bound.

As for your repute, you must know by absconding from familial and womanly obligations and rushing to the stage it is irreparably damaged. Never again will someone respectable, someone of stature, seek your hand. Gentle company is forever denied you.

It is unnatural for a woman to counter her father's will. It is unnatural that a young chit of your upbringing would seek the sort of ill-fame the theatre bestows. But you ever were unnatural. As a woman, you were born to submit to God and man. To be silent and obedient. You are not an exception; you are, as your name suggests, a Tribulation that your mother (God rest her soul), sister and I, praise be to God, no longer need bear.

You have chosen to follow in the footsteps of that Devil's slattern, Aphra Behn, and life-theatrical to a fine preferment. So be it. If I'd known the depths to which she'd fallen and has now cast you alongside her, kenned what she had become, I never would have allowed you to set forth.

Know this, Tribulation, there are consequences for what you've done, and you will be punished for your sins.

From this day forwards, you are no longer my daughter. Never again will you be acknowledged as part of this family, welcomed across my threshold.

You will quit all contact. If ever fate should deem our paths cross, I will refuse to recognise you. I will not address you. Bethan is forbidden as well. It will be as if you never were.

In my heart and mind, you have ceased to have meaning. You have ceased to exist.

God has spoken and so have I,
(Reverend) Howell Johnson

I didn't take my eyes from Aphra's face. I could tell she was doing her utmost not to react. I knew how that felt. I'd tried too.

And failed.

Dismally.

Finally, Aphra spoke. 'What cruel words; what unholy sentiments — and from a man of God; what utter heartlessness.'

My lips began to tremble. I pressed my teeth into them so they might still.

Unable to sit any longer, Aphra rose, Papa's letter clenched in her fist. 'I wish I could say I'm surprised. Shocked even. But, sadly, I'm not.' She shook the pages. 'This is woman's lot. Follow the script man has written, obey them in all things and you're a queen, a virtuous model of womanhood. Dare to deviate in action or words, and you're ordained a whore, a schemer who lacks virtue and respectability, a Jezebel who will lead men into sin. You're outcast.'

She sank back onto the bed. 'Your father has expelled you from his garden. His very own daughter. His flesh and blood. In his eyes, you're a fallen woman.'

My own eyes swam.

'But kitten, not only is he punishing you but Bethan as well by sundering any relationship the two of you might have. Forgive me, sweetling, my cousin might be a man of the cloth, but he's an utter bastard.'

I didn't dare say a word.

Aphra's colour was high, her eyes flashing brightly in the light that softened the contours of the room. She quickly read the letter again.

'It's … it's …' I began, inhaling sharply, forcing myself to a calm I didn't feel. 'I knew if he discovered what I was doing, his anger would be righteous, yet I never thought he'd take such extreme measures.'

A wave of fresh despair swamped me. Where was Papa's Christian charity? His acknowledgement of complicity in my supposed corruption? Had he not sent me to London? To Aphra? Knowing her as I did, her reputation — both the good and the bad, her fame, her infamy — how could he claim not to know Aphra wrote? That she was part of the theatre? How could he call her, his relation, such vile names? Not know her inherent goodness? Recall her cleverness? Had he severed himself so completely from extended family he remained in ignorance? Or was it wilful forgetfulness? It was possible, I supposed. Papa never, ever spoke of our cousins. As far as I could recall Mama hadn't either, nor Bethan. Not until she had to.

'I don't know what possessed your father, kitten, to write such dastardly things, and I can only imagine the hurt and distress he's caused you.' Aphra rose.

I slowly extracted the kerchief from where it was scrunched in my fist and blew my nose loudly. 'And you. As intended.'

Aphra nodded. 'As intended.'

'Why?'

Aphra let out a long sigh and placed Papa's letter on the table. 'The only answer I have is: because he could. He wanted to inflict the same degree of pain upon you that he feels you have caused him. But —' she held up her hand '— before I say any more, I'm going to ask Nest to bring up some wine and warm water so you might soothe your throat and wash your face. Is that alright?'

It was more than alright.

As Nest went about fetching what was required, Aphra quietly spoke of her own parents, her relationship to them. I knew what she was doing: offering me reassurance of sorts, reminding me I wasn't the first or the last child to incur a parent's displeasure or vice versa. Her father had been beloved and, when he died as the family were en route to an English sugar colony in the Americas called Surinam, it plunged Aphra, her mother and sister, who'd travelled to join him, into grief. The women were never the same after that. Of her mother, she gave scant account, simply saying that though they'd once been close her mother's propensity to drink and refusal to help her daughter when she was in dire financial straits (it was a long time later that I learned Aphra had been thrown in debtors' prison and, despite pleading with her mother to pay the monies owed, she'd refused) had cooled their relations, until they were completely sundered.

'Parents do not get to choose the child born to them just as a child does not get a say in who brings them into the world. Upon consideration, it's not surprising that sometimes a grave mismatch occurs.' She smiled and sidled off the bed, turning to gently touch my wrist. 'Just as well we can create bonds that make another family, is it not?'

Before I could reply, she went about lighting candles, then shooed me off the mattress and tidied the covers. I watched her out of the corner of my eye, wondering if the warmth inside me could be felt from where she stood. Once I'd washed, she insisted I change into my night shift and get into bed. While I did that, I saw her read Bethan's short missive once more.

Dear God, Papa's punishment was cruel. To forbid his daughters to communicate? Forever? Even for a vicar, that was severe. And what did Bethan mean by asking the Lord forgive *her* trespass? Did she mean sending me to London? To Aphra?

I glanced at her. Probably.

Aphra placed Bethan's note atop Howell's.

'Anything else, missus?' asked Nest. Guilt that she'd been downstairs and unaware of my distress made her more attentive than usual.

'No, Nest. Thank you.'

'Call if you need. I'll keep an ear out.' Nest shot one last anxious look at both her charges before closing the door soundlessly.

Aphra brought wine over, giving me the glasses to hold as she crawled onto the bed beside me. 'There,' she said, retrieving her drink and squirming into position. 'This is cosy.'

We lay side by side, propped up on pillows, me under the blankets, Aphra fully clothed above. The evening air circled the room, bringing with it the smells and sounds of the street — horse dung, the crackle and sizzle of braziers and the rich scent of bread and ale. Chickens clucked and squawked, while children shouted with excitement before a drum roll of running feet sounded. The deeper voices of men competed with those of women. The first stars were announcing themselves above the rooftops. An owl took wing nearby, its shadow falling across the window. A couple of gulls cawed.

Aphra sipped, one eye on me. I suspect she was gauging my mood. At least I'd ceased to cry — I'd no more tears left. My well was drier than the sands of Arabia.

'Do you want to talk about them?' asked Aphra, nodding towards the letters, gently straightening one of my curls and tucking it behind my ear.

'Aye. Nay. I … I don't know.' I was enjoying Aphra's maternal gestures, her closeness. 'I shouldn't be surprised by either. Not really.

I knew Papa would be furious if he ever discovered what I was doing. I just didn't expect him to …'

'Deny you?'

'Aye, like Peter did Christ.' I flashed a watery smile. 'And yet, in a way, it's a relief. I no longer have to pretend, to live with the burden of guilt. Yet, the timing is terrible, arriving so close on the heels of the theatre closing. It feels as if God is punishing me or, at the least, conspiring against me.'

'God always punishes the fairer sex, kitten. Even the *Bible* doesn't pretend otherwise. And His priests and the men who use and twist His words continue to collaborate to make our lot miserable.' She glanced up. 'And now I'm going to be struck down or turned into a pillar of salt. Make sure if I am you use me wisely and well — sell portions for profit.'

A giggle escaped. 'Oh, I will. I'll call it Dried Writer's Tears and make a fortune.'

Aphra grinned. 'Ah, that's more like it.' She bumped her shoulder against mine. 'I know you're beyond sad, but you must be angry too. I know I am.'

I huffed. 'Aye, I'm angry. I feel like one of Mr Oates's accused. My claims of innocence would be dismissed. I'm judged a slut with no chance to defend myself.' A quivery sigh escaped. 'I've done nothing wrong, not really … except ignore his instructions.'

'Which infuriates him.'

I paused. 'I've made a man angry. Do you remember when I said you do that? That's why they insult you.'

'And, if I recall correctly,' said Aphra. 'I replied "it's because they fear me".'

'You think Papa fears me?'

'Maybe.'

'I think he fears what I might become.'

'And what's that, kitten?'

'A woman who doesn't need a man … like you.'

Aphra finished her drink and, taking my empty glass, placed them both on the bedside table. She drew me into her arms, shuffling down in the pillows so my head rested against her breast and she could place her chin atop my hair. I'd never felt so … so … protected. So wanted. We faced the window. Aphra began to run her fingers through my curls, releasing them so they sprang back.

'You're right. I don't *need* men,' began Aphra slowly. 'But sometimes, I want them.'

I tried to sit up, but she held me tighter. 'Aphra!' I said in mock horror. She laughed.

'I said *want*, not need … There are times I desire a man in my life.'

'What for?'

Aphra burbled tenderly, hesitating before answering. 'For love, companionship. For conversation, to ease my path. For legitimacy. It would make things so much easier if there was always one present.'

'Instead, you have one some of the time — like Mr Hoyle.'

'Exactly. Though he doesn't ease my path so much as twist it.'

I pulled away slightly. I knew what she was referring to. It was a poorly kept secret that Mr Hoyle was a sodomite. 'If that's so, why do you want him?'

'Because I'm a fool and he's a clever, unattainable man. A fine writer who composes adroit, witty verses and who makes me laugh. I've told you he speaks seven languages, haven't I? How can one fail to admire that? Seriously, I enjoy the way he challenges me, encourages me to think harder, write better. I know you don't think so, but he can be excellent company.'

'In many languages too, apparently.'

Aphra chuckled and drew me back against her. Had my mother ever embraced me in such a manner? I couldn't remember. My heart filled with mellow, soothing waves that undulated and yet caused my very middle to ache and throb, to be off kilter in a disconcerting way. I was both light and yet terribly heavy. Was this what love felt like?

'Have you ever loved?' I asked suddenly.

'What?' asked Aphra.

'Have you ever loved a man?'

Aphra gave a sort of secret half-chuckle. She began to trail her fingers through my tresses again.

'I *will* start purring if you keep that up,' I said. The desolation in my voice was diminishing.

'Like the kitten you are.'

I sniffed. 'Well? Are you going to answer me?'

Aphra sighed. 'I'm always in love, Tribulation: it's my weakness. Or haven't you noticed?'

I had. 'Mr Hoyle?'

'Him. And Rochester. His Majesty, and the Duke. I love Elizabeth Barry. Today I love Nell Gwyn and Jacob Tonson, who finally paid me — not enough, mind. Sometimes, I love Thomas Betterton and Hortense Mancini. I always love Nest.'

'I don't mean like that.' I managed to tilt my head so our eyes met. 'I mean … you know what I mean.'

Aphra gave a low laugh. 'I do. I have.' She sighed. 'Once. A long time ago. In another country, another world …'

'Who?'

'A man who swept me off my feet, told me things I longed to hear, things which set my mind ablaze, my heart afire, and my passions aflame. A man for whom I lost reason and sense. And for whom I almost lost myself.'

This time, I managed to prise myself out of Aphra's arms so I could regard her properly. 'Was that your husband?'

'Oh, good God, no!' Aphra laughed. 'It was someone … someone who came into my life when I was young and mourning the loss of my father. A man I should never have trusted, should never have pursued.'

'You pursued him?'

'Later I did. Across the seas. And ever since have lived to regret it. For a whole range of reasons.' She met my curious gaze, holding my eyes for a long time. Gradually, her expression altered.

'Who was it?'

Unable to look at me any more, Aphra held out her arms and I fell back into them. 'Just as you don't *really* want to discuss your papa's letter — in fact, it doesn't deserve discussion — I don't want to talk about him. Not now. Not …'

I waited for her to say 'ever'. She didn't.

'Alright,' I said, reluctantly. There was a mighty story there, but tonight was not for telling. 'But if ever *you* change your mind …'

I snuggled closer. 'Aphra,' I said after a while.

'Hmmm?'

'Why do you think my parents named me Tribulation? Papa even refers to it in that …' I gestured towards the table. 'I mean, who names their child after trouble unless they're either expecting some or she caused it?'

Aphra considered her answer. 'I confess, I've had cause of late to ponder the same question. Clearly you know the story of Pandora.'

I rolled my eyes. '*Ad nauseum*. Papa would tell me — she's the nymph who disobeyed the gods and opened the jar they'd entrusted to her, releasing troubles or tribulations into the world.'

'That's only half the story.'

'Really? I never read it. I couldn't bear to.'

'Yes. Really. Trust your father not to tell you the rest, but I'm disappointed in Bethan. I would have thought …' Aphra shook her head. 'Pandora released evils into the world but, after they escaped, something remained behind.'

'What?'

'Hope.'

I sat bolt upright. 'Really?'

Aphra smiled. 'Really. You see, wherever there are troubles — or tribulation — Hope follows. She lingers in the gloaming, waiting to be called forth. Trouble summons her. So, maybe, your parents named you for that as well.'

I cocked my head, one brow raised. 'You don't believe that for a moment, do you?'

'No,' Aphra admitted, brushing the end of my nose with a finger. 'But I do believe that on trouble's heels comes hope. It has to. If it doesn't, then we're all lost.'

I rearranged the covers before resuming my position. 'Well, if not all, I certainly am.'

SCENE FIVE

All I ask is the privilege for my masculine part the poet in me (if any such you will allow me) to tread in those successful paths my predecessors have so long thrived in … If I must not, because of my sex, have this freedom, but that you will usurp all to yourselves, I lay down my quill, and you shall hear no more of me …

The Lucky Chance or, The Alderman's Bargain, Aphra Behn

As May slipped into June, bringing with it squalls of rain and a desperation borne of knowing the last weeks of the theatre season were slipping by — and, with the doors still closed, a final chance to make coin — Dorset Garden shareholders had no choice but to let some of the performers go. A few took temporary positions at theatres in Oxford and Cambridge where the students were a loyal if somewhat rambunctious audience. Some went to perform at private citizens' houses beyond the walls and further afield. Others returned to family businesses both within London and outside the city, while a few tried their hands at everything from selling elixirs to collecting scrap metal. As the days rolled into weeks, more and more left. In the end, we were a much-diminished group, all of whom agreed to being paid a percentage of what we once earned.

In order to warrant our keep, we were put to cleaning, repairing and sorting everything from costumes and associated tack to props and machinery: even the curtains and lights. It was filthy work and I'd taken to wearing my oldest shift and, on occasion, bringing Fabian's clothes and donning them once inside. It was hotter than Hell in the theatre — outside too as we melted towards summer and the blistering sun reigned. Sultry winds tossed detritus onto the street and we'd arrive windblown and cross. Sleepless, constantly pulling damp clothes from our moist flesh and always thirsty, our tempers frayed and words were often as heated and cruel as the daylight hours.

Never as cruel as Papa's, which, though I tried to push them from my mind, would arise at the most inconvenient moments, causing my spirits to deflate faster than a pigskin flask. I kept giving myself talkings-to: I'd a choice to make. I could either flounder in self-pity and let the words eat my soul or try and … not forget them, God knew I couldn't do that. They were too corrosive. But, by reminding myself of the people of whom I was so very fond (Aphra's face filled my vision), and who supported and encouraged me, I could build a barrier around them and shore up inner defences so they didn't hurt as much. I tried to convince myself I didn't need Papa or Bethan; what need had I of that family? As Aphra said, I could create another. Didn't I have her, Nest and the hodgepodge of remaining players to call my own?

Truth was, like Aphra with men, I didn't *need* my family. I wanted them. One that shared my flesh and blood. In defiance of Papa's decree, I wrote to Bethan — many times.

I never heard back.

I was grateful for work — any work — to distract me from my much-altered circumstances. Of course it wasn't only mine that had changed. Aphra's did too as the small allowance Papa sent abruptly ceased. In a brief, terse note to her, he explained he couldn't be expected to keep what he no longer had — a younger daughter. He also accused Aphra in many unkind (and unfair) words of leading me astray. As if I was a dog she'd happened upon or wasn't possessed of my own will.

'Not the first time I've been accused of corrupting innocence,' said Aphra, screwing up the letter and casting it into the fire.

I half-expected her to ask me to leave. On the contrary, she told me I'd always have a place in her household.

'You said you wanted a purpose, Tribulation,' she said. 'Now, you have a real one. Earning coin is no longer a choice, but a necessity, to support us.'

Papa's rage, his disappointment became easier to bear with each passing day. In a sense, I'd lived with it my entire life. It was Bethan's ready surrendering of our relationship that cut most deeply — though defying Papa's ruling and sending a final note had to mean something. I clung to that.

Gradually, as summer dragged on, visitors stopped coming to the theatre and we were left to ourselves in the echo chamber it had become. Without the other cast members, the hustle and bustle of rehearsals or performance, it was as though we were sole survivors of some catastrophe, like plague, fire or a marauding army. I suppose, in a sense, we were.

Then, one hot day midsummer, not long after the bells sounded noon, the Earl of Shaftesbury and his friends, Lord Grey and the burly vicar Robert Ferguson, paid an unexpected visit. Most of us were in the Tiring Rooms, sorting out costumes and knick-knacks, stacking them atop dressers. I'd only recently discovered some of the better-quality costumes were donations from the royal household — actual garments the King and his brother once wore. The jewels adorning them were real, the fabrics lush and expensive. They were marvellous to behold but sorely in need of repair. Aphra happened to be with us that day, having decided she'd had enough of sitting at her desk staring at bedroom walls. Her muses had retreated to cooler climes.

I was holding up a particularly extravagant cloak lined with mink, showing it to her, when we heard a familiar clack.

Mr Rickman, who'd also been kept on (Lady Mary declared the last thing she wanted was Killigrew to snap him up for, when our doors shut, Drury's immediately reopened), raised his head. 'Earl Shaftesbury and friends, if I'm not mistaken.'

He wasn't.

There was a collective groan.

The men and their servants entered and, after returning greetings, Shaftesbury spied a chair he liked the look of, sweeping his cane across the nearest dresser so his valet might set down a bottle of Spanish. The tinkle of breaking glass and thud of a book and jars striking the floor didn't raise so much as a brow. Lord Grey peered around like a regal bird on a perch, unruffled and all-seeing. The vicar leaned against the wall, half-buried amidst costume racks, nodding to Mr Rickman and watching us beneath beetling brows. The entire time, Shaftesbury couldn't stop smiling, the kind of smile you imagine a tiger wearing after devouring its prey.

I glanced at the Earl while he drank. Lord Grey, I couldn't read at all. Possessed of a rather bland but pretty face, like Mr Ferguson he made a point of listening rather than speaking — a habit Mr Rickman too had perfected.

Chatter gradually returned to the room, about Mr Pepys — the latest victim of the Popish Plot, who days before had been arrested and sent to the Tower accused of being both a closet Catholic and selling naval secrets to the Dutch, as if one crime wasn't enough. The King, the Scots, the fact the Commons had again passed a Bill to exclude the Duke from the royal succession (the Earl quizzed Mr Betterton and Mr Rickman for their opinions — it was expected the King would once more block it), were also discussed. But it wasn't until I wiped my brow for the umpteenth time that I became aware of a pair of calculating eyes watching me in the mirror's reflection.

I busied myself with renewed vigour, but not before the Earl poked Mr Rickman.

'Who's the scrawny giantess over there?' he asked loudly, swinging his staff towards me.

Mr Rickman frowned. 'The *lady* you're enquiring after, milord, is the Duke's Company book-keeper.'

There were some sniggers. Not all who'd been kept on were my friends.

I still hadn't turned around.

'Book-keeper?' His voice was loud. Abrupt. As if each word was cut to shape the moment it left his mouth. 'Ah, I'd heard of this *appointment*. What about you, Grey?'

'Temporary,' said Lord Grey, deigning a glance. 'A charity case.'

Shaftesbury forced a guffaw. 'Another woman. When will you learn, Betterton?' He turned to him. 'Papists and petticoats spell disaster … or should I say —' his eyes sidled towards me '— Tribulation?' There were chuckles. 'No wonder you were closed down.'

Prisca Smithton's and John Crosby's looks were barbed arrows. Aye, my two nemeses were still employed.

The Earl snapped his fingers in my direction. 'You. Come here.'

Resisting the urge to bark and bound over with tongue lolling, I put down the cloak. It wouldn't do to offend the likes of Shaftesbury — just ask Mr Pepys. Rumour was Shaftesbury was behind the man making the accusations against him.

I curtseyed. As if I was a horse he was trading, without uttering a word, he studied me top to toe, even using his cane to make me spin about then lift my skirts so he could examine my ankles. He looked at Lord Grey, who leaned over and whispered something. I gritted my teeth. Unbeknownst to the Earl, I considered him too, taking in his thin cheeks, long, bent nose and the crooked back not even his flowing golden periwig or heavy brocaded jacket could hide. The liberal scent he wore couldn't quite disguise a strange odour, cloying, sweet and not at all pleasant. He flapped a perfumed kerchief about, a flag, offering not surrender, but parlay perhaps. This was a proud man.

By all accounts, a treacherous one.

'Look at me,' said the Earl when I tried to pull my skirts out of reach of his cane.

I kept my eyes lowered. I was afraid if I didn't the sparks within them would set him aflame. I could feel Prisca's leer, and the concerned looks exchanged by Mr Harris and Mary Lee.

I finally raised my eyes and marched my lips into a smile.

The Earl stared, leaning forwards and squinting. 'By God, I think you're right, Grey. Where are you from, chit?'

'Kent, my lord,' I said wearily.

'Who's your father?'

My heart flipped. By rights, I no longer had one. 'The … the Reverend Howell Johnson, sir.'

He frowned. 'Johnson …' He searched the room. 'You're a Johnson, aren't you, Aphra?'

'I am,' said Aphra, drifting over. 'Tribulation is my cousin.' She gave me an encouraging smile and made a point of lifting her chin.

I copied her. *Half the battle in convincing people you can do something is pretending you can.* Including tolerating this man's interrogation.

He looked from her to me and back again, then over at Lord Grey, inviting him to compare us. 'And where's your father then?'

'In Chartham, sir,' I said.

'The docks?'

'Nay, sir. Not Chatham. *Chartham.*'

'You're alone in London?'

It was as if he knew which parts of me were bruised. 'Nay,' I said hesitantly. 'I've Aphra —' I was about to say I also had the players, but thought better of it. 'And Nest,' I added lamely.

'Nest? That's your woman, isn't it, Aphra? Still with you after all these years.' The Earl absorbed the information, pulling at his thin lower lip. 'So, you've no man to govern you,' he said disapprovingly. 'Merely women.'

'Hardly mere, sir.'

Mr Ferguson coughed.

The Earl's considerable brows furrowed. 'You've too much to say for yourself. No wonder, with Aphra as your guardian.' He caught Aphra's hand and pressed a kiss to the back of it as if to take the sting out of his words. She gave him a coy smile.

Why Aphra did that — on the one hand rebuke and criticise men for their shabby treatment of women, while on the other allowing them to undermine her, brushing aside their rudeness and vulgarity, and accepting with grace a courtly gesture — dumbfounded me. What a contradiction she was.

Mind you, her strategy, if that's what it was, worked, for the Earl appeared to soften. Who really had control here?

Prisca continued to enjoy my discomfort as I was questioned like a felon before the King's bench. Bored, the rest returned to their tasks, relieved they hadn't been selected for the Earl's particular brand of attention. Charlotte shot me a sympathetic look; Finnola and Mr Betterton winked. Mr Rickman gave me a brusque nod, a gesture of solidarity, before busying himself nearby. Listening.

'Come closer, girl,' said the Earl. 'Closer,' he said, indicating I needed to bend towards him. When I came within his grasp, he took hold of my chin and turned my face first one way, then the other. Heat began to flood my body, rise up my neck. If I thought it warm before, it was nothing to the furnace I found myself in now.

'I have to say,' he said softly, 'you've the most unusual eyes. Doesn't she, Grey?' He twisted my face towards his friend. 'Look at them, Ferguson. What say you?'

The vicar burrowed out of the hanging garments and approached. I tried hard not to squirm.

'Startling but marred by sin.'

I pulled out of the Earl's grasp.

'Why,' continued the Earl, undeterred. He peered up at Aphra. 'Yours are dark, Aphra, more like hot chestnuts. Whereas yours, yours are akin to jewels.'

'Turquoise seas,' said Lord Grey. 'With a dash of mud in one.'

The Earl laughed. I stepped back, rubbing where his fingers had impressed my flesh.

'Where've I seen a mark like that before?' Shaftesbury scowled. 'Grey? Ferguson? You can't recall either, eh? Damn. Tribulation *Johnson*.' He drawled my name, dredging the river of his mind. He gave a small growl of frustration. 'It'll come to me.'

Annoyed, he clicked his fingers and turned his attention to the wine. Dismissed, I gave a half-curtsey and went back to the dresser. Not before I locked eyes with Aphra, who was regarding me with a thoughtful expression.

About to drink, the Earl suddenly exclaimed, striking a knee, the liquid splashing over the lip of his goblet and onto his breeches, leaving a carmine stain. 'I know. It was that bastard, William Scot. Had the same discolouration. Remember, Grey? It was most off-putting.'

'The regicide's son,' said Mr Ferguson.

'The traitor,' added Lord Grey.

Mr Rickman stiffened, then turned and regarded me very carefully.

The Earl gave Aphra an evil grin. 'You recall *him*, don't you, my dear?' Without waiting for an answer, he continued. 'There was a scandal, wasn't there? Something happened years ago, in Kent.' He waggled his brows. 'It was quickly quashed. You wouldn't know, Aphra. It was when you were off gallivanting with the natives.' He patted her arm, arching a brow in my direction. 'Was Scot ever in Canterbury, per chance? I seem to recall he spent some time there.' He twisted his neck so Aphra was in his ken. 'Maybe his penchant for Johnsons began long before he met you, *cherie*?'

Aphra grabbed the back of the Earl's chair so hard, she tilted it. His laughter turned into a yelp.

'Forgive me, milord,' she said, as the Earl's arms shot out to maintain his balance. She let go of the chair as if it were a hot coal. It slammed back into position. 'I … I … there's somewhere I must be.' She mumbled an apology. 'I'll see you at home, Tribulation.' She forestalled any questions and, grabbing her hat and gloves, made a hasty curtsey and swept out of the room.

There was stunned silence before everyone began talking again. Finnola continued gathering scarves, Lady Mary drifted over to the Earl. Prisca and John Crosby made a poor pretence of not hanging on every word. Charlotte returned to decluttering a dresser. Mr Rickman began conversing with Mr Ferguson. It was as if nothing untoward had happened.

Only, something had. I desperately wanted to follow Aphra. Why had she reacted to the Earl that way? What did he mean about Chartham, Canterbury, and this William Scot having a penchant for Johnsons? The resemblance he remarked upon? Did this noble think Mr Scot was a relation of mine? Another cousin, perhaps? Or … God forbid, something more? The insinuation was apparent. I turned the splutter that escaped into a cough.

I had a father — *had* being the right word. Damn the Earl. I was simply being over-imaginative, over-reacting, making connections where there were likely none. Shaftesbury was nothing but a trouble-maker, wasn't he?

My gaze fell upon the mirror. An earnest face with a furrowed brow and bright, searching eyes — one with a golden smudge in it — stared back at me. Surely such imperfections weren't that uncommon, were they?

Words from Shakespeare flew into my head.

'They whose guilt within their bosom lies, imagine every eye beholds their blame.'

My hand fell away and my gaze strayed to where Aphra made her swift exit.

What did she suspect about this William Scot?

More importantly, what did she know?

SCENE SIX

He that knew all that ever Learning writ,
Knew only this — that he knew nothing yet.

The Emperor of the Moon, Aphra Behn

Gabriel Freeman paused just outside the Hope and Anchor in Hercules Pillar Alley and watched in bemusement as a man in a filthy greatcoat, bulging sack tucked under one arm, raced past, crawled atop a barrel, and then threw himself over a wall, desperate to avoid the whetted jaws of three wiry hounds chasing him. Deprived of their prey, the dogs bayed their frustration, hackles raised, only surrendering when a window above opened and the contents of a jordan were thrown.

'Oy, shut up, you salted bitches or I'll cook the lot of ye.' The window slammed shut.

The dogs ceased their howls and slinked off, tails between legs, wetter and smellier.

With a chuckle and hoping the dogs would soon have cause to wag those sad tails, Gabriel pushed open the door to the tavern. The rush of noise, the rise and fall of voices, clatter of tankards and tin plates, twang of a guitar and reedy strains of a singer enveloped him. So did the smell of rancid meat and grease. Grateful to be out of the rain, he stamped the excess mud off his boots, unclasped his cloak, hung it on a random hook, then headed towards his usual table at the rear.

Much to his relief, his friend Solomon van Kessel was already there. People were giving him a wide berth. Gentle by nature, a clever, well-read man who'd been a prince among his own, Solomon was terrifying to behold.

Almost as tall as Gabriel, he was twice as broad across the shoulders with a chest that would make a woodsman envious. Blessed with thick, dark curls, straight brows, and a wide flat nose, he had cheekbones so high and sharp they appeared to have been whittled with a blade. He was possessed of white teeth that flashed often, and not always because he was happy, but it was the tattoos which patterned his handsome face that turned heads as much as his cacao-coloured skin.

Snatched from their home in Coramantien decades ago, Solomon's mother and father had been enslaved and separated from their only child. Days later, a Dutch privateer found the boy hidden in a small burned-out hut near the shore. He'd been fending for himself. Under normal circumstances, very young orphans were either killed or taken to the Venetian markets to be sold to the highest bidder. For reasons unknown to his crew, who always thought Captain van Kessel a hard bastard, he took pity on the small, dark-eyed lad and brought him on board. Not as a slave to swab the sailors' shit and vomit, keep the weevils out of the flour and make sure the ale wasn't spoiled, or even as a cabin boy who'd sate the officers' desires. Van Kessel dressed the little blackamoor, who could have been no more than five, in fine linens he had modified and a solid pair of leather boots, and kept him in his very own cabin, though not bed, and taught him not just to read and write and the many languages he'd mastered over the years, but the ways of the sea.

Over time, word travelled about the Dutch captain and his caramel-coloured son. They earned the title 'Demons of the Sea'. Their reputation for fierceness was only exceeded by the fairness of their dealings. They were greatly feared, respected and, for a few years, hunted. That was until they were hired by the English Admiralty to patrol the borders of their briny territories. Reputable suddenly, their past was conveniently overlooked, then forgotten; such is the way of those who hold sway.

Twenty years later, Captain van Kessel was long dead, having bequeathed his ship and crew to the foundling he'd adopted. On a voyage to the Americas, the crew, resentful they'd been given a blackamoor master, mutinied and threw Solomon overboard. Near land, he swam ashore and after being revived and cared for lived for a time with the natives, gaining the tattoos he wore so proudly.

When an English ship ran aground on a nearby reef, it was Solomon who organised not only the rescue of the captain and crew, but repairs. He translated and helped smooth relations with the indigenous people. When it was time for the vessel to depart, the captain, persuaded by his first officer, a young man named Gabriel Freeman, invited Solomon to join them, and reclaim a position with his Majesty's navy.

This earned Gabriel, who not long after was promoted to captain himself, a life-long friend and loyal second officer, one who joined in all his ventures. Solomon understood he would be forever denied the rank that should by rights be his, and if he was destined to always be second, then it would only be to Gabriel — except when it came to intelligencing, in which they were as close to equals as their differences allowed.

For Solomon was excellent at ferreting out secrets. Folk oft underestimated him, something he used to his — and Gabriel's — advantage. Anyone with skin other than white was invisible — there solely to serve their Christian masters — and to believe them capable of doing or feeling anything, let alone thinking for themselves, was simply beyond most whites. Solomon knew how to profit from their ignorance: he wasn't only clever, he was also strategic.

'Still raining then?' he asked as Gabriel slid onto the bench beside him. They both had their backs against the wall, facing into the tavern. Old habits don't ever die, they become honed. Solomon pushed a brimming tankard in front of his friend.

'Pissing down,' said Gabriel, removing his hat and wringing out his hair. 'Cheers,' he said, lifting his drink and striking Solomon's.

They drank in silence, restless eyes roving the room, noticing the ruddy-faced lawyers trying to persuade one of the pretty maids to sit with them; the butcher and his son in their blood-spattered aprons, so deep in their cups they could hardly keep their eyes open; and the merchant and his older wife, thin-lipped and disapproving as her husband pinched the bottom of a buxom wench, almost causing her to drop a tray as she swung around to wink at him. Two cats sat in the rafters, their eyes mere slits but their heads turned in the direction of a half-eaten platter of food, temporarily neglected when the diners took to the floor to dance.

'Any word when the theatre will reopen?' asked Solomon finally.

Gabriel shook his head. 'The King is still aggrieved. Either that, or he's forgotten.'

'Pity. I enjoyed watching Jonathan Rickman perform. You're not half-bad, even if some of the audience up and leave midway.'

Gabriel gave a huff of laughter. Leaving mid-performance wasn't uncommon, nor was arriving then. When a patron only saw part of the play, they only paid part of the price of a ticket.

'The crowd oft do that,' Gabriel said resignedly. 'Take satisfaction from viewing a portion.' He shrugged. 'Can't understand it myself. It's like reading half a book or sailing partway to a destination and turning about. What's the point of starting in the first place?' He swirled his ale. 'At least the Company'll be ready to stage a few plays once the King reverses his decree.'

'You think that will be soon?'

Gabriel shrugged. 'Who can guess the royal mind?'

'When you do reopen, I believe it's a work by Otway followed by Etherege,' said Solomon smugly.

Gabriel turned towards him slowly. 'My, my. You're well informed.'

Solomon flashed his teeth. 'Just so happens, I discovered more than what plays are scheduled and that the theatre is cleaner than the royal chamber pot.'

'I expect nothing less from one of the finest intelligencers in his Majesty's service.'

While Gabriel masqueraded as the surly actor Jonathan Rickman, Solomon watched and recorded the activities of those suspected of working to have the Duke of York removed from the royal succession. It wasn't hard. Under the auspices of the Earl of Shaftesbury or any of his other titled allies, groups of men from all walks of life met in taverns and coffee-houses, above wine shops and houses, arguing loudly and long about ways to ensure a Papist never again held the throne. Bemused by their lack of caution, Solomon was kept busy. With the Licensing Act expired, the number of seditious tracts published increased a hundredfold, as had those eager to put their names to their words. Fools. A recent pamphlet entitled *An Appeal from the Country to the City* by Junius Brutus (which everyone knew was a pseudonym for the publisher Charles Blount) went so far as to suggest England was on the brink of a Catholic revolution and told readers to 'imagine the whole town in flame', claiming that troops of Papists would ravish wives and daughters, dash little children's brains against walls and plunder houses and cut throats. The images were barbaric and terrifying. Yet these authors persisted in making Solomon's work so easy. All he had to do was track down the writer or publisher and discover how deadly their intentions were. Most were simply full of bluster and hollow threats: men keen to be seen contributing to a cause they'd no intention of putting themselves in harm's way for. If the campaign was victorious, well, they could claim allegiance — their public words being proof. Others, however, were not so innocuous. They were playing a longer, far more dangerous game. It was these men the spymaster Joseph Williamson had hired them to find.

Find. Watch. Wait.

'So, what *have* you discovered, my friend?' asked Gabriel finally.

Solomon leaned over. 'Turns out Shaftesbury's funding most of the writers composing both the anti-Catholic diatribes and those seditious tracts demanding the Duke be excluded from the royal succession.'

'Is that so?'

'Including,' continued Solomon, 'this vicar, Robert Ferguson, who, as you well know, has grown fond of Dorset Garden Tiring Rooms.

They say he has the glibbest tongue in town and is a great listener who can sally forth on any topic.'

'Which explains why he's become indispensable to the Earl,' said Gabriel.

'According to gossip,' said Solomon, 'so has young Lord Grey, and a few low-life lawyers and printers.'

'Some odd choices of companions for a noble.'

'Depends what his motivation is — if it's to win support with the Lords *and* Commons, then maybe not.'

'Support for what?' asked Gabriel. 'Just the Exclusion Bill? Ensure his Royal Highness, the Papist Duke of York, never wears a crown? Or more?'

'To quote the Bard,' said Solomon, 'that *is* the question.'

The men sat with their thoughts.

Gabriel stretched his arms above his head and stifled a yawn. 'Looks like I'll have to accept an invitation to one of Shaftesbury's interminable dinners again.'

'Been playing hard to get, have you?'

Gabriel was about to be flippant when he changed his mind. 'Not hard enough.' He rubbed his jaw. Sometimes, he hated this, being an intelligencer, the way it made him not only behave, but think and look at people. Unable to accept anyone at face value, he was always second-guessing, searching for motive, believing the worst.

It made for poor relations. It made for a poor life.

It had made him a poor husband.

His throat caught as golden locks and a pair of sky-blue eyes awash with misery filled his vision.

An outraged scream followed by gales of laughter from the table of lawyers forced the image of his dead wife, Wait-Still, from his mind. The young maid ran from the taproom, her bodice torn, jeers and insults following in her wake.

Gabriel couldn't abide men who hunted women, especially in packs. To calm himself, he took a long, leisurely drink. 'Is there anything else?' he asked, smothering a belch.

'There is.' Solomon drew closer. 'It involves the woman playwright Williamson also asked us to watch — Mrs Aphra Behn. See a bit loitering outside the theatre, I do. Observe even more dallying on the street near her house. But following her has proved most fruitful — 'specially two days ago.'

Gabriel straightened, weariness sloughing from his body. 'Go on.'

Solomon quickly explained what happened when he shadowed Mrs Behn as she dashed out her door, clearly perturbed. She'd made haste to old Barnabas Harley, a former crewmate of Gabriel and Solomon's, who now ran the posting inn on the New Canal.

'She paid him twice the usual to ensure a letter was with the next courier heading for Dover. Naturally, Barnabas allowed me a look … for a fee.' He rubbed his fingers together. 'It was addressed to Venice and written in code.'

Gabriel recalled Mrs Behn's reaction to Shaftesbury's badinage in the Tiring Rooms. *There was a scandal. Something happened, years ago, in Kent. It was quickly quashed. It was when you were off gallivanting with the natives …*

A tic began working in Gabriel's left cheek. 'You kept a copy, I presume?'

'You presume correctly.' As casually as he could, Solomon extracted a folded page from his jacket and passed it over. Gabriel opened it and scanned the contents. He sucked in his breath. 'It's addressed to Sir Bernard Gascoigne.'

'You know him?' asked Solomon.

'We've had dealings in the past. He used to work for Williamson.'

'Another bloody intelligencer,' said Solomon. 'Does he still?'

'Likely. For others too, no doubt. Gascoigne shifts between Venice, Amsterdam, Rotterdam and now the Americas. I think he also has a house in Bruges. Mrs Behn must know he's still active if she's written to him in code.'

'It's suspicious, isn't it? Writing in code.'

Gabriel shrugged. 'Suspicious and cautious.'

Solomon grunted.

Gabriel continued. 'Mrs Behn herself invented this particular one when she was sent to Antwerp back in sixty-six to try and persuade Scot to work for the King again.' He placed the page on the table between them. 'See here? Mrs Behn is number 160, the English 156. The number 71 stands for Holland.' He folded the letter and passed it back to Solomon.

'And 159?' asked Solomon. 'That's code for William Scot, isn't it?'

'It is,' said Gabriel. 'She's asking Sir Bernard to help her locate him. Apparently, she has some important information that will alter his life.'

Solomon released a long, low whistle. 'Information? Isn't *that* code for an offer?'

'Maybe. But what on earth could Mrs Behn offer him? Why would she even want to? William Scot's a notorious double agent,' said Gabriel.

'His name was already a byword when I met you,' said Solomon.

'And not only because of his father's actions,' agreed Gabriel. 'It was thought for a while Scot was working for the Crown, trying to repatriate the family name, atone for his father's treachery. He soon put paid to that notion by defaulting to the Dutch. No-one is really sure where his loyalties lie any more.'

Gabriel sank back on the bench, deep in thought. He knew something of the time Mrs Behn — Aphra Johnson as she was then — lived in Surinam, in the West Indies: how she came into conflict with the replacement governor, a short-tempered man named Byam. It was there that she met the considerably older William Scot — a meeting that was to alter her life and sully her reputation, and not just because of what happened between them in the colony.

But what else had Scot done? What else was Shaftesbury alluding to? What was it he said to Mrs Behn? Something about him having a penchant for Johnsons …

You. Wouldn't. Know.

Only, from her reaction, it was evident that, if she didn't know, she suspected.

Gabriel's frown deepened. His mind churned. Mrs Behn hadn't been back to the theatre since bolting that day. The letter was undoubtedly prompted by what the Earl had said.

Christ's blood. He would have to take these latest developments to Williamson. Were there other letters? Ones to which they weren't privy? Had Mrs Behn been seeking Scot a while? And what did Tribulation *Johnson* have to do with it, if anything at all?

'We certainly won't be the only ones watching Mrs Behn if she's searching for Scot,' said Solomon.

'Indeed.' Gabriel ran his fingers through his hair. 'What possible life-changing information could Aphra Behn have for him? Why search for a regicide's son, someone whose reputation is irredeemable, at a time like this? When the question of the royal succession is causing such conflict, and her work is being debased as pro-Catholic? When one can't look askance at a crucifix without being held to account.' Gabriel's eyes swept the room. 'She's nobody's fool. And as far as I can tell, she's a loyalist. What's so important she takes such a risk? The fact she went to Barnabas rather than the official post office shows she doesn't want her correspondence interfered with or traced. It also suggests she suspects someone may be watching.'

'She didn't anticipate us then, did she?'

'She did not.'

Gabriel sat quietly, mulling everything over. He didn't like this. He couldn't believe Mrs Behn would be involved in something nefarious: that she would put herself, her reputation at risk — not again. Then there was Tribulation. The woman was clearly fond of the girl. More than fond. Yet lesser folk had done more and with less to lose. When there was a righteous point to make, a belief to sacrifice oneself to, a cause to fight for ...

This made no sense. He sighed. 'I thought her spying days were well and truly over. Considering the way her standing was reviled, and mostly by Scot, I'd have thought she'd avoid contact with him altogether.' He paused. Two burly-looking men he didn't recognise, though one had the bearing of a constable, were looking in their direction. 'Why reach out now? What's making her break years of silence?'

Solomon murmured into his beer. '*That* is the question.'

Gabriel glared at the men until they turned aside, muttering darkly. Were they just discommoded by Solomon? Mind you, he wouldn't put it past either Williamson, or the two Secretaries of State, Sunderland and Coventry, to have them tailed too. Or was someone else watching them? Killigrew? Or was it the Earl of Shaftesbury? It was beyond exhausting, all this observing, reporting, leaping to conclusions — mostly wrong.

He forced himself to remember what had been said in the Tiring Rooms. Shaftesbury all but humiliated Tribulation, claiming she reminded him of William Scot. The inference was both clear and offensive. Was it even relevant? Or was the Earl up to the usual, hurling offence like mud and seeing if it stuck?

Around the hazy room, men nursed drinks, flirting, gambling, either pretending indifference or examining each other brazenly, boldly, a gaze fixing or sliding away, estimating the threat.

'So, why is Mrs Behn seeking the whereabouts of a double agent?' repeated Gabriel, mostly to himself.

'That is *the* question,' said Solomon.

'Stop saying that,' said Gabriel.

'I thought you appreciated my efforts.' Solomon snickered.

Ignoring him, Gabriel continued. 'Until something else comes to light, it will be assumed Mrs Behn's doing this because she's embroiled in the Popish Plot or something equally heinous. Something that poses a danger to the throne.'

'Maybe she is. Is she a Papist?'

Solomon said the word with such distaste, Gabriel couldn't help but smile. Captain van Kessel, a stout Protestant, had taught him well. 'Mrs Behn prays to no God I know of. If she's reaching out to Scot, I can't believe it's anything to do with Catholics, Oates, or any plot for that matter.' He stopped. 'That is, unless —'

'She's acting on someone else's behalf,' finished Solomon.

Gabriel's mouth thinned. 'Shaftesbury's.' He recalled the way the louche had kissed the back of her hand, the way she'd fluttered her eyes. Had he communicated something? Was it a signal for her to reach out to Scot, make an offer, or was something else going on?

Shaftesbury was an avowed Republican who made no effort to hide his allegiances, nor his delight in stirring up trouble. In their many conversations, Gabriel had encouraged him to believe he was sympathetic to the Protestant cause — that he possessed the same mindset as the Earl and his followers. Not that the nobleman cared particularly. As Solomon noted, he shared his views with all and sundry; it was easy to be nonchalant when his rank and royal affiliations protected him. God damn the man. With Parliament still prorogued, and no bill regarding the royal succession ready to be debated by the Lords, let alone passed, and those in the Earl's pay stirring up emotions, fuelling division between those who were for the monarchy and those against, between Catholics and Protestants, high-born and low-born, there'd be strife. Word on the street was an uprising was being planned.

'Some say,' said Solomon, folding his burly arms, 'not only is Shaftesbury behind many of the pamphleteers, but he and Buckingham are the brains behind Oates.'

'Someone has to be: the man appears to be devoid of at least half his wits,' scoffed Gabriel. 'The Popish Plot is well beyond his capacity to have conceived alone. Shaftesbury's certainly the one throwing fuel on the Pepys fire as well. Things are looking very grim for him.'

'What about that cousin of Mrs Behn's, the tall one you can't stop talking about?'

The withering look Gabriel levelled at Solomon had no effect.

'Think she's involved?' asked Solomon.

Gabriel signalled for the maid to come over and ordered another round.

He waited until she was gone. 'I don't.'

'Maybe she's better at acting than you credit.' When no response was forthcoming, Solomon nudged him. '*You've* been acting strange about this Tribulation woman.'

'I have not,' said Gabriel indignantly.

The wench returned with their beer, placing it carefully before them, making sure they both had an eyeful of her generous décolletage. She slowly dropped the coin Solomon gave her between her breasts with a little wriggle, wink and cheeky smile. She was most becoming, with russet curls and wicked green eyes. If Gabriel hadn't been so preoccupied with a pair of turquoise ones, he might have been tempted. From the moon-struck look on Solomon's face, he was.

'It's all too easy to forget Mrs Behn is very clever,' said Gabriel, slurping the foam off the top of his drink.

'For a woman …' said Solomon, side-eying Gabriel. His friend failed to bite.

'Once a she-spy, always a she-spy,' Gabriel said thoughtfully. 'It's what Williamson says. It's why he insisted she be watched when the city's roiling with plans and plots and Catholics are the enemy. There's no doubt she's up to something. But does it involve treason? Papists? Does it involve anyone else?' He held up a finger. 'Don't say it.'

Solomon grinned. 'You're at the theatre to do more than leer at a chit from Chartham, no matter how comely you find her.'

'Speaking of Tribulation Johnson,' said Gabriel slowly, 'there could be trouble of a different kind brewing there.'

'Not just in your pants?'

Unfazed, Gabriel continued. 'One of the young actresses, Prisca Smithton, has been talking to those two cumberwolds either Spencer or Coventry hired to watch the theatre.'

'Aye, I've seen her with them by the river. A few times. Ruffians, the pair of them,' said Solomon. 'What of it?'

'She's no supporter of Tribulation, seeking to turn many of the company against her.'

'Has she succeeded?'

'Somewhat. People are fools. Keen to believe the worst of those they perceive have an advantage. Anyhow,' sighed Gabriel. 'I need you to watch Mrs Smithton too. Find out what she's telling them. Better still, find out what they're asking.'

Solomon nodded. 'Done.'

'Excellent,' said Gabriel. 'Very well. I'll inform Williamson about these latest developments. About Mrs Behn.'

Solomon struck his chest. 'And I'll add Prisca Smithton to the list of those I'm observing. I'll let you know the moment I learn anything.'

They clinked tankards and drained their drinks just as the lawyers found another hapless woman to taunt and corral against their table with tentacle arms and barrier legs. She had long yellow hair and blue eyes that widened in fear. Anger pierced Gabriel's chest. Anger, and something else.

'First,' he said, rolling up his sleeves, 'I have to teach some poltroons a lesson.'

He heaved himself off the bench, took two steps towards the drunken men and terrified woman and turned to Solomon. 'What are you waiting for, you scurvy turd? An invitation? Bring those mighty fists over here and help me.'

SCENE SEVEN

Who is't that to their Beauty would submit,
And yet refuse the Fetters of their Wit?

The Forc'd Marriage or, The Jealous Bridegroom, Aphra Behn

What remained of the Duke's Company stared at Lady Mary in stunned silence as her words were slowly absorbed. 'Because the theatre is still officially closed and we've no revenue coming in, I'm afraid we're left with no choice but to let you all go.'

Though not quite as bad as being disowned, it was a terrible blow, even if not entirely unexpected. The Company's resources were finite; the coffers weren't some cornucopia magically refilled.

With one last sympathetic but resigned look, Lady Mary rose and, gesturing for Charles and Alexander to follow, left the Tiring Room. They tripped behind her, keen to get away, the Bettertons and other major shareholders close on their heels.

No sooner had the door shut, everyone burst into conversation.

'What the fuck am I supposed to do?' Prisca asked, wringing her hands, echoing what everyone was thinking. 'I turned down an offer to join a troupe in Oxford. No-one's looking for performers this time of year!' There was a howl of agreement.

'At least you don't have children,' said Margaret, great tears rolling down her cheeks.

'At least you've only one,' said Mark Danvers, rubbing his jaw and raking his scalp, reminding everyone he had five, and elderly parents who lived with him as well.

Adversity became a competition.

A chorus of anger, frustration, but above all sadness and worry raged. How does one make ends meet when there's nothing to bind the middle? My heart ached for them — even Prisca.

Aware of Mr Rickman looking in my direction, I didn't dare acknowledge him. I wondered briefly what he would he do. Where he'd go. Once the salvation of the Duke's, he was condemned to the same penniless fate as the rest of us.

What would I do? I had to earn a wage, especially since Papa no longer supported me. Aphra could barely afford to cover her own expenses, let alone mine.

I'd some savings, but not as much as I should. Annoyed at myself for allowing Charlotte and Nest to persuade me to purchase some pretty neck kerchiefs and a second-hand gown a few weeks ago, I wished the coin back. Likewise, I regretted buying a copy of the Duchess of Newcastle-Upon-Tyne Margaret Cavendish's *A True Relation of My Birth*. Aphra recommended it as a way of making me feel better after Papa's letter. The Duchess was a bold, enterprising female who claimed women were men's equals: quick-witted, smart. The only difference, she averred, was that women were denied access to the same education. As if to prove her point, she dared write with great profundity about science, philosophy and many other subjects and even included some of her poetry. Just as Aphra hoped, I found her work inspiring.

On second thoughts, I didn't regret the purchase. It made me want to write, something I'd only recently started doing again — Papa's letter, his denial of me, had freed me in unexpected ways. I willed words to flow from my pen the way they did my mind. Aphra kept asking if she could read my efforts, but I was too embarrassed to show her. I told myself I just needed to find the right subject when what I really needed was confidence.

And practice.

And Aphra's gift for writing.

Perhaps the Bishop's Whelp might have some paid employ? Or maybe a printer? At least I'd stay abreast of news. There was always work sewing or washing. Imagine me a seamstress. The clothes would no sooner be worn than they'd fall apart. As for being a washerwoman … well, at least the lodgers would have no reason not to keep their garb laundered. Sometimes, you had to search for the best in a situation, didn't you?

A tear struck the dresser.

'What are you howling for?' said a sharp voice. Prisca.

It didn't help that Mr Rickman gave my shoulder a reassuring touch as he passed. The last thing I needed was consolation. It would completely undo me.

'You've got Aphra to take care of you, her what pisses coins the way a brewer does ale.' Prisca leaned against the adjacent dresser, arms folded, face a storm.

Pisses coin? I wasn't going to admit, especially to Prisca, that even though my cousin never ceased writing, she could barely summon a trickle.

'Leave off, Prisca,' said Charlotte, who sat the other side of me.

'Why? She's acting like the weight of the world's on those raw-boned shoulders when all she's got to worry 'bout is herself. With what she's been earning, she could hand us all some coin and make our lives easier.'

Much to my surprise, Mr Rickman spoke. 'Didn't you hear?' he growled. 'Enough.'

Prisca glared at him, chin jutting, mouth moving, but she didn't say anything aloud and levered herself away.

'She's right, though,' said John Crosby from across the other side of the room, his full lady-lips pouting. 'That girl,' he gestured to me, 'has no right to snuffles. Fortune's kissed her pert little arse. Only fair it sinks its teeth in now.' He gnashed his great yellow ones to prove his point. Pity he had so few in his head — it made for a small one.

'You seem to have forgotten,' said Mr Rickman. 'Matters not what role you play, be it queen,' he gestured to Elizabeth Barry, 'king,' he indicated Mark Danvers, 'pauper,' he looked pointedly at Prisca, who scowled, 'or prompter.' This time, when his fingers rested on my shoulder, I relished their weight. 'We're all affected by this, including the shareholders. If the theatre is shut, they're not earning either. Yet, they've creditors and more knocking at the door daily. If one goes hungry, we all do. Rather than fight between ourselves, we should be thinking of ways to help each other.'

'Gawd, you've become right gabby all of a sudden, haven't you?' hissed Prisca, hands on hips. 'Anyway, it's alright for you. You're a man. You'll never be wanting for work. Not like us women. Once we've trod the boards, all we're fit for is bawding. Fucked if I'll do that.'

'Again, you mean,' said Charlotte sweetly.

Prisca swept her cape off the back of a chair and plucked her hat from the table, pushing it onto her head. 'Think of helping all you like, Mr Rickman. 'Cause I won't. The only person I'm gonna help is meself!' There were some mumbles, whether of agreement or not was hard to tell. Charlotte opened her mouth to retort. I closed my hand around hers and shook my head. It wasn't worth it.

Prisca waited for John to precede her. She paused at the door and, with a dramatic toss of her head, left the room. Others trailed, necks bent, whispers fraught.

Elizabeth and Charlotte gathered their belongings along with Mary Lee and Elizabeth Currer. They offered quiet words of solace to each other, to me. Charlotte dropped a kiss on the top of my head. 'Ignore the spindle-shanked bitch. When you've finished, come join us. We'll be drowning our sorrows at the Whelp.'

Elizabeth offered a sad smile. She wouldn't want for work. Nor Elizabeth Currer nor Mary Lee. The King's Company, who'd benefited from our long closure, would shortly come a-knocking.

Soon, only Finnola, Juliet, Jacob, Mark Danvers, Pascal, Mr Rickman and I were left. The others sat quietly, hollow-eyed, trapped in their thoughts. It would be hard for them. Most had only ever known life with the Duke's Company.

It was all I could do not to bury my head in my arms and allow the tempest brewing inside me to unleash. It wasn't just self-pity, and sorrow for the others — though they were there too — but righteous anger at the unjustness of Prisca's accusations. John Crosby's as well. No doubt their views were widely shared, but everyone else lacked the courage, or had better manners than to express them, even those still in the room with me. God's breath, it hurt — as if I'd been whipped by a thousand tongue lashes. I might have accepted the position of prompter, a chance to prove myself, but hadn't I? And on a pitiful wage, despite what Prisca claimed. Jesus in a basket, I'd tried. I really had.

A quivering sigh escaped.

Mr Rickman cleared his throat, reminding me he was still there.

'What am I going to do?' I asked in a small voice. 'I can't go back home.'

'Back home? Why would you?' he asked. I'd told no-one at the theatre except Charlotte of my situation. Unexpectedly, he dragged over a stool and sat beside me, reaching over to press a large hand against my back. Something delicious and warm passed over me, settling in a liquid pool in my lower regions. I tried not to fidget. It was such a contrast to the way my head felt. 'There must be something you can do?' he said. 'The theatre won't remain closed forever.'

'We said that weeks ago and look,' I said, half-sitting up, opening my arms to the room.

His hand dropped. 'True. But you admitted once you never really sought to be here. You had other aspirations — writing, wasn't it?'

I didn't recall telling that to Mr Rickman. I was right; he listened to everything being said, even when he appeared not to. I'd confessed that in the first couple of weeks, and mainly to reassure others I'd no designs on their roles. Since then, I'd altered my opinion. Not only did I want to write but act as well. Should one preclude the other? Couldn't I do more than one thing? Or was that breaking some unwritten rule too?

'Aye,' I admitted reluctantly.

Though I'd begun to pen thoughts about everything from Titus Oates and the Popish Plot to the behaviour of theatre audiences, and reflect upon news about wars and skirmishes, as well as what I observed in the parish and ward, I didn't possess the finesse or learnedness needed to be printed. The more I read, the more I knew how naive I was — about the world, about people.

As Prisca and John Crosby kept reminding me, I was nothing but a country chit. How could I even conceive of writing let alone being published when I knew nothing?

The story of Socrates and the Oracle of Delphi suddenly came to mind. She told him he was the wisest of men because he professed how unenlightened he really was. Ha! Imagine a woman having that said to her, especially if she admitted her limitations. She'd simply have her worst suspicions about her own weaknesses and deficiencies confirmed. 'Silence, dullard! Of course you know nothing.'

Whenever I read the news-sheets or listened to Aphra and what was said around me, my ignorance was made apparent. I lacked experience, and intimate knowledge of people, court, the gentry and business — not through choice, mind.

'I can't help but wish,' Mr Rickman began, looking about the room, 'someone would write about *this*.' Finnola was folding clothes. Juliet was pretending to clean hair from a brush while Jacob scoured the floor with the toe of his boot. Mark Danvers and Pascal were on the cusp of leaving, their sadness palpable.

'You mean the impact the closure's having.'

Mr Rickman smiled. It lit up his whole face, banishing the gloom he oft wore in repose. Pity he didn't deploy it more often. Or, considering the way my heart fluttered, maybe it was a good thing. 'I do.'

Was Mr Rickman suggesting I put quill to paper?

My cheeks grew warm — not with modesty but a quiet thrill — as an idea took hold. This was something I *did* know; it didn't require formal schooling or knowledge of the classics and ancient tongues. Then, dammit, doubt made himself at home. 'I'm not sure I'd be able to interest the publishers, let alone readers,' I said, mostly in the hope he'd contradict me.

'I wasn't suggesting *you* should write it.' Mr Rickman's eyes twinkled.

Did he mean that? His eyes were so dark, like the night sky when the moon was absent, and the stars burned holes in the firmament. I was reflected in them, frowning, disconsolate, offended.

'But,' he continued, 'maybe Mrs Behn could? I heard she's writing a great deal of late.'

As if her life depended on it. Or so she could escape it.

'She is; though I'm not sure if this —' I jerked my chin '— is something she would tackle.' I paused.

'You're acquainted with the publisher Sir Roger L'Estrange, aren't you?' he asked.

'He's friends with Aphra.'

'Go and see him. Tell him what the King's decree means — not only to audiences who once flocked here and who still have Drury Lane to entertain them — but to those who depend on his Majesty's patronage, on his goodwill and that of his brother to survive. After all, you're living it. Not only am I sure Sir Roger'll write about it, but he'll pay you for the story.'

I quashed the flare of indignation that he didn't consider I could write such a piece. Though, he *was* correct. People didn't know the huge impact the closure was having on those employed here. How could they? All they saw were the bright lights, flamboyant costumes, and music. The dazzling smiles and false laughter. The actresses stepping out with the gentry. All they'd read and heard were the naughty goings-on, the royal rewards bestowed upon the likes of Nell Gwyn and Moll Davis, the parties, dinners, scandals. And, of course, the brawls. It was a diversion to them, a moral yardstick by which they measured their own sanctimony. They didn't understand or know about the hard work behind the scenes: the damage to reputations, deserved or not. What we were willing to tolerate, to sacrifice, to remain.

But why should I tell Sir Roger when I knew first-hand what was lost? Why should he or Aphra undertake a task I was perfectly capable of doing? Better, really, because, as Mr Rickman said, I was in possession of first-hand knowledge.

A frisson of excitement made my skin goose. How was the King supposed to know the repercussions of his decision if someone didn't tell him?

What if that someone *was* me?

Filled as I was with purpose, words began to take root in my head, growing and blossoming until my mind was a garden — one badly in need of weeding, but nevertheless in bloom. Before I lost my train of thought, let alone courage, I sprang from the chair. I could put something together and, if I was swift, have it to a printer before close of day. I grabbed my coat and hat and was about to leave the room when I raced back to where Mr Rickman sat.

He didn't know he'd lit a flame. He thought he'd merely given me an errand. Still, I owed him. I wouldn't be so tardy expressing my gratitude this time.

'Thank you,' I said and swooped to give him a kiss on the cheek. At the last minute, he turned, so my lips met his.

The warmth of his mouth, the way his lips accommodated mine was unexpected, shocking. I tried to withdraw but he raised his hand and tangled his fingers through my hair, drawing me closer. I fell onto his chest, my breasts flattening against the leanness of his frame. My heart thudded; my insides turned molten. Unable to help myself, I opened my lips to receive his. Paths of longing carved their way through my chest, along my thighs, merging in a hot centre, before I regained my senses and, with as much strength as I could muster, pushed away.

My face was flushed, my breath came in gasps.

'How dare you!' I hissed, praying no-one had seen.

'It was you who kissed me. I simply returned it.'

'I … I … I didn't mean for you … you weren't supposed to …' I didn't have the words to describe what had just happened. Enraged and hotter than a baker's armpit, I scooped up my cloak and was appalled to see his breeches had changed shape.

'Can't say I regret it,' rumbled Mr Rickman, glancing at his groin without a trace of embarrassment.

'Oh!' I said; my eyes widened before they slid away, and shame coursed through me. Igneous shame threaded with something else, something that made me squirm in a deliciously painful manner. The words in Papa's letter began to dance in my vision.

You are now reduced to a theatre-harlot by any reckoning.

I was not, and yet Mr Rickman had treated me as if I was.

Cold, hard fury descended.

All eyes were upon us. Once more, I was the centre of attention, only this time, stage-fright would not silence me.

I took a deep breath. 'I don't know who you think you are.' I kept my voice low. 'Or what you think *I* am, but I tell you now, sir, I'm no street strumpet you can manhandle or upon whom you can foist your unwelcome attentions.' He went to speak, but in a mirror of a gesture he once used upon me, I pressed a finger against his lips. 'Peace! You chose to mistake a friendly gesture of thanks and turn it into something more, not me. I'll wear the blame in this instance, but for this reason alone. I misjudged *you*.' I took my finger away. 'For all your curmudgeonly ways, I thought you to be a man of honour. Rest assured, sirrah, I'll not make the same error again.'

He tried to rise but became tangled among wooden weapons. 'Forgive me, Mrs Johnson. Tribulation. You're right, I'm a complete knave. I never meant to —'

Before he could offer another excuse, I pushed him back into the seat, snatched my hat and strode out of the room, trying to put distance between myself and what had just happened.

Once I reached the streets, I stopped, resting in the shade of a barber's awning. I was trembling. I took a few deep breaths, one eye on the alley, afraid Mr Rickman would appear, the other searching for where I would hide in the event he did.

Fortunately, he didn't follow.

My anger slowly cooled, yet what remained was indignation. How could men even know what women were capable of if they continued to not only tell us what we could and could not do, but treated us like chattels positioned about the place for their convenience? Feel like a kiss? Take one. A grope? By all means, sir, here are my bubbies. Proffer a compliment, sir, an insult, sir, I'm all swooning ears, sir! Take me against my will. Whatever sir desires … thy will be done.

As my temper diminished, clarity took its place. The person I was most cross at was myself. Why, I'd literally fallen into his arms, so eager had I been to receive his kiss. Not just receive it either but return it, dammit. I rested my palm against my chest. All the stories I'd read, the plays and poetry, even what I'd observed, hadn't prepared me for the physical reality of a man's embrace, how my body would respond. How much I would *feel*. How much I still did.

But was it for a man's touch, or was it because it was Jonathan Rickman's?

I didn't want to explore the answer. Not now. I'd a piece to write. Work that would focus my mind and cool my ardour. Push Mr Rickman and the memory of his mouth, his hard, lean frame and bloody dancing breeches far, far from my head.

From my tingling flesh.

I eventually left my temporary shelter, nodding to the cutler, who'd set up his barrow and grindstone, already looking forward to being ensconced in my room. There, I'd draw inspiration from Shakespeare's *Henry VI* and 'call for pen and ink and write my mind' and pray, that in committing to this, I was in my right one.

SCENE EIGHT

Patience is a flatterer, Sir — and an Ass, Sir.

The Feign'd Curtezans or, A Night's Intrigue, Aphra Behn

Held between liveried guards bearing pikes and wearing swords, and ordered to be silent, I was forced north along Dorset Street. Terror turned my thoughts into wire that scritched and scratched, shredding any sensible, rational answers. Why had soldiers seized me? Was I to be implicated in the Popish Plot? Was I about to be thrown in Newgate alongside poor Mr Medbourne, or the Tower, like Mr Pepys and other 'traitors'? Surely these uniformed men had the wrong person.

They had been lying in wait as I left the house just after six bells. Anyone who might have borne witness turned their backs the moment the guards swooped. Shutters were half-closed, faces retreated from windows. Urchins dived beneath carts. I didn't blame them. I just prayed someone would tell Aphra or Nest.

Then it struck me. I knew exactly why I was being marched ignominiously through the streets. It was because of what I'd written about the unjustness of the theatre closure. Oh, dear God in Heaven up above. I took a long, deep breath and tried to restore my calm, sort my galloping deliberations. For good measure, I uttered a prayer as well.

It had taken me three drafts to settle upon an article that pleased. Three drafts and two bowls of chocolate. I read it over many times, wishing I could show Aphra, ask her opinion. I couldn't. This had to be my secret. Aphra said women oft wrote from the shadows. I had to protect myself. Protect Aphra too. The last thing she needed was her detractors accusing her of producing literary offspring. Even so, I couldn't bring myself to sign what I'd written *Anonymous.* I briefly toyed with my own name, but then thought of Papa, remembered the crushing weight of his judgement, the consequences, and that merely after someone *else* printed my name in an article.

If I dared to claim these words, the denigration and retribution for my boldness would be fierce and endless.

I'd flicked the end of the quill against my chin a few times, thinking how lovely it must be to sign one's name, knowing at the very least with ownership of an opinion you were responsible for eliciting others; for stirring debate — for *reaching*, as Aphra said. It wasn't fair our sex had to always hide, or pretend lack of wit or ability — and why? To appease men.

Then it occurred to me how I would sign.

I quickly scrawled my nom de plume, and before I could change my mind, gathered my cloak and purse, and, shouting to Nest that I was on an errand, all but ran to Fleet Street. From there, I hailed a sedan chair. I wasn't brave enough to ask Sir Roger to consider publishing my piece. Mr Shale and his father were out of the question. But a woman publisher was an altogether different prospect.

Deposited outside St Paul's, I battled my way across the street and then through the crowds attending market and shopping within the grand church itself. Outside, there were laden carts filled with fruit, vegetables, second-hand pots and pans, clothes and furs. Beggars wandered aimlessly, hands outstretched; and children selling freshly slain chickens, coneys and all manner of other animals (I could have sworn I saw rats) pleaded tiredly with passers-by. Stalls were erected in every conceivable space and vendors shouted, beseeched, jigged, threatened, even sang (the threats were easier on the ear) to attract attention. Numerous speakers, most standing atop boxes, under pieces of scaffolding or on the plinth of a statue, cried across the square, drawing crowds with the latest headlines or predictions that God's Judgement was nigh. There were the usual anti-Papist railings and so much more. As I pushed my way towards the Gun, I fought the temptation to browse the carts and tables of books, resisted the lure of shops selling 'Arabian spices' and 'China-silks', and another claiming to have a book written by one of the Apostles. Thousands of reasons I shouldn't be there bickered with the stubborn little voice hammering inside my head, insisting I forge onwards.

I passed the sign of the Ship, the Black Swan and so many other booksellers — new and second-hand, practically on top of one another and competing for trade. Hard to believe so many books had been lost in the Great Fire years earlier as gowned and cloaked men bargained over a tome, others leaving with fresh purchases tucked firmly under their arms. On the look-out for Ivy Lane, one of the narrow, cobbled tributaries deviating off the main yard, I almost missed it.

People milled inside the rather gloomy interior of the Gun, ignoring the variety of noises issuing from the rear — a printing press. Pools of dim light revealed shelf-lined walls, the cases filled with books of all sizes and description. Three tables in the centre were crowded with reams of paper — blank and printed — and a few stacks of beautifully bound books and plays. There were small pamphlets, larger folios and boxes of inkhorns, oak galls, jars of ink and rows of quills finished with different feathers. There was an overpowering odour of dust, leather and paper. There was also the smell of something sharp, metallic, mixed with the stench of animal. I longed to linger, examine the books, read the pamphlets and tracts, browse the latest news, but upon seeing absorbed customers, and hearing the continuous thuds, clanks and voices coming from the rear rooms, I took my chance. I made my way to the long counter at the back where Mrs Joanna Brome stood.

Widowed recently, she was still garbed in black, a cap covering her head. Her face was intelligent. Her eyes, a pale grey, were sharp. She had thin lips and large hands. When she saw me, she put aside what she was reading and smiled in recognition. 'God give you good day. You're Aphra's cousin, aren't you? Tribulation Johnson. The one working at Dorset Garden.'

'May God give you good day, too, Mrs Brome.' I was relieved she remembered me from when Aphra had brought her backstage a few times after performances. 'I'm hoping you can help me.'

Before I could change my mind, I swiftly explained why I was there.

Mrs Brome frowned, drummed ink-stained fingers against the countertop and then held out her hand. 'Show me.'

Somewhat reluctantly, I handed the pages over, explaining the urgency — more so I didn't snatch them back and run.

Moving a lanthorn closer, she read them swiftly, sucking in her breath. 'My, my, Mrs Johnson. This is bold indeed.' She shot me a curious look. 'You wrote this?'

'I … I did.'

She pursed her lips, but not in a disapproving manner. 'It's very … provocative. You've addressed it to his Majesty — like a letter. Makes it personal.'

'Until it becomes public.'

'Indeed.'

'Do you think …?' I took a deep breath. 'Will you publish it?'

The furrows between her brows deepened. She cast a few looks towards the back room. Then, just when I thought she'd decline, she nodded. 'Especially if it helps Lady Mary and the Duke's.'

Relief flooded me. Relief and something else. 'No-one must know I wrote it, Mrs Brome.' I reached for her hand. 'It has to be our secret.'

'Joanna,' she said, squeezing my fingers. 'If we're to hold this secret, then I think we need to be on first-name terms, don't you?'

We shared a cautious smile. I returned her grip. Ink transferred to my fingers. I wiped them on my skirt. 'Thank you, *Joanna*. So,' I said, suddenly all businesslike. 'When can you print it?'

Joanna cocked her head. 'We're just finishing a job, but this shouldn't take long to typeset. I can do it myself. If I ask Rohan, one of our workers, to stay back this afternoon, we should have it ready to be distributed by tomorrow evening. The Mercury Women can do it, though you understand they'll take a cut.'

The Mercury Women hawked news-sheets, pamphlets and tracts all over London. Any they couldn't sell in bulk to booksellers and criers, they distributed at points around the city. Sometimes they stood on boxes and read the headlines, tempting people to pay a penny to see what was printed for themselves. Literate, cocky, with loud voices and able to repel those who sought to challenge the news or prevent them from continuing, they were all ages and sizes. Each carried a huge satchel and wore a grubby apron, smeared with newsprint. It oft marked their fingers and faces, and it was easy to mistake them for beggars, or even women of poor reputation. Aphra said one did so at their peril. A thrill went through me to think that not only would a woman be printing my work but distributing it as well. Was this how Aphra felt when the actresses performed her lines?

'If you use their networks, then your words will circulate further, be more widely read,' said Joanna, thinking I needed convincing.

We swiftly discussed payment and number of copies.

That had been three days ago. It never occurred to me I might be punished for my daring. Was Mrs Brome in trouble as well? I sincerely prayed not. Who was so offended they demanded my presence? Who could call upon so many guards this early in the morning? More importantly, how did they know who wrote the damn piece?

There was only one person who had such authority and the ability to uncover such information.

We turned into Fleet Street, marching against the traffic, most of which regarded us with great interest. We'd just passed a huge herd of cattle, their stinking turds spattering the road and being trudged into smears, when we halted by an unmarked but nevertheless fine coach outside Sergeant's Inn. Four horses snorted and stamped their hooves. People slowed to ask who it was for. When they spied me in the guards' midst, cries went up — boos and cheers.

Reminded of that first night on stage, I felt familiar ice crawling through my veins. Only, this was no play, and I wasn't acting. My vision grew dark before bright lights danced across it. I swayed and the officer in charge grabbed me.

'Inside,' he grunted, opening the door to the coach. He collapsed on the seat opposite, rapping the back of the driver's seat with his fist.

After what seemed an age, we rolled to a stop. The doors were flung open, and the captain, who'd hadn't uttered a word the entire distance, jumped out, turning to assist me. The sun's beams transformed the sky into a blue and gold dome. As I blinked against the light, I was astonished to see the verge of St James's Park. There was a glimmer from the canal that formed its glittering spine. Already, folk were meandering between the shady trees, picking fruit, sitting beneath verdant boughs or riding horses on the many paths.

I shielded my eyes.

'Here,' said the captain. 'Wear this.' He handed me a black and silver vizard with a small handle.

'Now?'

'No. Tonight, when I take you to the theatre. Of course, now.'

The captain urged me forwards, two guards walking either side — one short, the other my height. The rest remained with the coach.

'Where are you taking me?'

No answer.

'Upon whose orders am I here?'

Still, no answer. After a while I gave up and took comfort in being out in the open. A group of men and two women were playing a game of Pall Mall on grass studded with iron rings. A herd of cows grazed nearby, pretty milkmaids lolling beneath the trees beside them. Shaggy-muzzled dogs scampered about here and there. It was so very bucolic. Like a scene from Dryden.

The sun glistened upon the lake's surface, turning it into a sheet of bronze. From a small island in the middle sweet trilling issued. There was the faint scent of roses and lilac and the familiar waft of tobacco. On the lake, two odd-shaped craft floated, the passengers reclining lazily. Upon one, a musician played a viola, the music echoing across the water. Conversation rose and fell, punctuated by the occasional burst of laughter, or a cheer from a nearby group playing shuttlecock.

It was as we rounded the eastern end of the lake that my suspicions were confirmed. It was one thing to speculate who might have ordered my presence, but quite another to have such a wild surmise confirmed.

I saw his dogs first. Renowned for his early morning walks, it seemed King Charles also chose to have women abducted — abducted or arrested, I wasn't sure which. A fleet of spaniels came tearing down the grass towards the water's edge, pulling up short just when it appeared they were going to tumble in and disturb the waterfowl floating serenely by.

'Halt,' said the captain suddenly. I itched to salute. 'Wait here,' he said, abandoning me in the shade of a willow's lacy fronds.

I'd read and heard so much about his Majesty and here he was loping up the sward towards me. When I was a child, talk about him had been mostly very positive. Handsome, debonair, the hope of the country, Charles II embodied all the promise of England. By the time I was scratching my first letters into a horn book, the mood had shifted. Now, even his closest friends felt emboldened enough to write awful poems about him, to laugh, as Aphra and Sir Roger said, at their monarch rather than with him. Even the news-sheets were oft unkind. Lanky, he was very tall, his dark periwig adding to that perception. Possessed of a large nose, heavy cheeks and pouched eyes, he was also old.

'So,' he began, when he was but a few feet away, bending to pick up two persistent spaniels and holding them to his chest. Such an affectionate, everyday action made him both extraordinary and ordinary simultaneously. 'You must be Tribulation Johnson. You may remove the mask.'

Why were my hands trembling? I balled them into fists and hid them in my skirts, along with the mask. I kept swallowing. 'At your service, your Majesty.' I made a poor attempt at a curtsey.

'Are you? Shouldn't that be disservice? It's not every day one of my subjects calls into question my decisions. And yet, this is what you, a mere chit, took upon yourself to do.' He gazed over the dogs' heads. So much for a Merry Monarch. Melancholy or even Moody Monarch would be more apt.

I went to speak but he held up a dog-filled hand to prevent me. Then, perhaps realising how strange that looked, he handed the mutts to one of his attendants and snapped his fingers. A piece of paper was passed over. A copy of my published letter.

Butterflies with steel wings edged with barbs took flight in my chest.

'If I'm not mistaken,' he said, 'you're the author of this … this … what shall we call it?' He rubbed his chin in an overblown manner, a Wycherley villain made manifest. 'Letter? They're usually private affairs, are they not? So, let us refer to it as a *condemnation*.'

'Oh, nay, your Majesty —' I began, my thoughts whirling. How could he be so certain I was the author? After all, I'd signed it *One of the Fair Sex*. I might not own the work as an individual, but I would as part of an ignored collective. As Aphra said, it was only when we united and spoke as one our voices would be heard. I let the King know the closure affected everyone — women too. Actresses, aye, but also those who worked behind the scenes like Finnola and Juliet, as well as the wives, sisters, mothers and children of performers who relied on them for upkeep, never mind the men. Were not men providers? Hard to provide anything when there was no coin forthcoming. I also reminded his Majesty the theatre and its workers did not dwell in an empty parish or ward. What about the local shop-keepers and vendors, the inn-keeps and tavern owners, the coffee-house proprietors, the printers and news-sheet publishers who all relied on those from the Duke's Company to spend their wages in order that they too could keep their businesses flourishing? And what about those further afield who relied on these same businesses to purchase their stock? What about the mercers, cloth-makers, perruquiers, carpenters, foresters, brewers, and other trades who relied on the Company and those they patronised to buy their products? If there was no longer a demand, if coin wasn't exchanging hands, then, like ripples in a pond, it radiated outwards until, finally, all was still. And broke.

I wrote that in closing the theatre, his Majesty didn't just punish the Duke's Company … he punished *everyone*.

'I would never dare to —' I began.

'But you did, chit. You dared to write this.' He shook the pages and arched a dark brow.

I was going to say *condemn* … only, I had, hadn't I?

I would stand behind my words, even if my knees threatened to buckle. I began to understand why, when challenging the status quo, questioning mores, Aphra remained anonymous. Why other women writers did as well. God knows, anything Aphra put her name to (and even much she never penned) attracted opprobrium and insults. If every female was called to account for her opinion, slandered and denigrated, never mind brought before authority — before the King no less — and punished, then of course it was easier to remain anonymous. Better still, stay silent and in the shade. To tolerate injustice and pretend an acquiescence we didn't feel.

Too late, I thought as a beam of sunlight penetrated the canopy and struck me in the face. I may as well have lit a beacon. And I thought I was so clever.

Dear God. What was going to happen? To me? To Aphra? Swept up in my excitement, I'd thought myself her equal. A man's equal. My hubris was breathtaking. What about poor Mrs Brome?

The King was staring at the page. 'God's truth, I'd no idea the Company suffered so — nor that many others. If my sources are correct, not even Drury Lane has profited. No new plays, scant audiences. Seems we're all the poorer for it.' He screwed the paper into a ball and cast it to his man, who caught it. 'If only my lickspittle courtiers had half your courage, madam, then I'd be forced to examine my mind more often.'

'Your Majesty?' I met his eyes. They were dark, almost as black as Jonathan Rickman's. Funny he should come to mind, the man who, without knowing, had inspired me in the first place.

Close up, I could see the argent glint of whiskers the King's barber had missed, the silver bristles sticking out at peculiar angles within his neatly trimmed moustache. The pores of his face were large, and red webs tracked the sides of his nose and his chin. Within his gaze, I didn't see anger or a desire to punish. I saw a combination of weariness and regret.

All the time I'd been looking at him, he'd been examining me. 'Your eyes are a most unusual shade, madam.' He tilted his head. 'You have a disturbance in one.' He moved so close I could smell him. Musk, soap and wet dog. 'You're uncommonly tall for a woman. Why, if we were upon level ground, we'd almost be of a height.' He took a step back and studied me top to toe. 'Do you play the breeches part?' When I shook my head, he raised a brow. 'What part do you play?'

'I'm not an actress, your Majesty. I tried and failed. Dismally.'

'Ah.' The corners of his mouth lifted, as did a finger. 'I think I know something of that.'

I could feel my cheeks growing warm. 'I'm currently book-keeper.'

'I'd heard the Duke's had a female in the position. And Mr Downes? He's recovering, I trust?'

'Slowly, sir.'

'But he will recover.'

'God willing.'

'Yes, yes.' He waved a flounced wrist. 'God willing. Though, when Downes does, what will you do?'

I shrugged. 'I … I'm not certain, sir. Write some more?'

He froze then emitted a low chuckle. 'Oddsfish, but you're an audacious creature.' He looked me up and down once more, as if in the brief time we'd been talking I'd undergone some alteration. 'Now, replace the mask before those watching discover your identity. I assume you don't want it known?'

'It would be my preference, sir.'

'Very good. Well, let me say, madam, it's been a pleasure, but one I don't wish to repeat too soon.' Whistling to his hounds, he began to walk away. Our audience was over. I quickly dropped another curtsey. He'd only taken a few steps when he swung around, walking backwards.

'When you next write, missus, I'd advise more discernment. I only choose not to punish you because you achieved what very few ever have.'

'Your Majesty?'

He stopped. His men too, almost falling over one another. 'You managed to catch the conscience of a King.' With a half-smile, he turned and never looked back.

SCENE NINE

Told her, if she continued so bold,
That he would have a case made out of hand,
To keep her tongue in, under his command.

Anatomy of a Woman's Tongue

On Saturday 19th August, in a snowstorm of playbills and choir of criers, the theatre reopened. Thomas Otway's *Friendship in Fashion* was staged. Filled with deception and revenge, mistresses and gentlemen intent on seduction and the consequences, the characters were as tortured in love as the playwright himself. Parts of the production were quite outrageous, so it offered the best of diversions.

Saturdays were when the company usually mounted a new show, knowing the audience was generally leaner than during weekdays. It also allowed the author, in consultation with Lady Mary and the Bettertons, to make any adjustments — alter lines not working; tweak a character who didn't receive favour from the crowd; or even add another song. By Monday — after frantic rehearsals — any mistakes were generally rectified. All were aware we'd be watched closely, and Otway's script, despite having been performed before, was treated as cautiously as a new one.

Shocked by the play at first, its overt lasciviousness, I'd seen it in rehearsal so often I think I'd become inured, but also I began to appreciate it was just as much a satire of social mores as it was a tasteless, bawdy comedy. Certainly, the characters who most deserved it received their comeuppance. Mr Smith delivered the prologue and Elizabeth Barry gave the epilogue.

While enthusiastic, the audience wasn't large — as expected. The music was cheerful and loud, the songs excellent and the actors word perfect. No wonder, since they'd been put through their paces so many times. Given a reprieve of sorts, I leaned over the prompter's table, a lanthorn at my elbow, and allowed my mind to wander.

There'd been such relief when the King rescinded his edict. Actors and actresses were recalled from wherever else they'd managed to find work. Finnola and Jacob readied costumes (which, after all our attentions during closure, really only meant ensuring the correct ones were brushed and hung). Juliet checked the make-up again, discarding anything too oily or that had attracted mould or flies. Scenery was put into position, Pascal and Evan touching up any damage incurred during storage. Tuning instruments, chittering tongues, thudding boots, candlelight and smoke, the musty, interesting smells only people exude, filled the theatre once more. The worries of the last months were hidden behind too-loud laughter, extra-wide smiles and endless gossip.

The performers didn't fool anyone, least of all each other.

But the question on everyone's lips was: who wrote that oh-so-public letter to the King and made him change his mind?

Who *dared*?

Names were put forward, men's, despite the female appellation (folk assumed it was a clever ploy to mislead and deflect royal punishment), until it was concluded Aphra was responsible. If she was too modest to take the credit, well, they'd give it to her anyway. In the end, she'd no choice but to accept the outpouring of gratitude, to which, in order to defray suspicion, I added mine as well.

Aphra accepted it with a wry grin. My attempts to keep what I'd done from her had failed from the outset.

'You and I need to talk,' she said after I arrived home the very morning his Majesty confronted me, dishevelled, still reeling in disbelief. She waved a copy of the pamphlet in my face. My heart sank. What would she say? I began to prepare a defence.

She shooed Millie and Molly out of the kitchen and asked Nest to make us coffee. Then, she faced me. 'The King had a few words to say, did he?'

Surprised she knew who I'd been with, I carefully lowered myself onto a bench. I didn't know how she'd react, despite encouraging my writing — how she'd really feel about me trespassing on what was essentially her territory. In the past, any time Papa discovered what I wrote, it was denigrated, mocked, and ultimately destroyed. Not even Bethan's attempts to soften his criticisms, or Lady Adeline's insistence I persevere, had helped. As a result, I became wary of sharing my efforts with my elders, especially after Lady Adeline died.

'More than a few,' I admitted.

There it was: a grin. I began to relax … a wee bit.

Informed of my arrest by a couple of the shop-keepers opposite, Aphra had been about to depart for White Hall when Joanna Brome appeared on the doorstep. The evening before, the Censor, Henry Bennet, Lord Arlington, had come to her shop, soliciting the identity of the author of the tract about the theatre closure. After threatening Joanna (which didn't work) he guessed.

'How?' I asked.

Aphra waited until I'd had a few sips of coffee before continuing. 'He knew a woman wrote it. His men searched Joanna's shop and found the original. He told her because the style differed from mine and you've an intimate knowledge of the theatre, it had to be you. Relax, kitten. He wasn't after a revelation but confirmation. The man's no fool …'

My hands shook. Nest bustled in the background. Piles of laundry waited to be sorted at one end of the table; at the other, bunches of dried herbs and fingers of string sat. Lavender, lilies and the scent of chamomile were almost destroyed by the pungent aroma of the bitter Mohammedan gruel, as Nest oft called it.

Aphra placed the tract on the table between us and leaned back in the chair, arms folded, waiting.

'The King is going to rescind the decree,' I said. It came out in a defensive rush. 'The theatre can reopen.'

Aphra made a tsking noise. 'That *is* good news. But, Tribulation, it doesn't alter the fact you drew the attention of Lord Arlington and those who seek to restrain if not stop us. I don't think you understand what you've done. Yes, you've accomplished something positive, but at what cost? You're now in Arlington's ken.' She sighed. 'Which means we all are. Joanna. Me too.' Her face folded into planes of sadness and something more, something darker, deeper. What was she afraid of? An image of Lord Arlington, the ever-present black plaster stretched across the bridge of his nose, appeared. I shuddered.

I stared at her, then the page. Suddenly, the enormity of what I'd done struck me. If I hadn't already been sitting, I would have fallen. The words, *To his sacred Majesty, defender of the faith, suffering, unaware of the plight his action has caused, deliberately remote*, merged and became clear. A stubborn little nub of pride refused to disappear. After all, I hadn't waited for something to happen. I made it happen. I did *something.*

And trouble followed.

How Papa would enjoy this.

On second thoughts, maybe not.

'I'm so sorry,' I said meekly, the last of my vanity dissolving. 'I should have told you, shown you.'

'Why didn't you?'

'I don't know.' I threw my hands up in the air. 'Nay, that's not true. I thought …' I inhaled. 'I thought you'd discourage me.' Dear Lord, I sounded pathetic.

Aphra gave a gurgle of laughter. 'Why, you fool, I'd have *helped*.' She put down her bowl. 'When are you going to understand, Tribulation Johnson? I'm not your papa. But unless you share your intentions, ask advice or aid, then I can't offer anything.' She reached over and squeezed my fingers.

She was right. She'd only ever shown me encouragement and kindness, put me forward for employ which no-one, especially me, thought I was capable. If anyone knew what it was like to be overlooked, work against the grain, expect criticism and dismissal, it was her.

I hadn't given her a chance to show disapproval or support. I'd presumed to know how she'd respond. Colour flew into my cheeks. I felt ashamed. I tried to express remorse. Before I could, she spoke again.

'I'm so proud of you, Tribulation.'

'Y-you are?'

'I wish I'd thought to do something so … so … plucky.' She shook her head in admiration. 'I feel I owe you an apology.'

'*You* apologise to me?' I gave an awkward laugh. 'Whatever for?'

Aphra nodded when Nest held the coffee pot over her bowl. 'I didn't understand, didn't recognise the writer within you. I made no real effort to.'

I protested. She waved it away impatiently.

'When you made mention of your desire to write, I admit, I thought it nothing but a young woman's foolish fancy. I thought you blinded by what I do: that you were unrealistically optimistic. I was unfair. Every day you see what I endure. Hear it too — the good and the bad.' She rested her hand atop the pamphlet. 'This. You've real talent. What you wrote, it was direct, captured the crux of the issue, and you don't beg pardon of the reader. Or, for that matter, his Majesty.'

I could barely see as my eyes filled faster than a brewer's tun, but it was my ears I thought damaged. Was I hearing aright?

Aphra put down her bowl. 'You remind me so much of myself at your age. Full of ideas, ambition, passion, but with no-one to guide let alone share these with. I'd nowhere to go to learn, to develop and practise, let alone anyone to approximate or who could ease me into this writing life. I plunged in — for various reasons —' her eyes grew faraway, before she gave a flippant motion of her hand '— and almost drowned.' She waited until I wiped my eyes. 'I don't want you to have the same experience. I want to help. Question is, will you allow me to?'

There was a beat, then I scrambled to my feet and raced around the table, throwing my arms about her neck. 'Aye! Aye! Thank you, thank you,' I whispered into her hair.

'Ah, my bundle of trouble,' she said, a suspicious quaver in her voice. 'It's me who should be thanking you, isn't that right, Nest?'

''Tis indeed, missus,' said Nest and, much to my surprise, she threw her arms around both of us, holding tightly. She sniffed a few times. Loudly. Right in my ear. Turns out, it was in fine order.

With great reluctance, I released Aphra and Nest, but not before they'd both kissed me.

After that, we spent what remained of the morning around the kitchen table talking. Aphra and Nest insisted I describe every minute with his Majesty. We discussed how excited the Company would be when they heard the news, how long it would take to recall everyone and mount a play, how big the audience might be. We also talked about what inspired me to dare to write in the first place.

'With so many ordinary people having their opinions published — and not so ordinary, look at Titus Oates — I thought why not try at least?' I didn't admit it was Jonathan Rickman who first planted the idea in my head. To think of him conjured memories of that kiss and ... well, I'd worked hard (and unsuccessfully) to forget it.

'Sir Roger is beside himself about the state of the press,' said Aphra, frowning. She was none too pleased either. 'There are so many new-sheets circulating, some only lasting as long as it takes to read them. The government has lost any control over what's being published. On the one hand, they can no longer direct what people read and learn, or quash criticism of their methods. On the other, there's a great deal of false news being printed and taken as truth — and that's not healthy for anyone, let alone the nation.'

'As I came down Dorset Street, there was a man standing atop a box reading a satire about the Devilish He-Whore who lives yonder in Rome.'

'A He-Whore?' sighed Aphra. 'That's not very inventive.'

'Sounds like a donkey braying,' tsked Nest, joining us at the table. 'They were saying the same over by Cheapside. Folks were cheering and clinking pennies in the man's tin faster than his boy could count 'em.'

'The Tetchells brought home a poem last night entitled "England's Obligations",' said Aphra. 'It's addressed to that awful associate of Oates, the one who supported all his wild claims. Only, now he's being heralded as the one who uncovered them: "Captain William Bedlowe, the grand discoverer of this most horrid plot."'

Ah. The man responsible for the brawl that led to the closure of the theatre in the first place.

'Pride comes before a fall.' I heard Papa's voice as I said it.

'It does. The greater the pride, the harder the fall. Remember that, Tribulation.' She bopped the end of my nose. About to pass her bowl to Nest, Aphra paused. 'With that in mind —' At that moment, the noon bells rang, alerting us to the day's passing. 'You've saved the Duke's Company, the theatre, and those within's livelihoods, but —'

'They must never know,' I finished.

Aphra nodded gravely. 'Not if you wish to keep using that wonderful nom de plume. *One of the Fair Sex*. There're so many ways of reading that. Nevertheless, no-one can ever know you were the author.'

'Except the King.'

'Except Old Rowley.' Aphra smiled at my confusion. 'That's his Majesty's pet name.'

My brows rose in query.

'Named after a favourite horse,' she explained.

'A horse? Why?'

Aphra arched a brow at Nest before her glinting eyes slid back to mine. 'Surely, as a country chit, I don't need to explain to you about a horse's, err …'

'Plum tree-shaker,' supplied Nest helpfully.

We didn't stop laughing until Molly, concerned about the noise, stuck her head around the door.

'Everyfing all right, missus?' she asked.

For some reason, we found this hilarious too.

From that day forth, with Aphra's encouragement and guidance, I began to take my writing far more seriously, concentrating on subjects I felt confident about. I wrote short pieces, longer tracts and even some verses about everything from the state of the roads and, after three people in a week drowned, the way boats and other craft would collide and clog the Thames, making passage both a difficult and dangerous affair. I wrote trivial pieces about the stifling heat of the summer, examined the prognosticators' warnings about the months to come — I even wrote about the impact the Popish Plot was having on ordinary people, from shop-keepers to vendors, to those who, though not English, called London home. Because of irrational fears and suspicion, they were being hounded and abused. It was mainly the Dutch and French, but also Italians, Spanish and a Turkish family who lived near St Bridget's. Anyone with an accent or swarthy skin was considered fair game.

After multiple drafts, major and minor changes and rewrites, some of my work was even published — by Joanna Brome *and* Sir Roger. Aphra would deliver my pieces, refusing to divulge the writer. When my words did appear in print, it gave me such a thrill even if only a close few knew the real identity of the author.

Instead of signing *One of the Fair Sex* on all my work, I also chose to adopt the pseudonym women and those who feared repercussions for daring to have an opinion (after all, some authors' words had cost them their lives) oft deployed: *Anonymous*.

Aphra was so proud. When she'd read my work, offering sage advice and changes here and there, endorsing my ideas as well as critiquing them, encouraging me to hone and sharpen, argue more forcefully, find different words to describe my point, delete others, I'd shake my head in wonder. This was how I always imagined it would be — that I would find someone I could share thoughts with and who would listen, challenge me, and encourage my writing.

Believe in me.

It was a while before I understood Aphra was not only my teacher: she was everything I dreamed an older sister, mother or even father might be.

Would Papa have been gratified? Could he forgive me? I plagued myself with these useless questions — useless, because I already knew the answer: of course not. I was the weaker vessel daring to assert myself, stake a claim in men's domain. My tongue was unguarded, my voice raised. Papa would be horrified and ashamed and, if he hadn't already, he would have disowned me. Yet, there were nights I dreamed he folded me in his arms and whispered words of loving praise against my hair. Only, when I withdrew and examined his face, it wasn't Papa's I saw. It was another man, a stranger, whose features were shadowed, hidden, even if the love I felt pouring from him was not.

Daringly, on two occasions I did sign *One of the Fair Sex*. I wondered if his Majesty read my pieces and, if so, did he think of me, the bold creature who, once upon a time, caught the conscience of the King.

SCENE TEN

Say, from whence you owe this strange intelligence?

Macbeth, William Shakespeare

'There she is.' Solomon nudged Gabriel in the ribs.

Gabriel slowly unfurled from where he leaned against a disused barrel outside the Red Hart Inn. He watched as Prisca Smithton staggered out of the ale-house opposite, thwacking the hand of a man who lunged at her.

'Get orf, you poxy toad,' she slurred.

The man backed off, hands in the air.

She shook her fist before stumbling away.

'Is all in readiness?' asked Gabriel.

'It is,' said Solomon.

Over the last weeks, Solomon had not only kept an eye on Aphra, but managed to follow Prisca, learning her routine: where she went when she left the theatre, who she talked to, where she lived. Sometimes, she went straight to the two spies lurking by the riverside and spoke to them in feverish tones before slinking away. Each time they'd hand her coin and, twice, a meagre purse. After which she'd visit several businesses and, closer to where she lived, a maggot-ridden ordinary. Each call was punctuated by a trip to an ale-house.

While Gabriel knew the woman was making very real trouble for Tribulation, a part of him also felt sympathy. Responsible for an ailing widowed mother and a sister who'd lost her arm in an accident a few years earlier, Prisca was weighed down by what she perceived as unfair obligations. Instead of understanding such ill-fortune was no-one's fault, Prisca grew embittered — mostly towards her fellow humans. When life continued to pummel you, pushing you deep in muck no matter how hard you worked to try and crawl out, it was easy to blame others. To look to their successes, their smoother passages, as the reason yours miscarried. As if there was a finite amount of good fortune to be doled out and God, for His own reasons, had passed you by. As if by removing one obstacle, your painless path would be assured. In Prisca's mind, Tribulation was the obstacle, the reason her life was in such a sorry condition.

It didn't help that Prisca had never risen in her chosen profession either. He'd heard from the Bettertons, Elizabeth, Aphra too, that while the girl had a good voice and memory, and a pretty pair of calves for a skinny wench, it was her attitude preventing her being given better parts. If you constantly moaned, belittled others' efforts, found reasons why they didn't deserve their roles or disparaged their achievements, spread rumours (even those that were true), you damaged yourself far more than the intended target. People united in discord and resentment do not loyal allies make. Prisca's barbs didn't go unnoticed and not only by those they were aimed to strike.

Gabriel and Solomon followed Prisca, keeping their distance when, once again, she stopped to spend her clype-coin in an ale-house. If he was to mitigate the damage she'd already done, Gabriel had to stop her once and for all. While the information Prisca fed the men sent by Coventry had initially been inconsequential, she'd started inventing things that could cause great harm — to Tribulation and, potentially, his entire mission.

Falling in behind the men and women weaving in and out of the taverns and cook-shops, dodging barrows and carts, the odd hog or flapping chicken, Gabriel and Solomon, felt caps pulled low, wended their way to Fetter Lane, felt caps pulled low. The sky was darkening, and rain threatened. A flock of birds rose suddenly from a nearby church and flew in an arrow formation above, their warbling a chaunt that suited Gabriel's mood. Tired horses with knotted tails pulled drays towards Holborn, grubby-faced children slumbered atop flattened hay, while exhausted adults stared with glazed eyes as they trudged through milling traffic. Music issued from a tavern and two men tumbled out of another, tripping over a sack. Prisca narrowly avoided being struck by flailing fists and legs. She was luckier than one old man who, drubbed by a boot, toppled over. Gabriel and Solomon hurried forwards and scooped him up, depositing him on a log outside a house and then disappearing back into the crowd before the shaken gent could thank them.

They tailed Prisca to a narrow alley near Black Swan Inn. With a curt nod, they increased their pace and, before she sensed their presence, came up either side of her.

'Fancy meeting you here, Prisca,' said Gabriel smoothly.

She stopped in her tracks, hand flying to her heart. 'Why, if it ain't the great Jonathan Rickman hisself.' A calculated look transformed the fear into something else. Then, she saw Solomon.

'And who's this?' Her grin increased. 'Ain't this me lucky day?'

Gabriel took her arm and began to steer her into the lane. 'I was just thinking the same thing.'

'What —?' She tried to pull against him, but he was too strong. 'Whatcha doin? Where're yer takin' me?'

'I just want a chat, Prisca,' said Gabriel. 'Happens I know the owner of a cosy little establishment down here aways.'

'But if it's a chat you be wantin', there's a perfectly good ale-house just around the corner.' Prisca began to resist.

'Come now, Prisca. Surely, you're not frightened of an old friend? Not when you've been so keen to speak to strangers.'

'I don't know what you mean —' she began, eyes searching for an escape.

Solomon laughed.

'Oh, I think you do,' said Gabriel and, holding her steady, he rapped on a freshly painted door. A single light glowed through the thick glass of an adjacent window.

The door opened almost immediately and the smell of something heady and spicy wafted over them. A woman with beautifully coiffed hair coloured an unnatural shade of red, almond-shaped eyes a startling pale green, a large patch on her cheek and coffee-coloured skin, stared down at them. She flashed her teeth — the gold ones catching the light.

'Why, if it isn't my two favourite sea-dogs come for a visit. It's been a long time, Gabriel, Solomon.'

'Who you callin' Gabriel?' exclaimed Prisca.

The woman's eyes became slits. 'You know better than to bring your own entertainment, boys.' She flicked open a fan and began to wield it like a barber a razor, perilously close to Gabriel's neck. 'Some of us might take offence.' She pouted.

Gabriel dodged the fabric blade and deposited a kiss on her cheek before pushing his way in. 'No-one can compete with your charms, Cleo.'

Solomon did the same on the other cheek. 'No-one.'

'Oy,' snarled Prisca. 'I'm right here.'

They ignored her and shut the door. 'Anyhow,' said Gabriel, keeping a firm hold on a wriggling Prisca. 'Mrs Fallon is expecting us. We're to have the blue room.'

Cleo released a long sigh. 'All's prepared. Mrs Fallon will join you shortly.' She snapped the fan shut and, leading the way into a larger room, pointed towards a dimly lit corridor. 'Just don't disturb anyone. I imagine you want ale?' The men nodded. 'Supper too?'

'We won't be that long,' said Gabriel, and he gave Prisca a small push in the back. 'After you.' But Prisca was staring about the crowded room. There were plush chairs, small tables and velvet lounges scattered everywhere. Pastoral paintings were hung alongside those of naked goddesses enjoying the attentions of well-endowed satyrs and centaurs. Swathes of richly embroidered chintz and velvet draped the spaces between, all but hiding the soot-stained walls. Candles burned, the scent mingling with what the women had liberally sprinkled over themselves as well as smoke from pipes and the fire crackling in the huge hearth. In one corner a lone flautist exhaled plaintive notes. It was hot. Half-dressed women were splayed over chairs and reclined upon sofas, barely decent in sheer fabrics and bodices, breasts either pushed into impossible mounds or fully on display. There were a few men, sweating, drinking, puffing on pipes, their cravats undone, their breeches too, busy stroking or pawing flesh, while the women pretended to be enraptured, little moans and sighs of pleasure or giggles escaping.

'Next time the Duke's is in need of actresses, I know where to come,' said Prisca loudly. 'You lot'd give Mrs Barry a run for her money.'

Solomon dragged her away.

'Gabe,' said Cleo softly, before he could follow. She rested long fingers against his arm. 'We heard about Wait-Still … and the babe.' Her eyes filled with pity. 'May God watch over them.'

Gabriel could scarce bear it. 'Thanks,' he grunted and pulled away, aware of eyes other than Cleo's following. How many more times would he have to endure people's sympathy, let alone the memories it caused to rush like a current into his head, sweeping away his equilibrium.

Solomon cocked a questioning brow, ever vigilant.

Gabriel returned his silent query with a brusque nod. He was fine. He was; after all, as much as he might have once wished to, he couldn't change the past.

Three doors up the hallway was the Blue Room, so called because of the azure cover on the bed and the marine silk wrapped about the lanthorns. The walls glowed with ghostly light, making Prisca's skin look sickly and Solomon's positively scary. Monstrous shadows mottled the walls. The unmistakable fragrance of incense, juniper and even cardamom lingered, as did a slightly more pungent, salty smell that had a great deal to do with what happened within the space. With no window to release them, the odours sank into the mattress and covers, the fabric on the chairs, were inhaled by the paint. Above it all, hovering like avenging angels, was a thick pall of tobacco smoke.

'Sit,' said Gabriel to Prisca, indicating a chair and shutting the door. He was pleased to see paper, ink, sand and the quill he'd requested side by side on a small table.

Prisca clutched her bag to her chest. 'Not 'til you tell me why I'm here.' She looked pointedly at the bed. 'Clearly, it's not for *that*.' Her expression altered. 'Anyway, as I thought I made obvious, *you* wouldn't have to bring me here.'

Solomon rolled his eyes. Gabriel felt a wave of revulsion. If you didn't know what resided in Prisca's heart she could be mistaken for pretty.

Before he could respond, there was a knock on the door. A fresh-faced maid appeared with a jug and some tankards.

'My thanks,' said Gabriel, taking the tray and waiting while Solomon found coin. The girl didn't give Prisca a second glance. Mrs Fallon had her women well trained and, by the carriage of this wench, from a young age.

As if conjured by his thoughts, Lucinda Fallon, Madam of the Bower of Bliss, swooped into the room. Of medium height, with honey-coloured hair, clear grey-blue eyes and a complexion that belied her years, she offered her beringed hand to first Solomon, and then Gabriel. Both men bent over it reverently. When Gabriel straightened, he was delighted when Mrs Fallon bestowed a soft kiss on each cheek.

'You've been missed,' she said, her eyes scanning his face, her fingers holding his. 'Even if I understand why.' She tightened her hold momentarily. 'Nevertheless, I'd hoped to see you long before tonight. You don't need a reason to be welcome here, Gabriel. Wait-Still was like family and so are you.'

Gabriel led her to the chair opposite the one Prisca stood behind. 'I won't deny I've been tempted, Lucinda.' He gave a sad sort of smile. 'But work has contrived to keep me away.'

Mrs Fallon cocked her head. 'And much to my joy, it returns you to my doorstep.' She released his hand and then, with aplomb, rearranged her dress and sat with regal back and an imperial gaze. They were in her domain after all.

'Mrs Lucinda Fallon, may I introduce to you Mrs Prisca Smithton. The woman I told you about.'

Prisca watched the entire scene play out, standing, her lips twisted. Though she tried hard not to show she was afraid, Gabriel could see, from the way her eyes darted about the room, alighting briefly upon each of them, she was unnerved. 'What've you told the likes of *her* about me?' Prisca swayed slightly. He could almost admire her boldness. Almost. 'I don't want no bawd knowin' my business.'

'Rest assured,' drawled Mrs Fallon. 'This *bawd* is the poorer for being enlightened.'

Solomon swallowed a smile and perched on the end of the bed behind Mrs Fallon, resting an arm on the back of her chair.

'For God's sake, Prisca,' said Gabriel impatiently. 'Stop being difficult and damn well settle your arse.'

With no choice but to comply, Prisca gave a proud lift of her chin before sitting. While Solomon poured them each a drink, Gabriel dragged another chair over, placing it on Prisca's right. He reversed and straddled it. 'Now, let's have that chat, shall we?'

Prisca snorted. Mrs Fallon picked up her drink and looked from the men to Prisca and back. 'I don't have long. I'm expecting some important guests.'

'What am I doin' 'ere, hey?' asked Prisca. 'And why she's 'ere?' She jutted her chin towards Mrs Fallon.

Gabriel was hardly going to admit to Prisca that Mrs Fallon also worked for Sir Joseph Williamson. Among his most successful intelligencers, she and her carefully selected girls collected secrets and names as fast as they did devotees. Between eavesdropping at the theatre and by the river, and with the information the women at the Bower gathered, he and Solomon had been able to piece together exactly what Prisca had been up to.

'Because, hellion, these delightful men invited me.' Mrs Fallon raised her glass and drank heartily. Lucinda was a canny one, tough as a cobbler's last. Very little ruffled her feathers.

Nevertheless, Gabriel's patience was wearing thin. 'She's here to offer you a future.'

'I don't want no future this whore could offer,' blustered Prisca.

'Is that so?' said Mrs Fallon, unperturbed. 'And you haven't even heard what it is this whore offers yet.' She gave a polite laugh. 'But if you'd rather continue to take the pennies you earn on your knees in those back alleys and snickets, I'll waste no more of your time.' Mrs Fallon went to rise.

'Why you —' began Prisca, also standing.

'Lucinda,' Gabriel beseeched. 'Please.'

Mrs Fallon made a show of hesitating then sat back down with a mighty huff, but not before she shot him a wicked grin.

Gabriel rubbed his forehead wearily. 'You too, Prisca.' He waited for her to resume her seat. 'Believe it or not, we've not brought you here to frighten or hurt you, but help. *All* of us.' His arm encompassed everyone.

Prisca eyed them warily. 'How?'

'First, you need to answer a few questions.'

'Do I now?' Prisca seemed to wrestle with an idea, before abandoning it. 'Come on then, I haven't got all night. I've important guests.' Her imitation of Mrs Fallon was almost perfect.

Gabriel glanced first at Solomon, then at Mrs Fallon. 'Very well,' he began. 'We know you've been feeding certain information to men who lurk by the river. Men who, of late, have paid you for what you tell them.'

If Prisca's face hadn't already taken on the ghoulish hue of the room, he would have sworn it paled. She balanced her bag on her lap and reached for her ale. 'What if I have?'

She was going to brazen it out.

'We also happen to know you've furnished these men with complete falsehoods. What we want to know, is why?'

Prisca took her time draining her drink, putting down the tankard and swiping the back of her mouth. 'What's it to you?' She swung around to Solomon. 'Or you for that matter? Or you?' she spat at Mrs Fallon. 'What do you care?' She faced Gabriel again, then began to laugh. 'You've taken a fancy to Tribulation Johnson, haven't you?' She shook her finger at him, as if he was a lad she was scolding. 'I told John Crosby you was keen on her. Aphra's bloody cousin who can't fart without someone else taking the blame. The golden girl of Dorset Garden. Can't put a fuckin' foot wrong, can she? Nor nothin' else it seems.' She grabbed the jug and without asking refilled her vessel. 'Should have known she'd turn you.'

'Only, she didn't, did she?' She set the jug down with a thump. 'You're no more a boy-buggerer, a Molly Man, than I'm fuckin' Queen of the Ottomans.'

'Gabriel a sodomite?' Mrs Fallon's scorn was thick. 'I thought you said this one was clever?'

Gabriel remained silent. Inside, he could feel the familiar storm brewing. Flashes of anger punctuating the reserve of calm he worked so hard to maintain. He tried to staunch them. This woman had no idea who she was dealing with, the desperation of those men to whom she told dangerous lies, whose coin she greedily took. She didn't comprehend the havoc her words could wreak. Or maybe she did and that's why he was so furious. Still, losing his temper wouldn't accomplish anything.

Except making him feel better …

'Prisca,' he said, using his voice the way he did upon the stage, to silence the audience. 'We know what you've told these men, what you've accused Tribulation Johnson of being involved in. And, by association, those closest to her as well.'

'Do you?' She regarded him slyly. 'Well, watcha need me for, then? Why d'ya bring me 'ere? I've a reputation to protect, ya know.' She gave a dry laugh which became a cough. She took in the serious faces. 'Then, you'd also know I never said nothin' 'bout Aphra or the rest of the Company. That'd make me a fool, wouldn't it? I know which side me bread's buttered on.'

'I've no doubt you do,' said Gabriel. 'And while I don't think you're entirely stupid, drawing the attention of the authorities to just one of the Duke's Company implicates all, or have you so readily forgotten Matthew Medbourne?'

'How could I?' Her cockiness was beginning to desert her.

'If you remember what happened to Mr Medbourne and why, yet still level dangerous accusations, false inferences, at a colleague, then it makes you something much worse than the mere troublemaker I believed you to be.' Gabriel paused and took a breath. 'You've put good folk in grave danger. People are being put to death for far less than what you've accused Mrs Johnson of saying, of doing. So, I ask again,' said Gabriel steadily, 'why'd you do it?'

Prisca gave a careless shrug.

'Did someone put you up to it?' asked Solomon.

Prisca looked from Gabriel to Solomon and Mrs Fallon and back again, her eyes narrowing. 'Who the fuck are you lot? That tart back there called you Gabriel. Said you were a sailor.'

Gabriel rose, distracting Prisca momentarily. As he did, he signalled Mrs Fallon, who, swift as a fox, wrested her bag from her.

'Oy, bitch. Give that back.' Prisca tugged and pulled and appeared to consider crying out for help. When she understood resisting did her no good, she let go and fell back in her seat.

Mrs Fallon opened the flap and searched the contents. Within seconds, she withdrew a crumpled piece of paper and passed it to Gabriel, who did what he could to straighten the page. It had been carelessly ripped from a book and, if he wasn't mistaken, the book in question belonged to Tribulation. The journal she'd taken to writing in of late.

He scanned what was written and frowned. Then he laid it on the table before pinning it beneath a long finger. Mrs Fallon and Solomon leaned over to examine it.

'*You've* written this,' he said to Prisca in a quiet, deadly voice.

'Not me,' said Prisca. '*Her*.'

Mrs Fallon tsked in disgust. Solomon's eyes narrowed.

'This isn't Mrs Johnson's hand,' said Gabriel. 'I'm familiar with it from the prompter's book. Nor are these her words. A letter to —' he glanced at the page '— Brother Simon? A Jesuit. Asking permission to join a conventicle?' He gave Prisca an incredulous look. 'I doubt Tribulation knows a single Catholic, let alone a Jesuit.' He inhaled, counting in his head. 'And here I was thinking the worst you'd done was suggest she was a Papist sympathiser.'

'She is! That's no lie.'

'She's not alone in believing Catholics are being unfairly treated. That makes a person *sympathetic*, not a sympathiser. But this —' He slapped the page with the back of his hand. It fluttered above the table like an injured bird before coming to rest. 'This is entirely different. This would get her arrested, tried — if she's fortunate — and most certainly condemned.' He regarded her. 'Why, Prisca? Has someone ordered you to do this?'

Faint noises from the room next door penetrated the walls. A giggle, a groan, the sound of a bed creaking.

Prisca began to gnaw her lip. She looked from one man to the other. Her eyes lingered on Mrs Fallon, but she saw no support there. The last of her bravado evaporated. Finally, she spoke.

'No-one ordered me except meself.' She let out a long sigh. 'I never meant no real harm.' She plucked at her skirt then shrugged. 'I'm sick of the likes of her coming in and lording it over the rest of us. You understand, surely?' she pleaded with Mrs Fallon. 'Must happen to you all the time.'

Mrs Fallon regarded her with such pity, Prisca was forced to look away.

'I never meant to hurt her.' Her voice began to quiver and her eyes glistened.

Gabriel hardened his heart. The tears weren't for Tribulation, but herself.

'Well, not much,' admitted Prisca. 'I just wanted her brought down a peg or two. Better still, gone.' She sighed. 'It didn't matter what I told them coves by the river, they wanted proof.'

'And when you couldn't find any, you devised some.'

She shrugged again. 'Didn't have a choice, not if I wanted what they promised.'

'Which was?'

'Enough coin to get decent medick for ma. She's poorly and nothing I've tried has helped. Her cough grows worse each day, she bloodies the kerchief all the time. Then there's me sister …'

'And yet you spend this coin you claim your mother needs, that your sister could use, in taverns,' said Solomon dryly.

She whipped around, scowling. 'I'm entitled to a bit of fun, ain't I? Try workin' all day and then going home to sickness, misery and pain night after bloody night. Used to be the theatre let me forget a while; not when we were shut down and made to clean like drudges. Not when someone named Tribulation Johnson fuckin' well sucks the joy out of it.'

'You think removing Mrs Johnson will improve your life?' asked Mrs Fallon.

'Can't make it worse.'

Gabriel shook his head. Solomon exhaled. 'There's no accounting for some.'

Prisca made a disparaging noise. 'Whatcha going to do? S'pose you want me to fess up to Lady Mary? Tell Mrs Behn?'

'No,' said Gabriel.

'Well, that's a bloody relief.' She half-laughed.

'You're going to confess to my master.'

Prisca sat up, eyes widening. 'Your *master*? I knew it. I knew you weren't really one of us, *Gabriel*.' Her eyes became slits. 'Who's your master then? Or is it mistress? Is it her?' She pointed at Mrs Fallon.

Gabriel made the slightest inclination of his head. On cue, Mrs Fallon stood. 'Enough.' Her voice was steel. She rapped her rings hard against the table, making Prisca and Solomon jump. She leaned over Prisca, a menace of silk, satin, a king's ransom of jewels and a boudoir of perfume. 'Listen to me carefully, Prisca Smithton,' she drawled, placing one elegant finger beneath the woman's chin and tilting it towards her. 'I'm nobody's mistress but my own. His master —' she indicated Gabriel '— is another story. He's someone you want to pray with all your shrivelled heart and withered soul you never meet. For if you do, I swear on the hooves of Mephistopheles he'll be the last person you ever lay eyes upon.'

Gabriel's brows shot up and he turned a guffaw into a clearing of his throat. It had been a while since he'd seen Mrs Fallon in action. Prisca was right. She'd give Mrs Barry a run for her money.

Solomon stared at their old friend in round-eyed admiration.

Mrs Fallon slowly withdrew to her chair.

Prisca's mouth opened then shut. Dread entered her eyes and the last bit of blowsiness evaporated. She stared at Mrs Fallon, Gabriel then Solomon. 'Those coves down by the river,' began Prisca, her voice hoarse. 'They're nothin' but a pair of fools, I see that now. Put there like bait to lure small fish while you lot —' She raised a shaking finger. 'You work in the shadows until the real prey emerges: watch and listen and then strike.' She snatched at the air. 'We thought the authorities were watching the theatre, but they've been cleverer than that, haven't they? They put you, Gabriel, *in* it. Who you after then, eh? Who's the big fish? You after them Papists what's Mr Oates says is going to kill the King? Who is it? Who you watchin'?'

Time to put an end to this once and for all.

Gabriel extracted a piece of paper from the sheets on the table and pushed the inkhorn and quill towards her. 'Let's just say I'm watching everyone to ensure a grave injustice doesn't occur. Which means, Prisca Smithton, you're going to confess you not only embellished what you told "them coves" from the river but also told outright falsehoods in order to implicate Tribulation Johnson and besmirch the name of the Duke's Company for no other purpose than your own selfish ends.'

'What? I'll do no such thing,' said Prisca, wrapping her arms around her middle.

'Not even for silver?' asked Mrs Fallon, producing a heavy black purse from within the folds of her gown and dangling it before her.

Prisca eyed the purse, then Mrs Fallon. Her mouth moved; her eyes roved the room as she wrestled with her conscience. It was a one-sided match. 'S'pose I agree. What will happen?'

'What will happen,' began Gabriel affably, 'is you'll take the money and not only quit our sight, but the city. Along with your mother and sister, you'll go and never return.'

'Leave the city? But that means the theatre. I … I can't! I won't. You can't make me.'

'No, but I can,' said Mrs Fallon. 'As you've already gleaned, we're not what or who we seem. Believe me when I say I can make you do many things and none of them to your liking.'

Gabriel took the purse from Mrs Fallon and placed it in Prisca's shaking hand.

'Take it, Prisca. Cease your petty arguments, your defiance, and concede defeat while you can. You'll not get a better offer.'

'Nor will you get a second chance,' added Mrs Fallon.

'There's more than enough in there to start a new life far from the city, far from the grievous temptations it offers,' said Solomon helpfully.

'But …' Prisca's voice broke. 'What if I refuse?'

Mrs Fallon casually reached for her glass. 'Then, as I warned, you'll meet his master.'

Three pairs of eyes rested upon Prisca.

A few minutes later, a confession was written, signed and sealed. Moments after that, a silent Prisca, replete with purse and bag, firmly escorted by Mrs Fallon, was gone.

The men waited until the footsteps faded and Mrs Fallon's voice grew dim, then exchanged wry grins.

'Well, hopefully that's the last we see of Mrs Smithton,' said Gabriel, sinking onto the chair she'd just vacated, pushing a blank page around with his finger. 'I loathe this kind of thing, Solomon. Leaves a bad taste, strong-arming women like that — even poisonous ones.'

'It had to be done, my friend.'

'Did it?' His shoulders slumped. 'I suppose it did. Thank God for Lucinda. What a performance.'

'I almost gave her a standing ovation.' Solomon chuckled.

'Me too,' admitted Gabriel. He glanced at the door. 'Williamson has a strong ally there.'

'So do we,' said Solomon.

'We do indeed.' Gabriel released an enormous sigh and ran his fingers through his hair. 'After that, the last thing I feel like is attending this soiree at Rochester's house tonight.'

Solomon slapped his thighs and stood. 'But you will. Shaftesbury and his allies will be there. Duty calls.'

'When does it not, of late?' asked Gabriel, before taking Solomon's offered hand and being hauled out of the chair.

As they did a last check of the room, Solomon paused. Faint laughter followed by a squeal reached them. 'Hope you're right about Prisca Smithton, Gabe.'

'What do you mean?' asked Gabriel, opening the door and nodding at a gentleman staggering down the hall, an older plump woman trying, and mostly succeeding, in propping him up.

Standing aside so they could pass, Solomon didn't reply until they were out of earshot. 'In my experience, those types of people are like chipped coins, they pop up again and again and ruin good deals.'

SCENE ELEVEN

Love, like reputation, once fled, never returns more.

A Voyage to the Isle of Love, Aphra Behn

Before we'd even arrived at John Wilmot, the Earl of Rochester's house, I was regretting accepting the invitation. Resplendent in a costume Lady Mary permitted me to borrow, an emerald ensemble with tiny goldfinches and curlicues embroidered around the neckline and hem, I'd drawn eyes the way day-old oysters do hungry bumpkins. The bodice was a tight-fitting masterpiece of velvet. Paste jewels in a matching hue hung from my neck and ears. Nest had dressed my hair. I looked quite the lady — or whore, as a drunken sot roaming outside the house shouted when I alighted from the hackney carriage. Such a fine line between the two, it seemed.

It was my first invitation to a nobleman's house. Actually, it was my first invitation anywhere except Lady Mary's rooms, the Bettertons' apartments, the Bishop's Whelp and a couple of taverns in Bridewell and Fleet Street. Not that I ever felt the need to be social. Aphra, Nest, my writing and work with the Company were more than enough, especially now we'd reopened.

Nervous, having some idea of what to expect from Aphra, as well as the behaviour of the gentry who frequented the theatre, I prepared to stave off unwanted attention and reserve my blushes and disdain for all the vulgarities I'd no doubt hear and witness. Nevertheless, it would be a new experience and a part of me relished that.

Aphra was in a strange mood, quiet the entire ride, plucking at her gown — a lovely bronze dress that shimmered where the light struck and made her hair look lustrous. The moment we entered the already crowded salon and she accepted a glass of wine from a servant, downing it in one gulp and demanding another, I could tell she also rued coming. Part of the reason was because our host was quitting London awhile for his country house at Woodstock. It reminded her how much she would miss him. The other part was the presence of the Earl of Shaftesbury.

Those surrounding him parted as he raised his glass in our direction, a peculiar, knowing grin twisting his mouth. I repressed a shudder and promised myself I'd do all in my power to avoid him.

We were separated almost immediately, Aphra being led away by George Villiers, the Duke of Buckingham, leaving me with an actor from Drury Lane whose name I didn't catch. The Duke, a cousin of Barbara Castlemaine, his Majesty's longest-serving mistress, was a man with influence. Corpulent, with a broad face and double chin, he filled the space. His eyes, which latched onto to all the women in the room, were watery and round, and he gave off an air of innocence which was quickly dispelled the moment he opened his mouth. He always made me feel … counterfeit.

In many ways, that's exactly what I was — a fake. I didn't belong here.

Despite Aphra's assurances, I oft felt I didn't belong anywhere at all.

Melancholy, thy name is Tribulation.

Across the room, Charlotte caught my eye and waved. She'd borrowed a costume as well and looked lovely in sapphire and silver. The Bettertons were present, as were Mary Lee and Elizabeth Currer. As expected, Elizabeth Barry wasn't. She swore she'd never forgive Rochester for removing their daughter from her care over a year ago — a daughter he then left with a nursemaid and his wife at his country seat.

I smiled and nodded to those I knew, and though Charlotte attempted to join me, she was prevented by a rather well-dressed gentleman. She winked over his shoulder. Spared the philandering of Mr Pepys who, though no longer languishing in the Tower, was still under suspicion and declining invitations, she was free from monopoly and able to enjoy (if that was the right word) other men's attentions. Or not. Strangely, she felt enough pity for Mr Pepys to visit him where he had removed from his old residence at Derby House to the lodgings of his former servant, Will Hewer, in Cheapside. Desperate to fight new accusations (of selling maps to the French as well as popery and treachery) levelled at him by yet another disreputable character, Pepys had been grateful to see Charlotte.

'He has supporters,' she said when I asked why she was going to see a man she felt such ambivalence towards. 'But also detractors. What he needs is friends, Trib.' Charlotte had a kind heart. Some might say a soft one.

'Including you?'

Charlotte had given a sad laugh and shrug. 'I suppose I am.'

Invited to sit, I found myself next to the Earl of Arran. He was discoursing on the lands he'd recently acquired in Kent. At least I knew something of sheep and grass, coming as I did from that county. Not that anyone was really listening. They were too busy flirting with the other women present — wives, mistresses, actresses. There were a few from Drury Lane. I recognised Margaret Rutter, a comedian, Mary Corbett, by whom two wealthy gentlemen appeared to be enraptured, and the famous Mrs Elizabeth Boutel: according to some the first woman to grace the English stage. Quite wizened and heavily patched, she was enjoying an inordinate amount of attention, in no small part due to her habit of leaning forwards to display generous bosoms and touch whoever was conversing with her in an intimate fashion. Charlotte caught my eye, and when I made a 'cup runneth over' gesture against my own modest décolletage, she grinned.

For all Aphra tried to limit my exposure to what Papa would have called 'corrupting influences', it was a lost cause. Surely one chose whether to allow rogues of all ilk any sway. I liked to think I tolerated rather than was led by them.

The Earl of Arran was looking at me as if expecting an answer. What was the question? He put a hand on my knee, squeezing it. I jumped and would have moved but a burst of laughter drew all eyes and he withdrew his hand. It was the effervescent Rochester. Even before we arrived, he was cupshotten. Loud, lurching side to side and using his arms like windmills to make a point, he was clearly under the influence of wine and more. He was celebrated for claiming he could outswill Bacchus, and it was evident this wasn't a casual assertion. Not that it appeared to affect his ability to relate amusing anecdotes or proffer insults. He was unable to bear others receiving attention rightfully his and made certain it returned to where it belonged. He was the blazing star of this production, and no-one was allowed to upstage him.

God in Heaven, he looked ill. I caught Aphra watching him, eyes narrowed, her lips downturned in concern. The colour of his skin beneath the too-flushed cheeks, the poor application of patches to hide the festering sores upon his face: this was a sick man. The yellow eyes made him appear like a fox or owl. He was sweating a great deal, though in truth it was a warm night. Too many bodies even in this large space.

Distracted by a woman with a towering headpiece, the Earl of Arran twisted to address her. Ignored, I admired the intricate tapestries, the gilt-framed portraits staring down from the walls. If these ancestors were anything like Rochester, they'd be wishing they could peel themselves away and join us.

Two long tables dominated the room, laden with half-eaten platters swimming in grease, aspic and assorted sauces. Candelabras burned brightly, the wax melting down the sides of the silver holders to pool across the cloths. Some poor creature had to clean those. Chandeliers above shone. In the pockets of darkness nearest Aphra, some lord or other was pissing. I did a double take and screwed up my nose. Why couldn't the man go and use the hearth or, for God's sake, the corridor like the others? Even the garden was closer; one had only to go through the great doors at the other end. I tried to see who it was.

William Chiffinch, the King's procurer, and a law unto himself. I'd had an unfortunate encounter with him backstage on one occasion before the theatre closed. From what I'd heard, he wasn't likely to miss an opportunity to drink and dine. Maybe he was vetting women for the royal bed.

Listen to me, having internal conversations about those present as if I was accustomed to mixing with such people, attending fancy dinners, nattering with aristocracy. In a way, I suppose I was. The theatre had prepared me — not just the folk I met in the Tiring Rooms or auditorium and whose exploits I witnessed, but the plays themselves. Were they not studies in human nature? In the gentry, the wealthy and their foibles? Their contradictory morality? Dorset Garden was a prologue for life. Or was it the other way around? Or was it a mirror? It would have to be a crazed one. I began to muse which was which.

'Enjoying yourself?' A hand fell on my shoulder. It was Aphra. The Earl excused himself and gave her his seat. I tried not to show relief. She sat heavily, listing slightly in the chair. The darkness that affected her earlier had been lightened by wine. 'What think you of the company? Rochester's abode?' She swept her glass in a wide circle, ruby liquid washing over the rim.

A few whispered, their eyes lingering upon us. ''Tis most grand. The people are … interesting.'

Aphra gave a snort of laughter. 'That's one way to describe them, I s'pose.'

'Do you enjoy yourself?'

Aphra considered my question very seriously. About us, chatter rose and fell. Someone brought out a deck of cards and, commandeering a table near a window, beckoned men to join him. They fought over seats, laughing uproariously when a pot-bellied gentleman fell on his arse.

'There was a time,' she said, 'I would have been dazzled and worked hard to ensure I didn't show it. Now …' She paused. 'Now, I wonder what on earth I found so alluring.' She made a vague gesture. 'These men, the women, their conversations — though that's too generous a word. They don't converse. They draw verbal swords and joust, each parrying the other with phrases and witty one-liners, seeking to arouse the greatest laugh or offence. Preferably the latter. The larger the wound they inflict, the better. For they seek to vanquish their foes and claim the prize.'

'What's that?' I asked, relieved she too found it all a bit tedious and … what was the word? Staged.

'Isn't it obvious?' She thrust her glass in my direction. 'A woman.' She indicated those dotted about the room. Each one had a male or two attached. We were the only exceptions. Perhaps they were afeared they'd get skewered by Aphra's tongue. She shifted so her lips were close to my ear. 'They're all talking about who wrote the persuasive words that changed the King's mind.'

My eyes widened. 'Still?'

'It was quite the accomplishment.'

I tried not to preen. 'I guess they're surprised it's a woman?'

Aphra guffawed. 'They don't believe *that* for a moment. How could a mere female have the daring let alone the wit to challenge Charles Rex?' She drank. 'They credit a man with your words, kitten, but fear not. Even while they argue about which *man* wrote the piece, they still talk about the *Fair Sex*. Whether they know it or not, it's women they promote.' She fell silent a while. 'That used to be me. The one whose company was sought, whose laughter men fought to hear, whose attention they'd do anything to attract. No more.' She hiccoughed. 'Now, I'm just a used hag.' Her eyelids grew heavy. 'In their minds,' she gestured to the men, 'I'm as good as a whore and have been for a long time. Becoming a writer, sacrificing my reputation by writing bawdy material, being public and unashamed about it, *persisting*, just confirms it.' She clinked her glass against mine. 'But when men do the exact same thing, their reputations are made and even reinforced.' She shook her head. 'Be careful, my dear, lest what's happened to me happens to you. Writing, renown, comes at a great cost … for us women.'

She rose a little unsteadily, deposited a wet kiss on my cheek, and returned to Rochester's side, laughing uproariously at something he said. I watched, bemused. For all Aphra railed at the way men perceived and treated her, treated females, she also played the part they created for us very well. Same with the others — Charlotte, Mrs Betterton, Elizabeth Boutel. I thought of Bethan; she too was playing a part — dutiful daughter, in order to become an obliging wife. Was I any different? I said and did one thing, then thought another. I suppose we all performed for men in a way. For each other too.

Bells chimed, clocks ticked and course after course of rich food continued to appear. Haunches were pulled apart with greasy fingers; slices of venison were rolled and posted into slippery mouths. Banter rose and fell, uncaring showers of meat, vegetables and wine sprayed neighbours and table linen liberally. City folk were always held up by Papa as being the epitome of good manners and grace. If he could only see Rochester's guests, he might be forced to reconsider.

I sat quietly, sometimes trying to catch Aphra's eye. Restless, she moved up and down the table, finding others to talk with (especially since, as usual, Mr Hoyle, who arrived after we did, was all but ignoring her). Charles Sedley manifested before me, chatting as if we were longstanding friends. My heart sank. While I appreciated the man's verses, his reputation as a complete rake far outweighed any pretty prose. I was forced to continually step back, watch where he placed his hands, removing them from my waist, my hip and even my buttocks, all while smiling; to object was beyond consideration. What I wanted to do was stamp on his toes or kick him in the cullions. Known for washing his prick in wine and then downing the liquid, as well as a propensity to gad about the streets naked, Sir Charles was lauded and his company sought — but not by me. I prayed, as he breathed all over me, he wasn't about to disrobe. Fortunately, though his hands roved and his eyes too, he was mainly interested in quizzing me about whether Aphra was the author of the tract. After a time, he grew bored with my ignorance. When it also turned out I knew none of his neighbours in Kent, he exclaimed loudly, 'But these are important people!'

'Not so important I know them, sir,' I replied.

He blinked, then, with a malodorous huff, left. I tried not to pretend I hadn't just offended one of the King's inner circle. I looked around to see if Aphra had noticed. Across from where she stood was the Earl of

Shaftesbury. Beside him were Lords Grey and Sidney. Nearby was Mr Ferguson. They were conversing and nodding in my direction.

Unable to endure their scrutiny, tired of the gossip and susurrations, I went to the windows and turned to view the room. From this perspective, the scene was like an etching from Dante's or Ovid's poems about hedonistic gods or Hell. Men and women tossing back drink, shoving handfuls of food into their mouths, trying to outdo each other with a droll line, sarcastic remark, a disparaging observation, the promise of *amore*. Aphra was right. This was like a joust but with no rules. I briefly caught Charlotte's eye. The well-dressed gent had moved his chair so close he was practically atop her. His periwig had slipped, and his cheeks were so plump and red it looked like he'd swallowed a pair of apples.

Still, she beamed and nodded, all while her body twisted and turned like a contortionist in silent objection. I made my way over. 'Charlotte,' I said, touching her gently as if we hadn't already wordlessly communicated from across the room. 'I was wondering if I might request your help.'

'Ha, if it isn't the woman book-holder.' The man, who could barely focus, attempted to appraise me. His eyes were riven with veins and his mouth was stained. 'You can hold my books any day.' He chuckled, cupping his crotch.

'And with scarce one hand, sir.' I smiled sweetly.

He frowned. 'What's your name again?'

'Tribulation,' answered another. It was the Earl of Shaftesbury. 'Causing you some, is she Armstrong?'

I turned to Charlotte, desperation writ on my face.

She removed Mr Armstrong's hand from where it now slid along her thigh and stood. 'My friend here was just saying she feels ill. Actually, Tribulation, you look terrible. Are you going to purge again?'

I covered my mouth and made my cheeks bulge.

'Purge?' squeaked Mr Armstrong, trying to scramble out of the way. The Earl of Shaftesbury stepped back, using his cane to force a servant aside.

'She's cursed with a weak constitution, my lord,' said Charlotte, one arm flung over my shoulders. 'I'm sure you've heard the tale of her arrival in London? How she cast the contents of her stomach all over Dorset Street?'

'Oh, thank you,' she added once we'd escaped into the hallway. She pulled me out of earshot of the weary servants. 'I thought I'd never get away from that man. Honestly, he was pawing me like a puppy its master.' She shuddered.

'It's me owes you,' I said. 'I couldn't bear another conversation with the Earl of Shaftesbury. Studies me like I'm some experiment the Royal Society have unearthed.'

'I've noticed,' said Charlotte, rolling her shoulders and rotating her neck. 'Well. What do we do now?'

Servants moved to and fro, carrying everything from slimy half-finished platters to laden ones steaming with meat or drowning in sauces. They trudged up and down stairs to the kitchen. Heat and voices rose from below — as if Hades was located beneath this very floor. I glanced towards the dining room. Or upon it.

The hall was wainscoted with burnished wood and decorated with a variety of portraits, coats of arms and, unusually, a faded velvet cloak.

A doorman waited patiently to admit any newcomers, glancing over towards us to see if we required him. A burst of shrill laughter followed by the sound of breaking glass carried. I couldn't bear the thought of returning to the party.

'I'm leaving,' I said suddenly.

'What about Aphra?' asked Charlotte.

I glanced towards the dining room. 'I'll ask the doorman to inform her. I just can't —'

'Me neither,' sighed Charlotte, suddenly looking very young and vulnerable. 'Do you know, I actually missed Mr Pepys?' She sighed again. 'Shall we share a hackney? I don't live far from you.'

I looped my arm through hers. 'That would be excellent.'

The doorman summoned a boy who retrieved our cloaks. We waited inside while he sent the same boy to find us a vehicle.

When one pulled up outside, an avalanche of scat followed. The driver moved forwards a few paces before alighting and opening the door. The air was ripe as I turned to help Charlotte up the step.

'Oh, Lord,' she said, and dropped back to the road. 'My purse. I left it on the chair next to Mr bloody Armstrong. Sorry, Trib. Won't be a moment.'

She quickly explained what she was doing to the driver. With a shrug, the young boy who'd hailed the coach followed her back inside.

I rested my head against the back of the seat, trying not to inhale the musty smell. Jesus, someone must have carried sheep in here. Sheep with shit dangling off their fleeces. Maybe reposing wasn't such a good idea after all. I began to imagine lice crawling and started scratching. I was just thinking of unpinning my headpiece when I heard voices. There was the jangle of harness. The door opened. I was about to warn Charlotte not to recline when I stared in disbelief.

It wasn't Charlotte climbing in the carriage.

It was damn Prisca Smithton.

SCENE TWELVE

For thou hast made a very fiend of me, and I have hell within.

Love-Letters Between a Nobleman and His Sister, Aphra Behn

'Stop the coach —' I began.

Prisca lunged, clamping a hand over my mouth. 'Shut up,' she hissed, pushing me back into the seat. I wasn't frightened so much as angry. I couldn't see her face, just the glint in her eyes — eyes that regarded me with pure venom. I ripped her hand away, quickly looking to see if she carried a weapon. She reeked of ale, wine, and something far less palatable.

'What are you doing here? Don't —' I said, as she went to cover my mouth again. I could still feel the greasy imprint of her palm against my lips. The carriage rolled and we were flung closer. 'Don't you dare touch me.'

She lowered her hand; her breathing was rapid, shallow in the gloom. She was a shade come to life. Every instinct shouted 'get away'. Curse my curiosity, I had to know why she was here, what she wanted. But I also had to make sure she didn't injure me or herself.

I remembered the time Farmer Whittle was breaking in a new horse ill-treated by its previous owner. He'd spoken to it in a quiet, even voice that also exuded authority. Slowly, the horse ceased to buck and prance. Its ears, initially flat upon its skull, rose so it could hear what was being said, the reassurances, the firmness.

'We have to go back,' I said, trying to sound like Farmer Whittle. 'Charlotte is waiting; she'll be worried. Allow me to fetch her and then you can speak to both of us.'

'What I have to say is for your ears alone.' Prisca slid away from me. 'Anyhow, I paid the driver to travel a few streets then return.'

I took a quiet breath. 'Out with it, then.'

A link boy ran past and through the window the light struck her face. Dirt streaked her cheeks and her eyes were swollen. Blood dotted her mouth. At first, I thought she'd been struck, but from the way her teeth sank into her lower lip, it was evident she'd been gnawing it. She'd also been crying. Nay, sobbing. My heart, which was beating like a soldier's drum, swelled. I mightn't like the girl, I might loathe the way she'd turned many against me, but something terrible must have happened to upset her so, make her seek me out in such a fashion.

'What's so important,' I said softly when she still didn't speak, 'it couldn't wait until the morrow?'

'Morrow?'

'At the theatre.'

She gave a strangled laugh, then buried her face in her hands.

I wasn't sure what to do. Part of me wanted to offer comfort, the other to push her out the door.

The clop of the horse's hooves on the dirt was percussive, comforting, like a clock ticking. We passed by other coaches and chairs, the voices of their passengers carrying. Groups of men clustered outside ale-houses and some apprentices strode along the road hailing others, including a pair of constables. At least if I called for help, it would be close.

'Listen,' she said, finally, wiping away tears with the heels of her hands. 'I've something to tell you. You may not believe me, but God's oath, I swear on my mother's soul, it's true.'

There was a beat.

'Jonathan Rickman is not who you think he is.'

Of all the things I expected to hear, this was not it.

'Mr Rickman ...?' I blinked. 'What's he got to do with anything?'

She began to laugh. 'Oh, everything, Trust me.' Her laugh ceased as quickly as it began. 'For a start, his name's not Jonathan Rickman. It's Gabriel. I don't know his last name. Maybe it's Rickman. Point is, he's not an actor. Oh, he can act, only a fool would deny that, but that's not why he's at Dorset Garden. He's been put there to watch us. Watch you, Tribulation Johnson.'

'What nonsense is this?' I couldn't believe what I was hearing. I knew she was jealous of me. Seems she was jealous of Mr Rickman as well. Clearly, the woman was in her cups. 'I think you should get out. Driver!'

'Wait! You need to hear me out. Please.'

It was the please gave me pause. Prisca never said that.

Then, before I could utter another word, a story poured out of her. She told me what Jonathan ... *Gabriel* ... and a man named Solomon and a bawd named Mrs Fallon did: the bargain they struck with her. To prove it, she produced a generous purse.

Pole-axed by what she revealed, and not just about Mr Rickman and his strange associates, but about the terrible lies she'd told, what she sought to attribute to me, the lengths she went to, I was speechless. How could someone I barely knew hate me so much? Despise me for things beyond my control? I could barely give it credence. I couldn't stop staring at the nemesis I never knew I had — the enemy not at the gate, but within.

Even tonight, I'd heard Rochester lament how bad things were in London, that Titus Oates had made it a man might not turn his back for fear of being hanged.

Nor, it seemed, a woman.

As for Mr Rickman ... I couldn't bear to think about it. What it all meant. If she was right, and he was a spy, why was he interested in me? If he was an intelligencer seeking information, what could I possibly know? And what was he doing with a tattooed blackamoor and a bawd?

Then, it occurred to me. All the questions he'd asked about Aphra — and not only of me. The fascination with her writing, her opinions, who hired her services. How intently he listened whenever she spoke in the Tiring Rooms; how he noted who was with her in the audience. I burned with confusion. Why, I'd kissed the man. I pushed memories of that aside, rudely. My thoughts flitted and buzzed.

From the growing noise outside, we were approaching Rochester's house once more.

Prisca wrung her hands. 'I'm sorry I lied, that I told those men you were a secret Catholic. I never thought it would cause real harm.'

'*Real* harm? What other kind is there?' I said bitterly. 'How could you, knowing what Oates has done? After what happened to Matthew Medbourne? To Mr Pepys? Suggesting someone is sympathetic to Papists or worse all but spells their doom. You. Know. This.'

She lowered her face.

I made a scoffing noise. 'I can't forgive you. I don't even know what it is you're telling me, if it's even true. What I do know is the man you're maligning has done nothing to harm me. Nor has this Solomon or Mrs Fallon. Or, from what I can tell, anyone else. Unlike *you*.' I let that find its mark. 'If Mr Rickman is using an alias, if he's at the theatre to uncover a plot or traitors, then it's with good cause. He's working to protect his Majesty. From what you've said, he knows I'm no traitor and did whatever was in his power to save me. So did his accomplices. Save me from *you*. He's not my enemy. They're most certainly not. *You* are.'

Prisca's shoulders were shaking. At first, I thought she was crying then I realised she was laughing. 'You don't get it, do you? He doesn't give a damn about *you* or anyone else. He has a job to do. His role isn't to save you from me or anyone else. Who do you think you are? One of your cousin's heroines? Even they save themselves. The only person the likes of him is concerned about is himself. Himself, his bloody master — whoever that might be — and the King. For some reason, you're a means to an end. I just don't know what that end is. Do you?'

The coach rolled to a stop. The driver called out. I could hear Charlotte and another deeper voice.

Prisca flung open the door. 'Jonathan Rickman's the finest actor the fuckin' Company's got. Problem is, he saves his best performance for off the stage.'

She leaped out. There was no goodbye, no nothing. Without looking back, she ran off into the dark.

I sat there unable to move. My mind had become a hedge of brambles; my heart a weeping wound.

Two faces filled the open doorway.

'Was that Prisca Smithton I just saw?' asked Charlotte, looking over her shoulder in disbelief.

'The very same,' I said, noticing who was beside her. Words became imprisoned in my throat before, with a deep breath and a push, I freed them.

'Why, hello, Jonathan Rickman.' I leaned forwards so he could see my face. 'Or should that be *Gabriel*?'

Calmly, he looked at me, then Charlotte. He held out his hand. 'Come,' he said. 'You and I need to talk. Charlotte, do you mind seeing yourself home? I'll ensure the driver delivers you to your door.'

'Of course …' began Charlotte, confused, flashing me looks, mouthing *Gabriel?* Hesitantly, she climbed inside.

I wanted to refuse, to stand on high ground and be all moral and take umbrage. But I also wanted to know, *had* to know, what was going on. What this man — whatever his name — was up to. Why the actor with the molten voice had lied. More importantly, why he'd intervened in Prisca's plans to be rid of me. Her voice echoed in my mind. *I just don't know what that end is. Do you?*

I placed my hand in his just as Charlotte took my place. She gripped my other wrist. 'Is everything —' her gaze glided to Mr Rickman '— alright?'

'Nay,' I said, uncertainty thickening my voice. 'But I hope it soon will be.'

I allowed Mr Rickman to help me alight. We watched in silence as Charlotte was driven away, her face a mask of concern as she leaned out the window. Behind us, the laughter and shrieks of London's rakes and wits and the women who fawned over and entertained them rose and fell in devil-sent merriment.

Mr Rickman linked his arm through mine. To any onlookers, we might have been lovers taking a stroll.

After we walked a while, he spoke. 'I'm not certain exactly what Prisca has told you, but I pray you'll give me the chance to tell my side.'

'I'm here, am I not?'

He bowed his head in concession but said no more.

Wind whipped my cloak, disturbed my headpiece. People began to give us a wide berth, aware something was happening between the two tall, well-dressed people in the middle of the street. Mindful we were attracting unwanted attention, we increased our pace.

'What game is this you play, sir?' I hissed as he led me on. Hundreds of questions shouted to be heard in the echo chamber of my mind. They were so loud I almost didn't catch his answer.

'A deadly one, Tribulation Johnson,' he said. 'One of life and death.'

Deadly? Life and death? He was serious. It was one thing to accuse Prisca of putting me at risk, admonishing her for being cavalier when so much was at stake. But here was Mr Rickman using the same language to solicit my cooperation. Ice momentarily replaced my blood causing me to give an involuntary shiver, and my throat thickened. All the voices in my head grew quiet, except for one.

It screamed a single word.

Run.

SCENE THIRTEEN

Man is apt to think we were merely intended for the world's propagation and to keepe its humane inhabitants sweet and clean; but, by their leaves, had we the same Literature he would find our brains as fruitful as our bodies.

A Gentlewoman's Companion, Hannah Woolley

Conscious of the warmth of the arm tucked against his, the brush of silk and velvet against his breeches, the very smell of Tribulation, and resisting the urge to drink in her appearance, her undisputed elegance and beauty in such finery, Gabriel was most aware of her confusion and anger. It was like an extra companion wedged between them, making it difficult for him to concentrate. If he'd thought for a moment Prisca would run to Tribulation, he never would have let her leave Mrs Fallon's. Well, that wasn't quite true. But he would have had Solomon escort her home and ensure she left the city without speaking to anyone. What he hadn't anticipated was the extent of the loathing Prisca felt for Tribulation. It had outweighed her fear of what might happen should she not cooperate. They'd underestimated the woman; he wouldn't make that mistake again. But what if she told anyone else? Somehow, he doubted that. She'd given her final performance. After all, she wasn't out to damage him — just the woman by his side.

It was more good fortune than planning he happened to arrive at Rochester's the very moment Prisca jumped into the coach. Too far away to prevent it leaving, he was grateful he was there when it returned. Now, he had to do some fast thinking and talking.

Prisca had revealed his name, which meant she would have also told Tribulation his real occupation, likely Solomon's and Mrs Fallon's as well. Though Prisca didn't know their purpose, he'd no doubt she'd surmised something close to the truth.

Truth. That was what he had to rely upon now. But how much?

He slowed his stride as, side by side, they moved further away from the Earl of Rochester's house. The traffic on the street thinned; people became fewer. A cold wind blew up from the river, a refreshing change from his fevered thoughts. Light tendrils of mist accompanied it, hovering above the ground, entwining their ankles, veiling the cobbles. In silence, they passed mostly darkened houses. Part of him wished he was indoors, even in Rochester's — anywhere but here with Tribulation Johnson.

He'd no intention of bribing her or levelling threats to ensure silence or compliance, as he'd done with Prisca. Thus, he was worried once Tribulation heard what he had to tell her, she'd run straight to Aphra, Lady Mary or the Bettertons, and his cover would be ruined.

His mission would be.

What choice did he have but to put his faith in this woman?

Gentle laughter and the strains of a viol drifted from a small tavern, its door open to welcome the cool air. Gabriel gestured in its direction.

Tribulation shrugged acquiescence, and he veered towards the entry.

As they went through the door, for just a moment, chatter ceased, the music skipped a beat and heads turned. Just as swiftly, folk resumed what they were doing. A game of One and Thirty was being played at a table, dice at another. By the fire, a large, dusty dog splayed, its head resting on giant paws.

He led her to an overturned barrel close to the unlit fireplace, away from the players and soft music. He pulled up a stool and bade her sit. She did, drawing off her gloves, unpinning her cloak, gazing about, refusing to meet his eyes.

'Ale?' he asked. She gave a slight nod.

By the time he returned, Tribulation was patting the dog, whose tail was wagging and large, languid brown eyes shone approval. She'd not long whelped.

Unable to resist, Gabriel put down the jug and tankards and ruffled the hound's sweet head. The dog rolled over, paws wheeling, tongue lolling.

By the time he sat opposite Tribulation, some of the tension, the brittleness, had left her face.

'So ...' he began, pouring them drinks.

'So,' she repeated.

Gabriel licked the foam from his upper lip. He needed a shave. 'You've spoken to Prisca.'

The ale was good. Rich with hops.

Tribulation nursed her drink. 'It's more accurate to say she spoke to me.' She met his eyes. 'What she said can scarce be believed.'

'I don't doubt.'

Tribulation drank and then lowered the vessel. 'I also want you to understand I know she didn't seek me out because she's a friend. Rather, to inflict a fatal parting shot — on both of us.'

He was impressed. More than impressed. Most women of his acquaintance would be hysterical, firing accusations and blaming him (quite rightly) for Prisca's aggression, his deception. Instead, he was met with quiet dignity and reflection. He'd thought he alone had judged Tribulation's character correctly. He hadn't. Even he had underrated her.

'Though,' she continued, 'I gather there's truth to it or we wouldn't be here.'

Gabriel rested the tankard on the table, his hands a cage around it. 'You're right.' He released a long sigh. 'My name isn't Jonathan Rickman.'

Tribulation grew very still.

'It's Gabriel Freeman. Jonathan Rickman is an alias I oft use.' He paused. 'Among others.'

He could see her saying his name in her head. Wait-Still had teased him for being named after the archangel who appeared to the Virgin.

In Milton's *Paradise Lost*, Gabriel was chief among those who guarded Paradise. Quite the responsibility — in both cases. Pity he hadn't lived up to his namesake in real life.

'Pleased to meet you, Gabriel Freeman,' said Tribulation, holding out her hand. 'I'm Tribulation Johnson.'

A flicker of surprise crossed his face. 'I know.'

'Aye,' she said, a tad curtly, thrusting her hand forwards again. 'I only know Mr Rickman. Mr Freeman is an undetermined quantity; therefore, we need an introduction or this —' she indicated the tavern, their seating arrangements '— is most improper.'

Hastily, trying to hide the smile tweaking his lips, he took her hand. What a strange creature she was. 'Pleasure to meet you, Mrs Johnson.'

'Tell me about yourself, Gabriel Freeman,' said Tribulation. 'Where are you from? What brings you here, to work in theatre?'

He tried not to show his surprise at her apparent nonchalance, or was it concealed concern? He wasn't used to sharing his past. Sharing himself. How much should he tell her?

'Very well.' He swiftly ordered his thoughts, moving pieces here and there until satisfied with the arrangement. 'I was the son of actors in a travelling troupe. Oh, don't look so incredulous. It was back when Cromwell ruled, so no theatres were allowed.' He gave a wry smile. 'Not that it stopped performers pursuing their craft and mounting productions all over the country. When my parents died from a wasting illness, I decided to remain with the troupe — they were the closest thing I had to family.'

'I'm so sorry about your parents.' Tribulation studied him closely. 'You were happy acting then?'

'Happy?' His voice rose in pitch. He could not have been more surprised had she asked if he was a Fifth Monarchist. 'Why, yes, I suppose I was.' He eyed her curiously. 'It all changed, of course, the itinerant lifestyle, when King Charles was restored to the throne. Suddenly, theatre was no longer illegal. We began to look for somewhere to base ourselves. It was decided we'd try one of the larger cities like Oxford or Cambridge.'

His eyes anchored to the far wall while his memory drifted in time. 'We were passing through Bristol, intending to remain a few days, stage a production. Ships were in port and sailors always made a good if raucous audience. Warned to stay away from the docks, I didn't listen. I was thirteen, thought I knew everything and could deal with anything.' He gave a short laugh. 'Except sailors on the hunt for recruits. I was press-ganged and forced to serve with the royal navy.' He hesitated and, in that moment, a world of pain opened.

'Oh, Mr Rickman … or should I say, Mr Freeman?' Tribulation's hand closed over one of his. 'I've heard about young men kidnapped and compelled onto ships, treated little better than slaves, taken away from kith and kin. It was a cruel way for you to enter manhood.'

He stared at her hand, marvelled at its warmth, the way it entered his veins, his bones, and spread; the empathy in her tone, her eyes. 'It is what it is — what it was, at least. I could do naught to change it.'

'But it must have been … hard for you.' She withdrew her hand and a chill descended, as if a polar wind had swept the room. 'Going to sea. After performing as well.'

He clasped his drink lest she see the effect her touch had upon him, an effect that reached his hammering heart. Was she a sorceress? Dear God, those almond-shaped eyes that refused to look away from his face, the way she absorbed his every word, the way those perfectly formed, soft, soft lips parted just so, was enchanting. *Listen to yourself, Gabriel*, warned his inner voice. *Remember why you are here.*

'It wasn't all bad, not really. Not every sailor saw a press-ganged youth as an easy mark, especially one with height. Once I'd proved myself in battle and it became apparent I could both read and write, I was an asset, not just a commodity.'

So much was revealed in those two words: asset and commodity. He thought of the slaves he'd witnessed being transported and sold over the years. There was money to be made packing the holds of ships with blackamoors. The Royal Adventurers into Africa traded in human cargo, ripping natives from their homeland — men, women and children. They were treated as assets to be sold to make the slavers and ships' captains rich. Once bought, they were commodities, used to further advance the wealth of plantation owners. Worked unto death in some cases. Even in London, most blackamoors were considered property which, depending on how they were dressed and displayed, reflected their owners' status. Solomon would quickly disabuse anyone who made the sometimes-fatal error of presuming him anyone's property.

'Anyway,' he continued. 'I was more fortunate than most because by the time the Third Dutch War began, I was not only an experienced sailor, and had risen through the ranks, but served with none other than the King's cousin, Prince Rupert — the supreme Allied Commander. He gave me a ship to captain.'

'You were a captain?'

'Once upon a time.'

'But Prisca said you are a spy.'

He wondered how much more he should reveal. 'I prefer the term intelligencer.'

'Intelligencer.' She pursed her lips thoughtfully. 'And that's what you are now? Or do you still have a ship at your command?'

How did he explain he'd given up his old life because God had seen fit to cruelly punish him by taking away his wife and newborn daughter? Tribulation was waiting for an answer. Was he ready to confess his terrible sin? That though he'd loved Wait-Still, it wasn't enough to save her? Save their child? He should have been there; he should never have left.

Yet, when Prince Rupert sent him and his crew to haunt Dutch waters, raid and disturb the shipping, he'd never questioned his duty to the Crown. Solomon had tried to dissuade him, saying his responsibility was to his new family, but he'd ignored his friend, his wife's pleas, the inner voice tolling in his head, and convinced himself Wait-Still would be fine; her anxiety, her feelings of doom, were understandable. It was a natural, womanly worry, no more. He'd be home in plenty of time for the birth … to welcome his child into the world.

'Mr Rick— Gabriel,' said Tribulation gently. 'Are you alright?'

He coughed to cover his embarrassment. His guilt. Wait-Still and the tiny babe Patience, wrapped in their shrouds, floated in his vision. He brushed his fingers across his brow as if to move them on.

'Yes. Yes. I'm just thinking how to explain what I do. That I left the sea.'

'You left? Why?'

Because it no longer called him, not when the lament of his wife's and daughter's deaths was so much louder, when it demanded penance for his choices. He cleared his throat, his mind. Penance had come in the form of Sir Joseph Williamson and the chance to prevent more needless deaths, including the death of his monarch.

'When Titus Oates and his colleagues, Israel Tonge and then William Bedlowe, revealed this Popish Plot and concerns about how far it extended were raised at the highest levels, the Prince put his network of intelligencers at the disposal of Sir Henry Coventry.'

'The Secretary of State.'

Gabriel nodded slowly. 'Coventry mounted a few investigations, but the former spymaster, Sir Joseph Williamson — have you heard of him?'

'He was recently dismissed from his post, wasn't he?'

'Ah,' said Gabriel, and then he stopped. If he wanted to earn Tribulation's trust, ensure her cooperation, she had to know the truth. 'What I'm about to reveal,' he began, resting his elbows on the barrel and lowering his voice, 'I tell you at great risk not only to myself, but the realm.'

Tribulation said nothing, which was the most reassuring response of all.

'Sir Joseph's dismissal isn't what it seems,' said Gabriel. 'It's a ruse. The King ordered him to work behind the scenes to try and catch those involved in the Popish Plot — and any others that might be fomenting. As a consequence, Sir Joseph was given men of experience, some of whom were embedded within professions it's believed might harbour traitors.'

'Such as the theatre?'

Gabriel leaned back. 'The theatre is the ideal place to plot and plan. Pretend to be one thing while really being another.'

'Like you —'

He pulled a face. 'Touché. Yes. Like me. Once Matthew Medbourne was accused of being a Papist it wasn't a big step to assume there might be others.'

'You believe he *was* plotting against the King.'

'Doesn't matter what *I* believe. Nor does it matter if he was or wasn't. It's what he was accused of. Once it was thought the theatre might be harbouring traitors, it had to be thoroughly investigated,' said Gabriel softly. 'My background made me the perfect choice. I was recalled to London and sent to Dorset Garden to see if Medbourne was part of or, had indeed established, a network.'

'And?' Tribulation inclined towards him. 'You've found nothing, have you? No-one at Dorset Garden would consider being so disloyal to the Crown let alone plotting to —' she dropped her voice '— bring about the King's death, to help Papists to power, or anyone else for that matter. They're Royalists through and through. Just look at the plays, at the playwrights too.'

Gabriel had to decide, and fast. If his instincts were right about Tribulation Johnson, she could be a very useful asset. Closest to the person he had to either prove a traitor or clear, she could work on the inside in ways that weren't possible for him. If he was wrong, and she divulged everything to Mrs Behn, well, that would be another disaster he'd deal with.

He made up his mind. 'That's where you're mistaken,' he said.

Tribulation's eyes narrowed. Quiet conversation filled the background, interrupted by the gleeful cheer of a man who'd won his hand at cards.

Time for Gabriel to show his hand. 'Your cousin, Aphra, was a spy once,' he said slowly.

'Everyone knows that. Oh.' Tribulation's eyes widened. 'You think she still is, don't you?'

Gabriel inhaled sharply.

Tribulation sat up and struck the wood. 'You're watching Aphra, aren't you? You're afeared I'll expose you to her.'

'Will you?'

'Depends on what you tell me next.' Tribulation's cheeks paled. Her hand had a slight tremor. Gabriel wanted nothing more than to take that hand and still it between both of his, to smooth his fingers down that sweet face in the hope colour might be restored. Being sensible for the first time since he helped her from the carriage, he did neither.

'Of late, Aphra has written to a former ... friend. Someone she knew while she was in Lord Arlington's employ years ago. Did you know the chief Censor used to manage the King's spy network?' Tribulation shook her head. 'He also managed Aphra.'

Gabriel ceased talking momentarily as a weary-looking drinker slumped past. 'Aphra has written to this friend asking for help in locating a known turncoat.'

Tribulation inhaled sharply. '*What*? Who?'

'The name will be familiar. William Scot.'

Tribulation frowned. 'The Earl of Shaftesbury made mention.' It was evident from the way her eyes lost focus that she was thinking, assessing.

'At one stage,' he continued, 'William Scot was said to be Aphra's lover. Her reputation was sorely damaged by her involvement with him.'

Gabriel shifted uncomfortably. 'Now she's reached out to him, a known traitor to the Crown, and even though it's through a third party, such an approach can only harm her once again. The questions are, why is she doing so? And will her actions hurt anyone else?'

Before he could say anything more, Tribulation rested her hand on his arm. 'Mr Freeman, Gabriel, please. Stop. Cease your prattle.'

This was the second time Tribulation had sought to silence him. His brows rose, his eyes hardened. 'I beg your pardon, madam,' he said in formal, offended tones.

Tribulation withdrew her fingers. 'I think I might know why Aphra is trying to contact Mr Scot. The reason is not what you assume.'

'Pray,' said Gabriel, now more amused, picking up his tankard and taking a swill. 'How do you, Tribulation Johnson, know what the finest intelligencers in the King's pay do not?'

Tribulation took a deep breath. 'I believe Aphra is trying to learn if William Scot is my father.'

Luckily, Gabriel's reflexes were swift, otherwise he wouldn't have been able to right his tankard so quickly when he knocked it over.

In few words, Tribulation reminded him of the Earl of Shaftesbury's imputation of scandal associated with William Scot while he was in Kent. With a scarlet face, she confessed what had really brought her to London, about her sister, Sir Marmaduke, and his marriage proposal. Then, in an almost emotionless manner, how her father had subsequently disowned her and how he had forced her sister to as well.

'Not because of what happened with Sir Marmaduke, you understand. But because of what, in his mind, I've become.' She indicated the costume she was wearing.

There was no need for her to explain.

'Don't you see?' said Tribulation quietly. 'If Mr Scot *is* my father — and much was made of an uncanny feature —'

Gabriel remembered. The eyes have it.

'— it explains why Papa could so readily disclaim me. It also explains why, before I was born, the family not only left Canterbury, but ceased to have contact with our relations. Even Bethan who was once so close to Aphra lost touch … until I needed somewhere to go.'

'You've given this a great deal of thought,' said Gabriel, trying to quash his doubt, wishing he could take away her evident hurt.

'Aye, I have. My situation has induced a lot of wool-gathering. And, while there's no denying Aphra's timing is dreadful, I assure you, sir, this isn't about a Catholic plot or any other kind. It's about parents. It's about fathers.'

Gabriel stared at the flush-faced woman with her magnificent eyes, eyes enhanced by an aurous smudge. He took in her untamed curls, which even now were trying to escape the ridiculous headpiece. Her scent was so distracting, a sweet mist enveloping him, even in a tavern rich with odours. Tribulation was right. It did make a terrible kind of sense, but it was also a bit too convenient.

There was also the undeniable truth: this could be about both paternity *and* plot.

'Have you discussed this with Aphra?' asked Gabriel finally.

'Nay. I tried. She refuses to talk about him. She said he was a part of her past she had no desire to make her present.'

Not entirely, thought Gabriel, but refrained from articulating this. 'Do *you* think you're his daughter?'

'I … I don't know.' Her voice was filled with hope and something else, something without light. His heart lurched and, again, he wanted to fold her in his arms.

He smoothed his jacket instead. 'Whichever way you look at it, this alters things.' He took a long drink. 'But not everything.'

'What do you mean?'

There was the faint sound of rain hitting the mullioned windows. In the candlelight, fat droplets blurred into thick ribbons of moisture. The dog opened one eye and struggled to her feet as she saw her owner stir. Keen to avoid a drenching, people began to rise and don capes and hats.

With one eye on the departing patrons, Gabriel beckoned Tribulation closer. 'Despite what you've just told me, there are those in authority convinced Aphra is up to no good. Before you protest, they have their reasons. They think she's either working with the Dutch as revenge for the way she was treated by our government years ago or — and I cannot discount this — she's being forced to act by someone else, someone pulling her strings.'

'Aphra doesn't have strings. She's her own master.'

Gabriel bit back a quick retort. 'Seems to me the Earl of Shaftesbury knows how to make her dance.'

'You think he deliberately made mention of Mr Scot's name to goad her?'

Gabriel glanced around. 'Whether it's about an old lover, or to cast doubt on your paternity, Shaftesbury's a Whig extremist who's fought hard for the Exclusion Bill, trying to ensure Catholics can never take the throne. He would much rather instil a puppet Protestant he and his cronies can manipulate than see that happen.'

'You refer to the King's bastard son, the Duke of Monmouth.'

Gabriel nodded. 'I do. But back to Shaftesbury and Aphra. Look at it from my perspective: the Earl arrives at the theatre when it's closed, happens to mention a former traitor to someone who long ago formed an attachment to him and who has known Dutch connections. Within hours, regardless of her reasons, Aphra's using her old contacts to find out where William Scot is.' He swiftly told her about the letter.

'She doesn't even like the Earl of Shaftesbury.' Tribulation's lips narrowed.

'That means nothing. No-one does.'

Only a few patrons remained. The rain was loud, the accompanying wind moaned down the chimney. The serving wench was deep in conversation with a young baker over by the bar, the candle between threatening to scorch them.

Gabriel watched Tribulation watching them. It was hard not to stare. She was so completely unaware of her charms. Taught to believe because she was uncommonly tall and smart, she had nothing to offer, she was a catch easily missed — if one was fishing.

Fortunately, he told himself, he wasn't.

She swung back and he glanced away. 'What do we do now?'

'*We?*'

She glared at him. 'Surely you're don't expect me to do nothing after all you've told me? Once again, Aphra's reputation, one she's worked so hard to rebuild, is at stake. I can't just stand aside.'

More than that. He regarded her thoughtfully. 'Will you tell Aphra what we've spoken about?'

She started. 'What do you take me for?'

Gabriel hesitated. 'Someone who speaks her mind.'

She gave a sad smile. 'Papa was forever castigating me for such an unwomanly trait.'

Gabriel gave a click of consternation. 'Happens it's a trait I admire very much.'

'You do?'

'When the mind is as fine as yours, yes.'

Tribulation appeared lost for words. Then, her brow furrowed. 'What will *you* do?'

Gabriel sighed. 'Whatever needs to be done.' When he saw the look on her face, he quickly added, 'To prove Aphra's innocence.'

Tribulation sucked in her breath. 'You think her innocent?'

'As clever as your cousin is, she might not be aware she's being used. Especially if, as you believe, she has her own very personal reasons for wanting to find Scot. I also wouldn't put it above Scot, once he learns Aphra seeks him, to take advantage of her search to advance his own ends … again.'

Tribulation cupped her hand over Gabriel's. He stared at where it rested. Her flesh against his. 'Then, *please*, let me help you.'

The last thing he wanted was to destroy this sudden accord, insult Tribulation. 'That's not the way I work. Anyway, I can hardly ask you to spy on your cousin.'

'You didn't ask. I'm offering. I'd do anything to prove Aphra's intentions are benign; that she would never knowingly aid anyone seeking to harm the Crown.' Her turquoise eyes glowed. 'Please?'

Deep down, Gabriel knew what he was about to say wasn't wise. That something other than his mind was guiding his response. But, he reasoned, if it meant maintaining his cover, and perhaps finding the evidence needed, then he potentially had more to gain by at least allowing Tribulation to believe she was helping him.

'Very well,' he said with faux reluctance. 'But —' he held up a hand when Tribulation went to speak '— it will require you to do certain things you may find unpalatable.'

She baulked. 'Such as?'

He quickly explained the role Solomon played. There'd be time later to explain Mrs Fallon. Not that he expected their paths would cross. 'As to your duties, you'll have to open and read letters, keep me and my associate informed about who Aphra meets, where and why. You'll have to keep secrets — from Aphra, your friends.'

'I'm excellent at keeping secrets.'

'How will you explain tonight to Charlotte? You used my real name, after all.'

Tribulation thought for a moment. 'I'll tell her I heard you were trying for a role with Drury Lane — a character called Gabriel. I needed to know if this was true in case I had to recast forthcoming productions. How does that sound?' Her eyes sparkled.

Gabriel was impressed. 'It will also mean reporting anything you learn.'

Tribulation took a deep breath. 'I can do that too.'

Gabriel tried to convince himself this wasn't a huge lapse of judgement on his part. With an inward groan, he began to imagine what Solomon would say. As for Sir Joseph: well, his master didn't need to know everything.

Gabriel hesitated then raised his tankard. 'We have an agreement?'

Tribulation scooped up her drink. 'We do, Mr Freeman.' Their tankards touched, the hollow sound akin to an oath.

'Then, for God's sake,' he said, wiping his sleeve across his mouth, 'call me Gabriel. Except when others are about, then it must be Jonathan, or Rickman. Can you do that?'

Her smile was a sunrise in spring. 'Only if you call me Tribulation.'

Gabriel gave a crooked grin. 'I called you that the moment I laid eyes upon you.'

ACT THREE

Winter 1680–Winter 1681

From Teaching to Reaching or, Improper Spheres of Activity

The City's a grumbling, lying dissatisfy'd City
And no wise or honest Man regards what it says.

The City Heiress or, Sir Timothy Treat-All, Aphra Behn

... these women have so much contradiction in 'em, that 'tis ten to one but a man fails in the art of pleasing.

Sir Patient Fancy, Aphra Behn

SCENE ONE

Good God! what an age is this, and what a world is this! That a man cannot live without playing the knave and dissimulation.

The Diary of Samuel Pepys, Samuel Pepys

'So, kitten,' began Aphra, one evening towards the end of winter. A new year was upon us. Snow was thick on the ground, so too lurid gossip and the usual gripes about Papists, the succession, and the Dutch. After a quiet return to the boards, the Duke's Company had success with repeat performances of *Oedipus*, some of Shakespeare's and Ben Jonson's works and a new play by Thomas Shadwell, *The Woman-Captain*. For months, Aphra had been working on an adaptation of an older play by John Marston, *The Dutch Courtesan*, which she intended to rename.

Half-rising from her desk, she handed her manuscript to me. 'I'd like you to read through this draft for me.'

I took the pages from her. She'd taken to asking me to proofread her work. I loved being trusted with such an important task as well as the privilege of being among the first to enjoy her creations. I began to flick through the pages. The characters' names were typical of Aphra: Mr Wellman, Mr Shatter, Mr Trickwell (I could already imagine his role) and Marinda, Corina and Mrs Dashit.

'I think it needs something of the current mood woven through,' she said. 'Some anti-Catholic sentiment — as much as I grow tired of reading and hearing it all the time. And maybe another song or two.'

'You want my opinion?' I asked.

She arched a brow. 'Oh no, kitten. I want much more than that. I want you to finish it.'

'*What?*'

She grinned. 'Weave your ideas through, create new characters and scenes. You know the story, the original play too. Lord knows we've discussed it often enough.' She interlaced her fingers and regarded me. 'I want this to be something we work upon *together*.'

I could scarce credit what I was hearing.

She continued. 'I want us to explore the ways in which men and women dupe each other.'

I tensed. This is what my secret did — made every word, every conversation laden with double meaning.

'Men proclaim to love a woman, yet, when she surrenders her body to their entreaties and passionate declarations, to mutual physical cravings, call her "whore".'

I released my breath slowly.

'When women withhold their affections, staunch their yearnings for fear of losing their reputations, what happens?' Aphra threw her hands in the air. 'They're called the same thing. We cannot win in this game of flesh and desire. No matter how we play it, we always lose.'

Was she speaking of the play or herself? 'You're saying the game is fixed?'

She gave a huff. 'Fixed. Rigged. Predetermined. All those things. Against women.'

And so, over the next few weeks, in the little spare time I had, I spent the evenings on Aphra's play. Only each time I referred to it that way, she would correct me.

'You mean, *our* play.'

Our play.

How those words, one of them at least, tormented me. Here I was doing what I'd longed to since a child, writing without fear of disparagement or punishment. It was a complement of creative minds. I was being guided, encouraged, critiqued. I was *learning.* Aphra's generosity and imagination were, to me, a source of wonder. The way she urged me to be more daring with the characters' repartee, make the lyrics bawdier, take risks, suggested I delete dialogue, build a scene more swiftly. She pushed me in ways I'd never dreamed.

I basked in her support while, behind her back, I ear-wigged upon her private conversations, snuck looks at her correspondence, and generally kept track of her movements.

Guilt, but also a satisfying frisson, accompanied every action, my every dissembling word as I opened and read over letters I'd collected from the table in the hallway, asked glib questions about who she was writing to or if she'd had any guests or visits planned that day. Unaware my interest was anything but friendly, Aphra would casually tell me. Blushes would oft stain my cheeks and I'd avert my head or move out of her line of sight. Not that she paid much attention. Lost in the throes of work, Aphra could talk and write at the same time. Nothing appeared to disturb her ability to focus or, if she was interrupted, resume where she left off. I admired this enormously, especially as I had to work even harder than usual to concentrate.

News that Matthew Medbourne had died in prison plunged the Company into mourning and brought the cruel and serious repercussions of the Popish Plot and Oates's outlandish accusations home once more. Innocent or guilty, it didn't seem to matter.

Audiences remained scant throughout spring and grew leaner as summer flowered and the court and gentry left the stinking city for their sojourns in the country. Some of the major players also left to perform at court pageants, which gave the new hires a chance to step into bigger roles. A false joviality almost hid the intensity with which we staged each play. We were brought closer by an awareness of how fragile life was, how contingent on the whim of powerful others — audiences, royalty, and damned Titus Oates.

With Prisca gone, I no longer had to be as wary lest a prank was played or wait with bated breath to see what rumours were being spread. People still chin-wagged, of course they did, but without an adversary like Prisca to encourage spiteful talk or cast aspersions, the theatre was an altogether far more pleasant place to be. Just when I should have been able to relax, however, I couldn't. There was only one reason for this: Jonathan Rickman, alias Gabriel Freeman.

From the moment we departed the tavern the night of Rochester's party, our relationship altered. It wasn't obvious, not on the surface, at least I didn't think so. But for my part, the way I regarded him had changed. Jonathan Rickman had been quite the bounder — a talented one. Now I knew this was a performance, I found myself watching him more closely for signs of the man I'd met at the tavern. I would catch his eye mid-rehearsal, or across the Tiring Rooms and, unable to help myself, offer a secret smile. He would nod and, though he rarely returned my grin, his dark eyes would sparkle.

We'd worked out a system whereby after performance once a week I would wait outside an ordinary in Tudor Street, behind the theatre. There, another intelligencer, the man Prisca mentioned and Gabriel apprised me of, Solomon van Kessel, met me. I'd report on Aphra's movements and communiques. Gabriel decided it wouldn't do for him and me to be seen together outside the theatre often, especially as inside we maintained a professional distance lest tongues flap. Yet, it was perfectly feasible for me to engage weekly with a terrifying giant of a blackamoor with the gentlest of eyes and most brilliant smile.

Who was I to argue?

The first time Solomon approached me, I thought I was about to be murdered. Evening had fallen and there were a few stars straining against the firmament, the thick smoke from coal fires all but obscuring the sky. A cold, snapping wind rose off the river, filling it with whitecaps. Boatmen were cursing loudly as they tried to bring their wherries towards the stairs without damage. I'd walked swiftly along Water Lane, keeping my head down, my cloak pulled tight. This was a derelict area of tumbledown dwellings with broken windows and a foul ditch filled with human refuse and animal entrails, most of which, when the rains came, flowed into the Fleet. Uneasy, I wished the businesses and houses kept their torches lit to alleviate the growing gloom. I'd just passed two beldames smoking thin pipes on their stoops, nattering in a language only they understood, when I heard soft but nevertheless distinct footfalls. Normally, I wouldn't think twice, but I'd taken an unaccustomed route and the streets were deserted, draped in twilight and shadows.

I turned into Tudor Street, relieved to see light spilling out of the ordinary and a few folk loitering around a brazier, roasting something on long sticks of wood. I increased my pace, intending to join them, when the person following stepped closer. Before I could reach the safety of the group, a hand gripped my arm.

'I believe you've information for me.'

I spun around, fists raised.

There stood a huge, broad-shouldered man, concealed beneath a long, hooded cape. His palms were raised defensively, and he stepped back. 'Whoa, missus, whoa. I'm not here to fight but talk.' White teeth flashed as he regarded me.

I looked such a contradiction, gowned and swathed, adopting the stance of a pugilist.

'Mr Van Kessel?' I asked and lowered my arms.

The man swept a neat bow. 'At your service.'

After that first introduction, Solomon would linger near the ordinary in a variety of guises. A one-armed sailor, a blind soldier, a Mosselman, a vendor with a cart. Beneath the lone tree in a small garden in the centre of a courtyard I would sit and wait for the signal to approach, or he would wander over. Feet apart, we would exchange news in low voices. Because there was so little to relay, we'd sometimes simply chat. On three occasions, Gabriel appeared — in disguise. For all that I'd considered his appearance most distinctive, he was a master of camouflage. I didn't see him until he wished me to. And then, I scarce remember what I said, the thump of my heart drowning coherent thought; the way my body tingled and ached at his very closeness made action impossible. What must he have thought of my stammers, my verbal stumbles? That he'd enlisted an imbecile?

The first time it happened, I thought I was sickening with an ague. Yet, he was all patience and kindness and thanked me graciously. On these evenings, I had to tear myself away, resist the urge to seek extra information about the man I was discovering had more layers than a jester's costume. Perhaps foolishly, there were I times I felt I caught glimpses of the real Gabriel. This was a man I could not only trust, but, God help me, like very much as well. I chose not to examine the way my insides began to frolic whenever I saw him: as if bluebirds had been released to serenade the sun.

After he left, I would consider him and wonder, was I like the rest of the Duke's Company and merely being duped?

I prayed not.

Weeks followed days and vice versa. I grew impatient. Whatever Gabriel, Solomon and their master were seeking proved elusive. My only consolation as surveillance and snooping continued was that nothing manifested to link Aphra to the Popish Plot or any other. Thus, I could persuade myself what I was doing was right, noble even. I thought I was so clever; no-one else had an inkling of what I was up to.

'You notice anything different about Jonathan Rickman?' asked Charlotte one day.

'Different? How?' I asked, my movements measured.

'I dunno. He's not such a grumpy bastard any more, don't you think? Said good morrow to me — I almost fainted.'

'I hadn't really noticed.' My eyes drifted towards where he sat at a dressing table applying make-up. I had the strongest feeling he knew we were talking about him.

Charlotte gave me a suspicious look. 'Hadn't you? Why, he's practically a new man.' She glanced over her shoulder, then turned back, whispering. 'If I didn't know better, I'd say someone's captured his heart.' She nudged me and nodded with authority.

I gave a sharp laugh and brushed her words aside. 'Don't be silly, Charlotte. Everyone knows he doesn't have one.'

Jonathan Rickman might not, but what about Gabriel Freeman?

By mid-June, the play Aphra and I were writing together was finished. We called it *The Revenge or, A Match in Newgate.* The dialogue was bold, quite libertine, and didn't hesitate to be brutal. In the end, aware of the opprobrium we'd attract from some quarters, especially in the depiction of men and women's relations, Aphra made the decision not to claim authorship — for either of us.

'You may not earn praise as a playwright, kitten, but neither will you attract condemnation and the awful names that follow a woman who puts herself forward. Who dares to write like a man.'

Authorship was given to Anonymous. The joke was, Aphra was Anon and I was Mouse which, as I said to Aphra, was rather a demotion for a kitten. She laughed and reminded me how in fables, the mouse confounded a lion …

It was performed in late June; as word flew around there was a production so salacious even the author hadn't put *his* name to it, crowds flocked to see it. Of course, Lady Mary, Mr Betterton and a couple of the other shareholders knew Aphra had penned it, but as promised, she protected my reputation by not admitting my contribution. What she did do, however, was share the Author's Benefit. I'd never earned so much money in my life.

'Enjoy this success while you can, Tribulation. It doesn't happen often,' she said as I stared at the heavy purse in my hand. At last, I could start to replenish my exhausted savings.

When the book-seller and printer Narcissus Luttrell published the play a month later, we were paid some more. By then, people were claiming Mr Betterton was the author. A part of me longed to admit my part, but for once common sense prevailed and I kept quiet.

Papa would be pleased. I was learning discretion after all.

SCENE TWO

He was but lent this duller World t'improve.

Aphra Behn, on the death of John Wilmot, Earl of Rochester

July rolled in on a wave of scorching heat. Just like John Downes who, after spending months recovering, returned to his old job. A bit slower and weaker (to start with), he was still as sharp as a bodkin. His hands, which were terribly scarred, and the fingers webbed like duck's feet, were also very stiff. He needed someone to help him.

Fortunately, that's where I stepped in.

Unfortunately, it was for a fraction of what I used to earn. So much for my feeble efforts to save. Women, it turns out, can be beggars but not choosers. Officially, I was made Mr Downes's assistant; I felt more like a slave or navvy sometimes. I made certain I didn't overstep his authority or undermine him but did what needed to be done and what he might struggle to accomplish.

I half-expected Mr Downes to be resentful, listen to the grumblings of those who'd never accepted my presence. I waited for the barbs about my height to start, for him to suggest I give up theatre and become an attraction at one of the fairs held around the city. They never came. Far from being inclined to find fault, disregard my perspective, or want me gone, Mr Downes found me indispensable, something he readily admitted. I wondered if it was because, having been in the theatre all his life, he didn't feel that working beside a woman, let alone being reliant on one, diminished his manhood. Not only was he kind and easy to work with: he taught me so much — and not only about the theatre. He was a marvellous repository of gossip and stories. Often, when the play was in full swing, he'd spy someone in the audience and whisper sordid tales in my ear.

'Did you know the Earl of Shaftesbury has a copper tube in his side? He had a chirurgeon insert it to draw fluid from his liver when he was a young man. Stinks. That's why he covers himself so liberally with scent. They oft refer to him as Tapski in the news-sheets.'

'Tapski?' My eyes were as round as a plate.

'Like a beer barrel,' said Mr Downes, patting his side and mimicking pouring.

Conniving the Earl might be, but I pitied him for knowing that.

'See that woman over there?' he said one night during a rowdy performance of *The Princess of Cleve.* 'That's Hortense Mancini — Duchess of Mazarin. A Catholic.' He pulled a face. Mr Downes had very little sympathy for Papists. Initially, he'd thought well of Mr Oates and believed his claims, persuading himself the endless arrests and bloody executions were necessary. That was, until Matthew's needless death changed his mind. Nothing could alter entrenched opinions as easily as personal experience.

'It's said —' John's whispers continued '— her husband would knock the teeth out of their maids so they didn't catch a man's eye. He also ruined a magnificent art collection by painting over their ...' He held his hands over his crotch and then nodded towards my breasts. Very little embarrassed him, or anyone else at Dorset Garden for that matter. 'When the Duchess came to England, she became the King's lover. She's also rumoured to enjoy the favours of both men and women.' My eyebrows rose. 'Including, some say, your cousin ...' I'd heard that particular story before and could neither confirm nor deny. Mr Downes paused as if imagining them together, licking his lips. 'She's called the "great whore" — the Duchess, not Aphra. Not to her face, of course.

'She escaped her dreadful marriage by disguising herself as a man.' He looked pointedly at me. He knew I'd arrived in London dressed in my brother's clothes.

From John (as he insisted I call him), I learned that just like Tom Otway, the playwright, Nathaniel Lee, also tried acting and was useless due to terrible stage-fright ('it's far more common than you think'), and he confirmed what I had of course already heard: that John Hoyle was a man-lady — a sodomite.

We rubbed along very well together, John Downes and I. Me, handling paperwork, taking dictation, ensuring the cast members and Company were paid and the authors received their benefits — all according to John's calculations. He administered orders to cast and stagehands and was inordinately pleased I could fetch anything out of his reach. I would turn pages on the master script during performances and make any necessary annotations and changes during rehearsals. Those who'd been discommoded by my elevation into Mr Downes's role were far more accepting of me as his assistant. Invitations to join the cast post-performance resumed. In the Company's mind, I might still have been a freak and carbuncle on womanhood, but I was their freak. I'd assumed my rightful place. A helpmeet. I guess I should have been piqued. As it was, I was more relieved. After all, I'd much to occupy me.

A brother and sister — Kit and Grace Savage — were hired to replace Prisca and an actor who never returned from summer hiatus. From Bath, the Savages (and much was made of their name, as they were very genteel and sweet) were both in their twenties and had acted at Oxford and annually at Bartholomew Fair since they were in petticoats. Both were short in stature (though, as Gabriel pointed out, wasn't everyone to us?), with lovely golden curls and hazel eyes. Kit's smile was slightly marred by a scar that cleft his top lip; he said a dog bit him, but the way his eyes strayed to Grace when he told the story suggested otherwise. Grace's eyes were bigger, and she had a button nose. Both had lovely singing voices, honeyed and pure, like angels. Grace danced as beautifully as her name suggested. It wasn't long before they were cast in minor speaking roles and entrusted with songs. Charlotte was vexed, as she usually did most of the singing, but grudgingly acknowledged the siblings had better voices.

New productions were planned, including Aphra's next play, *The Young King*, old ones were staged, and the Company did well some days and others scarce covered costs.

I maintained my vigilance, watched my cousin and checked her correspondence, not only so I might alert either Gabriel or Solomon should something out of the ordinary arrive but so I could do whatever was in my power to protect Aphra.

It had been an unusually cool day for late July. Rain spilled from low-hanging clouds, like a dripping faucet. The wind nipped and bit, arriving in flurries that paid no respect to gowns, coats or breeches, but passed straight through. Inadequately dressed for the unseasonable weather, none of the cast felt inclined to go for drinks after the play was finished, so I headed straight home.

The house was quiet when I entered. Aphra and Nest were at the New Exchange. As the days grew longer, the lodgers had taken to dining at a new tavern up near Sergeant's Inn. Jonathan said it wasn't so much the quality of ale or victuals that made the place attractive as the two sisters who served customers. First listening for Molly or Millie and reassuring myself they were in the kitchen, I swiftly sorted through the mail.

There were a couple of bills for the Tetchell brothers, and quite a number for Aphra, for printing, books, food, wine, fabric and another pair of shoes. There was an invitation from John Dryden — the usual kind of missive. I was about to throw the pile back upon the salver when a heavily sealed letter with strange markings caught my eye.

My heart quickened. The growing shadows became sinister. I swallowed and snatched it up, secreting it in my placket, taking the stairs two at a time. Once in my room, I lit a lanthorn, carrying it to the table. I sat down, undoing my cloak, removing my gloves and wiping my sweaty palms. I took a couple of deep breaths and then, with a patience I didn't feel, examined the letter carefully, one ear upon the stairs, waiting for a tell-tale creak, the opening of a door, the sound of voices. None came.

Guilt swamped me. What was I doing? If I was swift, I could race back downstairs and replace the letter. No-one would know. I'd inform Gabriel and Solomon a missive for Aphra had arrived from overseas. Let the men deal with it.

But what if the contents were incriminating? I had to know.

I was both relieved and horrified when the seal flew off first flick of the dirk I'd wriggled beneath the wax. I carefully placed it to one side and stared before slowly unfolding the single page. My breathing was shallow and my heart behaved like a drunken tumbler. When I finished reading, I leaned back in the chair, arms dropping to my sides as if great weights were attached.

The letter was all but indecipherable: written in code. The numbers 159 and 160 predominated, as did 156. Number 62 also appeared. The name 'Astrea', which I knew was Aphra, featured, as did 'Celadon'. Who was that? Was that William Scot? Was he the author? There was no signature. My ears roared as I read it again and again. It made no sense.

My mind churned, my stomach too. Why was Aphra being sent a letter written in code? Only intelligencers or people with something to hide did that. Was Sir Joseph right and Aphra was plotting something? Absurd thought. As a writer, Aphra was always plotting something. It wasn't until I heard the shouts of men outside I was reminded of the precariousness of my situation. Swiftly, after chiding myself for levity, I melted the underneath of the wax and resealed the letter, praying Aphra wouldn't notice it had been tampered with. Then, I raced downstairs and jumbled it among the other correspondence.

Just in time. With a great clatter of boots and flurry of fabric, Aphra stumbled through the door, Nest just behind her. As she entered, Aphra emitted a strangled sound.

'What is it? What's happened?' I rushed towards her. Her hair was in disarray, her eyes swollen and red, bottom lip atremble.

She shook her head and pushed past me, blundering into the parlour, arms outstretched as if she'd suddenly been deprived of sight.

I turned to Nest. 'What is it?' I began, dread I'd been discovered rising.

'It's Johnny Wilmot,' said Nest, using the Earl of Rochester's name. Her voice was odd, her eyes glassy. She too had been crying. 'It's all over the streets.'

'What is?' I asked cautiously.

'He's dead, Tribulation.' It was Aphra. She leaned against the doorframe, her face twisted, her voice broken and weary. 'My blazing star will shine no more.'

In two strides, I took her in my arms and held her as she sobbed. My back turned to the letter I'd just opened and read.

Evidence of treachery — but was it mine, or Aphra's?

SCENE THREE

... only the brutish and degenerate part of mankind ... men of desperate fortunes ... Do commonly take up informing as a trade ...

A Sermon Against Persecutions Preached, Samuel Bold

Rochester's death hit Aphra hard. Months later, she was still sleeping poorly. Her skin was sallow; more lines creased the corners of her eyes and criss-crossed her forehead, which was oft set in a frown. Her lips were dry, her sweet smile rare. It made my heart ache to see her like this. Eyes dark with misery, her entire body was wrapped in a cloud of eternal gloom. The elegy she'd written for Rochester had been cruelly criticised, the Earl of Mulgrave and the Reverend Gilbert Burnet condemning her verses, reducing what she wrote out of love and admiration into something tawdry, calling her 'a vile woman', 'odious' and 'obscene'.

'Why can't they leave well enough alone?' she'd lamented through tears, taking to her room again for days after the attacks. Grief weakened her ability to brush off her critics, meet their scorn head on; grief and the sheer volume of public malice. I wished I could relieve her of the pain so evidently afflicting her — pain of the mind, body and soul.

Even weighed by wretchedness, she still wrote.

As Yuletide approached, we remained wrapped in a shroud of woe and, on my part, contrition. I'd told Gabriel about the letter I'd read, memorising the strange numerical code. All he'd tell me was that though it didn't prove Aphra's guilt, nor did it shore up her innocence.

'Aphra is custodian of a secret, one we have to uncover,' he said.

Just like my cousin, I too was a keeper of secrets and if I learned nothing else I did discern this: secrets not only grow in size and significance, but they also start to occupy space — and not just in my head. My secret moved into the house and theatre. It walked beside me on the street. It nudged me in the Tiring Rooms, draped itself over my shoulders as I sat at the kitchen table. It was ever-present as Aphra and I bent over pages making changes to lines, scribbling notes in the margins. It sat there, a great grey lump, staring at me with judgemental eyes. It hovered when Aphra read a draft of a play. It whispered in my ears as I sat in the parlour, the latest news-sheet open on my lap. It murmured sweet dreams as I pushed my head into the pillow, ensuring they were anything but. It accompanied me to friends' houses, to church, the bloody Bishop's Whelp after performances, on visits to the city.

I persevered with my prying because I believed what I was doing was right — right for the country, the King and, most of all, for Aphra. Only, sometimes, when I tossed beneath blankets and turned more times than a roasting boar, doubts and misgivings competed with ridiculous thoughts of triumph. When the night held me captive, I would dare to consider: what if I was wrong? What if the decision to help Gabriel didn't just hinder his mission, but destroyed Aphra? What if I wasn't a victorious Caesar, but a duplicitous Brutus?

Et tu, Tribulation?

Her critics, her adversaries — Henry Care, Wycherley, Shadwell, Burnet — were nothing compared to me.

I was another Prisca: the enemy within.

When Jonathan Rickman unexpectedly announced he was leaving the Duke's Company, ostensibly to deal with a family matter in the north, the Company took it in its stride. Actors and actresses left all the time. Replacements of Rickman's calibre might be hard to find, said Lady Mary, but there were plenty of men waiting in the wings to take up his part.

I had to pretend I was surprised, even though I'd known of Gabriel's imminent departure for weeks. He'd pulled me aside one evening after performance and explained the letter Aphra received revealed important information: William Scot was currently in the United Provinces — Dutch territory — but intending to make his way to London. Gabriel and Solomon were being sent abroad to track him down.

Disappointment and another emotion I was too afraid to examine filled me.

'But, if you know he's coming, can't you just wait until he arrives?' I sounded like a two-year-old denied a treat.

Gabriel shook his head. 'Sir Joseph is convinced if we find and follow him, and he's part of a plot, he'll lead us to his co-conspirators.'

Aphra's name hung in the silence between us.

After his last performance, Gabriel lingered by the prompter's table. A farewell (an adieu?) was imminent. I liked it not. Around us, the stagehands were shifting scenery and props back into position in readiness for the morrow's performance.

I sank onto the stool, pressing my hand over my heart to ease the ache. First looking over his shoulder, Gabriel moved closer. He was still in costume, a prince and hero no less. Damn. It was as if he had stepped out of the pages of an Arthurian tale. I'd always loved Sir Lancelot and quite understood Guinevere's preference for him over her husband.

I broke the silence. 'I thought I was meant to help you prove Aphra's innocence. Not send you away.'

'The results of our work can oft be … unpredictable,' he said kindly.

His face was in shadow and impossible to read. He rested his fingers on the edge of the table. The lanthorn, which was dull, managed to arouse a glimmer from the ring he wore. A black stone set in a silver band. I focussed on it, marvelling how the stone was the same colour as his eyes, only lacking their lustre.

'Well, I don't like this outcome.' I folded my arms.

He bent towards me, his lips a hair's breadth from my ear. 'Neither do I.' He eased himself away slightly.

Our eyes met.

A storm of confusion raged in my breast: howling winds, lashing rain and lightning that jabbed and pierced my ribs, leaving gaping holes and burned runnels. I was off kilter, exposed in a way I'd never felt before. It was all I could do not to grab the lapels of Gabriel's coat, draw him close and cling to his solidness.

Prisca's words tolled in my skull. *He doesn't give a damn about you or anyone else. He has a job to do.*

He did. And I did too. These strange longings, born of my wild imagination, my reading, writing, and too much bloody time in the playhouse, had no place in my head or heart. I'd cast myself in a role not written: Gabriel as well. My untamed thoughts had transformed our relations into something they were not and never could be. And yet … a small, clandestine part of me, those dark recesses buried in my fancies, encased by my dreams, dared to hope.

I saw that now. Now that he was leaving. God damn. I felt it too.

Gabriel still loomed over me; the guardian angel he was named after made manifest. He was neither my guardian nor my angel.

I bit my tongue and retreated to the comfort of words I knew by rote, those on the master script. Black lines wobbled and shimmered. Why were they so blurry?

'Tribulation,' growled Gabriel. 'Though I'll be gone, I pray I'll not be forgotten.'

He waited. I kept my head bowed.

'I'll be unable to communicate regularly,' he said. 'To do so would jeopardise the mission. As soon as it's safe, if I'm able, I'll write. You have my word.'

The stage was silent, dark. It was just me, Gabriel, and a small corona of light.

'Well,' I said. 'You'd best not tarry then.'

Did he step closer?

I shut my eyes, waiting for what came next. His hand closing over mine? Drawing me to my feet, and folding me in those strong arms?

Nothing.

There was a shift in the air. I opened one eye, then the other.

He was gone.

A week after Gabriel departed, talk in the Tiring Rooms was that we were better off without Jonathan Rickman. Swiftly forgetting how he'd drawn crowds and many admirers, the other players recast him as unreliable, a misanthrope who was never dedicated to the Duke's, just himself.

They may not have missed Gabriel, or perhaps they decided to survive his absence by altering history, but for me it was like a much-loved poem had been torn from a book or favourite lines were left out of a play. I tried to piece him together from memory, stolen and arranged moments, shared smiles, looks, conversations. It was a coverlet with holes and missing stitches, but it mostly sufficed. I would wrap myself in it and force myself to be content. What choice did I have?

Damn Gabriel Freeman. He'd made me feel important, necessary. He'd trusted me to report what I discovered, with his real identity, his mission, no less.

And curse my heart, I had let him in.

As a friend. A dear friend. Nothing more. Nothing less either.

Moses in a basket, I even missed Jonathan Rickman.

It was as if I'd lost two allies, not one.

It was merely because when in his company, I felt … what? What did I feel?

Seen. Heard.

Though Jonathan Rickman's name peppered my conversations (my inner voice uttering his real name each time), something Aphra noted wryly, I tried to fill the void he left by reading voraciously and writing. And what did I read but constant references to the dangers posed by Papists?

As the New Year approached, we clung to hope that the worst of the Popish Plot and Oates's fearmongering was over.

God and the angels must have been clutching their sides to prevent them splitting. They knew hope was a dangerous thing.

SCENE FOUR

Almighty Rabble, 'tis to you this day
Our humble Author Dedicates the Play.
From those who in our lofty Tyre sit,
Down to the dull State-Cullies of the Pit,
Who have much Money, and but little Wit.
Whose useful Pursies, and whose empty Skulls,
To private Interest make ye Publick Tools:

Prologue, *The Second Part of the Rover*, Aphra Behn

Aphra was putting finishing touches to a poem she'd been commissioned to write by his Majesty — not that anyone was supposed to know who her patron was. Designed to critique the Republicans among Parliament, a group who were now being referred to quite openly in the news-sheets, pamphlets and coffee-houses as 'Whigs', she was exposing how these men manipulated the King's bastard son, James, the Duke of Monmouth, for their own ends. Entitled *To a New Scotch Tune*, it referred to 'poor Jemmy' — a thinly disguised Monmouth. It was bold and to the point.

When I first read it, I was stunned. 'You cannot put your name to this.' Alarm was writ upon my face. 'The most famous Whig of all, the Earl of Shaftesbury, will lynch you.'

'Him and Buckingham and all the others who pander to the state-bullies of the pit.' Aphra was referring to the Parliamentarians. She slowly turned away from her desk, a cunning smile on her lips. 'What kind of fool do you take me for? Just as I advise you, I will remain anonymous. At least I've been promised a decent purse.'

'Are things so bad you have to take such risks?'

She'd put down her quill and pushed back her chair. 'Dire,' she said matter-of-factly and, with a groan, rose. 'We either have to find a way to increase our income, kitten, or move.'

We'd discussed relocating to another house over summer the year before. She'd been unable to write while gripped with grief over first her mother's anticipated passing (and remorse they hadn't been closer), then Rochester's death, and we'd been reliant on my wage. Not even a repeat performance of *The Rover* with its decent Author's Benefit — which like any payment received had to last weeks and sometimes months — was enough to cover Aphra's debts let alone the constant bills. We'd been forced to let Molly and Millie go. Nest and I managed their duties between us.

This was the second time she'd raised our finances of late. I glanced at her desk. She might be commissioned by the King, but payment from the Privy Purse was not guaranteed. One had only to remember how long the navy waited to be paid during the Dutch Wars. Aphra could be in pauper's prison before she saw a groat. She worked for his Majesty because, like everyone else, she couldn't refuse. But to leave Dorset Street?

As damp and sometimes dour as the house could be, I'd grown used to it. Used to the lodgers, the noise that filtered in from outside, the ever-present smells, the smoke-stained walls and ceiling, and Hecate. It was comforting: familiar if somewhat pungent.

'There's a place off Newe Street I've been told about,' said Aphra. 'It won't be vacant for a few months but ...' Misreading the look on my face, my sudden silence, Aphra threw her arm around my shoulders. 'What does it matter where we live? So long as we're together.' She leaned away slightly. 'Seems you're stuck with me, whether you like it or not.'

'Happens I like it, very much.' I kissed her on the cheek. A flash of conscience almost ruined the moment. 'But I like it here as well.'

She pinked and touched her face, her smile deepening. She squeezed tight before releasing me, staring in faux dismay at the sprawl of paper and quills. 'Unless I finish some of these projects, and get paid, we'll be forced to search for new lodgings long before winter is over.'

Determined to make up for lost time, of late Aphra had undergone a burst of creative energy. She was working on three plays, two translations and several poems.

The threat of moving meant I didn't need any more encouragement to ask Lady Mary and Mr Betterton if I might try out for a speaking part. Before Gabriel had finished his last role in *Timon of Athens* (or should that be as Jonathan Rickman?), and after auditioning to prove my acting skills had vastly improved (I never had found the time to join Lady Mary's classes), I was cast as a manservant named Harlequin in Aphra's next play, *The Second Part of the Rover*. This continued the English Cavaliers' misadventures from the First Part. The main character was named Willmore who, everyone agreed, was a thinly disguised portrait of none other than the Earl of Rochester.

My concerns that a play featuring exiled Cavaliers roistering in Catholic Spain and which referred to all women as whores might be good for the box office and for laughs, but would do little to enhance Aphra's social standing, proved well founded.

It simply fed her critics.

The Second Part of the Rover was staged in late January 1681, after Gabriel had gone, when snow lay thick on the ground and parts of the river froze. Whether it was the play or the promise of relative warmth in the theatre, the auditorium was full for five consecutive afternoons.

For a few hours spectators were hugely entertained, able to push the identity of the author from their minds as they wriggled with mirth at the profanities, the indecent goings-on, calling and cheering, jeering as well. Yet, the moment the curtain shut they donned Puritan minds as they discussed the play's merits or otherwise. In salons and coffee-houses, away from the guilty pleasure of Dorset Garden, men and women continued the long, slow flensing of Aphra's reputation.

It didn't help she dedicated the play to his Royal Highness, the very Catholic Duke of York. Excoriating Aphra became a sport carried on in the news-sheets, in poems, and in all manner of other tracts that were circulated, read, shared and discussed.

It was heartbreaking. It broke Aphra's — into rubble. Despondency descended once more, trapping her in its thorny embrace for weeks. Yet, every day, she fought hard against its pernicious hold, continuing to write, to create, even if it was only a few words.

'If I cease altogether, then my detractors are the victors,' she'd say.

And everyone else loses.

As winter blew itself into a temper of snowfalls, rain and freezing winds before the patient thaw of spring arrived, I was given more breeches parts, even a line here and there, a dance and songs — never solo. My singing voice was merely satisfactory, Mr Betterton judged, which was quite the compliment according to Charlotte. My confidence grew as I threw myself into whatever role I was given and helped Mr Downes.

What I relished was, upon the stage, I could be anyone — a servant, boy, man, maid, goddess, labourer, worker, nanny, princess — anyone except Tribulation Johnson, disowned daughter of Howell Johnson, forgotten sister of Bethan, potentially William Scot's bastard, and a fledgling, anonymous writer. I mainly kept to myself and was content. I wasn't liked or appreciated by all, but the occasional thanks or smile, never mind the cheers and applause of the audience each night, and even their ridicule and flung fruit, made me feel seen, alive.

It also reminded me of something. While it was gratifying to be seen, what I truly desired was to be a woman who was heard. Not just uttering words a playwright put in my mouth, or sweet nothings to pander to a man's pride, but like Aphra, sharing my own considered views and damn the consequences.

Time again to wield my pen.

Wield my words.

SCENE FIVE

I'll shew my self all woman in my Art,
(Puts the dagger and Pistol in her two Pockets)
But be a very Devil in my heart

The Revenge or, A Match in Newgate, Anonymous

'Have you heard?' Mr Pepys burst into the Tiring Rooms one afternoon early July, hands flapping, his periwig askew.

Ever since he'd escaped conviction for treason, Samuel Pepys made a habit of frequenting the theatre. From the expression on his rubicund face and the way he struggled to catch his breath, it was clear the news was of great import.

'Sam, Sam,' said Mr Betterton, attired in costume, striding over and escorting him to a chair. He clicked his fingers, and Jacob rushed over with a decanter and glass. 'You're in a state, sir. Quench your thirst then enlighten us. What news?'

Mr Pepys took the goblet and drank greedily, erupting in a volley of coughs and spraying some claret on Mr Betterton, who stared in dismay at his formerly white robe. We were minutes away from taking our places for Nahum Tate's *The History of King Lear* — described by one Wit as a more pleasing version of Shakespeare's tragedy. Mainly because there was far less death, more marriages, and a happy ending. Mr Betterton was playing King Lear.

Mr Betterton made a poor attempt to dab the droplets away, managing to smear them before he surrendered. By now, everyone was peering in Mr Pepys's direction. If only our players could command such rapt attention and so swiftly.

'Well,' said Mr Sandford impatiently from across the room, one eyebrow drawn darkly, a brush balanced between his fingers. 'Out with it.'

Mr Pepys drew himself up. 'The Earl of Shaftesbury has been thrown in the Tower.'

There was a beat. Then, talk erupted.

'I don't believe it.'

'Shaftesbury?'

'It's because of what he did at the Oxford Parliament back in March,' explained Mr Pepys, flapping his hands to quell the chatter. 'First he follows the court there with hundreds of armed men in tow and then has the hubris to stand in the House of Lords and insist Monmouth be made legitimate. No wonder the King dissolved Parliament after only a few days.'

'And no wonder he's been arrested,' said Mr Betterton. 'We heard the Duke of Monmouth and Lord Grey brought their own militia as well.'

'They did,' squeaked Mr Pepys. 'To support Shaftesbury. How there wasn't another civil war is anyone's guess.'

There was a buzz of excitement, the rush of disaster avoided. I thought back to that time. Though the news about soldiers marching towards the Oxford Parliament with the intention to influence votes had only reached London days later, after the crisis had been averted, it had still managed to dominate Tiring Room discussion. The fear of what might have transpired had been very real.

'What will happen to Titus Oaf now Shaftesbury, his main supporter, is locked up?' pondered Cave Underhill.

'Whatever it is,' said Elizabeth Barry. 'It won't be enough. Not after all the heartache and misery the wretched man has caused.'

That became the cue for everyone to put forward an appropriate punishment.

'He should be left to starve in Newgate, like Matthew,' said Finnola.

'Public beheading,' said old Jacob.

'So long as they use a rusty knife.' Susanna Mountfort held up a prop one.

'Or a blunt one.' Katherine Herbert ran her finger along a wooden blade.

'Disembowelling — with a spoon,' said Mr Underhill, reinforcing his macabre notion with actions.

There were cheers of agreement.

'May he rot in Hell,' said Samuel Sandford.

I'd become so caught up in imagining an appropriate fate for Mr Oates (beheading, disembowelling and rotting were simply the beginning), I forgot to give the fifteen-minute signal. It wasn't until Mark Danvers nudged me I remembered. I scooted about the room, ringing the bell, putting a stop to the excitement. There were the usual looks of horror, followed by a flurry of adjusted robes, crowns and garlands and a frenzy of paint being applied to faces. I left the room to alert the stagehands. By the time I returned to issue the five-minute warning, there were only a few actors remaining.

I couldn't help but wonder what the Earl of Shaftesbury would plan now. Being in the Tower would constrain most men, have them reconsidering their actions and possibly even regretting them and seeking ways to make amends and beg forgiveness from the King. Not Shaftesbury. If anything, he'd be busy plotting his next move and considering those best placed to make it on his behalf. The Earl, all knew, rarely dirtied his own hands, not when others were prepared to do it for him. It was hard not to wonder who he'd recruit to his cause this time. No doubt, it would be someone with nothing left to lose.

These were my thoughts as I ushered out the stragglers, ready to take my place. I was dressed as a soldier (with lines), as for this production I was both actor and assistant book-keeper. I glanced over my shoulder as I left the Tiring Rooms in time to see Mr Pepys pour himself another wine. Thinking no-one was about, he removed his feathered hat and with great aplomb bowed deeply to the mirror once, twice, and thrice, before nodding, smiling and offering a flourish to some vast imagined audience.

The mood in the city was incendiary. All everyone could talk about was Papists, the King, his brother, Shaftesbury, Monmouth, the heat, and the endless rain that did little to cool the air — or tempers, which were frayed and quick to ignite. Fights broke out: fruit, meat, jordans, rat carcasses, anything at hand was flung. When a dead body was found, bloated and stinking in the middle of a ditch two streets away, its throat cut, the only surprise was there weren't more. Papists were blamed, as they were for everything. Even the Great Fire was being attributed to them. Rumour was the engraving on the grand monument was going to be changed to reflect this.

Oft at night, lying in bed in that betwixt state where slumber hadn't yet taken hold and my thoughts were still mine to arrange, I would think over the day and the conversations I'd had. One evening, I'd come upon Aphra in her bedroom, working upon a new play set during Cromwell's reign. Using John Tathum's play, *The Rump*, she was adapting it for the Duke's and thinking of calling it *The Roundheads*. Thus far, she'd only had a basic outline and a prologue, but I admitted surprise she would seek to tackle something so obviously partisan when all about us debate about who should rule next raged.

'How is it partisan?' she asked.

'Well, it's set during a time when England rejected monarchy in favour of a Republic. So, couldn't it be seen as antagonistic to the Crown?'

'Only if the Republic had been successful and it wasn't. But —' Aphra stood, inviting me to take her seat and look upon her words '— what I wish to produce, to paraphrase Tathum, is a small mirror of the late wretched times. Just as they tried then, we have men determined to control everything — what we read, our thoughts, behaviour, even who should inherit the throne. The point I wish to make is they may think they have authority, maintain control, yet they only *appear* to do so. It's nothing but a fragile illusion.'

It was hard not to admire Aphra's determination to use her plays to teach and reach, to try and rise above the criticisms and continue. Yet I was often left uneasy and, honestly, a little dissatisfied with her efforts. The women characters, for all Aphra's talk about their right to liberty and freedom to desire whomever they chose, rarely if ever asserted those rights outside the bedroom. They mainly used the scant power they possessed — and it was most often physical beauty, what lay between their legs, or what had been bestowed through rank and wealth — to lure men into their arms and wedlock. Nay. I was being unfair. What was Aphra creating but an accurate portrayal of *our* times? Tathum's small mirror held up to show audiences and women where their so-called power really resided.

In the smallest of domains.

I wondered as I tossed and turned atop the sheets if Aphra would write a part for me to play. Those thoughts naturally led to the other thespians and then, as was my wont, to Gabriel. I'd oft dwell upon him, and Solomon, and not just when sleep was elusive. Even during the day, I'd stop and wonder where they were, what they were doing. Had they found William Scot and were they even now making their way home?

After being so involved (or feeling like I was) in their mission, it was hard to wallow in dark ignorance. Gabriel wasn't at fault for that, nor for the injury I felt at being cast aside; I certainly didn't blame him. Any wounds, which I occasionally picked at and reopened, were self-inflicted.

In order to distract myself, I was attempting (after much encouragement from Aphra) to write my own play. Tentatively entitled *Like Father, Like Son or, The Mistaken Brothers*, it was loosely based on Thomas Randolph's *The Jealous Lovers*, which dealt with the contentious topic of removing an unpopular ruler. Aphra was reading each scene as it was completed and suggesting improvements.

Nor did I forget my other writing. Every evening, I set aside time to consider what I might next pen for publication. I would pore over the news-sheets, discussing their contents with Aphra if she was about, Nest if she was not. Even the lodgers became excellent sounding boards. Not that they listened, not really. Like most men, they felt the public arena was theirs and my observations were for amusement, not serious consideration. What I noticed in a very short time was, after I'd added my argument to theirs, perhaps challenging or noting a fact they'd cited incorrectly or overlooked, they'd harrumph or flap their hands as if I was an irritating moth, sometimes chuckling indulgently at my temerity. To them, I was naught but a child who'd blundered into an adult conversation and said something almost intelligent. Less than five minutes later, Joseph, Michael or Robert would repeat my point, sometimes verbatim, and enjoy hearty congratulations for their perception and erudition.

I would grind my teeth so loudly, Hecate (who I secretly thought of as my second self) would raise her head and her golden eyes would widen before she'd yawn, exposing her little razor teeth.

When I mentioned this to Aphra, she brushed it off. 'They're the same as most men, kitten. Surely you realise that by now?'

If I did, it hadn't annoyed me to the same degree. Possibly because I hadn't sought to assert myself or my opinion with the same level of confidence before.

She gave a regretful sigh. 'Sadly, you become accustomed to such treatment. It used to rouse me to offence and then defence — which you've more sense than to deploy.'

Not in my head, I didn't.

She sat back and swept her hand over the paper before her. 'Now, I simply use their trite utterances and hackneyed behaviour as fodder for my plays, the foolish ways in which men speak to and of each other. The way they consider women is a lexicon and mode unto itself and has served me well. Little do the men in the audience know when they laugh at my characters, Willmore and his peers, chuckle at Philander or Sir Patient Fancy, they're laughing at themselves.' I'd drifted closer as she spoke. She drew me in. 'Nothing gives me greater satisfaction. It might be a small victory but 'tis one nonetheless.'

But was it the Pyrrhic kind? The question began to haunt me.

We both wrote — me when the theatre wasn't beckoning, Aphra rarely pausing of late. My cousin still had the capacity to make me marvel. If only she wasn't subject to the torments of melancholy, usually incited by the physical pains which beset her or the cruel words of her antagonists, she'd be a modern-day Hercules.

Nay, Hippolyta.

There were those among her more tolerable acquaintances who would call her Astrea, the name used in the letter that sent Gabriel and Solomon away. The men adopted it to position her as a goddess at whose feet they worshipped. Aphra deployed it ironically and to identify herself with its mythical and literary counterparts, especially the character of Astrea in Honore d'Urfe's *L'Astrée*, a book thousands of pages long. I'd read it to Lady Adeline years ago. She adored it. If Papa had known half of what I read, let alone such a scandalous tale, he would have forbidden me to ever grace milady's doorstep. It was the story of star-crossed lovers, a shepherd and shepherdess who lived hundreds of years ago and whose love is oft-thwarted by the ambitions and interference of others. To me, that was Aphra, who loved men like Rochester (who'd loved mainly himself), John Hoyle (who was wilfully indifferent to her affection and also unable to return it in the manner she desired), and even William Scot, her former traitorous paramour. Her feelings for them were doomed from the outset. Why she chose such complex, difficult, unreachable males, men who never appreciated her, I struggled to understand. Gabriel's image chose that moment to flash into my mind. I quickly pushed him aside. Though Aphra wrote about love and relationships with a jaundiced eye, she also possessed a heart filled with hope and, I knew, longing.

It was while I was contemplating men, women, the desires that haunt us, the wants that drive us, and the love we consistently search for, that not entirely unexpected news reached me.

SCENE SIX

'Tis a harder task to leap from a Lord to a Rogue, than 'tis from a Rogue to a Lord.

The False Count or, A New Way to Play an Old Game, Aphra Behn

I was in the Tiring Rooms when a couple of goldsmiths who'd joined us began discussing a wedding they'd blundered upon a few months earlier. They were waiting to take Grace Savage and Lily Palmer to a ball at their Guildhall. One of the gentlemen was quite rotund and dressed in a brocade jacket with beribboned breeches (a ridiculous fashion all the rage in London a few years earlier). The other was very lean, and possessed of one bright green eye, and one brown. He was wearing a periwig that looked as if moths had taken up residence. While they waited for the women to change, they drained glasses of canary.

Sat nearby, I was busy removing my make-up and thinking how well the performance had gone. The company had staged a spectacle: Thomas Shadwell's comedy *The Lancashire Witches and Tegue O'Divelly, The Irish Priest*. Even before the play was produced, it was causing controversy. Shadwell and Dryden, friends for a season and even collaborators, had publicly fallen out and were now using their work to mock and deride each other. The cast were trying to guess which character was meant to be Dryden — most of us bet on Father Tegue, a fool and rogue at best who led a coven of witches. No expense had been spared to mount the production: special machines had been built to help the witches fly across the stage, while trapdoors were enlarged to ensure they could sink out of sight when required. There was also a great deal of dancing and music.

Then, at our second rehearsal, Mr Betterton recast me from a soldier to a witch — with lines, songs and dances. When I tried to protest, he wouldn't hear it. Nor would Lady Mary, or any of the shareholders. They were deaf to me.

Mrs Betterton ignored my protests. 'You dance very well, my dear.' That stopped my objections. No-one had *ever* said that to me. 'And in this role, your height is a boon. The witches are powerful women. Enjoy.'

When I tried to argue surely witches didn't dance, as it would detract from their serious intent, it was Elizabeth Barry who looked at me with steely eyes and said, 'They danced in the Scottish play and, if it's good enough for that, then it's bloody well good enough for Mr Shadwell *and* you.'

It would also add to the comedy. The other witches were shorter than the King's spaniels. When I was part of the coven, I stood out like a lone mast on a raft. That was the point. Between acts, the witches moved around the stage with 'crouched bodies' and performed 'droll jumps'. I didn't like it, but it did mean extra coin.

Of late, I'd managed to earn a little bit through writing. After the Accession Day procession the previous November — which was meant to commemorate and celebrate when Queen Elizabeth took the throne and thus the country officially became Protestant, but had turned into little more than an anti-Catholic demonstration — I'd written about what I'd witnessed, laying bare my horror at the violence. Not only the burning of effigies of the Pope and Sir Roger L'Estrange (because of all the negative reports he'd written about Titus Oates), but between spectators and towards those unable to defend themselves; some even went hunting for victims. I made mention of the horrific immolation of live cats. I posited the question, *Shouldn't those ready to blame Catholics and aliens for ills whether real or imagined at least uphold a higher standard? How is burning live creatures and setting upon innocents any less horrid or barbaric than the unproven crimes of which many are accused?* While the words of *One of the Fair Sex* didn't set the town ablaze, or have me brought before his Majesty, they did generate discussion.

The day after the report appeared in the news-sheet *The Daily Courante*, I heard it being discussed in the Tiring Rooms, where Mr Sandford, Mr Harris and Jacob were debating the main points. That evening, the lodgers were still talking about it, saying it had been all anyone spoke of in Will's Coffee-House and among the stallholders at St Paul's. Aphra and I exchanged a somewhat smug smile.

Of course, the following day, it was yesterday's news and thus forgotten.

With the success of Shadwell's anti-Catholic play and my newfound confidence with the quill and on stage — even as an all-dancing, all-singing witch (both done badly — despite what Mrs Betterton said — and drawing much laughter) — it was easy to keep my ears peeled for news. With the playhouse full each of the six nights and the shareholders keen to run a seventh, the Tiring Rooms were cramped as members of the audience flocked to congratulate the cast and set up assignations with the actresses who'd been absent over the long, hot summer. Some men even attempted to flirt with me. I tolerated it awhile, until they lost interest. But what these men did do was gossip. My ears rang like clarions, my mind droned like summer bees and my fingers were like — well, itchy fingers.

Preoccupied with something I'd heard about Lord Grey, I hadn't paid too much attention to the goldsmiths until 'Chartham' was mentioned. It's not every day you hear your small parish come up in conversation. I thought at first I misheard and what they said was *Chatham*, the royal dockyard on the Medway. But when the men said how beautiful the bride was for someone not in the bloom of youth, and how her husband, a plain man of much greater age, should consider himself lucky to call such a vision wife, my blood first froze then began to burn.

I was about to ask for more information, not caring it would reveal I was ear-wigging, when the portly man continued.

'She was the vicar's daughter. Johnson, wasn't it, Hilary?' He turned to his friend.

'Yes. Yes,' said Hilary with the parti-coloured eyes. 'Something like that. From what we could glean, the vicar was glad to have her off his hands. I would have taken her off his hands and placed her straight on my rump-splitter.' He grabbed his groin and the men laughed uproariously.

Mr Harris looked directly at me. Like most of the company, he knew I'd come from Chartham and my father was the vicar. Thankfully, he didn't point out the connection to the rump-splitter and his parti-eyed friend. Quietly as I could, I finished removing my make-up and, having already changed out of costume, left the theatre.

'So,' said Aphra later that night when I told her what I'd overheard. She was tucked at her desk in the bedroom. 'Bethan is married.' She spun a wine glass glumly before draining the contents. If I didn't know better, I'd swear she was wounded by my sister's news as well.

'Aye,' I said, slumping onto the bed. 'Again. To another awful man — one who tried to bargain with Papa so he could marry me in her stead. I don't understand why she wed him … and after all this time.'

'Because, like most women, she'd no choice. Marriage is the only option if a woman wants social currency.'

'*You're* not married,' I pointed out.

'Ah, but I was. The best thing Johannes did for me was die, God rest his soul,' said Aphra. 'Oh, don't look so shocked. If nothing else, widowhood confers the freedom to make my own choices; I have relative independence, which at least reduces the constant pressure.'

'Pressure?'

'To snare a husband.'

Bethan had been a widow and she hadn't been pressured, not really. Not until Sir M appeared. If I'd remained at home, I too would have felt that pressure. Now, I'd ruined any chance of marriage by damaging my reputation inveterately. It didn't matter I rejected would-be lovers: I was an actress and thus a woman who'd fallen so far no ordinary man could resurrect me. That would require a bona fide miracle.

I fell back on the bed, arms stretched above my head, and stared at the ceiling. Blackened from years of hearth fires, it was like a glowering thundercloud, softened only by the radiance of the lanthorn and candles. A part of me always imagined I'd marry. One day. Bear children, have a household for which I was responsible. Mayhap, I would. I used to imagine the type of man I'd wed (taller, kind, thoughtful, someone who enjoyed reading and talking, oh, and listening — to me). Wealth was not a consideration, though I didn't want to be a pauper either.

Bethan, well, she'd not only married a man of means this time but been handed a title: Lady Marmaduke Babcock. Bile rose before an image of her long, dark hair, chestnut eyes and cherry mouth made it recede. Upon her head she wore a sparkling coronet, while a golden gown fell from her plump shoulders. I wondered if she was content? I prayed so.

Regardless, neither Papa nor Bethan had done the courtesy of informing me about her nuptials. I was indeed *persona non grata*. I was neither daughter, nor sister. I was barely a legitimate woman any more. What was I?

Aphra put down her drink and came and joined me on the bed. I sat up reluctantly and she wrapped an arm about my shoulders. 'That's not all that's upset you, is it?'

My head sank onto her breast. 'Ignore me, cousin. I'm indulging in some self-pity, wondering what I am now I truly have no family.'

'You have me,' she murmured against my hair.

I couldn't speak.

'Anyway, you're more than just a daughter or sister, dearling.'

'What am I then?'

'A woman of many parts.'

I made a choking noise. 'I was just thinking I'm hardly even a woman …' I pulled away slightly. 'I mean, look at how the men —'

Aphra put her fingers against my lips. 'If you judge your womanhood by the way men — especially those fops who frequent the Tiring Rooms — regard us, then you'll only find a very narrow definition of what we are, what we ever can be.' She ushered me back into her embrace. 'You're many things, Tribulation. Look at what you've experienced, what you've accomplished since you've been here, despite huge hurdles and gross objections — and not only from me.' She grinned. 'Why, you've trod the boards — and still do, more capably than ever. You bring my words, the words of other writers, to life and give pleasure to audiences. Despite what others say, it's a worthy occupation, for, mark my words, Tribulation, one day women will own the stage and without the baggage of narrow assumptions they currently carry. You are, like Elizabeth, Charlotte, the Marys, blazing a trail. And that's not all: you write as well.'

'Not as well as I'd like. And anonymously …' I was determined to be a martyr and loll in misery a little longer.

Aphra simply laughed. 'Of course! But you're improving — look at your recent success — and we've discussed over and over why you cannot lay claim to your words.'

'But —' I sniffed, banishing the looming tears '— what about when I can no longer perform or write? What then? All I've done is guarantee no man will want me for wife.'

Aphra sighed. 'Only a man who's not worthy of being your husband. If you wish to marry, then of course you'll find someone. One day. But is that what you want? To surrender your name, your body and, unless he's a rare kind of man, your mind?'

Her breast was so soft, and she smelled of lavender, candle smoke and rosewater. Part of me found the idea of surrendering myself attractive. The other wanted to resist it with every fibre of my being. Is this how Aphra felt?

'I know I don't want to be a poor spinster, reliant on the parish for everything. Invisible.'

Aphra made a noise deep in her throat. 'Listen to me very carefully, Tribulation. For as long as I breathe, for as long as I can use a quill — for as long as *you* can — you'll never be invisible. You'll always have a place, do you understand? I *am* your family. Push thoughts of marriage away for now. You've plenty of time before you need to sacrifice yourself on that altar.'

Suddenly, I was a virgin of old, garbed in white with a shimmering breastplate, draped across a great stone, a large, curved knife hovering over my heart.

'In the meantime, you can indulge in self-pity at least until … let me see …' she twisted around to look at the clock on her dresser '… nine of the clock. Then, you are to cease.'

Five more minutes. I didn't need that long. I unfurled, using my sleeve to dab my eyes. I sighed. 'I feel a little silly now.'

'Don't,' she said, looking at me with such a kind expression it almost started me off again. 'It's understandable you would think upon such things in light of the news about Bethan.'

'What most upsets me is I had to learn of it by accident.' My chest grew tight. 'I held out hope, you know — that somehow I'd be forgiven: reinstated as a daughter and sister. 'Twas a false hope.'

Aphra rose and poured us both a glass of wine. 'Has it occurred to you maybe your father is preventing Bethan from communicating with you?' She passed me a glass and sat back down. 'I would hazard a guess that not only are her letters never being posted, yours aren't reaching the recipient either.'

My heart skipped. I hadn't thought of that.

'Why don't you try and write again? If she's indeed married, then she's mistress of her own household. Mail will go to the manor. Your papa can hardly intervene there, can he?'

'You don't know Papa,' I said, but with a smile. All of a sudden, there it was again. Hope. I stood up. 'I *will* write. Right now.' I rose. 'Thank you.' I kissed the top of her head.

'You, kitten, are always welcome.' With a groan and slow unfolding, she stood and plodded back to her desk. Her hips had been giving her trouble again — all her joints, really. On occasion, her hands would swell, and her knuckles were developing ridges and lumps, misshaping her fingers, making it increasingly difficult for her to write. I paused in the doorway as she lowered herself into the chair, adjusting the cushion. I would talk to the local apothecary, Mr Franks, about making another unguent she could rub into her aching hands and thighs.

When I reached my room, I lit a few candles, drew the curtains and found a fresh sheet of paper. Fuelled by Aphra's words, I put aside my sadness and began to write. I congratulated Bethan and expressed hope that (even though she'd married an old louche who spat like a London docker and burped like a drayman) she'd find contentment. Nay, happiness.

Clearly my time helping Gabriel made me the best of dissemblers.

I returned to Aphra's room a short time later to show her what I'd composed. It was becoming quite the habit. Turns out, she'd also scribed something.

'Of you go, get some rest,' she said, giving me a slap on the arse. 'You can take them to the mail office before theatre tomorrow.'

At the door, I stopped to admire the picture she made as she picked up a sheet filled with writing. 'Thank you, Aphra.'

'What for?' She laid the page down and began to sharpen her quill.

'For everything. Sorry I interrupted.'

She gave that long, slow smile of hers. 'I'm not.'

As I closed the door, I somehow knew she wasn't just referring to tonight.

SCENE SEVEN

For Thou hast made a very fiend of me, and I have hell within.

Love-Letters, Aphra Behn

A month later, there was still no word from Bethan. There were even days I forgot I was yearning, praying for an answer. When a piece I'd written was accepted and then published, not in the *London Gazette* as I'd initially hoped, but as a separate tract, and distributed widely throughout the city, being sold on street corners, read aloud by criers and Mercury Women, all thoughts of Chartham were pushed from my head.

It had been inspired by the shambles that was the Oxford Parliament, the Earl of Shaftesbury's arrest and the ongoing machinations of his supporters — mostly the Green Ribbon Club. This was a group of like-minded men, Whigs, who not only supported Titus Oates, but were also known for their vociferous anti-Catholic leanings. They wore green bows or ribbons on their hats and were readily identifiable — even where and when they met was generally known. It was hard to reconcile the notion they were heavily involved in conspiracies and even sedition with their apparent openness. Perhaps that's what made them so dangerous: they simply didn't care. I'd penned a delightfully contentious piece (Aphra's opinion) questioning, among other notions, what exactly made a person a dissenter or for that matter loyal?

For a few days, there was talk of little else but the anonymous author who wrote *Intolerant Toleration or, May God Forgive Bigotry Unleashed.* While a few tut-tutted over the contents and the cowardly author who declined to put his name to it, there were many who agreed. It was all I could do not to preen in their presence. Some felt the King had been a fool to call for an acceptance of all faiths when he ascended to the throne — an impossible proposition in the first place (which was not the point of my argument, but one couldn't help how it was interpreted) — while others understood the piece was a stern rebuke of anyone who used the Popish Plot or any other scheme as an excuse to attack those weaker or less able to defend themselves. I was especially critical of those conspiracies real and imagined being used to stoke old fears and make enemies out of those who worshipped differently.

When I saw copies in the Tiring Room and the Mercury Women still selling it days later, I raced home to tell Aphra. The effect these words had on people, how they took them to heart and quoted them to each other, astounded me. How some were so furious, they almost tore the tract asunder. I couldn't decide which was better. My heart sang as words *I'd* penned echoed around me, repeated by familiar and strange mouths. It was a heady, addictive sensation and I relished it. Did all writers feel this way? Did Aphra? No wonder she didn't allow the spiteful observations of her foes to stop her. No wonder the men wanted to keep this thrill for themselves. The power it bestowed was dizzying.

Aphra urged me to use this triumph to write more, not rest on my laurels. I wanted to keep writing, but found I was almost crippled by the wondrous reception. I'd wanted to make an impact, have my words mean something. At last, they did. Yet, here I was, afraid anything I wrote from now on would pale by comparison.

When I didn't show Aphra anything new three nights in a row, she sought me out.

It was ten of the clock and I'd been sitting at my desk for over two hours without producing a single word. That's not quite true. I'd produced many only to strike them out and start again. Over and over.

'Ah … the muses have forsaken you.' Aphra used her hip to force me to create room.

Conscious my desk was even untidier than hers, I went to stack the news-sheets and pamphlets, but she stopped me. 'Leave them. Talk to me. What's wrong?'

I tried to explain how my brief success made me even more frightened of failing: that I was struggling to find a subject to write about that might be as well received as my last. Even as I spoke, it felt churlish, admitting this to her.

'Oh, kitten.' Aphra gave the gentlest of smiles. 'What you describe happens to all writers.'

It was the first time she'd included me as a member of the profession. My ribcage swelled, a little spark flickering to life within.

'We seek to be published, read and, frankly, appreciated. Not for ourselves so much — though there are those who pursue adulation.'

She was thinking of Rochester and the other Wits who composed to much fanfare — Buckingham, Sedley and the like.

'Rather, we wish to be appreciated for our minds, our imaginations, the tales we weave too. It means people value them, take them to heart, circulate and discuss our stories and ideas, that in turn makes what we do meaningful, important, because it lives beyond the page, beyond us. For that, we're oft loved. But it also means we risk censure, mockery and denigration for exactly the same thing. A hard-won reputation, a catalogue of wonder, can be scuttled with one blow — and not just those levelled by the critics.'

The pain in her voice was acute. She brushed a hand over my book of John Donne. I reached over and clasped hers in mine. She gripped my fingers then released them.

'If you truly want to be a writer, to have your words published, then you must put these worries aside or, at least, not allow them to inhibit you.'

I made a disparaging noise.

'Oh, it's not easy, I know.' She gave a bitter laugh, then inhaled and released the breath slowly. 'To compare our work – with that done by others, to their successes and our own – and despair, is a writer's lot. The men's too. And it can be utterly debilitating.' She twisted on the chair until she faced me. One arm ran along the back, the other rested on the desk. I felt embraced, held, as if the confidences we were sharing were a barrier between us and the rest of the world.

'But, kitten,' said Aphra, leaning over until our noses touched. 'If I've learned anything over the years it's this: each work should be a singular objective. Don't look back, don't look forward. Focus on now.' A finger alighted on the blank page before me. 'If I allowed everything that was said about me to dictate what I write, I would never pick up the quill. I write because I've no choice — not just to keep a roof over my head, and sustenance in my belly, but because something in here —' she thumped her breast '— doesn't allow me to stop.' She touched the place over my heart. 'I know you're the same.'

I nodded, hardly daring to breathe.

She took away her hand and rummaged through items on the desk. Finding a quill, she began to sharpen it vigorously. 'My advice to you, is cease thinking about the outcome.' She pushed the quill into my hand and rose. 'And just write.'

I dwelled upon Aphra's words for days, using them to inspire me, moving betwixt my play and more serious pieces — first about the Quakers being given land in Pennsylvania, then the Duke of York and what exile means for someone, not only those of royal blood. I even wrote about the importance of penning letters. Of how the written word can bridge more than physical distance. My anguish over Bethan didn't go to waste.

I was pondering this weeks later, during the performance of Aphra's latest play, *The False Count*. By now, another Accession parade had been and gone, yet another Pope-burning exercise that, like the year before, saw an effigy of Sir Roger burned beside his Holiness. Maybe that's why Aphra's play was a terrible flop — that and its very 'Whiggism', as Mr Shale, the lily-livered, (not so) Anonymous Critic declared. Aye. I'd recently learned the Anonymous Critic who often reviewed plays and enjoyed excoriating Aphra, who'd named me so cruelly in reviews, was none other than our neighbour — Timothy Shale. He didn't hold back about *The False Count* either. The almost empty pits, the half-full stalls. The only thing he failed to mention was that the audience talked so loudly throughout, lines were drowned and songs barely heard.

'Dear God,' said John Downes, as the second performance drew to a close. 'I don't know whether this is worth running a third night.'

My heart sank. No third night, no Author's Benefit.

I peeked into the auditorium, at the scant few who were easy to see in the glow from the footlights and chandeliers. The Earl of Shaftesbury, who, inexplicably forgiven by our tolerant liege and a jury of Whig sympathisers, had only just been released from the Tower, sat in his usual box. Next to him was Lord Grey. He'd taken a fancy to Grace, much to the delight of her brother, who believed she'd snared herself one of the gentry. This was partly because Sir Charles Slingsby had recently proposed to Mary Lee, and her husband dead only a few months. Thus the hopes of the other actresses were raised as they imagined their lustful dalliances translating into something more honourable. More permanent. Mrs Lee only agreed to marry Sir Charles on the proviso she could continue to tread the boards. Much to everyone's astonishment, he agreed. Not many men would be so accommodating. Beside Shaftesbury and Grey were men I'd grown used to seeing about the theatre and town — Robert Ferguson and Lord Algernon Sidney. Sat with them this evening was a gentleman I'd never seen before. Square-shouldered, with a chiselled jaw, he wore a grey periwig and a suit cut in the continental style.

'Who's that?' I asked John, who knew everyone worth knowing and many who weren't.

John followed the direction of my finger. On stage, the final act had commenced. It was set in a garden, and many of the characters were required on stage as a great dance took place. I really needed to make an entry.

'The man on the end? That's … oh, what's his name? An associate of Lord Grey's. A salter, originally from outside London somewhere. Josiah Keating? Keeling? A Baptist.' He pulled a face.

I didn't have time to probe further as my cue came.

I couldn't help glance in the stranger's direction as I skipped on stage, wondering at this man who'd come to see a play few felt had any merit, grateful he filled an otherwise empty seat.

SCENE EIGHT

I value not the censures of the crowd.

The Lucky Chance or, The Alderman's Bargain, Aphra Behn

Lady Mary left it to Mr Betterton to deliver the bad news. *The False Count* was being cancelled. Attendance was pitiful, a quick head count of the audience revealing there were more people on stage than in the auditorium. My thoughts flew to Aphra. Perhaps knowing her play was to be abandoned, she'd remained at home.

Depressed chatter rose and fell, some taking it in their stride (it wasn't the first show to end peremptorily), others confused and bitter. Discussions about roles in the next production had already commenced. Hugs were exchanged, sympathetic looks. It was always a blow when a play fizzled. Some didn't make it to the second night and, while it would be easy to blame the playwright, everyone accepted a degree of responsibility. There would be a detailed examination of the whys and wherefores of what went wrong: script, performances, the music, settings. In the meantime, the show would go on — tomorrow we'd be staging Dryden's *The Kind Keeper*.

I only half-listened as I contemplated how to tell Aphra (bluntness was best), when who should join us but the newly released Earl of

Shaftesbury and his entourage. They burst into the Tiring Rooms in a froth of lace, chortles and heady scent.

'What news?' Shaftesbury cried from the doorway.

Charlotte elicited a quiet groan. 'Can't they leave us in peace? Must they gloat?'

The men fell into empty seats or wandered about pounding backs, reaching down for kisses which we reluctantly provided. We couldn't afford to offend anyone this night. Footmen and servants trailed after them, tasked with pouring wine, lighting pipes and tending to their needs. The expressions on Shaftesbury's and Lord Grey's faces proved Charlotte's assessment correct — they were here to enjoy our misery — and not only because a play regarded as openly anti-Whig and performed by a company with a royal Catholic patron had failed to attract audiences.

'Where's the author? The wretched scold herself?' asked the Earl, craning his neck in an exaggerated fashion. 'I want to commiserate.'

And the devil desires a halo.

Samuel Sandford made a show of lifting various items on his dresser and peering beneath them. 'Not here, milord,' he said, eliciting chuckles.

'Well, where *is* the dulcet doxy?'

I knew damn well where she was but wasn't going to reveal her whereabouts.

I hunched on the stool, using the mirror as a barrier so the Earl wouldn't spot me. It was a squeeze in the room and, despite the bitter weather outside, rapidly becoming warm. Tobacco smoke began to insinuate itself about the place. More wine was poured, glasses being offered to the players. I declined. I needed a clear head. A couple of merchants appeared in the doorway, one carrying a beribboned box, but upon seeing who else was scattered among us, they made themselves scarce.

I pulled off the periwig that was part of my costume, rearranging it on the stand upon my dresser, and began to wipe the oily paint off my face, trying to suppress a cough. Out of the corner of my eye, I could see Lord Grey, who'd rushed straight to Grace's side, showering her with kisses, eager to undo her gown and assist with her toilet. With pink cheeks owing nothing to make-up, she stared at him the way the King's hounds did their master. She was well and truly moon-struck. I only hoped the rumours about Lord Grey proved unfounded or we'd have another broken-hearted actress to repair.

Hovering nearby, listening to the Scottish vicar and Mr Betterton, was the man I'd seen in the box earlier. What was his name again?

Long-limbed, he would have been able to look Gabriel in the eye. His face was shadowed by his large-brimmed hat and the dreadful periwig he sported, which sat low on his brow (or maybe the hat pushed it down). There was an impression of strong features and, when he briefly raised his head, this was confirmed. He was older than I'd first assumed, possessed of jowls and pouched eyes, but quite handsome nonetheless.

Then, he smiled — straight at me. I was taken aback. Just as I'd been studying him, he'd been examining me. I looked away, but not before I saw him nudge the Earl.

Shaftesbury's clipped voice rang out. 'Ah. Yes. That's her. Mrs Johnson. Aphra Behn's cousin.'

Before I could reply or disappear through a doorway, the man approached.

'Good evening.' The stranger swept off his hat and, in a tight area, managed to execute a neat bow. 'My name is Josiah Keeling. You're Mrs Tribulation Johnson.'

The Baptist salt man. Eyes that reflected the light of the candles so brightly they appeared to flame, briefly met mine in the mirror. The voice was a pleasing mix of accents, as if the world had been condensed into this man's pipes.

I twisted and would have stood and curtseyed, but he filled the space. Instead, I bobbed my head. 'I am, sir. Do you know my cousin, perchance?'

At that moment, the musicians entered the Tiring Room, all exclamations and disappointment. The volume increased and, though Mr Keeling spoke, I couldn't hear him. I cupped an ear and shrugged.

He replaced his hat and sank onto his haunches beside me. 'I said, that's a Kentish accent, is it not?'

'It is indeed, good sir. But you have the advantage for yours is difficult to discern. May I enquire as to its origin?'

Mr Keeling's smile broadened, and his arm described an arc — or would have except it caught Charlotte on the side of the head. She'd been leaning forwards, trying to gain an introduction.

Mr Keeling abruptly withdrew his arm and stood. 'Madam,' he said to Charlotte, grabbing her hand and bestowing a kiss upon it. 'Forgive me.'

Charlotte rubbed the side of her head and fluttered her eyelashes. She was incorrigible. 'All is forgiven, or would be over supper, sir.'

'Supper? Pity, I already have a commitment. Another time, perhaps?'

Before she could respond, he turned back to me.

'In answer to your question, Mrs Johnson,' he continued, unaware of Charlotte who, with an exaggerated puff, folded her arms and started to have a pointed conversation about the rudeness of foreigners with Juliet, who was tending to Lady Mary Slingsby the other side. 'My accent is a result of treading the stage of the world, Mrs Johnson, the stage of the world.'

I didn't think this man was entirely foreign; in fact, there was something vaguely familiar about him, only I couldn't work out what it was. He kept averting his face, nonplussed by the activity around us.

'Do you know my cousin, sir?' I repeated, turning back to the mirror and seeing I'd missed a patch of make-up. My cheeks began to redden. I grabbed the cloth and rubbed.

'I feel I do … from her plays,' said Mr Keeling. 'They're very … edifying.'

If that was his opinion of *The False Count*, he'd be the exception.

'You've seen a few?' I glanced at him. The brim of his hat cast a shadow over his face, masking the upper half and making his expression difficult to read.

'Only the latest. I've been abroad, thus not had the opportunity. The others I've read and imagined.'

I nodded. 'Well, sir I hope you won't judge my cousin's considerable talents on the reception of this one. Most of her plays have an excellent run. It's just there are too many distractions in London at present —'

I jerked my chin towards the window '— for people to find the usual solace from our entertainment.'

'Indeed. The chattering classes are currently most bothered. But is it because they fear a Catholic plot or a Catholic King?'

That was blunt. Surely he didn't expect a response. Questions like that let alone answers had landed better people in prison. I wondered why he would say such an unguarded, irresponsible thing.

He laughed and rested a long-fingered hand on my shoulder. I froze, keeping my eyes downcast. Desperate to alter the tenor of our conversation, to have him lift his hand but not daring to appear churlish, I was about to ask if he would be coming to see our next production when he removed his fingers. 'It's been a pleasure, Mrs Johnson,' he said with a small bow. 'I'll look forward to seeing you perform again and to your cousin's next effort. I pray it enjoys a decent run.'

Charlotte rose, pulling a face at Mr Keeling (who didn't see it), pointing in the direction of the tavern. I quickly found my feet and dropped a curtsey. By the time I straightened, the Earl of Shaftesbury had joined us.

'Nothing like her cousin, eh?' With barely a glance in my direction, he led Mr Keeling away.

I sank back down. What a peculiar interaction.

The men didn't linger. After a brief discussion with Mr Betterton and Mr Harris and an invitation to join them at a nearby coffee-house, the Earl and his friends departed, servants swiftly packing away the goblets and stoppering half-drunk wine.

Only as I was walking home did I recall the Earl's question to Mr Keeling. Why would he ask for confirmation I was nothing like Aphra if the salt man only knew of her through her plays?

SCENE NINE

In an Age when Faction rages, and different parties disagree in all things …

Dedication to *The Roundheads or, The Good Old Cause*, Aphra Behn

Though I fully expected Aphra to be crestfallen when I told her the play had been cancelled, ever contrary, she simply shrugged, asked how the cast fared, and then over the following weeks, worked hard to complete her next one.

'Sometimes, Tribulation,' she began, between bites of buttered manchet, 'failure can drive you to succeed, even if it's just so as not to feel the agony of defeat again.'

I also told her about the Earl's visit and my introduction to his new friend, Mr Keeling. 'Do you know him? He said he was familiar with your work.'

'A Baptist salt man? I think I'd remember if I'd met someone like that. Peculiar accent? If you see him again, you must point him out. Sounds like a welcome addition to the usual reprobates the Earl comports with, especially if he likes my work.' She grinned and turned back to her desk.

He hadn't said whether he liked her work or not, but I didn't correct her.

Encouraged by Aphra's energy, her determination not to be felled by bad news, I spent every spare moment trying to finish a draft of my play and some other pieces for publication, including one on what it was like to be rejected. I knew that particular pain first-hand, and not only due to what happened to Aphra or because much of my writing hadn't found a home.

Reduced income from lack of Author's Benefit and my own poor wage was compounded when our landlord, a merchant who traded in spices and bolts of cloth, announced he was going to raise the lease in the new year. The other lodgers moaned for a day or two and then promptly forgot — they had steady work, a set amount they could rely on each week. They didn't do the kind of piecemeal stuff Aphra and I were compelled to do. I could see why Aphra oft referred to it as 'working for bread'. We literally worked to earn enough so we didn't starve.

Or freeze.

December announced itself with a clamour of storms and icy blasts that pierced our coats like swords a Saracen's chest. Not a night went by when we didn't shiver ourselves to sleep. Not for the first time, Nest was invited to share Aphra's bed. I even thought about joining them under the covers.

What finally made us concede we needed cheaper lodgings was when Aphra was forced to ask Mr Hoyle for a loan to buy our share of coal to heat the house. According to Nest, it wasn't the first time the man had extended financial help. Invited to dinner, when he saw not only the simple and cheap fare provided and the threadbare state of the coat worn by Aphra, a woman who took pride in her appearance, he arrived unexpectedly two days later with fur-lined cloaks and gloves, not just for Aphra but for me and even a second-hand one for Nest as well. Astonished by his generosity, and softened a little by what Nest revealed, I was forced to reconsider all the negative thoughts I'd had.

When I tried to thank him, stroking the grey rabbit fur lining the lovely navy-blue mantle, he held up a hand to stop me.

'I can't have Aphra looking like a pauper in my company. Nor you in hers.'

Dumbfounded he could turn such an act of generosity into something so selfish, before I could think of how to respond he insisted Aphra join him for dinner. Not before she and I traded a perplexed look, one which, when I closed the door on them, keeping the frigid winds and sleet at bay, Nest also wore.

'That man is an enigma,' she muttered, shaking her head, and returning to the warmth of the kitchen. 'An enigma wrapped in coaldust. I'll never understand him.'

I mounted the stairs, determined to keep working. Aye, Mr Hoyle was a mystery — one I'd no inclination to solve — but as I sat in my chilly room, my new cloak draped over my shoulders, I was grateful to him.

Despite Mr Hoyle's beneficence (or as Nest murmured, because of it) the Sunday just before Christmas, after Nest and I attended service at St Bridget's, Aphra met us outside. Together, we forged our way through the snow-bound streets to Mr Jacob Tonson's shop in Newe Street.

Newe Street, though the other side of Fleet Street, was still part of Farringdon Ward Without. Draped in our fine cloaks and with fingers ensconced warmly in our new gloves, we crossed the busy thoroughfare and entered Shoe Lane, passing any number of shops (most closed for trade, though a few admitted customers discreetly). There were stationers, mercers, cordwainers, chandlers and scriveners as well as lawyers and the usual sprinkling of ale-houses, ordinaries and taverns. A few braved the streets, most returning from church.

Above us, clouds formed fantastical shapes, as if a heavenly army of grey and silver dragons and horned badgers were blessing our enterprise. Even as I looked, they broke apart and departed, off to fight other, more important battles.

Bells tolled mournfully as we passed Gunpowder Alley and headed towards Newe Street. Its name belied its condition. Three- and four-storey houses and shops in various states of dilapidation, mould and soot marking the exteriors, lined either side of a road awash with filthy snow and mud. Nothing was said between us, just a stiffening of shoulders, a sniff of the air and tighter gripping of each other's arms that had little to do with the icy wind and everything to do with shoring up confidence.

As we turned into the street, broken windows and untidy stoops awash with charcoal-stained melt met our gaze. A cart with a damaged axle blocked passage partway down. Whereas I first thought men had surrounded the contraption to repair it, the closer we drew the more evident it was they were stealing parts. Children observed from grimy windows, one licking the glass, while others, their clothes patched and outgrown, dashed about in the snow, their thin wrists and gaunt faces feverish as they pelted each other with snowballs or chased barking dogs. The smell of burned food and tobacco lingered. I could only imagine the stench that would wrap its thick arms about the place come summer.

The further we went, the lower my heart sank.

Three-quarters of the way, we turned into a wider lane and Aphra stopped. 'That's Jacob's shop there.' She pointed at the shingle swinging in the freezing wind that slapped our cloaks, threatening to tear them from our shoulders. 'The house is just around the corner. According to Jacob, it's next door to the sign of the Dragon's Heart.'

'We're going to be living next to an ale-house?' asked Nest despondently. 'Why, there's another over there too. There goes me slumber.'

Aphra pursed her lips. 'Please, Nest. We've no choice.' She led us into a surprisingly neat little courtyard filled with grey light. In its centre was a thick-trunked oak with gnarled branches shaped like antlers, overhanging a worn wooden bench.

Directly across from where we entered was the Dragon's Heart: a two-storey affair with casement windows and bright paint on its stoop. The door was wide open, strains of music and conversation carrying out to where we stood. Comfortably sat beside it was a three-storey house made of brick and wood. Dormer windows dominated the top floor and large curtained ones those lower. Smoke billowed out of the chimneys, disappearing into the firmament. For a moment, my spirits rose. Then my eyes alighted on the house on the other side.

With four storeys, the lower two of which groaned under the weight of the upper ones, making the entire building look like a collapsed loaf, the house was in a terrible state of disrepair. It had two chimneys, one of which worked like a consumptive louche. Snow was piled against the front door, a marauding force laying siege to the premises. The windows were cloudy with grime, dark as well. I just knew which house was our future abode.

What I wasn't expecting was the warm welcome we received from the owner, Mr Coggin. A mercer, he was short and balding, with a squint in one eye. He was nevertheless a friendly fellow. After he'd kicked much of the snow from the stoop, he ushered us inside, apologising as a great deal of slush drifted into the hallway. Then he escorted us into a cosy and surprisingly clean parlour, took our cloaks and ordered a young boy to fetch bowls of chocolate, shooing us towards the blazing hearth.

'Chase the chill out of your lady bones.'

My lady bones were very grateful.

Mr Coggin was an avid theatregoer, and it turned out the playwright Thomas Shadwell, not one of Aphra's favourite people, already had rooms in the house, as did another gentleman named Thomas Sprat.

'So, while you'd be sharing with two Toms, they keep to themselves … mostly,' assured Mr Coggin.

Other than the lodgers and Mr Coggin, there was his widowed daughter, Clara, who cared for him and served as a housekeeper. The young boy we'd seen and a cook slept in a room beside the kitchen, and an extra maid came in to work during the day. The Coggins lived on the first storey. Mr Shadwell and Sprat had two rooms apiece below the attic. We were to be offered the floor below them, on the second storey. There were four rooms for our use. The main parlour — he gestured around — kitchen and 'little house', which was in the backyard, were shared. The rent was a fraction of what we were paying in Dorset Street. I tried not to gasp when Mr Coggin named the price.

'Before you agree,' he said, rising and holding out his empty bowl. Clara, a smaller version of her father only with hair, dashed forwards to retrieve it, collecting ours on the way. 'Follow me and see if they suit yer purpose. I know you writers like light and heat and though the house is small and don't look like much from the outside, and though 'tis a mite draughty, and sometimes noisy, it has much to like within.'

If the parlour was anything to go by, he wasn't telling falsehoods.

We trudged up a narrow staircase that creaked and protested with every step. No sneaking home late. On the second landing Nest paused, breathing heavily.

When Aphra and I turned to offer aid, she waved us away. 'Stop yer fussing, I be fine.' Something her red face and wheezes belied. Fortunately, we'd reached our destination.

There were two small rooms, one of which was another parlour of sorts, next to a bedroom that also housed a decent-sized table and two chairs. Perfect for Aphra. The other two rooms were considerably smaller again, but both had a bed, table, chair, chest and, best of all, working hearths. It was all dusty and in good need of a clean, but Mr Coggin assured us this would be taken care of before we moved in. 'Clara be a fine mort. Very particular, like her blessed ma was. She'll have these in shape in no time what with Mabel our maid's help. You'll see.' He pivoted, studying the rooms as if he was the one considering a lease. 'So, what yer say?'

Even if what we found hadn't pleased us, we would have said aye. The price was too good to refuse. Though the walk to the theatre would be much longer and colder, and we'd likely shiver worse than wet dogs throughout winter, if I managed to secure some more roles and place my writing, I might even be able to afford the occasional hackney.

We trooped back downstairs and, over another bowl of chocolate (it was very good), came to an agreement. We would move in the New Year.

As we exited the house, abuzz with excitement because reality far exceeded our expectations, and Mr Coggin seemed the nicest of landlords, the ale-house next door had become quite clamorous.

Nest released a long, long sigh.

Snow had started to fall, a slow, gentle spiral alighting on cloaks and hats like a sprite's kiss. I looked skywards, a child again as I tried to catch flakes upon my tongue, a giggle erupting.

Upon seeing what I was up to, Aphra copied. Like childerkin, we twirled, arms outstretched, faces raised to the sky. Nest stood there shaking her head, trying not to smile.

'What if Mr Coggin should see?' she roused. 'He'll think he's letting the rooms to a couple of Bedlam loons.'

We only ceased when a group of men entered the court, doffing their caps. We nodded in return, suddenly formal as we took each other's arms, breasts heaving, cheeks rosy, taking a moment to regain our balance and breath.

'God's good day,' the men murmured, almost slinking over to the ale-house. Amused they were trying not to be seen imbibing on the Lord's Day, I only noticed another gentleman loitering outside when the men were almost upon him. His clothing was so dark, he'd practically blended in with the building. He was peering in our direction.

I raised a hand, but he swiftly turned away and disappeared inside. The other men followed, talking loudly, and the door closed.

'What's wrong?' asked Aphra, trying to lead me away.

'Thought I saw someone I knew.' I glanced over my shoulder.

'Ah,' she exclaimed, filled with enthusiasm now our accommodation dilemma was solved. 'You've truly become a Londoner if you cannot take ten steps without seeing a familiar face. Means there'll always be some bastard who can bear witness to your mistakes and, worse, tell the world. So which prigger did you see?'

'Mr Keeling.'

She looked at me blankly.

'The Baptist salt man,' I said as Nest took my other arm so she didn't slip. 'Remember? The one who was at the play?'

'The one with good taste? Well, if he's in this part of the city and on a Sunday, he's likely up to no good.'

Which was exactly what entered my head. After all, hadn't the man mentioned the two terrible preoccupations of the people? The Popish Plot *and* the succession — which were really about the same thing: Catholics.

As we sauntered back to Dorset Street, stopping to purchase some hot chestnuts, I found myself examining those we passed more closely, looking to see who else I recognised, wondering what they were about.

I *was* becoming a Londoner and, because of my work for Gabriel and Solomon, a suspicious one at that.

SCENE TEN

Beware the fury of a patient man.

Absalom and Achitophel, John Dryden

Across the choppy seas and in another country, an exhausted Gabriel, unaware he was very much on the mind of one Tribulation Johnson, slumped onto a bench in the smoky tavern, pulled his hat from his sweaty head and waited for Solomon to rebuke him. His fingers and toes burned as the rictus of cold holding them in an icy grip began to thaw. He looked down at his cape, which hung sadly from his shoulders to curtain his thighs. Heavy from the snow and sleet, the hem flanked with muck, its wool began to steam as it too felt the benefit a crush of warm bodies and a flaming hearth bestowed. He was like a chimney in need of a sweep, so badly did clouds of vapour rise from his frame. A few men glanced pointedly in his direction, some chuckling, others shooting sympathetic looks, while those closer screwed up their noses and turned away in disgust at the pungent odour. He didn't blame them.

Why Solomon insisted on meeting in this small, crowded establishment in Maastricht, when there were better ones along the Mus River, closer to the docks, he couldn't fathom. Maybe it was something to do with the sweet-cheeked serving wench making eyes at his friend. Still, he had to admit, it would be hard for anyone to overhear them. God's ear bones, it was difficult to hear himself think, the place was so noisy, filled as it was with sailors, dockers, merchants and those seeking to bargain with them.

It was as good a place as any to deliver bad news.

Voices rose and fell, the gruff cadence of the Hollanders jarring against the sing-song tones of the Flemish. It was like an orchestra tuning and some of the instruments were off pitch. He caught strains of French and Italian — that a Frenchman dared showed his face with the siege of the city still fresh in people's minds beggared belief. He listened for English, but no-one spoke it, not in his hearing. Not that the speaking of it should arouse suspicions — it was precisely why he and Solomon weren't out of place, not now hostilities with the Dutch were over … for the time being at least. Merchants from all over used Maastricht's port, their cargo travelling overland from the fortified city to Paris, Calais, Barcelona, Venice, London, Bristol, Dover and numerous major towns.

At the adjacent table a Hollander with huge forearms was breaking apart a haunch of meat, slapping chunks of the hot flesh onto freshly baked bread and passing it to his crew. Gabriel's mouth began to water. He hadn't eaten for what felt like days — nor slept. All he wanted to do was return to their lodgings and crawl into the flea-ridden covers and wait for Morpheus to claim him, carry him to that serene place where elusive traitors were caught, dead wives and babes ceased their haunting and a bewitching curly-haired woman possessed of unusual height stopped taunting. Where a man could just get on with the business of living. He pressed his fingers into his burning eyes.

Since that was but a boy-blind dream, he opted instead to pull Solomon's brimming tankard towards him and drain the last of the amber liquid, swiping his mouth with a greasy sleeve. The Dutch might be swill-bellied cheese-munchers, but by Christ and all the angels they knew how to brew beer.

Catching the attention of Solomon's doxy through the thick smoke, he signalled for another round.

With that irrepressible twinkle in his dark eyes, Solomon finally appraised his friend, recoiling as the smell reached him. 'Jesus's balls in a vice, Gabe. You could have at least changed.'

Gabriel rested his weary head on one hand, his elbow almost slipping under its weight.

'Could have. Didn't.' He lowered his nose to his armpit. 'God, I stink worse than a nightsoilman's apron.'

'I would have said a fisherman's breeches. It's like you've bathed in fish guts,' said Solomon, moving aside so the wench could deposit two brimming tankards on the table. 'Rotten ones.' He pressed coin into her palm. She captured his fingers, holding them a moment too long. He pulled his hand away, shooing her from his side with a brusque gesture. With a pout that would have done the King's mistress proud, she sashayed through the customers, slapping away groping hands, ignoring the lewd comments.

'I was about to order food,' said Gabriel wryly.

'You can eat later. Drink,' grumbled Solomon, lifting his tankard. 'Then tell me what you've learned.' He clinked his vessel against Gabriel's.

Gabriel drank thirstily, released a mighty burp, then stretched his legs beneath the table, wriggling the pins and needles away. 'Turns out, the information we were given back in Rotterdam was wrong. The bastard wasn't on board.'

Solomon sat up straight, all signs of annoyance gone. 'You certain?'

'I don't smell like this because I crawled around a boudoir.' Gabriel sighed and leaned over the table, lowering his voice. 'I hid on the docks while the crew disembarked. When the Moon Cursers had been and gone, I drew closer. Christ, it was colder than a duck's arse. I thought, if Scot's not going to brazenly stride about Maastricht, he must know he's being followed. So, he's either waiting until curfew to slip ashore or he's hiding onboard and sailing with the tide. When the nightwatchmen were distracted by cards, I climbed on board and searched below deck. Not a sign of him. I even searched the hull. Nothing but barrels full of herrings —'

'That explains the smell.'

'— wool, beer and cured leather.' He took another drink. 'By the time I'd finished, dawn had broken. I had to wait for the cover of darkness before I could make my escape. Here I am.'

'You, and your cologne,' said Solomon.

Gabriel ignored him. 'The blaggard Arlington vouched for, the one who told us Scot would be aboard *that* ship, either led us astray —'

'Or was bribed. Most likely by Scot,' finished Solomon.

'I'm inclined to think the latter,' said Gabriel, looking about. 'The man is more slippery than a Thames eel.'

'You think he knew we were on to him?'

'From the beginning. If he wasn't informed before we even left England, then he knew to be wary. He's always been cautious. It's in his blood.' Gabriel massaged the back of his neck. 'It also comes with being a double agent.'

'A bloody traitor, you mean.' Solomon struck the table. 'We saw him, Gabe. With our own bloody eyes. Even the official we … persuaded … eventually revealed Scot was travelling about as an English salt merchant. He was heading to Maastricht and from here to Rhineland.'

Gabriel frowned. 'In retrospect, it was too easy. Too neat. I think that official was bribed as well. Don't forget, in the past, Scot worked for the Dutch. What's more, I think Williamson is right: he still does. He's under the protection of a stadtholder, somewhere. Eluding our reconnaissance was no accident. Sending us off on this fools' errand as well. This was planned and now we've lost not only the man we were sent to find, but weeks.'

The brightness in Solomon's eyes dimmed. 'Fucking weeks.' He threw his hands up. 'He could be anywhere.'

'No, my friend, that's where you're wrong.' Gabriel drank the last of his beer. 'Not anywhere.' He rose, stamping life back into his numb feet. 'I know exactly where he is and it's where we need to be as well.'

Solomon finished his drink, wiping the foam from his top lip. 'Don't tell me. Mother bloody England.'

Gabriel shot him a grin. 'Alright, I won't. You coming?'

'Only if you promise to bathe,' said Solomon, throwing up a hand to prevent him coming closer.

'At least the winter storms have all but abated,' said Gabriel, gesturing for Solomon to lead the way out of the tavern. 'Should be able to find ourselves a Dutch privateer willing to make the crossing.'

'For the right price,' said Solomon, shoving a burly German aside with his shoulder. The man spun, face twisted in a scowl, until he saw who'd bumped him. He held up his palms in mock surrender, smiling and nodding, and created room.

'After I've washed, eaten and slept, we'll go find us one. Someone discreet,' added Gabriel, stepping into the gap. 'We can't announce our homecoming.' There was a flash of regret. 'To anyone.'

'You'll inform Williamson though?' asked Solomon.

Gabriel paused by the door and carefully pinned his cloak. The thought of admitting they'd lost Scot, never mind valuable time, pained him. 'We'll use the old Hanse network. Get word to him. He'll need to get eyes on English ports.'

Scot had avoided capture for now … that was all. Still, the man had a mighty lead. God Himself only knew what he'd manage to do with that, a double agent with contacts in London, treachery in his heart. Yet, what if Tribulation was right and this hazardous journey Scot was undertaking, all because of something Aphra wrote, with all its feints and decoys, the risk to his life, was about paternity? No. There had to be more: Gabriel knew it and his instincts were rarely wrong.

Even so, what did a man do with the knowledge he'd fathered a child? A child who was now a woman. Claim her? Or ignore her? What if, somehow, she imperilled the life he'd created? Gabriel and Solomon had learned Scot had a fine one in Middleburg; assuming a false name and thus past, he'd not only married well, but had children. Did Aphra know about them? Did Tribulation?

What would Scot do to Tribulation if he perceived her as a threat to his existence?

Worse. To whatever else brought him to English shores.

'I'll tell Williamson, if he hasn't already, to put extra eyes on Tribulation and Aphra Behn as well,' said Gabriel as he re-entered the cold moonless night, glancing up at the sable firmament.

'Good idea. Whatever he intends, Scot'll go to them at some point,' said Solomon, confirming what Gabriel believed. 'Mrs Behn's invitation, her insinuation, it's irresistible for someone like him.' Solomon hesitated, then slapped his friend on the back. 'Don't worry, Gabe. She'll be alright.'

Gabriel didn't even bother trying to pretend he didn't know to whom Solomon referred. The man knew him better than he knew himself.

Heads lowered, they hurried down the cobbled street. 'We can take over surveillance once we reach London,' said Solomon. 'Learn what we can about Scot's reasons for reappearing — who else he contacts and why.'

'We can also look to Tribulation and Aphra's safety.'

Solomon made a noise akin to a growl. 'Something big's afoot, Gabriel — why else would Scot dare show his face? Once we discover what it is and who else is involved, we can seize the seditious bastards.'

Gabriel glanced at his friend. What if Tribulation was wrong and Aphra *was* involved? Even unwittingly? Would he arrest her? Could he? Tribulation would never forgive him …

His heart quickened. Ever since Wait-Still and his daughter died, he'd done all he could do avoid thinking about them, his selfish choices. Done all he could to avoid London. There, his demons lay. Accepting ridiculous missions in countries where he scarce knew the language, taking unnecessary risks. Solomon too, even if it was only to ensure his friend didn't come to harm. When Williamson ordered him back to London, he'd made every excuse to refuse the commission. Now, all he could think about was returning. Maybe this time he could lay the past to rest, reconcile his guilt and protect the woman he'd come to care about.

Dark curls framing a pair of bright turquoise eyes swam in his vision.

How stricken she'd appeared when he told her he was leaving; how valiantly she tried to pretend an indifference he was certain she didn't feel. He'd wrestled with his longing to … what? Sweep her up in his arms? Make promises he didn't know he wished to until they formed in his head? What if she'd resisted? What if he was wrong and had misread her completely? What if he was gulling himself and she was the best of actresses? The thought made him smile. She'd improved, but she wasn't *that* good.

Nevertheless, Tribulation Johnson had done the impossible and caulked a hole in his damaged heart.

In a most uncharacteristic gesture, he sent a swift prayer heavenwards.

He asked God to keep her safe from both Scot and any trouble, knowing even as the unspoken words flew beyond the stars, that when one's name was Tribulation — and he recalled the way she spoke her mind, wrote it, was prepared to do whatever she could to protect those she loved — it was an impossible ask.

ACT FOUR

Spring 1682–Autumn 1682

From Proof to Punishment or, The Crooked Piece of Man

Better to reign in Hell, than serve in Heaven.

John Milton, *Paradise Lost*

Alas! a woman that attempts the pen,
Such an intruder on the rights of men,
Such a presumptuous creature, is esteemed,
The fault can by no vertue be redeemed ...

Anne Finch, Countess of Winchelsea

SCENE ONE

Lord what a house is here, how thin 'tis grown.

From the epilogue to *Like Father, Like Son or, The Mistaken Brothers,* attributed to Aphra Behn but written by her cousin, Mrs Tribulation Johnson

In less than five minutes, my first play, *Like Father, Like Son or, The Mistaken Brothers,* would make its debut. Though I'd co-written *The Revenge* with Aphra, in my mind it was this one, a solo effort, that would enable me, if only secretly, to add 'playwright' to my growing list of (meagre) accomplishments.

My thoughts were gnats, flittering here, alighting there. I could scarce utter a coherent sentence let alone calmly observe patrons entering the auditorium. Instead, I tried to imagine the cast preparing behind the curtain, muttering lines, exercising their vocal cords, tugging and pinning costumes and hair into place, gossiping about those filling the seats.

God in Heaven, please let the players be word perfect. Better still, let the play be a success.

The play was ostensibly about two men vying for leadership over an imaginary realm, and I'd worked hard to ensure no-one could accuse the author of writing libel or being partisan. One couldn't create a tale about a kingship under threat, regardless of inspiration, without being seen as writing about King Charles, his brother, or the succession. But when Lord Arlington passed the script without changes, confidence I'd succeeded in my intentions was renewed.

It was all I could do not to chew my nails as I fidgeted beside Aphra and Nest, waiting for the music to commence. Box office had been paltry all throughout winter, and not just at Dorset Street. The King's Company at Drury Lane was rumoured to be heavily in debt and struggling to draw a crowd. Actors had been let go; contracts weren't being renewed. It was a terrible situation that made everyone at Dorset Garden increasingly nervous. Work was only as reliable as a paying audience.

Already I'd had a setback as, the week before, the King left the city for his annual jaunt to Newmarket in the north-east. The Duke of York, recently returned from exile in Scotland, accompanied his brother. As usual, all the court sycophants and London elite departed too, which meant those we could usually depend upon to fill the theatre were absent.

Perhaps sensing my concern, Aphra reached for my hand. '*Beaucoup de merde*, kitten. If not tonight, then for those that follow. You've done what very few have achieved — put your name to a play.'

'Not exactly,' I whispered.

'You know what I mean,' she said.

Anonymous … thy name is woman.

We smiled cautiously at each other, both smiles laced with inevitability.

As I watched the few folk trickling in, brushing rain off their capes, looking a little windblown, my heart gave a series of strange manoeuvres, as if it had taken to perambulating around my chest. I prayed that, regardless of tonight's numbers, the play would have a decent run. So many failed to go beyond a third night of late — not because they weren't any good, but because the Company couldn't afford to stage a play few came to see.

Still, I hoped those who braved the brisk spring weather enjoyed themselves. It wasn't too much to ask, was it? Regardless, I'd relished learning about all the other aspects of mounting a production. Writers weren't only responsible for the script, including the many songs throughout, but helping cast it as well. I'd never been aware of quite how collaborative the process was. I knew the author could nominate performers to deliver the all-important prologue and epilogue (Charlotte was giving my prologue and Mr Gevan, hired in the new year, was delivering the epilogue), but I'd thought they merely endorsed the major parts. While the chorus and minor speaking roles were generally chosen by the Bettertons, Mr Smith (who'd taken over as a shareholder and manager when Mr Harris left) or even Mr Downes, the writer had huge input into who she thought might best carry a part and could request a particular player for a role or write one that best suited their talents. Their wishes were mostly fulfilled — at least for the first run.

No wonder so many performers turned themselves topsy-turvy to remain on good or better terms with playwrights.

For an entire morning, I'd sat in the pits with Aphra on one side, Lady Mary on the other, paper and quill in hand so I could make notes as players auditioned. Mr and Mrs Betterton and Mr Smith sat behind as John called actors and actresses to the stage and they read lines. My lines! As each performer exited, comments were thick and fast and I listened intently to what the others said.

'She lacks the intensity.'

'His timing is slightly out.'

'That can be adjusted.'

'He's not how I imagined that character.'

'Won't look right next to the servant.'

'Perfect.'

And so on.

Since all of us were regularly in accord, casting had been a relatively easy process. Once in rehearsals, roles were either confirmed or altered, as not only did the performances improve, especially once lines were conned, but sometimes, as was the case with Mr Gevan and Mr Sandford, another performer suited the part better and their roles were exchanged. I also monitored rehearsals and heard what lines and songs, what stage directions worked and didn't, and made modifications. I tried not to adjust the script too much as I'd been privy to how frustrating it was to accommodate repeated alterations (and that was before those made after the first performance) as both actress and book-keeper. It was why thespians generally enjoyed performing plays written by other actors.

'They understand the craft in a way a writer cannot,' offered Elizabeth Barry.

I felt Aphra might beg to differ but took it as a compliment. After all, was I not an actress as well? A very minor one.

What I also noticed was the difference in the way some of the company treated me. As the author, I was bestowed with a certain degree of respectability that saw my stock rise. It would have been humorous, the deference with which I was suddenly treated, the compliments, had it not also been so obvious and reflective of such desperation. In writing a play, I'd assured them of work — something the situation at Drury Lane reminded us all too sharply was precarious.

Before leaving the Tiring Rooms, I'd made sure to wish my leads *beaucoup de merde* and had given Charlotte a small token for good luck. It was a pretty beaded ribbon for her to wear after the show, when we would retire to the Bishop's Whelp for customary first night celebrations. After greeting Nest, Mr Coggin and Clara (who joined us in the box at my invitation) and the people below us, who I'd never met before, I rearranged my skirt. Aphra found my hand and wrapped it in hers. Unable to help myself, I imagined basking in the praise of the Company, of the public who, unaware of my womanly status, would heap acclaim upon the dilettante balladeer. My dreams of success were so grandiose, I'd organised with a Mercury Woman I'd become friendly with, Winsome Jones, to keep aside any news-sheets advertising or reporting the play. Visions of sending cuttings to Bethan or Papa and having them rush post-haste to London to beg forgiveness and welcome me back into the family bosom began to edge their way into my extravagant thoughts. They also strayed to wherever Gabriel Freeman might be, and I wished he was here, not only to perform my words, but to behold my triumph.

Lord what fools these mortals be.

The musicians had been a playing a while when, suddenly, the tune changed and the volume grew. The curtains were about to open. With a sinking heart, I scanned the theatre. There were a few people in the pits, more seated in the boxes and some making their way along the aisles to occupy the benches. I was gratified to see Samuel Pepys, who touched his cap with a look of surprise to see me this side of the curtain. John Evelyn was beside him. Apart from those two, there weren't many more known to me. A couple of booksellers from Paternoster Row, a cordwainer from Shoe Lane, the handsome silversmith and his wife from Dorset Street, and some lawyers from Lincoln's Inn. A cough echoed. Someone called out to one of the orange-sellers. Her wooden heels clacked as she crossed to him. There was a flurry of noise, hails and laughter as more people entered, among them Timothy Shale. Upon seeing me, he frowned. His father was beside him and he'd brought at least two more.

Thank the Lord they didn't know a woman was the writer or they'd exeunt as if pursued by a bear, never mind what the Anonymous (venomous, I thought) Critic would pen.

Finally, the music swelled and, as though controlled by the instruments' notes, the curtains floated apart. Charlotte appeared and head held high, strode to the very edge of the forestage. She looked magnificent with the candlelight capturing her high cheekbones and cupid-bow mouth. Her dress, a fitted gown of amber with gold edging, made her look both regal and desirable. With a huge grin in my direction, she opened her arms. There was a smattering of applause.

'Lord what a House is here, how Thin 'tis grown.' She paused.

There was some laughter. I gulped. The line wasn't meant to attract mirth.

Unperturbed, Charlotte continued. 'As Church 'ere Conventicling was put down, Since all the Brave are to Newmarket gone!'

I'd added that line last week.

'Declining states-men are abandon'd too,
Who scarce a Heartless Whigg will Visit now:
Who once had Crowds of mutineers in Fashion …'

As she continued, there were gasps, some objections and a very loud, 'You shove it up 'em, luv!' Maybe I wasn't as bipartisan as I liked to think. I'd made sure to avoid mocking Whigs directly, especially since of late the loudest and most dangerous of them, Shaftesbury and his friends, made a point of mainly attending and supporting plays by sympathetic writers. It was preposterous.

Needless to say, the Earl and his coterie weren't there and, as the play proper began, with few cheers, a little laughter, and light claps, I prayed they'd make the effort to come another time if just to fatten the painfully scant crowd.

Alas, it never happened. For all my foolish dreams of playwriting success, of emulating my cousin and bringing home an Author's Benefit to rival the likes of Dryden's or Etherege's, it wasn't to be.

Whereas I'd hoped to be *Like Kinswoman, Like Cousin*, my play, *Like Father, Like Son*, ran for one more night (and attendance was even more pathetic) before it too was cancelled.

Just like that, my playwriting escapade came to an abrupt, if temporary, end.

SCENE TWO

... a Woman, 'cause 'tis said,
The Plays she vends she never made.
But that a Gray's Inn Lawyer does 'em,
Who unto her was Friend in Bosom.

Ovid Travestie, Alexander Radcliffe

There's oft no rhyme or reason as to why friendships form. When *Like Father, Like Son* was cancelled, and I was doing my utmost to pretend I wasn't struck inert with doubt and humiliation, an unexpected one blossomed.

The day the termination was announced, the not-so-new actress, Grace, who'd only had a minor part, made a point of seeking me out. I'd been trying to avoid the Tiring Rooms. When you pin so much hope, so many vainglorious dreams upon something only to have it fail, sympathy, ridicule or even understanding were beyond my ability to bear.

We were in the midst of rehearsals for *Madam Fickle; or The Witty False One* by Thomas Durfrey, a comedy that had been successful when it first ran a few years back. It was hoped mounting it again would push the recent disaster from people's minds. Another show must go on ...

I busied myself helping Mr Downes and Mark Danvers, there being (thank the Lord) no role for me in this production. Grace found me marking up changes to the master script according to John's instructions.

'I just wanted to say, Tribulation, I'm so sorry about your play.' Her tone was sincere; her eyes kinder than a puppy's.

To my horror, the tears I'd refused to allow welled. I blinked and, when I went to speak, my voice came out all bubbly, like a little fountain.

'Oh, that's alright,' I said, keeping my head bent over the script.

'No,' she said, touching me lightly. 'It's really not. All that work and —'

Damnation. Empathy. I was undone. Tears slid down my cheeks.

'No-one able to appreciate it.' I sniffed. 'Or unable to, more likely.'

She gave a bark of laughter. 'It was a *good* play. A bloody fine one. Too good for the likes of them coves,' she said, jerking her thumb towards the pits. She grinned and I found myself returning it, in a very wavery, watery way.

Our moment was broken when John reappeared and ordered her back on stage.

With a sweep of her skirts and a wink, she returned to position, but not before she called, 'Meet you at the Whelp after and we'll drown your sorrow.'

True to her word, she sat beside me as I downed far too many ales and some wine, listening with relief as nearby patrons, who'd just come from Drury Lane, spoke loudly about how empty the theatre there was.

'Told ya,' said Grace, nudging me in the ribs. 'I told her,' she repeated to Mark, John and Charlotte, who'd accompanied us. 'Audiences are harder to come by than an honest wherryman these days.'

'She's right, Trib,' said Charlotte, who, though disappointed on my behalf, was already immersed in her next role. 'The cancellation had naught to do with the quality of the work and everything to do with the quantity — and quality — of patrons.'

'Doesn't help the fewer in the auditorium, the worse the echo,' added John. Always a problem, the acoustics at Dorset Garden made it difficult for actors to be heard.

That night marked the beginning of my friendship with Grace. She even insisted on accompanying me home. We walked, staggered really, arm in arm through the streets, ignoring the catcalls and improper offers from equally cupshotten men and, occasionally, offering the same, bursting into loud giggles that would have put the bawds at Charing Cross to shame.

Up until then, Charlotte had been my only real friend among the women at Dorset Garden. Most had overcome their initial resentment, and no longer perceived me as a threat, on or off stage, and now I could add 'flop' to my catalogue of accomplishments, why, I was practically one of them.

The news-sheets had been most unkind. The Venomous Critic went so far as to call the play 'execrable rubbish from the pen of a newly created eunuch — because he sits so firmly astride a political and social fence, his cullies have been severed'.

I didn't know whether to be upset at the 'execrable rubbish', seek out Mr Shale and introduce him to some, or be relieved town gossip attributed the play to a man. That was until it escaped that a woman *was* the author. Then, all the opprobrium fell upon Aphra. Just as quickly, the work was attributed to Mr Hoyle — apparently responsible for anything Aphra wrote. I wondered how he felt about that? The accolades he could wear like a coronet, but when the praise turned to rancour, his crown must have felt like it was made of thorns.

God forbid anyone consider a woman capable of creating anything remarkable — or unremarkable, as the case may be.

It was beyond exhausting.

It wasn't only because of Grace I was able to shuck aside the coat of disappointment I was inclined to don. Aphra also ensured I didn't wear it (for too long). Conveniently ignoring her own tendency to fall into melancholy when her work miscarried, she determined I use this latest setback as a spur for further creativity.

We'd been living in Mr Coggin's house a few weeks by now. It was altogether a fine arrangement and, though the distance to the theatre and the river was further, Fetter Lane was a matter of yards away and with it the benefit of ready transport. Mr Coggin and Clara, more often about than the lodgers of Dorset Street, were solicitous and inoffensive landlords who did their utmost to affect our comfort. If I didn't know better, I would have sworn Mr Coggin was sweet on Aphra — or Nest. It was difficult to tell as he was quite charming to both.

Mr Shadwell had been most displeased when he learned we'd shifted in and, within two days, he moved to new premises just around the corner. As much as I admired his plays and writing, he was arrogant, dull and boastful. He also had a terrible habit of picking his nose and examining closely his extractions before wiping them upon whatever surface was near at hand — collar, cuffs, a lady's skirt, curtains, cushions, a friend's breeches. He'd once referred to Aphra's friend and Dryden's brother-in-law, Edward Thomas, as the 'poet-ninny', and bestowed terrible names upon Aphra. Of late, Shadwell went about telling anyone who'd listen a decent play took over a year to write and those who spent less time were merely writing for 'profit'. This came about after he discovered Aphra had written *The False Count* in a mere five days.

Clearly, this was a man who didn't have to write for bread.

It didn't help that Mr Shadwell also counted the Earl of Shaftesbury among his close friends. They forever had their heads together (sharing lice and nasal excretions no doubt) and I'd seen them stumbling out of the King's Head Tavern on the corner of Fleet and Chancery Lane on many occasions, sporting those ridiculous green bows or bobbles on their hats to distinguish themselves.

The night we were told my play was cancelled and Grace escorted me to a home sans Shadwell, Aphra saw my new friend gone, then came and found me in my bedroom.

I was lying face down, unable to move any further, feeling nauseated by all the wine and ale I'd consumed and from the foolish dreams I'd harboured. My head was buried in the pillow, the ale-fuelled bombast having deserted me. I felt Aphra's weight on the bed, her hand warm on the centre of my back. Apart from a small fire crackling in the hearth (bless Nest), and the sliver of light from the moon coming in through the windows, the room was in darkness.

Both wishing Aphra gone and desperately praying she'd remain, I took a deep breath and, when she neither moved nor spoke, rolled over with a deep groan and tried to see her in the dim light.

'Can't even follow in your footschteps,' I said, deliberately melodramatic, flinging a hand over my eyes. 'My feet were always too bloody big.'

'So,' she said more firmly than I expected, 'you're giving up, then?'

I parted my fingers and pried an eye open. Her shadowed features swam. 'Giving up? Aye … I mean, nay,' I said glumly, thinking I'd do exactly that. 'All that effort for nothing. Not even a small purse.' I raised a leg and studied my shoes. They really were enormous. I let my leg drop and my hand flopped over my heart. I could feel its fluttering, so fragile, like a trapped bird, beating itself against the bones of its prison. 'God. It hurts, doesn't it? Failure.'

Aphra stroked the hair from my face. I could feel her breath on my cheek. 'Yes.' She dropped a kiss on my temple. 'That which is worth the trying oft brings pain. Whether it's people, causes, love, writing … I think that's partly why we do it.'

'What? Write?'

'Write, fall in love, throw ourselves into something, never knowing if we'll succeed or fail. With the possibility of disappointment and the pain that accompanies it comes an equal chance of victory and the glorious emotions that engenders.'

'What? Hand in hand, like trouble and hope?'

Aphra snorted. 'If you like. It's two sides of the same coin. It's the risk we're addicted to — which will it be this time? It's heady, dangerous and altogether unpredictable.' She gave a dark laugh and rose.

The acrid smell of flint filled the room and the glow of freshly lit candles stretched across the bed. I tried to sit up. The room began to undulate on steady waves. I clutched the bedding, regretting the wine … that I'd ceased drinking it.

Below, another door opened. There were low murmurs followed by careful footsteps on the stairs. We didn't speak until we heard Mr Spratt pass our rooms and move around above.

Aphra held out a hand. 'Come along. Let's go fetch some wine. Forget drowning your sorrows.' She heaved me off the bed. 'Let's pickle 'em and set 'em aside while we discuss the idea for your next play … what was it again?'

I smoothed my rumpled gown, catching a glimpse of my rather puffy face in the mirror. 'Really? It wasn't very good.'

'Really?' echoed Aphra, hands on hips. 'Don't start doubting yourself after one misfire. Good God, kitten. Wait until you've had as many as I have.' She winked. 'Seriously, be sad. Be disappointed. That's natural. But turn your feelings into something productive — use them. If you allow them to take over, then you'll do far worse than fail. You'll stop trying.'

We raided the kitchen and found not only some wine, but some manchet and cheese. We took it all back up to our parlour, stoked the fire and there, encouraged by Aphra and Nest (who wasn't yet abed and joined us), I revisited an idea I'd had about ancient tales of the Sabines and first Romans. Filled with unholy spirit, we threw outrageous plots and characters back and forth like a game of tennis.

An hour or so later, I'd pages filled with fresh thoughts and had quite forgotten the cancellation. When I caught Aphra and Nest giving mutually satisfied looks, I knew this was by design.

Later, long after Nest retired, and our aim of being utterly pickled was met, Aphra raised her glass and tried to look at me through the ruby liquid.

'Your friend, Grace? Decent of her to bring you home. She seems nishe.'

I giggled. 'Nishe? She does, doesn't she? Came and shought … *sought* me out. To sort me out too, methinks. Insisted on coming home with me.'

'You were cupshotten.'

'I was! What am I now?'

'Bottleshotten?'

I laughed. 'Jugbitten?'

'Swilled.'

'Toxed.'

We chuckled.

'She could have shtayed,' said Aphra, trying to manoeuvre the glass to her mouth. 'Had some wine with us.'

I sat up straight. 'Nay, she couldn't. She had a liashon.'

'Liashon? With whom?'

'Oh.' I did a complicated movement with my wrist, loving the action and repeating it three more times, staring at my hand as if I'd never seen it before. 'Lord Grey. Forde. Of Werk. Whatever his name is. Appar…ently,' I chuckled; such a long, pretty-sounding word, 'he's in love with her.'

'Ah. Shaftesbury's handsome fop friend.'

'The very one. If you like men with no chins.' I tucked my own chin into my neck and stretched my legs, waving my unslippered feet back and forth before the glowing embers in the hearth. They weren't *that* big …

'He's married. Most unhappily.' Aphra stifled a burp.

'She knows.'

Aphra gazed with bleary eyes about the room. The tolling of bells carried on the wind. I counted the rings. Eleven of the clock. It was late. I had to be at the theatre early on the morrow. Con lines for the new-old play, find out what roles I'd be cast in over next month's productions.

Aphra put down her glass, frowning. 'He can't love her.'

'Just becaush he's married? When's that ever stopped a man? Or woman.'

Aphra stood on unsteady feet. '*Because*, rumour has it, he's in love with his wife's sister.'

'Nay!' I exclaimed, all round eyes and open mouth.

'That's what the canters tell. Whether there's any truth in it …' Aphra shrugged, then leaned down and kissed me on the head. Once. Twice. 'Hypnos beckons, him and my pillows. Good night, kitten.' With a half-hearted wave, she tripped out of the room, leaning momentarily against the doorframe to steady herself before pushing herself through with a laugh.

I remained in the tiny parlour, waiting for my mind to stop spinning, enjoying the sounds of the night: the soft spit and crackle from the hearth, the creak and whispers of the house, the way the windows trembled as the wind whipped them. A gust blew down the chimney, making the melted stumps of the candles gutter. The room was cast in macabre shapes and shadows. My eyes grew heavy. Images of Lord Grey, Grace, Aphra, Samuel Pepys, Lady Mary, the Earl of Shaftesbury and, much to my astonishment, the Baptist, Mr Keeling began to parade through my mind, talking, praising, condemning, waggling fingers, applauding, booing. They were interrupted by Gabriel Freeman, bending towards me, a wicked look in those pitch orbs, his firm lips poised for my kiss, when he suddenly drew back and began to rebuke me.

Cross at him, at my stupid, stupid thoughts, I banished him with a snarl that grew deeper, slower.

Finally, my head slumped onto my chest and the infernal chittering ceased.

SCENE THREE

(I've been) disgraced by an inkhorn mate.

Henry VI, Part 1, William Shakespeare

Mr Betterton burst into the Tiring Room, a comet hurtling through the heavens. Whirling in his bright tail were Lady Mary, Charles and Alexander, and shareholder William Smith. A few looks of concern as well as a hubbub ensued. No-one wanted to appear lax in front of those who paid the wages.

'Who's died now?' muttered John Crosby.

With a mighty flourish, Mr Betterton removed his hat and the plumed monster flew towards Jacob, who promptly caught it. 'Gather around, gather 'round,' he boomed, waving us towards him, dragging a couple of chairs closer and bidding Lady Mary and her sons sit.

Nicholas, who'd poked his head around the door when he heard the commotion, was commanded to fetch the other stagehands and bring benches. Chairs were quickly rearranged in a semi-circle and Jacob and Juliet pushed the costume rack out of the way to accommodate the extra stools. Mr Sandford, aided by Mark Danvers, who appeared at the other door, shuffled a couple of dressers against the walls.

There was always news of late, but it must be important if we all had to abandon preparations an hour before curtain. Was Drury Lane about to shut? Had there been another attempt to alter the succession? Had bands of Whig militia taken over the streets? Had the King's condition worsened? He'd been unwell of late. News in the coffee-house, Garraway's, was that he was so ill he'd asked for his son, Monmouth, and his brother to attend him. The rival successors — a dire sign.

Swiftly, we took seats, me between Grace and Charlotte, directly behind Elizabeth Barry, Cave Underhill, and Mary Slingsby, now Lady Mary — another one. We had a trinity of Marys, minus the virgin (as James Nokes said). To my right were John Downes, Samuel Sandford, James Nokes and John Crosby as well as Kit, who winked at his sister. Behind us were the minor players, Pascal, Evan and the stagehands. Even the musicians squeezed in, naked without their instruments. The orange-sellers crammed into the space, their baskets of bright fruit sweetening the room, which quickly became stuffy. We waited expectantly, quietly chattering, most trying to guess why we'd been called together.

'Hope this won't take long. We've a play to perform,' said Elizabeth Barry, patting her hair.

'Maybe not,' whispered Charlotte.

My heart tumbled. I wasn't alone in assuming the play was cancelled. It was Friday May 5th — the second night of *The Duchess of Malfi*. Numbers had been very poor opening night, made worse because we'd just finished a successful five-night run of Aphra's comedy, *The City Heiress or, Sir Timothy Treat-All*. The full houses had astonished us, coming just when we'd begun to believe they were a thing of the past. But *The City Heiress* was an excellent play, recreated from an older one. The greatest drawcard was the character Sir Timothy Treat-All, a hilarious caricature of the Earl of Shaftesbury. Once word spread, the theatre filled with those keen to see the Whig leader mocked, even those who supported his cause. The Earl attended every single night, along with his cronies. I could almost feel his fury building with each line uttered, as each well-known gesture of his was emulated.

After performance, he'd sweep backstage with the usual suspects in tow — Lords Russell, Howard, Grey, Essex and Sidney as well as the Scottish preacher. Of Mr Keeling there was no sign which I thought odd, considering he'd claimed such interest in Aphra's work the last time I met him. The Earl made a point of seeking her out, bestowing a kiss on her hand and congratulating her fine work before promptly turning his back and failing to address another word.

Lord Grey headed straight for Grace's dresser, depositing a beribboned box of comfits and kissing her softly on the neck. Aphra caught me looking and cocked a brow. I hadn't said anything to Grace about the rumours involving his sister-in-law. I wasn't sure I had a right. It was scuttlebutt. Nasty tattle. I didn't want to destroy her happiness.

After downing a drink, the Earl loudly issued an invitation for the Bettertons, Elizabeth Barry, Mr Smith and Mary Slingsby (who was invited to all the grand houses now she had a title) to join him for supper at Thanet House. Needless to say neither Aphra nor I were included. Clearly, the Earl wasn't as sanguine about his theatrical alter ego as he pretended. Nor was he happy about the obvious Tory leanings of the play, complaining loudly to Mr Betterton every single night. It didn't help it was dedicated to Henry Howard, (great) nephew of Aphra's friend, the Catholic William Howard, who'd been beheaded because of the Popish Plot.

Still, said Aphra, as we all were forced to listen to Shaftesbury complain that a direct attack was preferable to one levelled from the stage where he had no recourse, the Earl was more than capable of defending himself. People had died for Shaftesbury's cause — and it wasn't over yet.

Talk was he was simply biding his time, sick and old as he'd become. I watched him limp about the Tiring Rooms, offering a touch on the back here, a whisper there, a calculated look and pointed finger elsewhere. I still recalled Mrs Betterton telling me the very first night he was a dangerous man. Everything I'd seen and heard since confirmed that. Not even his stint in the Tower had given him pause. Aphra was either very brave or foolish (and likely both) to lampoon him and his ideals in her play. She wasn't simply poking the bear: she was lashing him with more enthusiasm than a Covent Garden madam (or so Samuel Sandford said). Unconcerned or equally potty, maybe both, her friend Thomas Otway had written a reckless prologue.

Within days of the play's first performance, an anonymous poem, *The Tory Poets, A Satire*, appeared, denigrating both Mr Otway and Aphra. Everyone knew Shadwell was the author. Why, he even mentioned my play, *Like Father, Like Son*, incorrectly attributing it to Aphra and calling both plays shams.

Then, a man named Robert Gould published another diatribe calling Aphra impudent and her work a disgrace. He claimed she'd become *Sappho, famous for her gout and guilt*. Aphra laughed when she read it.

'Sappho, eh? Well, I've been called worse and by better. At least Mr Gould has me in good company. He called Dryden's wife a whore, Dryden a lecher, and Otway a drunk.' She paused. 'He's right on two counts.'

William Wycherley added to this lexical flogging. He equated Aphra and her work to prostitution — where she sold her *parts* (pieces of writing) for money and flaunted her body (of work) about town.

Why were these men not accused of plagiarising? They rehashed and recycled the same old phrases and labels, borrowing from each other in their relentless efforts to pour ridicule on Aphra and, by association, any woman who dared to dip her toes in their domain. They lacked originality and most certainly imagination, though that didn't stop their insults harming their target and maligning Aphra's reputation. I loathed them for it. Aphra gave the appearance of conciliation but was waiting for the right moment to attack and defend with her pen. Then, woe betide the textual poltroons. Their names and repute would fall beneath her rhetorical blows.

My thoughts were interrupted when Mr Betterton, standing near the doorway, clapped his hands and glowered at us beneath his great bushy brows. Immediately, the chittering ceased. He turned to Charles and gestured for him to take the floor. Mr Davenant stood, tugging uncomfortably at his jacket.

In all the time I'd been with Dorset Garden, I'd only seen Lady Mary's oldest son a few times. He rarely appeared backstage, leaving any dealings with the performers to his mother, the Bettertons, and now Mr Smith. Occasionally, I'd see him in his favourite box, to the right of the stage, often with guests. It was said he was content to manage affairs behind the scenes. If that was so, why had the cub emerged from his den?

'I've some important news I wish to share.' Mr Davenant gave a dramatic pause. 'Dorset Garden Theatre will, after many years and at the end of this season, cease to host the Duke's Company.'

There were gasps. Then everyone began to speak at once.

'No!'

'This can't be?'

'It's because the Duke's a bloody Papist, ain't it?'

'What am I to do?'

'What about my children?'

'I've debts to pay.'

Mrs Barry half rose and then sat down, her face working like a broken bellows. Lady Slingsby paled. Mr Nokes and Mr Sandford began spluttering and stammering. Jacob shook his head in misery. Juliet burst into tears and, with a flair that drew admiring looks from Anne Bracegirdle, threw herself into Finnola's arms. The stagehands looked as if they were either about to weep or flee the room. Perhaps both. The orange-sellers sat quietly, one picking lice from her hair, the other peeling fruit.

'Oh, no,' said Charlotte softly, leaning against me. 'Just when I thought we'd turned a dark corner.' I felt her searching for my hand on one side, while Grace did on the other. I clung to both, uncertain what to think. We were driftwood upon a tempestuous sea.

There was soft crying, a low keening. This was terrible news. I wished I could unhear Mr Davenant: that somehow, we could alter the inevitable.

'But, you can't,' protested Mr Underhill, finally. 'Why, our takings, poor though they've been of late, are still better than Drury Lane — the reviews as well.'

There was a loud flurry of agreement. A drying of eyes, collective straightening of spines.

'If there's no Dorset Garden, then what's to become of us?' asked Lady Slingsby in a voice so plaintive the whole room leaned in her direction as if trying to reach her.

Mr Davenant looked about benevolently. The other shareholders were very quiet. For an announcement that spelled the end of the theatre, they were oddly passive. What was going on?

'Stopper your tears; cease your complaints and worries. Listen,' said Charles Davenant, projecting his voice so it could be heard above the crying and muttering. He drew himself up. Being a short man, it was a small gesture. 'I said, *Dorset Garden* will cease to host the *Duke's Company*, not that *you* will cease to work. Instead, the two current companies — King's and Duke's — will merge and operate under a new title: The United Company.'

Charles Davenant had missed his calling — he was quite the dramatist after all.

There were gasps, this time of a completely different tone. Whereas before it was from a dearth of air now it was a surfeit. Faces turned towards one another like flowers to the sun, open, filled with wonder and light.

'From November onwards,' continued Charles, the birth of a smile transforming his face, 'the majority of our productions will be staged at Drury Lane. Yes. You heard aright. We're shifting to our rival's theatre, which will become ours.' His grin widened. It was contagious and passed from one player to the next. 'We will, however, continue to use Dorset Garden for productions such as operas and plays requiring special effects — like *The Lancashire Witches* and the Scottish play.'

'We're not about to lose our positions, then?' asked a minor player from the back of the room.

Mr Davenant gave a reassuring chuckle and shook his head. 'Not unless you wish to retire or end your contract — if you have one.' He was speaking to the male actors. Women couldn't be awarded contracts. 'Some of the King's players have already reached a decision.'

'They know about this?' asked Mr Nokes, aggrieved.

'They do,' said Charles. 'The impact upon Drury Lane and, indeed, the King's Company is far greater than upon us. For a start, myself and Arthur, with Mother's help and that of our actor-managers —' he indicated Mr Betterton and Mr Smith '— and minor shareholders, will continue to run the United Company much as we have this one. We'll hold both royal patents and move to bigger, better premises. We'll be a larger group with a greater range of stock plays at our disposal, many of which I know you've been longing to bring to the stage. We've fine actors and actresses to fulfil all roles. The King's Company, well, depending upon who is offered work, will be greatly diminished ...'

'What about Charles Hart, Edward Kynaston and Michael Mohun?' asked James Nokes, referring to the leading thespians of the King's.

'They of course will be invited to *apply* to the join the new company. Whether or not they take the opportunity is up to them and, of course, the shareholders.'

'What about Mr Downes?' asked Charlotte, turning to look at John.

Mr Betterton answered, spreading his arms in a benevolent gesture. 'Where we go, John goes.'

John gave a ghostly smile and pretended he had something in his eye.

'His job is as safe as yours, Mrs Butler.'

'That goes for the rest of you as well,' said Lady Mary, standing. 'Cease your worries. The merger is months away and, in the meantime, if there are no further questions, you have a play to perform and we have much work to do. We simply wanted to share this grand news.'

As swiftly as the celestial bodies of the managers had arrived, they left; the room was the dimmer for their absence. As soon as the door closed, talk exploded.

'Merger, my hairy cullions,' said John Downes, slapping his knees. 'This is a take-over.'

'Aye, but we're the ones taking over, so who cares?' said John Crosby, with a careless shrug.

'Possibly the actors and actresses being displaced,' I said quieter than a flea's sigh. I'd worked hard to get Mr Crosby back on side after

Prisca left and didn't want to undo my work. Grace shot me a warning glance and pressed her lips together. Clearly, I'd have to work on my sotto.

All the same, this was marvellous news for the players, but what of the playwrights? If the merger meant the Company gained access to works previously denied them, then surely the demand for new titles would be greatly diminished?

For the next few minutes, I put that thought aside as we shifted dressers and racks back into place, returned stools and chairs, and tried to comprehend what we'd been told. A new theatre? Drury Lane? A new company and name? I could hear Elizabeth and Lady Slingsby, Mr Sandford and Mr Nokes reeling off the titles of plays they'd at last be able to perform, their voices high with excitement. Even the stagehands were affected.

When John rang the fifteen-minute bell what seemed like moments later, there was a screech of panic. The show commenced on time and proceeded, if not quite as flawlessly as an old stock play should, with a few missed cues and lines, smoothly enough that all was forgiven. Tonight marked a new chapter in the history of not just Dorset Garden and the Duke's Company, but London theatre.

In name at least, we'd be United.

If only the King could do that for his country.

SCENE FOUR

Nature as wrong'd me when she made me Woman:
Or else when I was form'd, she heedless and hastily,
Snatch't the next Soul for me, and left my Sex Imperfect

Romulus and Hersilia or, The Sabine War: A Tragedy, by Anonymous
(alias Tribulation Johnson but attributed to Aphra Behn)

Summer entered, stage right, its heat so intense I imagined the Greek god Hephaestus, half-naked at his forge, working his bellows, sweat slick upon his twisted flesh, hammering the metal, shaping us into creatures that bore little resemblance to those who only a few weeks earlier had shivered through glacial days. Gone were the hunched, scurrying folk, enveloped in layers of wool, replaced by wilting wenches and languid gentleman, sauntering along streets, reclining in shade or by water as they fanned themselves, puffing and blowing ruddy cheeks. Whereas once talk had been of the succession or Popish Plot, now conversations were of a meteorologic kind, everyone offering their opinion about the weather, as if Mother Nature or God for that matter gave a damn.

The major players among the Duke's Company (the title had become more precious as its relevance raced towards its end) had long left

London, escaping the stifling heat and feeble audiences. Charlotte and Katherine Herbert had departed for Oxford, Lady Slingsby had been taken to her husband's country seat for a well-earned rest (his words), and the Bettertons had taken Elizabeth Barry, Susanna Mountfort, Elizabeth Currer, James Nokes, John Crosby and young Anne to give command performances at Hampton Court.

The theatre was an altogether different place without the more important players present. Grace and Kit and young Madoc Osborne, a talented singer who'd joined the company after our demise was announced, were all cast in major parts. Sal Gibbs strutted the boards as did Margaret Collins. Already, some of the King's players had sought to join our ranks. Three were given parts — Joanna Cross, an older woman content with small roles, and two young men, both named Joseph, and though not related, bearing striking resemblance to each other. They were simply happy to have work.

Because John Downes left with the Bettertons, I became sole bookkeeper once more. With no new plays, just familiar and popular ones for which everyone knew not only their own lines but everybody's, my work wasn't onerous and it gave me time to complete the play I'd told Aphra and Nest about.

Every evening after performance, I'd head home, shut myself away and write. There was a brief break for supper, when Aphra and I would discuss what had happened at the theatre — how the performance unfolded, the behaviour of the audience, and any news we'd heard. Determined to be topical, I also wanted my play to amuse and beguile sophisticated London crowds. The recipe was simple: the more bawd and low humour, the better chance it had. God forgive me, as I wrote about wanton women and lecherous men (and noble and pure ones — I wasn't yet completely depraved), I even relished the notion.

There were evenings when the lines poured from me with ease and then other occasions where finding a word, let alone enough to construct dialogue, was like pulling a tooth — a great deal of pain and blood — and just as tedious and messy. Then, I would simply cast my mind back to that supper at Rochester's house or recall many an hour in the Tiring Rooms and the mix of wits, louches, mountebanks, women of poor fame and those of renown I'd encountered. Thus, dialogue flowed and my characters began to take shape, and though I could say for certain I didn't set out to replicate any one person of my acquaintance or of wider reputation, there were aspects of the characters that might, if one squinted or stretched their fancy, be deemed recognisable — but more as a type than specific. I was like one of those birds that collects scraps to make a nest, only I collected expressions and idiosyncrasies and crafted characters with them.

By mid-July I'd finished a first draft, which I passed to Aphra, doing everything I could, including helping Nest repair garments (when I was at the theatre, she'd unpick my stitches and pass the garment back to me in the evening. I began to understand how Penelope in the *Odyssey* felt tackling the same piece of weaving day after day though with far less patience), to distract myself as I awaited her opinion.

Four days later, Aphra handed the pages back. I could see a series of bold markings and my heart sank. If there was this much wrong on the first page, it didn't bode well for the remainder.

'Why so glum?' she asked, giving my long braid a gentle tug. 'I've made a few suggestions, but overall, this is good, Tribulation. You've drawn on the Sabine legend and the foundation story of Rome to create a tragic tale of love and vengeance.'

I'd already convinced myself it was unworthy and was quite prepared to cast it upon the flames. 'Really?'

'There it is again. Doubt.' She patted my cheek. '*Really*. How about we discuss it?'

My limbs were ready to detach themselves from my body and float about the room I felt so light and relieved.

Aphra led me to a chair in the parlour. 'Sit, sit.' She fell into the chair opposite, then hesitated. 'I can guess where you drew inspiration for your less savoury characters and their foibles, but where did you learn to write about love so … so … feelingly?' She touched the pages. 'Feliciana's shattered heart, her forlorn hope, Hostilius's pain: why, they're achingly lovely. Very moving. I wondered …' There was a knowing look in her chocolate eyes. 'Have you …?'

Perched on the edge of the chair, I rearranged my skirts. 'Felt such love?' I gave a small laugh. 'Alas. What I wrote is drawn from what I've read and witnessed. From you — your plays and poems,' I added quickly. 'And others. Shakespeare, Jonson, Marlowe — they all write so poignantly about love, as do Ovid and Homer. Never mind the countless plays I've seen at Dorset Garden. It's the one theme that unites them — love.'

Or lust.

'Well,' said Aphra, 'this reads as if *you've* felt it.'

My cheeks reddened. Caterpillars crawled up my insides, their long spiky backs tickling and making me fidget. Aphra spared me further questioning.

The faraway look she sometimes wore appeared. 'You're right. One doesn't have to feel something to describe it; one needs only imagine.' She released a long, heartfelt sigh. 'Even so, I hope one day you not only feel such passion — but that it's returned.'

I wanted that too, I thought as my caterpillars metamorphosed into butterflies, each one with Gabriel's face on their wings. I batted them away.

Aphra flicked through the pages. 'Have you considered who might play the roles?'

'Oh, aye.'

Gabriel. Gabriel. Gabriel.

'I was thinking Elizabeth Barry for Hersilia, Susanna Mountfort or maybe Mary Slingsby for Tarpeia. I'm still not sure about Feliciana. Mr Betterton for Romulus.'

'Of course.'

'But … I don't know about Hostilius.'

Aphra scratched her chin. 'Pity Jonathan Rickman isn't about: he'd have made a perfect Hostilius — manly, noble … and that voice.' Aphra clutched her hands to her bosom and fell back in her chair.

I struck her lightly just as the last butterfly gave a cheeky flutter before being vanquished with a slow blink. 'He's all those things. But he's also not *here*.'

Aphra chuckled and passed the script back. 'Have you thought about who might write the prologue?'

I had, but …

'Perhaps,' continued Aphra, almost shyly, nodding at the pages in my hands, 'you might consider me?'

If I could have transformed into a starling and swooped about the rafters, I would have. Or trilled like a robin. Unable to do either, I did the next best thing. I thrust the manuscript aside, launched out of my chair like a fletched arrow and shot into Aphra's arms.

'Consider it done!'

The chair rocked back with my additional weight. Before either of us could retrieve our balance, it toppled over, flinging us both to the floor, limbs entangled, skirts askew, shrieking with laughter.

That was how Nest found us, lying side by side, legs and arms akimbo, chuckling madly.

'I've said it before and I'll declare it again: loons, the pair of ye!' She righted the chair and picked up the scattered pages.

As if to confirm her assessment, we simply laughed harder.

Much later, as the sun set and a breeze, though not cool at least refreshing, wafted through the window, we sat, side by side, poring over Aphra's written comments.

We tackled each page and scene, every character and their dialogue, making little changes here, adjustments there, even altering stage directions. As we worked, a part of me broke away and hovered above watching and listening, as if I were a spirit or angel (not the avenging kind). I saw an older, experienced woman, hair tucked behind her ears, a furrow between her brows, lines fanning from the corners of her eyes and at her mouth, paths of experience along which she determined to lead me. Patient with her young protégée, the baby bird in her nest, believing in her, instilling confidence and inspiration, she offered ideas for improvement, and prodded the young one to discover them herself and fly. The chick absorbed everything, clucking and chirping, with feathers sometimes ruffled but more oft puffed with excitement. They debated, argued, agreed or didn't.

Every spare moment for over a week, I rewrote and refined. Then, I did it again, and then again. I kept thinking about what Aphra said long ago, how plays were 'secret instructions to the people, of things 'tis impossible to insinuate into them in other ways'. And so, with one ear on the current news, and the other on theatre and street gossip, snippets of conversations overheard in alleys, shops, church and riverside, and neighbourly disagreements, my play about the past, which I also hoped was entertaining and heart-wrenching, became as much about the present and the people I lived among as I could possibly make it as well.

'Oh, I meant to tell you,' said Aphra one evening after I joined her in the parlour, 'do you remember a while back there were rumours Lord Grey was having an affair with his wife's sister?'

How could I forget? Since then, I'd hardly been able to listen to Grace opine about her lover. How, whenever he was in London, he'd collect her in his carriage after performances, take her to Thanet House for supper with Shaftesbury and the other fine lords and wealthy gentlemen, or hire a tilt boat and glide upriver, downriver, across the bloody thing, on a Sunday. He'd even taken her to Newmarket overnight. Usually loquacious, when I pressed her for details about the men and Thanet House, knowing they were all Whigs and likely discussing ways to alter the succession and hoping I might be able to include something of this in my play, she'd not only become uncomfortable and even reticent, but, I could have also sworn, afraid.

'Nothing worth repeating,' was all she would allow.

'Why?' I asked Aphra now.

She passed me a glass of wine and sank into the chair beside me. 'It gives me no pleasure to relay this, but I have it on excellent authority Lord Grey, the scoundrel, is indeed involved with his wife's younger sister, Henrietta Berkeley. I know!' she added at the expression on my face, which was akin to biting into a plum and finding half a maggot. 'It's partly vengeance against his wife, who has made quite the cuckold of him with the Duke of Monmouth — his friend, no less. The Wits have been lampooning Grey for a few weeks now and it's goaded him into being very indiscreet. Which means he's been gulling your friend all along to avert suspicion from this tawdry affair. The man is a louche and rogue. The sooner Grace finds out, the sooner she can remove herself from his sphere and try and shore up what remains of her reputation. For, once his real intentions are exposed, there'll be little left for her to salvage.'

Aphra didn't remain long after dumping that pile of dung in my lap, summoning Nest to help her prepare for bed. I sat in the parlour, trying to ignore the stench of the story. My appetite fled as I watched the sky change from dove-pearl to silver to lovely shimmering violet. It would have been quite soothing except the firmament was overlaid with images of wide-eyed Grace, and chinless, boneless Lord Grey and his faceless sister-lover.

By late July, *Romulus and Hersilia or, The Sabine War: A Tragedy* was finished, accepted for performance by the Duke's Company and sent to the Lord Chamberlain for approval. If I thought waiting for Aphra's opinion had turned my mind faster than a Flemish spinner's wheel, waiting for Lord Arlington's verdict was a different kind of giddy that left me aswoon with possibilities — all bad.

In less than a week, the play passed the Censor and, with the return of the major players from their summer activities, it was soon cast and in rehearsal.

This time, I prayed, as I oversaw practice from the pits and even took a role as one of Hersilia's women, the play would run more than two nights. Once again, my head was firmly in the clouds and my dreams grander than a king's palace.

If only I'd heeded Aesop who, in his fable of 'The Old Man and Death', warns, 'be careful what you wish for lest it come true …'

SCENE FIVE

I want to be doing something with the pen, since no other means of action in politics are in a woman's power.

Harriet Martineau

In my defence, I didn't arrive at the theatre on opening night of my play with the *intention* to tell Grace what was being said about Lord Grey. But damn if it didn't leap into my mind and creep into my throat the moment I laid eyes upon her. When the rogue burst into the Tiring Rooms, presenting her with a veritable garden of fragrant flowers, a large box of comfits and a dazzling bracelet, my tongue, upon which the wicked tale sat, swelled to monumental proportions. A part of her had to know, surely? And not only because, as Winsome the Mercury Woman had shown me that very morning, some gossip had written that Lord Grey, 'as the report goes, saith he married the eldest sister and expected a Maidenhead, but not finding it, hee resolved to have one in the family, if any be left' and distributed it all about the city.

If everyone was on the cusp of knowing about the rogue, then surely Grace deserved to as well.

Throwing a pointed look in Lord Grey's direction, Aphra, who was there to support me and wish us *beaucoup de merde*, left. Her words echoed in my head. 'The sooner Grace finds out, the sooner she can remove herself... and try and shore up what remains of her reputation.'

The moment Lord Grey departed, I took a deep breath and, trying to consider best how to tackle such a sensitive subject, and being aware it wasn't my strongest suit, sidled over to Grace. First tolerating her recital of the man's devotions and then being forced to examine the proof, I reached a point where I could no longer stomach what I was hearing and seeing. I took her hands. I waited until she met my steady gaze and, in as calm and measured a way as possible, told her what I knew. At least, that was my intention. Rather, much like I had on Aphra's doorstep the day I came to London, I purged. I cast the dreadful story of her lover's affair all over Grace and then sat back and waited for her reaction.

Grace didn't say anything at first; she simply snatched her hands away. Then, much to my surprise and great discomfort, she burst out laughing.

'Oh, Tribulation! Is it not enough you write tragedy without making one of my life?' She turned back to the mirror and began to powder her décolletage. Clouds of talc billowed, making me cough then sneeze.

Regarding me through narrowed eyes, she continued. Each word was a needle that stuck me so fiercely, I was amazed there were not pinpricks of blood all over. 'Lord Grey loves *me*. If he loves his wife's sister too and certain people choose to interpret that in a salacious manner, it's hardly my fault, or his. Rather, it speaks to the person capable of turning it into lascivious and immoral goings-on.'

I stared at her reflection, but having unleashed her defences, she refused to meet my eyes. Flattened and feeling rather foolish and mean and, yes, salacious, this certain person retreated to her dresser, but not before I'd seen a look of doubt cross Grace's lovely features.

It was far too soon to describe *Romulus and Hersilia* as a success, but when, upon the second night, the house was full, I allowed a tiny crackle of confidence. This time, at least, I would earn an Author's Benefit.

While I wanted to believe it was my tragic story of doomed love and the performers who brought it to life attracting audiences, I was wise enough to comprehend it was Aphra's provocative bookends — the prologue and epilogue. Patrons left the theatre abuzz. Charlotte opened the play and Mary Slingsby closed it. They were the first to be seen and heard — and the last. Women were the real heroines of this performance both on stage and off.

Like a brilliant beacon, only with glossy locks, Charlotte delivered Aphra's fiery prologue with aplomb, ignoring the audience's interruptions, the howls of protest. In a daring move, Aphra took to task Protestant Whigs (the Green Ribbon Club were even named), decrying them as a bunch of rats and weasels who gnawed at the lion's (the King's) beard and who, when he roared, skulked away like the vermin they were. They were described as knaves and fools, as 'bully braves' possessing 'lawless tongues' and relying on 'arbitrary Juries', and accused of swearing 'Burlesque Oaths' (some men stood at those words and shook their fists). Aphra's scathing assessment and Charlotte's steady delivery hit home. Words were sharp, precise weapons wielded by a sweet-mouthed woman, and they fell with deadly precision.

From the wings, I could see the Earl of Shaftesbury, Lord Grey, and the other Whig hangers-on — including someone I hadn't seen a while: Josiah Keeling. I would have recognised him from his height alone. Throughout Charlotte's soliloquy, Shaftesbury struck the floor over and over with his cane, his brows drawn in such a furious scowl his eyes were all but shuttered by hairy awnings. Those surrounding him howled like wolves – or disloyal nobles hearing unpalatable truths — objecting as if this was the House of Lords, but failing to silence the speaker. I was thrilled. Was this not what a playwright's words were designed for? To challenge, move, inspire, poke, provoke and entertain? As the Tories in the audience cheered and clapped, the Whigs tried their utmost to drown them out with hisses, heckles and boos. Aphra had provided a marvellous entree to the play.

The reaction to the epilogue was quite different. Perhaps they were exhausted by what had unfolded — the sad story of two races united and torn apart by love, family, friendship, betrayal and war — for when Lady Slingsby finished, there was a moment of silence, before the audience erupted. Shouts of outrage, disbelieving laughter and calls for the author to be either crowned or lynched ricocheted off the walls and ceiling, landing with mighty echoing thumps on the stage. We were a castle besieged. If I wasn't yet teaching, I *was* most certainly reaching.

'The King will hear of this,' said John Downes, lowering his head into his hands and shaking it back and forth. I was standing beside him, raised on tiptoes so as not to miss a word or gesture.

'You think he'll make an appearance then?' I asked, hope flaring. If his Majesty showed, the place would be full to the brim with wonderful, stinky shit.

'If he doesn't shut us down first.' John peeked between splayed fingers. 'Doesn't matter he's the face of the Whigs: you can't just refer to the King's bastard son as treasonous and ungrateful, claim rebellion is brewing, and not expect the wrath of White Hall to fall upon us.' He craned his neck to peer at the audience, still on their feet, arms raised, mouths open. 'Though,' he added, his hand falling way, 'at least until we hear from his Majesty, we're guaranteed a good crowd.'

After helping John secure the master script, I made haste to the Tiring Rooms intending to congratulate the cast and not-so-secretly hoping they in turn would applaud me. A few knew I was the author, though the shareholders had advised my identity be kept close. After seeing the audience's reaction, and hearing John's words of doom, I was ambivalent about their caution. Surely, a little infamy couldn't hurt … too much.

I ducked and weaved between those who'd clambered onto the stage to praise the players, ignored as just another theatre lackey. The Earl was conspicuous by his absence. Wending my way between the flats and through the wings, I headed towards the Tiring Rooms, chin up, shoulders back.

I hadn't gone very far when I was grabbed and, with surprising strength, pulled behind a piece of scenery. It was Grace. She stood in a pool of mellow light cast by a lanthorn she'd placed upon a plinth we'd used in the play.

'You scared me,' I exclaimed, laughing to cover up my genuine fright.

Grace kept her head bowed; she was shaking. I thought at first it must be from the cold as her costume was very flimsy, but as she raised her chin and her eyes met mine, I saw it was flaming rage.

'How dare you?' she said with such venom I took a step back. 'You tried to ruin my only happiness with wicked lies, with spite and cruelty.'

'Nay, Grace. That's not so. Please —' I began, reaching for her. The dim light cast her features into hollow planes, and her eyes were huge, great moons in which the stars swirled.

She slapped my hand away. 'Don't touch me. I believed you my friend, but you're a malicious creature, one who has never known love and never will.' She gave a bitter laugh that dissolved into tears. 'You're doomed to only ever write about it, make a poor copy of what you sense in others. Stay back, I say! I was warned about you, told you were nothing but trouble. I should have listened, but no, I gave you a chance and look what happens? You repay my kindness with spiteful gossip and cruelty.' Her chest heaved as she held up her palm to stop me approaching.

All I wanted to do was say how sorry I was — not that I told her about Lord Spineless. It was just never my intention to hurt her though, of course, what I told her had. I did it to save her … from a mountebank. From Lord Grey. From a grievous error of judgement. From herself. How could I make her see that?

'Don't you ever speak to me again, do you hear?' said Grace finally. 'Unless it's to issue an instruction, something to do with work. Otherwise, as far as I am concerned, you're *persona non grata*. You're dead to me.'

The words were like a punch to my stomach, a vicious blow to my soul.

Grace whipped around, almost colliding with an errant sandbag. I watched her vanish into the gloom of the corridor, the white of her gown making her appear like a spectre of tragic roles past.

Unable to face her or anyone else, lost in an evendoon of doubt and regret, I doused the lanthorn and sat quietly. When I was certain everyone was either in the Tiring Room celebrating, or had left for the tavern, like a quick-fingered conjurer at Bartholomew's Fair, I did a disappearing act of my very own.

Aphra found me later that night sitting in the dark by the parlour window. A great big bat in a gloomy belfry.

'Where were you, kitten?' she said, in a voice too loud for the quiet house, before shutting the door. 'I expected to see you at the Whelp.' She dropped a kiss on my head. She smelled of wine, ale and the perfumes of many excited embraces.

I waited until she'd pulled up a chair. Then, taking a deep breath that I drew from the very ends of my toes, I told her.

'Oh, Tribulation,' she said when I finished, excavating my buried hand and holding it. We both stared out the window. It was a still, humid night. The moon had risen, carving a crazed silver path across the crooked rooftops. Mullioned windows released the lambent glow of candles. The hulking shadows of the occupants moved back and forth, lending the houses an eerie quality, as if they were inhabited by mythic monsters or ghosts. An owl hooted a dirge, the faint music from the tavern a fitting counterpart to the creature's song. A man and a woman crossed the square, heading towards Shoe Lane, when a cat darted across their path causing the woman to squeal. There was quiet laughter, the offer of an arm.

Aphra pressed my hand tightly.

'I … I thought I should tell her, that she … she'd want to know. I couldn't bear that she was being … gulled. Used.'

'I know,' said Aphra quietly.

'And he a lord, and she an actress and wanting to believe not just in him, but in everything he promised — a better life, a respectable one … I couldn't bear it, Aphra. Not Grace. Not him. It was imperative she know what he offered was false. That he, it, was a chimera. But now … now I'm the fiend … I'm being punished for his sins.'

It was Bethan and Sir Marmaduke all over again. Even the consequences were the same. 'You're dead to me.' God! Would I never learn? Was I doomed to always repeat mistakes?

Aye, if good women made fools of themselves over worthless men.

Aphra kneeled at my feet and took me in her arms. I wept a tempest and not just for Grace. A part of the sorrow was for me. For Papa had been right all along. What a broken, unnatural woman I couldn't help but be.

When my sobs began to subside, Aphra spoke. 'Sometimes, people don't want to hear the truth. But, sometimes, kitten, though you feel compelled to tell them, they don't need to either.'

I knew that. Deep down. 'When you gave that look, in the Tiring Rooms, I … I thought you were instructing me to tell her or, at the least, suggesting I do. I'm not blaming you — please don't think that for a moment. This was my doing, my choice. A poor one, it seems.' I nestled my face in her shoulder again.

'I would never have advised such folly.' Aphra pulled me away, hands atop my shoulders so she might regard me.

Aware my eyes were swollen dams on the cusp of breaching their walls again, I wiped them.

'Sometimes, kitten, a lie is kinder. Sometimes, it's easier for people to bear than candour. We all live with lies — lies we tell ourselves … and others.'

'I don't,' I sniffed.

'Don't you?' She smiled kindly. 'I can think of a few. Isn't writing under a pseudonym a lie of sorts?'

'But … it protects me: you said so yourself.'

'Exactly. Lies are sometimes told because they do less harm than the truth. It doesn't make them evil or wrong. There are occasions when it even makes them kind. Or at least preferable.'

My lips began to tremble. Once again, my runaway tongue was being schooled by the sweetest of mistresses in the gentlest of lessons. 'I was unkind.'

Aphra shook her head. 'Not deliberately. But Grace has taken it that way. Knowing the truth (even if she claims not to believe it) she's still chosen to live with a falsehood. Both the falsehood that is Lord Grey and that you're what she claims, something she must make of you to justify dismissing your warning. Dismissing you.' She sat back on her heels. 'The truth will out. Lord Grey cannot hide what he has done and, when he's exposed, then you can be the friend you want to be to Grace.'

'How? She has me a corpse, our friendship shriven and buried.'

'By forgiving her.'

I paused, then nodded miserably. I hoped I was generous enough to do that.

With a mighty groan, Aphra tried to stand. 'Dear Lord, I'm getting too old for floors. For late nights and debauchery — even in the best of causes.' She hiccoughed and flapped a hand for me to assist.

When she was back in her own chair, and wine was freshly poured, she raised the glass in my direction. 'I loathe seeing you so sad, and on a night when you should be celebrating your triumph.'

'*Our* triumph.'

'*Ours*.' Aphra purred. 'You don't know how much pleasure that word gives me.'

Oh, I did.

'In future,' she said softly, 'warn me of your intention to speak the truth. That way, I can either caution or do my utmost to protect you.' She faced me in the gloom. 'That's a promise.'

'I'll hold you to it,' I said, never intending for a moment that Aphra would ever have to keep it.

Little did I know how her words would come back to haunt me.

SCENE SIX

Write on! and let not after ages say,
The whistle or the rude hiss could lay
Thy mighty spright of poetry …
Silence will like submission show:
And give advantage to the foe.

Aphra Behn, advice to Edward Howard after the failure of his play *The New Utopia*

They came for Aphra while I was at the theatre. According to Nest there were six soldiers, armed and dressed in the King's livery, pikes gleaming, swords drawn. They arrived on horseback, a small carriage in their wake, managing to attract onlookers like a Southwark fisherman's catch does flies. First making them wait while she dressed in her best gown and had her hair groomed, Nest added gleefully, Aphra, head held high, went without complaint.

At Dorset Garden, similar events unfolded. Waiting until Mary Slingsby delivered the last line of the epilogue (and to a packed house), soldiers charged onto the stage from the pits (where we later suspected they'd been watching the entire performance) and arrested her. Thinking it was scripted, the audience went wild, shouting, throwing fruit and other missiles, striking the soldiers and poor Lady Slingsby, who was all atremble and confused. It wasn't until one gallant, understanding the livery was genuine and the weapons the guards carried real, leaped to her rescue — his sword drawn — that things turned ugly. He demanded the guards release the 'poor maiden immediately'. Being neither poor, nor for that matter a maiden, Lady Slingsby began to object. Fortunately, before the gentleman could inflict or receive fatal injury, one of the pikemen knocked him senseless. The gentleman keeled over like a felled tree, and was kicked unceremoniously into the audience, dousing candles and breaking glass as he went. John and Mark had the presence of mind to dash on stage with buckets of sand whilst I ordered the curtains closed.

There was no time to defend Mary Slingsby, especially once Lady Mary Davenant appeared, demanding to know what was going on, and was presented with a royal warrant. Defeated, and knowing what the arrest of one of our lead performers meant for the play, we watched as a cowed Lady Slingsby was led away.

Afterwards, we sat glumly in the Tiring Rooms, refusing to admit any of the fops or Wits — even the Earl of Shaftesbury, who kept rapping his damn cane on the door, no doubt to exult. It wasn't hard to guess who'd ensured word of the play had reached the King — more accurately, reports about Aphra's damning contributions had sullied royal ears and twisted his resolve. One had only to see the charges, which Lady Mary passed to Mr Betterton. He unfurled the document and read aloud.

'"Whereas the Lady Slingsby and Mrs Aphra Behn have by writing and acting at his Royal Highness's Theatre committed several misdemeanours and made abusive reflections upon persons of quality, and have written and spoken scandalous speeches without any licence or approbation to those that ought to peruse and authorise the same, these therefore require you to take into your custody the said Lady Slingsby and Mrs Aphra Behn and bring them before me to answer for the said offence, and for so doing this shall be your sufficient warrant. Given under my hand and seal this 12th day of August, 1682."

'"Charles Rex".'

It was the first chance I'd had to consider Aphra. Of course she'd be indicted as well. Without excusing myself, I left the theatre and hailed a hackney. It rocked and bounced as he took me up past Fleet Ditch and across Fleet Street to just where Ludgate began to slope; shouting and swearing at any in his path, he careened up Harp Lane before swerving into Shoe Lane. Flung from side to side, I clung for dear life, developing a sudden affinity for my tortured bedclothes. In future I would peel them away from my body congenially every morning.

Alas, as I burst in the front door, calling for Aphra, the moment I saw Nest's crumpled face, I knew I was too late.

Too late to warn Aphra and far too late to save the play.

For, once again, the theatre was ordered closed.

By the time reports of the arrests appeared in the *Newdigate Newsletter* and *The True Protestant Mercury*, both Aphra and Lady Slingsby had been returned home and the theatre reopened — on the proviso *Romulus and Hersilia* didn't grace the stage. Lord Arlington made it clear that when and if it did again, it would be sans prologue and epilogue. Relieved the King hadn't punished the Duke's Company by keeping the theatre doors shut long, I felt thoroughly chastened, nonetheless. After all, Aphra may have written the words that attracted such vituperation, and Lady Slingsby uttered them (unsurprisingly, the King wasn't offended by what was said about Whigs — the same couldn't be said for the Earl, who both possessed a long memory and bore grudges — just his bastard son), but it was because of my play.

I couldn't understand why I hadn't also been arrested. From experience, I knew using a pseudonym or signing a work 'anonymous' didn't stop the likes of his Majesty or Lord Arlington knowing who the real author was. I began to suspect Aphra had done what she promised and protected me. Either that, or she'd struck a bargain of some kind.

Grateful she'd simply been shown to Lord Arlington's rooms at Westminster, made to wait over twelve hours, then threatened with Newgate and, after a thorough dressing down and a fine (for which she borrowed the money — presumably from Mr Hoyle), sent home, Aphra recounted everything to me and Nest the following day.

'I couldn't have tolerated a moment in prison, not again,' she said wearily. Neither of us had slept the night before: Aphra waiting to learn her fate; me conjuring cells, torture and worse for her. 'I'd have agreed to anything to avoid that.'

Turns out, she did. Less than a week later, Aphra was on her way to Paris.

Mysterious as to why she was going, all she'd reveal was the other Secretary of State, her old acquaintance Sir Leoline Jenkins, had suggested the trip in lieu of more serious consequences.

'I'll work upon my French and, while I'm there, visit the salons and meet Mademoiselle Scudery and Abbe Paul Tallemant, both of whom you've heard me talk about endlessly.'

Nest pulled me aside and told me not only would she be accompanying Aphra (I was glad) but while in the city, Aphra intended to seek medical attention for her worsening ailments: her gout and contorted fingers, and mercury for a disease that would, on occasion, strike her lady parts and cause great discomfort.

It was only after they left in late August 1682, with a bustle of packing and promises to write, I realised that, for the first time since I'd come to London — nay, in my entire life — I was quite alone.

Glad I'd the theatre and the Company (even if Grace and the others she'd clearly told of my so-called cruelty pointedly ignored me) to keep me occupied during the day, I came to relish my solitary evenings. I was St Gerasimus only without a lion (I did miss Hecate), St Paul or better still, Julian of Norwich. Not only was she a hermit, but a writer too. Every time a clock chimed or a cough or footsteps resounded, never mind noises from outside, the illusion of seclusion was quite destroyed.

Solitude, I found, was something to which I could grow accustomed. Well, for a time at least. The success of *Romulus and Hersilia* (arrests and closing aside) should have inspired me to more productivity. Alas, I found the muses once again packed their luggage and deserted me. The hours I should have dedicated to writing were instead spent thinking — very busily — about doing exactly that.

As the days passed, despite my pleasure in being alone (Mr Coggin and Clara, the servant, and Mr Sprat were akin to wraiths — out of sight if one went searching), I came to miss Aphra and Nest. Weary after being at Dorset Garden, I'd lounge in the parlour, arm draped just so, and gaze out the window, imagining myself trapped in a great tower; granted, one of rotting wood and crumbling bricks. The sky would alter from either blue or slate to the darker hues that preceded nightfall. Flocks of birds warbled their swansong as people disgorged from their houses or returned, shucking off their day and embracing evening. Men, some with women in tow, pushed through the doorway of the crowded ale-house. Much later, they'd stumble out, voices raised in liquid joy or ale-induced fury. Sometimes, fists were involved. Then, blood would flow, whistles sound and constables arrive to lug the offenders, and ofttimes the victims, away.

I'd try and imagine what Aphra and Nest were doing. Were they exchanging witticisms in some crowded salon? Were they perambulating along the Seine as Aphra promised? Watching the moon ascend and shed its lambent light over Notre Dame and the cobbled streets? Being entertained by aristocrats and philosophers? Or was Aphra immersed in baths of salts or mercury to lessen her suffering?

I declined invitations from Charlotte, Katherine Herbert and Mark Danvers to drinks at the tavern. Instead, after performances, I lingered in shops, buying quantities of ink galls I didn't need, surplus quills, and paper I'd every intention of filling, someday, just for someone to talk with. No-one awaited me at home or worried what might be delaying my return. In a sense, I was truly my own woman, at liberty to spend time as I chose. It was remarkable. Remarkable that what I most chose to do was watch the clock mark time. Aware I was wasting an opportunity, when Winsome and some of the other Mercury Women asked me to join them in their favoured ale-house, the Unicorn's Horn, by the river, I accepted.

When I woke the following day to the clashing toll of Sunday bells, I decided not to attend church. My head ached but I also thought it was about time I ceased wool-gathering and put my purchases to good use. At least, that's what I told Mr Coggin and Clara, who, along with the servants, looked at me in a most disapproving manner, envisioning the wrath of God falling upon the household as they left to attend service at St Andrew's.

I was just setting out the paper and sharpening my quills when came a knock on the door. At first, I thought I must be mistaken: after all, who calls on a Sunday? When the knock sounded again, I wondered fleetingly if it might be Gabriel returned or even, in a flight of complete fancy, Papa or Bethan. This is what being alone does — your mind makes implausible leaps.

The bells were knelling nine of the clock when I reached the door. Whoever was on the other side was midway through another volley when I wrenched it open.

'Mr Keeling!' I exclaimed, taken aback. 'What can I do for you?' My astonishment could not have been greater had it been his Majesty standing there. Not quite true. Nothing the King did could surprise me any more.

Though he was tall, because Mr Keeling stood at ground level and I upon the doorstep, we were almost eye to eye. He'd removed his hat and, for the first time, I was able to discern his features properly. Possessed of a rather florid face, he'd eschewed his usual periwig to reveal a shaven head of grey stubble. Few men could carry such a style, and certainly not this one. With little hair and no periwig to provide a distraction, his face became the hero … or not. He had a long straight nose, arched dark brows and a full mouth. Broken veins riddled the corner of his nose and cheeks, giving his face a rather ruddy hue. His skin was nevertheless of a darker complexion than most, which made his eyes, which were the most unusual colour, stand out. Lead roles in the making.

More so, because one eye had a golden smudge interrupting its azure surface — just like mine. What a peculiar coincidence …

When he stepped forwards, seeking to enter without an invitation, I opened the door wider. I didn't resist or rebuke him; it was as if I was briefly mesmerised.

'Forgive my intrusion, Mrs Johnson,' he said. There was that strange accent again. Flavoured with spices and faraway tones.

'I'm afraid there's no-one here to greet you, sir,' I said, remembering to speak. 'Mrs Behn is abroad and, if it's Mr Coggin you're seeking, he's at Sunday service.'

'I'm aware, madam. It's not them I've come to see.'

A little warning chimed in my head. 'Oh?'

'I'm here to see you.'

My palms grew sweaty, and my eyes travelled to the other houses in the court, most of which would be devoid of all their God-fearing residents, goddammit. I glanced at the tavern. Though it was not yet open, the landlord, Mr Brogan, should be about. If I slammed the door and ran fast, I could reach its relative safety if required.

'Please,' said Mr Keeling quietly. 'Don't be afraid. Upon my word, I mean you no harm.'

'What do you mean then, sir?' I asked, not yet ready to close the door.

'I've information that might be of interest to you.'

'About what?' I gripped the handle tighter. 'Is it Aphra? Is she well?'

Mr Keeling held up his hands. 'I know nothing of Aphra. Not any more.'

Any more?

Mr Keeling took hold of the door. 'How about we close this and find somewhere to speak privately?' Clearly, he thought the servants were still here. I wouldn't disabuse him.

I loosened my hold as the door clicked shut. I could no more resist him than ignore the frantic scramble of my thoughts. An unsteady hollow thudding filled my ears. I gestured awkwardly to the stairs. 'The parlour is this way. If you would like to proceed, I'll arrange refreshments.'

Mr Keeling bowed and began to ascend. His frame was monstrous on the stairwell. As soon as he was out of sight, I flew to the kitchen, found a tray, glasses and some small ale and arranged them. There wasn't time for coffee or chocolate. I would let the man say what he came for, then bid him leave. I had to.

I mounted the stairs, tray balanced, both dreading and longing to hear what he would say.

Mr Keeling sat with hands clenched into rocks on his knees while I poured drinks. Slightly turned towards each other, facing the window, we sat in the same chairs Aphra and I had occupied the night she told me she was off to Paris. The sun, which was a glorious sphere in the pale blue sky, shone brightly, making the dirt of the court look like Arabian sands — at least, how I imagined them.

Mr Keeling didn't immediately speak, but drank slowly, studying me above the rim of his cup. I avoided looking in his direction, willing him to talk. It was wrong he was here, with me, unchaperoned. He must know if we were discovered, this would damage my already fragile reputation, a reputation I'd worked hard to ensure couldn't be sullied more than my work demanded.

Anger began to mount. I turned to him only to note with astonishment his eyes were brimming with unshed tears.

'Mr Keeling? Are you quite well?' What is it about men and tears that makes a woman's resolve vanish? She becomes all weak-kneed, forgiving and quivery — unlike men, who are repulsed by women's water.

'No, Tribulation Johnson, I fear I'm not. For a start —' He put down his drink. 'I have you at a disadvantage.'

'Oh? How is that, sir?' I wasn't certain what to do.

'My name is not Josiah Keeling.'

I froze. The chime became a clarion. 'And what might it be then, sir?'

He paused. There was a drum roll. A cymbal clashed. 'My name is William Scot.'

That was why he seemed so familiar. Why, when I looked at him, there was a sense of knowing. They *were* my eyes I saw, replete with the distinguishing dash of umber in the right one. He wore a version of my face, albeit masculine, older and worn with experiences I could never hope to share or know. He was a distorted mirror that reflected aspects of myself — with a history about which I remained ignorant. He held in his huge hands a part of me — a part I longed to know.

'Are you my father?' I asked simply.

He hesitated a mere moment. 'I believe I am.'

My chest expanded to admit a lifetime of possibilities. Of alternate memories that, far from being bleak and dark, were so radiant and bright I had to shield my eyes.

He rose and opened his arms. 'And I'm here to tell you my story … *Our* story.'

Call it foolish, a feminine compulsion. The actions of a lonely woman, a daughter alone. Perhaps it was ingrained obedience. Perhaps it was a dream I'd never known I held being fulfilled. Instead of questioning his statement, doubting him, I stood and flew into his embrace.

SCENE SEVEN

Children are so much the goods, the possession of their parents, that they cannot, without a kind of theft, give away themselves without the allowance of those that have the right of them.

Guide to the Female Sex, Hannah Woolley

'I do not know what you've been told,' began William Scot.

We'd returned to our seats, slightly clumsy with each other after we'd clasped. This man was my father. This tall, broad-shouldered man with a winnowed field for hair and a lived-in face with eyes the colour of foreign seas. While in his arms, pressed against his firm chest, aware of his chin resting upon my hair, a wave of sadness had engulfed me. Not once could I ever recall Papa holding me in such a way — closely, tightly, protectively. Not with love — it was too soon for that, but in a manner filled with rainbow promise. Promise that never again would I feel an outcast. Or alone. I drank in the sight of him, sitting so close our knees almost touched, and thought how he was like a book, or a play I was about to read, to watch and yet, this time, I was also part of the performance. I was all atingle, a shivery bundle of anticipation. And yet, there was also something odd about it all, something that didn't sit quite right. Why did he wait until I was by myself to tell me? Why not reveal who he was earlier, when he was at the theatre for example? He could have easily made an excuse to speak there. Why not let Aphra know he was here? Had she not sought his whereabouts? I understood as a man with a dubious past, an alleged traitor, he'd adopted an alias to avoid the attention of authorities, and yet he'd managed to dwell in London and consort with the likes of the Earl of Shaftesbury and other members of the Green Ribbon Club without being arrested for weeks. Did they know who he was? They must. Why, the Earl was around the same age. They must have known each other well before the King's restoration. No doubt, these men protected him. A tiny, inner voice warned me to quash my excitement, temper my longings, and maintain as much objectivity as I could.

After all, this was also a man who'd betrayed his country, his King and, worse, Aphra. I'd needed to understand why.

'Very little,' I answered. That wasn't completely true. I also knew I should be reporting his presence to the authorities. I would … just not yet.

Maybe …

He was my *father*. Presumably, he'd loved my mother. He must have learned of my existence; he must care. Why else was he here? At the very least, he deserved a hearing. A chance — from me.

'Good.' He gave a soft smile. The lines around his eyes folded into creases. This was a man used to smiling, treating life as one grand entertainment. Or being in the sun. 'Then,' he continued, 'all I ask is that you set aside the little you think you know and lend me your ears. It may conflict with what you've heard, but this is my version and I would tell it.'

'Please,' I urged.

And so, William Scot, the man who claimed to be my father, told me his tale.

Apart from rising to refill Mr Scot's — my father's — glass, I didn't move the entire time he spoke. When he finished and enfolded me into his arms again, the initial excitement and confusion I felt at his presence was somewhat tempered. I had to fake a comfort, an acceptance, I didn't properly feel.

Whatever I'd expected him to tell me, it wasn't what I heard. Nay, that's not quite right. Nothing he said astonished me, not really. How could it alter the fact of the man himself? The son of a regicide who'd spent time in Canterbury, fallen in love with my mother, fled when the authorities came aknocking — and when they followed him to Surinam and then Holland, he unashamedly sold his services to the highest bidder.

But it was the manner in which he told his story, the emphasis he gave parts, what he omitted as well as his readiness to shower me with effusive praise, that left me uneasy. I would consider what it all meant later. As I fetched him another drink, grateful the Coggins and servants remained absent, it occurred to me there was a still a great deal I wished to know.

And, frankly, some things I wished I didn't.

It was most peculiar hearing him talk of Papa, Mama and even Bethan almost as if they weren't real people, but props in the performance of his life. Oh, he waxed about how Mama made him feel, but not once did he express remorse or guilt for cuckolding Papa. Nor did he pause to consider how my family's lives were irrevocably altered by actions he initiated. I'd no doubt he instigated the relationship with Mama. He was far too confident, too aware of his own status, even as a fallen man, not to have seduced a mere vicar's wife. The fact he admitted he could move in Canterbury society with relative ease, but chose folk who were, to use Charlotte's phrase, 'easy pickin's' to guarantee his acceptance, exposed a slyness that made me most uneasy.

Was I being too cynical? Were the news-sheets I read, gossip I heard, plays I performed and helped to stage beginning to affect the way I viewed even my own father? Never mind awareness that he'd betrayed Aphra, that he was sought by Gabriel and Solomon as well.

It didn't help he sounded much like the Wits when they barged into the Tiring Rooms, using predictable words and hackneyed phrases to pander to actors' and actresses' vanity. My father may have observed me, may have thought he knew me, but he did not.

Why wasn't I dizzy with delight? I had a father! Papa was relegated to a minor role. But, as the morning wore on and we spoke — well, Mr Scot did most of the speaking; I listened — my feelings of ambivalence grew. When I asked why he'd risked coming to England, he admitted, while I was the main reason, he also had business to attend, business that could alter his life. More he wouldn't say, but he grinned continuously, joggling his brows as if to indicate a great secret. He was staying in rooms at Robert Ferguson's house. He admitted he was sympathetic to the Whigs, whose cause, in his mind, most closely aligned with his father's ideals and the Commonwealth. We turned to less inflammatory and dangerous topics such as the theatre, Mr Coggin's house, St Bride's, the state of the river over summer, even how the horrid Popish Plot and Titus Oates appeared to have all but fizzled ('like a fuse that never takes', he said and I thought of all those who'd died or been hounded, arrested, beaten, had their homes and livelihoods taken, been exiled, all because suspicion landed on them, and wondered what they'd think of such a description; surely, their lives had exploded as a consequence of Oates and those who encouraged him — many of whom were among those my father counted as friends). He asked about Aphra's and Lady Slingsby's arrests and then, much to my astonishment, queried if it was because they were suspected of being involved in a plot themselves.

'Another plot?' I said, wriggling in my seat. 'I don't think so, sir. While I know there have been several sham plots in the wake of the Popish one, Aphra made no mention of any such accusation. Why? Have you heard something different?'

My father gave a laugh which sounded false even to my amenable ears. 'No. Only, that so many — including women — have been called to account for even a whisper, such is the volatile mood of the city. It wouldn't have surprised me if Aphra was held for more than writing words deemed treacherous. Her intentions have been called into question in the past.'

His tone was conciliatory but his words provocative. Did he expect me to agree? To be a turncoat and admonish Aphra and her choices? Puzzled as to his motivation, I rose. 'Only to those who choose to interpret them so. Aphra is and always has been loyal to the Crown. She does not suffer those who seek to overturn the rightful succession, regardless of whether the heir is a Catholic or not. To her, the King is God's anointed and his faith should not forbid him his sacred right. If she offends anyone with her words then it must be your friends who she sees as —' My hand flew to my mouth. Here I was talking about offending people and I was doing that to my own father.

Rather than rebuke, my father chuckled. 'You're right on that score. My friends, and by that you mean Anthony Ashley Cooper, the Earl of Shaftesbury —'

It flashed across my mind how odd it was my father said the man's name and title in full, as if reminding me he had powerful associates.

'— Lord Grey and Mr Ferguson, find Aphra's constant attacks both tiresome and reckless.'

'Because she gives a voice to those who lack one — a voice that disrupts and challenges their authority, forcing them to listen.'

My father made a show of considering his response. 'It's the tone of the voice that most disturbs them. It's offensive and oft bellicose. The Earl genuinely cares about ordinary folk and their desires, despite what Aphra writes.'

I stifled a snort. It wasn't just Aphra calling the Earl and his allies to account. 'Forgive me, sir, for I know he's your friend, but if the Earl really cared about ordinary people and what they want, wouldn't he encourage his associates to make legitimate changes, using Parliament and the people's representatives, instead of provoking anger and unease on the streets, inciting rebellion?'

'Sometimes, Tribulation,' said my father condescendingly, 'the only way to instigate change is by burning down the old order so a new one might rise.'

'Like the phoenix out of the ashes.'

'Exactly,' he said, failing to pick up my sarcasm.

'And yet, the phoenix rises only to burn again and again. It repeats the pattern of its death and rebirth.'

My father began to splutter. 'Until such time as the King holds another Parliament, and honours its outcomes, the will of the people, then what else can the bird — the people — do but torch existing structures so better ones replace them?'

'Replacement doesn't always guarantee improvement,' I muttered and moved to the window. Neighbours were returning to their houses. Services must have concluded, which meant the Coggins would be home soon. I didn't want them to find Mr Scot there. Perhaps sensing my mood, as I turned from the window, he stood.

'While this has been delightful, Tribulation, I must make haste. I can see from the expression on your face you'd rather not be found entertaining a man without a chaperone, even if he is your father.'

Nor an accused traitor, I thought, but kept that to myself.

We bade each other farewell and, as he brushed his lips against my cheek, he made me promise we'd meet again soon.

'You understand, Tribulation, my presence, my identity, must be kept secret.' He wrapped a hand around my forearm. 'I've come here at great risk to myself.'

'I understand,' I said, while all I could think was, *What about the risk to me? To Aphra?*

I shut the door and raced up the steps, taking them two at a time so I might watch him leave. He cut a fine figure as he wove his way past those eager for their Sunday dinners or, I thought as the tavern opened its doors, ales. He doffed his hat to a group of well-dressed women who curtseyed and giggled, one turning to watch as he disappeared around the corner. Not once did he look back. I felt a combination of relief and disappointment.

So, I thought, resting my elbows on the sill, any thoughts of writing swept from my mind, that was my father. As I followed his passage across the court, it occurred to me: if William Scot was in London, where on God's good earth was Gabriel? How could I learn *his* whereabouts? Should I?

Nay.

If I'd learned one thing working with Gabriel and Solomon, it was that I'd only be given as much information as needed to perform any duties — and, for the time being, they were finished.

I gave a forlorn sigh and sent a swift prayer that wherever Gabriel was, he was safe. Oh, and Solomon too, I thought chiding myself for almost omitting him. The best thing I could do until they returned was carefully consider what I did know — about William Scot, the man who claimed to be my father. I would keep the secret of his presence, at least until I could tell Aphra and seek her advice.

As I swiftly revisited all he'd told me — the travels he'd undertaken, the things he'd done, the opinions he'd offered — it occurred to me that not once, during the entire three or more hours we'd conversed, had he asked about me.

SCENE EIGHT

Since Man with that inconstancy was born,
To love the absent, and the present scorn,
Why do we deck, why do we dress
For such short-liv'd happiness?

'To Alexis, in answer to his Poem against Fruition',
Aphra Behn

Over the next couple of weeks, I saw my father a few times, never for very long. It was usually after a performance or, on a Sunday, after service. We went for a walk in Covent Garden and St James's Park. Once, we lingered by the river enjoying a rare hour of tepid sunshine. A small ale-house was chosen on another drizzle-bound evening, where we partook of broiled pigeon and cheese. I would look forward to seeing him, only to find that afterwards I was left somewhat disappointed, as if hungry after a banquet or given an incomplete book to read.

My father would greet me with an enveloping hold and 'What news?' and then immediately embark on a recounting of what he'd done since we'd last seen each other. He'd regale me with long-winded stories of when he lived in Surinam, Antwerp, Bruges, Amsterdam, and Middleburg. I mostly enjoyed these tales of unfamiliar cities and places, the people, customs and geography. The United Provinces dominated, understandably since it was where he now lived. He spoke about elegant stone or wood buildings adorning streets, how lilting music oft filled the air, mingling with the smoke or morning mists to make it appear as if the clouds themselves were singing. He described the change of seasons, the unusual character of the light, which was such a contrast to what shone in London even though the same sun beamed down upon us. Rivers meandered lazily through many of these places, and he'd describe the large barques or galleons, or the smaller boats and barges filled with coal, wood, wool, fruit, vegetables, grain and livestock that glided atop the waters; how, just as in England, rivers were the lifeblood.

'Every time I was upon the dark green waters —' he began the afternoon we spent by the Thames. The river was abubble that day, choked with wherries, tilt boats, barges and the larger ships destined for faraway places. I'd have liked to have sat in quiet companionship, drinking in the animated portrait of the waterway, but my father had other ideas.

'— I would imagine the very same brine wending its way to the ocean and then on to England. Upon the sea, the rivers, was when I felt most connected to my homeland and was struck with grief that I could never return.'

I didn't point out he was here now, so it seemed he could. All the same, I couldn't help but wonder, were we being watched? Were intelligencers shadowing my father's every move? I would casually take in the surrounds, my eyes alighting on those who lingered close only to observe my father doing the same. Aware of potential peril then, his apparent ease was but an illusion.

'Tribulation,' he sighed. He did that a great deal. Drawn-out exhalations of a weary spirt — or a performing one. I was beginning to think my father was the consummate actor. 'Sometimes, recognition of longing, of need, doesn't manifest until the object of desire itself does.' He reached for my hand and gripped it in his own, his meaning apparent. A couple sitting nearby threw us disapproving looks and I wondered if they believed us to be lovers. Judgement would fall upon me, not the man. I sought to alter their perception.

'Ah, Father,' I said loudly and was relieved to see their expressions change from reproof to benevolence. 'Verily I do appreciate your meaning.'

My father struck his chest with his fist and gave a rather soggy smile. 'That's the first time you've addressed me as such. How it plucks my heart strings.' I half-expected him to press the back of his hand to his forehead and expire in one … two … three … He played his fingers across his ribs as if to demonstrate. '*Father*,' he sighed again. 'Another longing made apparent. When we're together, in private, I would you always call me so.'

Damn if my bruised heart didn't chirr. It wasn't an imposition. Not when the man I'd believed my papa denied me.

Most days, William Scot would come to the theatre, sitting in a box and watching whatever was being staged whether I had a role or naught. Sometimes, the Earl of Shaftesbury was with him. Once, Lord Grey. Most often, it was Robert Ferguson. It gave me a peculiar mix of pleasure, pride, regret and disgruntlement to see him there. I chose not to consider his choice of company too deeply, more's the pity. How was he not ashamed of what his daughter was? Did they know what I was to him? Did it matter? He might forbid me from acknowledging who he was to me in public — after all, he was still a wanted man and, as he made mention, to reveal his identity would place him in grave danger. And, as he failed to mention, me as well. I told no-one and, as a consequence, there were those among the cast who naturally believed I was his mistress, unable to conceive of a relationship that didn't involve a woman surrendering her body and reputation, especially when that woman also trod the boards. I found it tiresome but, for the time being, convenient.

And yet, this man, my father, who was unknown until he became a faint possibility, was both all I'd hoped for in his bold and regular assertions of affection and pride and a strange disquieting disappointment. He'd revealed something of his past, his life (though he was curiously reticent about time spent with Aphra and dodged my questions with unnerving skill), but he still exhibited a remarkable lack of curiosity about mine. Of Mama, Papa, Bethan, he never asked, so I never told. In some ways, I felt protective. It was as if by not recounting or demanding he hear of them, I was shielding them from further hurt or harm. I had to believe William Scot was speaking truthfully when he claimed ignorance of my existence until recently. But a tiny, reedy voice deep inside my head would occasionally raise its concerns, forcing me to wonder. If he loved Mama as much as he'd declared, why had he never bothered to reach out and at least enquire as to her wellbeing? How her life unfolded (collapsed)? Was it to protect her? Out of consideration for Papa's dignity? Was it he feared the dreadful justice of the Crown should his whereabouts be known? Or was it something else altogether?

And why, if he was sought for crimes about which he wouldn't speak, was he able to walk abroad? Admittedly, with a false identity, a disguise of sorts, and in select company who all worked to conceal his history. And not without a preference for the crepuscular comfort of evening and darkened rooms and theatres. But he was about nevertheless. What had changed? To what end were Shaftesbury and the others protecting him?

When sleep continued to tease me, I'd lie awake and catalogue the days, ponder these questions but, as with a great deal to do with William Scot, the answers continued to elude me.

And then Aphra came home.

I welcomed her return like the city spring zephyrs. I'd become quite wretched in her absence. By simply reappearing and holding me tight, showering kisses and declarations of the space I'd taken up in her heart and head each day, repeating how much she'd missed me, she reminded me I belonged *somewhere*.

And with someone.

I didn't intend to blurt out the miracle that had manifested while she was away but, perched on the bed while Nest unpacked her bulging bag, Aphra snatching up mementos as fast as they were removed, each with a story attached which she began to regale, bestowing magnificent gifts, I could wait no longer.

A colourful neckerchief was draped across my shoulders, a book by Abbe Paul Tallemant, *Voyage de L'Isle d'Amour*, was pressed into my hands. Like a conjurer, she extracted from her case a glistening bottle containing a beautiful, heady fragrance made from jasmine and musk. I was quite overcome. No-one had ever thought to purchase me such extravagant presents before.

'See this?' She held up another book. '*La Montre. The Watch*. Given to me by none other than the infamous Balthazar Bonnecourse himself. Look. He's even inscribed it. What say you?' She pushed it towards me. '*Mon Dieu!*' Her speech was peppered with expressions in dulcet French, a language she'd always been able to speak, albeit clumsily, but her grasp on it was markedly improved even in a short time. 'What's wrong, kitten?' She paused midway through unravelling a wondrous piece of lace.

I slowly placed the unopened book down. 'William Scot is here.'

Her face paled and she slumped onto the bed, books, shawls, shoes and other fripperies tumbling to the floor. Nest froze, a long peach-coloured garment falling from her fingers. 'Are you certain?'

I took a deep breath, inhaling clarity and conciseness. 'While you were away, he introduced himself. He's been here, in London, a while. Under a false identity.'

Aphra's dark eyes glimmered. 'Who?'

'Josiah Keeling.'

She frowned then her brow smoothed. 'The Earl's Baptist friend.' She dragged her fingers though her hair, uncaring of the pins raining upon her shoulders in a shower of metal.

'That's not all.' I waited until I had her attention. 'He claims he's my father.'

Aphra inhaled sharply. 'Oh, my darling girl. He told you that? How? When?'

Nest gave up all pretence of unpacking and, first caressing my face with a dry thumb, pulled up a chair next to the bed. Holding my hand tightly, Aphra listened as I told her just about everything William Scot had said and done since the day he came to the house. I didn't admit to my ambivalence — about the man, or about whether to alert the authorities. Not then.

After I finished, Aphra sat quietly, eyes scanning my face, as if to exhume any forgotten detail. My hand was still enfolded in both of hers. With a long sigh of inevitability, Nest heaved herself to her feet and returned to unpacking, but not before she'd dropped a kiss upon my head and squeezed my shoulders.

'Oh, Tribulation,' said Aphra, rising. She moved to the window and gazed out, a prognosticator looking to the future. No wonder, when her very home now bore the stain of a past she'd thought forever behind her. The view from her room was slightly different to mine. Whereas mine overlooked the court, Aphra's faced Holborn Hill. Waves of rooftops, billowing smoke and teeming streets merged before thinning into structured rows of orchards and verdant rolling hills. 'This is my fault.'

'How?' I joined her. 'How is it *your* fault?' Where the grey light struck her face, it rendered her ancient, like a crone of myth. I began to imagine her as the Oracle of Delphi, condemned to eternal life by Apollo who, though she first agreed to his advances — providing he grant her immortality — later reneged on their deal. Unable to break his promise, the god ensured she'd live forever, but age. Such a cruel punishment, condemning the woman who spurned him to a living death. Is that how William Scot made Aphra feel? Every year she'd been on God's good earth showed: a life tempered by bitterness, sorrow and regret.

The day, which had started with insipid blue skies and a cowardly sun, was now being swallowed by a bank of clouds creeping from the south. Washing strewn over hedges and fences was being haphazardly bundled by distracted maids. I could just spy vendors in the streets further up the hill, erecting canopies over their produce with practised ease. From where we stood, snatches of conversations carried, along with faint bleating and bellowing and the eerie whistle of approaching winds.

Finally, Aphra found words. 'Because … I should have told you what I began to suspect the moment I set eyes on you but refused to acknowledge until … until …' She lowered her head.

'The Earl of Shaftesbury,' I finished. 'That day in the Tiring Rooms.'

I remembered how uncomfortable his words had made her, made me: his crafty, knowing looks and coarse barbs like a woollen garment against bare skin.

She bit her lip, her teeth leaving marks that refused to fade. 'Not only did he see what I had, he *knew.*' She gave a harsh bark of laughter. 'Why, you even asked me what he meant by his sly insinuations. Who William was. What did I do? Instead of being direct I … I …'

'Wrote to a friend to discover William Scot's whereabouts so you might confront him yourself.'

Aphra's eyes narrowed, and a small, shrewd smile flashed. 'Ah … I wondered if you'd been reading my letters.'

A lance of guilt pierced my body. My cheeks filled with the colour of guilt. 'You *knew*?'

'You forget, Tribulation. I was once a spy. I was taught how to open letters, reseal them so no-one suspected. You were very good. It took me a while to realise what was happening.'

'Why didn't you say something?'

Aphra gave a half-hearted shrug and turned away. 'Because I thought you had a right to know what I lacked the courage to tell you.'

The lance was withdrawn and the wound miraculously healed. I stared at her in wonder.

'I mean,' she continued, 'what if my suspicions, if the Earl's, were wrong? What trouble would we set in motion? I needed answers and I thought if I went straight to the source, I would find them. Only, so many years had passed, I didn't know how to locate him, just someone who might know how I could. What I never considered was that William would discover I was searching for him and come here. Part of the reason I agreed to go to Paris was I thought, hoped, I might get word of him there. That was a wasted effort and now I know why.' She slumped into a chair. 'I think I need wine. Nest, can you, please?'

Nest nodded reluctantly, not wanting to be severed from the discussion. She shut the door behind her.

Deep furrows rent Aphra's brow and her eyes were the colour of slate. She'd been honest with me; it was time to furnish her with all the truth.

'Aphra,' I said, kneeling beside the chair, holding the arm, wanting to hold hers. 'There's something else.'

She smoothed my hair from my forehead. 'From the look on your face, one would think you'd murdered someone.'

I swallowed. 'Not murdered.'

Aphra's brows rose.

'I didn't open your letters to assuage *my* curiosity alone.'

Summoning courage from the depleted stores inside me, as I crouched beside her, at one point dragging over a stool to ease my cramped legs, I told her everything. I told her about Jonathan Rickman who was really Gabriel Freeman (ensuring my tone was measured even as my shining eyes betrayed me); and about Solomon and Sir Joseph Williamson. How I agreed to help them so I might prove she wasn't involved in any plot to harm the King.

'A plot? Hurt his Majesty?' Aphra scoffed. 'As if I would consider such treachery. The only plots I'm involved in are the written kind.' She shook her head sorrowfully. 'Shaftesbury and his cronies, Titus Oates and his, have much to answer for: their accusations have ensured the words and actions of even the most blameless of people are thought suspect. And now you tell me Jonathan Rickman was an intelligencer?' She whistled and her head moved in admiration. 'He had everyone fooled. A fine actor indeed. Pray, continue.'

I explained how I had to check any correspondence she'd written or received and report back to Gabriel or Solomon who, in turn, told Sir Joseph.

Aphra sucked in her breath.

'I only did it to prove your innocence.' My excuse sounded weak even to me, becalmed as I was on this ocean of trouble, one of my own making.

Nest returned, and would have left again, but I asked her to stay. There were to be no secrets between us, not any more.

'So, you have done nothing to forgive, Aphra,' I said. 'Nothing.' I inched my way towards her, my eyes never leaving her face. 'It's I who must beg yours — for breaking your trust, betraying your generosity and goodness.' I could barely see for the tears that suddenly welled. I prayed she would see them for what they were — not a device to elicit sympathy but torn from my heart in shame.

Aphra didn't say anything at first. Nor did she move. Instead, she turned towards the window. Rain had begun to fall. Great, heavy drops of utter sorrow that fell on the roof even as they coursed down my face. Was discovering my real father worth tearing asunder the wondrous family we'd made here in London? Nay. Yet, the blame didn't lie with William Scot, as much as I wished it. This was my fault, my doing, my choice. If Aphra wanted nothing more to do with me, I would understand. I would pack my belongings and quit her sight this day. Lord, I sounded like a stage direction, yet this was no performance, but life. My life.

Just when I thought I had to break the impossible silence, she rose and pulled me to my feet. With a broken, guttural groan, she folded me in her arms.

She felt smaller, frailer, despite her pleasing plumpness — a bird flung from the nest. I could feel her trembling … or was that me?

'I'm only going to say this once, kitten,' she whispered, her words feathery against my cheek. 'There's *nothing* to forgive. You did what you thought was right, to protect *me*. It's more than anyone, Nest being the exception, has ever done.' She cupped my face with both hands and stamped her forehead against mine. 'You did what you thought was right.' She took a deep, shaky breath. 'Know this. I love *you*, Tribulation Johnson. It matters not who your father is, what your mother did, how or why you came to me. The point is, you did. You whirled into my life — oh, alright, cast yourself upon my doorstep. You found me and, in turn, we found each other. There's nothing you could do or say that would alter my feelings, except to perhaps make them stronger, if that was even possible. Do you hear me? Do you? William Scot might be your father, but to me, you're the daughter I never had and, until I met you, didn't know I longed for.'

I was sniffing in a most unladylike way as my eyes and nose streamed worse than Dorset Ditch. My chest ached with a glorious wonder. Filled with relief, with warmth and radiance, like a thousand suns, I swear I became a beacon lightning all of St Bride's and beyond.

'Oh, Aphra … I don't know what to say.'

'Aye, you do,' said Nest, standing and rubbing my back. I'd almost forgotten she was there. She wrapped her arms around us both.

'You're right. I do. You, Aphra Behn,' I began, searching for the right way to put my emotions into words, 'you're more than a mother or sister to me. They're accidents of birth — oft happy ones, but sometimes, as I have cause to know, not. You're much more than a friend, though you're that as well — a friend like those described in tales of yore, magical and terrible all at once.'

She laughed.

'You're … you're … You're my soul-kin. My heart-kith. And, I … I love you too … With every single strand of my being.'

Aphra didn't move for a long time. None of us did. Then, she kissed me softly on the mouth. 'I know you do, goose.'

'What happened to kitten?' My voice was cracked, as if my words had sundered it.

'She became a protector and grew claws and wings …'

'That makes me a griffon.'

We both burst out laughing.

'Griffon it is, then.' Aphra gently released me. 'My very tall griffon.'

I turned to look at Nest. 'I love you too, Nest. You know that, don't you?'

Nest's face lit up. 'Just as well, chit. One-sided affection is rarely agreeable.' She hugged me tightly.

Aphra brushed hair out of my eyes and when Nest released me held my face a moment longer. Her smile was a treasure found — rich and beautiful. 'Come now.' She patted the bed. 'Sit back down and, while Nest finishes unpacking, let us talk further about this father of yours. For, if William Scot has dared to return to England, I'm sorry to say, it's not only because of you.' She brushed my hand. 'I don't say that to infer you're not significant to him.'

'I didn't take it that way.' I flashed a smile. 'The thing is … from the moment he revealed himself, I've had this feeling there's something else at play, another reason he's here. Whatever it is, he won't tell me.'

Aphra nodded solemnly. 'If he's in the company of Shaftesbury and Lord Grey, the reason is dubious. And he's staying with Robert Ferguson?'

'That's what he told me.'

Aphra rubbed her chin. 'Why do known Whigs risk fraternising with a regicide's son, a traitor who sold his country to the Dutch and is a wanted double agent, eh?'

'He was very curious about your recent arrest. Wanted to know if it was for more than offending the King. He even wondered if you might be involved in a sham plot or something similar.'

'Now, I've no doubt he's up to something. He was trying to see where my loyalties lie. And, I suspect, testing yours as well.

'The question is,' said Aphra, after taking a long drink. 'What's he hope to gain by coming home now, apart from introducing himself to you? What can Shaftesbury, Ferguson and that damned Green Ribbon Club offer him? They either need William for whatever they're planning next or they're hoping his presence will distract whoever is watching them from their real intentions. They must be making it worth his while for him to take such a risk.'

'You think the Earl is up to something?'

'The Earl is always up to something,' said Aphra dismissively. 'His plan to use Titus Oates to overturn the succession has failed. Parliament appears to be permanently prorogued, so he's left with no choice but to attempt something dramatic.'

I thought of William Scot brazenly declaring the only way to bring about change was to burn existing structures down.

Aphra drummed her fingers on her bottom lip. 'How far would someone determined to overturn government and the succession go so their plans succeed? Why bring William into the mix? What can he possibly do? What does he hope to gain?'

She rose and began to pace. Nest returned to unpacking. I watched Aphra, nursing my wine, trying to deduce answers to her questions.

Finally, she stopped. 'What we need to do is try and discover not only the real reason your father is here, risking his life, but what Shaftesbury and his friends are up to as well.'

'You don't think we should let the authorities know he's here? I confess, Aphra, the question has been plaguing me since he first revealed himself and I've felt so divided.'

Aphra gave a secret sort of smile. 'Trust me when I say we don't need to alert anyone. I've no doubt the regimen know he's here — and if for some reason they don't, then when we're ready and if there is something to divulge, we'll inform them.'

'Not before?'

'What if, perchance, William *is* here for you? What if I'm wrong and he's a changed man after all? Shouldn't we give him the benefit of the doubt?'

'But how do we find out?' I asked.

'By using the only things at our disposal and which men always underestimate — our wit and wiles.' Aphra held up a cautionary finger. 'Not that it will be easy, mind. There's a reason your father has managed to evade the authorities for so long. Why he was able to outsmart me all those years ago. He may come across as somewhat guileless and even honourable, but —' She paused, one brow arched.

'I don't foster illusions about him,' I said quickly. But I had. More than I realised. Illusions that were being shredded faster than a woman's reputation.

'Very well then. If you're certain, kitten. Let's see if we can't discover his other reasons for being in London.'

She was too tactful to say 'real'.

'And when we have them?' I asked, the essence of a warrior entering my veins.

'Then, we take what we know to the authorities.'

So be it.

Aphra continued. 'It's a pity your man Gabriel Freeman isn't still about to advise us.' She helped herself to more wine. 'I'll arrange to meet William as soon as I can. I doubt he'll be forthcoming. Though I'm not the ingenue I once was, he knows me too well. But you, you

Tribulation, are a foreign land. And from what you've told me, William fancies himself quite the explorer. If William is going to let down his guard and allow something to slip, it will be to you, his daughter.'

Aphra was asking me if I was prepared to betray my father. It was the question that haunted my waking dreams.

'But, as you said, we must also consider he might be innocent,'

'Yes. We should. So, how about we treat our investigation the way you did yours for Mr Freeman? We'll set out to prove his innocence.'

I could live with that.

'But, if he's not, kitten —' she was serious suddenly; I could see echoes of the spy she'd once been, a woman charged with protecting her country, her liege '— then you have to be prepared to do whatever it takes not only to save the Crown but to bring those who would harm it to justice — even your father. Can you do that?'

At that precise moment, we were interrupted by a knock on the door. Nest scurried to open it. Clara Coggin stood there beaming.

In the flurry of welcomes that followed, the gushing adoration of Aphra's souvenirs and gifts, and insistence she relay every detail of her travels, I prayed she'd overlook one.

I failed to answer her final question.

SCENE NINE

The mind is its own place, and in itself
Can make a Heaven of hell, a Hell of Heaven

Paradise Lost, John Milton

In his lodgings in rooms above a shop in Witch Street, Gabriel nursed a jug of ale, sitting in the one chair the room could accommodate, what with the large bed occupying most of the space. Bored, he gazed out the rickety crack-paned window towards the river he couldn't see but would have sworn on a Bible he could smell.

Below him, the old clockmaker, the landlord, a Hollander named Maarten van Beek, could be heard closing his shutters and giving his long-suffering apprentice instructions. A recent widower, van Beek was trying to soften his grief with wine and failing. After a few drinks, he was oft found sitting upon a stool, the supper the maid prepared uneaten, a puddle of abject misery. Now and then, understanding his state of mind, Gabriel tried to keep him company, but he had his own problems, the greatest being that damned mountebank, William Scot.

It still annoyed Gabriel the man had managed to slip past them and make land in England like a royal returnee. He'd always prided himself on his powers of surveillance and disguise, but in such a case it didn't matter what precautions were taken — if the target knew you were coming, evasion wasn't hard. There was no doubt: Sir Leoline had a leak. Williamson had warned the Secretary but, damn his pride, Sir Leoline refused to credit the notion and blamed the former spymaster's men for incompetence instead.

'I suspect it was Buckingham,' said Williamson to Gabriel upon his return. 'Or that pickaroon, Shaftesbury.'

Gabriel didn't disagree.

Once Williamson learned from Gabriel that Scot was back, the new spymaster failing to notify the old one, it hadn't taken long for his men to locate him. He'd been observed making contact with Tribulation but was yet to meet with Aphra. Now they were back, he and Solomon would take over reconnaissance. Though he was concerned Scot appeared to be spending a great deal of time in Tribulation's company, it did give credence to her insistence that Aphra only reached out to learn the truth about her parentage. But it also meant Gabriel was forced to watch without intervening as the treacherous bastard inveigled himself into Tribulation's graces. He felt like a pottage left too long upon the stove, everything stuck to the insides, scarring the metal.

Gabriel would sometimes marvel that the heart he thought forever torn asunder by Wait-Still's and Patience's deaths had repaired itself — that he was able to feel something other than anger or despair again. From the moment he saw Tribulation standing in the wings of Dorset Garden, dressed in that flimsy white robe, dreadful make-up disguising her lovely face, shaking with cold and apprehension yet doing her utmost to bury it, he knew she was a danger to him. More accurately, a danger to his sworn commitment to never, ever love again. He didn't deserve to. He'd rather be stabbed, shot or even tortured than know the pain of handing over his heart to another's keeping and losing her. But when he'd collected Tribulation in his arms during that first performance, surprised at how comfortable he felt holding her, and looked into those lustrous turquoise eyes, one with a splash of amber, as if God added a dapple of liquid gold when forming them, he was lost.

On top of everything, she was also a deep thinker, a weaver of marvellous, clever stories. Like Aphra, she was a woman from whom tales, accounts, observations, flowed. It was wondrous to think Tribulation had composed not one play, but two thus far. Not even calling herself 'Anonymous' had kept her identity safe from him. And then there were the few astute tracts she'd had published — Aphra wielding her influence. Now they were both involved in another story — one Scot had invented to hide his real intentions. Intentions Gabriel was determined to expose.

If only he could warn Tribulation, tell her to be careful. But the whole operation now depended on her not knowing she was being watched — Scot and Aphra as well. If he was to discover what Scot and the other men he met with — Shaftesbury and Lords Grey, Russell and Essex, Algernon Sidney, the vicar Robert Ferguson and, of late, the barrister Robert West and an old Cromwellian, Colonel Rumsey — were planning, and prove that neither Tribulation nor Aphra were involved, then she must remain in ignorance of their surveillance. They all must.

Problem was, he suspected Aphra was also seeking to discover Scot's reasons for returning to England. Why else hadn't she come forward about Scot's presence to the authorities? Or maybe it was for Tribulation's sake. God knows, he was equivocal about it all.

Were Shaftesbury and his cronies plotting an uprising, as Williamson suspected? Or was it something else? Only time and watching and bloody waiting would tell.

So, here he was, back in London, a matter of streets away from the theatre, White Hall, Westminster, and Tribulation. She'd moved since he left. It was a shock when he loitered about Dorset Street only to learn that the 'woman writer and her daughter' (as one local shopkeeper described them) had removed to the other side of Holborn in St Bride's. It hadn't taken long to find them lodging with the mercer Coggin. A ramshackle house in a small court with a tavern and some disreputable neighbours. The number of times Gabriel had followed Tribulation home from the theatre didn't warrant counting. If he wasn't able, Solomon stepped in. The irony of being unable to guarantee her safety while she was with her own father rankled him terribly.

Alone and disowned and all because she trod the boards. What would her family make of her being published and performed? You couldn't disown someone again, could you? It was such a spiteful gesture.

Thank the Saviour she had Aphra.

It was no wonder Aphra safeguarded her. They were birds of a feather, a pair, hatched from the same clutch and huddled in the same nest.

Ah, Nest. He smiled at the thought of the old lady. According to Williamson and Arlington, she'd been clucking around Aphra since they could remember. He was glad she was still there to chirp around Tribulation.

He just wished he could as well.

Moses in a basket. Listen to him. Chirping. That was most definitely not on his mind when he was around Tribulation …

Forced to lurk in the shadows, in the boxes of the theatre, the entries and doorways in alleyways and snickets, to become invisible in the crowds always milling across the bridge, his duty was to see without being seen. To observe from nearby tables inside inns and ale-houses, the back of the church. From the window in the ale-house opposite the Coggins'. Whenever he wasn't keeping an eye on Scot, he was watching Tribulation. Maybe he should be grateful the man was spending time with his daughter: made his job easier.

He took a long draught of ale. It had grown warm. He swiped a hand across his mouth and willed Solomon to return.

For once, his powers of mind worked. There were footsteps on the stairs. A sharp rap, and the door creaked open.

'I'd offer you a drink,' said Gabriel. 'But it's not very appetising.'

'Forget that,' said Solomon, shutting the door and flopping onto the bed. 'I've news.' He took some deep breaths and mopped his brow with an enormous kerchief.

'Did you run the entire way?'

'Only part,' said Solomon. 'I had the hackney take me towards the river and Steel Yard.'

'That's in the opposite direction.'

'Exactly. Then, I hired a wherry to take me to Arundel Stairs and, from there, I made my way on foot. Those following me are hopefully still on the tail of that hackney. I paid him to continue to Seething Lane.'

Gabriel burst out laughing. 'A wild goose chase.'

'Have you ever seen a wild goose?' asked Solomon. 'Me neither. But I want to know what the bloody bird's after and why he's never caught.' He smacked his lips together. 'On second thoughts, give me a drink. I'm drier than a miller's fingers.' He accepted the tankard and downed it in three gulps.

'What do you have?' asked Gabriel.

Solomon's dark eyes twinkled. 'You know we were certain that group from the Green Ribbon Club were planning to interfere in the election of the London sheriffs, only we couldn't confirm it because the bastards moved their meeting place? Well, I found their new location, Gabe.'

Gabriel straightened. 'Where?'

'They're in rooms above a wine shop of a certain Mr Shephard, who also happens to own a tavern out Hoddesdon way.'

'I know the one. It's near the bridge at Rye House.'

'That's it,' said Solomon.

'Who's gathering? Is it still Shaftesbury, Grey and the like?'

'Them, and others — a one-eyed fellow.' Solomon covered his left eye. 'They call him Hannibal.'

'Richard Rumbold,' supplied Gabriel. 'Ex-military.'

'There's Mr Wildman, a Leveller, from what I can gather. Richard Goodenough — the newly elected sheriff — has started showing his face, along with his brother. They'd hang about the theatre sometimes when you were performing. There's a couple more I'm yet to identify.'

Gabriel hesitated. 'Was William Scot among them?'

Solomon sighed. He knew it was something Gabriel didn't really want to hear. 'He was.'

Gabriel nodded slowly.

'Turns out,' continued Solomon, 'Williamson's right. They're planning an uprising — either Accession or Gunpowder Day. They're talking thousands of men, putting London in arms.'

Gabriel let out a long whistle. 'They've only given themselves a few weeks to set the impossible in motion.'

Solomon poured himself more ale. 'Time enough to be foiled too.'

'Did they see you?'

Solomon laughed. 'Ja, of course, every one of them. I bribed the wench pouring drinks in the tavern next door to let me serve them. They didn't hold their tongues before a blackamoor, did they? What would an ignorant savage like me understand?' Solomon made a scoffing noise.

Reinvigorated, Gabriel leaped to his feet and clapped him on the back. 'Come on, let's go tell Williamson.'

'So he can arrest them?'

'Williamson will hold back. This group of misfits won't be content with just an uprising — especially when it's still so far off and risks failure. My bet is it's another distraction. They're plotting something riskier and far more dangerous. Something involving fewer men. Once we learn what that is, *then* Williamson will strike.'

'With deadly force,' said Solomon, finishing his drink.

'With deadly justice, at any rate,' said Gabriel, trying not think of what such a verdict would mean for Tribulation and her newly minted father.

SCENE TEN

Dar'st thou upbraid the faults thou hast created?

The Revenge or, A Match Made in Newgate, Anon (Tribulation Johnson with help from Aphra Behn)

I wasn't privy to Aphra's first meeting with William Scot in sixteen years. But when she entered the parlour after having been in his company, she was at sixes and sevens, forgetting to remove her hat and coat. Nest didn't wait to be told: she fetched wine.

Aphra began to pace, wringing her hands, pinching the fabric of her skirt and staring at the walls, out the window, at her feet. Vaguely aware of my regard, she flashed a smile, holding up a finger to let me know she was collecting thoughts, like a spindle wool. As patiently as I could, I waited and gazed towards the lofty heavens. It was quite late, the bells having tolled ten. The moon was aswim on violet seas, caressing the city with silvery beams. September was almost abed and the nip in the air was a stark reminder autumn was well and truly upon us and winter, its close brethren, would pay a visit all too soon. A small fire crackled in the hearth, just enough to keep the chill at bay.

Finally, after Nest brought a jug of claret and fresh glasses, and a hot chocolate for herself, Aphra spoke — but not before she'd enjoyed a restorative mouthful.

'In so many ways,' she began in the middle of the conversation she'd evidently been having with herself, 'he's still the same, but in others, it was as if I was addressing a stranger.'

'Strange the man is,' mumbled Nest.

Aphra shot her a withering look. Nest met it, daring a contradiction.

'So many years apart, so many changes.' Aphra passed a hand over her face, resting it lightly on one cheek then the other, indicating the kind to which she referred. 'And yet, when I saw him again, aged, carrying more flesh than I recall, my treacherous heart skipped and fluttered like a maiden about a maypole. Ugh.'

Aphra was the first to admit she was ever susceptible to male charm. My father likely was aware and had set out to disarm her. I prayed it hadn't worked. After Paris, she'd sat me down and told me everything about her relationship with him — how he'd befriended her at a time when she was grieving her father's unexpected death, so far from home and desperately in need of succour. How he seduced her.

'Though,' she added swiftly, 'that implies I wasn't entirely willing. I was.' She sighed. 'What's apparent to me is, while I always thought our meeting in Surinam was a happy coincidence, it's unlikely William stumbled upon fellow expatriates by chance.' She paused. 'I'm now convinced he deliberately sought us out to learn if anything had resulted from his dalliance with Jacquetta. Rumour, gossip or …' her eyes rested gently upon me '… a child.'

I didn't know what to say. Instead, I listened as Aphra explained how, in the months they were together, he'd stolen her heart — a heart that fractured when he left. Years later, when she tried to reclaim it in Antwerp, where she was sent by his Majesty to persuade William Scot to work for the English again, he told her it had been safe in his keeping all along. Then, he betrayed her. He told anyone who would listen, whispering in ears, spreading gossip in salons, conveyances, writing letters, that she was unfit to be a spy. Loose-tongued, foolish, a deceitful woman: he did everything in his power to traduce her reputation with not only other intelligencers — English and Dutch — but among her English masters and the King. To what end, whether to bolster his standing with the Dutch or the English, or simply to be cruel, Aphra was never sure. Even though I already knew parts of the story, I didn't know it all, and certainly not from Aphra's perspective. It was hard for Aphra to tell me. To think, had she been a lesser person, weaker, William Scot might have succeeded in utterly destroying her.

'What William appears to have forgotten,' she continued, 'is that I'm no longer the naive young woman he swept off her feet. Oh no I am not,' she added, as if to remind herself.

I waited for her to cease fidgeting. 'Did you learn anything?'

Aphra held her glass towards Nest, who refilled it. 'Only that he still likes to talk about himself.'

Something I'd learned as well.

'Oh, and that he's not above attempting seduction.' She laughed at my expression. 'Naturally, he failed. Other than that, he's been living in the United Provinces these last years, working for the Dutch —' she pulled a face '— and, I suspect, certain factions here in England. Only he wouldn't admit to that.'

'It's true, then. He's a traitor? Even now?' The thought my father would undermine his own countrymen, work with our enemy, sickened me … and yet … I wanted to find reasons why he might, make excuses. Was that how all children of traitors felt? About fathers who failed to meet expectations? They sought to soften their deficiencies with ready excuses or construct defences to make the truth more palatable. I barely knew my father and I was torn betwixt truth and fancy.

'I'm sorry to say, he is. To the core. Only he would not see it that way. None of those who betray their countries, their fellow countrymen, ever do. They find justifications for their behaviour and lay the blame for their choices at others' feet.'

We sat quietly, thoughts whirring and wheeling.

Finally, Aphra spoke again, hesitantly. 'Were you aware he was married and had children, kitten?'

'He said he was once married.'

'Still is. Her name is Joanne. A scold by all accounts — his, of course.'

'He …' My heart threw itself against my ribcage. How much more damage could it sustain? 'I was led to believe he was a widower. There are children?'

'Four. Living.'

'Sons?'

'All daughters.'

Unbidden, an image of him sitting next to me by the river formed. I recalled the words he'd spoken with such feeling. *How it plucks my heart strings … Father … Another longing made apparent. When we're together, in private, I would you always call me so.*

I'd wrongly, foolishly, in my desire to belong, to be acknowledged, assumed I was his only child. Dunce! Why, just as he had Aphra once upon a time, he'd played *me*, not the instrument that was his heart. I took a deep, deep breath, mining my reserves. It was time to ask the question I'd been longing to. 'Did … did you talk about me?'

'Of course, kitten. How could I not?' She finally remembered her hat and began to pull out the pins. 'I believe him when he says he knew nothing of you. How could he when until Bethan's letter arrived, I knew nothing either. You were both a shock and delight —'

Not such a delight he didn't pour falsehoods into my ears. Into my heart.

'— and he's very taken with you.'

'He doesn't know me.' Bitterness clipped my words.

There was a beat. Aphra ran her hands along her thighs. 'No. He does not. And I would, to the best of your ability, keep it that way. Men like William have a way of turning that which you allow them to know, to see, to their own ends. I know from experience. And I don't want you getting hurt.'

Too late for that.

I sat back, spinning my glass. Candlelight caught the liquid, making it glow like a carmine lanthorn. 'Is he involved in something sinister?'

Aphra began removing her coat. Nest helped her shrug it off.

'He's in something up to here.' She drew an imaginary line across her neck. 'Along with Shaftesbury and his crew. I like it not, Tribulation.

I've seen that look on William's face before, the way he behaves. He becomes too loquacious, too ready to agree to anything.'

'To what did he agree?'

'Spending more time with you. There's something he wishes to tell you.'

'That he's a traitor, plotting the King's downfall,' I said, po-faced. 'How easy would that be?'

Aphra gave a guffaw. 'Far too easy for the likes of you or me. I couldn't wrest it from him. I just know when I was telling him about why you were in London, I mentioned Howell disowned you so completely you found out about Bethan's marriage from an unrelated source. How it broke your heart. He became quite overcome and said he would talk to you. I'm worried he intends to use this as an excuse to exploit your sorrow —'

'Again.'

'— and try and draw you into whatever scheme he's involved in. You'll be careful, kitten, won't you?' She sat back down. 'William might be your father, but he's also a wanted man.'

Guilt that by remaining silent about his presence we were complicit in whatever he was planning gnawed at my calm.

Nest busied herself lighting a few more candles. Dull noises floated from below — Mr Coggin and his daughter had guests tonight. There was a roar of laughter, a stamp of a boot. The sweet notes of a viola tickled the air.

Aphra studied me. 'You might be able to use his concern to our advantage. Play to his sentimentality.'

I could. 'Did he say when he wants to meet?'

'Only soon.' Aphra took both my hands in her own. 'If this is too much, kitten, I'll understand. It isn't fair to ask this of you, let alone expect it. The man, whatever his past, his present, my entanglement with him, *is* your father. You deserve to know him as such. Just deal with him as a daughter would, only in a manner that doesn't harm you, or your heart. Leave it to the likes of Jenkins, Williamson or Arlington to manage William Scot the traitor.'

I wished it were that easy. For William Scot was both — traitor *and* father. While I was clear on what made him a turncoat, how was a father supposed to behave? I'd only ever known Papa, the fathers in the village, or those I read about in stories and plays. They were all so different. Or indifferent. Some were violent, some weak and easily led. Some saw their daughters only as commodities to be sold in the marriage market to better their own wealth and standing. Most saw their girls as burdens to be shed. I sighed.

For that matter, how *did* a daughter conduct herself? According to Papa, I'd ever been unnatural. William Scot had four others to compare me to. I never fared well in the comparison stakes …

God in Heaven Up Above. It was fast becoming apparent that it would have been better for everyone, especially me, if William Scot had never reappeared.

SCENE ELEVEN

How fatal are forced marriages,
How many ruins one such match pulls on.

The Lucky Chance or, The Alderman's Bargain, Aphra Behn

In the latest issue of the *London Gazette*, an advertisement for a missing person appeared. While that was nothing extraordinary, this particular one caused quite the hubble-bubble. After all, it wasn't for anyone common, but a noblewoman — none other than the woman Lord Grey was said to be having a torrid affair with, his sister-in-law — the very young but not-so-innocent Henrietta Berkeley.

The news-sheet was pushed into my hands the moment I entered the Tiring Rooms.

'Read this,' said Charlotte triumphantly. 'Looks like Grace's lover, that scoundrel Lord Forde Grey has eloped with his bloody sister-in-law. The girl owes you a mighty apology.'

I stared at Charlotte then sat and read. A huge reward of two hundred pounds was being offered for the runaway, described as 'a young lady of fair complexion, fair-haired, full-breasted and indifferent tall'. Someone wanted their property back.

I looked up from the news-sheet and was relieved to see there was no sign of Grace.

'She hasn't appeared,' said Charlotte, craning her neck as if she might suddenly. 'Mr Downes is already searching for a replacement for today's performance.'

Poor Grace. She'd be filled with bitter remorse, terrible shame and anger. For all she'd levelled harsh words towards me, we'd been good friends and I wouldn't want her hurt for the world.

I wondered if Aphra had it right all along and Grace was nothing but a foil to distract people from the identity of Lord Grey's real lover. Or was he, like so many of his ilk, a perfidious womaniser?

'Maybe she doesn't want to face you,' said Charlotte, flicking the pages. 'Or anyone else.' They were peremptorily snatched from my hands by Juliet, who shoved them into Sal Gibbs's as she flounced through the door.

Gossip washed over me as I slowly changed into my rehearsal costume. *An Evening's Love or, The Mock Astrologers* was currently being staged, but we were also preparing to mount the popular *Man of Mode* again in a few days and Mr Betterton had insisted on a full run-through.

I shut out the chitter, the calculated cries of 'What news?' every time someone entered. It was just an excuse to regale them with the lascivious story of Mrs Berkeley. The words 'rogue', 'scoundrel', 'slut', 'wanton', 'whore' and 'fool' were flung about like mud beneath a horse's hooves. I didn't admit to Charlotte I already knew much more about the sordid affair than was revealed in the missing person's advertisement. When Aphra returned from the continent, she'd not only been bursting to the brim with information about the fascinating people she met, the conversations she'd enjoyed, the places she'd seen and the food she'd eaten, but also with gossip about Lord Grey and Henrietta Berkeley.

From an English expatriate who was distantly related to Henrietta's mother, the entire tale spilled at a salon Aphra attended near the Seine. Lord Grey's affair with his wife's younger sister, who was less than eighteen, had been going on for years. Years! Shamed by his wife cuckolding him with the Duke of Monmouth, Lord Grey had ordered her to their country estates, allowing her only a day to pack. After that, he was free to carry on with her sister Henrietta who foolishly had written a letter to her lover, which her mother intercepted.

'She'd written that her older sister never suspected they'd fallen into each other's arms and that she was deaf to their love-making in an adjoining room.' Aphra pulled a face. 'They were fucking right beneath her nose. Tasteless on so many levels.'

It was, I thought miserably, tucking my shoes beneath the dresser and pinning my hair back. And now another person, a good person, was going to be injured — all because of unchecked lust and petty revenge.

Aphra said telling the truth wasn't always a worthy enterprise.

Neither was being right.

I felt horrible.

Not horrible enough to spoil rehearsals. The performance was flawless as well, apart from the audience, who more than made up for their poor numbers by being extremely boisterous, throwing oranges at each other throughout and, during curtain call, at the cast.

'Hope they paid for the fucking things,' said Mr Betterton afterwards, uncharacteristically sharp. He lifted strands of pulp from the periwig he'd worn and threw it at the floor in disgust. 'Someone needs to make a living from this place. May as well be the orange-sellers.' He tossed the ruined periwig to Jacob and stormed upstairs.

The sorry, sordid affair that was Grace and Lord Grey was still on my mind as I dressed. I'd brought my Sunday best to wear, which simply meant it was less stained and patched than my other gowns, as I was to meet with my father for supper. He'd arranged a room at the well-patronised Ox and Plough near Covent Garden and organised a hackney to pick me up.

'You're looking rather lovely tonight,' said Finnola, who was helping Charlotte style her hair after removing the peruke she had to wear onstage. 'Meeting yer new man again, are ye?'

'You mean, *old* man,' countered John Crosby, elbowing Samuel Sandford, who obligingly chuckled. Much had been made of Josiah Keeling being elderly and my youth.

'Thank you,' I said to Finnola cautiously, choosing to ignore Mr Crosby.

Charlotte shot me a sympathetic look. Of all the Company, only she knew who Josiah Keeling was to me — though not his real identity. Ever since Aphra and I had tearfully confessed we'd been keeping secrets from each other, I could no longer bear Charlotte, my only real friend at Dorset Garden, not knowing at least part of the story. I'd already lost so many people because of lies and deceit. I'd no doubt a few more would fall by the wayside before the whole truth was out.

It was not long past seven by the time I alighted from the plodding, worn hackney. The Ox and Plough was a fine-looking establishment of brick and wood, with newly painted doors and windows; it had stables and even a small garden filled with late blooms and a burbling fountain. I regretted being indoors on such a fine evening. The air was redolent with woodfires and the pungent smell of scat. The sky was a wash of rose, gold and lavender, a queen's bracelet. Folk strolled around Covent Garden or stood outside the many taverns and ale-houses. Music added piquancy and the urge to quicken my step overcame me. Dancers had cleared a space in the centre of the square, tapping toes and clapping hands. A magician in a long cloak held up something bright and sparkling in one hand while his other twisted and turned to ooohs and ahhs. Not as many as were given to the man making fire dance across spinning batons. It was terribly exciting, heady.

My father was seated at a pitted table in a darkly wooded room to the right at the top of the narrow stairs. There was a smouldering fire in the hearth, and candles burned, casting miniature halos. There were two lush sofas and a great many chairs covered with lots of soft cushions. Thick curtains garlanded the windows. I could see the flash of flames every now and then and hear a smattering of applause and cheers. The odour of tobacco was strong, as was a musky scent in which my father liberally doused himself. A platter of cold meat, freshly baked manchet and sweetbreads sat upon the table along with a pewter jug and two ruby glasses. I could see from my father's complexion he'd already enjoyed a glass or two of claret.

'Tribulation,' he said, jumping to his feet and wiping his hands on his breeches before taking my cloak and hat.

As I sat, he arranged my garments neatly over one of the sofas. 'Wine?'

Before I could answer, there was a splash and burble. I noticed a slight tremble to his hands. Palsy? Or something else. A tinny knocking began in my head. A warning bell that set me on edge. I finished perusing the room to find my father's gaze resting upon me.

'By God, you're really quite lovely in an unconventional way. Amazing to consider you're mine,' he said.

I didn't contest his assumption, though it rankled.

He lifted his glass. 'To family, Tribulation. To us.'

'Shouldn't you include the rest?' I asked, somewhat snippily.

'Oh, you mean my other daughters?' he said as if their existence was something I'd always known. Well, two could play at that game.

'My *sisters*,' I said and was pleased to see him falter a little. 'And your wife, of course. Joanne, isn't it?'

'It is.'

'I would know all their names,' I said.

My father lowered his glass slowly and shifted to sit sideways in his seat, leaning partly across the table. 'Yes, yes. And you will. But first, please, you must be hungry. Eat. The food here is always excellent.' He broke off a leg of chicken and handed it to me. Was he biding time or could he not recall his daughters' names?

Regardless, I *was* famished and, first rescuing a napkin, took a bite.

Father was right, this was delicious. But I was also hungry for answers. 'Pray tell, what are my sisters' —'

'It's been brought to my attention, Tribulation,' he interrupted, almost sternly: a schoolmaster quieting unruly pupils, 'for all we've spent time together, there's a great deal I don't know about *you*. It's awfully remiss of me. I've a tendency to talk about myself, a terrible flaw, I know.' He gave a smile that was anything but sorry.

It was hard not to laugh.

'Aphra told me about Howell and his terrible decision to disown you. You didn't really furnish me much detail.' He steepled his fingers and looked at me accusingly over the top of them. Me? Lacking detail?

Pot. Kettle.

'I cannot imagine anyone, let alone someone you thought your father, choosing to forsake you.'

Surely, he was being ironic.

I put down the piece of chicken and wiped my hands. 'Please, don't perturb yourself on my account. Aphra took me in before Papa and my sister abandoned me. The truth is, ever since my mother died, I've struggled to fit into the family. I —'

'What say you?' William Scot's face paled. 'Your mother is dead? When? When did this calamity happen? I thought …' He lunged for wine. In two gulps his glass was empty. 'How?'

Oh dear. I'd made a grave error of judgement. In my efforts to be clever, to brush aside his faux concern so as not to let him hurt me, I'd inadvertently injured him.

'I'm so sorry,' I began. I wanted to touch his hand, close my fingers over it, but didn't feel I had the right. 'I thought you must know.'

'Know … I … I? How?' He reached over and hastily poured wine, more missing the glass and splashing on the table. He didn't seem to notice.

'It was a long time ago,' I said softly. 'I was but six.'

William Scot froze. Then, ever so slowly, he put the bottle down. He looked at me strangely, frowning, his mouth moving, but no sound issuing. 'B-but,' he spluttered finally, 'how is this possible? Aphra told me she's only recently married. That you found out when you overheard some men in the Tiring Rooms discussing the wedding.'

Cold like the middle of January entered my chest and began to spread like a crazed hoar frost, rendering my centre, my limbs, my very heart completely numb. It was if the world was rapidly turning to ice. 'She was referring to my sister.' The words came from a long, long way away. As if I was underwater or in a tunnel. 'My older sister, Bethan.'

William Scot looked at me with a mixture of relief, pity and leaden guilt. He eased back in his chair, fingers spread wide on the table. 'Oh, my sweet child. Of course you don't know. You cannot. Nor Aphra.' He grabbed my hands before I could hide them. 'No wonder you're so lost, so confused. No wonder we both are.' He took a deep breath and his blue-green eyes with their dash of smut met mine.

'Bethan isn't your sister, Tribulation. Oh, dear Lord no. Bethan is your mother.'

ACT FIVE

Winter 1682–Winter 1689

From Loving Absence to Scorning Presence or, Such Short-Liv'd Happiness

... and where men build on false grounds, the more they built, the greater is the ruins.

Leviathan, Thomas Hobbes

A woman writing a play is a novelty and that every female 'I'th' upper Box, Pit, Galleries' is a spy to hold men in 'wanton Complement That ... you may not censure what she's writ.'

The Forc'd Marriage or, The Jealous Bridegroom, Aphra Behn

SCENE ONE

What would love signify, if we did not love fervently? … in matters of love, excess is a virtue, and all other degrees of love are worthy of scorn alone.

Aphra Behn

Lady Bethan Babcock
Horton Manor
Outside Chartham
Kent

Dearest Bethan,

Forgive me writing when I know I'm forbidden contact. I would not cause you trouble for my disobedience (again), but I have, of late, learned something of momentous import from a gentleman who, I believe, is known to you: Mr William Scot. This man, who recently appeared in London, did announce not only is he my father, but that you, Bethan, are my mother.

I cannot begin to describe the maelstrom of emotions that overcame me when my connections, first to Papa, and now you, were revealed as immeasurably altered. I know you disapprove of what you describe as my 'florid language' and propensity to embellish everything, so I will speak as plainly as I am able.

I must know: is what Mr Scot told me true?

On the one hand, if it is, the way Papa has treated me my entire life, why he was so ready to disown me, suddenly makes awful sense. Even my name, Tribulation, carries a weight I'd never accorded it. On the other what doesn't tally, is if you're my mother as Mr Scot claims, why have you not admitted our relationship before, at least to me? Why have you maintained the pretence of being my sister? As Isaiah asks, 'Can you feel no love for the child you have borne?' Especially now you're married and no longer beholden to Papa for succour and protection? Is it because your husband knows naught of this? Or is it because Mr Scot is indulging in some cruel deceit, the purpose of which I cannot fathom? Which is it? I implore you, Bethan, please don't allow me to dwell in the darkness of ignorance any longer.

Mr Scot does protest how much he loved you, and yet not once have I heard you mention him; he who must, at some time, have meant so much you risked your reputation. I understand having a child out of wedlock must have been a dreadful, scandalous burden. Papa and Mama protected both you and me and our futures by claiming me as their own — I should be grateful. I am. But, Bethan, if you are my mother, then surely the time for deceit, at least between us, has passed? The time for silence as well.

I promise, I'll not reveal anything of what I've been told (except to Aphra, with whom I shared this allegation), until I learn from you the truth of it. I would not embarrass or disgrace you or risk the esteem in which you're held for the world. I pray you do not see me, your loving sister (daughter?), as an object of mortification, despite the conditions of my birth.

They were not of my making, and I fail to see why I continue to be punished for them.

I would be your daughter in name and deed, even if it is to be a closely held secret.

Please, write to me, Bethan. Let us end the silence between us. We have many years for which we must compensate.

With God's blessing and all my love,
Tribulation

London was abuzz again as gossip flitted here and there, alighting upon one set of lips before being transferred to a pair of ears and so on. Now, instead of religious divisions and accusations of heresy being levelled, a far more degenerate matter was on everyone's tongues.

Lord Grey was arrested for conspiring to 'commit whoredom, fornication and adultery' and flung in the Tower. His wife's sister and his lover, Henrietta Berkeley, was found in a milliner's house near Charing Cross not long after the advertisement seeking her whereabouts was published.

I found it hard to even feign a modicum of interest. I was preoccupied with my own drama.

It had been more than six weeks since I plucked up the courage to write to Bethan. Despite my earnest entreaties, no word had yet come. Bethan, it appeared, didn't want to know let alone speak to me about truth, lies or anything at all. I was still, whether sister, daughter or theatre-whore, outcast. I lay awake at night, staring at the blotched ceiling, listening to the owls' haunting cries or the link boys scooting along gloomy alleys, crying out in their reedy sing-song voices. Throughout the long, dark hours, when the cold would nip my cheeks and make me huddle further under the covers, I would relive scenes from my childhood: Bethan scolding me for falling in the river when I ventured too close; bandaging my hand when I scalded it on a hot pot the maid had left on the kitchen table. I recalled her whisking me away from Papa's fury and suggesting I take over reading to Lady Adeline, even though I knew in my heart it was something she relished doing. Over and over, I revisited these moments and understood them through a different set of eyes, an aching heart forever changed. I kept asking myself, God, the shadows that squeezed into the room, and my wretched, shiftless soul, 'Are you my mother?' I was like a baby bird abandoned in the nest, starving not for food, but truth.

Looking back, it was apparent Bethan oft protected me, in that stiff, almost indifferent way she had, intervening to ensure I didn't land in more trouble. What I thought was an older sister interfering, domineering, or siding with Papa against me, was more akin to a rescue mission, even if what she was saving me from was myself. And yet, no matter how far back I delved, what memories I dusted off and pummelled into shape, I could scarce recall affection. Bethan and Papa rarely embraced or caressed let alone praised me. I'd always believed it was because they weren't inclined or because somehow they thought there was a finite amount of love to be distributed and it had already been used up. I couldn't recall them holding or expressing fondness for each other either. Maybe they had before Mama died? Before Fabian? I tried to dredge up remembrance of Mama … my grandmother? She was the one person who had seemed to tolerate my presence. Or was that a kind illusion? Something I'd invented?

I dashed away tears I didn't even know had begun to fall until they became rivulets. Annoyed I should allow something I could never change to upset me so, I tried to imagine what the future might hold if Bethan was indeed my mother. I began to envisage our reunion. She would hold out her arms, a beatific smile upon her lovely face, her troubled, angry brow smooth, and I would fall into them, and she would express all the pent-up love and devotion she'd never been able to before for fear her secret would out. Then, arm in arm, whispering, nattering, ever in each other's sight, we would do all we could to make up for lost time. Mother and daughter, side by side, inseparable, united at last …

Still, no letter arrived.

Other times, I wondered if Bethan even received my missive. What if it had landed in Bethan's husband's hands and I'd lived up to my name and caused irreparable strife between them? Or what if he'd intercepted it and given it to Papa? Dear Lord — *that* didn't bear thinking about. I should have been more careful with my wording, more subtle. Too late. All sorts of sensible and wayward reasons as to why I hadn't heard from her flew through my head as I tried to lose myself in writing, in the work of the theatre, and the gruelling task of moving the entire Company to Drury Lane.

At the beginning of the month, the Duke's and the King's officially merged and became the United Company. Our last production as the Duke's had been Thomas Otway's *Venice Preserv'd* — a play filled with dastardly plots and betrayal and heated sexual liaisons. Because it was highly critical of the Whigs, it passed the (Tory) censor without change — unlike other plays that had been refused performance rights. It was a huge success and a fine way to bid Dorset Garden adieu.

Two weeks later, after spending long, sweaty days loading carts and shifting boxes and racks of old and dusty costumes, props, numerous gewgaws, make-up, hairpieces, furniture, lights and so much more, then finding new places for everything in Drury Lane, we staged our first production there, John Fletcher's *Rule a Wife and Have a Wife*. It was an older comedy about men, women and the seemingly endless problems of marriage, and was, as John Downes said, a relatively safe option for a debut. The cast, mainly Duke's Company actors in major roles with some King's Company members in minor ones, had already performed for a select group at Inner Temple Hall.

Resentment ran higher than a moon-tide, especially among those of the King's Company who missed out on speaking parts and felt they deserved more than carrying and unpacking their rival Company's laden boxes or cleaning old wax out of footlights — even if the former Duke's Company members also completed identical tasks. Arguments about whose dresser was positioned where, whose stool was whose, even who had precedence when entering the Tiring Room, raged for days. It wasn't until Lady Mary stated categorically where dressers, costumes, chairs, benches, and even pots of make-up were to be placed that an end was put to it — at least in her hearing. When roles were assigned, I swear, the room felt like London when a storm was about to break. The air was so thick and heavy it was hard to breathe, and not just because Mr Mohun and Mr Tate puffed away on their ivory pipes. The objections that broke out when the Davenants, Mr Betterton and Mr Smith left the room were so loud and great Mr Crosby said it was like being in a coffee-house during a candle auction.

When the sly insults (poorly dressed as gracious observations) started, former King's Company leads free with their opinions about who from the Duke's had robbed them of their rightful parts, Charlotte leaned over and whispered, 'More like tom-cats fighting over a bitch in some stinking snicket.'

For all we were meant to represent two royal companies brought together under the one title, the United Company made a mockery of its name. It also had many more Duke's Company actors than King's, and the latter felt in their diminished positions the way an only child might after the arrival of a new sibling: usurped. We may have been in *their* theatre, but this was now very much a Duke's business. The United Company was owned and managed by Charles Davenant, Mr Betterton and Mr Smith, and many of the King's Company actors, despite glib promises, were never recontracted. Not even Charles Hart, said by some to be the finest actor of the King's, had been rehired. Afflicted with stone and gravel and in much pain, the poor man should have felt relief at being released from his contract and still paid his weekly wage of forty shillings so he might seek physick and thus regain health, but it turned to bitterness. Other actors were forced to find work elsewhere, most leaving the city and joining troupes in the provinces. Michael Mohun — called Major Mohun — Edward Kynaston, Mrs Corey, Mrs Cook and Mrs Bowtell were among those few who remained.

The poisonous mood in the Tiring Rooms during the changeover spread, took root and grew, an uncontrollable weed in an unruly garden. Gossip, forever rearing her ugly head, reigned. Jealousy was the face most oft worn as actors and actresses maligned each other. Confidence was continuously undermined, making working together most uncomfortable. Grateful I was too unimportant to attract much attention (though a couple of the former King's Company men thought they were within their rights to grope my breasts when I was carrying an armful of furs back to the costume room; I soon disabused them), I was reminded of my first awful months as book-keeper at Dorset Garden, when nasty pranks were played and talk would still in my presence. It was testimony to the quality of the acting, the invisible vizards donned, that audiences remained largely oblivious, even when in the Tiring Room afterwards, smiles, praise, friendly banter and bonhomie between the cast were as false as the perukes and jewels they wore.

Despite this, even the most jaded and embittered had to admit that Drury Lane was a much better theatre. Burned to the ground ten years earlier, it had been redesigned and rebuilt on the same site. The dreadful tinny echo we'd been forced to tolerate at Dorset Garden was now a thing of the past. Here, not only were the acoustics excellent, the forestage a good size and the lighting brighter, but the auditorium, though smaller, was raked like an amphitheatre, meaning there were no more complaints about women with hairpieces and hats that soared into the heavens or libertines in their monstrous periwigs hindering the view. Backstage, there was a veritable warren of rooms including a huge and well-equipped Tiring Room, another for hosting guests, and still more for storing scripts, props and costumes, and even a room dedicated to copying. I was like Sir Francis Drake, still discovering rooms and cupboards weeks after we'd reopened.

The building itself, which wasn't quite as grand as Dorset, but lovely nonetheless, was accessed by patrons from a narrow passageway in Bridges Street (which gave one the effect of entering a cave or some illicit gambling house, according to a delighted Mr Betterton). The stage entry was from Drury Lane itself. Though the theatre was further back from the river, it was located partway between White Hall and the city walls, so it was easy for the gentry to access. Covent Garden was also close.

Even with all the envy and spite being parried and thrust in a never-ending duel that would have made the Montagues and Capulets blush, relocating and reopening was just the distraction I needed. If not for that and Aphra, I don't know what I would have done, as whenever I'd a moment to myself, my wounded, confused heart and head were filled with crazed thoughts of William Scot and Bethan.

The night I came home from *that* supper, I'd woken Aphra who'd fallen asleep atop her bed and told her. We'd spoken into the early hours until I fell asleep beside her. The following day, she'd encouraged me to write to Bethan, to seek the truth, whatever it might be. She offered to send a letter too, but while I appreciated her support, this was something I had to reconcile. Anyway, she'd work to get on with.

Ever since Aphra returned from Paris, she'd been furiously busy. Commissions had flowed in the wake of her arrest over the excoriating epilogue and prologue she'd written for my play. Those who'd once dismissed her as a 'petticoat author' were now prepared to pay excellent coin if she'd just contribute to their publications, her notoriety guaranteeing sales. Flattery and promises came thick and fast — much like men, Aphra said. Never one to refuse a mannerly gent showering her with praise and compliments, especially one with a purse, Aphra was in her element. Others procured satires and verses, mainly criticising the Whigs but also her beloved Tories.

When I asked how she felt about being paid to disparage Royalists, she shrugged. 'I take work where it's offered, Tribulation. I don't have the luxury of being particular or partisan. Plus, it keeps those who would deprecate my efforts guessing, does it not? They continue to wonder where my loyalties really reside.'

Inspired by the people she'd met in Paris and works she'd read while away, she was also writing poetry. Poems about sexual obsession and unchecked desire flew from her pen, including those written on behalf of others, earning a pretty penny and, as was expected, a barrage of insults and degradation. Aphra would attempt to shrug them aside. 'Remember, in their minds, I'm a whore — one who is loose with her words. May as well be paid for them, kitten.'

Around this time, Aphra also commenced writing something manifestly based on the scandal holding London in its grip, entitled *Love-Letters between a Nobleman and His Sister*. It was to be a long work of prose, not a play. By altering the names and making the setting French, she turned the tawdry Grey affair into a work of fiction, while still managing to discredit a well-known Whig. I never did find out who was paying Aphra to embark on something so topical and dangerously risqué, though the fact she couldn't say pointed to either the King or one of his Secretaries of State.

Aphra also worked on some translations. This was becoming the vogue — young scholars translating archaic, inaccessible works from Latin and Greek into English for modern readers. Due to the disparity in women's education, Aphra, like me, had never been taught to read or write in the ancient tongues, and this vexed her deeply. So, she set about retranslating the scholars' rather dry and dull efforts into something far more exciting — with no small degree of success.

No matter what I did, how I tried to occupy myself (writing was beyond me at this time), what Aphra or the constant dramatics playing out at Drury Lane — on stage and off — offered, everything led me back to consideration of my parentage.

Of William Scot, I saw less. After he delivered the news that floored me, I didn't see him for weeks. Notes would arrive at the house at all hours, oft accompanied by a small gift — ribbons, gloves, a woollen scarf. He'd apologise for not being present, writing that while he was busy with pressing matters, I was always in his thoughts. It was hard not to be gratified by both the notes and the pretty gifts. Maybe I was more like Aphra than I thought.

Nor did I hear from or see Gabriel. Not that I really anticipated either.

Truly.

Well, maybe I did … a little.

From Kent, there was nothing. Not a word.

I began to wonder if I should take matters into my own hands and make my way to Chartham, force a reckoning — only, if I did that, and Bethan's husband remained unaware, I could cause an unforgivable rift and not just in their relationship. I wasn't yet ready to risk that.

Not when I held out hopes of what yet might be …

SCENE TWO

If we be weak by nature, they strive to make us more weak by our nurture. And if in degree of place low, they serve by their policy to keep us more under.

The Woman's Sharp Revenge, Anonymous

Lord Grey was trialled before the King's Bench on 23rd November. What made his reckoning more memorable than most was that when his lover, Lady Henrietta (full breasts, indifferent tall), emerged from the house in which she'd been hiding to attend, another phrase was added to her description: 'swollen with child'.

It was all anyone could talk about even days later as we prepared to stage Ben Jonson's *Bartholomew Fair*, one of those plays denied the Duke's Company and which Mr Betterton and Mr Smith, united in intention, had longed to produce.

I only half-listened as Charlotte, Katherine Herbert, Mrs Ann Quin and Mrs Katherine Corey (the latter formerly of the King's Company and who was a good friend of Mrs Quin, who used to work under Mr Killigrew), chewed over the details of the trial.

'My sister,' began Mrs Corey, a stout woman around my age, with eyes that bulged in a rather unbecoming way, as if she was permanently startled, 'said that when Lord Berkeley stood up and demanded his daughter come home with him, she declared she would go nowhere but with her rightful husband.'

'Husband!' exclaimed Charlotte. 'But Lord Grey cannot be married to her — he's married to her sister.'

'Exactly,' said Mrs Corey, a knowing smile upon her wide face. 'Turns out, while she was in hiding, she married none other than Lord Grey's factotum, Mr William Turner.'

'No!' gasped all three women.

'What? The short fella with no hair and all them pox marks?' Mrs Quin screwed up her face.

'Yes!' said Mrs Corey, delighted at their reaction. 'Him.' She began to apply liberal quantities of powder. 'Talk about an arranged marriage.' She winked.

'Arranged to suit his lordship,' said Charlotte.

'What happened then?' asked Mrs Quin.

'A right barney erupted between father and daughter,' said Mrs Corey.

The women laughed.

'Anyhow,' continued Mrs Corey, applying still more powder, 'she was taken off to Marshalsea for a night. As for Lord Grey, well, what could anyone do? No-one was prepared to debauch her ladyship's reputation further by suggesting the child wasn't her lawful husband's, were they? Not even Judge Jeffreys. But that didn't stop swords being drawn and threats levelled in the courtroom. My sister said she thought there'd be bloodshed.'

'Well,' said Mrs Quin, 'I think Lord Grey should consider himself very fortunate.'

'One rule for the toffs and one for us,' huffed Katherine Herbert.

'One for the men and another for women,' said Charlotte.

There were murmurs of agreement before the women ceased their chitter and concentrated on readying themselves for curtain call.

I put the last touches to my own costume, a servant's. I'd no lines, just discreet entrances and exits. I was also a member of the crowd in a few scenes. Instead of being focussed on the performance, my thoughts reached out to Grace. Ever since news of Lord Grey's affair broke back in September, she hadn't returned to the theatre. Nor had her brother Kit. Whither are they? I thought. I wished I could comfort her. She'd been so besotted with his lordship, dizzy with gratitude for his attentions, she'd seen in him not only a considerate lover, but a means of escaping the life she'd entered. He was her ticket to respectability: a bridge to gentility. The irony: that such a disreputable man could ever have accorded lovely Grace status.

Grace was still on my mind as I headed home hours later. It was a cheerless night and the warmth acting always instilled had long dissipated as a freezing wind howled up the streets, blowing over trestles, rocking empty barrels and flinging hats, papers and bits of detritus along the dirt, biting and stinging and dispersing people faster than constables a group of unruly apprentices.

The evening was unusually dark, the moon concealing itself behind thick clouds. I'd been forced to hire a link boy to light my way, but there were a few moments where it seemed the wild wind would douse the flame. The pitch torch growled like an angry dog and the shadows created by our passage loomed and capered in a sinister fashion. The link boy, no more than ten years of age with a shock of red hair making him resemble the torch he carried, kept starting and stopping at every noise, making me jump as well. Shapes shifted in doorways, moving into the darkness of alleys as we approached. It was easy to believe in spectres and ghosts if not men with bad intentions following. I shivered and not only because I was cold. This was not a night for the faint-hearted.

By the time we reached the end of Newe Street, I put the boy out of his misery and gave him a generous tip. 'Bless ya, missus,' he said, biting down hard on the coin and offering a black-toothed smile. He scampered off before I could thank him or check he hadn't lost another tooth.

I held my cloak tighter as I strode through the court, relieved to hear the whine of music and deep voices carried on relentless gusts. Torchlight flickered in sconces and candlelight behind thick-glassed windows. I looked forward to being on the other side of one.

I almost reached the door when I became aware I wasn't alone. With shaking hands, I tried to turn the knob, but my fingers were so chilled, my body so atremble with dire imaginings, they wouldn't cooperate. Just when I managed to find a grip, a hand curled around my shoulder.

I tried to call out, but my voice deserted me.

The moon chose that moment to appear and in doing so revealed who had accosted me.

'Grace!' I exclaimed on a wave of relief.

Her face was thinner and cast in sadness. She grimaced. 'Aye, 'tis me. Sorry I startled you. I've been waiting. I don't know where else to turn.'

I opened the door, and light from inside spilled out. 'Please, please, come in.' I gestured for her to precede me. 'Let's get out of the unholy wind.'

I shut the door and almost at once, warmth stole over us. I began to remove my outer garments and then boots. Grace stood gazing about. 'I'd forgotten how nice it is inside, compared to the exterior.'

I took her cloak and was shocked at how gaunt she'd become. Her shoulders were sharp, her cheekbones too. Even her hands resembled large barn-spiders. 'Have you eaten?' I asked as she inhaled, her eyes half-closing. The smell of cooked meat wafted from the kitchen. My stomach growled.

She shook her head. 'Not properly, not for … weeks.'

Heels clacked across the floor above us. Somewhere in the house, a door opened and then shut.

Grace looked about nervously. 'I … I shouldn't have come. I … forgive me …' She reached for her cloak.

'Nay. Wait.' I stopped her. 'It's only Mr Coggin and Clara.' I deployed Farmer Whittle's tone again. 'We can go upstairs to the parlour. Aphra is out; Nest will be abed. It will just be you and me. Please, Grace. I'll settle you and then fetch something for us to drink and eat. Then you can tell me whatever it is that's brought you out on a night like this.' I waited.

Grace glanced towards the ceiling, still in two minds, before, with an apathetic flutter of her hands, she acquiesced.

We mounted the stairs. I made sure she was ahead. She was like a fawn, ready to bolt at the slightest provocation.

When I finally sat her by the crackling fire, blanket spread over her knees, a trencher of meat and bread in her lap, as well as a small ale which she downed thirstily, I filled the silence with talk of the theatre, the weather and the outrageous price of wool and cloth while she ate.

Satisfied she was settled and more at ease, I drew my chair closer. 'It's good to see you, Grace, though it dismays me greatly you haven't returned to work. Do you need help? Whatever is in my ken, you have only to ask.'

Grace put down the bone she'd been picking and removed her plate from lap to table. She wiped her mouth with the napkin I'd supplied. 'No,' she said softly. 'At least, not the kind you may think.' She lowered her head and let out a long sigh, her hand resting lightly on her stomach. 'Everyone knew Forde was involved with his sister-in-law. Everyone except me. Though I suspect I *chose* to remain in ignorance.'

I clicked my tongue.

'But you, Tribulation Johnson, you were the only one brave enough, kind enough, to alert me.'

'I'm so sorry, Gra—'

'Don't be. Please. I was a fool not to listen, to turn upon you the way I did. Can you ever forgive me?'

I gave a dismissive wave. 'Already done.'

She flashed a smile. Ah, there she was. 'You're the only person I can tell. The only one I trust.'

A sick, heavy feeling entered my chest. I stared at her, at the position of her hand, and I knew. 'Oh, Grace. I'm so, so sorry. Anything I can do to help you, the babe, I will.' No swelling — yet. A protective urge swept over me as I thought of the life it would lead, the difficulties it would face as a bastard, something my papa and mama had at least spared me.

Grace lowered her head. 'Punishment for my sins.' She stroked her stomach. 'But that's not why I'm here.'

Wisely, I remained silent.

She searched my face, the light of the fire casting hers into a mask of darkness and amber. 'I think, no, I *know*, Forde, Lord Grey, is involved in a dreadful plot.'

Not another bloody plot. 'Really?' I said, swallowing my disappointment she was revealing something so commonplace — at least in these times. 'Against Catholics? Or is it non-conformists this time? Quakers? Jews?'

'I'm being serious.' Grace cleared her throat. 'I know for a fact that Lord Grey is part of a plot being hatched by —' she held up her hand and began to count off each finger '— the Earl of Shaftesbury, Lord Algernon Sidney, Lord William Russell, Sir Thomas Armstrong, Robert Ferguson, the Duke of Monmouth and others.' Her hand curled into a fist.

I was all ears now — like a coney. 'To do what, pray?' I asked when she faltered.

She paused. 'To assassinate the King.'

My veins became molten. Heat sped through my arms and legs and pooled in a heaving mass beneath my breasts.

'That's not all,' said Grace softly. 'So is a man who claims to be your father, Tribulation Johnson. A man who calls himself Josiah Keeling, but who I know for a fact is really the traitor Mr William Scot.'

SCENE THREE

What in strong manly verse I should be exprest
Turns all to womanish tenderness within.

from 'To the Unknown Daphnis on His Excellent Translation of Lucretius', Aphra Behn

As the sky lightened and the streets beyond sprang to life, I watched Aphra trying to calm her feverish thoughts. Tired from arguing with John Hoyle all evening then crying herself to sleep, she could scarce believe what I had to say when I woke her and shared what Grace had revealed.

Grace had refused to remain the night, insisting on returning home to where Kit anxiously awaited. I'd no choice but to reluctantly let her go.

After she left, sleep had eluded me, my thoughts dominated by the same questions. Was Grace right? Could William Scot really be so foolhardy as to be involved in some nefarious plot to not only destroy the throne, but *kill* the King?

The only conclusion I could reach was that Shaftesbury and his associates, unable to change the succession, were now making plans to remove King Charles permanently. Seems they'd drawn my father in — but how?

Aphra stopped and snapped her fingers. 'Of course!' She faced me. 'That's it.'

'What?' I asked, shucking off my weariness.

'I think I know why William is working with the Green Ribbon Club. Why he's prepared to participate in something so evil.'

I waited. Aphra plonked herself on the edge of the bed beside me. 'Through Shaftesbury, Grey and the rest of the Whig ringleaders, William is being given a means of returning home to England: one that doesn't make him beholden to the current regime, but a hero of the new one *if* a coup is successful. After all, if they achieve their murderous ends, there'd be a new King and government — ones he'd helped install. They would be indebted to him. All his past sins would be erased. He would be able to start over.'

I stared at her, momentarily speechless. It had an appalling logic. According to Aphra, it's what he always wanted — to come back but on his terms, terms that wouldn't see him imprisoned, a pauper, or some nobleman's lackey. I was just a pleasant distraction, a convenient and legitimate (ha!) cover should his presence be discovered (and no doubt it had: he was being watched; we all were).

And what was Aphra but another reason to be here — he'd obeyed the summons implicit in her letter. I could hear him now: 'She did entice me here, your honour, with her eloquent, compelling words.' He'd no doubt produce a copy of her original and coded letter to Bernard Gascoigne and implicate her in whatever he was planning, especially if it meant saving his own skin.

I bunched my fists and pressed them to my forehead.

'Are you alright, kitten?' She rested a gentle hand on my knee. 'Your mind must be in a worse turmoil than mine. First, you learn William is your father, then Bethan, your mother. Now this.'

Rain struck the glass. I raised my head. It had poured all night, as if the very heavens were mourning an inconceivable future loss. In the silvery light, I caught my reflection. My sleepless night showed. Shadows ringed my eyes and my skin was pale.

'I wish I could take you away from all this — that we could pack our bags and flee.' She glanced towards the window.

'Only, we can't.'

'No. We cannot.'

Aphra stood and resumed her perambulations. I could almost hear the cogs of her mind whirring and clinking.

Grace had come to me, revealed what she did, because she believed Aphra knew what to do with this information. She knew the right people and how the intelligencing community worked. Or she once had.

'Did Grace give you any indication of *when* these men might act?' asked Aphra, looking about for paper and a quill. 'Exactly what they might do?' She moved to her desk.

'Nay. But she was under the impression they were in disarray now the Earl of Shaftesbury has left the country.'

Arrested last year for high treason, he had been released soon after because the jury was comprised of mostly Whigs. When word reached him that he was going to be arraigned again, this time over planning another uprising, but would face a jury weighted in the Tories' favour, Shaftesbury couldn't risk the outcome and fled to Amsterdam. Tiring Room gossip said the Scottish vicar, Ferguson, and others had joined him. I suspected that's where my father might be, given his recent absence.

I joined Aphra at the desk.

She snaked her arm about my waist. 'This is too great for us to hold onto, kitten. We need to alert those who can throw men and resources at it, find out if this scheme's real, how far it extends and exactly who's involved. With the principal plotters overseas, time is on our side.' She removed her arm and, finding a quill, dipped it in the inkhorn. 'I'm going to request an audience with Sir Leoline Jenkins. I daren't put what we know on paper lest it falls into the wrong hands.'

'Will you make mention of William Scot?'

Aphra paused, moving the quill to prevent the ink dripping. 'God's truth, Tribulation, I haven't made up my mind. What do you think?'

I gazed at a point outside the window, pressing my lips together. 'I ... I want to know for certain the extent of his involvement. We only have Grace's word. What if this is her vengeance against Lord Grey for what he did to her and has no basis in fact? What if we accuse my father and he's really innocent?'

Aphra schooled her face. 'Yes,' she began cautiously. 'There is that … possibility.' She sighed. 'Very well. For the time being, I won't mention him. But, Tribulation, you must promise me you won't alert him.' She circled my wrist and gave it a meaningful squeeze.

'I won't, if you promise the same,' I said and in Aphra's eyes saw my own ambivalence reflected.

'Goddamn the man,' snarled Aphra. 'He doesn't deserve either of us.'

Aphra began to compose. When she'd finished the note, she handed it to me for approval, then sanded and sealed it and sent Nest with a coin to find a boy to deliver it.

'Tell him to wait for a reply or at least a receipt,' said Aphra.

I slumped into a chair as Nest left the room. 'What do we do now?'

'What women always do, kitten.' Aphra studied me over steepled fingers. 'We remain quiet and wait.'

Though we were given proof Aphra's letter was delivered, a summons to White Hall didn't manifest until the New Year.

Rather than dwell on that, or on the fact that still no word had come from Bethan, with Aphra's encouragement and under her watchful eye, I threw myself into work at the theatre. Instead of leaving after I'd removed my costume, or locked away the master script for John, I offered to con lines with the players again. Acquiring all the plays we'd never been able to perform was a boon for the Duke's actors and actresses, but for many of them, it meant learning entire parts from scratch. They were eager for help and I was keen to provide it. Anything to keep my mind off not just fathers and mothers, but bloody plots. Nevertheless, I kept my ear to the ground for any whisper of a threat to the King.

For any whisper of William Scot.

And, God knows, Gabriel as well. Never before had I wished so hard for him to appear: enter, stage right. Alas, he missed his cue. Aphra and I were alone in this.

But at least we were alone together.

Grace and Kit never did come to the theatre to ask for their jobs back. When Charlotte and I went to their lodgings, we were told by their landlady they'd returned to Bath before Christmas.

'Sometimes London gives, other times it takes. With them two, it drained the life from them. I hope they're happier back home,' she'd said with a sad smile.

It was my hope for them too.

Then, just when I thought Sir Leoline must have either forgotten Aphra's request or never received it, we were summoned to White Hall.

SCENE FOUR

Soft winning language will become you best;
Ladies ought not to rail, tho' but in jest.

The Ladies Defence, Lady Mary Chudleigh

We approached by river, disembarking at White Hall Palace stairs. It was a blustery day. The earlier rain had given way to heaving grey clouds that glowered as we were rowed up the dark green waters. Dressed in my finest clothes, I was grateful yet again for the thick cloak and fur-lined gloves Mr Hoyle had given me. Aphra's brown eyes were alert, taking in everything as we showed our summons to the guards at the end of the pier and were escorted by a squat one, with bowlegs and an imperious manner, through the sprawl that was the palace.

I'd been to White Hall a few times, always for royal command performances in the Great Hall. Each occasion, we'd arrived by road in carriages laden with props and costumes, not via the river. Entering the grounds from the water was a very different experience. I spied the roof of the Banqueting House and, whereas the first time I came I admired its grand façade, all I could contemplate this day was that my grandfather had been one of the men responsible for beheading the King's father there. I imagined the crowds, cheering, baying for blood and weeping for the doomed liege. The triumph and sorrow. I walked beside Aphra in distracted silence as we were led along a wide cobbled path, past a pretty chapel and then a series of higgledy-piggledy buildings and narrow, dank passages.

Despite the cold and threatening downpour, the place was filled with people. Elaborately dressed noblemen and women strolled about, arms linked, heads close together. There were aproned maids, footmen and pages scurrying here and there, wearing their importance like livery. Couriers dashed past, men with documents tucked under their arms, frowning and looking officious. Some lords were stumbling home from a night of drinking, others were still carousing, neckties and jackets askew, faces bloated and food stains splashed all over their shirt fronts like medals. Held upright by these cupshotten gallants, women staggered with them, hair unpinned, bodices open, tripping over squawking chickens and uneven stones. It was hard not to stare, though no-one else was, clearly accustomed to such unruliness so early (or late) in the day. Everywhere I looked there were uniformed guards, weapons glinting in the argent light. I'd never seen so many armed men except in a royal procession.

Aphra grimaced. 'Ever since the Popish Plot, the King had the number of guards doubled, if not tripled.'

The Office of Secretary of State was a series of beautiful, darkly wainscoted rooms overlooking the Privy Gardens. The smell of beeswax and lemon was strong. The guard left us waiting while Sir Leoline's man notified him of our arrival. Portraits adorned the walls, interspersed by shields and banners of noble houses. Spaced at equal intervals, intricately patterned cabinetry sat beneath them, topped by colourful vases and decorative objects. Some resembled human shapes, but many I couldn't even attempt to identify. But it was the elaborate geometrical design of the floor that attracted my eye. As if to make up for the apparent randomness of White Hall, the interior and gardens were an ode to symmetry.

I was drawn to a large window through which green and orderly gardens could be seen: a series of squares and rectangles divided by paths, each shape showcasing a statue. To think, this was where the King's spymaster watched over the realm. How could he concentrate on secrets and plots with all this beauty around him?

'Lovely, isn't it?' said Aphra quietly. 'I was relieved we were asked to meet Sir Leoline here instead of his rooms at Westminster. They're altogether different and very gloomy. Filled with squint-eyed undersecretaries and clerks who've forgotten how to smile let alone laugh. There it's easy to believe dungeons riddle the floors below.'

Before I could ask her if the old, rather plump woman in the garden I saw angrily dressing down a young lady was Barbara Castlemaine, there was the militant sound of heels. Waved forwards by a man of middling years sporting an ill-fitting periwig, we obeyed.

We passed through a series of rooms that, while not quite filled with secretaries and clerks, nevertheless contained several men working busily at desks, the scratch of their quills, the low chitter of exchanges, as well as the comforting flutter of paper like background music. No-one acknowledged our passing, though I was certain they were aware.

As we entered the office of Sir Leoline Jenkins, a clock on top of a bureau struck nine. We were punctual. The room was long and narrow, the walls painted a deep auburn. Bookcases lined one and, as we walked the length of the chamber to stand before a desk which had two comfortable chairs facing it, I resisted the urge to examine the shelves and touch the books. Tobacco smoke lingered in fragrant wispy clouds, and the smell of wine, grease and the faint scent of old parchment could also be detected. A fire burned in a large hearth, keeping the room warm.

But it was the man behind the desk who caught my attention. He was chalk in complexion with a long, bony nose, and when he raised his head, I couldn't help noting how impenetrable and dark his eyes were. He was younger than my father, but not as old as Papa, and yet there was something about the way he held himself, hunched over his desk, arm circling the papers strewed before him as if to prevent us peeping, that made him appear both older than his years and yet ageless. With the lace spilling from his neck and his elaborate sleeves and voluminous jacket, he was like a sorcerer from a tale. His mouth was wide, shapely, and yet, as he gestured for us to come closer, gave no hint of a welcome. We were an inconvenience at best, an utter nuisance at worst. How that could be conveyed by a mere look and gesture was quite an accomplishment. Mr Betterton would be envious.

'Sir Leoline,' said Aphra, curtseying. 'Thank you for agreeing to see us. This is my cousin, Mrs Tribulation Johnson.'

I curtseyed and would have sat, but Aphra gave a slight shake of her head. We hadn't been invited.

'I wasn't in a position to refuse you, Mrs Behn,' he said. His voice was sharp. 'Nor you, Mrs Johnson.' He extracted a page from amongst those in front of him. Aphra's note. 'Not when you write you need to urgently discuss business pertaining to the King's wellbeing.'

'I think my exact words were "a threat to his life", sir,' said Aphra, showing her teeth in what might be mistaken for a smile. 'I also think our notion of "urgent" differs greatly. I sent that weeks ago.'

Sir Leoline lowered the parchment. He linked his hands, resting his chin on his knuckles. He gave a long, weary sigh. 'Mrs Behn, if I agreed to see everyone who claimed to have knowledge of a threat to the King's life, urgent or otherwise, I would never leave my office.'

Aphra inhaled patience. 'Perhaps so, sir. But what I — we — have to relate is most serious.' She stepped closer. 'And, I like to think that, considering my previous service to the government, you know I wouldn't dream of wasting your time.' She placed a hand against her heart as if to steady it. I reached for her other hand and gave it a reassuring press.

Sir Leoline leaned back in his chair and his eyes swept first Aphra and then me. 'Pray, tell, what "urgent" intelligence have you come by?'

For the next few minutes, Aphra told Sir Leoline not only what Grace said (without revealing her name) but what both she and I had since surmised. Careful to leave William Scot's name out, she nevertheless revealed the other suspected plotters — the Earl of Shaftesbury being first and foremost, Lords Sidney, Russell and Essex, the Scotsman, Robert Ferguson and finally the Duke of Monmouth.

'There are other men involved too.'

'There always are,' drawled Sir Leoline. He slowly scraped back his chair, stood, and walked to the window. Rain had begun to fall again, obscuring any view of the garden. Lightning forked, illuminating the room with a terrible intensity before fading. Moments later, thunder grumbled like a cross old man.

Unperturbed, Aphra continued, asking me to clarify a couple of the details, including the code names Grace mentioned.

'In their meetings,' my voice sounded as if it had been tangled in wire, 'they refer to his Majesty as "Slavery" and the Duke of York as "Popery".'

Aphra nodded approvingly. When she'd finished, we stood, side by side. Sir Leoline remained with his back to us, hands clasped behind him.

After what seemed an age, he turned and leaned casually against the sill. 'Let me be sure I have the facts straight. These men you've identified are plotting to at least overthrow the government, at worst, assassinate the King?'

'Yes,' said Aphra.

'But, when it comes to specific details, what this plot actually entails, you're ignorant.'

'That's right,' said Aphra cautiously.

'Do you know *when* they plan to act?'

'No. Only that they've tried to organise uprisings and failed.'

'So you said — Accession and Gunpowder Plot days.'

'Yes, milord.'

'I see. Maybe you can tell me *where* this assassination will take place?' He waved his arm about. 'Here? Hampton Court? On the Thames? At the theatre perhaps?'

Aphra stiffened. I could feel the heat of her growing anger.

I answered. 'There was mention of intercepting his Majesty on the way back from the races.'

Sir Leoline deigned to see me then. 'Newmarket? But you've no confirmation. No proof.' He folded his arms. 'Of any of this.'

'No, milord,' said Aphra. 'But surely, the names of those conspiring alone are enough to —'

'Mrs Behn,' snapped Sir Leoline, levering himself off the sill and striding to his desk, 'if you knew how often these exact names are mentioned in relation to plots to overthrow his Majesty, poison him, the Queen, his current mistress, his dogs … How many plans these same men have been accused of hatching and by better people than yourself, all of which, when thoroughly investigated, have amounted to nothing, you wouldn't have wasted your ink —' he swept aside her note: it fluttered to the floor; he didn't retrieve it '— or your time coming here.' He sat down heavily and regarded us both darkly. 'Do you really think I don't have eyes and ears on these men all the time? That I wasn't aware of these code names? That I don't know their every move, their every thought?'

Aphra bit back a caustic laugh. 'That's just not possible, sir.'

'I'll tell you what's not possible!' shouted Sir Leoline, thumping the desk and half-rising out of his chair. 'It's not possible a doxy like you and this young —' his fingers tried to catch the air, his mouth twisting as he searched for a suitable word '— *chit* know better. That you have access to better intelligence than my men.' He leaned across the desk, his cheeks flaming. 'You have too much to say for yourself, Mrs Behn. You always have.' He pushed himself upright. 'Your reputation *is* well established here. Think we haven't forgotten Antwerp here in White Hall? How *you* failed miserably?'

Aphra opened her mouth, but his raised finger warned her to close it.

'I know what this talk of plots and assassinations is. Like Oates, you seek to ingratiate yourself with his Majesty. Well, I tell you now, madam. It won't work. Not with the King, nor me nor anyone else with the sense to see you and this cousin of yours for what you are … fabulators, just like the Salamanca Doctor. You're nothing but foolish women with too much to say.' He gave a bark of laughter. 'Save your ridiculous plots, your dangerous ideas and slander for your plays. Don't try and make a drama of real life with yourself centre stage. There's only one way that will end.' He threw a sinister look in the direction of the Tower.

Aphra began to shake. Not with fear, but with a fury I felt mirrored in my own body. Why, Sir Leoline was going to discount everything as female prattle.

I went to defend Aphra, defend what we, in good faith and hope, had brought to him. Before I could say anything, Aphra spoke.

'If that is all, Sir Leoline?'

'It's not. Though you made much of the Earl of Shaftesbury being a part of this plot, I'm afraid that's impossible.'

'He's more than capable of controlling men from Holland, sir.'

'I'm sure you're right, Mrs Behn. But the same cannot be said if he's dead.'

Aphra stiffened in shock. 'The Earl is dead?'

For all I disliked the man, the news was unexpected. Awful. Crippled, short in stature, followed by that unpleasant odour issuing from the wound in his side, Anthony Ashley Cooper had been larger than life. Able to coerce men and women to act with him, even against their own best interests, he'd been both the best friend the King ever had and his most cunning enemy.

'Indeed,' said Sir Leoline. 'Breathed his last on January 21st, in Amsterdam, or so my informants tell me. The news will soon be on the streets. Maybe you need to invent another figure to lead your band of killers?' He looked from Aphra to me and back again. 'Do not waste my time or anyone else's again, you hear?' He picked up his quill, found a piece of paper, and, without looking up, brandished a lazy hand at the door. His man opened it at that exact moment. He must have been listening. Soon, our humiliation, our curt, callous dismissal would be all over White Hall. We'd be laughing-stocks.

We made our way back to the river, our escort doubled to ensure we didn't linger. As if we'd wish to. We walked through the rain. Distant thunder rolled across the skies. Hot with shame and rage, I couldn't believe Sir Leoline had been so ready to discount us. Did he really receive so many reports of plots? The news-sheets carried information about any that'd been foiled or which partially succeeded, but it had been a while since any new ones had appeared. Maybe Sir Leoline censored them?

And what if we *had* mentioned my father? Would the name William Scot have made the Secretary sit up and take notice or would we have been made to feel even more like we'd been cozened?

The trip back was a wet, sombre affair. When the hackney rolled to a stop as we approached Fleet Street, Aphra said, 'I shouldn't have expected anything less. It's Antwerp all over again. Not even when I warned the court the Dutch intended to attack the fleet in the Medway was I heeded. What happens? A few months later, they did, sinking every ship and capturing the King's flagship, the *Royal Charles*. Then, the court conveniently forgot I'd forewarned them; that disaster could have been averted if only they'd listened. I'm like the Trojan prophetess, bloody Cassandra, a clarion of truth no-one hears let alone believes.' She sighed. 'I'm so sorry, Tribulation. I shouldn't have brought you.'

'There was nowhere I'd rather be than by your side.' I lifted her hands from where they were clenched in her lap and laid my cheek against them. 'We did the right thing, Aphra, I know we did.' I hesitated. 'Only, if Sir Leoline is right and the Earl is dead …'

'It means someone will have taken his place. There are moves afoot: I know it. Your concern Grace is saying these things to seek vengeance is legitimate,' she said gently. 'But I'm convinced William's here to ensure he can return permanently and the only way to do that is to end the Stuart brothers. For while either of them live, he will forever be the son of the man who killed their father.' She gazed out the window thoughtfully.

The rain was steady by the time we turned up Shoe Lane. Vendors were shouting to attract the few customers deliberately ignoring them. Messengers darted across the road, satchels slapping their thighs, while women lugged heavy baskets with sodden cloths draped over them. Deep puddles and dripping roofs made walking most unpleasant.

'What do we do?' I asked.

'For now? Exactly what Sir Leoline said his men are doing. Watch, listen and ask — carefully. Only, unlike the spymaster's men, we have an advantage they lack. A way of finding out things that, no matter how good or clever his intelligencers are, they could never be privy to.' Her eyes sparkled.

'You mean …'

Aphra smiled, slow and wide. 'Yes, kitten. Once William Scot returns from wherever he's gone, he'll seek out our company again. In turn, we'll keep our eyes and ears primed lest he let something slip. The authorities have chosen to not only disbelieve what we told them but dismiss us as well. They've left us no choice but to find the proof we need — proof they can't ignore. Not if we wish to prevent a tragedy. What say you?'

I halted just a few steps away from the house, disregarding the rain thrumming against my cloak and weighing down my hat. 'I say the Trojans *and* King Agamemnon ignored Cassandra at their own peril and look what happened to them.'

Aphra grunted. 'True. But I haven't forgotten what happened to Cassandra either,' she said, and opened the door.

I waited a beat before following. Neither had I. After all, she was murdered for telling the truth.

SCENE FIVE

The haste of a fool is the slowest thing in the world.

The True Widow, Thomas Shadwell

Either my father was an excellent agent who kept his secrets close and never dropped his cover, or he was indeed as virtuous as a Puritan's palate. He reappeared a few days after our encounter with Sir Leoline, keen to resume our acquaintance. We were eager he did as well. Yet, it didn't seem to matter how hard Aphra and I tried to extract information about the business he was undertaking in London, he never veered from his original story: he was seeking to invest in the Hudson's Bay Company on behalf of a Dutch merchant who specialised in furs. When Aphra asked if he was intending to meet with the Duke of York, who upon Prince Rupert's death had taken over management of the company, he said that was yet to be arranged.

Aware how long it took to meet with Sir Leoline, I thought he might be waiting until doomsday.

'Aren't you worried you'll be recognised?' I asked one bitter morning as we strolled by the river. 'Seized and taken to the Tower? Especially now the Earl is dead.'

My father paused to look at the fleet of stalwart swans, back upon the water now the ice was breaking. He shrugged in a rather nonchalant manner. Shaftesbury's death left him unruffled. 'One thing I've learned, Tribulation, is people see what they wish, believe for the most part what they're told. To those I've encountered since returning, I'm Josiah Keeling — the Baptist salt man. Where I'm from (I tell them East Smithfield via the world), why I'm here, doesn't really interest them. I'm simply the convivial stranger who buys them ale, orders meals, meets with his daughter and old friends, and is altogether inoffensive. I hide, if you can call this hiding —' his arm swept the embankment '— in plain sight. There's no reason for anyone to suspect me guilty of crimes others have unfairly attributed.'

'But you admit you worked for the Dutch. You still do. I know that years ago, Aphra tried to recruit you back to the Crown …'

'And, as Aphra will tell you, my dear, it's no felony to work for bread.'

'Doesn't that depend on who's baking it?'

He didn't answer.

Indifferent to any dire fate awaiting him, William Scot eagerly accepted our invitations to perambulate even on the coldest days, attend theatre, join us for supper. Together or apart, we couldn't extract anything of import, anything to prove what Grace said was true.

He was word perfect.

After winter grudgingly allowed spring to show her shy face, it was easy to convince myself Grace had been hoping for vengeance after all. Sir Leoline had everything under control and my father, while not a good or honourable man, was in the city to conduct legitimate business. Maybe the Earl's death had put an end to any plots. Maybe my father was as changed as he claimed.

Not everyone felt that way. I couldn't shake the sense eyes were upon us, watching our every move because of William Scot. Sometimes, I'd catch a swiftly turned head at the edge of my vision, a man with his hat so low on his brow and his cape so high that all I could see of him was the tip of his nose. Men in long coats swerved into nearby streets only to loiter aimlessly the moment we swung towards them. Other times, it was merely a prickle on the back of the neck, a shiver down my spine: the hollow ring of footsteps in a deserted courtyard. The notion we were not alone but observed and heard was constant. Not that anything we did or said, or any action by my father, was worth reporting let alone arresting him for. It was all so innocent.

Too innocent.

Usually one to forgive men their many slights and their ever-growing catalogue of sins against womankind (or at the least excuse and attempt to understand them), when it came to William Scot and guilty intentions, Aphra was as unbending as a bargeman's pole. I should have trusted her judgement.

While Aphra toiled over her latest project, I agreed to meet my father after finishing work at the theatre.

We took a hackney to Covent Garden and a lovely little tavern that served delectable coney pies and the softest bread imaginable. Night had fallen and although the silvery moon was abroad she was a lucent glow behind a thin veil of gauze clouds. It was icy. Late snows meant passage was slow, as slush and mud caught in the wheels, and not just of our conveyance but of every other person's which seemed, as we continued to grind to a halt, trapped in an endless maze of vehicles, to be most of London.

In the great square of Covent Garden, stalls had been erected, braziers breathed tongues of orange warmth and people milled about, wrapped in layers of wool and fur. It was nice to see children playing and dogs cavorting.

We entered the Boar and Raven just as the bells tolled six. The place was asqueeze with revellers and toxed workers. Fortunately, my father was on good terms with the owner and was shown to a table near the fireplace. We wasted no time ordering and soon were enjoying their buttery pies, the meat so tender it melted in the mouth. The beer was very tasty too, with a lovely froth and a score of sweet notes in the amber liquid. My father's companionship may not have been all I hoped for, but he knew how to choose a good venue.

After he asked about my week and how the performance went, I asked him about his own week. For the first time since I'd known him, instead of launching into a detailed description of almost all the places he'd been (I didn't believe half — I mean, how many times could you go to the Tower to view the jewels there? Or be invited to sail to Gravesend with a foreign Admiral?) and the many fascinating, dull or unattractive people he'd encountered lately, his face closed and his eyes grew wary.

'It was quiet,' he said.

'Oh.' I'd quite prepared myself for a long and tedious story. 'Still no word from the Duke then?'

'The Duke?' He frowned. His tone was sharp.

'You're seeking an audience with him, are you not?'

'Oh. Yes. Yes. Soon, I hope.' His gaze alighted on a group of men in dark clothes who were silently eating. They all wore hats and I wondered if they might be Quakers. Brave to be about when the mood in the city was so intolerant.

When one of them noticed and returned his curiosity, my father looked away, troubled. 'Are you well, Father?' I asked. He was rather pallid and the lines between his brow were deep as canyons. He wasn't smiling nearly as much as he usually did either.

'Well, yes. Fine. Only …' He paused. 'I'm afraid I've some bad news.'

My heart beat a tattoo. 'Oh?'

'I have to go away a while.'

'Again?'

He nodded brusquely.

'Business?'

'Yes. Business.'

'Where?'

'Where?' He pushed his tankard about with his thumb and fixed his gaze on a large dog that was looking up at its owner, a cooper from his garb, liquid eyes pleading for a morsel from the plate. 'Um. Bristol. Yes. Bristol.'

'Are you meeting traders then?'

'Yes. Traders.'

He was behaving most strangely. I fidgeted with the remnants of food. 'How long will you be gone?'

His eyes flickered a few times. 'As long as it takes.'

'As what takes?' I asked curiously, almost scared of the answer.

He drank noisily, wiping his sleeve across his mouth. 'You ask too many questions, Tribulation.'

'There was a time you didn't mind.'

'Well, that time has passed.'

Who was this man?

He banged the table with his knuckles. 'Have you finished? Good.' He stood before I could object or ask anything else and attracted the attention of the serving girl. 'Gather your cloak. We best be going.'

As the young woman quickly added up the cost of our meal and drinks and gave him a total, he reached into his pocket. As he pulled his hand out again, a piece of paper escaped. I grabbed it. It was blank. Strange. I went to return it but, as I did, my hand drifted close to a candle. As the paper passed over the flame, words began to appear.

Before my father saw, I scrunched it up and buried it in my placket.

'Ready?' he asked, gesturing for me to proceed.

He hadn't noticed a thing.

The trip back to Newe Street was silent apart from the noise of the streets and the splash of melted snow on the sides of the coach. The earlier congestion had cleared, and passage was swift. My mind was racing. What was my father doing carrying about notes written in invisible ink? There was no doubt this is what I'd taken. I'd even smelled the lemon.

Fortunately, my father was in no mood to linger, though he did hold me tightly when he said goodbye at the entrance to the square.

'Tribulation,' he began, 'forgive me. I've not been good company. I've much on my mind. I promise to make it up to you.'

'You don't have to make up anything, I —'

'I do. I will. In time, you'll understand.'

I withdrew from his arms. 'What will I understand?'

He went to speak, then changed his mind and shook his head. With a brief, last hug, he returned to the carriage. He never looked back.

The moment the vehicle disappeared, I ran across the square, ignoring the lurid invitations from those idling outside the tavern, and burst into the house. I took the stairs two at a time, shoving open my bedroom door and shutting it with a clang. With shaking hands, I lit a candle and, unfurling the paper, positioned it carefully above the flame.

Bit by bit, partial letter by letter, words slowly formed.

When they were revealed, I could scarce believe what I read.

Slavery and Popery returning from Newmarket 1st April. Men to be in position Rye House, Hoddeson, before 28th March. Hannibal and The Tamer will lead. Weapons and instructions to follow. The time is nigh for the old order to die.

God be with us.

This was an order to ambush the King and his brother on their way back from the races — just as Grace claimed the men discussed all those weeks ago.

I reread it, no longer in any doubt.

Whoever was behind this intended to kill the Duke of York *and* the King.

And so did my father.

SCENE SIX

I had rather have a plain russet-coated captain that knows what he fights for, and loves what he knows, than that which you call a gentleman and is nothing else.

Letter from Cromwell to Sir William Spring, September 1643

'We've no choice,' said Aphra, her face blanching as she reread the note. 'We have to go to the authorities.' She passed it over to Nest who, with a small cry, sank upon the bed. We were in Aphra's room.

'What if they don't believe you again?' asked Nest hoarsely, looking from Aphra to me, confusion and fear upon her aged mien. 'Look at the way you and Tribulation were treated by Sir Leoline. Never mind years ago when all those terrible things were said about you, Aphra. Not only were you never paid for everything you did for King and country, all the risks you took, you ended up in debtors' prison.'

Aphra made a scornful noise and pointed at the incriminating words. 'They'll have no choice but to believe me now, won't they? We have this note.' She stared at it, then pressed her fingers to her forehead. 'On second thoughts, they're just as likely to claim I composed it as a form of revenge — to make a fool of Sir Leoline.'

I sat beside Nest. 'Look at the dates. This is in less than two weeks. We have to do something.'

Aphra drew in her breath and went to her desk. She began searching for a clean sheet of paper. 'You're right, kitten. But, as much as I'm loath to admit it, even with this evidence, we're not in a position to do much, not without help. We need someone who'll take us — and that note — seriously.'

I raised a brow. 'Who?'

'There's only one person I can think of after Sir Leoline treated us the way he did, and that's your friend Gabriel's master. Sir Joseph Williamson. He's had me watched for months, if not years. He at least takes threats against the King's life seriously. If anybody will move on this swiftly, it's him.'

'I wish Gabriel was here.' It was out before I could censor it. I tried to mollify my words. 'He would make sure Sir Joseph acted.'

'Well, he's not. So, it's up to us.'

Aphra pulled a chair close to the desk. After a moment, she began to write. When she'd finished, she passed the page to me.

Careful not to smudge the ink, I read.

Sir Joseph,

The King's life is in immediate danger. There's a plan afoot to kill him and his brother as they return from the Newmarket races. We have evidence and will hand it to you in person at a place you nominate.

His Majesty's loyal subject,

160

'Was that your code name? 160?'

It was always hard to imagine Aphra a spy, carrying secrets, travelling abroad, conspiring with dangerous agents, doing the bidding of men like Sir Leoline or Lord Arlington. Yet seeing the number writ on the page, a proxy for the woman before me, made it suddenly real and very, very alarming.

I shivered, nodded my approval and handed it back.

'Less said —' she murmured as she sanded then folded and sealed the note. She stood, straight-backed. 'We must make certain this is delivered into Sir Joseph's hands.'

'I'll take it,' said Nest, rising stiffly to her feet.

Aphra pushed her gently back down. 'No, my friend, you won't.'

'I will.' I held out my hand.

Aphra looked me up and down. I waited for her to refuse my offer. 'Do you still have your brother's clothes? The ones you were wearing when you first arrived?'

Understanding dawned. 'I do. I also happen to know where Sir Joseph stays when he's in London. He rents rooms in High Holborn — Robin Woods Court off Dean Street. I heard Solomon make mention of the Golden Alligator.'

'That's a tavern,' said Nest.

'How do you know?' asked Aphra.

'You don't know everything about me, missus,' tittered Nest.

'Very well,' said Aphra, shaking her head fondly at Nest. 'Head to Holborn. Make some discreet enquiries. Find out exactly where his rooms are and deliver this message straight to him.'

I nodded solemnly, all seriousness and darkness.

'I just pray anyone watching won't suspect the lad who leaves the house is anything but another Coggin worker,' said Aphra. 'Go change, kitten. It's time to play the breeches part again. Never before have you played such an important role.'

I didn't have be told twice.

The bellman's voice was faint as I half-ran into Newe Street. '*Oyez, oyez, oyez* … Six of the clock and all is well … God Save the King!'

All was not well, though I did mean to try and save the King, I thought, as I darted down a small alley, intending to steer clear of the busier roads and head west. There was no moon and a faint spitter had started. The laneways were muddy and quite slippery and I was grateful for my sturdy boots. Groups of men and women lingered around fires, some in silence, others chatting and chuckling, all enjoying a final ale before heading home. The plaintive notes of a viola sounded from a window above. A horse whickered nearby and the grind of carriage wheels on the cobbles of Chancery Lane was faint. The air had sharp teeth.

I'd just crossed Fetter Lane, my breath escaping in long white plumes, and was about to enter a narrow, dingy snicket when a hand clamped over my mouth. I was roughly bundled through a doorway.

Panic seized me. It wasn't until whoever snatched me had trouble closing the door and holding me that I acted. I went limp in my captor's arms and, at the same time, tried to bite the gloved hand across my mouth.

'Oh no you don't.'

I gave a startled exclamation. 'You!'

I was released and stumbled away, the wall the only thing preventing me from falling.

Taller than I remembered and just as roguish-looking, he sported a neatly trimmed beard. His clothing was ill-fitting and made from coarse fabric. He smelled of brine, sweat and tobacco. He could have been a dock worker, a sailor, a builder. Only he was none of those things. He was Gabriel. There was so much I wanted to say, to ask.

What I did instead was throw my arms around him.

'I'm so glad to see you!' I pressed myself against him, loving the way the top of my head fitted so neatly under his chin.

He gathered me to him tightly. 'And I you.' He held me at arm's length and in the dim light coming through the open doorway, searched my face. 'If you knew how hard it's been seeing you, knowing we couldn't talk — I couldn't let you know I was back —'

'Back? Since when?' I began, then shook my head. 'Later. Tell me later. I need to find Sir Joseph.'

'Williamson?' asked Gabriel, surprised.

'Aye, Williamson.' I stepped closer. 'Oh, Gabriel, there's a plot to kill the King!'

'There's always plots to kill the King.' His tone was gently mocking.

I stamped my foot. 'Not you too. Sir Leoline scorned me and Aphra when we told him. But this time we have proof.'

Confusion sat upon the face I'd missed so much. The face that invaded my dreams and would have coloured every bloody waking moment if I'd allowed it.

As quickly as I could, I told him — about Grace, what she'd revealed, how we thought it serious enough to tell the Secretary of State.

'But he didn't see us for weeks and weeks, Gabriel, and, when he finally did, he was as dismissive as you're being.'

Gabriel threw up his arms. 'Forgive me. I didn't mean —'

'Wait.' I pressed my fingers against Gabriel's lips. God, they hadn't changed. Soft but firm. Warm, like my insides. I shook myself and took a breath. 'That's not all.' Taking a deep breath, I told him how Aphra and I decided to find proof by focussing on the one person we thought might provide some.

'So, William Scot *is* your father.' Why did the thought he already knew knock at my perturbation?

'It matters not who he is, not when he's plotting to kill the King.'

'Are you certain?'

'About his paternity or murderous inclinations?' I gave a defiant thrust of my chin. 'A note fell out of his pocket as we were leaving a tavern this very night. A note scribed in invisible ink.'

'What does it say?'

'The King and his brother are to die on their way back from Newmarket on April 1st. Assassins have been ordered to Rye House near Hoddeson.'

Gabriel looked incredulous.

I tugged his lapel. 'Sir Joseph must send troops. Arrest them and foil the plot.' I placed my palms against Gabriel's chest. I could feel a deep thrumming.

I lowered my voice. 'That's why I'm dressed like this; I was on my way to tell Sir Joseph, bring him to Aphra so she could show him the note and prove what we claim is true.'

'I wondered why you were gallivanting around in male attire.' Gabriel smiled.

My insides clenched. 'I'm not gallivanting, Gabriel. This is serious.' I needed to keep my thoughts uncluttered, my purpose clear. 'But if you're simply going to mock and delay, then I'm wasting time. *You're* wasting my time *and* your master's. Either take me to him or, if you have doubts, I'll go to Holborn myself.' I made to push past him.

'I *do* believe you.' He grasped my upper arm, preventing me leaving. 'Solomon and I have been in London for weeks watching for signs of another uprising or plot. We knew there'd been attempts to rouse rebellion, but thus far they've failed. Not even Shaftesbury's death has prevented others proceeding with plans.'

'Aye. This Rye House scheme.' I waved Aphra's note about. 'Please, Gabriel, help me reach Sir Joseph.'

'I would, only he's not in Holborn.'

'Where is he?'

'At his residence in Cobham, in Kent.'

'*Kent?*' My heart sank. 'But he cannot be. It will take a day or more to reach him and days to organise soldiers from there.' I leaned against the wall, the wind leaving my sails. I buried my head in my hands. 'What are we going to do?'

It was cold in this house. Now I'd stopped moving, it stole over me, chilling me to the very bone, even though I'd donned Fabian's thick coat. A small pool of light allowed me to see Gabriel and a hallway, but the rest of the house was plunged into darkness. I could sense it was deserted though it had a feeling of having been occupied. Through an open doorway, I caught nebulous glimpses of furniture, a rug upon the floor. Books sat upon shelves.

'Whose house is this?' I asked.

'Mine,' said Gabriel quietly. He paused. 'I … I purchased it for my wife …' He scanned the walls, the ceiling, gazed at the open doors, the staircase, his face drawn with sadness. 'For Wait-Still. But after she and Patience, our daughter, died —'

I sucked in my breath. A daughter too. I hadn't known.

'— I couldn't bring myself to use it.' He looked about wistfully.

'Gabriel. I'm so sorry.'

What else could I say? *Oh, Gabriel.* No wonder he never wanted to return to England, to London. Even so he'd accepted the mission at Dorset Garden. Why not? There he could be anyone he wanted, anyone except a grieving widower, a forlorn father. No wonder he'd been so angry, so distant all the time. All those rumours about him, the cruel and ridiculous assumptions. Ironically, the truth had been the strangest and most painful of all. A widowed spy; a grieving father; a bold intelligencer. How shallow we all must have seemed. I longed to take him in my arms, hold him to my heart. Hold his heart … repair it.

'Exactly how long *have* you been back?' I asked after a moment.

'A few months,' he admitted. 'Before winter last year.'

A long time. And I never knew … 'And you've been living here?'

'Not really. I simply use it when needed. I hired rooms elsewhere. More convenient for … work.'

The silence was a tangible thing, expanding to fill the space between us. I could hear my own breathing. I imagined the house with light, laughter, warmth; with Gabriel, his wife and child … children. A lifetime of memories … only they never had a chance to begin. A yearning rose in me, a yearning tinged with jagged pain. I looked at the man who'd bought this house dreaming of a future, a future that was ripped cruelly away. My body tilted towards him. I wanted to offer comfort, solace … Truth told, I wanted to offer more …

This was not the time.

'We need to act,' I said, reminding myself as well as him why I was here, the bearer of urgent tidings. Important ones. I was one of the few people in possession of knowledge that could either destroy or save the monarchy.

Save the country.

He took a deep breath. 'Alright. Here's what we'll do. First, we'll return to your cousin. I'll make copies of the note. Then, we'll take them to Sir Joseph. While men head to Rye House to prevent this catastrophe, others will set out to Newmarket to warn the King. An ambush returning from Newmarket won't come as a complete surprise. But there must be no doubt how serious this threat is.' He glanced towards the doorway. 'It's too late to leave tonight. The gates will be shut. Solomon and I —'

'He's here?' I glanced about.

'He's conducting surveillance.' Gabriel hesitated. 'Upon many of the men you mentioned … including William Scot.' He paused. 'I'm sorry, Tribulation.'

'Not as sorry as I am.' I gazed into Gabriel's sable eyes. 'If I can prevent my father from doing something foolish, reach him before the authorities, I would.'

'You'd save him?'

I considered his words. 'I know it's wrong, but aye. He may not be a good man or much of a father, but he's the only one I have.'

Gabriel's lips thinned. 'You may already be too late.'

'That's what I fear.' There was a beat.

'At first light, Solomon and I will ride for Cobham and alert Sir Joseph, then rally troops to ride to Rye House and await these assassins. The last thing they'll expect is an attack upon *them*.' Gabriel held my chin gently. 'Thank you, Tribulation Johnson. Not only are you beautiful and clever, but you're brave as well.' He smiled. 'Like a heroine from a play.'

'I'd never be cast as one,' I said, with a brittle laugh. *Beautiful? Me?*

'You oft are … at least, in my imagination,' said Gabriel. We stared at each other, the distance between us rapidly contracting. He was the sun and I was a planet swimming into orbit. His dark eyes glowed as his mouth lowered.

I could feel his breath upon my cheek, the warmth of his body. Mine began to tingle and shake as rivers of molten heat raced through my veins. My eyes flickered shut as the moment I'd longed for began to unfold and his lips collected mine.

'Gabriel!'

We broke apart as a huge man burst into the house holding a lanthorn aloft. Solomon stood panting, looking from Gabriel to me and back again, a silly grin on his face. 'I didn't know you sailed in that direction, captain — Oh!' His dark eyes widened. 'Tribulation.' Before I could speak or move, he lunged and crushed me in his great burly arms, the lanthorn swinging dangerously behind me, making shadows cartwheel. 'If you knew how often I'd longed to do that,' he purred.

'Enough of that, Sol,' said Gabriel. 'We're on the move.'

'So are Grey, Ferguson and Sidney,' said Solomon, releasing me reluctantly. 'That's what I came to tell you. They've left Shephard's rooms and are heading out of town. I'm yet to learn where.'

'Rye House,' said Gabriel and I in unison.

'What house?' asked Solomon.

'I'll explain on the way,' said Gabriel.

'To where?'

Gabriel retied his cloak. 'Mrs Behn's.'

'Will she have food? I'm starving,' moaned Solomon.

'Food and a story like no other,' said Gabriel, looking in my direction.

'Well, what are we waiting for? Lead on, MacDuff,' said Solomon, indicating the door with a flourish.

'I wish you'd stop doing that,' grumbled Gabriel, as he followed me into the alley.

SCENE SEVEN

God save the King

Against Gabriel and Solomon's wishes, Aphra and I left London at first light in a hired carriage that rumbled and rocked as we rolled out the city walls and through the countryside. It had been difficult to persuade the men that not only should the original note be taken straight to the King, but Aphra and I should deliver it.

'We'll get there faster than any men Sir Joseph dispatches, and if the plotters *are* on the look-out for government agents, the last people they'll suspect to be carrying proof of their intention is two women,' I argued.

I knew Gabriel was softening to our idea, but what he said next gave us pause. 'What makes you think his Majesty will listen to you when others refuse?'

Aphra bristled but only because she knew it was true. 'This,' she said, and held the note aloft. 'If he doesn't believe the words of two women, then maybe he'll believe the seditious threat of one man.'

As the wheels trundled over the crackling and groaning roads, the thin film of ice splintering as we progressed, I thought about Gabriel — Solomon too, riding east, towards Sir Joseph's. I prayed not only that they'd reach him promptly, but the soldiers would arrive in time to surround Rye House and capture the culprits — before they had a chance to act. A small part of me also prayed my father would either be absent, or escape.

After Gabriel and Solomon relented on us travelling to Newmarket, we sat up late into the night, trying to work out who exactly was involved in this deadly scheme. It was evident that while there were nobles implicated, they were the puppet-masters or, as Gabriel said, directors and stage managers.

'The main performance is being left to others,' he said. 'Directed, now Shaftesbury's dead, by none other than Algernon Sidney.'

The others, from what we could glean, were a rag-tag mob of merchants, ex-soldiers, parliamentarians and Whig-idealists if not zealots who bore huge grudges against the House of Stuart, were committed Protestants who feared Catholic rule, or believed passionately the time for a monarchy was over. Sometimes, all three. And my father was one of them.

'The Earl of Shaftesbury might be deceased —' said Aphra.

'May God rest his soul,' said Solomon quickly.

'— but he engineered this. If we manage to halt this travesty, it's still his doing. Men will hang for a heinous crime he couldn't even remain in the country let alone alive to see committed.' She looked at Solomon. 'You can ask God to rest his soul, but I hope it burns in Hell.'

Solomon stared at Aphra wordlessly, his eyes reflecting the flickering fire.

When it was time to part, I'd been reluctant to say farewell, scared Gabriel would vanish from my life again. For months I'd believed him abroad, risking everything, but he'd been here in the city observing, reporting, waiting … not for me. Well, maybe he had been, just a little. Waiting for the right time to make his presence known. And thank the good Lord he had.

My thoughts were as busy as the road to Newmarket. The journey was supposed to take two days, but great ruts of dried mud, and broken-down carts and carriages, were making headway slow. Aphra and I were thrown against each other in the carriage continuously and I began to wonder if my rump and shoulders would survive. Aphra's groans each time we connected were becoming louder and more guttural. Not even the sights we glimpsed, or the endless passage of farmers herding cattle, laden carts and the trudge of boots heading in the opposite direction, were enough to distract us from our ever-growing misery.

We rode past Waltham Abbey mid-morning, following the path of a fast-flowing river. Its joyful chuckling and bubbling over rocks and sand made mockery of our torment. Nest, who remained behind, had packed us dinner and, when we stopped at Hoddeson to change horses, we clambered out stiffly and sat outside a small inn in a patch of weak sun and gratefully shared the cold meat, bread, flask of wine and some fruit.

It was with reluctance we resumed our journey. Needs must, I recited over and over, like a Papist novice's mantra.

On the other side of Hoddeson hulked the now infamous — in our minds at least — Rye House. Aphra asked the driver to slow and we both hung out the window, gazing at the large former malthouse and its outbuildings. More like a castle, Rye House was possessed of high walls and wide lazy moat. Ivy and mould clung to the stonework like a desperate lover, lending it a mystical but also forlorn air. One could well imagine a knight in gleaming armour riding forth on a charger brandishing a sword and defending his liege lord before being brutally vanquished.

All too soon, the road running by the side of the manor house narrowed sharply before a toll gate forced us to a complete stop. A spectral mist floated, and it was easy to picture the spirits of the building's ancestors waiting impatiently for those who would join them in death.

Once through the gate, we followed the part-cobbled, mostly dirt lane, and were plunged into a world of gruesome shadows. We jounced over a field, then paused while the driver paid toll at yet another gate; nearby stood a lumbering guard with an enormous wen on his forehead and a few broken teeth, paying scant attention to us as he was too busy scratching his balls. I wanted to shout: Where is your pike? Your sword? Your blunderbuss? All I could think as I stared at the grey stone of the outbuildings, the entwined copses, was, *Who is lurking there?* Or were they yet to converge on this place? Who would be responsible for killing his Majesty and the Duke? What about the oblivious postillions? The poor, loyal horses? From the look on Aphra's face, similar thoughts were occupying her as well.

'This would make the ideal place for an ambush,' she whispered.

I pointed out the window. 'Men could hide in the hedgerows this side, and behind the walls that one. They could even shoot from the house if they had to.'

'The arrow slits in the old building would make the men firing hard to hit,' agreed Aphra.

We shared a long look once we were clear of Rye House and the few cottages and farms built in the surrounding fields. We crossed a rickety bridge where a rather dilapidated tavern sat. This was the one owned by the London vintner, Mr Shephard, one of the conspirators. Was he inside? Was my father?

I withdrew from the window. I'd seen enough.

We stayed overnight in a small, reasonably clean posting inn in the small village of St Chesterford. My dreams were filled with splatters of scarlet, piercing screams and the dreadful thwack of falling bodies. Out of it all emerged his Majesty, his hooded brown eyes heavy with sadness, his swarthy skin stained with gore as he pressed a gaping wound upon his chest. 'You were too slow, Tribulation. Too slow ...'

We arrived dusty and weary in Newmarket at dusk on Sunday the 21st of March. I wasn't sure what I expected, even knowing how much time the King spent in the place, but certainly not a bustling town crowded with courtiers, servants and sightseers, most of whom were gadding about, drinking, carousing and altogether having a frivolous time — especially on the Lord's day. Once again, I felt like running about and screaming warnings. A Bedlam loon.

The first inn we tried was fully booked. Apparently, the place was always teeming when the King, his entourage and other hangers-on were in town. From the way the landlord's face glowed and the many patrons in the taproom raised their tankards at the mere mention of the King, it was evident he was very popular. Why wouldn't he be? He had brought prosperity to Newmarket by not only favouring it with his and his courtiers' presence, but by holding races every spring.

A tiny room in the loft of the Courtier's Charger, a smaller inn on the edge of town, was available. The owner, Mr Brown, was a bald man with a sizeable belly who, when he learned we were there to see his Majesty, couldn't stop apologising for not having better accommodation. We quickly reassured him we didn't mind sharing a bed, even a single one with a thin mattress, nor the fact I had to bend almost in half so as not to bump my head on the low beams.

After washing the worst of the road from our faces and necks, fixing our hair and brushing our clothes, we shucked off the vestiges of travel-ache and tiredness, and went down the two flights of stairs and into another crush in the taproom. The noise was deafening. It took a while for Mr Brown to understand we didn't want his delicious, cheap supper yet, just directions to the King's residence. If we hadn't been told where to find it — the opposite end of the village from where we were — the clamour alone would have alerted us. Crowds of well-dressed (and some barely clothed) people were clustered around firepits, downing ale after ale and wine, and dancing. The music was loud and raucous. There was such a celebratory air. Both Aphra and I were swung off our feet by young men who also tried to foist drinks upon us. Laughing, we declined (Aphra with more than a little regret) and pushed and twirled our way towards the long path that, after diverging into a lower and upper road, led to the King's Newmarket residence.

Nothing like a royal palace, it comprised two storeys of stone and glass sprawled across nicely kept gardens which were ablaze with torches and filled with roaming figures. Light spilled from every single window. There was more music, shrieks of ribald laughter and resounding guffaws. Revels were in full swing.

Aphra approached some liveried sentries standing outside a small gatehouse and, using her voice to full effect, announced who we were and demanded to speak to his Majesty. Our duty was to gain the King's ear and, if possible, persuade him and his brother to leave Newmarket post-haste. They took one look at us, two slightly dishevelled, journey-worn women, and burst into gales of laughter. It wasn't the reaction I expected or hoped for. Undeterred, Aphra stood before the chuckling men.

'We're not leaving until you inform his Majesty we're here.'

With much rolling of eyes and palpable resentment, the sentries ordered us to follow them towards the house. Left unattended in a spacious hall, we perched on a polished bench and waited. From the knowing looks and winks exchanged by other guards scattered around the huge hall, most standing either side of the many doorways, I didn't expect to see the King any time soon.

Aphra gave an impatient sigh. 'I'm not sure this is going to work, kitten. I fear neither my name, nor yours, holds any sway. But I don't know what else to do.'

When William Chiffinch staggered out of a doorway, giddy laughs and jeering in his wake, my heart sank into my boots. Of all the men to fetch, they picked the King's bloody procurer — the man I'd once kicked in the cullies backstage and told if he wanted to keep his ladyware in working order to never come near me again. We stood as he staggered across the hall.

'Mrs Behn,' slurred Mr Chiffinch, the reek of sweat, wine and lustful thoughts reaching us before he did. 'I wasn't sure I heard aright when I was told you was awaiting. I'd say what a delight, only I'd be telling a falsehood, and I well remember how you disapprove of those.' As he spoke, he was looking me up and down. 'Don't I know you?' He bent towards me, bloodshot eyes narrowing.

'Maybe, sir.' I resisted the urge to clamp my nostrils.

'Please, Mr Chiffinch,' said Aphra, as patiently as she was able — which was barely. 'By all you hold sacred and dear, it's imperative we speak to the King immediately. Tell him we're here. We have some urgent information to impart.'

'Well, missus,' drawled Mr Chiffinch, stepping so close we were forced to step back lest we keel over. 'I'm afraid that's for me to decide, not for you or this doxy to tell me.' He rubbed his crotch.

Maybe he did remember me after all.

'So, out with it. What is it you must tell him?' He went to throw an arm around my shoulders, but I dodged and he stumbled against the bench, falling to one knee. A few of the guards sniggered.

'What you lot looking at, eh?' he shouted as he heaved himself upright. 'Keep that up, and you won't have eyes to see let alone heads to lower.' He turned back to us, the mask of tolerance removed. 'Well, *ladies*,' the word meant something else on his lips, 'either tell me *now* or leave. Your choice.'

Aphra and I looked at each other. I urged her to say something.

'May God give you good evening,' said Aphra, and she curtseyed.

Mr Chiffinch's eyes widened, his face turning the most remarkable shade of puce. 'Why, you fuc—'

'Quiet now, Mr Chiffinch,' said Aphra, resting a hand on his arm. He looked as if he was going to slap it away. She removed it before he could. 'You said it was my choice. If you don't like it, then I suggest you complain to someone who cares.' Before another word could be exchanged, Aphra took my wrist and dragged me away.

'Make sure those strumpets are escorted off the grounds,' yelled Mr Chiffinch. 'And never admitted again. They're henceforth banned. Do you hear?'

'Yes, sir.' The guards came to attention before two peeled away to walk either side of us. Two more took up positions front and back.

'What are you doing?' I hissed in Aphra's ear as we were marched back down the grand path, towards the revelling folk on the street.

'Hush. Don't say anything more, not until we're clear.'

The guards pushed us into the crowd of cupshotten men and women, most of whom failed to notice the rude manner of our dismissal. Aphra and I shoved and weaved our way through the merriment, but not before we'd been groped and pinched, begged for a dance or kiss, preferably both. It was a relief when we were the other side and spared any more ale-laden words or wet, sour lips.

The air was frigid, the sky a dazzling coverlet of stars that twinkled and appeared to join hands and frolic. I could have sworn I saw a few of the court nobles skipping and waving ribbons, arms linked with a couple of very young maids, as they wended their way towards the King's residence. It was as if Newmarket itself was one grand party to which Aphra and I were most firmly uninvited.

It wasn't until we finally reached our rooms, where the landlord, surprised by our swift return, promising to bring supper, that Aphra finally vented.

She flung her hat aside and sank upon the bed like a deflated sail. 'Goddamn it, kitten. I'm so tired of always being thwarted by bloody men.' She ran her hands over her face, wiping away the anguish.

I was busy trying to light a fire in the small hearth. I paused and turned.

She raised jaded eyes. 'There was no point telling Chiffinch anything. The dullard had already determined to dismiss us: didn't matter who we were or if the King deigned to give us an audience. We could have said a comet was about to strike, and he would have shrugged as it careened towards us in a fiery blaze, declaring it but a heavenly spark, and returned to his roistering.'

'So, what do we do?' I asked quietly. The coals finally began to smoke. I pushed open the small window before the room filled.

'We have to outsmart those who think they know better. Who always seek to undermine and most certainly underestimate us.' Aphra flung herself back on the bed, arms outstretched. 'Dear God, look at that,' she said, pointing at the ceiling. 'It's disgusting.'

I glanced up at the huge patch of black and grey mould, an old man's beard.

She covered her eyes. 'I'm like the men. If I don't see it, I need never address it. Oh, kitten,' she groaned. 'We need to come up with something—*anything*—that will force his Majesty to leave Newmarket early and well before the Rye House assassins are in position. You heard what Solomon and Gabriel said — that's imperative — even one could spell death for the royal brothers. In the meantime, pray they've reached Sir Joseph. And that he believes what they tell him. Show him.' She pulled the original note out of her placket and held it before her. 'So much for having proof. Hasn't made a damn bit of difference.' Her arm dropped and the paper drifted to the bed.

I stared outside. Even as far away as we were, the noise and music carried. I could see the dancing lights from all the braziers and bonfires lit to celebrate the King's presence. Though we'd only stopped in the taproom a brief time, there'd been talk of more courtiers arriving and the races to be held in a few days' time. If that was the case, it would be nigh on impossible to persuade the King to leave. It would take a disaster …

A disaster.

Suddenly, my father's words came to me.

The only way to instigate change is by burning down the old order so a new one might rise.

I looked upon the dazzling flames capering and whirling, sending showers of golden and silver sparks towards the firmament. They were so close to the buildings … It would just take one errant flame … One stray scintilla …

'Aphra.' I twisted around. 'I think I know how to make the King leave.'

SCENE EIGHT

The King's survival was later attributed to the intervention of providence ... but the conspirators would not have been ready even if he had returned as planned.

State trials, 1683

Setting fire to Newmarket by design proved more difficult than I'd thought.

The following day, we first attended a service at St Mary's, the local church (me to compensate for missing Sunday service; Aphra merely to remain by my side), then we spent the remainder of the morning strolling about, mimicking the many visitors by admiring the shops, the windmill, the fine racehorses being led to better grazing, and downing an ale or two in a tavern, all the while searching for somewhere to start a blaze. We had to ensure it would cause enough destruction to send the King back to London post haste but not enough to cause injury to the village or its inhabitants.

Newmarket was divided by a main road, one side being denoted as the Cambridge side, where the finer houses, including the King's residence, sat; the other was the Suffolk side, where commoners lived. There was also a marketplace on one side of the High Street and another, narrower road on the other, which led towards Mill Hill. We'd no choice but to set the fire on the Suffolk side. Unlike the Cambridge area, the houses on the Suffolk side were huddled very close together and the wood was old. The flames would spread quickly and cause the sort of alarm needed.

Unprepared to admit how reckless our plan was, or desperate, we ignored its enormous flaws and prayed for the best. Well, I prayed. Aphra hoped.

Just on sunset, as arranged, I hid in a farmer's stables. It was one of the few places with easy access, slightly back from the main road. There were great gaps and holes where wood had rotted or the palings simply fallen into disrepair. I half-buried myself in straw and waited until the farmhands retired for the evening. Lingering nearby to first make sure I wasn't seen, Aphra returned to the inn and made a point of having supper sent to our rooms, behaving as if we were both there.

When night had thrown its dark blanket over the countryside and humans and animals were, if not abed, at least indoors and unlikely to roam (all except the King's revellers at the other end of town), I released the two old nags, who'd tolerated my presence, and piled hay next to the ramshackle walls. I struck a flint I'd swiped from a table at the inn, and the sparks fell on the chaff. Smoke flew into my lungs and I began to cough. Tears sprang to my eyes. The flames, hesitant at first, suddenly burst to life. I fed the blaze, huffing and blowing.

Before long, tongues of fire were licking two sides of the building. I could hear the faint whinny of the horses, free upon the heath, but so accustomed to their stables, they hadn't yet run. The heat was intense. I slipped through a gap in the planks and bolted towards them, waving my arms, leaping like King Lear on the heath, urging them to bolt.

I'd only just assured the horses were safe when I heard footsteps. I squatted behind a drystone wall at the same time as a man crossing the field from a tavern found one of the horses. Then, he saw the flames.

'Fire!' he shouted. 'Fire!' He ran forwards then changed his mind, turned and fell. Stumbling to his feet, he began to race towards the nearest houses and pound on the doors. 'Wake up! Fire!'

I prayed the families would escape but be slow to respond to the blaze. We needed the barn and outbuildings to catch, for the nearby trees as well. Unexpectedly, wind rose, whipping my clothes, my hair. Where had that come from? It almost dislodged the cap pulled down on my head.

Figures appeared on the crest of the hill. There were more shouts and then some disappeared, while others ran towards the barn.

'Quick, rouse Farmer Downing. Tell him to move the King's horses. Save his herd.'

'Get the vicar,' someone else called.

'Alert his Majesty!' The cry was taken up.

Panicked voices rent the air. Men, women and children ran helter skelter. Dogs tore about, barking their fear and confusion. Some folk carried buckets, others blankets and besoms, darting forwards to try and douse the cinders landing on the grass, the sparks threatening to ignite. Too late: the wind, which blew from the north-east and fiercer than I'd accounted for, whipped the flames into a roar. I watched in distress as a row of houses we'd never intended would catch began to sizzle, then flame. People burst out the doors, babes in arms, women sobbing, men wailing their puzzlement, their terror. It was awful.

I was about to offer help, but a hand grabbed me.

'You must away, kitten.' It was Aphra.

I fell against her. 'What have I done?' I whispered as yet more houses and an ale-house whooshed alight.

'What needs must,' said Aphra, her face grim in the crazed golden light. She was a warrior queen sacrificing her people to the gods for a greater good. She tugged my clothing. 'We cannot be found here.'

When we finally emerged from our rooms some time later, the other side of the high street was a great wall of flame. It was shocking to behold. There was nothing that could be done to control it. The wind governed the fire now, stirred it into disorder and commanded it run amok. Efforts to fill buckets were useless. The one stream running through the village was filled with sewerage and partly frozen. Abandoning the water supply, people concentrated on getting each other and their livestock to safety. Furniture and clothes were piled on the Cambridge side of the road, the paltry wealth of the commoners on display. Everyone prayed the wind didn't change direction.

As Aphra and I ran down the road, towards the central part of the inferno, I tried to shut out the sobbing and howls of those who'd lost their possessions, their homes. It was useless. Their wails and prayers, their accusations and promises to God flew into my head and wedged in my heart. I held their filthy hands, staunched their tears, drew them away and offered words of comfort. I was thanked, blessed. Me. A devil-sent hypocrite.

When we were still some yards away from the centre of the conflagration, the King and Duke suddenly appeared. Members of their court surrounded them in a corona of jewels and silk. Following orders, some of the King's guards broke away to assist the villagers. The rest of his men were billeted so far out of town, they hadn't yet heard about the fire.

We drew closer to the as-yet clean arrivals, but not so close the King could see us. Mr Chiffinch was nowhere about. Aphra plucked at my sleeve. 'I pray this works, kitten, or all —' she nodded towards his Majesty '— is lost.'

My cousin wasn't above appeals to the Highest Authority after all. The situation was dire.

I gazed around at the despairing faces of those whose homes and belongings were nothing but fire and ash. 'For some, it already has been,' I whispered.

After doing all he could to direct those who tried to control the fire (one couldn't fight it), as he had the great one that ravaged London almost two decades earlier, the King conceded there was no more to be done. Instead of leaving for London immediately as we'd hoped, his Majesty remained to ensure his horses were safe and to render what aid he could to the people who lived in a place he clearly loved. Then, to our further dismay, the following day, he retired with his followers to the Earl of Suffolk's house nearby. When the wind changed again (thus saving the rest of Newmarket) and blowing ash and the stench of burning towards the Earl's residence, King Charles finally made the decision to return to London — a week earlier than originally intended.

I could neither rejoice nor feel triumph our plan had succeeded. Not when over sixty homes and three inns were destroyed. Despite my best efforts, some livestock perished. All this, in just over four hours.

Exhausted from helping douse and ameliorate what I'd started, offering solace and aid where possible, taking ale and food to those in need and finding canvas and blankets for the families forced to bed down on the heath, I felt a mixture of terrible guilt and complete despondency. I sent endless prayers of thanks to the Lord no human lives were lost; I don't know what I would have done had even a single person died.

By the time we saw the royal retinue with its endless rolling carts and carriages, servants, guards and hangers-on leaving two days later, the King and his brother had long gone.

The people of Newmarket would never know their sacrifice had likely saved the King's life. At least, I hoped he was safe. Until word reached us from Gabriel or Solomon, we wouldn't know.

Thus, when two filthy and weary horsemen rode into Newmarket four days after the fire, and rumours spread a mighty blackamoor was in town, I knew who'd come.

I didn't care my clothes and face were covered in more smuts than a chimney sweep's or my hair resembled a tavern wench's besom. When I saw Gabriel striding up the street, head swivelling one way then the other, aghast at the devastation, Solomon beside him, both attracting looks and whispers, I threw down the cloth I'd been using to clean some boots found in the debris and ran pell-mell.

If the good folk of Newmarket were curious regarding the relationship between the wild-haired, grubby wanton who flung herself into the tall man's arms before spinning and embracing the broad-shouldered blackamoor, they were satisfied that night when Aphra (she-who-knew-the-King) claimed we were family. An odd one, but one nonetheless. The people expressed gratitude to the men for the loan of their women, who were angels to have worked so hard to help the poor villagers who lost so much. I could scarce bear their praise. It was like a blazing brand upon my soul.

Confused at first at why I was so evidently uncomfortable with the acclaim, Gabriel and Solomon stared with wide-eyes and what I thought was distaste when Aphra quietly explained what we'd done to ensure his Majesty's exit — what we were left with no choice but to do because of Chiffinch.

Solomon was the first to break the silence. 'Remind me to keep flint away from you, missus.'

I stared at my lap, hands clenched tighter than a sailor's knot. Gabriel reached across and covered them with one of his own. 'I know you feel the pain of these people keenly,' he said softly. 'But you have saved the King and, in doing so, saved *them* from a much worse fate — civil war. That's no small thing and, if you explained what you did and why, they would beg you to burn their houses down all over again.'

'Shhhh,' I said, looking around frantically. 'I doubt that, Gabriel.'

'I don't,' said Aphra with newfound confidence. 'Gabriel is right. They love his Majesty. Look how quickly they've rallied. He's promised them coin to help rebuild. That has given them both hope and something to look forward to.'

'Let's pray he keeps *that* promise,' said Gabriel, letting go of my hands. 'He can be free with promises, especially when it involves money he doesn't possess.'

'He's too fond of Newmarket and the races not to keep this one,' said Aphra, confidently.

'In the meantime, they freeze on the moors.' I was the life of this small party.

'Tribulation,' said Aphra firmly. 'Stop being maudlin. It does not become you. We both knew what we were doing when we happened upon the —' she waved her arm towards the outside '— solution. Of course there are casualties. There always are. But, as Gabriel says, the alternative was much, much worse.'

I raised watery eyes to Aphra and saw Gabriel and Solomon also regarding me. What I'd thought distaste was empathy. They too had been forced into unpalatable but necessary decisions. I had to shuck off the guilt and accept what I'd done and ensure the consequences were worth it.

To the faint sounds of wood splintering, shouts as the partially ruined walls of houses were pulled down to tired cheers, and timber still considered sound enough to reuse was heaved to one side, Gabriel and Solomon filled us in on their news.

'We know the King and his brother are safe. But, tell us,' said Aphra, sitting up like a schoolboy, 'did you apprehend the plotters?'

Gabriel and Solomon exchanged a strained look. 'I'm afraid the news there's not so positive,' said Gabriel.

An icy breath gusted through my body, turning my veins to frost. And just when I thought to reconcile my actions. 'What do you mean?'

'Sir Joseph acted upon our information immediately,' said Gabriel. 'Thirty troops were dispatched from London. It took us a couple of days to reach Hoddeson and get into position. We surrounded the property, lay in wait and watched. The following day, when there was no sign of any assembly — of plotters or armed men — we'd no option but to search the premises, top to bottom.'

'We tore Rye House apart,' added Solomon.

Gabriel nodded grimly. 'We uncovered a cache of arms — blunderbusses and some muskets as well as ammunition, but nothing else overtly suspicious. Colonel Rumbold and his wife *were* in residence, along with a friend from Cromwell's time named Thomas Walcott. Their names are known to us. Rooms had been made ready for visitors, and according to local farmers there's been a great deal of comings and goings of late. That's hardly out of the ordinary, as Rumbold pointed out. The place is a resting point for travellers.' Gabriel sounded resigned.

'My father?' I asked tentatively. 'Was he there?'

'If he was, there was no sign. But …' Gabriel hesitated. 'Nor was anyone else we suspected of involvement.' His eyes grew distant, as if he was viewing an alternate scene.

'No-one?' Aphra covered her face with her hands.

'Apart from those Gabe mentioned,' said Solomon.

She harrumphed. 'I can only imagine what Sir Joseph had to say about that.'

I could scarce credit what I was hearing. After all the tension, the swiftly made plans, the journey to Newmarket, the thwarted attempt to see the King, never mind the nail-biting horror of the fire. The drafting of soldiers, the surveillance and raid on Hoddeson. All done because of a conviction we were going to apprehend the plotters; save the King. Yet what was it all for?

Naught.

It was a play built to a crescendo, setting up false expectations in an audience and then leaving them cheated and dissatisfied. I could hear the jeers, the boos.

'Was it all a hoax? Were we gulled?' I asked faintly. My wretchedness was almost complete.

Aphra appeared equally glum. 'What about the note? The meetings between the conspirators? The deadly intent expressed?' She looked from Gabriel to Solomon. 'Is it possible you arrived at Rye House too soon? Before the plotters had a chance to rally?'

Solomon grunted.

'That's what we believe,' said Gabriel. 'Whatever the reason they hadn't yet assembled, Sir Joseph wouldn't wait. He couldn't afford to, not when the King's life and the future of the realm were at stake.' He shook his head. 'At the least, we expected to find "The Tamer" Wildman if not a few others there.'

'Where were they then?' I asked.

'Who knows?' Gabriel shrugged. 'En route? Suffering a change of heart — which wouldn't be out of character. Maybe when Scot found his note missing he warned the others to abandon their plans? These Whig plotters do a great deal of talking, but rarely act, as the record shows.'

'The look on Rumbold's face when his Majesty and the Duke rode past while we were searching the premises, and with only half a dozen outriders to protect them, told its own story,' said Solomon.

Gabriel nodded in agreement. 'He was heard to mutter, "Free flies Blackbird and Goldfinch" — yet more code names for the royal brothers,' he explained.

'And that's not enough to arrest him?' I asked.

'It is not,' said Gabriel gravely.

'Was all this for nothing then?' My voice was small.

'No,' said Gabriel swiftly. 'The main objective was to save the King and his brother. That's accomplished. We know from our own intelligence, weeks and weeks of surveillance, this plan *was* real. Something prevented it going ahead.'

'Us?' I asked. 'This?' I swept a hand to the window.

'Maybe,' said Solomon. 'Or, as Gabe said, knowledge that Scot's note was lost. Or, like us, those en route to Rye House to take up position either heard about or even witnessed the King and his brother riding back to London early and knew their plan was compromised so returned home.'

I sank back against the chair, plucking my lip. 'It's like a play without a climax, no proper ending.'

'Only because we haven't reached the culmination yet,' said Aphra. 'To even plan the death of a King is treason, Tribulation. Punishable by execution.' William Scot occupied her thoughts too. 'There *will* be an apogee, and a dénouement; this isn't the end, kitten, as much as you might want it to be.'

'This wasn't for nothing, Tribulation, it wasn't,' said Gabriel earnestly. 'If for no other reason than with his Majesty secure, we now have the time to uncover all the culprits. More than ever, we know exactly who to watch.'

'God,' sighed Aphra. 'It's the Medway all over again, isn't it? I warned the government, but they ignored me, became complacent, even though the evidence was right there.' Aphra turned to Gabriel. 'Whatever happens now, we can't become apathetic. What does Sir Joseph think? Does he share Sir Leoline's mindset, believing I'm making up plots to draw attention to myself?'

Gabriel shook his head. 'He agrees something's afoot. The stage is set.' He gave me a weak smile. 'We were fortunate this time: we were alerted. King Charles is out of danger. We may not be so lucky next time.'

'Nor might his Majesty,' added Aphra.

We sat in silence, food forgotten, drinks too. Birdsong drifted through a window, and the giggles of children. A cow bellowed in the distance. I couldn't look outside. All I saw was charcoal monuments to haste.

'What happens now?' I asked, finally, pushing a piece of meat around on my trencher.

'To you?' Gabriel picked up his tankard. 'Nothing. You go home, return to the theatre, to writing, your life. Both of you.' He raised his drink in Aphra's direction. 'As for us, we continue to watch and gather evidence.'

'In order to apprehend these men, let alone prevent another attempt on his Majesty's life, you need more than overheard mutterings or an incriminating note, don't you?' Aphra shut her eyes briefly.

'We do,' agreed Gabriel. 'What we really need for arrests, let alone a conviction, is to either catch them red-handed, which we tried, or a confession. For someone to have an attack of conscience and profess everything — names, locations, dates. A signed deposition.' He stroked his beard. 'Despite the Popish Plot debacle, it still carries weight.'

'How likely is that to happen?' I asked.

Silence and dubious looks were my answer.

With a stifled groan, Aphra pushed back her chair and stretched. 'Come, Tribulation. We'd best pack and be on our way. Mr Betterton gave you a week's leave. If we don't depart on the morrow, you could be in trouble.'

'Well, that *is* my name,' I said wryly. *Just ask the people of Newmarket.*

Gabriel touched my arm. 'And where trouble comes, hope follows.'

Had Aphra said something? I looked into his obsidian eyes, eyes that were so hard to read and yet were filled with something that made me think of the starry sky I'd been lost in only a few nights earlier. One that swirled with prancing light, faith and optimism. How lovely he should offer solace by saying that to me.

In that moment, it was easy to forget the destruction I'd wrought, and believe anything, even hope, wasn't a foolish conceit, but possible.

SCENE NINE

I pray you, in your letters,
When you shall these unlucky deeds relate,
Speak of me as I am; nothing extenuate,
Nor set down aught in malice …

Othello, William Shakespeare

For days after we returned to London, my dreams were wracked by vivid images of gold and copper flames, heart-wrenching screams, and the tortured faces of the villagers of Newmarket. The sensation of being trapped in a furnace, my skin slowly burning, crackling, the flesh being flensed from my bones, would startle me awake: bathed in sweat; tangled in bedclothes; the smell of smoke and cooked meat strong in my nostrils.

Apart from sleepless nights, life returned to normal faster than I credited. Easy when your waking mind holds tight your darkest secrets. Work at the theatre continued apace, and I took on small speaking parts and committed to both help John Downes and assist Mrs Betterton with her school. In the end, I wasn't needed for the latter as Mrs Betterton had decided to step back from acting and focus more on teaching aspiring performers, so had the time to dedicate to it. Aphra encouraged me to write more, to reflect on what had happened back in March as a form of catharsis for my guilt and regret — both having been made worse when Rye House offered no results. I wrote an anonymous eyewitness account of the fire at Newmarket, focussing on the bravery and resilience of the townsfolk, their determination to make the best of the worst and help each other. It went a small way to assuaging my remorse.

We'd heard from some theatregoers who, in the ghoulish way so many people do, went to Newmarket in the aftermath of the fire to ogle at tragedy and soak up misery. I could never understand how people chose to become sightseers of the macabre, tourists of sorrow. But they did pass on the news that rebuilding had commenced and the people were very welcoming.

Aphra was able to plunge back into writing. She'd taken it upon herself to introduce Mr Creech, the translator of Lucretius's *De Rerum Natura*, for which she'd written an introduction, to those she felt could offer him advancement: Sir Roger, Mr Dryden, Mr Pepys and of course, Mr Hoyle. She was also working furiously on her *Love-Letters Between a Nobleman and His Sister*, which would be published in separate volumes. Lord Grey may have escaped arrest for his involvement in what we privately referred to as the Rye-House Plot, but Aphra wouldn't allow him to escape public condemnation for his other salacious crime.

For a few weeks, as April arrived and gentle spring coaxed away the frosts, and fragrant blossoms unfurled on trees and in fields and the rains fell with renewed vigour, it was easy to be persuaded life could go on. Even the fuming, foaming agitator, Titus Oates, was a much diminished figure. Sir Roger maintained his relentless pursuit regarding Oates's and his colleagues' damning testimonies. Every other edition of his news-sheet, *The Observator*, exposed inconsistencies and fabrications in the so-called 'evidence'. Whereas once, such dogged determination had earned Sir Roger nicknames like 'crackfart' and 'Towser', saw him accused of being a secret Catholic and forced to flee town, now he was heeded. The Mercury Women, Mr Tonson and Mrs Brome could not keep up with demand for Sir Roger's publications. There was fortuity in that — unlike other fly-by-night publishers and correspondents, who changed opinion faster than a weathercock in a summer storm, Sir Roger reported facts, stayed his course and was reaping rewards: a renewed and solid reputation.

Recently, Oates had the gall to try and claim a share of the Jesuit property seized during the Popish Plot. He was unsuccessful. With his pension from the King withdrawn and having been ousted from his accommodation at White Hall, the man was living on Christian charity — the irony. Once he was a person of note whose words were acted upon with virulence and speed, but with his staunchest supporter Shaftesbury dead, Buckingham licking his wounds or biding his time, Algernon Sidney being closely watched, and the Tories in ascendance, Oates was reduced to nothing, to being a nobody, or worse, a scorned relic.

Yet, I couldn't shake the sense of something bubbling away just below the surface, waiting to explode.

I was returning home after a very successful performance of John Dryden and Nathaniel Lee's *The Duke of Guise*. The Company had tried to perform it the previous autumn, but the censor had banned it. Though it was set in France, back then, it was felt the events depicted mirrored too closely what was happening with the King and his bastard son, Monmouth. As I'd had cause to reflect before, time altered everything — including perceptions and memories.

Bells tolled a merry six and I waved to a sweet-faced flower girl who, like her blooms, was enjoying the late sunshine. I was thinking how delightfully balmy the evening was. Perhaps I could persuade Aphra away from her desk and out into the not-so-fresh air.

As I wandered down Newe Street and into the court, I saw our front door was open. This was unusual, as Clara didn't like dust blowing into the house: not that anyone else did either I supposed. Then Nest appeared on the stoop and frantically waved me over.

I ran the last few steps, my chest tight.

'Is it Aphra?' Of late, she'd been complaining how much her limbs ached and of a sharp pain in her middle.

'She's out and about. Cease your worries on that score.' Nest ushered me inside and closed the door. 'You've visitors.'

'Mr Scot?' I asked, my body becoming taut. Since the events at Newmarket, I hadn't seen William Scot. There'd been a note, a few scrawled lines saying he was travelling north for a time.

'They've come from Chartham.'

My heart lurched.

Nest held my shoulders, forcing me still. 'It's Bethan, Tribulation, and she's not alone.' She hesitated. 'I've put them in the upstairs parlour.'

The room disappeared, and if Nest hadn't been holding me, I think I'd have staggered. Bethan, in the house. Who with? Papa? Nay, Nest would have said. Who then? Nor Sir M, please God.

Thoughts of both Bethan and Papa — whatever I was to them — were like an aching tooth I tried to ignore but would occasionally prod and poke until the pain was too great. And now she was here. My mind pirouetted: feelings of excitement, foreboding and so many other emotions collided and collapsed.

She was here.

'If you need me, Mrs Tribulation, call,' said Nest, drawing me into her arms before releasing me reluctantly. 'Mrs Aphra will be back later.'

I gave a tremulous smile. 'Thank you. Please, Nest, tell Aphra to join us the moment she arrives.'

I ascended the stairs slowly, clutching the banister. What would I say? What would *she* say?

It was easy to be bold and brash, demand truths with a pen, when you didn't have to face the person you were asking … This was different. My stomach churned, a cold sweat enveloped me. After I had waited so long to hear from Bethan, she'd come.

When I reached the landing, I stared at Aphra's closed door, wishing she was here.

Only, this was something, someone, I had to face alone.

Before I could change my mind, I took a deep breath and entered the parlour.

SCENE TEN

(A Medium, I confess, I hate,)
For when the mind so cool is grown
As neither Love nor Hate to own,
The Life but dully lingers on

Lydicus or, The lover in fashion, being an account from Lydicus to Lysander, of his voyage to the Island of Love, Aphra Behn

The first thing that struck me when I saw Bethan, rising from a chair, was how content she looked. Never before could I recall seeing her mouth upturned nor her eyes so bright. Always lovely, today she was beautiful.

'Tribulation,' she began. 'You look well. B-better than well. London life suits you.'

I paused halfway across the room, not knowing quite how to greet her. Did I kiss her, hold her?

I did neither.

She stepped towards me, then stopped. The arms she'd held out dropped to her side. I wasn't alone in my confusion.

'You look … well too, Bethan.' We were so formal, so proper … on the outside. Inside, I was a roiling, boiling ichorous mess. I wondered if Bethan felt the same.

I gestured for her to sit again. A chocolatier and two half-empty bowls waited on the table. Only then did I become aware of a figure standing unobtrusively near the hearth.

'Mr Parker!' My astonishment was complete. What on God's good earth was Papa's curate doing here? Turns out, he wasn't as thin, old or ungainly as I remembered. In fact, with his hair longer, and tied at his nape, a clean collar and neat jacket, he was almost handsome.

'Walter's my husband,' said Bethan swiftly. She smiled sweetly at him.

'Your *husband*?' I stared from one to the other. 'You didn't marry Sir M then?'

'I did not,' said Bethan, firmly. 'After you left, despite Papa's unashamed urging, Sir M never renewed his offer for my hand and, in time, found another more suitable candidate.' There was no sign of regret.

'Thank the Lord,' said Mr Parker, eyes travelling to the ceiling.

Poor woman, whoever she was. 'Then, you have my congratulations, Bethan … Mr Parker.'

'Please, Walter,' said Mr Parker, grinning sheepishly.

I sank into the chair opposite Bethan, trying, failing, to gather my thoughts, my wits. 'While your arrival is a surprise, I'm glad you've come. It's been over four years.' I tried to keep the rebuke out of my voice. I think I mostly succeeded. '*We've* a great deal to talk about.' I looked meaningfully at Mr Parker.

'Walter knows *all*, Tribulation,' emphasised Bethan softly. 'Which is why I'm here. It's time you did as well.'

All. Such a little word to hold so much.

'I see,' I exhaled quietly. Was I ready for this? I had to be. Without further ado, I ploughed ahead – before courage deserted me. 'Why didn't you answer my letters? I wrote … I —'

'I never received them,' said Bethan quickly. 'Not one.' She lowered her head. Walter came to her side and placed a gentle hand on her shoulder. She reached up and covered it with hers. The gesture was so loving, so natural, it made my heart fill.

'Papa?' I asked.

She nodded. 'I'd no idea you'd written so many, let alone the one you must have been waiting desperately for me to reply to.'

'About William Scot.'

Bethan raised her head. 'Aye, that one. It went to the manor and Sir Marmaduke; well, upon seeing who it was from, he must have given it to Papa. I never saw it — I never saw any of them.'

We locked eyes. In Bethan's, crouched just behind the contentment, I saw unaccountable sadness, anger and, much to my astonishment, a little fear. What was she afraid of? Me? William Scot? Papa?

'Did Papa finally give my letters to you then?'

Bethan glanced at her husband. 'Nay. I found them hidden in his study.'

I frowned. Since when did Bethan rifle through Papa's drawers?

'I'm afraid we've some terrible tidings, Tribulation,' said Walter.

Before he even said the words, I knew.

'Your father is dead.'

'You mean, my grandfather,' I said automatically, wincing at my harsh tone.

Bethan inhaled audibly. 'Aye. Your grandfather. He died over a month ago.' She paused. 'He'd been sick a long while, attacks of apoplexy affecting his ability to talk and walk. In the end, he could barely communicate. Walter took up his duties in the parish over a year ago.'

Over a year, yet I'd known nothing of Papa's ailment.

As if reading my mind, Bethan reached for me. 'I wanted to tell you, Tribulation. Truly. He wouldn't let me. Just as he wouldn't let me write to you. I tried, at first, I really did, but he had the servants watching, waiting, taking my letters straight to him, no matter what means I used to avoid detection. After a while it was easier not to write and for that, I pray you'll forgive me. In my defence, the entire time, I thought it your preference too, that you'd rather forget me, us.'

I made a quiet noise of protest.

'Not that I'd have blamed you,' she added. 'Not after what Papa wrote. I couldn't forgive him that. Not only for sundering *his* relationship with you, but mine as well.'

'I never really had one with Papa,' I said with a half-hearted shrug. Yet, the news of his passing hurt far more than I thought. *Papa is dead.* 'It was you I missed.'

Bethan edged forwards. Walter took up position behind her chair, both hands folded over the back. 'That's why,' she began earnestly, 'among other reasons, I'm here. I want to try and make amends for what's happened — for everything. To do that, I need to tell you about … about William Scot.'

'Was what he told me about you the truth?' I held my breath.

Bethan bit her lip at the same time as she gave a single nod. 'Aye. I'm your mother.' She started to reach for me, but her hand fell away. 'You must be furious with me. My cowardice in keeping our relationship a secret all these years, pretending to be your sister. It must be so confusing for you. Hurtful too.'

'Furious with you?' I shook my head, frowning. 'Nay, I'm not furious at all. You didn't even come into my life until after Mama died, and I was what? Six? You were so grown up — already a widow and in your twenties. I never questioned who you were to me, just *how* you were. I thought you resented me, resented being forced to help raise a little sister. You were so distant sometimes, so remote … and yet, I also remember kindnesses, the small gestures — and big ones.' I contemplated my surroundings. 'You sent me here.' I could feel tears beginning to muster. I blinked them back, forced them down. *Not now.* 'What I don't understand, is why didn't you tell me once I was living with Aphra? Why continue the charade? Were you ashamed of me?'

This time, Bethan took my stiff hand in hers and looked me directly in the eye. The satin of her gloves felt smooth and artificial. '*Ashamed* of you? Never. The only person I was ashamed of was myself.'

Bethan released me and smoothed her skirts, tugged at the gloves she hadn't removed. 'This isn't easy for me, Tribulation.' She hesitated. 'I've no doubt, God played a hand bringing William Scot into your orbit. I just wish I'd been brave enough to admit what I'm about to tell you sooner. Unlike you, I lacked the courage to speak my mind, forge my own path.' She gave a shuddering sigh. 'But Walter's love, Papa's death, and reading all your letters have, together, helped me see it's time to tell you what's been kept from you, from everyone. But, Tribulation, I need to know: are you ready to hear it?'

What was Bethan about to tell me?

'I am.' The words were out before I could stop them.

She nodded grimly and took a deep breath. In a quiet voice, she continued.

'You wrote that William Scot told you he loved me; that consequently, you hoped there was mutual affection between us.' She gave a bitter sound. 'William Scot did ever deal in deception and duplicity, something Aphra's well aware of and learned to her detriment.' She hesitated. 'Despite what he may have inferred, when we were introduced in Canterbury all those years ago, I'd no regard for him except in the way a young woman does for an older, well-bred man who pays her attention. He worked hard to earn the family's trust; to earn mine.

'Even so, he didn't love me, Tribulation. He didn't *make love* to me. That implies a reciprocity of feeling. There was none. The truth is …' She stopped. She closed her eyes momentarily. When she opened them again, she said five words that will be forever seared into my memory.

'The truth is, he forced himself upon me.' Years of pain, torment and nightmares accompanied her statement. 'He waited until I was alone and followed me into our garden and he … he …' Her chest began to heave, her hands to shake. She bit her lip, the colour fleeing where her teeth impressed it. Determined, she lifted her chin, gave a little flick of her head, clenched her fingers, resolute, tenacious. 'He did take me against my will not once, but twice. From that violent act, God did see fit to make you.'

I fell back in the chair as if I'd been pummelled.

Bethan was raped?

My father *raped* my mother?

I pressed a fist into my stomach. My throat thickened.

I stared at her. She met my gaze unflinchingly, pity upon her beautiful features. Pity for me.

He. Forced. Himself. Upon. Me.

How did I reconcile this? How does anyone?

Oh, poor, poor, Bethan.

My poor mother.

My thoughts were blazing, bright twirling cinders alighting in different parts of my mind and setting them aflame. It was Newmarket all over again.

Dear God. This beautiful, quiet woman, my sister-mother, was abused, by William Scot. Her honour trammelled. Not only by him. My mind was raging. *She was also desecrated by her first husband. And by Papa. Then, she was denied her child.*

And, in turn, I was denied her.

Bethan may not have cried, but I did. Sorrow cascaded down my face: sorrow for her, for myself that I was born of such a vicious, appalling act, a constant reminder of pain, violation and humiliation. But Bethan wasn't finished. I forced my tears back, determined to listen. It was the least she deserved.

'When I told Papa what happened, what William Scot had done, he refused to believe I wasn't a willing participant. That I hadn't foregone all my principles, my morals, and committed the most heinous of sins. As for William Scot, he vanished. When it was evident I was with child, it was assumed *I'd* seduced William Scot.'

I beheld her in horror.

'After all,' she continued, 'does the church not teach that if a woman is truly raped, a babe will not ensue? Only consensual relations produce a child.' She gave a disparaging huff. 'What a misguided assumption, invented by men so women continue to pay for their sins.'

'You paid for William Scot's,' I managed croakily.

'So did you, Tribulation. So did you.' She waited a beat, then continued. 'Papa would have sent me away, but mama refused to condone this and begged him for an alternative solution. They wouldn't allow me to try and cast you from my womb, though I pleaded with them for that too and, may God forgive me, did attempt the same with the help of a wisewoman. I imagined the child, you, as a homunculus, a miniature version of the man who destroyed me. You were poison in my womb.

'I was, thank the Lord, unsuccessful.'

I sucked in my breath. Bethan tried to rid me from her body. Jesus Christ, but hearing that did wound. Burrowed through the flesh to lodge where it cannot ever be extricated. I was like a soldier crossing a lexical battlefield, knocked down, bloodied, forced to rise and dodge the slings and arrows of outrageous revelations and pray I reached safety.

I was a poison in her womb.

'You would oft ask,' she said, unaware of the effect of her words, or perhaps not wanting to see, 'why the family moved to Chartham. Why we gave up the joys and excitement of living in Canterbury to retreat to a backwater in the country. Why we cut ourselves off from family, from kin. *You* are the reason. My disgrace was hidden until such time as you were born and Papa and Mama could acknowledge you as their own and as my much younger sibling. Then, of course, before uncomfortable questions could be asked, I was shunted off in marriage.

'After a time, I was grateful for their intervention, their choice, even if my first husband was a brutal man. By then, I thought he was nothing more than I deserved. Becoming Mrs Pratt, moving away, also meant I need have nothing to do with you, a constant reminder of what *he* did. The only part I played was to name you. That was another question you would ask over and over. Why were you christened with a Puritan name that held such negative connotations? I named you for what you were to me, what you signified for the years ahead — trouble. The moment you opened your eyes and the mark became apparent, my heart froze.

'By the time I returned to Chartham a few years later, a reduced widow, you looked like him. The resemblance grew as you did.' She gestured to me. 'You're tall, slender, with that blight in your eye. You're possessed of the same long fingers, fingers that did horribly use me. I could scarce bear to be in the same room as you, a living reminder of my degradation.'

I shut my eyes. *I* could bear no more. I started to rise.

'Wait. *Please.*'

I sank back down.

'You see, Tribulation, despite the defences built around my heart, my resistance to your affections and blandishments, I grew to love you.'

Bethan was naught but a shimmering outline.

'Oh, I was never good at showing regard, not after William Scot, and for that I beg your forgiveness. I tried to show it in other ways — protecting you when I could, watching from afar to make sure you didn't come to harm, giving you to Lady Adeline, who I knew would nurture your wild imagination and cultivate your clever mind.

'As the years passed, I came to understand Papa had protected neither me nor you but imprisoned us with his deception. We were both being punished for something neither of us had done: the crime of William Scot.

'When Papa accepted Sir Marmaduke's suit, I thought at last, I can escape from my relentless gaol and take you with me. The man may have been a buffoon —'

Walter coughed.

'— but at least I'd have had a modicum of liberty as his wife. I know you didn't understand. When he retracted his offer and asked for you in my stead, I was appalled. I had to find a solution. If we couldn't escape, I determined you at least would.

'I remembered Aphra. I'd sometimes hear of her from travellers and, when she started writing plays, I read about them in the news-sheets. Papa, thank the Lord, remained in ignorance – of her profession, of her married name. When I saw an advertisement for one of her plays, a way of helping you presented itself. I persuaded Papa to send you to her so we might alter Sir Marmaduke's mind.'

Oh Bethan …

'When you left for London, I was relieved beyond measure. I knew it was only a matter of time before Aphra would wield her influence and you would find your place. You have, haven't you? You're happy?'

Poor Bethan. She needed me to be.

I found a kerchief, wiped my face and blew my nose. I felt almost shy with her — my sister, my *mother* — who I'd never really known. Who'd been so badly used and who'd sacrificed so much. For me.

She was watching me cautiously, a look of sorrow and something else on her face.

'I am. I have.' I smiled. It was a poor attempt as my mouth was still atremble and my eyes kept filling. But Bethan saw and returned it.

'Thank you for telling me the truth … Bethan …' I couldn't call her Mother. I hoped she understood. It occurred to me, I'd spent my life trying to replace the Mama I thought I'd lost — first with Lady Adeline, even with Aphra. Ironically, my mother had been there all along. 'I know it wasn't easy for you to tell me.'

'Nor for you to hear,' she said.

Aye, well, she had that right. 'And what about you?' I added quickly, ashamed I even thought listening to the dreadful tale compared to living it. 'Have you found your place?'

This time, Walter placed both hands on Bethan's shoulders and she tilted her head back and beamed at him.

'I have. As wife to a man I love. But,' she hesitated, 'there's something else I need to tell you. God has also seen fit to give me a second chance at being a mother.'

My heart shrank and then just as quickly expanded.

'I'm with child, Tribulation, and it's my hope that this time I can be what I never could to you.'

I think I might have waited a beat too long and my bright smile might have appeared forced, but finally, I managed to blurt, 'Congratulations. God bless you both — and the babe. This is marvellous news.' It was. And I mostly meant it. But a tiny part of me, in a wedge of my heart, felt such injury. I tried to patch it quickly, cover it to examine later, when I was alone.

The afternoon passed swiftly after that. We talked of Papa's funeral, the theatre, Aphra's health, the King, and what was written in the latest new-sheets. Nest replenished our bowls, but when she enquired whether Bethan and Walter would be staying for supper, they declined.

'We have to go,' said Bethan too quickly. 'We've arranged to stay with a cousin of Walter's.'

I couldn't help but feel relief.

We said goodbye awkwardly, but with affection, nonetheless.

Bethan held my hands. 'One day, Tribulation, I hope we'll come together as a family and you can meet your younger sister or brother.' She touched her stomach. 'I pray there'll come a time when I'll call you daughter, and you can find it in your heart to forgive me for being less than what I should be, and far less than you deserve. I pray one day you might call me Mother.'

Stunned by her words, by her insight, I couldn't move.

Walter, who'd barely said a word the entire time, took the opportunity to fold me in a crushing embrace. 'She does love you, you know,' he whispered.

As Nest and I stood on the stoop, watching them cross the square, Bethan suddenly turned back. In a few strides, she stood before me.

'One last thing, Tribulation.'

My heart began to do strange manoeuvres. What now?

'You were never "unnatural", simply "unconventional". A woman for whom life is a series of adventures to be savoured. May it always be so.'

She stood on tiptoe and kissed my forehead.

She rejoined Walter, waving back towards us, and I raised my arm in reply. Nest pressed me to her tightly.

'*Au revoir*,' I whispered.

Aphra found me about an hour later, sitting in the growing darkness, dry-eyed, unable to utter a word. Concerned, she kneeled by my side. 'Nest said Bethan was here.'

'She was.'

She slowly sank into the chair close to mine and over the next while I recounted our entire afternoon, leaving nothing out.

When I'd finished, Aphra rose, lit a candle, and paced back and forth, back and forth, wearing a path in the floor.

Then, she stopped, retrieved the jug from the table, and poured us both drinks. 'Well,' she said and sat back down.

'Well,' I repeated.

'I'm not sure what to say,' she continued after a beat. 'I've no words. As for William … I always knew he was a misbegotten, despicable jackleg, but this …' She gestured to the world. 'This is the act of a complete whoreson. I didn't think he could stoop any lower, be more depraved or wicked. I was wrong. Poor Bethan … All those years, such a brave performance: such a difficult masquerade.' She reached for my hand and held it.

For someone who had no words, Aphra was doing well. Some were slithering about in my heart, in my soul. Poisonous deadly ones.

'You do know I'm here for you, kitten?' Aphra's dark eyes were pools of sympathy, of sorrow too. 'Always.'

I had to look away before I fell into them and drowned myself. It was hard enough to keep at bay the sobs I felt climbing my chest, rib by rib, crawling into my throat. 'I know.'

In the short time since Bethan and Walter left, I'd done some thinking. Oh, I needed to do a deal more yet. And while there was good to take from what Bethan revealed, much understanding, the heart of her story, of my creation, was beyond horrifying. I was struggling to comprehend what it meant.

Would it alter me? Should it?

The notion tormented me.

If I wanted to continue to enjoy the life I was making, my work at the theatre, my fledgling writing, and seek to improve my circumstances, it was apparent I'd a choice to make. I could either welter in self-pity and let Bethan's shocking admission, my new knowledge about my birth, my father, that my entire life had been founded on lies, reduce me to dust, or I could use this information as scaffolding to build a new life, a better one. Bethan had done so. Despite all she'd endured, all she'd suffered, she'd chosen to put the awfulness behind her and embrace happiness. And love.

All the same: poor, poor Bethan. I couldn't cease thinking of her that way. That had to change. She deserved so much more than such a weak appellation. Deserved more than my sympathy. No wonder she'd been such a withdrawn figure in my childhood — literally and metaphorically. To have a reminder of Scot's violence, his abominable act, thrust upon her day after day. I might have been called sister, but I was never that to her, or daughter. I was poison: the embodiment of shame, pain and sin. I was trouble in every single conceivable way.

And yet, she came to love me. I would hold on to that as my truth. *My* hope.

These were the thoughts that cluttered my head until, hours later, I reached a decision.

There was only one person I held accountable for everything that had happened to the Johnsons. It was the man who'd lied to me from the start — about himself, what he'd done, what he still did. From the outset, he'd lied to Bethan, to Aphra and even the King.

The tears that finally surfaced and fell, striking the hearth and hissing, weren't of sadness, but borne of utter rage. And, if I didn't find a release for them soon, I was scared that, like parts of Newmarket, I'd be reduced to ash.

SCENE ELEVEN

If it be you that strip these daughters' hearts
Against their father, fool me not so much
To bear it tamely; touch me with nobel anger,
And let not women's weapons, water drops,
Stain my man's cheeks

King Lear, William Shakespeare

June was always an unpredictable month, the contrary child of the calendar year. Younger sister of midsummer, it provided days of warmth and sunshine or lashings of rain and chilly mornings — but I barely noticed the weather this evening as I hurried home from the theatre. Unable to secure a hackney or any kind of conveyance as all were hired, I walked as swiftly as I could, scarcely acknowledging those who greeted me. I had a great deal on my mind.

A note had been waiting when I arrived at Drury Lane. It was from Gabriel and written in the code he'd taught me. We'd been communicating regularly since the events surrounding Newmarket. William Scot had been sighted heading back to London. Gabriel warned me to be cautious lest he made contact.

I could only pray the man did. There was much unspoken between us, and I would alter that.

I wanted to let Aphra know about Gabriel's note. She'd unfinished business with Scot as well.

By the time I reached the house, the bells had chimed seven and the bellman promised clear evening skies. The place was quieter than a charnel house. Nest had taken to keeping a look-out for my arrival each day, waiting on or near the stoop under the pretence of feeding the chickens that bobbed and pecked in the square. She wasn't there. Nor were the usual sounds of hustle and bustle.

I slowly removed my jacket and hat, hung them, undid my boots and wriggled into my house slippers.

'Hello?' I called. 'Nest?' I waited. 'Mr Coggin? Clara?'

Not a whisper. I checked the kitchen. Empty except for the odour of onions and something else unpleasant, the table was devoid of the usual clutter, the hearth cold. Strange.

'Aphra?' I tried as I mounted the stairs.

All the doors on the landing were closed, even the one to my room, which I didn't recall shutting. I'm not entirely sure why, but I opened it and had a quick look around. Nothing out of the ordinary.

I left the door ajar and rapped on Aphra's. 'Aphra?' When there was no answer, I turned the handle and pushed against it slightly. It too was empty. The desk was decorated with its usual scatter of pages, ink and quills while stacks of books towered on the floor, the tabletop and anywhere else they could. Maybe Aphra was out after all. I was about to go and change when a clattering noise from the parlour followed by a thud drew me.

'Aphra! I've news.' Relief I wasn't alone with restless spirits flooded me and I burst through the door — and froze.

Nest was crumpled in a heap. Blood oozed from a wound on her temple. I dropped to her side, not knowing where to touch, terrified she was dead. I looked about helplessly. Then I saw Aphra, tied to a chair pushed into a corner, gagged.

'Aphra! My God!' I abandoned Nest and, ignoring Aphra's wide-eyed appeals and shaking head, the sounds issuing from behind the gag, began to untie her. Firm fingers closed around my arm, wrenching me back.

'Not so fast.'

William Scot was unwashed, unkempt. His clothes were in complete disarray and a terrible horse-hair wig sat askew on his head. There were deep scratches down one side of his face. Blood spattered his shirt. He'd not subdued Aphra or Nest easily.

Before I could protest or even struggle, he flipped me into another chair. My hip struck the arm before I fell clumsily into the seat, crying out.

Aphra strained against her bonds.

'What are you doing here?' I began.

He said nothing.

'Why is Aphra bound? What have you done to Nest?'

'Hush,' said William Scot, wild-eyed and panting. 'Not another word or I'll bind and gag you as well. If you want answers, then you'll be a good daughter and obey your father. Sit silently and listen.'

Good daughter? Obey my father? I gazed in disbelief as he threw burning faggots on the smouldering fire of my rage. Aphra shook her head slightly, casting me a warning look. I understood. Better to humour him — or give that appearance.

He pulled up another chair, alighting on the edge of the seat as if we might share a tale or drink, uncaring that Nest lay bleeding on the floor. The rise and fall of her chest told me she was still alive, but it was evident she needed attention.

'Please,' I said quietly. 'I'll do as you ask. Just let me tend Nest.'

He lowered his head into one hand and with the other gave a dismissive wave of permission. I flew from the chair and, first rolling Nest onto her back, examined her wound. I went to the cabinet for a napkin and poured some wine from the jug upon it. I knelt and began to daub her temple. Nest groaned but didn't much stir. When that was done, I grabbed a cushion and placed it under her head. As soon as she was able, I'd make her drink.

The entire time, I didn't once look at my father, though I was all too aware of him hulking over me, of Aphra trussed. Why? What had she done? What had she said? What was he thinking?

I risked a look. 'The authorities know you're here.'

'Not in this house they don't.' He raised his head and smirked. How had I ever been thrilled by his presence? The wonder of him being my father?

My only solace was the doubt inflecting his words. He didn't sound entirely certain. I didn't reassure him.

'Sit there,' he said, pointing at the chair I'd vacated, as if I were a hound in training. Reluctantly, and with one last check Nest was at least comfortable, I did as he bade.

He went to the window and, careful not to let his entire frame show, searched the square. I took the opportunity to study Aphra. Apart from being tied, she didn't seem harmed. Not like Nest. I tried to piece together what had happened.

When he still didn't speak, but remained with his back to us, confident he'd be obeyed, I spoke out again.

'Why are you here?'

He crossed to the cabinet, found a glass and lifted the jug from where I'd placed it beside Nest. Indifferent to her recumbent form, he poured generously. 'Two reasons,' he began and resumed his seat. 'First, to say farewell. I could hardly leave London without saying goodbye to my old lover and daughter, could I?'

Aphra gave a muffled growl.

'Secondly.' He shot her a silencing look. She returned with a glare that would have done Medusa proud. 'I need help.'

'Help?' I couldn't believe his audacity. The presence of a known traitor and plotter in the house put me, Aphra and Nest in grave danger. Now he wanted us to aid and abet him? A fugitive from justice? Aphra was right: the man only cared for himself.

'Since Aphra refused to proffer assistance or anything else,' he said. 'You'll have to do.'

I tamped down the anger igniting my veins. Play for time, I thought. Play for time. 'Help with what? Another assassination attempt?'

'So 'twas you found the message. I only realised later it must have fallen out of my pocket when we were at the tavern.' He glared and stood again, prowling the room, examining objects on the mantelpiece, turning them over, stroking a book here, a candlestick there. I watched him the way one did a feral animal. 'Because of you, we were forced to abort our plans. Because of you —' his gaze included Aphra '— we're being hunted like rabid dogs. As a consequence, I need to get away. Leave the country. To do that, I require money and papers. My usual contacts are no longer … available to me. Aphra knows many printers and publishers, and they in turn know those who, shall we say, operate on the shady side of the law.' He faced me, stroking the feather of Aphra's favoured quill. 'It's the least you owe me.'

His hubris, his narcissism, was breathtaking.

'We owe you nothing, sir.' I stared defiantly. He was the first to look away.

'Why's Aphra tied up? Gagged?' I finally asked.

William Scot put the feather down. If I could have reached over and slapped the look off his face, I would. I curled my hands into fists. How had I ever thought the man roguish, handsome even? 'Because,' he drawled, 'like most women, she had too much to say. Always been your downfall, hasn't it, my once-lovely Astrea?'

'He groped her.' Nest groaned and her eyes fluttered open.

I started. 'Nest.'

Uncaring what William Scot commanded, I flew from the chair and tried to help her sit up.

'He wouldn't take no for an answer,' panted Nest, shuffling on her bottom until she could lean against the settee. 'Claimed it would be just like old times. So I did to him what I wished I'd done back then. Hit him over the head with the fire tongs.' She looked pointedly towards the hearth. They were lying, broken apart, either side of the grate. She must have hit him hard, explaining the blood on the side of his face, staining his shirt. 'Only, gentleman that he is, he hit me back.' She touched her head, pulling her fingers away and staring at the blood as if she couldn't quite believe it was hers.

Aphra struggled against her bonds, the rope marking her flesh. There was blood under her nails. She'd been defending herself *and* Nest.

My mind worked furiously. I knew from Gabriel that men were following my father, watching his every move. Aye, like hunters, waiting for the right time to close the trap. Problem was, as Gabriel and Solomon knew first-hand, William Scot excelled at evading scrutiny. Sweet Jesus. I prayed if the house was under surveillance that Gabriel or Solomon or even Sir Joseph — those who would know William Scot wasn't here because we were his allies, or part of any conspiracy — would be alerted. Then, I prayed, if men were watching, they wouldn't act on instinct and orders and burst through the doors and arrest us all.

The room fell quiet. The house fretted and grated, its regular sighs and murmurs unusually loud, an old woman fussing.

'Where's the rest of the household?' I asked suddenly.

William Scot's face broke into a triumphant grin. 'It wasn't hard to persuade Mr Coggin he was required at his sister's house. His daughter as well — a small accident about which I was vague. The servants didn't argue when they were told they had the evening off.'

A semi-regular visitor over the months, he'd relied on the trust extended to a familiar face. He'd been cunning. No doubt charming too. Something he was practised at. Anything to get his own way. I felt sick. But I had to bide for time, do what I could to keep him here. Give Gabriel and Solomon, anyone, the chance to assemble reinforcements.

But it was also my one and only chance to make sure William Scot, my father, was held to account for his past actions. If not by the authorities, then, at the very least, by me.

It wasn't the wisest decision I'd ever made, but neither was it the most foolish. I glanced at the door. I had to do it before anyone else arrived.

Before I lost my courage.

I watched him out of the corner of my eye as he drained his glass and refilled it. A selfish host at dinner. I despised him with every pump of my heart, every breath in my body. It wasn't only for what he'd done to Aphra, to Bethan — that was shocking enough — but this very day he'd attacked Nest, an old woman. It was also because of what he'd done to me — inadvertently, aye, without knowledge, but also with a devil-may-care attitude. Somehow, that made it worse.

Confident of my help, of his power over us, he returned to his seat and prated on and on about what he required in terms of paper and coin, how he'd outsmart and outwit those searching for him, boasting how powerful he and his friends were. How, though their last plan to alter the succession hadn't worked as intended, they'd managed to foil those seeking them. He blethered about how their next plan was assured of success; then they'd have the means to change everything. But what kind of power was achieved through violence, threats and sustained indifference to suffering?

I'd read enough myths, plays and poems to know it was only ever temporary. It only lasted until someone with more power usurped you. What I also knew is that power comes in different guises. Aphra had allowed me to see that. Her capitulation to men was most oft used to get her own way — an authority of sorts. She used her wiles, her wit and beauty, her connections, to steer her own course. She also used words.

They were my weapons too. My power.

I took a deep breath. It was time to hold William Scot accountable. *For everything.*

'I know what you did to Bethan,' I began.

He paused mid-diatribe. 'Excuse me?' He appeared genuinely confused. He scratched the periwig then picked something off it, squashing it between his finger and flicking it aside.

'In case it's slipped your mind, she happens to be my *mother.*'

'I know who she is,' he said haughtily. 'And I happen to be your father, young woman. And I'll be shown proper respect —'

I stood up slowly, unfurling to my full height, eyes flashing. I urged my knees to cease their shaking. 'You *raped* her.'

He stared, open-mouthed. I could see his mind working, the way thoughts flashed across his face, how they ticked like a broken clock, counting down to his doom. Denial rearranged his features. Cunning set them. He stood as well, trying to use his greater height. It was an advantage wasted here.

Then, he dared to sneer. 'Is that what she told you?' he rasped.

I folded my arms.

'I'd hardly call what happened between us rape.' He laughed. It was hollow.

I took a step closer. 'What man ever does?' I thought of what I'd heard month after month in the Tiring Rooms, casually boasted of at soirees, in taverns. Performed in plays. Men priding themselves on how many chambers of Venus they'd invaded, heavenly sanctuaries they'd opened, Chapels of Ease they'd enjoyed. Not once had they ever acknowledged the woman, her desires, her needs. I wanted to rage. 'The woman asked for it.' I closed the distance, prodding him in the chest with a finger. '*She* seduced *me*. Or what's the other line you men so casually throw? Oh aye, she *wanted me to* — that's it, isn't it?' I glanced towards Aphra — she'd wanted him so badly, he had to tie her up and muffle her.

William Scot (I couldn't think of him as my father) followed the direction of my gaze, then flicked my finger aside and twisted away.

I didn't care; turning his back didn't stop me facing what he did. 'You took Bethan against her will.'

He raised his hands in surrender. 'If that's how she chooses to see it, well —'

I balled my fists. 'See it. Feel it. Live it.' I took a deep breath. 'Do you know what your selfish desire, your unchecked lust did?' I didn't wait for him to answer. 'Nay. How could you? You committed heinous, sinful acts and then left Bethan to pay the price. Not only did your lechery destroy a shiny future, but she was deemed a whore by her own father. *A whore.* Shunted away, blamed for *your* sin. She was in disgrace. She lost her papa's love —' I paused and thought of Mama. Mama had always been kind to me but, from what I recalled, aloof with Bethan. At least, I could scarce recall them together … 'Her mother's too.' He turned around slowly, his face a picture of sympathy. I wasn't fooled. 'But.' I held up a hand to prevent him speaking. 'She wasn't the only one to pay for your crime. Oh no. You see, William Scot, *Father*, I paid too.'

With each word, each announcement, I grew in stature, in voice. It was as if I were upon a stage, delivering lines I'd written in my head over and over: burning thoughts, unchecked by men or anyone but my heart, flowed. I became Elizabeth Barry, modulating then projecting my voice just so, the way Mrs Betterton taught her pupils, the way Gabriel — Jonathan Rickman — had shown me. I used my words, my voice as a sword and was pleased to see every dark utterance, every thrust and parry, was not only heard but felt.

'Look at me!' I demanded.

He slowly raised his head. I was shocked to see his florid cheeks were wet. But were his tears for Bethan? For me? Or were they for himself?

'I, a mere babe, was denied a mother, father, a family. I was the embodiment of *your* sinful act, my mother's shame, and therefore barely tolerated, most oft spurned. I was given a name that ensured no-one would ever forget what *you* caused, what I represented. Tribulation. But you were the real trouble. You were, you are, William Scot, a tribulation I no longer wish to bear. None of us do.' A great wail rose. I tried to push it down, to deny it a life. But it came forth in a great heaving mess.

William Scot reached for me. I jumped away. The last thing I wanted was his Judas touch.

'Don't. Don't pretend you care. I don't want your false remorse now. Don't you dare offer *me* solace. Look at what you've done.' My arm described an arc. 'Look at Aphra, at Nest. Don't you understand?' I wiped my hand across my nose. 'You're a poltroon. A coward, sir.' Between glaring at him in defiance, daring him to stop me, I'd gone to Aphra and, pulling and shoving the chair so I could squeeze behind, untied the gag from her mouth, loosened the rope around her hands and ankles. 'Bethan *and* Aphra have thrived despite your callous efforts to reduce them. Aphra *has* succeeded despite all your falsehoods, your countless attempts to traduce her. And for what purpose? To make yourself appear stronger, more powerful. But it's all a show — like something we mount at Drury Lane. It's a performance you're giving, only one with no substance.'

I left Aphra's side and bent over where he sat in the chair I'd abandoned. My arms caged him. My face was inches from his. 'And I want you to know,' I hissed. 'I will succeed too. Despite you. *Without* you.' I drew myself up, dashed my hands across my eyes. 'You disgust me, you turncoat, you traitor. You *rapist*. You're no hero, despite what you might think. Have you ever performed a single action of which you're proud? That would enable your daughters —' I hesitated. Was not I one too? '— to hold you in esteem?'

His eyes flickered, but he remined mute.

'I didn't think so.' I made a soft noise of disgust. 'The moment you quit our sight, *I'll* not waste another thought upon you. You will be as smut upon furniture.' I ran a finger along the arm of the chair, collecting residue, and wiped my hand down the side of my skirt. 'And as easily banished. You will be nothing more than a forgotten character in a play with no audience.'

With slow deliberation, I returned to Aphra's side.

There was silence. Deep, dark, chthonic.

Though my heart was leaping about like a crazed coney, my mind was finally at peace. Aphra found my hand and brought it to her mouth. She was weeping.

William Scot sat there gazing at me, unmoving. I wanted to feel something, anything, but could not. Would not. I didn't look away.

Nest managed to stand and stumbled over to join us.

The three of us, Macbeth's (I dared to think the name) witches manifest. Maiden, mother and crone stared at William Scot without saying a word.

Evening had fallen, the sky transforming from lilac to a deep purple. Stars pierced the firmament, their merry twinkle a reminder that out there, life continued. Laughter carried from the tavern. There was the bark of dogs at play, children calling.

Like an old man, William Scot clambered to his feet. He looked at me with such pathos, such regret, I almost felt sorry for him. Almost. He locked eyes with Aphra, then Nest, and lastly, me.

'It was a mistake coming here,' he said. Then, with a touch of his head, a salute perhaps, he left the room.

We heard his boots on the stairs, the rattle of the front door and then the click of it shutting.

The three of us went to the window and stood side by side, arms around each other, watching as he crossed the square, neatly dodging two drunken men, the children kicking a ball. The tumbling dogs. In the blink of an eye, he was gone.

I made it to the hearth before I fell to my knees and vomited.

SCENE TWELVE

About the 19th (of June) was discovered a dangerous and treasonable conspiracy against the person of his Majestie and the duke of York by some of those called Whiggs.

A Brief Historical Relation of State Affairs, Narcissus Luttrell

Was it what I said that drove William Scot to reconsider the trajectory of his life? I like to think that somehow, just as I'd pricked his Majesty's conscience with my written words, those I spoke in passionate rage prompted Scot to act in the manner he did.

A few days after he left Aphra, Nest and me standing at the window and walked out of our lives, he used his alias, Josiah Keeling, in a message to Sir Leoline Jenkins, claiming he wished to speak to Lord Dartmouth, a naval commander who was good friends with the Duke of York. Why this man, we never did learn. Perhaps it was an attempt to distance himself from those he sought to harm. Before these important men, William Scot, still known as Mr Keeling, admitted to not only the Rye-House plot and a series of planned uprisings, including placing armed men in Drury Lane theatre so they might fire upon the King while he watched a play, but provided the names of every single conspirator as well.

Only much later did I learn he bargained with his confessors, extracting a promise of immunity from prosecution. Not quite the honourable or compensatory gesture I'd briefly thought it.

Arrests were swift and the punishments merciless. Lord William Russell, the Earl of Essex, Lord Howard, Algernon Sidney, a man named John Hampden and a John Wildman were hunted down ruthlessly and sent to the Tower.

Not all those identified were caught. Still seeking to shore up a future by weighing the odds, William Scot managed to warn a few of his confederates of the storm about to break. Lord Grey, Sir Thomas Armstrong and Robert Ferguson escaped (Lord Grey later provided a detailed confession in order to extract a pardon). Colonels Rumbold and Rumsey — those who were at Rye House, no less — and a man named Wade went into hiding, as did the Duke of Monmouth when it was revealed he too had plotted against his father.

The King, either aghast or more likely wearied by these weak men who worked futilely to undermine him, became involved in questioning the captured suspects. Fearful of his Majesty's wrath, they squawked like farm chickens, revealing the identities of yet more men — men who sought to capture the Tower and from there attack the city. Many Whig businessmen and nobles fell as a consequence of others pleading and striking bargains for their own lives.

Despite the King's impossible magnanimity, not everyone escaped justice.

Lord Russell was the first to be tried on 13th July 1683. On the same day, Essex was found in the Tower with his throat cut from ear to ear. Suicide was claimed. For months after, whispers he was murdered refused to be quashed. Word was the wound was so deep and long, he was practically decapitated.

'Bloody hard to cut off your own head,' Charlotte said. I was inclined to agree.

The Duke of York and even the other Secretary of State, Robert Sunderland, were suspected — not of striking the fatal blow, but of having a hand in Essex's death, if for no other reason than to remove a final rival to the throne.

Lord Russell was found guilty of high treason and sentenced to be hanged, drawn and quartered. On bended knee and with bowed head, he pleaded for clemency, but the King only commuted his sentence to beheading at Lincoln Inn Fields. According to the news-sheets, his Majesty said, 'If I do not take his life he will soon have mine.'

Just before Christmas that year, Algernon Sidney was also beheaded. In total, eleven men and one woman were executed, imprisoned or fled. Many more men were implicated, including the anti-Catholic publisher, Henry Care.

As for Josiah Keeling (who was never formally revealed as William Scot), talk in the theatre and coffee-houses and reports in news-sheets blustered different outcomes for the man who revealed the Rye-House Plot was legitimate, and had come very close to success. If the King hadn't left Newmarket when he did, catching the attackers unprepared, there was no reason to think it wouldn't have been carried out. When I wasn't considering the ways in which I detested the man, I admit his confession went some way to assuaging my guilt over the Newmarket fire.

Fortunately, not even those at Drury Lane realised Josiah Keeling was actually William Scot. Gossip I'd been courted by a traitor didn't last long (and thank God, they didn't know his real relationship to me), as I wasn't the first, nor would I be the last actress to have her head turned by a rogue. Just look at Grace.

It was from Gabriel that Aphra and I finally learned what happened to Scot. Waiting until most of the fuss and recriminations had died down and brief updates were buried in columns and had ceased to leave town-criers' mouths, Aphra invited Gabriel to Newe Street to give him a copy of her latest publication — Volume One of the *Love-Letters* she'd worked so hard upon.

It was a bitterly cold day in mid-December. Snow was already thick upon the ground and had been falling steadily. I prayed it would have stopped by the time I went to Drury Lane on the morrow. It was so difficult for horses and carts let alone conveyances to make passage when the roads were blanketed and drifts made them unpassable, requiring shovels and strong arms to clear. Traffic was oft badly congested around the gates and tollways. If it wasn't a snow-bound carriage, then it was a cart with a broken axle or a hackney tipped over. Arguments among vendors, drivers, farmers and couriers were rife, as was always the way when time and money were involved. Blood was occasionally shed. Indifferent to the woes and ways of men, the sky kept shedding snow. Even the mighty Thames, the lifeblood of London, had frozen over, stranding passengers, bargemen, wherries and tilt boats for days.

Huddled in the parlour, close to the hearth and away from the windows, we were enjoying a cup of chocolate while Gabriel apprised us, as he'd taken to of late, on anything to do with William Scot and the plotters. I'd almost become inured to the capacity men had to work against not only their liege and country, but their own best interests. Almost. For what he said next took my breath away.

'For turning King's evidence against the plotters, William Scot was given the richly sum of five hundred pounds.'

'Five hundred!' I gasped.

Aphra shook her head. 'That blaggard always lands on his feet.'

'Maybe,' said Gabriel. 'While his purse may be full, it's not all in his favour. His feet must remain in Holland, and his devious mind is to be turned towards Dutch activities. He's ordered to report anything he learns to Sir Leoline.'

'He's agreed to be a double agent.' Aphra threw her hands up. 'Again. When is the government going to learn? It's not the first time he's made promises like that — and failed to keep them.'

'Indeed,' said Gabriel. 'But Sir Leoline and my master have resolved to ensure this time at least, Scot keeps his word. If not, there'll be swift and dire consequences. This really is his last chance.' Gabriel fell strangely silent and it was some time before I learned how the former and current spymasters were going to guarantee such a slippery man's cooperation. As for the swift consequences, there was no second-guessing what they'd be.

As the night wore on, I wondered who'd be sent to carry them out when Scot once more proved traitorous for, like ravens atop the Tower, collaborators were constant in their plumage, despite appearances to the contrary. They just, as Gabriel said, demanded bigger purses.

'I think it's time to reveal why I asked you here, don't you?' said Aphra a little coyly. She passed Gabriel a copy of her book, which she'd asked Nest to wrap.

'A present?' exclaimed Gabriel, his face stamped with surprise and pleasure. 'But it's not Yuletide.'

Aphra chuckled. 'I wanted to give you an early copy before it's published next month. Anyhow, you've given us the greatest gift of all — not only did you never doubt me and Tribulation when we asked for help, but you've kept us informed about William and, in doing so, set our hearts and minds … maybe not at ease, but you've made them less troubled than they might have been.' She gave me a reassuring look. 'For that, we're ever indebted to you.'

'Amen,' I said, smiling warmly.

Touched by Aphra's words, her gift, Gabriel carefully opened it.

'Your book,' he said to Aphra wonderingly, smoothing the cover, gentle fingers turning pages, admiring the fine print. 'This is the one you based on the Grey affair, isn't it?'

'It is. But it's *your* book too.' Aphra reached over and flicked to the dedication. She'd made it out to Captain Thomas Condon, another alias Gabriel used.

He scanned it quickly and his cheeks coloured. Then, he raised his eyes and held mine for a long time.

I'd read the dedication and, apart from praising Gabriel's ruggedness, which she described as masculine beauty, she'd urged him, well, Captain Condon, to not be a lazy lover, but like her book, go into circulation …

Aphra couldn't resist interfering in matters of the heart, especially when her own wasn't at stake.

Later that night, when Aphra pleaded bed and Nest had long retired, Gabriel and I were left together in the parlour. It wasn't the first time we'd been in each other's company without a chaperone: a most improper situation by conventional standards, but then, we were hardly conventional. We'd been talking about Christmas — to which he and Solomon were invited, along with Sir Roger and his wife, Charlotte, Mr and Mrs Downes and a few others — before tripping onto equally safe topics — the theatre, the deaths of the plotters and the fates of those who'd escaped. Any subject except for the one spinning in my head, teasing my tongue and making it difficult to concentrate.

Snow fell, silently, secretly, caressing the glass before gathering in pockets, making it feel as if we were deep in a cave, far away from the hustle and bustle of the world. The fire crackled merrily, releasing clouds of smoke and, occasionally, a rain of molten sparks. We were both nursing wines when Gabriel spoke.

'I've something else to tell you, Tribulation.'

I held my breath.

'I'm to be sent to Holland. In the New Year. Solomon as well. As soon as the seas allow passage, we depart.'

So, this was what he'd been wanting, needing to say.

I nodded carefully, forcing the information to enter my head, blocking it from my damn unsteady heart. I worked hard to control my voice. 'To watch William Scot.'

It wasn't a question.

Gabriel sighed. 'Him, and we're to join forces with other agents and track down the remaining conspirators. Bring them to justice.'

Justice, thy name is a sharp dirk, a poison tonic, a deadly bullet. Kinder sometimes than the hangman's noose or the brutal axe of the executioner.

I knew it was always a mistake to expect Gabriel would be content to remain, to return to the theatre, call London home. He was someone who, like a fine wine, I had to appreciate while I could, and hope like Hell I'd happen upon another in the cellar one day. I couldn't help but feel the spectre of William Scot still hovering over my life, determined to cause it damage in unforeseen ways. Was this revenge for what I'd said?

I turned my face away slightly so Gabriel couldn't see the frown marring my brow or the sadness shaping my mouth as I imagined the days folding into one another, an endless procession, without him.

Not that I didn't have plenty to fill them — I did. But somehow, just knowing Gabriel was there inflected them with more colour, more life, made everything richer, better, and far more interesting. Gave me something to both cherish and anticipate.

I didn't realise he was standing next to me until he took my glass, put it down, and pulled me to my feet.

'Tribulation,' he said, examining my fingers one by one. 'I've also something to ask.'

I swear, my heart took flight. It left my body and began to flutter against the window, curious and filled with yearning. 'Oh?' I asked as coolly as I could. I failed. Dismally. 'What might that be?' I dared to look at him.

Ever so slowly, he drew me into his arms. The candlelight flickered within the stygian depths of his eyes, as if little fires were lit within.

As I pressed my body against his, a spark flew from him to me and ignited. I began to smoulder. How neatly we fitted. I began to burn.

His fingers gently pushed my hair behind my ears, away from my forehead. He lifted my chin, and his thumb, so hard and callused, brushed across my lips. They opened. I wanted to bite him, lick him, kiss him.

'I was wondering, Tribulation Johnson,' he growled and lowered his head until his brow rested against my mine, 'whether you might consider coming with me. To Holland. As a Freeman … or should that be, Freewoman?'

Before I could answer, he tilted my chin just that little bit further and his mouth captured mine.

Waves of longing rushed through me, roaring, dashing against the years of restraint, of hard-earned pretended detachment. My ears filled with sound. My heart returned to my chest, a painful collision, thumping, thumping. His lips opened further and his tongue swirled in my mouth, liquid, smooth, and oh so hot. I did what I dreamed for so long, twined my fingers in that thick, black hair and pulled him closer, closer, soldering us together.

How long we stood there, his lips travelling down my neck, exploring my ears, and venturing lower still as I pressed mine to the pulse in his throat and along that strong jawline, I don't know. The moon could have fallen out of the sky and flung the world into eternal darkness: I cared not. The stars were in my soul, dancing, sparkling, singing, setting me ablaze.

When we finally drew apart, our breath coming in gasps, my face sore from his bristles, my mouth pleasantly bruised, we still had our arms around each other. I never wanted to let go.

'Tribulation Johnson,' he purred in his leonine voice, 'you are full of surprises.'

'Pleasant ones, I hope.'

He kissed me again. Fiercely. 'Pleasant is not the word I'd have used.'

We laughed, harder than his observation deserved, both knowing when we stopped, an answer was forthcoming.

'Will you come with me?'

A noise beyond the door made us both turn. A hollow thud. Aphra had dropped a book. Either she'd fallen asleep, or her hands, which were slowly becoming more twisted, had made it impossible for her to hold it any longer. More and more, she was needing my assistance.

'Well?' Gabriel asked again, rubbing his nose against mine.

Dear God. I wished with all my heart, my soul, I didn't have to hurt him, hurt myself. That I could reply differently. 'Oh, Gabriel. I cannot.'

He inhaled deeply. 'Forgive my pride, but I thought, I felt that we —'

'Oh, you think correctly, sir.' I wriggled out of his embrace and drew him towards the seat he'd recently vacated. I pushed him into it then climbed onto his lap, looping my arms about his neck. 'Don't misunderstand, Gabriel. I want nothing more than to come with you to Holland, to the ends of the earth if you asked — as a Freewoman.' I gave a sad smile. 'It's just that,' I sighed and glanced at the door, 'I cannot leave her. Frankly, I don't want to. Not after everything she's done for me. She was there when there was no-one else. She has supported me, believed in me, loved me in a way that … I don't think I even understand. I love her too. And, for now, she needs me more than you do. I … I hope, I pray, you'll forgive me.'

I rested my cheek against his, curling into his body. He wrapped his arms around me.

'Damn Satan's hairy cullions,' he growled. 'There's nothing to forgive. I can't pretend I like it. Not one bit, dammit. Damn you, Tribulation Johnson, for being a woman worth waiting for, however long it takes. And while I'm at it, damn Aphra Behn as well.'

'Stand in line, sir, there are plenty of others waiting to do that.'

We both laughed quietly. I wanted to cry.

'I still have to leave,' he whispered. 'I cannot remain.'

'I know.' I bit my lip.

'But —' he moved so we faced each other again '— I promise you this, Tribulation. I *will* wait for you. And, one day, I'll come back. One day, when all this plot business is over, when those men are no longer a threat. When Aphra no longer needs you. Then, I hope, I'll even pray, that then, you'll be with *me*.'

I took his beautiful, strong face in my hands and pressed my mouth to his. 'When Aphra no longer needs me, I'll be with *you*, Gabriel Freeman, for always and forever. That, I swear.'

It was as good as a vow.

SCENE THIRTEEN

Envy, malice, and all uncharitableness, — these are the fruits of a successful literary career for a woman.

From a Letter to Mrs Hall, Laetitia Landon

The following year was a difficult one. Everyone said the winter was the coldest in memory and, certainly, the snow was thick, the air transforming into something heavy and hard. The days were so very short and the torrid winds bitter.

As if to make up for all the terrible news, the plots and conspiracies exploding everywhere, the executions and arrests, people celebrated the freezing conditions, parading around the streets, engaging in frenzied snow fights, sledding, skating, bull-baiting, much of it upon the glassy surface of the Thames. The river froze for weeks, its muddy surface altered to an opaque pane, creating a pristine space upon which canny people saw the opportunity to conduct business and, more importantly, play.

Dubbed the Frost Fair, it was the fashionable place to pass time.

Vendors erected an array of stalls, and artists such as jugglers, acrobats and impossible contortionists travelled from all over the country to perform under colourful canopies for dazzled crowds.

Out-of-work actors (some formerly from Drury Lane) staged plays in tents upon hastily erected stages for appreciative audiences. Hot food sizzled upon enormous braziers sitting upon the ice, offering extremes of heat and cold at once. There was tippling, coach races, puppet shows — all manner of entertainments for young and old. Horses, dogs, bears, even chickens shat and slid all over the glassy inert water. How could Drury Lane compete with that?

Audiences at the theatre diminished steadily, but instead of our usual complaints, we'd finish the play, change into warm clothes and then head down to the river to take part in the short-lived revelry.

When we mounted a production of *The Tragedy of Valentinian* by the late Earl of Rochester (adapted from an earlier play by John Fletcher and Frances Beaumont) and for which Aphra wrote the prologue and I penned the epilogue (I used the alias, 'A Person of Quality' — being ironic), competing against the allure of alternate winter entertainments, it was a surprising success. A lovely tribute to Aphra's old friend.

Mr Betterton said we'd stage it again soon, once the Frost Fair was over. I even played the small role of Marcellina, a lady attending Elizabeth Barry's tragic character, Lucina.

With the river solidified, all the usual water traffic had to adapt to wheels and use the roads, which then became even more congested than usual. Not a day went past reports of accidents didn't reach us. At least half a dozen times, a performer was either held up by or caught in one. Plays often started with actors and actresses (including me) filling in for the absent performer. Fog drifted about the city like an indolent cat, making conditions dangerous and providing the ideal cover for thieves, cutthroats and lovers. When it mingled with all the smoke from the fires lit on and by the river, plus all the coal burning in hearths and rising out of chimneys, it made visibility difficult. It was the perfect environment for enemies to be dispatched, including unwanted wives and husbands. Bodies were found in ditches, by the river, left in the middle of roads. The city charnel house was full to bursting.

Aphra was working steadily, doing all she could to earn enough to keep us warm and fed. Yet to be paid by White Hall for the supposedly secret work (writing pamphlets and verses) she'd done for them at the height of the Exclusion Crisis (the *Love-Letters* being among it), she'd written to the Exchequer and Lord Arlington in the hope they might put her petition for monies owed before the King. Predictably, there'd been no reply.

I wasn't surprised when, one morning before I left for Drury Lane, she announced she was tired of waiting and intended to seek an audience at White Hall that very day. Afterwards, she was going to visit her printer, Jacob Tonson, and see if she couldn't beg a few more pounds for something of hers he'd published.

'I've asked John Hoyle to meet me there at five of the clock.'

When she didn't arrive home by eight bells, I assumed she'd decided to stay with Mr Hoyle. Nest and I were snug in the parlour, reading, when there was a loud rap on the door. Footsteps pounded up the stairs and Mr Coggin appeared in the doorway.

He was wringing his hands like Pontius Pilate.

'Sorry to disturb you, ladies, but there's a gentleman who says Mrs Behn's been badly injured.'

I didn't hear the rest. I raced downstairs. There, in the doorway, looking rather dishevelled and discommoded, was Mr Hoyle.

'Ah, Tribulation,' he began. 'Come, help me. You too, sir,' he ordered Mr Coggin. 'Aphra's hurt. She's in the conveyance.'

Bundled in threadbare blankets which only served to press her sodden clothes against her, chilling her to the very bone, Aphra was pale and weepy.

'Oh, Tribulation,' she whimpered, her arm flailing as she tried to reach me.

As we carried her inside, Mr Hoyle explained the coach Aphra was travelling in between the palace and Charing Cross overturned on the icy road just past the Pope's Head Tavern and Temple. Upon hearing of the accident, Mr Hoyle had run straight there. After finding a physician to examine her and administer potions, and ensuring she wasn't mortally injured, he secured a hackney to bring her home.

'She's to rest. Rest, and on the morrow the doctor will administer an emetic and possibly leeches.'

Mr Hoyle was clearly shaken. I'd never heard him talk so much in all the years I'd known him. While Nest undressed Aphra, I encouraged Mr Hoyle into a chair and pushed a glass of wine into his hand.

'I feel so foolish,' said Aphra, trying to cooperate as we pulled off her shirt and unrolled her stockings, drying her legs vigorously, trying to rub some warmth back into them. 'When the carriage rolled the door fell open and I was flung into the slush at the sides of the road, my skirts flying over my head.'

Nest and I made sympathetic noises. 'Are you hurting anywhere?' I asked for the umpteenth time, failing to get a coherent answer. Finally, I placed my hands either side of her head. 'Aphra, listen, are you hurt?'

Her teeth were chattering, her lips blue. 'Mainly my pride.'

'She's injured her arm — her hand,' said Mr Hoyle helpfully. He had one eye on our ministrations, uncaring of Aphra's modesty. Not that she minded; she'd insisted he remain.

Looking like it belonged on a different body, her hand was swollen to almost three times its size.

With a squeal, Nest left the room, muttering about Charing Cross quacks, and promising to go wake the apothecary and get bandages and a poultice.

'I'll accompany you,' said Mr Hoyle, leaping up, draining his glass. Anything to escape the conversation and woes of 'petticoats'. His tolerance only extended so far.

When he'd gone, Aphra let out a long quivering sigh and fell back on the pillows, all bravado fleeing her poor, injured body. She'd stopped shivering, but her face was a terrible colour and there was a bruise forming on her cheek. I'd also seen a large one flowering on her hip.

'Oh, Aphra,' I said, lying down carefully beside her and kissing her shoulder. 'Will you be alright?'

'Of course, kitten,' she said, her eyes full of unshed tears. 'So long as my hand heals, and my mind is intact so I can continue to write. It's only my body, isn't it? I just wish the King would pay what he owes. I mean, the engraving he ordered as a reward for unnamed services, which we *know* was to do with Newmarket and Rye House, was all very well and good, but it doesn't buy bread, does it?'

Indeed, it did not. If only the King had asked Aphra to be his mistress, then she would have been endowed with titles, a pension, houses, and a parliamentary debt worth of jewels. Instead, she saves his life and gets an etching. That was King Charles all over: his life was worth less than his prick.

I pressed my lips together so I didn't say what I was thinking. The artist, Mr Robert White, while a very nice man whom I sure did excellent work, failed, in my mind, to capture her. In all fairness, neither of the other two portraits I'd seen of Aphra did. They were … unadventurous. Aphra maintained a painter was limited in what they could convey with colour and brushes: that the representation would always be shallow. Turns out, it was the same with an engraver. A writer, on other hand, could give depth and dimension with a mere word, a phrase or description. When I looked at Mr White's efforts, I saw a woman like so many others. Pretty, younger than she actually was, with an inoffensive turn of the head and demure brow. Where was my clever, kind cousin who could animate a corpse with her wit?

'I never had the chance to persuade Tonson my work is worth at least the same as the men's,' said Aphra softly. 'The coach overturned before I reached him.' She was still fixed on her earnings. 'I mean, why should Dryden receive ten shillings and me a mere five?'

I didn't say, 'Because he has a cock.' That would be stating the obvious.

'Worry about Mr Tonson when you're healed,' I said, helping her under the covers, pulling them up to her chin.

'Then, I'll deal with him on the morrow,' said Aphra, trying to smile. 'I intend to be fully recovered by then.'

Before I'd finished banking the fire, she was sound asleep.

Aphra never really recovered from her accident. It wasn't anything physical, though her limp became more pronounced, and she would occasionally moan that her hand ached and the fingers were stiff. Rather, it destroyed her confidence. She became wary of conveyances, chary of walking through the streets and less likely to travel anywhere further than the city walls or river. Even venturing to the theatre, which she occasionally graced, became a journey to foreign climes. Her world diminished thus — mostly, to her room and the parlour, where she wrote as if her life depended on it.

And it did.

As she'd always maintained, she wrote for bread. For mine and Nest's besides. Not that I didn't contribute to our paltry purse.

My writing ventures weren't altogether unsuccessful. I continued to pen tracts for various publications. Nothing to set the world afire, which is just as well as I'd seen first-hand what damage flames could do. I commenced work on a couple of plays. I continued to work at Drury Lane, not only assisting John Downes, but taking on slightly larger roles in various plays, particularly as actresses left, becoming the mistresses of rogues and rakes, occasionally a disreputable or credulous young lord, or married. While I'd never be an Elizabeth Barry, Anne Bracegirdle (who was becoming an outstanding actress), Mrs Cook or even a Charlotte, I held my own. At least it was a regular if small wage and I was working with people I mostly liked. They were an extended family of sorts, with all its foibles, flaws, failures and familiarity.

With the Rye-House Plot exposed, and the conspirators' names made public, the last strong Whig resistance and protest was brushed aside. A tide of loyalty swept the country as people became aware they'd almost lost their King. He may not be perfect, a man who loved fucking and was 'the sauciest prick that e'er did swive', as Rochester once wrote, but he was *our* sauciest prick. Even the Duke of York felt confident enough to return from Scotland and insist some of the Catholic lords who'd been languishing in the Tower were released.

Barely a murmur was raised.

Maybe this was why Titus Oates tried one last time to resurrect the power he'd wielded for a few short years. First, he demanded an audience with the King. When that was denied, he wrote a lengthy complaint about Sir Roger L'Estrange for everything he'd published against him over the years.

I brought home a copy for Aphra to read.

When she'd finished, she passed it back.

'I hate to say it,' she began. 'But the man has a point. I dislike he attacks Roger so vehemently — at least Roger has been consistent. He never believed in the Popish Plot. The government, as Oates states, not only announced its beliefs many times, but people died because they persisted in the falsehood that Oates was right: there was a sinister Catholic conspiracy. As he argues, how can they now deny what they once supported so rigorously, let alone executed men for?'

When news reached us in late May that Oates was arrested for defaming the Duke of York, calling him a traitor no less, it seemed the foolish man had, finally, overstepped some invisible boundary, and put an end to his reign of terror. Arrested for debt and fined the impossible sum of one hundred thousand pounds, he was thrown into the King's Bench Prison. His trial was set to take place in some unforeseeable future. The general feeling was the man would rot in there for life.

'One can only hope,' said Aphra, turning back to her latest work, a book of wondrous, daring poetry.

Just as I thought Aphra was rallying, King Charles, her beloved monarch, suffering the same condition as Papa, was carried to his bed. The city waited with bated breath as he was ill-used by a parade of physicians who attempted to save him. Alas, they failed and rumours afterwards were not only that he died a painful death, but that he converted to Catholicism in his final hours.

Aphra was quite nonchalant about the King's conversion. I couldn't reconcile it, not after all the fear, accusations, bloodshed and executions over the years. While King Charles may not have wielded the swords and axes that lopped heads and limbs, held the keys that kept so-called traitors in cells, or levelled verdicts that ruined or killed men and destroyed families, he was nevertheless responsible. Why hadn't he demanded the toleration he once promised? I would never understand and my memories of him would be forever tainted by the knowledge he'd always been a secret Catholic yet failed to give those who shared his faith any allegiance, let alone protection.

Despite the dangerous and foolhardy efforts of Shaftesbury, my father and their Whig allies, James, the Duke of York, the Catholic brother so many fought and died to have excluded from succession, ascended to the throne.

Aphra wrote a wonderful Pindaric to King James, not caring about his Papist faith, simply content the royal lineage was upheld. After James became King, she had a burst of creative energy, writing many plays, marvellous poems, challenging tracts, and loyal dedications. She even penned translations, including a very well received one on plants. Two works of prose were finished, and that on top of the three volumes of the *Love-Letters*. She also finally wrote the story she'd long wished to tell, of a slave she knew back in Surinam, the noble and tragic Oronooko and his wife, Imoinda. As if she knew her time was running out, she never stopped, despite the pain and fatigue, the megrims, the effort. I don't think she could have even if she'd wished. She was a writer — not just to the bone, but to her very soul. The act of putting words on paper, creating stories, expressing emotions, defined her.

Naturally, the critics still attacked, flocks of them descending and pecking and clawing, disliking her bawdiness, her satiric turn of phrase, her biting intellect, her acknowledgement of women's passions and desires and insistence they mattered as much as men's. Despising her, a woman, for daring to continue against their onslaught.

In the autumn of 1687, Nest and I managed to persuade Aphra to take a trip to Tunbridge Wells. Ever since John Hoyle had been arrested she'd refused to leave her bed, never mind the house. Though their relationship hadn't been the same since the accident (apparently the man didn't cope with invalids), when he was charged with sodomising a poulterer, a William Bristow of Gracechurch Street, something shifted in Aphra. It was if the scales fell from her eyes. It was not new knowledge that the man was inclined to his own sex — all knew that (Aphra had even written a poem about his inability to love her the way she desired in a bold poem called 'The Disappointment'). It was more she finally saw the darkness in him. When the charges were dropped, she expressed neither joy nor, much to my and Nest's relief, a desire to see the man again.

After Tunbridge Wells, Aphra retreated to her room. She was despondent about her deteriorating health, the state of her body, how her legs swelled and ached, the way her hands were now so crooked and puffed they could barely hold a pen (and she stubbornly refused to let me scribe — 'You're not a scribe, kitten, you're a writer. Never forget that.'). Her breathing was often coarse and shallow, and her stomach bloated, even though her appetite was less than a sparrow's.

When I returned from the theatre each day, I'd relieve Nest, who'd remained by her bedside unless she was running errands for medick, more paper, quills and ink, dispatching finished work to various publishers or chasing payment. Nest and I would take turns to keep Aphra company. She may have been ill, but she was still prolific. Rarely complaining and determined to keep up appearances, she also welcomed the loyal friends who called, or those who sought her creative advice, insisting we brush and style her now mainly grey hair, powder her thinning cheeks and apply her favourite scent — rose and musk. Then would she reign over the parlour, entertaining the likes of poets, playwrights, publishers and reverends with her amusing and oft scathing observations, her rich laughter hiding her increasing pain.

When, in 1688, King James abdicated in favour of an 'upstart Hollander from the United Provinces', it was almost more than Aphra could bear, despite his Protestant faith and the fact that his wife, Mary, was King James's daughter. To us, it was if various Kings and Queens were dancing through White Hall like Macbeth's ghostly vision, they changed with such frightening regularity. Would England ever know stability again? Commissioned to write a tribute to the new monarchs, she deliberately made no mention of the alien, William, choosing instead to sing Queen Mary's praises most effusively. It was brave move and a clever one — for who could fault her this time?

Of course, many still did.

Her patronage and care for me, even as her body weakened, were boundless, especially as I grew older and could no longer fall back on the excuse of my youth (not that I ever had — that was an indulgence left to others). Though my reputation was considered by some to have been irreparably ruined by treading the boards, suitors nevertheless sought my hand. It would have amused me had I not disliked causing undue pain by refusing them. Aphra would laugh at the antics of besotted merchants, young lawyers, even a pastor, calling them conceited coxcombs if they thought for a minute they had ascendancy over me ('They fall short, kitten,' she'd crow), or any woman. I was happy to humour her, let her believe I'd no need of a man, but we both knew my heart was with Gabriel and always would be. As Aphra once said, I didn't need him, I wanted him. I'd think of him often; sometimes when I'd no intention of admitting him, he'd wander into my reverie, look around, offer consolation or congratulations. At those moments, when my heart was newly afire, my body as well, I would torment myself over never having consummated our love. Oh, we'd discussed it, but after what happened to Bethan, I was loath to risk a child, even though I knew Gabriel was no William Scot. He respected my choice. Our letters were passionate but few, some of mine taking months to reach him, while his had a tendency to arrive in a bundle which I'd have to sort. I read them over and over.

As the years passed, I even saw him oh-so-briefly a few times when he returned to England with runagates from justice in tow. Then, when his commitments allowed, we'd squeeze every drop of time his work (and mine) allowed. I found my dedication to him was stronger than ever, despite our bodily denial. I couldn't help but wonder each time he returned to the continent: what if the gaps between visits, between letters, were too great and he found his mind altered or, worse, his heart? After all, I was surrounded by faithless, inconstant men — in verse, performance and real life. At those moments, I would shunt him from my mind lest I fall into melancholy.

As much as I longed for Gabriel and took much solace from his coded missives, I didn't once regret declining his offer of leaving with him.

Well, maybe once. Or thrice.

I never revealed to Aphra the nature of my promise to him, but she knew. Sometimes, usually in those moments when he was proving a great distraction to my compositions, or I'd drift mid-conversation, she would tap her quill against her mouth and smile at me.

'"Oh! Soft intruder on my solitude, Charming disturber of my ease, That hast my nobler fate pursued, And all the glories of my life subdued",' she'd whisper. Sometimes, I'd pretend not to hear when she quoted her love poems at me or urged me to follow my passion, follow Gabriel. More oft, I'd throw her own words back at her.

'"How strongly does my passion flow, Divided equally 'twixt two?"' I'd retort.

She'd chuckle in delight and open her arms. I'd wander into them gently, and hold her close, trying to ignore the ache in my heart, the fear thrumming in my soul at how skeletal and frail she felt.

SCENE FOURTEEN

Who can be happy without love? For me I never numbered those dull days among those of my life, in which I had not my soul filled with that soft passion …

Love-Letters Between a Nobleman and His Sister, Aphra Behn

It was the rain that woke me. After a steady fall throughout the night, a sudden squall struck the window, disturbing my exhausted slumber. For a sliver of time, I didn't know where I was. Then, I felt the bedclothes beneath my cheek and remembered. I was in Aphra's bedroom, maintaining a vigil that had started two days earlier.

I sat up slowly, stretching quietly, rubbing sleep from my eyes. I could just make out Nest as she slept in the chair the other side of the bed, her head slumped to one side, her hands folded over her middle. Between us, Aphra lay beneath the covers, her breathing loud and shallow. I stroked her cheek before I rose to open the curtains, trying not to think upon the doctor's final words the night before.

'She's only hours remaining,' he'd said.

An entire lifetime brought to its conclusion.

Outside, dawn had broken, and the city stirred. It was 16th April 1689. The air was filled with dark plumes of coal-fire smoke. The wind generously shared the acrid stench of the tannery and the pits outside the walls with the entire parish. Dewy flowers were bowed with the weight of the downpour now reduced to level thrumming, their colours fiercely and defiantly bright, their fragrance, ever so sweet. Wheels creaked and groaned as nearby traffic ground its way over worn cobbles, through the puddles and down pitted roads, under the city gates, past struggling shops, tumbledown and newly built houses, slumbering taverns, rancorous law courts, awakening theatres, grand monuments, gaudy palaces and even gaudier bawdy houses — not that there was much difference between the two. In the distance, traffic rolled past, people, high born, low born, unborn and the lumbering furred and plucked creatures that blasted, bellowed, clucked and snorted sharing passage with them. Bored dogs snapped at the steady droplets falling from overflowing eaves. Cats shook and shivered, trying to rid their coats of moisture. Children sat miserably beneath wagons and carts while their parents tried to lure harried customers over and spruik their wares. As I stared out the rain-drenched window, trying to see beyond our humble parish, towards the verdant hills and fields, taking in the wavering steeples, the blurred rooftops and chimneys, the congested roads, I thought how much Aphra was going to miss this — how much this city was going to miss her.

How much I would …

I returned to the bed, willing her to open her eyes, to speak. She'd barely said a word the last day as her body concentrated all its strength on simply surviving. Though I knew this day must come as her body wasted away and her agony increased, despite the regular administration of willow bark and a medicine called laudanum, it was an intellectual exercise I kept confined to practical thoughts of how best to treat her symptoms, alleviate her suffering. I avoided exploring our approaching separation and how it would fell me, but every time I looked at her, I felt like a tree being struck by a woodsman's axe. My ability to remain upright, linked to the earth, became precarious.

I sank beside her on the bed and pushed the hair Nest and I had lovingly tended away from her face. Was there something different we should have, could have done? A part of me still blamed those attending for misdiagnosing her and causing undue distress — the additional doses of mercury, of emetics and leeches. I had drawn a line when a foolish doctor wanted to try the new treatment of hot dung. Aphra had chuckled throatily as I unleashed my fury and disbelief upon the corpulent young fellow, who was clearly unused to being disrespected — and by a woman. If I were him, I'd get used to it.

Nest snorted and wriggled in the chair. I prayed she wouldn't yet awake. Selfishly, for just a while, I wanted Aphra to myself.

All the colour had fled her face, leaving it an eerie white. Her beautiful dark eyes were closed: curtains were drawn on what was to be her final act. The full-lipped, clever mouth was quiet. God, how I would miss hearing her. The years of pain, which had been carved upon her face of late, had all but vanished. She looked — not young, but neither did she appear old. She was simply Aphra. My Aphra. I found her dry hand buried beneath the blankets and drew it into my warm one. I'd already wept a tempest, a veritable storm that left me battered and bruised. Nest and I had together — but never in front of her. Aphra deserved better than our snuffles, our utter gloom: upon that we'd agreed. Especially when her life, her very spirit, had been so full, rich and meaningful. A challenge she rose to meet time and time again.

'Kitten?'

Her voice made me start and I quickly blinked back the damn tears that were never far away.

'I'm here, Aphra.' I pressed my lips to her forehead. She felt so very cool, despite all the blankets, the fire in the hearth.

'There's something I want to say,' she began. The words were breathy, hard to form between rapid exhalations. Her chest was rising and falling, her mighty heart beating, beating, fighting against what it knew was pending.

'I'm … I'm listening,' I whispered, moving my face above hers so she could see me.

A small smile flickered. She attempted to squeeze my hand, but there was no strength. I raised it to my mouth and held it there, afraid if I didn't a fierce keening would escape and never cease.

'P … promise me, that when I'm gone …'

A sob rose.

'... you'll keep writing.' She inhaled, a great shaky breath. Her eyes fluttered.

'Aphra?' I began.

She exhaled. 'That you'll continue now I no longer can. Write, kitten, like there's no morrow —'

I couldn't stop my cry, nor the tears in its wake.

'— and ensure your voice, *our* voices are heard. Don't let us be buried in the dry dust of history ...'

'I won't, Aphra. I won't.'

'*Promise* me.'

'I promise. I swear.' I glanced up towards Heaven and asked the angels and God to take my words into their safe-keeping.

I was unaware our quiet whispers had disturbed Nest; it was only when I felt her arms around me I knew she was there too.

'Climb up and lie beside her, Tribulation,' she said, urging me to stand so she might pull back the blankets. 'Like you always did.'

I didn't wait to be told twice. I scrambled onto the bed and, sitting up beside Aphra, with Nest's help, hauled her into my arms. She gave a groan, whether of approval or pain, I knew not. But she quickly settled as we rearranged the covers, and released a long, breathy sigh of contentment.

We were like an inverse Pieta: the child holding the mother.

Her hand fluttered weakly. 'Nest?'

Nest enveloped her fingers. 'I'm here, missus. Body, heart and soul. Always.' Her words were tremulous, last leaves on a winter tree.

I lowered my head and pressed my mouth to her head. 'I love you, Aphra Behn.'

'And I you, kitten,' said Aphra, her words rattled. She slowly shut her eyes.

Her chest, which had been working like a blacksmith's bellows, rising and falling at impossible speed, calmed. Her breathing too.

I glanced at Nest in panic.

Just as I was compelled to say what I had years earlier to William Scot, just as Bethan felt compelled to state the truth to me, so I must to Aphra.

'Nest, I need to — there are things I have to tell her.'

Nest gave me a look of such understanding and sorrow. She cupped my cheek. 'Then you must do so.' She nodded at me to start.

I inhaled to find strength. It was deep and shuddering. A part of me knew this wasn't necessary. Aphra had always known how I felt about her. But this was my very last chance.

'Thank you, Aphra,' I began. Shocked at how much my voice wavered, how inaudible it was, I drew on my stage-training to keep it steady, to ensure Aphra, wherever she drifted at this moment, heard me. 'You've been everything to me: mother, sister, dearest friend, mentor and most beloved. I came to you unfinished, a broken young woman who wasn't aware she needed repair. You made me whole. You completed me in ways I never foresaw. You gave me what no-one else before had — a place, a home, a belief in myself and what I could accomplish. You gave me the strength to not only try, but be unafraid of failing; to keep endeavouring until I succeeded.' My lips began to tremble. I held her tighter, drawing the last of whatever remained of her spirit into me and giving mine back as well. 'You gifted me and the rest of the world, your beautiful words, your imagination, your daring and wit. You did what you always sought to do — you *did* teach and reach. But, beyond all that, you gave me the most precious of gifts — you gave me your love.' I paused, momentarily unable to continue.

Her breathing had all but ceased. Her chest was still.

'I don't have the words to properly thank you — but they're also all I have. I also know they're all you'd want. So, Aphra, my Aphra, with all my shattered, heavy heart let me say so God and His angels hear, I love you. Always will. Now and forever more.'

She gave one last final sigh. A butterfly's wings.

It flew above her, circled over her desk, then out the window and into the grey, heavy skies.

She was gone.

Later, after Nest and I had rearranged her body, placing Aphra's head upon the pillows, and tucked her in, we brushed her hair again, weeping softly. Only after that did Nest go to fetch the doctor and coroner. Left alone, I returned to sit beside Aphra, wanting to take advantage of every moment I had with her, knowing once Nest returned with the men I'd never see her again.

God knew, I'd never hear her again.

I touched her cold lips gently with my fingers. Nay. That wasn't so. Aphra would never be silenced. Not so long as I lived, as her words, her ideas continued to be read and spoken. Not when they affected, inspired, amused, enraged and provoked anyone who heard or read them. Not when she'd shared all this and more with me and, along the way, taught me, everyone, so much.

I would not let her be forgotten.

I made up my mind then and there, as I rested against her oh-too-quiet breast, I would compose a portrait of her — not in paint or an engraving. I would do it the way Aphra would want: in words, so people would truly know her. I would include some of her finest poems and plays, and excerpts from her letters and longer works. I would celebrate the woman who dared to write for bread and who, in doing so, ensured other women writers, like me, could — would — follow in her bold, indelible footsteps.

I shut my eyes and prayed with all my sorry soul that one day, some time in the future, long after Nest, Gabriel and I were in our graves, beyond the theatre, the players, the Company, after all the kings and queens of England were dead, what I was yet to write would be read by different eyes and heard by different ears. That Aphra would come to be loved and, in turn, love again and again. She would be celebrated in times of which I couldn't even begin to conceive but knew in my lady bones would arrive.

They must, surely?

This would be my last and greatest act of love, of devotion to the woman who was everything to me and, without whom, I feared, my life would be forever dim …

EPILOGUE

My intimate Acquaintance with the
admirable Astrea, gave me, naturally,
A very great Esteem for her;
For it both freed me from that Folly
Of my Sex, of envying or slighting Excellencies
I cou'd not obtain; and inspir'd me with a noble
Fire to celebrate that Woman, who was an
Honour and Glory to our Sex; and this reprinting
her incomparable Novels, presented
me with a lucky Occasion of exerting that Desire
Into Action

The History of the Life and Memoirs of Mrs Behn,
One of the Fair Sex

The applause was more modest than a Puritan's blush, the cheers fainter than a newborn's sigh. Still, the play had made the third day and thus there would be an Author's Benefit. Aphra would have been pleased. *The Widow Ranter or, The History of Bacon in Virginia*, one of the last plays she wrote, was essentially the Company's eulogy to her. No-one cared the boxes were only half full. We threw ourselves into the characters with a gusto and verve that would have left the hawkers at Bartholomew Fair agog. None more so than Elizabeth Currer, who played the title role.

I wished Aphra could have seen her. I deluded myself that maybe, just maybe, the widow who dressed in men's clothes, strode about with grit and determination, verbally fencing with men and winning, who fought in several battles, might have been inspired by me.

Determined to soak every ounce of appreciation from the sorry crowd, Samuel Sandford and Anne Bracegirdle led us forwards in yet another bow, beckoning the minor roles to the forestage enthusiastically so we could have our moment in the spotlight. Unaccustomed to being so close to the pits, except when mid-performance, I held the hand of the cast member next to me tightly, blinking back the tears that had suddenly sprung to my eyes.

This is for you, Aphra.

How I missed her. Life had been so very quiet since she died. Nest and I remained at Newe Court. When I asked Nest if she would rather return to her family now Aphra was no longer there, she looked at me as if I'd suggested she marry a cockerel. 'What else are you but my family, kitten?' she asked.

The use of Aphra's pet name almost undid me and I threw my arms around the old woman, grateful that, if I no longer had Aphra, I had Nest. We had each other.

It was easy to forget that in the wake of Aphra's death, I still had a family. Bethan had become a part of my life — not as the mother she was, but the sister she'd tried to be. At first, we'd naively believed we could embrace our God-given roles, but it wasn't until we considered the judgement and stigma that would fall upon us like a crumbling edifice should we make our real relationship public that we agreed not to. And now there wasn't just us to consider, but her husband, and, of course, her sons.

Women pay for everyone's sins and so do those who love them.

When I saw Bethan again at Aphra's funeral, along with Walter and their two sons (aye, two), Charles Walter and Michael Fabian, I knew we'd made the right decision. It was too complicated, there was too much at risk if we didn't keep it a secret, not for me — who had nothing to lose, not even a reputation — but for Bethan. Her evident joy in being able to embrace the motherhood long denied her, along with respectability, went a long way to extinguishing any injury I felt. I was happy for her. I truly was. I also understood, as I watched her chiding the boys, consoling Charlie when he fell over on the street and skinned a little knee, Bethan could never be a mother to me — the time for that had passed.

So I continued to play perhaps the greatest roles of my life: younger sister to Bethan, sister-in-law to dear Walter Parker and aunt to their sweet boys. After all, if you tell a lie so often, live it every day, does it not become truth?

With that, I had to be content. To a great extent, I was.

Most evenings Nest and I spent in the parlour, me working on the book I was determined to write about Aphra, Nest telling wild tales of their adventures in Surinam, in Antwerp and London.

As once Nest had served as Aphra's conscience, she now decided I needed one. Not only how to dress and behave, but also when to school my tongue. You'd think I'd have learned such lessons by the ripe old age of twenty-eight. Alas. Nay. But one doesn't work in theatre without learning to use words (and the great and rich variety at our disposal) and voice to great effect. I loved her for caring enough to persist.

As news of Aphra's death spread, men appeared like flies in the carcass-strewn Shambles. Now the woman they perceived as my protector was dead (I hadn't understood how hard Aphra worked to keep men at arm's length from me), they arrived uninvited at the house, the theatre, accosted me in the street. I took to asking various actors to accompany me home. I even begged one, Mr George Powell, a lady-man, if I could call him my lover to deter ardent pursuers. At first, I was a little flattered and wondered that so many men would suddenly find me desirable and marriage-worthy (not all wanted to wed me — just bed me — as Mr Pepys helpfully pointed out one night in the Tiring Room after a few persistent suitors were removed by John Downes and Mr Betterton). But then it became apparent they thought Aphra had accrued some wealth and I was a woman of means.

Not so ardent after all.

I took great pleasure in informing them of their misguided pecuniary beliefs and that, far from being wealthy, I was struggling to pay off Aphra's debts. Few bothered me again once word got around.

'It was the same with Aphra,' Nest said, trying to comfort me. 'These men thought because she was related to Lord Willoughby they'd an heiress to swoop upon. Ha! She soon put them straight, just like you, kitten.'

There was only one man I longed for, one man I wished would appear and take me for supper, a ride on a tilt boat or a walk around St James's Park or Covent Garden. I half-thought he might come in the wake of Aphra's death. I wrote to tell him, as always care of his master, Sir Joseph Williamson.

Alas, he never came.

When summer ended and autumn drifted into winter, I began to think maybe Gabriel *had* changed his mind. Maybe he had found someone else. The thought was a thorn lodged in my heart. Maybe he was dead. The thorn became a dagger. A part of my thoughts was eternally cordoned off and allocated entirely to him — and Aphra. Just like my bloodied, wounded heart.

I think that's why, as I stood blinking in the footlights and taking another cheeky bow at the final performance of *The Widow Ranter*, I thought for a fleeting moment I spied him sitting in one of the boxes. It wouldn't be the first time my damned eyes had played the cruel jester. There, in part shadows, was a very tall man with long dark hair and a hooked nose. He wore a large hat with a white feather which curved over the brim and framed one side of his face. His arms were folded as he rested on the edge of the box.

When I looked again, holding up a hand to shield my eyes, there was no sign of him. The area was completely empty. The rest of the cast left the stage in a fuss of chatter and clutter, and the men in the pits were casting suggestive looks in my direction, studying me head to toe. I quickly turned and went to help Mr Downes douse the lights and pack the master script away.

I was just making my way to the Tiring Room, plucking at the laces on my vest, thinking of Aphra, wishing the audience had appreciated her work more. True, it was a challenging play, being about a rebellion in the Americas. Maybe it was too close to the bone — the way Aphra liked it. I began to smile.

'I hope that's for me,' said a voice that made me stop in my tracks, so deep, it was an animal growl; my reaction was always visceral.

I slowly raised my head, my heart playing a wild tattoo. There, striding out of the shadows, his long jacket flapping against his calves, his grin wide and white, his black, pirate eyes flashing, was Gabriel.

'You came,' I whispered.

He stopped a few feet away.

'I said I would.' He ventured closer. 'I'm so sorry about Aphra.'

I lowered my head in acknowledgment. 'She's buried in the East Cloister of Westminster Abbey. I think she'd be pleased about that. Though perhaps not so happy with what's inscribed on her tombstone.'

'Oh?' Gabriel moved nearer.

'"Here lies Proof that Wit can never be Defence enough against Mortality."'

It still stung these harsh words marked her resting place. Words I hoped my tribute to Aphra as well as her own work would disprove over and over.

'Let me guess,' said Gabriel with distaste. 'John Hoyle.'

'The very one. Not even in death could he offer Aphra praise or be gracious to the woman who, against all reason and sense, loved him.'

'Reason and sense oft have little to do with love, I've noticed.'

I wanted to close my eyes and inhale the smell of him. Sea, leather, velvet, smoke and the scent that was his alone. My body ached as heat stole through it.

'Why are you here?' I asked. Though, I prayed, I hoped, I knew.

'To hold you to that promise you once made.' He closed the distance.

'Oh? What was that?' I could not resist teasing him.

His arms, which had been about to encircle me, froze. 'Don't play with me, Tribulation.' His words were dark, perilous. I shivered. 'I'm in no mood for games. I've waited for you for so long, travelled the seas, biding my time. *Your* time.' He gave a half-laugh. 'You know she told me to come for you? Not once, but a few times over the years?'

I did.

'I knew not to heed Aphra's siren call. It wasn't hers to make. It was your song, your call. All I had to do was wait until *you* were ready. You and Nest. Your letter suggested it was time.'

I melted against him, thinking how apt it was he should find me here, backstage at the theatre, among the props and scenery for Aphra's last play. I glanced back at the stage.

'You're late,' I said.

He pressed his lips to mine gently. My body rose to meet his, but he pulled away. 'Come. We've much to talk about.' He took my arm and began to lead me towards the Tiring Room.

I baulked and began pulling him in the opposite direction, towards the stage door. 'I don't want to go there and face the others. Not now, not tonight. Tonight is for us.'

'You're still in costume.'

I quite forgot I was still garbed in men's clothing. Once again, playing the breeches part.

'Do you object?'

'Object?' He purred and planted a soft kiss on my neck. 'I'll take you any way, Tribulation Johnson. Dressed as a man, a woman or —' he leaned close, his lips touching my ear '— without any dress at all.'

'Mr Freeman,' I exclaimed, and slapped him playfully.

The exit lay just ahead, the light from outside forming a corona around its frame. Already, some of the cast were leaving. I could hear them planning to meet at the Rose and Crown nearby.

Before we followed them out the door and into the rain, I spun on my heel and drank in the theatre. The shadows, the glimmer of flickering lights, the melange of sounds. The way the words of the actors and stagehands carried and echoed: how they lingered like acoustic motes. The smell of tallow, grease paint. Of costumes, perfume, smoke and so many other odours. I thought of how far I'd come since opening night at Dorset Garden and my first performance, when this hulk of a man had literally swept me off my feet and carried me to safety. Is that what he was doing now? Nay. I'd felt safe for a long, long time. Aphra had seen to that. Just as she'd seen that my future lay with this solid, courageous and ever-so-patient man.

With him, and words.

'Gabriel,' I began, pausing as Mr Betterton and Mr Sandford's uproarious laughter carried. 'You're right. We do need to talk. Perhaps it's better I say what I must here.'

'You can tell me anything, anywhere, Tribulation Johnson.' He paused and a look of uncertainty crossed his face. 'So long as you don't tell me you've changed *your* mind.'

'Gabriel, nay, oh, nay.' I pressed myself against him, forced him to look at me. 'I haven't changed my mind — not about you. Never. How could you even think that for a moment?'

'What am I supposed to think?'

As carefully and swiftly as I could, I told him about the promise I'd made Aphra. How I believed I owed it to her, to all writers, to women ones especially, to continue on the road she'd started, that she'd paved. Regardless how difficult or bumpy the path, I must walk it so others might follow.

'That's why I want to remain here, in London. I want to remain in the theatre, to write, to publish.'

He didn't say a word.

'Do you know,' I continued in a rush, 'the United Company are mounting two of my plays this year alone? I've three tracts coming out soon and my work on Aphra is progressing. Oh, Gabriel, there's so much I want to do — so much I need to.'

Gabriel studied me, lifting his hands to hold my face as if it were made of glass. His rough thumbs caressed my cheeks. I longed to shut my eyes, lose myself in his touch. I must not.

'I've no intention of asking you to give up your work or to leave the theatre. Just that wretched lodging in Newe Street.'

'What?' I half-laughed.

'You and Nest cannot remain there. Not when there's a house awaiting you. Us.'

I thought of the house he'd bought for Wait-Still. Empty, forlorn. Not for much longer. In honour of her and Patience, we'd fill it with everything he'd intended and more. My heart soared. 'Is that what you wanted to talk about?' I took his hand in mine.

'Partly. What I also wanted to tell you was I've fulfilled my official duties — all the conspirators who could be accounted for have been brought to justice.'

I inhaled sharply. 'William Scot?'

'He's currently awaiting trial in Holland — ironically, not for his crimes against the English Crown, but for those committed against the Dutch.'

'Oh.' I waited for concern, sympathy or even empathy to pay a visit. They didn't arrive. Instead, a feeling akin to pity combined with a sense of rightness did. After all, William Scot, rapist, traitor, betrayer, was only getting what he so richly deserved. Was I a heartless daughter to think so? Nay, just an abandoned, used one. Along with the other women he'd deceived and brutally abused. Nevertheless, I was glad he wasn't languishing in an English gaol. I was also glad Aphra wasn't alive to learn of his ignominy. Maybe she already knew. I glanced upwards.

'Which means,' said Gabriel, taking me by the waist, 'I'm free to be whatever I want.'

'What's that?'

'Apart from with you?' He lowered his head and rubbed his nose against mine before pulling away. 'Why, I thought I might follow my other passion.' His eyes scanned our surroundings.

'You mean?' My heart began to sing.

'Someone once told me I was a fine actor,' he purred.

'A few someones, more like.' I took a step back, unable to quite believe what I was hearing. 'You mean it? You would tread the boards again?'

'You think I'd tolerate another actor being cast in the best parts you write?' He grinned. 'Seriously though.' The smile fell from his face.

'I'm weary of spying, Tribulation. Of traitors, of administering justice.' He sighed. 'Laws are arbitrary things, made by those in power, who are swift to alter them when it suits their cause or when the so-called criminal has a title or heavy purse. They're casually upheld and oft broken — least of all by felons.' He brushed a tired hand across his brow and I saw a newly formed sadness deep in his eyes, something I would seek to banish.

'I'd rather choose my own roles from hereon, aliases that last a few days, not months on end. I'd rather my false identities begin and end right there.' He pointed to the stage and laughed, then, just as quickly, became very serious. He held me by the shoulders and stared straight into my eyes. 'Truth be told, there's only one role I want. I'll do whatever you want or need me to so I might share your life, Tribulation Johnson. You *are* my life.'

How could this man be so … so … decent? So unexpected in every single damn way. Already, I looked forward to discovering his flaws.

'There *is* one other thing,' said Gabriel.

I waited.

'Do you think the Company might have work for Solomon?'

'That *is* the question,' I said, and we both laughed. 'I know it does. We're in desperate need of stagehands and so much more. He'd be so very welcome.' And not just by the United Company. 'I gather he's giving up intelligencing too?'

'For the time being.'

I gave a long sigh of contentment, of dreams being fulfilled. 'How I wish Aphra was here to see us.'

Gabriel swung me back towards the stage. 'Are you sure she's not? Look.'

The props from *The Widow Ranter* sat in the flickering lights. The scenery, which Aphra had described in her notes accompanying the manuscript, was still in place. How fitting my latest performance was in a play about a roistering woman, for that's what a ranter was — just as Aphra had been. Just as she encouraged me to be.

'Be proud of your name, Tribulation,' she'd say. 'Be nothing *but* trouble. One day, a man will come into your life who won't see you as difficult, unwomanly, or a challenge where he must emerge the victor, but who will embrace all that you are. All that you can be. He's the one worth loving.'

Aphra was right: he was.

I raised my welling eyes to the heavens, a smile forming. 'Oh, Gabriel. I can feel her.' I opened my arms, inviting her in, longing to feel her embrace one last time. 'You never really left me, did you, Aphra?' I waited for a response.

I leaned against Gabriel, staring at the reminders of her scattered about the stage, the legacy her wonderful words had created and, if posterity was generous and wise, always would. I hoped I'd be talented enough to continue it, to pass the baton.

Still, there was nothing.

As if to remind us of where we were, the stagehands appeared and began to close the curtains.

Disappointed my fancy had cruel limitations, I lowered my arms and had started to turn away when I heard it. A faint susurration, a soft, warmth breath against my ear, a swelling in my soul.

No, kitten. And I never will.

CAST OF CHARACTERS

*Denotes a real historical figure

Tribulation Johnson: daughter of Howell and Jacquetta Johnson, sister of Bethan and cousin of Aphra Behn

Abstinence Gumble: distant cousin of the Bishop of Canterbury and Tribulation's chaperone

Reverend Howell Johnson: Tribulation's father

Bethan Pratt nee Johnson: Tribulation's widowed sister

Joseph Pratt (deceased): Bethan's husband

Walter Parker: Reverend Johnson's curate

Sir Marmaduke Babcock: Bethan's suitor

***Bishop of Canterbury**

Lady Adeline (deceased): landowner in Chartham

***Aphra Behn (nee Johnson)**: Tribulation's cousin and infamous London playwright

Fabian Johnson (deceased): Tribulation's older brother

Timothy Shale: publisher at the Quill and Ink and Aphra's neighbour

***Thomas Otway**: playwright

***Charles Hart**: lead actor, King's Company, Drury Lane

***Thomas Betterton**: lead actor and manager, Duke's Company, Dorset Garden Theatre

***James, Duke of York**: brother of King Charles II, successor to throne and pre-eminent Catholic

***King Charles II**: ruler of Scotland 1649–1651, and then Scotland, England and Ireland, 1660–1685

***Titus Oates**: failed priest and fabricator of the Popish Plot, a Catholic conspiracy to assassinate King Charles II

***Edmund Berry Godfrey**: magistrate who recorded Titus Oates's affidavit outlining his accusations against prominent Catholics, who was later murdered

***Nest**: Aphra's maid (Aphra Behn did have a companion who shared her life, but her name is lost to history; the name Nest is an invention)

Millie: housemaid, Dorset Street

Molly: housemaid, Dorset Street

Jonathan Cross: lodger, Dorset Street; an apothecary

Michael and Robert Tetchall: brothers, lodgers, Dorset Street; scriveners

Roger: former lodger, Dorset Street; a printer

Jacquetta Johnson (deceased): Howell Johnson's wife; Tribulation's mother

***John Hoyle**: London lawyer and Aphra's sometime beau

***Johannes Behn (deceased)**: Aphra's husband

***Sir William Davenant (deceased)**: husband of Lady Mary, poet and playwright; former licensee of the Duke's Company

***Hannah Woolley**: author, *The Gentlewoman's Companion*

***Lady Mary Davenant**: Theatre Manager, Duke's Company, Dorset Garden Theatre

Farmer Whittle: resident in Chartham

***Charlotte Butler**: actress, Duke's Company

***John Downes**: book-keeper and prompter, Duke's Company

Mark Danvers: stage manager, Duke's Company

Nicholas Brown: stagehand, Duke's Company

Tom Brown: stagehand, Duke's Company

Michael Mortimer: junior stagehand, Duke's Company

Pascoe Bodley: scene painter, Duke's Company

Evan Marbury: scene painter, Duke's Company

***Mary Betterton**: wife of Thomas Betterton, actress, Duke's Company

***Henry Harris**: shareholder and actor, Duke's Company
***Samuel Sandford**: actor, Duke's Company
***Thomas Gilloe**: actor, Duke's Company
***Elizabeth Barry**: actress, Duke's Company
***Elizabeth Currer**: actress, Duke's Company
William Smith: actor Duke's Company
***Susanna Mountfort**: actress, Duke's Company
***Margaret Collins**: actress, Duke's Company
Prisca Smithton: actress, Duke's Company
Lily Miller: actress, Duke's Company
***John Crosby**: actor, Duke's Company
***James Nokes**: actor, Duke's Company
***Anne Bracegirdle**: actress, Duke's Company
Jonathan Rickman: actor, Duke's Company
***Katherine Herbert**: actress, Duke's Company
***Mrs Mary Lee** (later Lady Mary Slingsby): actress, Duke's Company
***Samuel Pepys**: Secretary of the Admiralty, diarist and ardent theatregoer
***John Evelyn**: famous diarist
***Anthony Ashley Cooper, Earl of Shaftesbury**: passionate Whig, leader of the Green Ribbon Club
***Lord Forde Grey**: peer of the realm, friend of Shaftesbury
***Robert Ferguson**: Scottish minister
***John Wilmot, Earl of Rochester**: friend of Aphra's, infamous louche and witty poet
Finnola: seamstress and dresser, Duke's Company
Juliet: make-up artist and dresser, Duke's Company
Jacob: general hand and dresser, Duke's Company
***Elizabeth (Izzie) Wilmot**: Earl of Rochester and Elizabeth Barry's daughter
***John Dryden**: playwright and poet laureate
***Nathaniel Lee**: playwright
***Charles Davenant**: Lady Mary's son
***Alexander Davenant**: Lady Mary's son
***Cave Underhill**: actor, Duke's Company
***George Villiers, Duke of Buckingham**: cousin to King and playwright
***George Etherege**: playwright
***Thomas Shadwell**: playwright

***Charles Killigrew**: son of Sir Thomas, manager Drury Lane
***Hortense Mancini**: King Charles II's mistress
***Barbara Castlemaine**: King Charles II's mistress
***Stephen Mortimer**: actor, Duke's Company
***Sir Roger L'Estrange**: former Licensor of the Press and publisher; friend of Aphra's
***William Wycherley**: playwright and harsh critic of Aphra
***Nell Gwyn**: former actress and King's mistress
***Charles Sedley**: writer
***Robert Boyle**: writer, theologian, scientist and founder of the Royal Society
***Moll Davis**: actress, King's Company
***Joanna Brome**: publisher
***Henry Brome**: publisher and Joanna's husband
***Chief Justice Scroggs**: main judge who presided during the Popish Plot
***Henry Care**: anti-Catholic publisher
***William Bedlowe**: compatriot of Titus Oates and an informer
Mandy Fitts: orange seller
***Jacob Tonson**: one of Aphra's publishers
***William Scot**: regicide's son, traitor, spy and once, Aphra's lover
***Lieutenant-General Byam**: governor of Surinam when Aphra lived there
***Henry Bennet, Lord Arlington**: King's Censor
***Thomas Corney**: English spy
***Sir Bernard Gascoigne**: friend of Aphra's and British agent
***Sir Joseph Williamson**: spymaster
Gabriel Freeman: former navy officer (captain) and, currently, intelligencer
Solomon van Kessel: former captain and Gabriel's friend and fellow intelligencer
***Charles Blount**: publisher and writer who uses pseudonym Junius Brutus
Wait-Still (deceased): Gabriel's first wife
Barnabas Harley: former crewmate of Gabriel and Solomon; runs posting inn on the New Canal
***Henry Coventry**: Secretary of State Southern Department, 1674–1680

***Robert Spencer, Earl of Sunderland**: Secretary of State, Northern Department,1679–1680 and 1683–1684 and Secretary of State, Southern Department, 1680–1681 and 1684–1688

***Sir Leoline Jenkins**: Secretary of State Northern Department 1680–1681 and Secretary of State Southern Department 1681–1684

***Israel Tonge**: Colleague of Titus Oates who kept the fears of a Papist Plot alive through accusation and testimony

Cleo: prostitute at the Bower of Bliss

Mrs Lucinda Fallon: Madam of the Bower of Bliss

***Will Hewer**: servant of Samuel Pepys

***Earl of Arran**: guest at Rochester's London house

***Margaret Rutter**: actress, King's Company, Drury Lane

***Mary Corbett**: actress, King's Company, Drury Lane

***Elizabeth Boutel**: first woman upon the English stage

***William Chiffinch**: Master of the Wardrobe and King's procurer

***Oliver Cromwell**: English General who ruled the English Protectorate, 1653–1658

***Prince Rupert**: cousin to the King

Patience Freeman (deceased): Gabriel and Wait-Still's daughter

***James Scott, the Duke of Monmouth**: King Charles II's bastard son

***Narcissus Luttrell**: book-seller and printer

Kit Savage: actor, Duke's Company

Grace Savage: actress, Duke's Company

***Earl of Mulgrave**: critic of Aphra

***Reverend Gilbert Burnett**: harsh critic of Aphra

***Lord Stafford**: executed for involvement in Popish Plot

Mr Franks: apothecary, Dorset Street

***Sir Charles Slingsby**: nobleman who married Mary Lee, actress

***Algernon Sidney**: associate of Shaftesbury and member of Green Ribbon Club

***Josiah Keeling**: a salt man and acquaintance of Shaftesbury

Mr Coggin: landlord
Clara Coggin: his daughter
***Thomas Sprat**: lodger with Mr Coggin
***Mr Gevan**: actor, Duke's Company
Winsome Jones: Mercury Woman, Farringdon Ward Without
***Edward Thomas**: John Dryden's brother-in-law
***Robert Gould**: critic and writer
***Edward Kynaston**: actor, King's Company
***Michael Mohun**: actor, King's Company
Madoc Osbourne: singer, Duke's Company
***Sal Gibbs**: minor actress, Duke's Company
Joanna Cross: actress, Duke's Company, formerly of King's Company
Mr Brogan: proprietor, The Dragon's Heart
Maarten van Beek: clockmaker, Witch Street
***Robert West**: barrister
***Colonel Rumsey**: member of Cromwell's army and staunch Republican
***Mr Shephard**: owner wine shop, London and tavern, Hoddeson
***Richard Rumbold**: retired army officer
***Mr Wildman**: a Leveller and plotter
***Richard Goodenough**: sheriff
Joanne Scot: William Scot's wife
***Henrietta Berkley**: Lord Forde Grey's sister-in-law
***Mrs Corey**: actress, United Company
***Mrs Bowtell**: actress, United Company
***Ann Quinn**: actress, United Company
***Katherine Corey**: actress, United Company
***William Turner**: Lord Grey's factotum, husband to Henrietta Berkley
***Judge Jeffreys**: presiding judge in trial of Lord Grey
***Thomas Creech**: translator of Lucretius's *De Rerum Natura*
Mr Brown: owner, Courtier's Charger inn, Newmarket.
***Thomas Walcott**: associate of Colonel Rumbold
***Robert White**: artist who did an engraving of Aphra around 1684

*__William Bristowe__: a poulterer who charged John Hoyle with sodomy

George Powell: actor, Drury Lane

Michael Fabian Parker: Bethan and Walter's son

Charles Walter Parker: Bethan and Walter's son

PLAYS PERFORMED OR MENTIONED THROUGHOUT NOVEL

Please note, when mentioned, these are as close to the actual performance months and years as was possible to realise.

Aphra Behn
The Forc'd Marriage or, The Jealous Bridegroom: A Comedy
Sir Patient Fancy: A Comedy
The Feign'd Curtezans or, A Night's Intrigue
The Lucky Chance or, The Alderman's Bargain
The False Count or, A New Way to Play an Old Game
The City Heiress or, Sir Timothy Treat-All
The Young King or, The Mistake
The Rover or, The Banish'd Cavaliers
The Second Part of the Rover
The Roundheads or, The Good Old Cause
The Widow Ranter or, The History of Bacon in Virginia
Attributed to Aphra Behn but written with Tribulation Johnson
The Revenge or, A Match Made in Newgate
Tribulation Johnson
Like Father, Like Son or, The Mistaken Brothers
Romulus and Hersilia or, The Sabine War: A Tragedy
William Davenant
The Wits
John Dryden
The Spanish Friar
Troilus and Cressida
The Kind Keeper

An Evening's Love or, The Mock Astrologer
John Dryden and Nathaniel Lee
Oedipus
The Duke of Guise
Thomas D'Urfrey
Madame Fickle or, The Witty False One
George Etherege
The Man of Mode or, Sir Fopling Flutter
John Fletcher
Rule a Wife and Have a Wife
Ben Jonson
Bartholomew Fair
Nathaniel Lee
The Princess of Cleeve
Thomas Middleton
Timon of Athens (adapted from Shakespeare)
Thomas Otway
Friendship in Fashion
Venice Preserv'd
Thomas Randolph
The Jealous Lovers
Earl of Rochester (John Wilmot)
The Tragedy of Valentinian
Thomas Shadwell
The Virtuoso
The Woman-Captain
The Lancashire Witches and Tegue O'Divelly, The Irish Priest
William Shakespeare
The Merchant of Venice
Othello
Hamlet
Nahum Tate
The History of King Lear (adapted from Shakespeare)
John Tathim
The Rump
John Webster
The Duchess of Malfi

AUTHOR'S NOTE

All women together ought to let flowers fall upon the tomb of Aphra Behn for it was she who earned them the right to speak their minds.

A Room of One's Own, Virginia Woolf

I always enjoy reaching this part of the book — the part where I can explain not only the motivation behind it, something of my own relationship to the story and the research I've done, but also where fact is interwoven with fiction and vice versa, where reality and imagination collide.

I wish I could start by telling you, dear reader, that ever since I was a child, I have loved Aphra Behn and her work. The truth is it wasn't until I was studying Virginia Woolf at university in my late twenties that I first read her name (see epigraph) and learned something of her work. I don't know if this is a reflection on me or the wilful degradation of her work and reputation that continued well into the twentieth century, but decades would pass before I encountered her again.

When I wrote an earlier novel, *The Chocolate Maker's Wife*, set during the heady, early years of Charles II's return from exile and the restoration of the monarchy to England, I read about the brave new world of English theatre — brave and new because, for the first time, women were allowed to tread the boards. I knew back then I wanted to write about the stage and the lives of actresses, actors and playwrights at some point. I also understood I couldn't write about these things without giving Aphra Behn a starring role. The prospect both excited and daunted me.

What I didn't expect, as I deep-dived into Aphra's life, her works and the social and historical context in which she lived, was how utterly fascinating she was, the woman who was a spy, playwright, Tory-propagandist and, as one of her biographers Janet Todd describes her, a 'punk-poetess' (love that). She was also, I was to discover, talented, intelligent, contradictory, complicated, deeply flawed, kind and loyal.

So, here's what we do know about Aphra Behn — and most of this is revealed throughout the novel. She was born a Johnson, in Kent, and was related to Lord Willoughby. She was fairly well educated, and her family had reasonable social and political connections. When she was a very young woman her father (who may have been her adopted father – there's debate about this as well as other aspects of her life) was posted to Surinam in the West Indies. Sadly, he died en route, but the family settled briefly in the English colony. While there, Aphra met William Scot, the regicide's son and already, it's believed, a double if not triple agent, and embarked on a scandalous affair with him. She socialised with various expatriates, fell out with the lieutenant governor, and became fascinated by the nobility and travails of the slaves, including Oronooko and his wife Imoinda — a tragic, terrible tale which Aphra wrote in novel form years later. (Despite the fact that she wrote *Oronooko*, a novel, thirty-seven years before Daniel Defoe's *Robinson Crusoe*, Defoe is still credited with producing the first novel in English — Google and you'll see. What acknowledgement she now receives is due to the dedicated work of revisionist historians and feminists.)

Sometime after leaving Surinam, Aphra had a short-lived marriage to Johannes Behn, who likely died of the plague. Just before the Great Fire of London broke out in 1666, Aphra was sent as a spy to Antwerp. Her mission was to try and recruit William Scot to the English network. While there, she was undermined, denigrated (and not just by Scot) and her work dismissed. She was paid a fraction of what she'd been promised, and her costs weren't covered. On returning home she was flung into debtors' prison and her warnings about a proposed attack by the Dutch on the English fleet in the Medway were ignored (the fleet was subsequently destroyed).

Her reputation was in tatters. Forced to earn a living, she turned to the pen and began to write plays, poems, tracts, translations, political polemics — whatever she could to earn coin. The pay was piecemeal, and a fraction of what men earned, so Aphra was often in debt. According to her biographers (there are three to date), even though she worked so hard and through rampant and toxic criticism, misogyny, and vilification of her reputation, she also had supporters. As she grew older, she suffered chronic physical pain (likely arthritis and other ailments) and illness, dying in what was tantamount to poverty.

She wrote broadly and quickly about love, sex and politics and, as Janet Todd in the excellent *Aphra Behn: A Secret Life* says, 'sexy politics and political sex'. Todd adds, that Aphra was 'a hack as well as an artist, needing to eat before she could write … Behn is remarkable for keeping herself through her work'. As Aphra oft stated: she wrote for bread. And Aphra knew she wrote as well as any 'appreciated man', refusing to let those who scoffed and scorned her work stop her.

As depicted in the novel, Aphra did appreciate men (she felt sexual desire was an expression of love and that men and women should love freely as equals) and counted a few among her closest associates. John Wilmot, the Earl of Rochester was one, as was John Hoyle. It was widely known Hoyle was gay and it's evident that Aphra's relationship with him was complex and mostly one-sided, though he must have done enough to earn her affection and trust. Often, her work was attributed to him or one of her other male friends, a situation which must have stuck in her craw. Roger L'Estrange, the writer and publisher, Jacob Tonson and the Bromes were also close associates as well as the Bettertons, Lady Mary Davenant and her sons, Nathaniel Lee and John Dryden. Aphra was also a sounding board and mentor to young male playwrights such as Thomas Otway and Nahum Tate, who she also counted as friends.

More than that, she was an inspiration to the women writers who immediately followed her. There were other women writers about at the time, such as Margaret Cavendish — an aristocrat — and even two female playwrights, Frances Boothby and Elizabeth Polwhele, each of whom had only one play performed before, as another of Aphra's biographers, Angela Goreaux in *Reconstructing Aphra: A Social Biography of Aphra Behn*, describes it, 'lapsing back into obscurity'. Other women wrote under a male name (often a relation) or using the nom de plume 'Anonymous', and were unlikely to have been paid for their efforts. There were at least five female playwrights who emerged after her death, each one, according to Janet Todd, seeing Aphra as her most important precursor. Aphra's distinguishing choice and what managed to offend the establishment so deeply (apart from being female) was the fact she wrote for money and was unabashed about it.

Thus, as Woolf wrote, Aphra blazed a trail that, even centuries later, other females, including women writers today, are following. How could I not at least attempt to honour such a woman?

It's also true that a biography and compilation of Aphra's work was written by 'One of the Fair Sex' (identity unknown) who claimed to have intimate knowledge of Aphra and her writings. It was published a few years after she died. This was a gift for this historical fiction writer. I began to wonder who this woman was and what her relationship to Aphra — personally, professionally and to her work — might have been. From these imaginings, Tribulation Johnson, a long-lost cousin, was born. A woman who has her own dark secrets and dreams, but is also talented, flawed, loyal, clever and, I hope, kind. Through Tribulation, we come to know Aphra — at least those parts of herself she allows us access to — but I also hope Tribulation stands as her own fully realised character.

How Aphra (and Tribulation) wrote, let alone continued to write under such constant personal and professional attacks, when there were so many vindictive and cruel things said about her and her work is remarkable. The linking of public writing, being a professional writer, with sex work was continuous. The traducing of her reputation was both depressing and enraging to read. It's testimony to her strength of character (and necessity) that she continued, though she suffered bouts of melancholy (depression), self-doubt and frustration, interspersed with occasional triumphs — much the same as many writers today.

Criticisms of Aphra as being 'vile', 'a whore' and 'failing in feminine modesty' weren't confined to her own century either. They continued down through the ages, ensuring her work — fourteen novels, numerous plays, poems, letters, tracts, pamphlets, lampoons and translations — was decried and then shunted aside. When some of her work was republished towards the end of the nineteenth century, a male critic, under the heading 'Literary Garbage' wrote the following in 1862.

> *... Mrs Behn's works had a scandalous reputation ... it is true that this did not prevent her from attaining honourable burial in Westminster Abbey but it is a pity her books did not rot with her bones. That they should now be disinterred from obscurity into which they have happily fallen is surely inexcusable.*

In 1888, a Dr Doran wrote:

> *Intellectually, Mrs Behn was qualified to lead the playwrights of her day through pure and bright ways; but she was a mere harlot, who danced through uncleanness, and dared them to follow. Remonstrance was useless for this wanton hussy.*

In 1913, Ernest Bernbaum even discredited the biography by 'One of the Fair Sex', claiming it had been written by a man and that Aphra had never been to the West Indies, nor a spy, and that there was no Mr Behn either.

It's hardly surprising then that, as Goreau concludes, 'for nearly two hundred years after her death, she disappeared almost entirely from the pages of biography, literature, of history itself'.

You just can't make this unjust, dreadful stuff up, can you? Naturally, it was fuel to the fire burning in my belly as I sought to repatriate Aphra Behn, and present a real working woman — two of them! — seeking to simply earn a living wage and contribute creatively and intellectually to their society.

Much of Aphra's body of work isn't what we'd call literary — she wrote what was popular at the time and crafted her plays according to the successful formulae of the day. They were bawdy and entertaining and written to be performed. I read all of them and found them amusing, somewhat predictable, clever at times, dull at others. Her poetry is excellent, her political writing can be scathing and her ability to lampoon is exceptional (her epilogues and prologues are wonderful). I didn't read any of her translations, but loved the fact that, though she oft bemoaned not having access to the kind of education a man received — specifically classical languages — she translated the translators and thus made their works even more accessible.

While Aphra's work *was* accessible, the real woman is a different matter. She is an enigma, someone who wore many faces or masks and who worked within the systems she also condemned. I could really relate to how Goreau felt when first embarking on her biography:

> *[Aphra] was not the heroine I thought first to discover; for that Aphra who so well understood, articulated, and raged against the oppression of women nevertheless found herself contradicted ... One Aphra could not live without independence, the other could not give up her dependence ... Her weakness, her desperate need for approval, are ours too.*

Janet Todd examines Aphra's life brilliantly, analysing and critiquing her work and known facts of her existence. Yet, she also acknowledges that Aphra is a complex and difficult subject.

This puzzling, inconsistent woman became an irresistible figure who I longed to get to know. What lay behind the public mask of her work, her responses to critics? Who better to tell us than 'One of the Fair Sex'?

While Tribulation is a fiction, what she lives through, what she experiences at Dorset Garden and among the actors and actresses, as a young writer, a daughter-sister, woman of the period, is not.

To the best of my ability, almost every play mentioned being staged at Dorset Garden was performed when described and with the cast mentioned. Though I have invented a few players (Prisca Smithton for example) and the stagehands, the rest are real historical figures, the Bettertons, Elizabeth Barry, Charlotte Butler and Anne Bracegirdle being just some examples. The prompter, John Downes, was also a real person and while he was never injured in a fire (that was a narrative necessity — sorry, John), I am so indebted to the meticulous records he kept of the two major theatres and the plays performed and the players taking part. His small book called *Roscius Anglicanus* kept me on track. Whenever I veer it's because Downes lumped together some years or plays, so I felt I'd the freedom to be flexible.

Likewise, the fight that broke out and shut down Dorset Garden for a time happened, and the figures who started it were real, though I adjusted the length of the closure.

For the camaraderie as well as lack thereof among the players — the competitive and sometimes vicious nature of relations — I drew not only on some fabulous histories of the theatre — including the *Time Traveller's Guide to British Theatre* — but on my own experiences as a young actor and one-time playwright.

I've had an enormous passion for the theatre for as long as I can remember (I first appeared as Puck in *A Midsummer's Night Dream* at North Sydney Independent Theatre when I was nine years old). I spent many, many years in professional and amateur theatre and taught drama. I also had my first professional play produced — a children's play — when I was twenty, at Marian Street Theatre in Sydney. It was called *An Adventure in Toyland.* Ironically, this very play saved me years later. I was a penniless single mother, struggling to make ends meet and living in Bendigo, Victoria, when my stepmother, Moira Adams, responded to a Missing Person advertisement in the *Sydney Morning Herald.* It had been placed by Marian Street Theatre, who were searching for my whereabouts as they had royalties from a second season of my play held in trust for me. Like receiving an Author's Benefit, it was a much-needed boost to barren coffers.

As I lost myself down the various deep rabbit-holes of research, I was also led to consider something I hadn't before by the fascinating *Treading the Bawds: Actresses and Playwrights in the Late Stuart Stage* by Gilli Bush-Bailey. She discusses how having a woman playwright like Aphra, actresses and a female theatre manager in the form of Lady Mary Davenant meant staging plays at Dorset Garden throughout those years was very much a female collaboration. Not only was there the undoubted support women gave each other on stage and off but the men were a part of that as well. And yet, as Bush-Bailey warns, in acknowledging this, I also had to consider these questions: 'Which story of women do we choose? An all too familiar tale of oppression or an equally tired romance of feminine skill triumphing against all odds?'

I chose to present both and yet challenge them too, which reflects reality.

As for the religious turmoil, the many plots and plans to assassinate the King and the shocking schism that tore the city apart, it's all true. While I wrote many of those scenes, I watched in despair as our own world was being torn asunder — people were again being encouraged to takes sides: vaxxer versus anti-vaxxer, one political ideology or leader against another, those pro lockdowns, those against, those who 'believe' in climate change (it's science, not an article of faith!) and Covid, and those who don't. We were encouraged to be polemical, to lob grenades at each other and build fortresses around our positions, instead of building bridges. Conspiracy theories went into overdrive — just like they did in England in Charles II's day. As the adages go — history repeats itself and truth is stranger than fiction. That was certainly the case here.

The 'Horrid Popish Plot', and the magnificently named Titus Oates and what he claimed and the turmoil he created all occurred. The former priest (who falsely boasted a Doctor of Divinity, earning him the sobriquet, 'the Salamanca Doctor') made the entire plot up, and people — good people, important people — died as a consequence. The murder of the London magistrate Edmund Berry Godfrey, who took down Oates's testimony and then was brutally killed, put the plot firmly in the public consciousness and not only gave credence to many of Oates's outrageous claims, but stoked irrational fears and responses to those.

The Popish Plot wasn't believed by everyone, including the King, but became a convenient way for certain factions within government — especially the Green Ribbon Club (which was also real) led by Shaftesbury and including Algernon Sidney — to ensure the Catholic Duke of York never ascended to the throne in the event of his brother's death. Many believed the Earl and his associates were behind the Popish Plot and Oates was their puppet. Thus, the 'Exclusion Crisis' — where two large factions in government (and members of the populace) were either for or against the Duke of York inheriting — dominated English politics. Whigs (against the Duke) and Tories (pro-royals) came into being.

The impact of the Popish Plot upon the theatre (and Matthew Medbourne was a genuine figure who was falsely accused of being involved in the plot and thrown in gaol, where he died) cannot be underestimated. Goreau describes it this way: 'The Popish Plot put an abrupt end to the merry days of the Restoration: wits, pranks, and the prosperity of the theatre were all to vanish in the atmosphere of universal hysteria and accusation.' Audiences became scant, and livings hard to make.

In case you're wondering what happened to the man responsible for all the deadly hysteria, I thought I should explain. Titus Oates's fate was not only to be discredited, accused of perjury (for which there wasn't a sufficient penalty) and fined, but he was imprisoned for life. Every year, he was to be paraded through the streets and placed in a pillory for an hour at various points in the city. During the first year, a crowd of ten thousand gathered at a pillory and pelted him with rotten eggs. Later, there were various attempts to free him, some of which almost succeeded, but how's this for injustice — he didn't remain in prison long. He was eventually released and paid a pension and later married a wealthy widow. He became a preacher at a Baptist church in Wapping, but after the church expelled him in 1701, he died in ignominy on 12 July 1705. For someone who caused so much death, upheaval, terror and suspicion, turning the city on its head, he ended not with a bang but a whimper. Was it fair? I'll leave you to decide.

Lesser known than the Popish Plot is the Rye-House Plot. Once I learned about this and how close it came to being successful and what happened in its aftermath, I knew I had to use it in the novel. In many ways, it was a far more serious attempt to assassinate the King and his brother. Many powerful people were involved and used all the anti-Catholic fear and anger aroused by the Popish Plot to make their plans — which also included many attempts to incite armed rebellion, including in Scotland.

One of the reasons the plot failed was because an inexplicable fire did break out in Newmarket, forcing the King and Duke to leave the town a week early and thus foil the conspirators. The description of the fire and its destruction are as accurate as records allowed. Josiah Keeling, presumably to save his own skin (as intelligence agencies were watching the plotters) confessed to everything and named names — he also warned some friends who escaped. A flurry of executions followed and those who could went into exile, including Lord Grey. There is an argument to be mounted that the discovery of this plot and those involved are what ultimately led to a reduction of Whig power and opened the way for James to succeed his brother without resistance. It also, according to Tim Harris's book *Restoration*, led to 'an intensification of the drive against dissent'.

While Josiah Keeling was a real person, it wasn't William Scot's alias. As far as I know, they were two different people. That's a liberty I took. History doesn't know the fate of William Scot — after betraying Aphra in Antwerp, his movements and death are unknown, a great gap this fiction writer sought to imaginatively fill.

The entire affair of Lord Grey and his sister-in-law is also true as is Aphra writing the book *Love-Letters between a Nobleman and His Sister* about it. It's assumed she was paid by the King or supporters in his government to do this to discredit the Whigs. She also dedicated the first volume to Captain Thomas Condon, praising his masculine beauty and telling him to find love.

Intelligencing, the information around the former spymaster Joseph Williamson, the covert and not-so-covert operations, disguises, assumed identities, code names (Slavery and Popery, Blackbird and Goldfinch) and codes, including the one Aphra invented, are all fact.

With the collapse of the Licensing Act came the end of censorship and government control over the presses. As a result, news-sheets and reporting not only flourished, but with this came so much false information or, as it was then called, 'false news'. People reading these fake reports could be easily misled and, certainly, when you read some of the stories and headlines, there was a real push to demonise Catholics and encourage discrimination against minor faiths and immigrants to the city — to attribute all kinds of dangerous behaviours, plots and deadly mischief to them. Roger L'Estrange was one of the few who, though capable of writing rubbish as well (!), did stand fast when it came to insisting the Popish Plot was a fabrication. This earned him many enemies and a great deal of public wrath. An effigy of him was indeed burned at the Ascension Day Parade two years in a row and the nicknames he was given in the novel were genuine. But he was proven right in the end.

Before I complete my note, it wouldn't be right not to mention the entrenched sexism of the era. I wish I could say it's difficult for us in the twenty-first century to understand, but as many recent movements have attested and as reactions to women in positions of power and influence constantly reveal, it's still alive and well. Nevertheless, what Aphra, Tribulation, the actresses and other women must have endured — well, it just makes me admire them more. But I'll let historian Ian Mortimer, in his wonderful book and essential reading, *Time Traveller's Guide to Restoration Britain*, describe it. When discussing this period, he writes: 'there is great inequality between the sexes. It amounts to sexism on a scale that you will barely be able to countenance …' On the following page, he continues: 'This is the amazing thing about sexism in Restoration Britain: the prejudices against females are so deep-seated that many women share them.'

I wish I could say that kind of thinking no longer exists. Alas …

Once more, I am indebted to so many fantastic, erudite historians, gender and feminist academics, journalists, theatre historians and specialists and so many more. Wonderful analyses of Restoration plays and writings were invaluable as were the biographies of Aphra I read — two I have already mentioned, the third was *The Passionate Shepherdess: The Life of Aphra Behn* by Maureen Duffy. Each offered unique insights into the woman, her work and the times in which she lived.

I am also hugely grateful to the marvellous documentaries, films and TV dramas produced and to YouTube videos of some of the plays, as well as unputdownable fiction set in the period.

As I write, I listen to the music of the era and burn candles associated with scents I might have smelled. My olfactory senses are eternally grateful modern candlemakers haven't yet designed ones that smell of shit, piss, blood, offal, tobacco, hearth smoke, tidal estuaries and overflowing ditches, never mind all the odours unwashed and unclean human bodies exude.

Thank you to everyone mentioned above for all the rabbit-holes you shoved me down — I loved them … a bit too much. Anything I have correctly imparted is due to your diligence and erudition. All mistakes are, sadly, my own, and I beg your forgiveness and that of my readers, and claim creative licence!

ACKNOWLEDGEMENTS

This is where I finally get to thank all the wonderful, generous people who knowingly and sometimes unknowingly helped with this book. For all writing is a solitary act, getting to the finished product isn't — it's as much a collaborative process as the plays at Dorset Garden Theatre. But delivering thanks also leaves me feeling quite anxious — sort of like sending out wedding invites and just knowing you've missed someone important. If I have, as I've said before, it's merely from these pages, but not from my heart.

First, I want to thank my agent, Selwa Anthony. This book was written not only during Covid and the long lockdowns so many endured, the fear and frustration, but during a very personally difficult time for me and my family — the death of my younger brother from brain cancer. I will return to that. Selwa not only kept in touch to make sure I was travelling as well as could be expected, but ensured I had the time and emotional and mental space to write. She's so caring and yet professional, so pragmatic and yet kind. I am eternally grateful you're in my life, Selwa, not just as my agent, but as a very dear friend who believes in me and this book, and who loved Tribulation and Aphra from the outset. Thank you.

To my wonderful, patient and magnanimous publisher, Jo Mackay … Where do I begin? Much like Selwa, you knew what I was going through and when I was so damn late with this manuscript you accommodated me. You held the door open and ushered me through it gently and compassionately. You offered sensational feedback on an early draft of the book — guided me much like Aphra does Tribulation — and I love you for it. The book is better for your sage input and I'm better for knowing you.

Now, when I talked about Gilli Bush-Bailey making me think about the supportive network of women that would have existed in Restoration Theatre she made me think further afield, about the females I rely upon. I've already mentioned Selwa and Jo. Well, there's a few more yet to come. There's the brilliant Annabel Blay, editor-in-chief, who shepherds me and the novel through the changes and the various stages of polishing a rough draft into a shiny finished work. Annabel is also very patient, liberal with her praise, considered with any critique and always, always available. Thank you, Annabel.

For this book, I was given a new and fabulous editor to work with — Kate O'Donnell. Kate — it has been wonderful working with you and look what we've accomplished together. Kate is funny, so insightful and thorough, chatty — everything you want an editor to be. She was also passionate about the story, the characters and plot and understood from the outset what I was trying to accomplish. How lucky am I? I hope, dear, readers, you can feel the joy that went into not just (most of) the writing — some parts were NOT joyful, but certainly the tremendously collaborative editing process was. It's been a labour of love — and that's down to you, Kate, and what you've brought to the manuscript. Thank you.

I also must thank Kate James for her shrewd finishing touches and incredible eagle eye. I am so very grateful. Then there's the whole wonderful, enthusiastic and talented team at HQ/Harper Collins: they help get the book designed, marketed, reviewed, onto shelves, into readers' hands and social media feeds. The gorgeous Natika Palka, Eloise Plant, Jo Munroe and everyone at HQ — I cannot thank you enough for all your support and hard work.

I also want to thank the talented Micaela Alcaino for another superb cover. When I first saw it, I was rendered speechless, it's so perfect. It gives me goosebumps – thank you so much. Likewise, thank you to Alex Hotchin for the amazing map of Tribulation's London. Compiled from images of contemporary maps I used, a very ordinary mud map I drew, this marvellous miracle was produced.

I also want to thank my delightful US agents, Jim Frenkel and Catie Pfeifer — you've always been so incredibly supportive and patient, communicative and kind. Jim's emails are full of information, humorous and warm, and I look forward to them along with the ongoing and avid encouragement.

When I first finish a draft of a book (it's actually about a tenth draft) I give it to Selwa and my two beta readers for initial reactions and feedback. Stephen, my husband, is one and the other is my beloved friend, Kerry Doyle. I'm always astonished at how she can critique what I've written, pinpoint its flaws and strengths and deliver suggestions with such consideration and wisdom. Thank you, Kerry — I know what I ask is a huge and daunting task, but you always tackle it with aplomb, professionalism and, above all, generosity. My heart is full.

I want to say a huge thank you to my Hobart friends: Lucinda Wilkins (my nerdle and book buddy) and Simon Thomson; our gorgeous neighbours and second family here, Bill, Lyn and Jack Lark; Bob and Christine Wilson; Mark Nicholson and Robin Maclean; Rosie and Clinton Steele; Robbie, Emma and Harvey Gilligan; Terry and Rebecca Moles; and our other delightful neighbours, Associate Professor Katrina Schlunke and Susan Brock. I also want to thank the ever-terrific Fletcher Austin, our utterly delightful Brewer, Daniel Moro Galindo and his partner, Aline Hidaka. Also, Mimi McIntyre, Jeff Francombe, Helen Shield, fabulous Donna Williams and Kerry Ashwood — who look after me and our house — what would I do without you all?

I also want to thank, from the bottom of my heart, my oldest and dearest friend, Catherine Miller. And to Peter Goddard (Kerry's partner), my grocery shopping partner, holiday-planner and all-round best bud — thank you. Also, dear Stephen Bender, Pat Brooks, Moira

Adams, the incomparable, Professor Jim McKay, Dr Frances Thiele, Grant Searle, Kirsten Macdonald, Angela and Billy White, Sheryl Gwyther, my old army mate, the lovely Shelley De Courcy Lys, my academic friends, Helen Johnson, Liz Ferrier, David Rowe, Linda Martello, and Janine Mikosza — a magnificent and successful writer who is also the sweetest of souls.

A huge thanks to my talented writer friends and HQ/ HarperCollins stablemates. Your support, sharing of information, successes and failures (there aren't many of those!), concerns and counsel, how you are so ready to offer solace or congratulations, tell your stories, is simply wonderful, uplifting and restorative in so many ways. You know who you are — thank you.

I also want to sincerely and lovingly thank my Facebook and Instagram friends, for touching base and supporting me through some very dark and sad times as well as the joyous and celebratory ones. You make such a difference and often without knowing you do — thank you.

I also want to thank my readers — where would I be without you? You are what keep me and my writing peers going. Thank you for reading and loving our books, our stories. Thank you even more for sometimes reaching out and telling me. Your words are like a ray of sunshine on a dark day and I bask in their warmth for a long time.

And a huge thank you to all the booksellers and librarians who put books into the hands of readers. I've said it before: you are the custodians of stories, the gatekeepers of the imagination. Thank you. I wish I could individually tell you all how much what you do means to me.

Thank you as well to all the reviewers professional and non-professional — those with book blogs, web pages, who review on Goodreads, Amazon, Instagram, YouTube and BookTok and wherever else you can share your love of reading. You support books and writers, readers, libraries and booksellers. Your passion, your drive keeps me motivated and inspired to keep writing.

I also want to give a big shout out to all the friends of Captain Bligh's Brewstillery. I'm not there as often as I should be, but when I work at our monthly bar nights, you're always so lovely and pleased I'm there — I am too. Thank you for your support for what it is Stephen, Adam and I do. Books and booze, hey, what a combination!

I also want to thank my much-missed inspiration and cherished friend, Sara Douglass.

It wouldn't be right not to thank my furbies — my beautiful furry pooches and felines, who are often curled up around my desk as I write. To Bounty, Tallow and Dante and Baroque. I am so fortunate you chose me to be one of your humans.

Now is the moment I've been dreading. I need to talk about one of the darkest times in our recent family history — the death of my younger brother, Peter Adams, from glioblastoma. There's a reason, apart from the fact she's the best sister anyone could wish for, that this book is dedicated to mine, Jenny Farrell.

Peter was diagnosed during Covid and when Tasmania and much of the country was locked down. After his initial surgery and hospital stay in Sydney, Peter was able to live independently. However, he couldn't drive or take himself to appointments, so Jenny would travel the couple of hours, sometimes a few times a week, to not only ferry Peter around, but cook food, ensure he took his medicine and generally care for him. When it became evident he could no longer look after himself and his care would be palliative, Jenny refused to let him go into the only available option — a nursing home (I know, I know — he was only forty-six) — and insisted he come live with her and her beautiful husband, John. Jenny and John not only rearranged their house to accommodate Peter and his needs, but Jenny, a nurse, stopped work in his last six months to look after him. As soon as she could, our stepmother, Moira Adams, came from Queensland to live with Jenny as well. Jenny was tireless in her care for Peter. We were able to receive help from the NDIS. I know a great deal of negative things have been said about the NDIS, but after a rocky start, which was to do with the provider, not the NDIS itself, we ended up with the most wonderful and caring team anyone could wish for: Life With Purpose Home Care, led by Farirai. They could not do enough for Peter — and tried to do more for Jenny, but she was determined to give our brother the kind of personal care only a loving sister could.

Peter was only hospitalised at the last, when it was evident Jenny could no longer look after him, and we maintained a vigil by his bed the final days of his life. Peter was incredibly brave, never complaining, always smiling, until he no longer did. Even so, his big heart refused to stop, and his last hours were very, very hard. I still wake sometimes, reliving them. I would not wish them upon anyone — least of all my endlessly optimistic, tall-story-telling, chuckling brother.

But what Jenny did, what she also did for me when I had cancer, wasn't exceptional — not for her. Jenny is the most unselfish, amazing, kind, uncomplaining and generous person I know. She always sees the good in everyone — even when it's bloody impossible for anyone else to see it. Dedicating this book to her is the least I can do. I am forever grateful to her for what she did for Peter, what she still does for me and the family. I may be the older sister, but Jenny is the rock, the glue that binds our wee family together. I adore you, Jenny, I really do. Thank you, my love, thank you for just being you.

It was hard to think let alone write in the aftermath of Peter's death, even though we knew it was inevitable. Jenny and I had talked every day — sometimes a few times a day — for months. It was a hard habit to break, and we still needed that touchstone. We grieved for a long time (still do) and yet, I am also so grateful that I had Tribulation, Aphra, Gabriel and bloody Restoration religious battles and politics to distract me from my sadness. We all learned how important the arts are to emotional and imaginative wellbeing and mental health during lockdown, how we turned to stories — written and visual, art, dance and music, performance — in order to get through something so unexpected and challenging and scary. What I learned was creating stories was also a welcome and necessary diversion. In so many ways, this novel is very, very special, as it was the light that led me through some very, very bleak spaces.

But I was never alone. I had my amazing, diverse and different, considerate and talented children, Adam and Caragh, and their lovely partners — Hugh (Caragh's) and Zak (Adam's) — to comfort me and share the sorrow. We told tales, laughed, cried, shook our heads in disbelief. Many of my darling friends played a similar role — especially Kerry Doyle and Peter Goddard — thank you.

But I'm not quite finished. The person who was by my side the entire time, not only sharing the burden of grief and the weight of expectations, but trying to lift them from my heart, was my magnificent husband and partner in life and everything, Stephen. My beta reader, my dream-believer, my sounding board, my Yoda, my reality check, the man who makes me cry with laughter. We're not always on the same page — except when it really counts. Every hero in my tales has something of you in them — the best part — your passion for life, your bloody beautiful soul. We've shared many escapades, my love, some fun, others, not so much. But not for anything would I trade a single damn second, not if you weren't there to experience every last one of them with me.

Love you more.

talk about it

Let's talk about books.

Join the conversation:

facebook.com/harlequinaustralia

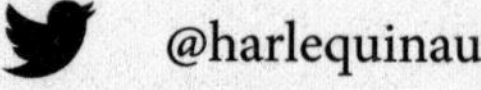
@harlequinaus

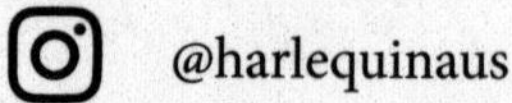
@harlequinaus

harpercollins.com.au/hq

If you love reading and want to know about our authors and titles, then let's talk about it.